IT COULDN'T BE Z...

As Shannon was sipping... to scan the crowd in the... Royal Enclosure. She suddenly... at a very particular profile. As her heart lurched wildly she turned abruptly away. But as she heard the unmistakable voice not far away she realized that something she had told herself could never happen in a million years was about to occur.

"Letitia, darling, how lovely you look."

"Zan, darling, hello. This is Shannon Faloon. Shannon, may I introduce Zan Fitzherbert."

Shannon felt herself turning as if by remote control. Wrestling with her sudden loss of poise, she faced him.

"How do you do, Shannon," he said, slowly extending his hand.

"How do you do," she murmured.

His eyes met hers with the power of a hammer shattering glass. The blurred handsome image she had carried of him, resolving to forget, came into focus with pulsating clarity, breathing life into the emotion she had tried to kill. Verdant memories of Australia fled before her impassive eyes behind the veil, and from the tremor in Zan's smiles Shannon wondered what he was thinking. . . .

JEALOUSIES

Other books by Justine Harlowe
Ask your bookseller for the books you have missed

MEMORY AND DESIRE

JEALOUSIES

Justine Harlowe

BANTAM BOOKS
TORONTO • NEW YORK • LONDON • SYDNEY • AUCKLAND

JEALOUSIES

A Bantam Book / March 1986

ISBN 0-553-25570-3

Published simultaneously in the United States and Canada

PRINTED IN THE UNITED STATES OF AMERICA

O   0 9 8 7 6 5 4 3 2 1

*To Helen Ritter, Kay Fonseca
and William Pinckney Harvey,
with profound love.*

The authors would like to thank the following people for their invaluable help and advice: Guy Robert, Elizabeth McCrum, Leila and Mac Mureson, Philip and Judy Petley, Jean Harvey, Jose Fonseca, Dr. Guy Bailey, Tina Mackenzie, His Excellency Francesca Bengolea, Laura Bennett, and Charles Milnes. Thanks also to Norman Parkinson, the Honorable Desmond Guinness, and the Baroness Thyssen, who were incomparable resources.

BOOK I

Chapter 1

County Limerick, Ireland, 1985

By the weathered stone wall of Kilgarin Castle, its turrets blurred by mist, the Kilgarin Hunt was gathering for the first meet of the season. The cawing of rooks carried for miles across the green landscape, as if heralding the ritual repeated for centuries in the courtyard of the castle, where now the barking of restless hounds mingled with the clatter of horses' hooves on the worn cobblestones.

It was difficult to believe this was 1985. The mounted huntsmen and -women, some in pink coats, others in black riding habits, looked like throwbacks to their nineteenth-century ancestors as they helped themselves to silver goblets of stirrup cup held high on trays by footmen, who also offered hospitality to ruddy-faced Irishmen in hacking jackets and Wellington boots. These Irishmen were farmers, and they would follow the hunt on foot. Their eyes betraying emotions as stormy as the Irish Sea in winter, they stood apart from the local gentry and landowners. As they drank mulled wine, they cast glances at the handsome women mounted on powerful geldings, who acknowledged their frank admiration with flirtatious smiles. The electric atmosphere was further charged by flying whispers that their host at the meet, one of the foremost peers of Ireland, was about to wed Shannon Faloon, and heads turned in curiosity as she entered the courtyard astride a glossy black hunter.

"Well, Zan, here goes," Shannon said to the Earl of Kilgarin, riding at her side. Clearly, she needed reassurance.

"Darling, it's only natural that everyone is staring at you. They all want to see the future Countess of Kilgarin. You have nothing to worry about, believe me. You look magnificent." Zan had time to say nothing more as the master of the hunt came up to greet him.

Her head held high, Shannon trained her eyes on the rolling green landscape shrouded in mist, trying to calm the nervousness welling up inside her. This land was as much hers by birthright as it was theirs, and she was reluctant to

3

admit that the approval of these strangers was necessary to her future happiness. Her veil concealed the expression in her dark eyes as she strained to achieve an air of confidence while holding tight the reins in her gloved hands. She wondered if anyone would guess that she had been born on the other side of the world in very different circumstances. Preoccupied, Shannon missed the look of shock on Zan's face when he sighted Kerry Van Buren mounted on a bay that fretted at the edge of the gathering. She had come uninvited to the castle, and he turned away abruptly, pretending not to see her.

Kerry reined in her impatient horse as she tried to catch sight of the woman who it was rumored would soon marry Lord Kilgarin. When at last she glimpsed Shannon's arresting figure, Kerry couldn't keep her thoughts from reeling back to the desperate night all those years ago that had culminated in Shannon's flight from home, an event that had so dramatically altered both their lives. Surely this privileged group of people gathered at the castle would find it difficult to connect the two of them with the reality of their origins, she thought ironically. Did everyone here know about Shannon's relationship with Amadeo Benguela, about Patrick, Rosemary, and the mystery that still surrounded her accident? Feeling her horse shift restlessly once again, Kerry moved to the edge of the dew-soaked grass, toward a knot of villagers, where she would be less conspicuous. She had twenty-four hours to win back the place that had been hers so briefly, and she regarded the misted fields and woodland beyond the castle that would be her battlefield. She watched as Shannon reached down to accept the note Kerry had given the footman to deliver. Hearing someone call her name, she turned with a start of anxiety to see a woman whose face seemed vaguely familiar.

"Kerry—I didn't know you were coming. I thought you'd be in London. We're all so sorry to hear about you and Mark."

Seeing the woman's arched eyebrows raised in curiosity behind her veil, Kerry's heart pounded involuntarily. She was saved from a reply by the blare of the huntsman's horn calling the riders to attention. Suddenly they were away, and the horses thundered over the lush turf after the baying hounds, leaving echoes resounding in the castle courtyard.

* * *

Later that afternoon Shannon left the hunting party as they sped toward a distant wood. Tiredly, she made her way back home along the path they had traveled earlier, past a ruin shielded by a grove of gnarled trees. Water dripped from the lichen-covered trees, and a dense mist rose from the earth, casting a gray-green gloom on the horizon. Reaching into her pocket, she withdrew the unsigned note she had received in the courtyard that morning.

Meet me in the ruined castle near Kilgarin at four, to discuss a confidential matter of the greatest importance to your future. . . .

Shannon had decided earlier to ignore the mysterious summons, but she was so close to the ruin now, and she *was* curious. . . .

Urging her horse to a gallop, she took the low stone wall that bordered the road. Then she cantered up a wooded path, her eyes fixed on a crumbling arch that rose darkly in the wild parkland, framing the skeleton of a once grand house. Glancing up as she passed underneath, Shannon was astonished to see a swan and a shamrock carved in the span of stone. It was the Faloon coat of arms, marking the entrance to Castle Shannon, a place that had loomed in her imagination since childhood. Now, on the verge of an assignation there, she felt a tingle of premonition race down her spine.

She guided her horse toward the ancient remains of the great Faloon dynasty, whose proud kingdom was now ruled by creeping ivy, moss, and wild, crooked trees outlined against the lowering sky.

She dismounted, tied up her horse, and walked through the undergrowth, acutely aware of the silence. Standing on the threshold of the great hall, she recalled the stories her father told of balls and feuds, great exploits and petty deeds. She had always assumed he'd concocted those tales to amuse a child, but the sight of the crumbling walls suddenly gave them substance. The central staircase climbing to the sky was a fragment of a vanished world that reminded her she had never explored her own past.

A sudden clicking noise startled Shannon, and, whirling 'round, she saw a woman across the ruined room in a riding habit, leaning against the chimney, lighting a cigarette.

"You startled me," said Shannon with a sudden intake

of breath. "Who are you? Was it you who sent me that note?"

Even as she spoke, a feeling grew within her that she knew the woman.

"Don't you recognize me, Shannon?" said Kerry, her smile full of provocative defiance.

"Kerry!" She gasped in shock. "What are you doing here?"

"You might say that I've come to claim what's mine."

Koonwarra, New South Wales, 1975

The day broke at Koonwarra with the kelpies barking somewhere beyond the woolshed, just before the pale light of a winter morning began to seep through the canvas blinds. Shannon opened her eyes and gazed up at the ceiling before sliding from bed so as not to wake Kerry. When her feet hit the cold floorboards, she instinctively curled her toes, shivering not from the chill morning air but from excitement when she remembered that Bob Fremont must be on his way back from fetching Charlie and his friend from the airstrip at Wishbone.

She dressed as quietly as she could in a pair of cords and a warm sweater, glad to see her sister was still sleeping soundly. It would give her a moment to herself to experiment with her heavy dark hair. She wanted to look special that morning, without appearing to have taken the trouble. First she twisted the heavy mane into a chignon, then, dissatisfied, put it in a ponytail, sighing with exasperation. It looked a mess, and all she could do was put it in the usual braid, which she finished twisting just as Kerry stirred.

At seventeen, Shannon had become acutely conscious of every detail of her appearance, and this morning in particular she found fault with the un-Australian cast of her own features, so in contrast with Kerry's brand of fair good looks that predominated from Darwin to Adelaide. Reflected in the mirror, she saw Kerry's coppery curls appear through the top of a sweater. Almost thirteen, she was small but enviably curvaceous for her age, and even her breasts were much more developed than Shannon's.

"Hurry up, or we'll be late," Shannon urged.

"I can beat you easy-peasy, anyway. Want a cuppa?" chirped Kerry.

6

"No time for that."

"Why didn't you wake me up?" called Kerry, grabbing her stock whip.

With the instinct of sisters who knew each other's habits and thoughts, they pulled on their boots and, charged with excitement, sped out of the small house, letting the screen door bang behind them.

"Come on—I'll race you to the stables," Kerry cried.

They clattered down the steps of the wooden bungalow built high over the dry creek. The clapboard house roofed in white asbestos was in need of a coat of paint, but it had an aura of privacy as well as a clear view of the blue hills that bordered Koonwarra.

Arriving at the stables in a state of breathless laughter, batting at the blowflies that swarmed around the station in summer, they gathered up the riding tackle and carried it across the yard sheltered by a long line of gum trees skirting the paddock. Shannon saddled up her taffy-colored mare, Butterscotch, and leaping onto her, she turned to look for Kerry, who joined her on Splendor, a roan gelding that was easily the finest horse on Koonwarra.

"Let's go," called Shannon impatiently.

Since the day they had heard that Charlie was bringing home a real English lord for the summer, they had both tried to affect a blasé manner, partly in defense against their father's searing comments about Anglo-Irish pillagers and partly because they were secretly convinced Zan must be the worst sort of pommie snob. Still, the name alone, Lord Alexander Fitzherbert, conjured up all the glamour of a storybook prince and they were bracing themselves for the excitement of seeing him for the first time.

As they trotted past the big house, Shannon caught a glimpse of Mattie Fremont on the wide veranda. The mistress of Koonwarra waved at the girls riding by. She of all people on the station was looking forward most to Charlie's return from Oxford. He was the firstborn of her three sons, and her favorite. Feeling the fresh wind against her face, Shannon stared back at the rambling low white house shielded by big old trees; in her mind there was nothing that could compare with it.

Ahead, the vast pasturelands of Koonwarra carved out of New South Wales sloped gently into the distance as far as the eye could see. The horizon, broken by gum and scrub oak, was populated with thousands of grazing sheep that from a distance were merely cream-colored clusters. The roustabouts on horseback had been mustering them since dawn, and their father, Brendan, was probably among them. As the girls skirted the barbed-wire fence that marked the home paddock, Shannon kept her eye trained on the narrow road, which disappeared into infinity between the blue hills that ringed the station, until finally she caught sight of the Land Rover making its way swiftly toward Koonwarra, leaving a cloud of billowing dust in its wake.

"They're here—they've arrived!" whooped Kerry. She couldn't contain her impatience, but galloped ahead on Splendor.

Inside the Land Rover, Charlie Fremont stared out the window like a caged animal returning to the wild. He could hardly contain his excitement at returning home—for good.

"Well—what do you think of it?" he asked the young man in the backseat.

"It's certainly big."

Zan, Lord Fitzherbert, had replied with such understatement that both Charlie and his father laughed.

Zan glanced at Bob Fremont's profile. The strong lines etched deep into his permanently suntanned face, his big-boned, spare frame conformed to the Australian stereotype, and though he was the owner of one of the richest and oldest sheep stations in the district, Bob's hands were as sinewy and rough as any of the ringers who ruled the bush on horseback.

"Looks like you've got a welcoming committee." Bob nodded in the direction of the two figures on horseback who had just appeared on the empty horizon.

In a sort of angry panic, Shannon found herself tearing after Kerry at full gallop. Now that they were in sight of the Land Rover she had no choice but to follow Kerry's lead, though for weeks she had imagined herself coolly greeting Lord Fitzherbert on the terrrace of the big house. She could have died of embarrassment. It was Kerry's intention to race brazenly alongside the Land Rover, and the closer Shannon got, the more her mortification increased. This wasn't how she wanted to appear, like some damn cowgirl, her hair whipping across her face, so desperate to meet the boys she couldn't wait until they got home.

In wild contrast to her sister, however, Kerry raced

madly parallel with the Land Rover, enjoying the exhilarating illusion that she was going to win the race. Reveling in the sensation of performing before an audience, she ignored Shannon's shout behind her and waved and smiled flirtatiously at the young man she knew must be Lord Fitzherbert.

Inside the Land Rover Charlie and Zan were fascinated by the sight of the girls on the racing horses. Charlie hardly recognized the wild banshee of a girl, her dark hair thrown back by the wind, struggling to hold her own with Kerry.

"You would never know they were related." Zan remarked.

"They're only half sisters—isn't that right, Dad?" Charlie asked.

"Yep." Bob nodded. "Their father hooked up with some native woman from New Caledonia before he married Kerry's mother, so I'm told. Shannon's a nice enough girl—but Kerry's a real hellion."

Bob Fremont shook his head, and when the speedometer hit forty he made a mental note that he would have a word with the Faloon girls about racing like that in the home paddock. It was a dangerous place to ride a horse pell-mell, and he was sure they both knew it. But after all, he reasoned, you had to allow for youthful good spirits. It was only natural. Casting a sideways glance at the young Lord Fitzherbert, kitted out in brand-new moleskin trousers and a felt hat, he wondered how the lad would fare in Australia. No doubt three months in the Southern Hemisphere would chisel substantial changes on the character and smooth handsome face of the young aristocrat.

Zan was avidly watching the girls. In contrast to Kerry, Shannon stared stoically ahead, and it intrigued him that she never once smiled in their direction.

"That cheeky little redhead has changed a lot since you've been away, Charlie," said Bob. "I'd say she's thirteen going on twenty-three."

"That says it all," said Charlie with a laugh.

"Damn, I wish those girls would slow down," Bob remarked as they rounded the last bend. "I've had to tell Kerry off several times this winter. I'm beginning to wish I'd never let that girl have a free hand with Splendor. She lives on that horse when she's not in school."

"Mum wrote me that she's been winning all the gymkhanas around."

"That's true enough. Kerry holds her own with the best—"

"My god—she's been thrown," Zan interrupted, causing

9

Bob to brake hard in instant reflex. The Land Rover skidded to a halt.

"I knew it," Bob said angrily.

Swirling dust clouded their view for a moment, and when it cleared they saw Shannon's riderless horse galloping free.

It took Kerry a moment to realize that the Land Rover was no longer following alongside. Bringing Splendor to a rearing halt in midgallop, she turned anxiously to see the men leaping from the Land Rover. Charlie dashed across the paddock to grab the reins of the twitching Butterscotch, while Bob stooped over the motionless figure that from Kerry's vantage point looked like a rucksack dumped on the ground. The sight made her go cold.

"That a boy, Splendor," whispered Kerry, patting the nervous animal. Her heart pounding in fear, she returned to the group around Shannon. Charlie walked toward her, holding out the reins of the horse.

"Here—take him back to the paddock."

There was no greeting, no smile of welcome. Charlie, she saw in one glance, was no longer an overgrown boy but a man, and he was glaring at her disapprovingly. She hardly dared look at Lord Fitzherbert.

"I'll speak to you later," called Bob sharply without pausing to cast a glance in her direction.

Lifting Shannon carefully to the backseat of the Land Rover, the three men crowded into the front and drove off in a cloud of dust, leaving Kerry by the roadside. Hot tears of humiliation coursed down her cheeks. She jerked the reins of Shannon's horse and trotted toward home, the very last place she wanted to be. Shannon was going to die, and she wished she could disappear suddenly and be transported to the other side of the earth.

When Shannon regained consciousness, it took her unaccountable minutes to recall what she was doing in this cool, dim bedroom papered in pink roses. Her head throbbed painfully, and the room spun when she tried to focus. But gradually she became aware of Mattie Fremont's strong face, her eyes clouded with concern.

"Now don't move or try to speak, dear. Just lie still. Everything is going to be all right," Mattie murmured, touching her cool hand to Shannon's forehead.

The girl fumbled for the vague memory of being carried

10

up the steps of the house in Bob's arms, of being surrounded by a jumble of voices that belonged to no one in particular.

"Mattie—the doctor's on the phone. I think you ought to have a word with him." Bob spoke from the doorway.

"I'm coming. I'll be right back, Shannon. Remember now, just lie still."

She nodded, slowly taking in the details of a room furnished in soft cream-and-green-striped chintz with splashes of pastel. It was like being inside a muzzy watercolor. The heavy curtains had been drawn against the light, and she could just make out a clock on the mantelpiece that now began to chime. The slightest movement made her head spin.

"I thought you may have drifted off for a moment," said Mattie. "You're a very lucky girl," she scolded softly, settling in a chair by the bed. "Doctor Watkins says you're to stay put for forty-eight hours or more, depending on how you feel. He'll be out as soon as he can."

"I've spoiled everything for Charlie's homecoming, Mattie," Shannon began weakly.

"Enough of that—it was an accident. Anyway, you're not to worry, but to rest and keep quiet. I'm afraid you can't eat anything for a bit in case of concussion, but by tonight we'll have you eating steak.'

The bliss of being cosseted in such unaccustomed comfort gave Shannon a sense of utter tranquillity. Just as she was about to fall asleep, the memory of Zan Fitzherbert's pure English voice nudged her back awake. The timbre of every syllable summoned up worlds that had filled her imagination since she was old enough to look at the English magazines Mattie subscribed to. Trying to fit an image to the voice, she had opened her eyes and found herself looking into a pair of serious blue eyes full of concern.

Later that morning Kerry escaped to the solitude of the little wooden chapel beyond the orchards of Koonwarra. When she'd returned with the horses she had hung around the stables nervously, waiting for Bob's summons. Hungry and miserable, she had been grooming Splendor when he strode into the yard. His reprimand had been swift and humiliating. Tersely he'd told her that she was forbidden to ride for the rest of the week and that she would be expected to muck out the stables after school. She had stoically refused to give in to tears in front of him, and now she slumped sobbing across a

11

tombstone. To be deprived of her horse, even for a week, was the worst possible punishment Bob could mete out, even worse than the beating she would undoubtedly receive from her father when he came back at sundown. Pressing her face into the brown grass, wet from sun-melted frost, Kerry gave vent to a passionate outburst of fury laced with tears at the injustice of being blamed for Shannon's carelessness. Her shame in front of Charlie and Zan Fitzherbert was too much to bear. She would never be able to face them. Rolling over on her back, she stared dismally at the hard blue sky. At this very moment pale, beautiful Shannon was probably being spoon-fed breakfast by a solicitous Lord Fitzherbert. She felt her stomach twist with jealousy at the thought. Tormented by the suggestion, Kerry leapt up and gathered a handful of stones, which she threw forcefully toward a tree, causing a flock of surprised birds to take flight.

The chiming clock woke Shannon from a dreamless sleep. She didn't know whether it was morning or evening, and it took her a moment to remember why she was nestled in this soft bed. When there was a tap at the door she called, "Yes, come in," thinking it was Mattie coming to look in on her.

As the door opened she was amazed to see Lord Fitzherbert carefully balancing a tray laden with dishes.

"I was elected to bring some sustenance to the invalid," he announced with an engaging smile. He set the tray down on the bedside table with an exaggerated care that suggested he was unaccustomed to waiting on anyone.

Overcome by acute self-consciousness, Shannon watched his every move. Propping up the pillows behind her head, he laid the tray before her and with a flourish unfolded the linen napkin. The moment she saw the scrambled eggs and buttered toast on a delicate china plate, her shyness dissolved a little.

"I hope you've got an appetite. You're expected to eat the lot. Mattie's orders."

"I've just realized I'm starving," she admitted.

"Oh, by the way, I haven't properly introduced myself. I'm Zan Fitzherbert."

"And I'm Shannon Faloon."

"At least you haven't lost your memory," he said teasingly, and she couldn't resist giggling shyly.

"Do you mind if I stay and keep you company?"

"No, of course not," she lied. Her appetite vanished,

and her self-consciousness returned as he sat beside her on the edge of the bed.

Her first snatched glimpses of Zan Fitzherbert as she tried to eat told her little of the young man who had been the subject of intense speculation at Koonwarra for months. They had all half expected him to be the worst sort of upper-crust stuck-up pommie, and it was generally agreed that he would need pulling down a peg or two. All that time Shannon had been determined to regard Lord Fitzherbert critically and without stars in her eyes, but now her resolution vanished. Physically, she had to admit, he easily surpassed the handsome image she had nurtured of him. In her imagination his face had been as immobile as a photograph, but the young man before her was animated, full of life, which added a great deal of charm to his handsome, classically English face. She found herself sneaking glances at his mouth, which had a laconic sensuality. And when, involuntarily, she imagined what it would be like to feel that mouth on hers, she flushed, certain he could read her most private thoughts. She looked up to see him studying her with concern.

"How are you feeling?"

"Much better, thanks to you for bringing me this tray."

"You took quite a tumble. I saw it, you know. I was looking at you the moment you hit the ground."

"I don't usually fall off my horse," she said, trying to sound casual.

"You were going like the wind. I didn't think anyone could survive a fall like that. I know I couldn't."

"Is Bob furious?"

"No, just worried. You gave him quite a scare."

"If you see my sister, Kerry, please tell her not to worry."

"I will. I think the poor girl got an awful scolding from Bob. He thought it was all her fault. Charlie mentioned she's a bit of a daredevil and that maybe this has taught her a lesson."

She stared at him, now without awkwardness. In just a few moments' conversation, an unexpected familiarity had been established between them. Perhaps he sensed it, too, for he turned away for a moment and fidgeted with the dial of the telephone on the bedside table.

"I'll take the tray if you're finished."

"Thanks—and please thank Mattie. It was very good," she said.

13

He paused to look at her as she lay back, her black hair strewn on the pillow. Pale from the shock of the accident, her face was dominated by eyes that were like dark pools intersected with light. Fringed with the lace of a borrowed nightgown, her slender wrists were fragile and fine, her full mouth unsmiling.

"Your face is going to turn ten shades of purple." He reached out to brush her bruised cheek. "I'll look in on you with the others to say good night. I expect your father and sister will be along later."

She watched him leave, awed by his self-possession. He paused in the doorway, looking back at her.

"Do you know, you look really lovely lying there."

Shannon reacted to his parting words with a little laugh of disbelief. Was this the way real lords behaved, or had he really meant what he said? She couldn't believe she looked lovely, now or ever, but just the same she reveled in a moment's unparalleled pleasure at the compliment.

Later she was happy to see Mattie when the older woman came in. Mattie gave off a comforting aura of self-assurance that appealed to the child in Shannon. She had felt infinitely at ease in Mattie's presence from the moment she saw her waiting for them to arrive on the steps of Koonwarra three years before. And Mattie, who had always wanted a daughter, had taken to the Faloon girls right away, especially Shannon. One of the legendary breed of wives of sheep station owners, there was a strong dose of common sense in Mattie's character. Yet for all her practicality she was not lacking in kindness or sentimentality when the occasion arose. She had the weathered skin of a woman who had lived at the mercy of the elements all her life, but her eyes were the same pure, unclouded blue as the sky on a clear day.

"No temperature," she said, taking a thermometer from Shannon's mouth. "It would seem the brain is intact, but your face certainly took a battering." She glided her fingers over Shannon's swollen cheek and forehead. "I'll fetch you a steak for it later on."

"Surely that doesn't really work," said Shannon, laughing at the idea of wearing a hunk of meat on her face.

"Well now, it could be an old wives' tale, but I've always used it, just like mustard plasters for chest colds." She brushed Shannon's hair back from the bruises. "My word, your hair looks pretty like that. Why do you always yank it back in that braid? It's so severe."

14

"Oh, it's such a mess—and Dad won't let me cut it." She sighed, and Mattie remembered that Brendan had several fixed ideas about his daughters.

Not long after Mattie had gone, Shannon heard footsteps at the door, and her heart began to race. Perhaps Zan was returning. Instead the tall figure of her father filled the doorway.

"Well, well, is milady receiving? And from her bedside, no less," Brendan called with cheerful sarcasm.

With an instinct that she was almost ashamed of, Shannon gauged her father's voice to see if he had been drinking. A little coil of apprehension relaxed inside her when she realized he was in one of his sober and loving moods.

"Well, what have we here, then? Mattie's giving you the royal treatment, that's for sure."

Pulling up a chair by the bedside, he looked at her with mock sternness for a moment, but his blue eyes reflected anxiety when he saw how frail she looked against the pillow. "Are you in pain?" he murmured, taking her hand, a gentle gesture that seemed to make the big man uncomfortable.

"I'm fine if I just lie still." Shannon noticed that he hadn't paused to take off his boots or change his shirt. He had come directly from the woolshed, where every day at Koonwarra a mob of sheep was mustered and weighed, dictating the relentless rhythm of his life.

Brendan radiated a dark, rugged glamour which he had passed on to Shannon in a finer and even more striking form. His Celtic blood had bequeathed him thick dark brows that bordered blue eyes of blazing intensity set in a face burned mahogany by the unrelenting sun. At forty-five the flame of passion no longer burned as brightly within him as it once had. Yet the wicked twist of a smile that might turn malevolent after too many drinks could still command unabashed female admiration, and one raised eyebrow could set a woman's heart beating faster.

It was hard to believe, Shannon thought, that the same man who talked so gently to her now could smash chairs over the kitchen table in a drunken fury. And though his anger seemed directed at the world in general, Kerry and Shannon always lived under the menacing cloud of his temper, like a savage animal hidden in their midst.

While Brendan related the trivia of his day, he found the picture his daughter made against the white pillows quite disturbing. The association it brought hit him with painful vengeance, tearing back the thin membrane that had blurred the memory of Françoise. Never before had Shannon looked so like her mother. There was something about the way her dark, unruly hair surrounded that small, perfect head, the way her hands rested on the blanket in the enormous bed, that recalled the most intense passion he had ever known. In the course of his lifetime, no other woman had aroused him like Françoise, and now the past seemed resurrected in Shannon. He didn't often think of Françoise—and when he did, he drowned the memory in alcohol.

"Where's Kerry?" Shannon asked.

"She's been sent to bed with no supper. I came straight over here to see you when Mattie sent word you were awake. Kerry's going to get a licking when I get back," he said darkly.

"Please, Dad, don't punish her. It wasn't her fault." When Shannon tried to rise she fell back as the ceiling whirled.

Brendan looked at her with concern. "Now, girlie, you're not supposed to excite yourself. That's what Mattie told me. Do as you're told."

Seeing the firm set of his features, Shannon knew there was no point in protesting over Kerry's punishment. For some reason Kerry always bore the brunt of Brendan's wrath, and not even Shannon's tears would change things.

Brendan whispered an affectionate farewell, then strode down the long hallway hung with botanical prints. A stranger stood at the end of the passage in the entry hall. One glance at his arrogant profile told Brendan who he was.

"Damn pommie," he muttered. If it hadn't been for the visitor, the accident would never have happened.

"Hello—I'm Zan Fitzherbert. You must be Shannon's father." He extended a hand, which Brendan ignored. "I'm sorry about your daughter, sir."

The "sir" enraged Brendan but immediately took the wind out of his sails. He suppressed the tart comment on the tip of his tongue.

"I'm sure Shannon will be all right, sir—there's nothing seriously wrong. I thought she had rallied wonderfully when I saw her a while ago."

Brendan peered at Zan narrowly; then, muttering a terse "Good night," he strode from the house.

All the way home he seethed with rage at the encounter. The Englishman's patronizing manner—thinly disguised as

16

familiarity—had opened up an old sore, one he thought had healed long ago when he'd left Ireland in the fifties after the war. It had been a long time since he'd been in contact with a member of Zan's breed, the typical Anglo-Irish aristocrat who had brought the country to ruin, and he reflected bitterly that they were still being churned out true to type.

"Damn the pommie bastard," he muttered to himself as his boots crushed the dry, frosted grass. Passing through a shimmering copse of silver gums illuminated by the moon, he brooded that Fitzherbert would be underfoot the whole summer. Then, in contradiction, he found his pride rising to combat the pointed insult. A Faloon could hold his own alongside a Fitzherbert any day of the week, with blue blood that went back to Elizabeth I. Things he felt he'd escaped from in Australia suddenly came back to plague him. If it hadn't been for the likes of Fitzherbert, heir to some half-breed title that had been a reward for groveling to an English king, the Faloons would still be in Castle Shannon. Its name-sake, his own daughter Shannon, would be comfortably ensconced in a grand room of her own instead of sharing a double bed with her sister in a wooden bungalow. The bitterness of gall rose in his throat as he conveniently ignored one crucial fact—that both he and his younger brother, Jack, had been born on the wrong side of the blanket and therefore could not inherit even what might remain of the Faloon estate. The creamy, freckled skin and titian hair of his mother, Kathleen, had attracted the attention of the philandering Earl of Shannon when she was up to her elbows in soapsuds in the laundryhouse of the castle grounds. During the troubled twenties, which had brought the estate to ruin, she had borne him two bastard sons. Then she'd changed her name by deed poll from O'Mally to Faloon; and with the aid of a small pension from the earl—who had long since tired of her—she'd moved to Dublin, where Brendan and Jack grew up.

By the time Brendan had reached home he had worked himself into a frenzy. In the center of the shabby room stood Kerry, her arms folded defiantly as she waited to defend herself.

"I don't know what they told you, Dad, but it wasn't my fault Shannon was thrown. Everybody's blaming me, but I can't see what I have to do with it. Bob Fremont is completely biased. . . ."

"Biased? What's that, Miss Fancy Talk?" he retorted.

17

The very sound of the word infuriated him, like a red flag before a bull. The small copper-haired Kerry standing so obdurately before him broke the fragile bolt holding back his wrath.

The thunder in Brendan's eyes paralyzed Kerry, and she began to tremble as he undid his belt.

"Come here," he commanded. "I'm going to whip you senseless for what you did today. You could have killed her."

Kerry was shaking with dread, but she refused to beg forgiveness as Brendan approached her. She had submitted to his beatings many times, but her spirit was more than equal to his own, particularly that night, as he planted one blow, then another, on her. Unable to keep little screams of pain from escaping her lips, she seethed with anger at the monstrous injustice of her punishment. There was an unprecedented savagery in the way Brendan gripped her arm, the way he lashed at her repeatedly, and when he finally released her she swallowed a sob.

"I hate you! I despise you!" she spat out venomously.

"Go to bed, or there'll be more where that came from," he snarled, and turned his back on her.

Kerry bolted to the bedroom and slammed the door behind her. Flinging herself on the bed, she buried her face in the pillow and gave a muffled scream that brought no relief. The only thing that could ease her humiliation, her sense of outraged dignity, would be uninhibited shrieking that could be heard as far as Wishbone. Instead, she had to content herself with sharp, impotent little spasms of release. The residue of her anguish collected in a pool of resentment centered on Shannon, who seemed to possess some magical immunity to Brendan's wrath.

Ignoring the sounds from Kerry's room, Brendan headed for the kitchen. There was a joint of mutton in the refrigerator, but his appetite was gone. Instead, he went to the cupboard, where he always kept a bottle of whiskey.

He wandered through the comfortless, functional living room. There was a bleakness about the furniture, the absence of personal possessions that created a dead atmosphere with no suggestion of a home. Shunning his usual spot by the television, he went determinedly to the screened porch, hugging his bottle. There he flopped into a chair in the corner and got down to the serious business of getting blind drunk as quickly as possible.

Whenever his maudlin Irish side took over, Brendan

18

Faloon indulged himself in a bout of solitary drinking very different from the kind of weekend drunk he sought in the town of Wishbone. There was a sort of ribald pleasure in the kind of binge he shared with roustabouts and shearers from miles around in his favorite smoky pub, and he usually ended up in bed with a woman for the night. It was a kind of forgetting that was the nearest thing to contentment he knew. But tonight his heart was as black as a sky with the stars plucked out. He gazed at the silhouettes of the trees, unable to keep his eyes from wandering to the big house ablaze with lights, a sight that reminded him of his own failure and isolation. After a full tumbler of whiskey, he turned with inward aggression on himself, meeting the thought that had tormented him for the last hour. Françoise's face returned to haunt him, and a wave of sentimental tears stung his eyes.

He had seen her for the first time in a bar in Brisbane, only weeks after he and his brother, Jack, arrived in Australia on a ten-pound passage from Southampton. He couldn't believe his eyes as he watched her pulling pints of beer for a crowd of brawny, thirsty men. She was like a white jade statue in a coal hole. Her slender arms reaching across the bar seemed much too fine to work so hard, and she kept her dark eyes cast down as if the sight of the men terrified her. From her jet-black hair and the exotic cast of her features to her delicate build, he guessed she must be part Polynesian or Oriental, a mixture that sent his blood racing. She was without doubt the most exquisite thing he had ever seen. Jack, at his side, laughed when he saw the look of naked desire on his brother's face, commenting that a girl in such a place could be little more than a prostitute. Brendan was enraged. To him, her feet didn't touch the sawdust-strewn bar floor, and he saw her as moving in a kind of bubble that protected her femininity and innocence.

When she finally met his blatant stare, the noisy bar fell away and the two of them stood alone, guarded in silence. As he softly asked for a beer, she looked at him curiously. In those days Ireland still clung to his coattails, and she seemed to sense that he was different from all the rough customers who tried to chat her up. His fascinated gaze left no doubt that his feelings were real, even though they were sudden. By the end of the evening the atmosphere between them was so highly charged that Brendan was mad with desire, a kind of wanting he had never experienced with a woman of his own blood.

19

When he finally possessed her in her room at the back of the pub, the myth of her fragility exploded. Françoise used every inch of her superbly honed body to make love to him. Her teeth, her tongue, her eyes, and even her heart coaxed forth sensations in him that he hadn't known existed. Locked to each other throughout the nights they spent together, they shared a passion that by day seemed dangerous. It wasn't long before Brendan's obsession led to a rift with Jack. When they had come out to Australia, the brothers had thrown in their small capital fifty-fifty, intending to amass a fortune and then buy a station of their own. But it became apparent that Brendan's energies were sapped by his lust for the barmaid, who refused to leave the bright lights of Brisbane, and he was tormented by thoughts of what she was doing when he was shearing in southern Queensland. The money that he should have saved he spent lavishly on her, dissipating his valuable fund of dollars. He was only half tempted to marry her, aware of the climate of bigotry that prevailed in Australia. Jack never ceased to remind him that she was a half-caste, ignoring that she was French on her father's side. Brendan consoled himself that when he had made his fortune he could build a barrier of wealth between him and a critical world. But he knew that Françoise began to brood because for her the only proof of enduring love was a wedding ring.

When she became pregnant, everything changed. Brendan hadn't bargained for a child, but he assumed responsibility and persuaded Françoise that she must accompany him to a station where he had a job for the spring shearing. The move was a disaster from the start. The other itinerant shearers left their women behind in the cities, the presence of Françoise set him apart from the others who lived in single men's quarters.

Françoise loathed life on the station—the heat, the dust, the flies, her isolation. The withering looks she received from the station women wounded her, and Brendan soon realized that the glances of undisguised lust from the men had created a rift between them. But in spite of their shared misery, he never anticipated that Françoise would leave him. His jealous rages, his drunkenness, and his absences finally broke her spirit. One day he came home to find the six-month-old Shannon wailing in her cradle. The note pinned to the baby's pillow pierced his heart.

Dear Brendan:

    This isn't the life you promised. If I stay, I'll die. I just can't help it. Please take care of our baby girl for now. I'll come for her soon when I have a place.

                                    Françoise

He blamed himself for not marrying Françoise, vowed that he would when she came back. But she never did.

Over the years Brendan's memory became clouded. His remembered love grew to monumental proportions that reality had never matched, and with it came bitterness. In rare moments of clarity he understood why Françoise had left him. As an immigrant, an outsider himself, he half understood her loneliness. She was only fulfilling the yearning of every woman who had languished in the Outback, but he couldn't find it in his heart to forgive her.

The easiest way to discourage Shannon's questions about her mother was to lie. He had simply told her that Françoise had died and gone to heaven.

Three years later he met Doreen, a kind, capable widow scarred by hardship and disappointment, but she had grown up in Australia and had the Outback woman's stoic acceptance of a life bare of anything but necessities. She was just over thirty, but the sun had added years to her broad Irish face. In Brendan she saw the raw material of a husband and father, and she turned her hand to keep him from drinking, trying to create a home. Even though she could only give him a pallid version of the passion that had welded him to Françoise, they had a period of stability together. They sometimes fought violently, for Brendan, soured by his experience with Françoise, came to think of women as a necessary evil, a judgment compatible with his Irish upbringing.

When Doreen died in childbirth on the remote Queensland station because the flying doctor couldn't get there in time, Brendan was left with a squalling infant an hour old and the four-year-old Shannon, who stroked his hair and tried to comfort him.

"Never mind, Dad, I'll look after the baby," she had murmured. Her hair was as black as a Tahitian Vahine's, and her dark-fringed eyes were serious beyond her years.

When the wool boom declined, Brendan had to go where his work took him. He farmed out the girls wherever he thought they would be cared for. He tried to make another go of his partnership with Jack, but the brothers soon discovered they had drifted too far apart. The hardworking Jack, who had inherited a natural gift for handling horses, had always kept his eye shrewdly trained on the brass ring, while Brendan had somehow let it slip away. One day Jack wrote to say he was managing a big stud farm south of the Darling Downs and that there was a place for Brendan; but when Brendan moved south with the girls, he was disappointed to find the job wasn't what he'd hoped it would be. Jack's easy luck embittered him, and when Jack landed a job at a prestigious stud farm in America, Brendan cursed him jealously and told himself he was glad to see the back of him. After all, hadn't Jack even tried to charm tiny Kerry away when he'd recognized her talent for handling horses? Just when Brendan thought his luck had run out, he applied for the job of manager at Koonwarra. On the strength of a background that ran the gamut from repairing a windmill to shearing a hundred and fifty sheep a day, Bob Fremont had hired him.

Inhaling a deep breath, Brendan wheezed at the cold air. Half the bottle was gone now, and his hand was no longer steady, but with a lifetime's experience he knew almost to the drop the definition of excess that would prevent him from getting up at five the next morning. The moon that always set the kelpies barking cast a pure white light on the screened veranda. His thoughts went to Shannon tucked up in the big mahogany bed. Was this the first step of a long journey toward brighter lights that would take her away from him? Her rare and exquisite beauty, her sweet nature, would prove irresistible to an Anglo-Irish lord like Fitzherbert, who would feed her with pretty words and compliments, plucking her bloom only to discard it as carelessly as had the earl with his own mother. Boiling with hatred, Brendan vowed to himself that if the pommie bastard dared lay a hand on Shannon, he'd kill him.

But Kerry was another matter. Unlike Shannon, she had never needed anyone's protection, and would twist a man like Fitzherbert around her little finger. From the time she was a baby she had proved to be headstrong, always rebelling against him. The strap was the only thing she understood, he thought darkly, fending off guilt at his own brutality. Yet she continued to challenge him at every turn, never even attempting to hide her contempt for him. The thrust of her chin, the fire in her eyes conveyed her fearless nature. Looking at Kerry was like looking at himself when young. There

22

was much of him in her to remind him painfully of his own bitter failures. She had the same wild, free spirit, the same thirst for life he'd had before he'd strayed off-course. He felt a deep primeval recognition of his own kind whenever he looked at his younger daughter. It was an emotion he could never articulate—and that some people might call love.

When Bob took the potholes on the road to Koonwarra at full speed, Mattie braced herself against the dashboard of the Land Rover.

"The rain is playing havoc with this road. We've got to do something about it," she said, her eyes narrowed at the sun-drenched paddocks daubed with the green that followed the violent spring storms that had shaken the land to life again.

"You say that every damn year, Mat," said Bob with a tolerant smile. "There's a million other things that come first now it's lambing."

"It makes my teeth loose." She winced as they took another violent bump.

Bob looked askance at Mattie, somewhat surprised. It wasn't in her nature to complain, and at a glance he saw what had set her off. She was watching two distant figures on horseback, racing toward home. Zan was following while Shannon took the lead.

"She's having a whale of a time now school's out. Like a bird let out of a cage," he commented. "I told her to show Zan every square inch of Koonwarra, and she took me at my word. I sure haven't had the time, and neither has Charlie or the boys."

"I wish you hadn't asked her. Bob, I think you ought to have a word with Charlie about those two."

Even though their relationship was innocent enough, Mattie had a feeling of foreboding about the two of them. They seemed to have taken to each other right away. It was a heady thing for a girl like Shannon to be noticed by a man of Zan's rarefied background, especially when every girl in the district had set her cap unsuccessfully for him.

"Are you sure you're not just getting upset over nothing, Mat? He seems all right. Anyway, what would a chap like Zan want with a girl like Shannon when he's got the pick of the bunch? He's a guest here on our station and wouldn't do anything out of line. And after all, he's a gentleman," he said with a touch of sarcasm.

"Well, Bob Fremont, I never knew you were so trusting."

"Let's face it, Mattie. He's unlikely to get involved with a girl who's supposed to be part abo."

"Nonsense. Polynesian," she corrected him. "That's why he might think he can treat her differently from other girls. And anyway, what if she were part abo? She's fresh, young, and pretty, and I don't want her feelings hurt. They're all going up the hill tonight for their barbecue, and I want Charlie to have a word with Zan before then."

"They won't get into mischief. There's going to be a whole mob of them."

"Well, if you won't do it, I will. If you ask me, Shannon's become too pretty for her own good."

"For hell sakes, you act as if they've been rushing off to shack up at a hotel in Wishbone or something," he said with a laugh. "Whatever happened to her and Jimmo? She'll soon be thinking of getting a husband now she's out of school."

"That was all over in five minutes," Mattie said. "She doesn't seem to take to anyone around the station, but that's not surprising. She has a right to be fussy, I suppose, but I don't want her head filled with impossible dreams."

She searched the shimmering distance, but the two riders had disappeared.

They sped through the gateposts that marked the entrance to Koonwarra. The name was displayed in simple letters, but the long and impressive drive was sheltered by Russian olive and maple trees that wove a canopy overhead. As they rounded the bend, the house flashed into view, giving a first impression of a clean white canvas brilliantly splashed with the pink and mauve of roses and wisteria. The lines of the low, rambling house suggested its origin. Built as a simple one-story sheep station, the house had grown over the years to accommodate a large family. It had an understated aura of stylish prosperity that had solidified over the generations, and the architecture was uniquely Australian, from the pitched roof of white asbestos that created a deep veranda encircling the house to the double windows hung with shutters that were closed in summer against the dust and heat. Four generations of Fremonts had lived there, beginning with Andrew Fremont, a retired English naval officer who had come to New South Wales to take a land grant in the 1850s. He'd called his domain "Koonwarra," an aborigine word meaning "black swan," a creature of rare beauty that had impressed him when he'd first landed in

Perth. Though the station was reduced in size from what it had been in the nineteenth century, it was more prosperous than ever, for the land was fertile and the climate one of the most favorable in Australia. Summers were long and hot, and drought was a constant worry, but the winters were short, and sophisticated farm management had eased the risk from year to year.

Mattie headed for the kitchen, a spacious addition to the main house that was reached by means of a closed-in walkway. Dottie, who had helped out in the house for years, was already preparing the picnic supper the party of young people were taking up to the hills.

"You haven't been out of this kitchen since sunrise, have you?" said Mattie with a smile. Intending to help Dottie, she reached for her apron. Then, remembering something she wanted to do, she walked down the long, carpeted corridor to the huge cedar doors of the main drawing room.

Though it was a sunny day, only a dim light crept through the shutters, kept half-closed to protect the rare Persian carpet. She turned on the lights of the chandelier, remarking that several bulbs needed replacing. The heavy Victorian furniture would have to be moved back or placed in the library if they were to accommodate two hundred for the party she was planning, which would neatly combine Henry's twenty-first birthday celebration with Charlie's homecoming. There were a thousand details she had to see to in the next weeks— the music, the flowers, the food, the champagne. She hadn't yet ordered her own dress. It had been a long time since the Fremonts had entertained in such style, and every detail had to be perfect.

Closing the doors behind her, Mattie crossed the hall and gazed through the latticed windows bordering the front door. She could make out two figures on horseback, and realizing they were Zan and Shannon, she frowned. Returning to the kitchen, she saw Charlie drinking a cup of tea. Lathered with sweat, his hair tumbling on his brow, he acknowledged her with a grin.

"Just nipped in for a cuppa, Mum."

"I'm glad you did. I want to have a word with you."

Carrying his cup, he followed her into the sunny room adjacent to the kitchen that served as her office.

"There's something I want to mention about Zan, Charlie."

"What about him? Has he been pinching the silver?" her son teased.

25

"Don't be flippant. It's about him and Shannon. I'm concerned about how much time they spend together."

"She's been showing him around, that's all. What's on your mind, Mum?"

"I think you can guess."

"Oh, no, you're wrong there. Zan's not interested in Shannon. He's more or less engaged to a girl in England, anyway."

"There you are. He doesn't care a bit about her, and he might hurt her feelings."

"If you ask me, it's done Shannon a world of good to meet someone like Zan. She hangs on his every word."

"I want you to talk to him before tonight. Explain to him what the problem is. He'll understand, I'm sure."

"Didn't you ever have a kiss or a cuddle yourself?" he said with a grin.

"When I did I sought a mate from my own background. And when the time comes for you to make your choice, I hope you'll remember that."

"All right. I'll have a word with Zan," he said, patting her on the shoulder affectionately. "But you're just being an old fusser."

Long shadows streaked the plain when Zan and Shannon had raced the last half mile toward Koonwarra. He could hardly keep up with her on the bay mare that Bob had assigned to him for his months on the station. Dashing through the gates of the approach to the house, Shannon wheeled sharply, heading for the willow-fringed waterhole and bringing her horse to a halt at the edge. She leapt down with a triumphant smile as Zan followed in pursuit, ducking to avoid a low-hanging branch that barred the way.

Shannon fell on the soft grass near the edge of the pond, laughing and out of breath.

"You got the best of me there," he called.

"Too right."

"I'm going to ask Bob to change old Shirley for something with life in it." He tied the mare to a tree, then stretched out beside Shannon, who lay on her back looking thoughtfully at the cloudless sky.

"Would you be having dinner with the Queen tonight if you were home, instead of going to a bush barbecue?"

He couldn't help but laugh. "My sweet girl, not everybody has dinner with Her Majesty. In fact, very few are so fortunate."

They glanced at each other, smiling. All day Shannon had been in a fever of excitement whenever she thought about the barbecue that night. She had now fully recovered from her fall, and the bruise on her cheek had faded to a violet shadow. Knowing it was expected of her, she had jumped back on Butterscotch at the first opportunity.

"Anyway, you know perfectly well I don't have dinner with the Queen. You're just sending me up," he said in the familiar way he had fallen into within moments of meeting her.

"All right, then, what *would* you be doing?" She leaned over to trace a pattern of ripples on the water with a stick.

"I might be in Greece now it's July—or probably in Cap d'Antibes. I often spend time there in the summer with friends of mine who have a villa there."

"Cap d'Antibes," she repeated wistfully. "Where is it? What's it like there? Tell me."

"It's a little fishing port in the south of France."

There was a seductive quality about her curious smile, so different from the knowing looks of blasé debutantes he dated in London. Shannon's eagerness to know every detail of a world he had always taken for granted had immediately beguiled him, and her ingenuous innocence had begun to weave a spell that he selfishly had no wish to break. As they talked he was distracted by the downward swoop of her dark lashes, the rich abundance of her dark hair, the delicate line of her throat. The enchantment that had begun the moment he saw her was now complete.

It was a challenge to try and describe Cap d'Antibes, just as it was to tell Shannon about Ascot or the Rose Ball in London. As images sprang to his mind, he told her about ancient ramparts that guarded the village against the foaming blue sea, pastel houses piled against each other, the sweeping view of snow-covered mountains to the east. He conjured up the great sweep of the Baie des Anges, where huge yachts bobbed like toys and the aroma of succulent herbs and garlic wafted through the narrow streets—looking all the while into her dark eyes, which had seen nothing but the vast and empty landscapes of Australia, sensing that the images he spun transported her to the other side of the world.

"Oh, Zan, you make it all sound so glorious," she said, hugging herself. "When you told me about the fires blazing at Kilgarin Castle and the lights of Harrods at Christmas, I could actually see them, but when you describe France I'm

27

really there. You know, my mother was half French. Maybe that's why I have a kind of feeling that France is waiting in my future. It may sound farfetched, but I have a premonition that I'm going to live there one day. That's my dream—or at least one of them. But first I'll conquer Sydney, like I said," she remarked with a disparaging laugh. "When I've done that I'll move on to Europe."

"That's quite a chunk of the globe you've laid claim to." Shannon's thirst for experience made all her dreams seem possible, but he couldn't help wondering uneasily what would ultimately happen to her. She was a desert flower blooming in this harsh landscape.

"I know what you're thinking," she said, drawing herself up defiantly. "You're thinking I'll never get out of here, that I'm stuck in the Outback, but you're wrong, you know."

He had in fact at that moment been fantasizing about the lines of her body beneath the corduroy and flannel. Taken by surprise, he searched for words that would encourage rather than disillusion her. "You know, the streets of Sydney and London aren't paved with gold. Earl's Court is filled with Australian girls working as waitresses, trying to make ends meet. It's a pretty rough life sometimes."

"That may be, but I'm different from all of them, and I know I don't belong here," she said impatiently.

The tremor of her voice revealed only a fraction of her fierce determination. She had confided some of her most private thoughts to Zan, and gradually she was beginning to sense that her most improbable dreams were his realities.

"You're lucky to know what you want. That's something," he mused.

"Am I? *You* have everything you want, don't you?"

"It might seem so, but I'm only the custodian of a title that happens to have a castle to go with it. It's a hell of a responsibility."

"Oh, come on, what a ridiculous thing to say. You're just trying to get sympathy," she said indignantly.

"Well, it's true. That's how I see it."

She smiled and shook her head incredulously. Zan's arrival had quickened her thirst for beauty, for experience, for life itself. All her life she had suffered from a hunger for every mundane thing that most people took for granted, including a decent pair of shoes—and her hunger, born of intense deprivation, was something Zan could never understand.

"Tell me about your family," she said. "You've never mentioned if you have any brothers and sisters."

"I'd much rather you told me what you imagine my family is like."

She paused. "All right. I think you have lots of brothers and sisters. You all live in the castle, and there are dogs and horses everywhere. You all play croquet on the lawn in summer—it's always summer in my imagination—and the butler serves tea at four under a huge chestnut tree. I can just see the table set with damask and silver and china. When you were little your sisters played with pretty dolls, and every afternoon you and your brothers played toy soldiers in a tower of the castle. And your mother, your beautiful mother, came to say good night to you when you were tucked up in bed. She always wears splendid ball gowns and smells wonderfully of lavender. I know exactly how your father looks, too. He's tall, and has a huge handlebar mustache, and he has kind eyes like yours. When you were little, he came to say good night wearing all his medals, and told you stories about your ancestors."

When she had finished he said laughingly. "Good Lord, what an imagination you have! Where did you get all those ideas?"

"From books or movies, mostly."

"You're priceless—but you couldn't be farther from the truth. My father is a total eccentric—a bit gaga, and wanders around an unheated castle. So much for that myth. He lost a leg during the war and has to be strapped to his horse when hunting. He didn't meet my mother until he was nearly fifty. She was what they used to call a Society Beauty, and she didn't stick around long. I haven't seen her for six years—not since she last invited me to tea at the Ritz. She's on her fourth husband—an impoverished Italian count—and they live in a derelict villa in Tuscany somewhat like Kilgarin." he said wryly. "So, you see, there was no tea on the lawn, no croquet, not even any brothers and sisters. I was alone with my nanny most of the time until I was sent to boarding school at five, where one was beaten for bad handwriting. Life was certainly no bed of roses, and certainly nothing like your storybooks. In fact, I think you and I might have more in common than you'd imagine."

Spoken without a trace of bitterness, Zan's frank description of his family life took Shannon completely by surprise.

He suddenly seemed touchingly vulnerable, and for a moment she hardly knew what to say.

"You're right, we do have a lot in common," she said quietly, moved to disclose facts about her past that she had never shared with anyone. "I never knew my mother, either. She died when I was a baby. Dad won't talk about her, and all I know is what Uncle Jack told me. She was half Polynesian. Her father was French and her mother from New Caledonia."

"Why did your father name you Shannon?"

"Oh, that's typical of Dad. You'd never know it, but somewhere in him there's a strong attachment to Ireland. He says that the Faloons owned a castle somewhere called Shannon." She gestured airily. "Underneath, he's a bit of a romantic. He used to tell me and Kerry the most fantastic stories, but now that I'm older I realize he's got a touch of the blarney in him."

"It could be true, Shannon. There is a castle by that name not far from Kilgarin. It's in ruins, but it's a beautiful old place."

Considering this unexpected possibility, Shannon's eyes widened in surprise.

"If you come to Europe, I'll take you there."

"*When* I come to Europe. Not if," she corrected him.

Zan smiled and drew her to him. She was unprepared for the devastating effect of his lips pressing hers in a kiss as tender as it was passionate. Her heart hammered wildly against her chest, and when he released her she experienced the exquisite sensation of infinite power yet helplessness as she lay weightlessly in his arms.

"Beautiful Shannon," he murmured. "Now I know why Gauguin went to Polynesia and never came back."

Zan was closing the gate of the paddock when he saw Charlie sauntering toward him.

"Have a good ride? Where's Shannon?"

"Fine, thanks. She went home. We rode as far as the river today. It's overflowing its banks, so we came back."

As they headed toward the woolshed, Charlie began with an air of apologetic boredom, "Listen, you can tell me to belt up if you think it's none of my business, but Mum has been on my back about you and Shannon."

"What do you mean?" Zan asked.

"I know it's absurd, but Mum thinks Shannon might

30

have a crush on you, and I suppose she's afraid she'll get hurt or something. Just thought I'd mention it. Mum's awfully fond of the Faloon girls, but she's a bit overprotective. I told her not to fuss and that Shannon's not your type."

"I didn't know I had a type," said Zan with a laugh.

"Sure you do. It's the same as mine, isn't it?" At Oxford and at house parties in Gloucestershire they had competed good-naturedly for the same girls, fair English roses with the same background as themselves.

"I'll take heed to sit on the other side of the bonfire tonight, in that case," said Zan flippantly. If Mattie was protecting the Faloon girls like prize lambs, he would have no choice but to curtail his friendship with Shannon. Even as he gave his assurance to Charlie, however, his heart stirred uneasily.

That night after sundown everyone, including a number of young people who had come over by car from a neighboring station, congregated on horseback near the stables. Waiting to follow was a pony hitched to a wagon loaded with food. Astride Butterscotch, Shannon watched the activity with a sense of mounting anticipation. There was a full moon, and it was far too late for frost now, though the night air had a sharp tang. She heard the laughing call of a kookaburra in the distance. Filling the open space with chat and laughter, they cantered into the darkness in twos and threes on the trail to the favorite picnic spot at the base of the scrub-covered hills, passing through glades of whispering jarrah trees that perfumed the night. Shannon wasn't far from Zan, who rode next to Charlie. Earlier in the evening he had chatted for a moment with her, setting spark to what seemed a pile of dry tinder inside her, and now, lulled by a promise of perfect first love, she enjoyed a blissful sense of calm interrupted by the burning memory of their first kiss that afternoon. For the first time in her life, she wasn't hoping for the days to rush by. Rather, she was savoring every delicious minute leading to the time when they would be alone again.

Above the picnic clearing, far from Koonwarra, the Southern Cross sparkled with the same primeval clarity that had charted the wandering of the aborigines and had acted as signposts for generations of stockmen. The gentle hum of yellow mondays was drowned out by laughter as everyone hurried to dismount.

While the boys got the fire blazing, the girls waited with

31

big pans of damper that Dottie had made, and they put the billy on for tea. Charlie and Zan were in charge of the steaks and chops, and now and then Shannon caught Zan regarding her from the other side of the fire as she helped cook the bread. Her face flushed from the heat, she paused now and then to brush back a tendril of hair from her forehead. Neither noticed Kerry observing Zan curiously as he studied her sister.

The aroma of eucalyptus leaves thrown on the fire, mingled with the tang of sizzling meat, filled the air as everyone heaped their plates. Shannon moved to a log at the edge of the fire and waited for Zan to join her.

He never came. Unable to comprehend what was happening, Shannon sat with her untouched plate on her knees. At Charlie's side, Zan ate and drank beer with relish, not once looking in her direction. Shannon sipped her tea distractedly. Normally she found it the most delicious brew on earth, but now it was tasteless.

As the evening waned, Shannon was forced to behold the picture of Zan, his face flushed with enjoyment in the firelight. He had dropped her as quickly as he had swept her up. The singing around the fire became intolerable, and by the time they began clearing up the rubbish from the party, she was trembling with confusion and wounded pride. When Zan finally approached her as they were loading the cart, she reacted coolly, not bothering to acknowledge him at first. Though her heart was pounding, she was determined not to let him see the hurt in her eyes.

"This was the best picnic I've ever had," he commented, searching for something to say. When she didn't reply he added lamely, "The stars are so bright out here, aren't they?"

"It's not surprising, is it? After all, the Outback is the middle of nowhere," she replied tartly. Turning on her heel, she headed for her horse.

Later, numbly brushing her hair, Shannon only half heard Kerry's excited prattle. She was perilously close to tears, which she was too proud to let fall in front of her younger sister.

"Why were you ignoring Zan tonight?" asked Kerry provocatively as she bounced into bed. Hands clasped 'round her knees, she stared directly at Shannon with pretended innocence.

"Was I? I didn't mean to," she said, turning to fold her jeans with exaggerated care.

"I thought you were really rude to him. I don't know how you could be so mean. I know I couldn't," she said with a sigh.

"I've come to the conclusion he's a bit shallow, if you want to know the truth."

"Shallow?" Kerry fell back with a peal of laughter. "Who are you trying to fool? That's not what you said yesterday. Then it was 'Zan this, Zan that.' Personally, I think he's the most interesting, best-looking chap I've ever met. He's ten times handsomer than Charlie or Henry or James or anybody."

"He's all right in small doses," Shannon replied in a tight, impatient little voice. "I finally discovered he's very stuck-up. Like I thought he'd be before he came. People aren't always what they seem at first," she said with an air of adult wisdom she scarcely felt.

"All I can say is, if you don't want him, I'll take him any day. *I* think he's a dreamboat."

"Aren't you a bit young to be thinking along those lines?"

Kerry leapt out of bed and began to sweep dramatically in front of her. "My dear," she began with an exaggerated English accent, "I may have the mind of a child, but I have the body of a woman."

Shannon ignored this remark, which normally would have sent her into peals of laughter.

The two of them had always had their differences. It had been a test of wills from the time Kerry was in her cradle and wouldn't stop crying until Shannon picked her up. She had started to give in to her early on, finding it much easier to capitulate than to resist, having had no idea how to care for a baby. The difficult child had grown into a willful teenager whose challenging smile sometimes seemed to dare Shannon to love her. Shannon's reaction was to retreat into her own inner space, a move that infuriated Kerry; but their lifetime of shared hardships bound them together in a united front that outsiders could never penetrate—until now.

"If you ask me, he gave you the brush-off," said Kerry cruelly, hurt that Shannon hadn't laughed at her joke.

Shannon spun 'round and faced her sister furiously. The careless remark had slashed through her façade, exposing the pain underneath. "Why, you little bitch!"

Kerry pretended not to hear. "I didn't want to mention it, but he was giving me the glad eye across the campfire."

33

"Good night," said Shannon tersely, turning off the light.

Even after Kerry fell asleep, she lay wide awake, still burning with anger. It was the first time Shannon could remember anyone coming between them. Kerry, her ally, had abandoned her when she was most vulnerable, leaving her to cope with an intolerable new emptiness.

On Sunday morning Shannon was setting out the cups for breakfast when the unshaven Brendan stumbled into the kitchen, followed by Kerry, who slid into a chair and hurriedly began spooning sugar into her oatmeal.

"Tea ready?" muttered Brendan without looking at the girls.

"In a minute," Shannon replied curtly. She was accustomed to his abrupt conversation in the morning, but she hadn't been sleeping well the past three weeks, and was out of sorts lately. Her eyes were circled by shadows, and she felt—and looked—tired.

"More milk, Shan," chirped Kerry, emptying the pitcher.

"Get it yourself," she retorted.

The sisters exchanged a hostile look, which Brendan ignored as he slurped his tea. The kitchen was barely large enough to accommodate the table and chairs, and this morning Shannon felt acutely claustrophobic. The smell of mutton chops and eggs frying in the pan physically revolted her as she went about her tasks like an automaton.

Since the barbecue she had taken every opportunity to escape from Koonwarra on her horse, going up into the hills as soon as she finished tidying up the house. Most of the time she spent thinking, propped up against a tree. It had begun to dawn on her that her life was drifting by aimlessly, and she had come to the conclusion that Zan's arrival had caused her to shelve all her dreams and plans about going to Sydney, as if they had never existed. Quietly she had resolved to put her pocket money away from then on, to achieve her dreams, which had somehow become tarnished from exposure to ridicule. She wished with all her heart that Zan's holiday were over, but it wasn't simple to stick to her resolve. Every time she saw him from a distance, the very ground she walked on seemed to slip from beneath her. The one thing that kept her at Koonwarra was Henry's twenty-first birthday party. Not because she didn't want to let him down, or Mattie or Bob. But it was one last thing she had to do to satisfy her own pride. Munching an apple as her mind wandered away from

34

War and Peace, Shannon had entertained herself with the fantasy of making a triumphant entrance into the big sitting room at Koonwarra under the blazing chandelier just as the orchestra struck up "Some Enchanted Evening."

"What's eating you, Shannon?" asked Brendan as she absently set his breakfast before him. "You haven't been yourself for a week."

Kerry smiled knowingly as she stirred her tea. "Shannon wants to be a lady with a capital 'L.' Didn't you know she was in love?"

"Shut up, Kerry," cried Shannon, tossing the dishcloth on the table, then rushing from the kitchen.

A black look from Brendan was enough to silence Kerry. His eyes, dark with reproach, fixed her to the spot as he shoved back his chair.

"I was only joking," she called after him.

Brendan found Shannon on the screened porch, struggling to fight back tears.

"What is it, girlie?" he asked helplessly. "What's troubling you?" He pulled up a chair opposite her and waited for her to look at him.

It was a moment before she could bring herself to speak. Leaning forward into a shaft of warm sunshine, Brendan reached out with a broad rough hand and patted her on the knee.

"It's nothing—it's just that now school is out, my life seems so pointless," she said tearfully.

"What's all this about you wanting to be a lady?"

"Nothing. It's nothing, Dad." She shook her head.

"That young Lord Muck hasn't been trying to fool around with you, has he?" His blood began to boil at the thought.

She hastened to deny it. "Oh, no, Dad. Nothing like that."

"Then what's all this about you being in love?"

Shannon lifted her eyes. There was a terrible rage written on her father's face, but there was also a sympathy that showed itself all too seldom. The depth of Brendan's blue eyes in his weather-beaten face offered a rare compassion, and Shannon became poignantly aware for the first time that he must have experienced the same painful emotions as herself. At that moment father and daughter seemed to understand each other as never before. Close to confiding in him about Zan, something held her back. She wanted to tell him every-

35

thing, let out all the pain inside her, but she was aware of his hatred for the upper classes. Moreover, years of self-reliance made it all but impossible now to unlock the suffering that was exclusively hers.

"Kerry's just a tease. What I'm feeling has nothing to do with Zan Fitzherbert, believe me."

Unconvinced, he replied, "Well, I hope not, because if I catch that stuck-up pommie within ten feet of you, I'll kill him with my bare hands."

The very thought of Brendan confronting Zan struck terror inside her. She would never live down the humiliation. Brendan's temper was as unpredictable as lightning in a storm, and there was no telling how far he would go.

"I'm just feeling depressed about Henry's twenty-first, to be truthful. I haven't a thing to wear, and all the other girls will be dressed to the nines."

He gave a little laugh. "If that's all it is, I don't know why you didn't tell me. Go into Wishbone. Buy yourself something pretty to wear."

"There's nothing in Wishbone," she protested.

"Send away for something, then. Get Mattie to help you. Whatever it costs, I'll pay for it. There now," he said, rising, "shoes, too. Get what you want."

"Are you sure?" she asked hesitantly. "It might cost a lot of money."

"Don't you worry about that. This is a special occasion. And anyway, our luck's about to change. I feel it in my blood. We Faloons are going to be back in the velvet, where we belong."

Kerry, who had heard every word as she hovered at the screen, interjected, "What about me, Dad? Can I have a new dress, too?"

"You've caused enough trouble for one day, girlie. And anyway, you're much too young." With that he dismissed her, then strode from the house, tipping his felt hat against the sun.

"I'm going for a walk," said Shannon when he had gone. "It's your turn to do the dishes," she called to Kerry.

"It's not fair," Kerry shouted after the disappearing figures of Brendan and Shannon. "It's not bloody fair!"

Later that morning Shannon walked up to the big house. Leaping over the puddles like mirrors scattered on the path,

36

she crisscrossed to the edge of the path to keep her boots dry, but her mind was filled with ideas of the dress she would buy for Henry's twenty-first. Approaching the big white house hugged by dark cedars, she looked back. A deep blue haze on the horizon meant that another storm was fast approaching, which was confirmed by an indefinable stillness in the air. She opened the kitchen door, and the delicious aroma of steak and kidney pie wafted out.

"Are you coming for lunch?" asked Mattie. "I'll set another place."

"No thanks, Mattie. I just wanted to ask you something."

The excitement in her voice made Mattie take notice. "Just go in my office. I'll be there in a jiff."

Shannon went in and sat on a button-back chair by the fireplace, her eyes roaming to the tempting pile of catalogs Mattie kept on the shelf.

Mattie's office was Shannon's favorite room. It was as important to Koonwarra as an engine room to a ship. From there Mattie managed all the details that made life run smoothly on the station. There was a breezy femininity about the carved pine desk piled with papers next to swatches of cloth and a vase of dried flowers. The framed prints of Victorian ladies contrasted with a chipped metal filing cabinet, and the worn chairs were a reminder that this was a working room and not a frivolous retreat.

When Mattie came in, Shannon said, "I've come to ask your advice about a dress for Henry's twenty-first. Dad said I could order whatever I wanted."

"How nice! Here, you can start with these," she said, handing Shannon a pile of catalogs. Mattie watched her, pleased to see her so happy about the party. There were a dozen young men coming from Wishbone and other stations, and the girl would have her choice.

When Mattie returned in a few moments, Shannon was triumphant. "I've found it. This is the one." She pointed to the dress she would wear to her private debut, her coming out, announcing she was no longer a girl from the Outback, but a woman with a taste for sophistication.

"Isn't it a bit daring?" Mattie asked gently when she saw the strapless black bodice and flaring coral skirt.

"No, I've made up my mind," she said adamantly.

"Well, if you're sure, fill out the order form. There's no doubt that you'll be danced off your feet in that frock. And now that's decided, what about lunch? The men will be here any minute."

"Thanks, but I'd better get back," Shannon said evasively.

"You're too late. It's going to pour buckets any minute," said Mattie, glancing out the window.

Absorbed in the catalogs, Shannon had failed to notice that the approaching storm had overtaken the last remnants of sun in a mantle of darkness. There was a flash of lightning, followed by a roar of thunder that shook the house.

There was nothing she could do but put on an apron and help Mattie and John, the aborigine houseboy, as she nervously thought about confronting Zan.

Bearing a steaming bowl of potatoes, she walked into the dining room and placed the dish in the center of the table—a massive mahogany antique, covered now with an oilcloth, that could accommodate up to twenty. As soon as the succulent steak and kidney pies had been laid on the table, the men began filing in, stamping their boots outside. Lean and sinewy to a man, their faces were etched with a distinct line where they pulled down their felt hats. Shannon knew everyone well, but expecting Zan to appear at any moment, she suddenly felt as ill at ease as she had on her first day at Koonwarra three years before.

The dining room was in such contrast to the way the Faloons lived at home that she could never quite get accustomed to it. The Fremonts used old willow pattern china and silver every day, luxuries that were a natural part of their existence. Shannon had often wondered what it would be like to live in such style. Her eyes wandered to the silver candlesticks on the sideboard and the painting of horses and hounds above it, but without her usual admiration of these elegant details. Her mind was on the empty seats opposite her, waiting to be filled.

When Zan and Charlie trooped in, they were both laughing. They had been caught in the rain, and now they slicked back their wet hair and rolled up their shirt-sleeves.

"You can't come in like that. You're soaking," said Mattie.

"It's all right, Mum. We've got to get back soon. Zan can't wait to shear another sheep, can you, Zan? He's really got the knack."

As he pulled up a chair opposite her, Shannon caught a glimpse of Zan, then looked away, her heart pounding.

"Hello, Shannon. What a nice surprise to see you here."

Zan helped himself to a large portion of pie. "I've worked up the appetite of a wolf this morning."

"How did it go?" asked Mattie.

"I managed to shear about a quarter of one sheep. The rest of the time I was trying to hold it down. It isn't as easy as it looks."

There was laughter around the table, followed by the amused comments of the men who had watched Zan struggling with a three-hundred-pound merino that had no intention of letting herself be sheared.

Shannon couldn't resist laughing, though she avoided Zan's eyes. The conversation revolved around the day's shearing, and when he spoke she found Zan's voice painful to bear, making her wonder if she had fallen for the sound of his voice before she'd even seen him. She hadn't seen him close up since the barbecue, and now that her chance came to observe him unawares, she was surprised to find the weeks of hard work on the station had hardened the lines of his body and given new definition to his face. The sun had bleached his hair, which at the moment was attractively tousled. A suntan suited him, she decided. It was not the cultivated bronze of a young man who had idled the summer away on the Riviera, but of someone who worked for his living.

"A penny for your thoughts?" he said when he caught her studying him.

"I was thinking that you're beginning to look like an Australian," she said, meeting his eyes frankly.

"We'll make an Aussie out of him yet," Charlie remarked.

"Too right," said Zan, laughing at the suggestion. "Both the sheep and I were lucky to get out of there alive this morning."

"It's the funniest thing you've ever seen, Shannon—Zan trying to grip a sheep with one hand and balance himself with the other."

"I must admit I thought it looked dead easy until I tried it."

"Come to the shed with us after lunch," said Charlie.

"Some other time," she replied evasively.

"Oh, come on and see me make a fool of myself," urged Zan.

When Shannon saw Zan's mischievous smile, she said, "All right. I'll come for a minute."

As the men began rising from the table, Mattie said,

39

"You go on. We'll clear up." Shannon found herself trooping to the woolshed like a reluctant pony balking at a fence.

The storm had cleared as rapidly as it had come, leaving sparkling puddles all over the yard, and the sky was a freshly washed blue. The strong aroma of wool and sheep hit Shannon's nostrils, and as they approached, the cacophony of the penned animals filled the air.

"I saw your father shearing yesterday. I was fascinated how good he was. Bob tells me he was a gun shearer in his heyday. What an amazing chap he is."

Shannon turned sharply, feeling a fierce pride well up inside. Brendan Faloon had never given Zan Fitzherbert the time of day, and the young man's generous compliment could only be interpreted as a patronizing insult.

"That's right. There's nothing on this station or any other that my father can't do, and that's more than a lot of people can say."

"Well, excuse me for speaking," he said sarcastically, then marched off in another direction, burning with indignation.

Shannon stared after him. Who the hell did Zan Fitzherbert think he was? Her father was right: he was just another arrogant Lord Muck after all.

Seeing Charlie motioning to her, Shannon felt condemned for a few moments at least to watch the shearing, and she entered the woolshed, a nightmare of heat, dust, and flies. She passed the stalls, where the shearers were already warming up for the afternoon's work. A few already had sheep in a stranglehold and were peeling off the pure white wool from their bellies, leaving trails of pink skin as smooth as a baby's.

Charlie and Zan had removed their shirts, but, angered, Shannon felt unmoved by her first sight of his muscular arms and torso. Charlie dragged a bleating sheep up from the pen, and Zan grasped it beneath the forelegs as the animal stared up at him stupidly. He seemed to be coming to grips with the sheep when he lost his balance and fell backward, so that Charlie had to come hurriedly to his rescue.

He lay there stunned for a moment, a bemused grin on his face. Zan had never looked as appealing as he did now, sprawled on the boards of the woolshed. He was such a ridiculous sight that Shannon couldn't help but burst into laughter.

"Go on, laugh," he said, pointing a finger at her in amusement. "And that goes for you, too, Charlie boy."

Shannon left the woolshed aware that somehow the rift between them had healed. With her she carried the indelible image of his strong bare arms.

Chapter II

Adjusting her black velvet riding hat—a Christmas present from the Fremonts the year before—Kerry tilted her head down in front of the mirror, then picked up her crop and struck a pose. For an instant she became the heroine of every horse story she had ever read, from *My Friend Flicka* to *Misty*. A corner of the bedroom she shared with Shannon had become her private shrine, decorated with pictures of various breeds of horses and the rosettes she had garnered at local meets. Whereas Shannon's most precious possessions were a bone mirror and a porcelain box on the dressing table she had made her own, Kerry prized a photograph of the Australian equestrian gold medallist at the Rome Olympics. Shannon's favorite photograph—of the famous cover girl Jean Shrimpton in a ballgown at Versailles—was a striking reminder that the two sisters couldn't have been more different.

Regarding her worn cord trousers and faded shirt with dissatisfaction, Kerry fantasized that she was wearing instead a proper English hacking jacket and cream bisque jodhpurs. This was the riding ensemble she dreamed of owning, described to her by Uncle Jack, who used to entertain her with stories of the Castletown Hunt and tales of the past when the Faloons had ridden to hounds. But no riding outfit was complete without exquisitely made riding boots, their polish so high she might be able to see her own reflection. Looking down at her scuffed cowboy boots, Kerry reminded herself she would soon have such a pair of boots, and made in England, too. She might even have them in time for the next picnic race meet in Wishbone.

Dashing from the house, Kerry broke into a run. Bob Fremont had lent her a corner of the home paddock to take Splendor through his paces during the summer, and she was determined not to waste a minute. She went to the tack room and hoisted the saddle and reins over her shoulder, then walked to the field where Splendor was grazing. She readied the horse in a flash and could have done it blindfolded.

"Hey, there, my beauty," she crooned as he nuzzled impatiently at her face. "You're even more anxious to get out there than I am, aren't you, gorgeous?"

Splendor was her first real triumph. He was a powerful horse—one-quarter Arab—and Kerry had taken him on not long after he'd been broken in. Determinedly she'd won the battle of wills with this beautiful animal, just the way her Uncle Jack had taught her, thus earning the respect of the boys at Koonwarra. She and Henry and Jamie had made a formidable trio at the local meets, she in dressage and jumping, they in flat racing.

With one graceful leap she mounted, then cantered toward the home paddock, a fenced area that was nearly a hundred acres. When Kerry gave Splendor his head, he made for the distant corner where she had set up a series of rusty old drums to practice her jumps. She took him through his paces until late morning, pausing now and then for a rest. Occasionally her perfect concentration would break, and her eyes would stray to the blue hills in the distance. A slight twitch of Splendor's ears alerted her that someone was approaching, and she glanced up to see Zan galloping toward her.

"Don't let me stop you," he called. "Carry on."

She smiled happily. In all the weeks he had been there, he never seemed to find time to watch her jump, though whenever she caught him alone she plagued him with questions about hunting and racing in Ireland. Her hero worship for Zan knew no bounds when she discovered he had done eventing in Ireland, and she was always hungry for more details.

Kerry took the first jumps effortlessly and was in the process of repeating the course when Zan motioned to her.

"How was I? What do you think?" she said, cantering up to him. The cocksure tomboy had disappeared, and in her place was an ambitious, talented young rider.

"Not bad at all," he remarked, impressed in spite of himself. "Your hands were a bit high, though."

"That's always been my problem. Uncle Jack used to remind me all the time. It's maddening."

"Well, let's work on it and a couple of other pointers."

After she had concentrated on his suggestions, Kerry

42

returned, exhilarated, to where Zan was leaning against the fence.

"He could clear at least five feet if I let him," she said, patting her horse.

"I don't doubt it," said Zan, amused by her brash, competitive spirit. "Where did you learn to jump like that?"

"Uncle Jack taught me everything I know. He put me on an orange crate when I was six to practice my first jumps. He said right away that I looked like I was born on a horse."

"You must be very fond of your uncle," he remarked when she had finished.

"Oh, I am. He knows everything there is to know about breaking and training horses, and there's nothing you can teach him about jumping or eventing or even hunting. We used to dream about going to the horse trials in Melbourne and Victoria."

"And where, may I ask, has this paragon of knowledge on horseflesh gone?" he couldn't resist teasing. Surely Jack was too good to be true.

When she told him, he said, "Pity he had to leave." Zan knew exactly what kind of man Jack was from her description. Ireland was full of this type of character. Almost raised on mare's milk, adaptable, hardworking, and sure of themselves, they had a sixth sense about horses essential to the breeding of highly strung thoroughbreds. Zan could imagine such a man wouldn't be content breaking mustangs in the Outback, or even breeding horses here. He must have taken pleasure in tutoring Kerry in the finer points of dressage and show jumping, but her ambitions had all the poignant hopelessness of a Scottish crofter heading for the bright lights of Mayfair.

"Well, Splendor seems like a good all-round horse. I don't see why you shouldn't win another rosette at Wishbone—and I'll help you," he added.

"Will you really?" she said breathlessly.

"We might fit in an hour tomorrow morning."

"Thanks a lot, Zan," she gushed.

They cantered off home and stopped at a gate, which Zan opened. When he turned to let Kerry pass he gazed up, and there was a moment of mutual appraisal between them. Kerry's glance was distinctly provocative, and as he met her gaze he privately registered surprise. As her hair passed before him like a coppery blaze of fire, Zan remounted and followed her.

Nearing the station, they rode side by side. "Isn't that Shannon?" he said when he saw a lone figure in the distance.

"It might be," said Kerry flatly, annoyed by the look of interest in his face. "I'll race you back," she said to distract him.

"Better not. You'll tire Splendor out, and we want him to be fresh for tomorrow, don't we? Meet you at the same time," he called over his shoulder, cantering off.

Sick with jealousy, Kerry stared after him.

Zan galloped up to Shannon, who was already disappearing into a glade of grass. "Where are you going?"

"To the shepherd's hut," she said, turning with surprise. "Mattie asked me to collect the pots of honey Bluey gathered yesterday. There were so many he couldn't bring them all down." Her voice was guarded, revealing none of her pleasure and excitement at seeing him.

"Who's Bluey?" he asked by way of conversation as he followed alongside her.

"He lives up at Bramble Cottage. You couldn't miss him. His hair is even redder than Kerry's."

"Ah, yes, Australian logic," he said with an amused smile. "I'll come with you."

"Right on. You can help me carry them."

The trail between the trees was just wide enough for two horses. New grass so brilliantly green that it almost hurt the eyes still covered the open spaces, giving the landscape a false lushness that wouldn't last.

"It won't be long now before you're on your way to Sydney and then heading for home," she remarked.

"You know, I can't help thinking that I'd enjoy what time is left if a certain person were a little friendlier."

"Oh? Who would that be?"

"She's a girl with an enigmatic smile who has intrigued me since the day she fell off her horse."

Her reply was an embarrassed laugh, and he knew he had won a point. Regarding the enticing picture Shannon made on her horse, all Zan's desire suddenly came alive after these weeks of abstinence in the Outback. He longed to know the scent of a woman's perfume and feel her soft, giving body in his arms. He suddenly wanted it enough to ignore the puritanical line Mattie had drawn between him and Shannon. Absence had only served to augment the force of attraction that still flowed between them, now making her well-nigh irresistible.

44

They tied up the horses and walked toward the wooden hut sheltered in the trees.

"The hives are farther up, in a grove of acacias. You can't see them from here." She mounted the steps to the hut, while he waited outside. "Here, you take the pots and put them in the bag, and I'll hand them to you. They're sticky, but we can wash up in the stream afterward." To hide her discomfort, she said, "Acacia honey is supposed to be one of the most fragrant in the world." Her hands touched his as she handed him pot after pot, but she refused to meet his eyes. When the last pot had changed hands, she waited for him to step aside.

"May I taste it?"

"If you like," she murmured, pausing on the step above. He dipped his finger in the pot, then touched it to her lips.

They stared at each other for a long moment. From the brim of a shadow where they stood came the harping of yellow mondays and the twittering of birds. Then all sounds gave way to the pounding of Shannon's own heart when Zan pulled her down and kissed her, gently at first, then hungrily, as the sweet taste of honey dissolved in their mouths. The brilliance of the day was darkened by an abyss of passion that left Shannon gasping. Her every nerve was flayed to life as Zan's strong hands played across her back with passionate gentleness.

"Oh, Shannon, my darling," he murmured.

She craved the power of his lean body as he pressed urgently against her. Falling back in his arms, she reached up to touch his hair, something she had longed to do from the moment she'd first seen him. Her fingers rekindled the fire, and he swept her into his arms for another passionate kiss, then another. He gazed at her in amazement, held captive by her exotic beauty as well as her gentleness.

They left the clearing in shaken silence, aware their worlds had changed. As they galloped toward home there was a new danger in the scented air that made Shannon profoundly quiet; but whenever their eyes met, a tremor of desire passed from one to the other.

"I should have been back before now," she worried as they neared Koonwarra, touching her hand to her tousled hair and burning cheeks. Her voice was breathless and hurried.

"When can we see each other?" he said urgently.

"I don't know. It's going to be difficult. I must go," she said, then reluctantly turned away with a brief wave.

45

He watched her until she disappeared. The sun was now high overhead, and everyone would still be at lunch. Luck was with them.

When Shannon rushed into the kitchen Mattie whirled around with an exasperated look on her face. "Where on earth have you been? I thought you'd be back ages ago so we could glaze these hams. I could have done it while Dottie was clearing up lunch if only you'd come back when you said you would." Mattie broke off scolding, her lips pursed in anger.

"I'm sorry, Mattie," she mumbled, quickly setting the jars on the table but taking care not to meet her eyes. When she glanced up she saw John's black eyes boring into her, and for an instant her cheeks colored guiltily as she imagined he must be reading her mind. The image of Zan was still etched so clearly before her that she thought it must be plain to others. She brushed her hair from her forehead and looked around in a daze, wondering what to do.

"Come on, now. No time to dawdle," scolded Mattie. "While I get the glaze ready, you can help Dottie put the sheets out on the beds. Then we can make them up tomorrow morning early. That's one thing out of the way."

Mattie paused reflectively as she went over the hundreds of details for Saturday's party. Wednesday had crept up quickly, and there was still a great deal to be done in addition to the normal routine of the station. She could have used a dozen extra pairs of hands that morning. Seeing Shannon's flushed face and dreamy-eyed expression, she decided she would never have had the patience to cope with daughters.

"By the way, your dress arrived," she called, and when Shannon turned with an excited smile added, "It's in my office. You can see it later. When you've finished upstairs, go and find Kerry. We can use her to cut out the vol-au-vents."

A while later Shannon went to Mattie's office to collect her package, then dashed out the kitchen door, taking a detour to the stables. Seeing Kerry's horse in the paddock, she called out to the Fremont boys nearby.

"Have you seen Kerry?"

"I think she hitched a ride into Wishbone with one of the hands about an hour ago," Henry replied.

"She did?"

Whatever Kerry could be doing in Wishbone on a Wednesday afternoon was a mystery, and Mattie would be livid when she found out. Shannon headed home and made straight for the bedroom, where she impatiently ripped the

46

box open and flung back the tissue paper to see the dress she had been dreaming about for so long. Shaking it out, she held it up to herself before the mirror. In the catalog the airy coral skirt had floated like a cloud, and the sculptured bodice had seemed the last word in elegance. The reality was somewhat different. The limp skirt looked like nylon rather than silk, and the bodice had a cheap sheen. She was so disappointed she couldn't bear it. The black patent shoes seemed all right, but they couldn't make up for the dress. She folded the frock back in the box and shoved it under the bed out of sight. Normally she would have despaired, but this afternoon she was quickly diverted by far more important things. In a state of euphoria she fell back on the bed. What was happening to her? she wondered. Her whole life seemed to have changed since that morning. Suddenly remembering Zan's description of her smile as "enigmatic," she leapt up and looked for the word in the dictionary. "Difficult to understand and mysterious," it said. This definition of herself amazed her. To be thought difficult to understand and mysterious was the highest accolade Zan could pay her, for it indicated that she must be as different from other girls as she had always felt. Strangely, too, this was exactly how she felt about him. She drifted around the room, hugging herself as she relived every wonderful detail of the afternoon. Pressing her fingers to her lips, she tried to recapture the explosive sensation of Zan's mouth pressing on her own.

"My darling," she whispered. "He called me 'my darling.' " She laughed at how absurd her own voice sounded as she repeated the words he had murmured. This could only mean that Zan loved her.

She seemed to have been waiting all her life to be discovered, to be understood. Her shyness with men had always come about because the man concerned hadn't been right. When thoughts about the future darted into her mind to destroy her elation, she pushed them away. "Lady Shannon Fitzherbert," she found herself whispering, but realized that this grand title had nothing to do with what had happened between them. A shepherd's hut was as far from the turrets of a castle as could be imagined, and for the first time she wished desperately that Zan wasn't a lord. A terrible thought intruded on her happiness, one that had hovered at the back of her mind all these wasted weeks they had been apart. She recalled Brendan's bitter, twisted expression whenever he mentioned Zan, and she was now sure her own father must have been the one who had warned Zan away from her. His vicious parodies of Zan's accent, his biting criticism of his visit on the station were all the proof she needed. She knew Brendan would stop at nothing to keep them apart.

When the Land Rover pulled up in front of the savings and loan in Wishbone, Kerry jumped from the backseat the moment the wheels touched the curb.

"You be back here in forty-five minutes, do you hear?" the driver called after her as she vanished.

She rushed headlong down the pavement, basking in the heady sensation of being in a metropolis, pretending that she was just passing through Wishbone on her way to Sydney. Stockmen with narrowed eyes and sun-creased faces studied the goods in shop windows, and their wives, easily identified by their weathered brown arms and shapeless clothing, indulged themselves in window-shopping. A good chunk of her boot money burning a hole in her pocket, Kerry felt a sense of superiority that she was actually out on a shopping spree. A crowd of aborigine shearers leaned against the frosted windows of the Horse and Boots, where Kerry caught the cool, beery air of the pub and heard gales of hearty laughter as she passed. She knew this was one of Brendan's favorite watering holes—that and the betting shop nearby. Heading purposefully for her destination, she ignored the stares of men collected near the granite war memorial. Their shirtsleeves rolled up, their hats pulled down, they passed the time by sizing up the women. Arriving at the corner of Prince and Cooper, she looked up at the fussy logo that spelled out "June's Modes," the best dress shop in Wishbone. Kerry plunged in, and when a saleswoman heard the bell tinkle she came to the counter.

"May I help you?"

"Yes—I'm looking for an evening dress," Kerry announced breezily.

The woman looked her over. "This way, please."

She was shown to a rack where a hodgepodge of dresses hung limply. The first to catch her eye was a bright green sheath in cheap brocade. The moment she slipped into it in front of the fitting room mirror, Kerry knew that it was the one. It was a knockout, and she loved the color. Striding up to the counter, she said, "Wrap it up, please. I'll take it," feeling her heart pound at her own brazen arrogance. As she counted her hard-earned dollars, Kerry felt a sudden pang of doubt, but it was too late. Now she would have just enough for shoes, and maybe a lipstick.

Laden with packages, she headed for the savings and loan, unable to keep herself from glancing at Purvis's and the words printed beneath the prestigious names: "suppliers of fine leather goods." Now it would take forever to save enough for handmade English riding boots.

On Friday night when Shannon went up to the house to watch the men hanging the lanterns for the party, Kerry pretended to be completely absorbed in reading the last chapter of *Misty of Chincoteague*. The moment she heard the screen door slam she leapt from the bed and dragged out her dress box. Her eye caught the billowing skirt of Shannon's frock hanging on the closet door waiting to be worn, and it was like a red flag of challenge. Taking a deep breath, she boldly cut four inches from the hem of the green sheath that was about to launch her new image.

Clipping on a pair of pearl earrings, Shannon gave one last adjustment to the hibiscus flower she had tucked into her chignon. It was the end of September, and the nights were warming up. All the windows were open, admitting the fragrant air of the bush, alive with crickets. Hearing the front screen slam, Shannon knew it must be Kerry.

"Where have you been?" she called impatiently. "It's almost time to go. I'm not going to wait for you, you know."

There was no reply from the living room, and she turned to study herself in the mirror one last time. "You'll have to do," she whispered to the dark image, half-familiar, half-strange, that insolently returned her gaze. Above a cloud of coral tulle lifted by a borrowed petticoat rose the tight black bodice cleverly altered by Mattie and now tied with a sash of watered silk. Shannon's abundant dark hair had been artfully swept up, and a touch of mascara and lipstick was enough to highlight a face already alive with excitement.

Hearing the click of Shannon's heels on the floor, Kerry pretended to be immersed in her book as she slumped in the chair under a lamp.

"Kerry—you're not getting ready! Come on. You've got to hurry up. I told you I wouldn't wait."

"You don't have to," she mumbled. Then, looking up, she gasped in amazement. "You look simply stunning,

49

Shannon," she whispered, swallowing a stab of white-hot envy.

"Do you really think so?"

"Yes, I do," she replied, reverting to a mood of pretended sullenness.

"Are you coming to the party or aren't you? What's come over you, anyway?"

"I haven't made up my mind if I'm going yet."

"Come on, Kerry. Quite playing games. I've washed and ironed your pink dress, now hurry and get into it. Dad's been up at the house for ages, and I told Mattie we'd be there early to lend a hand before the guests come."

"It's all right for you, isn't it?" said Kerry defiantly. "You got what you wanted, didn't you? A new dress, shoes, and I don't know what-all. . . ."

"Oh, come off it," Shannon flared. "This is the first real party dress I've ever had, and you know perfectly well that you'll get your turn when you're my age."

"Well, I'm not coming, and that's that."

"All right, have it your way. Stay home and sulk."

The moment Shannon's footsteps had died away Kerry snapped her book shut, then jumped up to get ready.

Koonwarra was a blazing sphere of light carved out of the midnight-blue sky that enclosed the plains and hills. A few Mercedeses and even Rolls-Royces were already sweeping up the drive to deliver their passengers at the front entrance of the house. Shannon knew tonight was going to be the grandest party ever seen on a station in New South Wales. When she reached the veranda, where all the French windows had been opened, she paused to drink in the sight of the reception hall, its crystal chandelier blazing with light. The historic room glowed with an unprecedented elegance that night, casting its spell on a throng of guests, most of whom rarely encountered such opulence. Like a dark vault, the treasure room of Koonwarra had been flung open, flaunting its gilt, lace, silver, and fine cherrywood furniture, and its richly patterned Persian carpet. At the center of all the grandeur was Mattie, who had shed every trace of the grazier's practical wife to become the chatelaine of a house fine enough to compare with any. Her dress, magnificent to behold, was of beaded blue satin, and at her throat she wore an heirloom diamond necklace that competed with the prisms of the chandelier for brilliance. She and Bob received friends from as far as five hundred miles away. Some of the women had dressed with a lavishness that would have suited the opera in Sydney, with satin gowns that swept the floor, frills and furbelows billowing up to their chins. Many wore long white gloves, and there was even a tiara or two. Starved for glamour, they had indulged in an orgy of finery that contrasted with their sunburned arms and faces. The men, too, wore what they fancied, from plain suits to white tie and tails.

Feeling gloriously elegant, Shannon swept down the terrace. She couldn't wait to surprise Brendan, who was busy packing cans of beer into a tub of ice behind the bar.

"Dad, what do you think?"

He froze when he saw Shannon standing before him. By the softness in his eyes and his mellow smile, she guessed he already had a few drinks under his belt, but she sensed it didn't dim his appreciation of her. For a moment he seemed overcome.

"Girlie, you look the image of your beautiful mother," he said in a voice full of emotion. This rare reference to Françoise took her by surprise.

"Thank you for the dress and everything, Dad."

"You're going to wreak havoc and break hearts tonight without even trying," he said with a bittersweet pride. It made him feel both old and young to look at her.

"Don't be silly," she whispered in embarrassment, though she had become aware of the knot of staring young men that had already begun to form at the edge of the dance platform erected on the lawn for the evening.

"I'll be keeping an eye on every one of them," said Brendan in a joking manner, but Shannon was uncomfortably aware that he meant it.

The orchestra that had come all the way from Canberra was tuning up, and couples were drifting from the house. Henry accompanied by Jamie, the youngest Fremont son, came to the bar and stopped short at the sight of Shannon. They were too astonished to speak, but the appreciation in their eyes spoke for itself.

"What did I tell you? You've got a following already," said Brendan as he handed them glasses brimming with beer.

Shannon hovered near the bar, pretending to arrange some glasses. Now and then she glanced through the open windows toward the crowd in the reception room, hoping to see Zan, when she spotted Charlie with Mattie and Bob. She suppressed a twinge of jealousy when she identified Hilary and Heather McNabe from the neighboring station of Caerleon. The pretty blond sisters went to Frensham's in Sydney, and

51

their polished manners and expensive dresses automatically made them rivals. But Shannon tried not to take any notice. To her surprise, they, too, seemed to be regarding her, but their eyes reverted to the double doors of the room as they stared star-struck at Zan, who had just walked in. Shannon's face lit up with a smile when he came directly toward her, not pausing even to speak to anyone, a moment after the music had struck up the first melody.

"Good evening, sir," he said, nodding to Brendan. "I've come to ask your daughter for the first dance, if I may."

With a triumphant sneer on his face, Brendan fixed his eyes on Zan.

"That, I'm afraid, is a father's privilege. Come, Shannon," he said, offering her his arm.

With boorish pride Brendan had shattered her glittering world, and as he towed her onto the platform filled with dancers, all color drained from the evening. She knew she would never forget the surprised look on Zan's face or her father's uncouth behavior.

She foxtrotted in Brendan's arms like a doll. All the fight had gone from her as he whirled her around the floor. He was smiling proudly as he displayed her like a prize possession, but she could hardly utter a civil hello to the dancers who greeted her. Over Brendan's shoulder she saw Zan lead Heather McNabe onto the floor in a strapless black evening gown that Shannon knew must have come from the most exclusive shop in Sydney. Brendan wouldn't release her until she had danced again, and this time she saw Zan dancing with Hilary, who was nearly as pretty as her sister. One of the roustabouts cut in on Brendan, and from that moment on Shannon was passed from one man to another in succession until she couldn't remember whom she had danced with last.

"You're the belle of the ball," said Bob proudly when they ended up together after a reel.

This, coming from him, was a rare compliment indeed, and if it hadn't been for the incident between her father and Zan, Shannon knew she would be having the time of her life. Just when she had nearly given up, she felt a tap on her shoulder.

"May I have the next dance?"

"Zan—of course," she replied with a rush of happiness.

The moment he claimed her Shannon felt she had been rescued from a wall of thorns woven by Brendan to keep him away. It would take an act of violence to pry her from Zan's arms, he clasped her so tightly.

"Every minute today has seemed like an hour," he whispered in her ear. They were safe in the center of the crowd, sheltered by laughter and music. The effortless way Zan glided her around the floor was such a contrast to the rough style of the roustabouts she had been dancing with that her head spun. When the music ended he still held her lightly in his arms.

Shannon glanced quickly around, looking for Kerry. Brendan was going strong and had become quite popular at the bar, where he was lashing out double measures, not forgetting himself. He was already well away and would be drunk as a lord by the time the cake was cut at midnight. When he broke into a gale of inebriated laughter, she looked away in contempt. She no longer cared if he saw her dancing with Zan.

"I could have died earlier this evening," she murmured.

Zan knew from experience that behind Brendan's raucous gaiety lay a deep melancholy. The pubs in Ireland were filled with disappointed men like Brendan, whose sullen faces were often as strikingly handsome as his. It seemed that their inimitable charm was compensation for the cup of bitterness they were forced to drink. Poets and dreamers to a man, they vented their rage at poverty and injustice on the nearest whipping post. He remembered seeing their faces through the rain-splashed windows of the Bentley when he sped through the village of Kilgarin to the castle.

On the terrace Charlie paused to put his arm around Mattie, who was fanning herself vigorously after jitterbugging with Bob.

"It's a great party, Mum."

She acknowledged the compliment happily, observing the swarm of people.

"May I have this dance?" asked Zan, extending his hand.

"You certainly may," she said with a bright smile, and they swept onto the floor.

As soon as he saw she was free, Charlie made a beeline for Shannon. When they were on the floor he held her away from his arms and took a long look, definitely liking what he saw.

"You look simply sensational tonight," he pronounced. "Where have you been all my life, you gorgeous girl?"

"Here at Koonwarra," she said, laughing. "What on earth has come over you, Charlie?"

His attempt at flattery hadn't disturbed the poise she

53

seemed to have been born with, a trait he'd always found a little disturbing; tonight, however, there was a sensual bloom about Shannon that he hadn't noticed before.

"What are you going to do with your life, Shannon, now you're out of school? Have you given any thought to tomorrow and the day after?"

After a few drinks Charlie always felt himself a bit of a philosopher, and now, as he began to appreciate the exotic quality of Shannon's allure, he thought about Rosemary, the English girl Zan was destined to marry. Her beauty had a cold, untouchable quality about it that suggested breeding and money, as far away from the dark, rich beauty he held in his arms as could be imagined.

"Oh, I've got plans," said Shannon in reply to his question. "First, I've got to get to Sydney."

"How are you going to do that? Have you thought it through?" he said doubtfully. Though Shannon might stand apart from other girls in the Outback, her dreams of escape were identical with theirs.

"I guess I'll just get on a train and leave."

"Any idea when?" he persisted.

"I'll know when, the moment comes, believe me." Her eyes wandered to Zan, who was still dancing with Mattie.

Charlie suddenly brought their dance to an abrupt halt. "Wow—get an eyeful of that!"

Shannon turned to see Kerry languidly dragging on a cigarette in the company of a brawny shearer, whose arm was draped around her. Now she understood what her sister had been doing in Wishbone. Kerry was trying so pathetically, and so unsuccessfully, to appear a woman of the world that Shannon flushed with hot embarrassment. The tight green sheath that had been badly taken in to fit her curvaceous little figure clung in all the wrong places, and her suggestive manner had fallen far short of the mark. She couldn't know that she seemed like nothing more than a little girl playing at dressing up.

"Charlie, you've got to help me get her out of here before Dad sees her," Shannon whispered. "All hell will break loose, and he'll ruin the party." Looking frantically in his direction, she saw he was still presiding grandly over the bar.

"She's a little fool," said Charlie. "She's got more than she might have bargained for with Dan Roper. He's one of the biggest skirt chasers around."

Her heart thudding in fear, Shannon could wait no longer but went straight to Kerry and took her by the arm.

"Kerry—I want to talk to you."

She turned with calculated slowness at the sound of Shannon's voice. "Leave me alone. Can't you see I'm busy?"

"Put out that cigarette and come here. Do you realize what will happen when Dad sees you?"

"Some of us just grow up faster than others, Shannon," she drawled lazily, turning her provocative smile on Dan. "And there's nothing you can do to stop it."

"Please, Kerry—listen to me. Dad will cause a scene that we'll never live down. He's already well away. . . ."

"Nope—I'm not coming, and that's that. Now piss off," she said, shrugging off Shannon's arm.

"All right, you little fool, have it your way."

As she stormed away, Shannon was intercepted by Zan, who had been waiting for her at the edge of the floor.

"What's the matter? What's happened?" he said, catching her arm.

She shrugged and turned toward Kerry.

"It can't be—is that Kerry?" said Zan incredulously. He burst into amused laughter. "What a transformation!"

"Dad will kill her when he sees her," she said helplessly. The suspense was like waiting for a bomb to drop.

Shannon braced herself when she heard a dull roar, like the charge of a wild animal, coming from the direction of the terrace. It was Brendan making his way through the crowd like a raging bull. Someone must have made a remark to him about Kerry, Shannon thought. He swept past her, his face contorted in rage, and people stepped back to give him room. Most of the guests were more irritated at the interruption than shocked, though a few were amused. All eyes were fixed anxiously on Brendan and his obvious target, Kerry, who had frozen at the edge of the floor by Dan Roper's side. Brendan came to a swaying halt a few feet away, his feet planted wide, his eyes blazing with fury.

"Come here, you little tramp," he bellowed.

At the sound of his voice the siren in green visibly shrank to a whimpering, frightened little girl, but she didn't budge.

"Did you hear what I said?" He yanked her toward him.

"No! Let me be!" she screamed, clinging to Dan. "I won't go home," she cried, her voice trailing off into a sob.

"You bloody well will. You're coming with me."

Suddenly Dan Roper awoke from his drunken indifference. "Who the hell are you?" he snarled.

At this remark Brendan's fist shot out with a punch that sent Dan reeling backward.

"Why, you . . ." he raged, recoiling swiftly. He was just as drunk as Brendan, but he had the advantage of being twenty years younger. In moments the two-man brawl broke into a free-for-all.

"Oh, no—good Lord," moaned Mattie, who was on the terrace when it all began to happen. It had just turned midnight, and Dottie had come out to tell her the champagne and cake were ready. "It's Brendàn, drunk as Chloe," she said in disgust. "Bob! Henry! Jamie! Where are you? Charlie—do something!" Mattie called.

She didn't need to be told that Brendan Faloon was the cause of it all. When she had seen Kerry earlier on, she had registered a note of surprise at her outrageous appearance. Now she realized she ought to have acted at once.

"Don't worry. Every good party needs a fight," said Dottie resignedly.

Mattie shook her head. There was such a mixture of people at Koonwarra that night, from the shiftiest roustabout to the richest grazier in the district, that it wasn't surprising the highly charged atmosphere had boiled over into a fight. When after a moment it suddenly broke up, men brushed themselves off, amidst confusion and embarrassed laughter. Bob had grabbed Brendan, and someone had pulled Dan off him. It looked as if the fight was over—at least for the time being—but Mattie winced as she caught Brendan's parting words.

"No daughter of mine is going to look like a trollop. You're going to get a real hiding for this," he shouted, planting a blow that knocked Kerry sideways.

The last that was heard from the humiliated Kerry was an anguished sob as she ran from the party down a tunnel of darkness.

"Well, that's the end of it," said Bob with a reassuring smile as he approached Mattie. "Brendan's in one hell of a temper. What got into Kerry, doing a thing like that? That little hellion just asks for it."

Mattie clapped her hands. "Come on, everyone," she shouted above the din. "It's time to cut the cake and make a few speeches."

"How about cutting the speeches and making for the cake," someone retorted, causing laughter.

Everyone left the garden and flocked into the reception room, where a huge cake was waiting to be cut and glasses of champagne were being circulated on silver trays.

Feeling physically ill after the sordid incident with Brendan, Shannon stood close to the Fremont family as the speeches began. Never in her life had she felt so ashamed. At the touch of a hand she turned to see Zan, gesturing for her to follow him. While the group was rocking with laughter at one of Bob's jokes, she slipped away into the cool night, where she made out the figure of Zan, silver with reflected moonlight as he leaned against a tree.

"Hello," he called as she approached, raising a bottle of champagne and two glasses. "I thought we should have a little celebration of our own, away from the crowd."

Retreating from the noise, they drifted into the liquid night emblazoned with stars.

"Are you all right?" he asked when they had walked silently for some time.

"Yes, I'm fine."

When he scooped up her hand, she responded by tightly intertwining her fingers in his, letting the empathy flow between them. As they meandered through the shadows it seemed to Shannon that she could walk away from her problems, as she was doing now.

"You must have been disgusted with what happened tonight," she said finally.

"Disgusted? Not really. You should meet *my* father."

"Don't tell me he gets drunk at other people's parties and starts fights. I wouldn't believe it," she said with a sarcastic laugh. In spite of all Zan had told her, she still retained her own portrait of the Earl of Kilgarin: he was wise, distinguished, and gentle. An older version of Zan.

"He once raced whippets in the ballroom at Kilgarin, and to amuse himself he had a yew tree in the garden sculptured like a naked lady. So you see, darling Shannon, every family has its black sheep. And it would be a dull world if they didn't. Come on—please cheer up."

She sighed. "I don't know what comes over Dad sometimes. Or Kerry, for that matter."

They had arrived at the last box of the stables, and Zan kicked the door open. Tossing the bottle and glasses in the hay, he reached out and took her in his arms.

57

His touch sent a shiver of anticipation through Shannon, obliterating every care that had been weighing her down. The sweet scent of horses, hay, and early summer seduced her senses, and when she felt his impatient mouth on hers, a bolt of pleasure, as unexpected as it was powerful, leapt like a current, welding them together. They tumbled into the hay, embracing passionately. He drew away, compelled to devour with his eyes what he would soon savor with every inch of his body, instinctively realizing that he was the first to know her untouched splendor.

"I adore you, Shannon," he whispered, caressing her temples. "Your mouth, your eyes, your laughter, everything about you. You're beautiful and fine. I wish I could take you away somewhere, and that we weren't in a stable. It's not good enough for you. This isn't where you belong. I don't know how or why or what there is on God's earth that has brought us together, as different as we are."

He had expressed all that she had longed to utter, and when he released her from a deep kiss, her words came of their own accord.

"I love you, Zan," she said, almost with a sob. It was a futile gesture, tossed to the wind, but she no longer cared as the pent-up yearning of the past months spilled into kiss after kiss.

"Trust me," he said, gently pulling her dress down. His hands were shaking as he removed his trousers and fumbled with the buttons on his shirt.

Robbed of the power to deny him the thing she herself wanted most, she felt a surge of happiness at his impassioned murmurs, and seeing his shadowed face suffused with desire, urgency coursed through her. Zan's hand delicately traced the line of her thigh, and when his fingers rested between her legs she didn't shrink away but reached out to explore his muscled torso. Discovering the root of his manhood, she stifled a moan of wanting.

"Shannon—Shannon, my love," Zan exulted, clenching his hand over her own.

"Zan, I want you, want you," she chanted.

Instinctively, her limbs wound around him when she felt him nudging against her. Their kisses grew deeper and more urgent, and soon Shannon's own passionate birthright commanded the even rhythm of her hips, willing him with all her heart to love her as ardently as she had ever dreamed possible. Impatiently he forged his way inside her, causing her a

58

spasm of pain; nevertheless, she continued to thrust against Zan as if she would never let him go, bringing him to a convulsive climax in moments.

When their lovemaking had subsided into tender murmurs and kisses, Shannon opened her eyes, almost surprised to find they were in the stables. They lay without speaking for a long while, content to let successive waves of sensation wash over them.

Zan lay at her side, drugged by a desire that was completely new to him and had nothing to do with hurried lovemaking in the backseat of a car or by the riverbank, where everyone played by the rules. The encounter with Shannon bore no resemblance to the kind of arousal he felt when he danced with his fiancée, Rosemary. It was the difference between the flame of a candle and a bush fire, and he was at a loss to comprehend it.

"The next two weeks are going to be hell. We won't always be able to meet like this," he said.

"I know," she replied, stroking his hair. Nothing could diminish her utter happiness.

"I can't bear the idea of leaving in two weeks, Shannon. Listen—what you said about going to Sydney—I was thinking, why not make the break now? I'll be so much freer when I'm there, and we can spend days and nights together. I can help you find a flat and even a job. If you really mean to go, why not do it now? What do you say?"

"Are you serious?" She pulled herself up as she watched him open the champagne.

Handing her a glass, he said, "I've never been more serious in my life. You don't belong here, Shannon. You know that, I know it. It's meant to be that you come away with me. Let's drink to it," he whispered, leaning over to kiss her.

She didn't need to think. "Yes, I will come," she cried exultantly. Zan had the power to make reality from fragments of dreams.

They talked for a long while, making plans about what they would do in Sydney. Finally they fell asleep, nestled warmly together, Zan's coat over them.

Shivering, Shannon awoke toward early morning and peered outside. The moon was now a pale shape on the vibrant horizon, reflected in the pale light of dawn. In a panic she leapt up and began to brush the hay from her dress, pausing to take one last glimpse at the sleeping Zan before she knelt to kiss him. Leaving the stables, she prayed she would make it home unnoticed and saw with relief that her father's bedroom curtains were closed. She was sure he was still in a deep, drunken sleep. Slipping the screen closed behind her, she tiptoed toward the bedroom, her shoes in her hand. She gasped when she saw Brendan staring at her from the kitchen, madness in his eyes.

"Where have you been?" He staggered toward her. As she heard the drunken slur in his voice, the words died in her throat.

"I know where you've been!" he roared.

"Dad, I can explain if you'll let me."

"Why, you little slut. You're just like that whore of a mother of yours. You—you and your tramp sister. Look at you—Jezebel in all her finery. The dress you tricked me into buying so you could offer yourself like a cheap whore."

"Dad, please." She backed away as he began to undo his belt. "We were having a drink, that's all, and we were so tired we fell asleep."

"What a load of crap," Brendan snorted. "You're just a bitch in heat, like your mother. She'd open her legs to anyone, and now you're doing it. . . ." His voice broke as the angry sentiment took hold of him. Raising his arm, he struck a violent blow that glanced off the table.

"Dad—don't. Please don't!" she screamed, her eyes wild with terror.

He came at her furiously, lashing the belt at her bare arms.

"You were my little girl. I loved you, like I loved your mother. There's a curse on you, Shannon. You're nothing but a common slut!" he shouted as she tried to break away. "I'm going to beat you to within an inch of your life, and then you'll be locked up until that bastard lord has left Koonwarra. Do you hear?"

Shannon writhed in pain as his belt bit into her flesh. Stumbling to the floor, she stifled her screams, burying her face in her arms. There was no one to help her, there never had been, and she clung tenaciously to the last shred of her pride, unwilling to cry.

When at last he stopped, the tempest still raged in his eyes as he stood over her. Fearing he would kill her if he could, she coiled herself up protectively.

"Go to your room," he said, yanking her up roughly.

For a moment their eyes met, Shannon's stricken with

agonized incredulity, Brendan's glinting with the compulsion to murder. Shannon was stunned to perceive a piercing ray of father's love—tormented, destructive, and agonized—directed at herself like a beam. It was a love that aroused pity and repulsion, horror and awe, and it was so anguished in its expression that she struggled to free herself from its suffocating grasp.

Shannon escaped into the dim bedroom, and slamming the door behind her, she leaned against it to brace herself from the shock. As her tears began to fall she saw Kerry huddling like a frightened kitten on the bed. The look of sly triumph she had worn earlier in the evening had vanished, and when Shannon fell on the bed with a heavy sob, Kerry rushed to comfort her. The two of them wept in each other's arms until they could cry no more. At last Shannon fell back, stricken and exhausted. Kerry bent over her and stroked her forehead sympathetically, trying to soothe Shannon's crushed spirit with an instinct that reached far back into their lost childhood.

"It's all right, it's all right," she whispered. "He'll have forgotten it all by tonight."

Shannon's immunity to Brendan's wrath had been a wedge between them for as long as Kerry could remember, but she felt no sense of triumph at the violent change of events.

As Shannon quietened and the first rays of sun filled the room, even the memory of the sublime pleasure of lying in Zan's arms the night before was obliterated by what had just happened.

"But why? Why did he do it?" whispered Kerry.

Shannon told Kerry the story she'd related to Brendan about falling asleep in the stable.

At the thought of Shannon and Zan lying together in the hay, Kerry felt a spasm of jealousy that she fought to suppress.

"Kerry," began Shannon, "I've decided to go away—today, now. To Sydney. I can't stay here another minute."

"I'm coming with you," cried Kerry as Shannon took her suitcase from the cupboard.

"No, Kerry. You can't," Shannon said gently. Seeing the stricken look in Kerry's face, Shannon took her by the shoulders. "You've got to stay here for the moment. I know we always planned to go away together, but let me get a job first, find some place to live. . . . Please," she pleaded, seeing the hurt in Kerry's eyes, now drained of the precocious Irish

61

spirit that enlivened her personality. The pale, shocked little face staring up at her touched Shannon deeply.

"But I can get a job, too. I can pass for sixteen any day. Dan Roper thought I was eighteen last night," she continued excitedly. "Anyway, I don't want to finish school."

"I don't know where I'm going to be, what I'm going to do. I don't even know if I have enough money to get myself to Sydney, let alone the two of us."

"Do you swear you'll send for me as soon as you can?" Kerry asked doubtfully.

"Yes, I promise. We'll find a nice little apartment, buy furniture. It will be just like we always talked about." Shannon began opening drawers and flinging clothes into her suitcase.

"You're not going to forget about me when you get there, are you? Please, Shannon!" she cried in desperation. "You know what it's like here."

"Listen, I know what you're worried about. If Dad tries to get at you, go to Mattie. She'll protect you, and Bob will, too. Promise me you'll go to them. Knowing that, I won't worry so much about you."

Shannon had by now changed into a thin cotton dress that hid the livid red welts on her fragile arms. Retrieving her money box, she took out the precious store of dollar bills that would have to last until she found a job.

As Kerry watched Shannon's every move, she felt as if her sister were about to catch hold of her destiny and disappear over the horizon . . . into the unknown. She struggled with an overwhelming sense of helplessness as she regarded Shannon standing there resolutely, her suitcase at her feet. The frail mantle of courage she had gathered about her seemed little protection against the world beyond Koonwarra, which, in Kerry's imagination, ended at Wishbone.

"Here—take what's left of my boot money," she said, leaping to fetch it.

"Thanks. I'll send it to you as soon as I can."

"No—don't do that. Save it for my ticket. And anyway, I won't be needing boots in Sydney."

"One last thing. Promise me you won't tell a soul where I've gone—except for Zan. Find him this morning and tell him, and warn him about Dad. I'll write as soon as I know where I'll be staying." She clasped Kerry to her in a desperate hug. "It won't be long before we're together again," Shannon murmured. "I'll send for you as soon as I can. You know

I will. If I go now, I can catch the mail truck as it goes back to Wishbone."

Fighting her last minute doubts, Shannon turned to go as if the wind were at her back. The last look between the two sisters was like a cord stretched to breaking point. Kerry wept silently as she watched Shannon go down the steps, and Shannon paused just once, to wave at her.

It had taken a long time for things to get back to normal at Koonwarra after the party, and as Mattie closed the door of the reception room, she could almost hear the echoes of laughter and music that had made the room come alive. The party was still being talked about far and wide as the best for years, and, she reflected as she walked into the cool hallway, it had unraveled a skein of events in the lives of people that was still evolving.

She went outside, where late afternoon shadows lay upon the garden, and absently began to pick the dead blooms from the hedge of lilies that bordered the terrace. Zan came to her mind, and she realized with relief that he would be leaving in a few days. Not until then, she felt, could they close ranks and resume life as it was.

Since the party Brendan had been on a continuous bender, and rumor had it that it was something to do with Zan and Shannon. Mattie would be glad to see him go for Kerry's sake, too; even though Zan had worked to help her in dressage, keeping her mind off Shannon's sudden departure, it would be better for her once he was back where he belonged. The attraction between Shannon and Zan had brought nothing but harm. It was inconceivable that a young man who played polo with the Prince of Wales would do more than amuse himself with a girl like Shannon—a young doe, a pretty dove who had enchanted him for a moment. Zan would go home to marry his fiancée, who would become the mother of his heirs and hostess in his castle. And the sweet-natured, capable Shannon would eventually find her way in the big city and would surely marry someone suitable and settle down in the suburbs to raise a family. That was how it would be, and though Mattie missed her, she was glad Shannon had found the courage to leave the Outback.

The next day, as Zan watched her in the paddock, Kerry was aware it might be the last time she would see him. After each round of jumps she cantered to where he was sitting, his felt hat casting a shadow over his eyes. Zan seemed restless and bored, and she had put her heart into every jump to secure his attention. A look of approval from him, a word of praise, was enough to make her wildly happy, in spite of the misery of living in the same house as Brendan. Since Shannon's flight he was like a defeated man, and he sometimes disappeared to Wishbone for days at a time to drink and gamble. As each day passed and no letter arrived from Shannon, Kerry became more and more agitated. There was a constant question in her mind every time she looked at Zan, wondering if he was feeling the same anguish she was.

On the morning Shannon had left, Kerry had sought him out to pass her sister's message. He had received the news in stunned silence, and since then there had been a tacit understanding between them that the subject was best avoided.

"I think Splendor is whacked," said Kerry, making excuses. It was nearing noon, and she was anxious to get back to Koonwarra before the mail arrived, desperately hoping there might be a letter from Shannon. With Zan leaving so soon, she was particularly anxious for news of Shannon's whereabouts, as she had hatched a plan that would enable her to slip away to Sydney with Zan. Once she had escaped, he would invite the two of them to dinner at the Wentworth Hotel, and perhaps even ask them to stay with his aunt at Rose Bay. But it all depended on getting Shannon's letter in time.

Lean and suntanned from his months in Australia, Zan was indescribably handsome to Kerry. Each time she looked at him she felt a sense of weightlessness, and she began to dream that he would choose her, love her.

They cantered across the paddock toward the house. The grass had already been fried in patches by the sun, and the hooves of the horses kicked up dust instead of mud. A mob of grazing sheep moved out of their way as they galloped toward home.

"Race?" Zan called.

"You're on."

Spurring Splendor on, she quickly outpaced Zan. She took the gate beautifully, although it was easily a foot higher than the horse was accustomed to, causing Zan to give a shout of admiration as he caught up with her.

Kerry excused herself as soon as they had put the horses away, and eagerly ran home. Dusty and breathless, she slipped unobserved through the veranda and sneaked down the hall to where the mail was always laid on a table. Anxiously she thumbed through the pile of letters, and her heart stopped when she saw Shannon's handwriting on an envelope addressed to Zan. She sorted through the envelopes, but when she realized there was none for her, she instinctively pocketed Zan's.

On the way home she wondered indignantly why Shannon hadn't written to her as well, when she must know that every fiber of her being was tense with waiting. She put the kettle on the stove, intending to steam open the letter and read it, then reseal it and hand it to Zan.

It wasn't nearly as easy as the detective novelists described to open a sealed envelope, and she made a mess of it. Bolting to the bedroom, she began to read, her hand shaking. First she scanned the lines for a mention of her own name but found none; then she carefully reread each phrase as the meaning of the letter sank in. "Sydney is beautiful . . . I can't wait for you to come. . . . I want you to know that I don't regret what happened. . . . I'll be waiting to hear from you. . . ."

Kerry threw down the letter as the scalding bitterness of betrayal rose in her throat. It was undeniably clear that Shannon and Zan had already decided to meet in Sydney and that their plans didn't include her. Perhaps Shannon had even provoked Brendan's anger to find an excuse to leave home, she reasoned wildly. For all Kerry knew, perhaps the two of them were even planning to run away together and get married, and were keeping it a secret. She was crushed they hadn't let her into their confidence.

She tore the letter into tiny bits and threw it like confetti on the bed. The pieces couldn't be small enough to obliterate every tender word the lying Shannon had intended for Zan. She fell into a rage on the bed, flailing her hands and legs as hot tears coursed down her cheeks. In one instant all the admiration and love she had for Shannon were drowned in a wave of hatred. She almost laughed through her tears when she remembered she had given her all of her hoarded boot money.

Tears exhausted, Kerry rose from the bed. She seemed to have spent a lifetime sobbing her heart out for no reason. The squalor of the house closed in her as never before. She envisioned Shannon and Zan living it up in Sydney and wondered how she could bear to continue living at Koonwarra. But at least she had one consolation: Shannon's letter to Zan had disappeared without a trace, and no one would ever know what had happened to it.

A few days later Kerry finished what she had started at Henry's twenty-first, losing her virginity in a hayloft to Dan Roper. He took her with a lusty roughness that perfectly suited her defiant mood, and as she watched though half-closed eyes Dan's rugged face suffused with desire, she reveled in the new sensation of power that was hers, wondering why she had waited so long.

Chapter III

Sydney, Australia, January 1977

Countess Elena breezed along Ocean Street, glancing now and then at a boutique, always mentally comparing it to her own establishment. As usual, she concluded with satisfaction that it was puerile to even put "Elena's" in the same category as other dress shops. Every detail about Elena reflected the impact her taste had made on Sydney society women, from her bold chunky jewelry and sleek blond chignon to her chartreuse dress bright enough to stop traffic.

When revolution convulsed Hungary in 1956, Elena's shop in Budapest had been destroyed. But she had built a kingdom for herself as far away as possible from political upheavals, in sun-drenched, prosperous Australia. For her the black-and-white-striped awning with her name swirled in elegant gold letters was a continual reminder that in a few short years she had not only survived, but triumphed in the brash city of Sydney. Pushing open the heavy glass door, she stepped into the cool interior that breathed European chic. Elena's had become a catchword for the latest trends in *haute couture*, and she credited herself with having single-handedly molded the image of the most influential women in Sydney, turning their attention to the importance of beautifully made accessories from Italy—crocodile handbags, kid gloves as supple as silk, and fashionable shoes, all elegantly displayed in rococo gilt cabinets.

Bracelets jangling, Elena paused to fuss over a huge

spray of white lilies in a crystal vase. Lavish bouquets were her trademark, one of the subtle details that suggested Elena's was not really a shop, but reminiscent of a salon on a Parisian boulevard. The oval room was furnished with Empire chairs, a crystal chandelier, and a rare Aubusson carpet in muted colors that recalled the delicacy of a Fragonard. All was peace, beauty, and order.

The countess noticed every detail of the shop in one practiced glance, assured that her assistant, who opened at nine, was as meticulous as herself. Taking her white leather diary, she scanned her engagements, then went to the work-room at the back of the shop.

"Darling, before I forget, would you book a table for two at La Causèrie around one? Something in a quiet corner. Jonquil and I want to talk," she called in a heavily accented voice.

Her assistant was just hanging up a ball gown that made Elena gasp in amazement when she saw it. It was a bubble of gold lace over organdy by Gina Frattini, and her mind immediately scanned her list of special clients, pinpointing two who would kill to own it.

"Isn't it the loveliest thing you've ever seen?" breathed her assistant as she gently brushed the golden folds of the dress.

"Sensational!"

Elena gazed approvingly at Shannon. The girl was a perfect assistant. She was intelligent, hardworking, and she was always dressed like a dream. The countess had gone through at least a dozen girls, and they had all left to get married within a year—or they were unwilling to work on Saturdays. Shannon, however, seemed to have no private life and would happily work until midnight if the occasion demanded. Yet it astonished Elena that she appeared to have no life of her own. Shannon was one of the most striking girls she had ever come across in Sydney. There was no doubt that the girl possessed the image that sold *haute couture*. From her emanated an aura of mystery in sharp contrast to the hearty freshness of Sydney girls, who, whether dark or fair, had all sprouted from the same tree of Nordic peaches. Shannon's cropped hair fell like a dark wing across her cheek, framing huge, expressive eyes that held a glimmer of the Orient; and her pencil slimness displayed clothes to perfect advantage.

How on earth she had ever been moved to give the girl a

job was something the mercurial Elena had often wondered. Then there had certainly been no hint of the stunning creature she would become. The moment she'd walked in the shop Elena knew the girl had come fresh from the Outback. And it wasn't her beauty that had impressed Elena, but her bold aplomb in announcing that her only experience had been a job at Woolworth's, as if she had been a vendeuse at Chanel. Elena had guessed just how much courage it had taken for her to walk through the formidable doors of the shop, and she'd set about polishing Shannon like a piece of tarnished silver, sensing she had made a good bargain. Little by little the value of what she had acquired began to shine through.

"Shannon!" cried Elena, rushing to the bell of gold on the rack. "I know who must have the Frattini—Charlene McDonald!"

"Oh, madam, you're quite right," she agreed. "What an inspiration!"

"I'm sure she'll be lunching today at La Causèrie. What could be more convenient? I'll whisk by her table and drop the hint."

When Elena had gone from the back room in a whirlwind, Shannon set about unpacking the rest of the large boxes airfreighted from Europe. She smiled to herself, knowing Elena was always in the best humor when she combined pleasure with profit. Shannon wondered if now might be the time to ask the notoriously tight-fisted Hungarian countess for a raise. As much as she owed Elena, life on a shoestring was a constant struggle. There was no question that she would have to have more money if she were ever to save for her passage to Europe, the goal that shone ever brighter as her lodestar.

Hearing the melodious bell that announced the arrival of a customer, Shannon decided it would be best to tackle the delicate subject of money when the countess had returned from a long boozy lunch.

When Elena came back in the afternoon, however, she was dragging her friend in tow.

"My dear," Elena called melodiously across the shop, "Lady Fortesque is *desperate* for something to wear to a ball tonight. I told her I was sure we could come up with just the thing."

"Hello, Shannon," called Lady Fortesque with a wave. "My, you look as pretty as a picture," she said.

The astonishing Lady Fortesque had fascinated Shannon from the moment she had stepped into the shop weeks ago. She had never met anyone remotely like her. Pink, plump, and blond, she was always outrageously dressed. Today she was wrapped in a froth of white ruffles that made an instant impression of fussy femininity. Her round china-blue eyes held a childlike quality of surprise, and her perky, upturned nose gave her face a happy aspect. Here was a woman who enjoyed life to the hilt, and it was impossible not to like her at once. She was as different from Elena as a cockatoo from a falcon, but the two women shared a breathless, dramatic approach to life that drew people to them irresistibly.

"As always, this shop is to dream," Lady Fortesque said with a sigh.

Bouncing from alcove to alcove in search of the perfect dress, Lady Fortesque infused a welcome light relief into the business of fashion, something that Sydney women tended to take very seriously. Shannon looked on as Elena paraded dress after unsuitable dress in front of Lady Fortesque, circumventing her eccentric taste. She had waged an unceasing campaign to tone down the Englishwoman's flamboyant image since she had arrived that summer for a visit.

"This, my darling, I have saved for a woman who is confident enough to dominate the room she enters," said the countess, unfurling a gown of black chiffon. "A Valentino, and the last word in elegance."

"No, no." Lady Fortesque's face puckered distastefully. "You know I detest black. I may be a widow, but I'll never wear her weeds. Why, poor Freddie would turn in his grave if he saw me in that."

"But it's so chic!"

"Chic?" she snorted, pirouetting from rack to rack. "No, Elena, I only want to look that chic when I'm pushing up daisies."

Elena rolled her eyes at Shannon in exasperation.

"I want something to express the inner me," interrupted Lady Fortesque while Elena was extemporizing on the importance of line in fashion.

"Line is wasted on my round figure. I want something outrageous—outré."

When dress after dress failed to please her, Shannon interjected, "What about the Gina Frattini, madam?"

The countess waved her hand. "No, no, it's too small, and anyway, I've already promised it to Charlene."

Lady Fortesque wheeled around. "Oh, let me see it, please," she begged.

At Elena's nod, Shannon fetched the cloud of gold lace. The moment she entered the room Lady Fortesque let out a squeal of delight.

"It's me! That's it!" she cried excitedly, rushing up to Shannon.

"No. This is not for you," Elena decreed. "You'll look like a goldfish in a goldfish bowl."

"But that's exactly how I want to look," Lady Fortesque protested.

There ensued a polite little dispute over the dress, and as both of them became more intransigent, Shannon awaited the outcome. The countess rarely failed to wield her judgment over a customer. The women who came to Elena's relied on her infallible instinct, and her dictatorial manner reassured them.

"I'm going to try it on!" announced Lady Fortesque.

"All right—have it your way," Elena said, sighing dramatically.

Shannon went into the mirrored fitting room to help her into it. Once she had eased herself into the dress, Lady Fortesque bit her lip in disappointment when she realized the zipper wouldn't close. She looked woefully at Shannon. "Elena was right. I was so sure I could squeeze into it."

"Don't worry—it can be let out just here. I had a look at the seams."

"Do you really think so? You're an angel." She charged out of the fitting room with Shannon in her wake.

"Shannon says it can be let out, but the thing is, can it be ready by tonight?" she asked, with pleading eyes.

Elena regarded her critically. "I really don't see how it can be done, unfortunately. I usually need at least twenty-four hours for that kind of alteration."

"I could do it, if you like," interjected Shannon.

"Oh, would you? You treasure, you!" cried Lady Fortesque, looking to Elena.

"Well, I suppose it is possible," Elena replied grudgingly. "If Shannon drops everything else, and Lord knows she has a lot to do today, we could deliver it by seven. She'll come over to Double Bay in a taxi."

* * *

That evening Shannon left Elena's shop with a huge dress box beside her on the seat of the taxi, Lady Fortesque's address in her hand. "Witterings," she repeated the name of the house to herself.

What a long way she had come in nearly a year and a half, she thought, watching as the gates and walls that protected some of Sydney's grandest mansions flew by. The last time she had been there, her frame of mind, as well as her circumstances, had been utterly different. Then, she had walked aimlessly in the dappled shade of plane and jacaranda trees like an orphaned child, but now she had become another person. The well-dressed, poised woman who carried a passport to open the high gates of Witterings had never dreamed that she would ever get any farther than an appetizing glimpse of the secluded villas passing by. In those days, when she had just arrived in Sydney, she hadn't been prepared for its breathtaking beauty, or its indifference. Still swimming in her own boundless naiveté, she had gone for days without speaking to a soul. Then, she had spent far too much time being embarrassed by her own gaucheness, acutely aware that the Outback clung to every detail of her appearance, from her clothes to her wild hair to the exaggerated twang of her speech. That was before she had discovered there were such things as skillful hairdressers, boutiques, and elocution teachers. The only thing she had managed to learn at once was that it was hopelessly impractical to even think of bringing Kerry to live with her when she had no room, no job, no idea of how she was going to survive. At that point, all her precarious hopes had been pinned on Zan's visit. She had fed on the wonderful things they would do when he got there—until he had let her down so callously.

Now, as the car approached Double Bay, she was aware that she still carried a little knot of pain around with her from the day she'd seen Zan's photograph in the *Sydney Morning Herald*. She'd been sitting on a park bench, combing the want ads for a job, and she'd recognized him at once—standing in the foyer of the opera house, in white tie and tails, surrounded by the cream of Sydney society. The gossip column that described him as one of England's most dashing bachelors mentioned that he was leaving at the end of the week and that he was staying with friends in Double Bay. Shannon had sat there motionless for a long time, staring sightlessly at the photograph; then the pain had come in waves, intense and almost unbearable.

71

In desperation she had gone for a walk in Double Bay the very next day, not with the intention of trying to contact Zan, but from the need to be near him. One glance at this exalted enclave of the rich was enough to convince her that the two of them had been doomed from the start. The huge glittering houses were cut off from the rest of the world by iron gates and fences, as impenetrable to outsiders as Buckingham Palace. All the tender dreams that had flourished in the remoteness of Koonwarra seemed absurdly naive in her new surroundings. She and Zan lived in two different worlds, she concluded once and for all. Facing the truth stripped of sentiment, she realized how little their night together must have meant to him when all Sydney worshiped at his feet.

Catching a glimpse of the harbor washed pink by the evening sun, Shannon wondered again how Zan could ever have been so cruel as to encourage the conviction in her that she could be his equal, even in love. She now understood that he must have been bored at Koonwarra and had needed something to amuse himself. She wasn't angry or bitter, but she hoped she was much wiser. The blow of his betrayal had jarred her to her senses, giving birth to an extraordinary craving for success that she hadn't known she possessed. After working in Woolworth's in downtown Sydney for three months, she had quit and resolutely headed for Elena's, determined to ask for a job. She was driven by the realization that if you started at the bottom, the chances were you stayed there. She had already passed Elena's a dozen times on her solitary walks, and it had become a powerful symbol of everything she wanted for herself.

No dream had ever seemed more wildly impossible than her desire to work for the famous countess, but the moment she gathered her courage to enter the shop, the obsession to belong there took hold of her. The very air in the shop was perfumed with intoxicating odors of fine, expensive things, and as her eyes scanned the massive bouquet of white roses on the gilt counter, the French carpet, the frothy lingerie carefully folded in an open commode, Shannon tossed aside all her disappointments and apprehensions and made a bold bid for the top.

The haughty Elena had terrified her. But, much to Shannon's astonishment, when she'd blurted out that she wanted a job, Elena had paused only a moment before saying yes. Her reply had been almost whimsical, as if she might change her mind if the mood passed.

"And don't think that working here will be all clover," she had scolded in her Hungarian accented English. "I'm a very hard taskmaster."

Delirious with happiness, Shannon had scarcely heard. Now, as the taxi moved up the long drive of Witterings toward its grand central portico illuminated by floodlights, Shannon forgot the obstacles of the last eighteen months. She had survived Elena's terrible temper, her miserliness, her exacting standards, even the unremitting loneliness in her little room in Paddington; moreover, she had undergone an electrifying metamorphosis—she was a butterfly released from its chrysalis. And now and then, as tonight, she caught the sweet, elusive scent of success.

She had never been to a house in Double Bay, or even to Elena's posh apartment in neighboring Vaucluse, for that matter. Alighting from the taxi with the box under her arm, Shannon stepped firmly onto the turf that had always been closed to her.

An Italian butler met her at the glass doors and led her into a wide entry hall that funneled into a grand staircase of marble railed with brass. The huge house seemed entirely deserted, and she guessed its inhabitants were already dressing for the party. She peeked into the living room, where a solid wall of glass doors led to the garden bordering the sea. The expensive modern furniture was covered in oatmeal-colored leather, and huge abstract pictures in vivid colors dominated the walls.

"Lady Fortesque asks you to please go upstairs," announced the butler.

As she advanced up the dizzying staircase, Shannon heard Lady Fortesque's irrepressible voice echoing from above.

"Yoo-hoo, I'm up here, dear. Come on up."

The petite Lady Fortesque was wrapped in a frothy blue negligee, and her hair had been teased into a mass of tinsel curls. Shannon was surprised to see how young-looking and slender her legs were, narrowing to a pair of satin mules.

"There's some champagne on the table over there. Please help yourself," she called. "I can't wait to try it on."

The palatial bedroom was like something out of a movie set, and Shannon had never seen anything like it. All the furniture was white, and the vast bed was a sea of quilted oyster satin strewn with pillows. Compared to the subdued elegance of Elena's, the suite Lady Fortesque inhabited was unashamedly ostentatious, and Shannon understood why Elena

73

hadn't been able to talk Lady Fortesque into a basic black dress when she glanced at the riotous colors and fabrics spilling from the wardrobe doors.

Shannon shyly poured herself a glass of champagne and wandered toward the doors that led to a balcony overlooking the shimmering lights of Sydney.

"Would you like me to help you on with the dress, Lady Fortesque?" she called toward the dressing room.

"Please call me Jonquil. I can't bear being called Lady Fortesque. It's much too grand," she said, dashing to the dressing table to rummage through a drawer. "I changed my name to Jonquil when I was fifteen. You see, I started life as just plain Gertrude. Imagine me as Gertie!"

She powdered her face furiously for a few seconds, then teased a lacquered curl. "Now," she said, turning to Shannon, "let's get down to the business of getting me into that divine frock."

Shannon was kept busy fetching several pairs of shoes to try on with it, clasping Jonquil's diamond necklace, and sorting through her glove box for a pair of long white kid gloves. Finally she fastened the last hook.

"I'm staying here with my old friend Eloise, whom I've known since I was a girl. She ended up marrying an Australian, and I try to come out here once a year. But this time, of course, I had to come without Thelma. It was bound to happen, wasn't it? That terrible Nigel popped the question to her after keeping her on the string for years—couldn't bear to see her going off again by herself, if you ask me, and anyway, I think he did it just to spite me, wretched man. The passage was booked, but there was no one to take her place. The voyage out was a nightmare. I can't bear flying. I don't know how I'll get along on the way back. Of course I carry far too many clothes, and some of them are just impossible to get into, like this one. And my jewel case"—she waved her hand—"why, it's a complete jumble. As you can see, I really need someone to look after me," she said, her eyes resting on Shannon.

There was something appealingly helpless about her innocent smile, her questioning blue eyes. For all her apparent self-indulgence, Jonquil exuded a warmth and charm that drew Shannon to her. She sensed that in spite of her wealth and title, Jonquil didn't know the meaning of snobbery, unlike Elena, who lived by a shrewd hierarchy of values, rating people in an instant according to purse and background, in that order. Jonquil's gaiety, tempered by kindness, must have been irresistibly attractive to the distinguished gentleman whose photograph, framed in silver, had pride of place on Jonquil's night table.

"That was my husband, Sir Freddie," Jonquil said when she saw Shannon looking at the picture. "We had thirty idyllic years together. He passed away ten years ago. I simply adored the ground he walked on," she added nostalgically. "We adored each other."

Somehow Shannon knew this statement was true.

"The little pooch in the other frame is Buggles, and I miss him so. But it won't be long before we're together again."

When it was time for Shannon to go, Jonquil kissed her on the cheek and said, "Why don't you come to lunch on Sunday? Oh, it will be just a lot of boring old fuddy-duddies, but Elena is coming, too, and if you're not doing anything, it might be fun."

"Why, I'd love to. Thank you very much," Shannon replied, taken aback.

"Good! You've been an absolute angel tonight. In fact, I don't know what I would have done without you."

One evening two weeks later, Jonquil summoned Shannon to Witterings.

"You must come at once, my dear. I have a proposal to make to you," she said on the phone in a breathy, mysterious voice.

All the way there Shannon wondered wildly what it could be. When she arrived, and the two of them sat cozily on the chaise longue in the bedroom, Jonquil wasted no time in broaching the subject.

"Have you ever thought of leaving Australia?" she said with a little gleam in her eye, one bejeweled hand playing with the sash of her shocking-pink lounging robe.

"I've thought about nothing else all my life," Shannon admitted. "And I will, too, when I save up enough for my passage. It's taking a lot longer than I hoped, though."

"The thing is, I had a wonderful idea the other day. This will explain it for me." From her pocket she withdrew an envelope, which she handed to Shannon. "Go on, open it," she urged, seeing the puzzled look on her face.

Shannon had never seen a P&O liner ticket before, and it took her a moment to comprehend that she was holding a first-class passage booked in her name, one way from Sydney to Southampton.

"I don't understand—what is it supposed to mean?" Already her heart had begun to flutter with excitement. It couldn't possibly be true, she told herself.

"Oh, do say you'll come, darling. You can see how I need organizing. It would be a perfect arrangement for both of us. I knew how you wanted to go to Europe, and you looked after me so beautifully the other day that I couldn't help envisioning you in Thelma's place. You'd be like one of the family, really, and you could have her sweet little room at the top of my house in Chester Square."

Jonquil had delivered her invitation to go halfway 'round the world with the same wild-eyed nonchalance she had displayed when inviting Shannon to lunch at Witterings.

"You can't mean it?" Shannon enunciated in stunned astonishment.

"Oh, but I do. And there's the ticket to prove it. Oh, of course, I could always get a refund. But I thought it rather an amusing way to tell you, just to hand you the ticket like that," she said merrily.

Shannon took a deep breath. The news had hit her so hard she was speechless for a moment. Every dream of escape she had ever cherished was about to come true! As the implications thundered down on her, she burst into tears, then just as abruptly laughed with joy and confusion. "I'm sorry—it's just that I still can't believe it," she gasped.

"I can only take it that that means yes."

"Oh, yes, yes," Shannon said in a rush, in case she changed her mind.

"I think this occasion calls for something stronger than iced tea," Jonquil remarked, ringing the bell.

When the butler brought drinks, they toasted the future, then Jonquil sank into her chair and began to tell Shannon something about herself.

"If dear Freddie hadn't seen me across the lights of the Lyceum Theatre, I don't know what would have become of me," she mused, toying with her pearls.

Shannon's face was a study in surprise.

"Oh, yes, my dear, I wasn't born a lady, you know. I was made one. I entered the world as plain Gertie Cottle in Cable Street, in London's East End. My sister Flossie and I started dancing in the street for pennies when we were tots, and that's how we went on the stage. As my life changed, so did my accent—just like yours is." Seeing Shannon's uneasiness at the frankness of this remark, Jonquil continued, "And if I want a good cut of meat, I go down to Smithfield Market in my diamonds and pearls, but when I slip into Cockney everything costs half as much. I never forgot who I am—remember that, and you'll save yourself a lot of trouble in life," she said, wagging her finger.

It had never crossed Shannon's mind that this butterfly of a woman, who seemed to thrive on frivolity, had begun her life in the poorest quarter of London. Her pretty round face was as unlined as a baby's, suggesting she had never had a care in the world. As she continued her breezy, light-hearted account of her impoverished childhood and her climb to wealth, Shannon began to feel that the two of them were going to get along famously. Woven into her poignant story were tales of secondhand clothes, a drunken father, and a lack of decent shoes—laundry hanging on poles in the cramped sitting room, and children sleeping four to a bed—details that revealed a common background and instantly established a rapport between them. From that moment on Shannon set about absorbing everything she could from Jonquil, just as she had with Elena; this time, however, she would not learn the paradox of elegance or how to run a business, but how to leap from one mishap to the other while still keeping her feet firmly on the ground.

She could never have foreseen the battle that would ensue the moment she announced to Elena her departure to Europe as Jonquil's companion, maid, and secretary rolled into one. From the moment she breathlessly delivered the news, and gave her notice to Elena, she was the victim of the countess's vitriolic temper, heralding the battle royal that was to follow. From then on Shannon found herself bounced like a tennis ball between the two women. Jonquil's spun-sugar frivolity proved more than equal to Elena's ferocious possessiveness. Elena veered from one extreme to the other, at first abusing Shannon for ingratitude, then weeping on her shoulder and calling her "my daughter." Finally, after opening her heart, she opened what she prized even more, her pocketbook, and offered to double Shannon's salary. For a week the battle for Shannon was the talk of Sydney, ending in an explosive scene between the two contenders at the races at Royal Randwick. A photographer recorded the countess throwing a drink in the face of the Lady Fortesque with the acid comment:

"There, you jumped up chorus girl."

Unmoved, Jonquil had replied, "Bring me some goggles. You never know what the Hungarian goulash might do next."

Shannon was shocked to see the ridiculous photograph of the two of them splashed in the *Sydney Morning Herald*. Of course, when she looked back on the incident she had to laugh, realizing that from now on, as Jonquil's companion, her life was going to be full of surprises.

They were to sail in February, which gave Shannon just enough time to go home to say good-bye.

When the train pulled out of Wishbone station, Shannon stood alone for a moment, letting the other passengers drift away. Picking up her smart new suitcase, she began to walk along the dusty platform in the brilliant sunshine, the dress of pleated lawn she had changed into moments before her arrival already clinging to her back in the midday heat. Her new shoes resounded on the empty platform as she walked toward the lone figure waiting in the shade of the station. Even at a distance she recognized her father, his hat characteristically pulled down over his eyes, his thumbs hitched into his belt loops. She could tell he wasn't sure it was really she, and smiling hesitantly as she approached, Shannon felt a twinge of shyness under his scrutiny. All the way there she had harbored what seemed like a childish desire to show everybody, including Brendan, how far she had come, but through her veneer of Sydney sophistication, her heart pounded with nervous anticipation. She hadn't expected to be so profoundly moved at the sight of her father, and her throat tightened with emotion as she approached him. Within a few yards of him her self-possession broke, and she dropped her suitcase and rushed toward him with arms open wide.

"Dad!" she cried.

A smile broke across his face as he hugged her. Laughing and crying at the same time, she clung to him, safe for a moment in his solid embrace. All their old differences were forgotten. Brendan's eyes were closed, his jaw clenched with inexpressible joy, as he held Shannon fast.

"You know, for a minute there I wasn't sure it was you," he said with a gruff laugh as they walked along. "Wait a minute—let's have another look at you to be sure," he said, standing back appraisingly.

"Just who did you think I was, then?" she asked with a laugh.

78

"Well, well. You look fine, Shannon. Consorting with lords and ladies now, I heard," he teased, picking up her suitcase. "I can see from now on we won't be nearly good enough for you."

"Oh, Dad, you know that's not true." His blazing blue eyes communicated his pride in her and the love he was unable to express aloud.

Clinging to his arm as they walked to the Land Rover she said, "It's so good to see you. I've missed you, Dad."

"And I've missed you, Shannon," he replied with a conviction that told her everything was all right between them.

A crooked smile crossed Brendan's face as people stared at him and Shannon; nobody would have guessed that this weather-beaten drover and this beautiful girl were father and daughter.

"Couldn't Kerry come?" asked Shannon, sliding into the front seat of the Land Rover beside Brendan.

"You know what she's like. Couldn't miss some gymkhana or other, but she'll be home soon after we get there."

Shannon was relieved in a way that Kerry hadn't come; she was dreading her sister's reaction to her departure for England. As soon as she had accepted Jonquil's offer, she'd dashed off an exultant letter to Kerry, adding that she was coming home for a visit. Still, she knew that Kerry would be crestfallen at the distance her departure would put between them.

During the long drive back to Koonwarra, Shannon regarded the endless landscape, glittering beneath a dome of blue sky. The unforgiving brown land, dotted with slow-moving herds of cattle and sheep, seemed bleak and empty after the electrifying buzz of Sydney. A hot wind blew through the noisy cab, bringing a fine dust that settled on her pretty new clothes; with every mile they sped toward home she felt herself dragged back in time by the powerful undertow of the Outback. Just the sight of Brendan's strong hands on the wheel made her feel like a child again. She could feel her father weighing up the change in her, a change she knew he found disquieting. Perhaps she ought to have come home in jeans and a T-shirt, she thought. But then she told herself that she hadn't come so far, climbed so high in eighteen months, to back down now. For once she wanted to flaunt her success, to show everybody that she hadn't slipped into obscurity and poverty in the melting pot of Sydney.

They passed through the gates of Koonwarra as the light

79

slanted in long strokes across grass burnt dry during summer's unrelenting heat. Brendan slowed down as they passed some hands mustering sheep, and Shannon noticed with affectionate amusement that he had the proud regard of a father escorting his prodigal back home.

"Nothing's changed much, has it?" he commented, nodding at the familiar landscape. "Lightning struck that big old gum over there a few months back, and we cut it down. Bob's extended the shearing sheds and drilled a new bore, but other than that everything's about the same. Buck Jones has left, and so has Neil Peak, but that's about all. Henry's at school down in Melbourne, but I guess you know all that from Kerry."

"Yes, she writes me all the news."

"I'm no good at writing. I guess you know that. But I'll try to do better when you're in England. I was thinking— maybe I could make a trip over sometime. That is, if you want me to."

"That would be wonderful, Dad," she said with genuine enthusiasm. "Maybe Kerry could come, too, and the three of us could make a trip over to Ireland."

"Now, there's an idea," said Brendan, his eyes gleaming. "Wouldn't that be something?"

But the moment the thought entered his head it seemed to die like an impossible dream, and Shannon found it hard to visualize it, too. A trip back to Ireland took more than money: it took the burning desire to return to what Brendan had so gladly abandoned many years ago.

Shannon smiled affectionately. "I'll come home when I can, Dad. You know that."

He replied with a look of sad skepticism, and then changed the subject. "Your sister has grown up a lot. You won't know her."

Shannon wanted to ask him how they were getting along, but something held her back.

"Well, here we are, home at last," said Brendan, pulling up in the shade near the bungalow. Shannon hopped outside while Brendan collected her bag from the back.

"Blackie," called Brendan to a passing shearer. "You remember my daughter Shannon. She's just back from Sydney for a visit."

"Hello, Blackie," said Shannon with a smile.

The double take he gave her made her look to Brendan with an embarrassed laugh.

"Shannon? Is that you? I don't believe it," he muttered, pushing back his hat. The gaping astonishment on the shearer's face made her feel like an imposter. "She looks just like royalty or something," he commented to Brendan as if she weren't there.

As they climbed the stairs to the bungalow, Brendan said with a chuckle, "Did you see his face? He couldn't believe his eyes. A lot of people are going to be surprised when they see you." Setting her suitcase down on the screened veranda, he slipped his arm roughly around Shannon's shoulder.

"Honestly, Dad. I haven't changed that much. It's all on the surface."

"I know that. Just the same, I'm proud of you. You've made something of yourself. That's something I never did," he said, his voice dropping.

The pause between them was full of unexpressed sentiments, broken when Brendan said in a cheerful voice:

"Well, girlie, how does it feel to be home? This place must be a change after what you're used to."

"My little room in Paddington is nothing fancy," she said, looking around at the shabby sitting room that seemed even smaller than her memory of it. From the moment she had fled Koonwarra, she had put it all out of her mind, from the worn chair cushions to the rugs puckered around the edges. She had conveniently forgotten the fine dust that covered the scratched tabletops, the drab flowered curtains, and now she struggled to conceal her dismay at the utterly depressing shabbiness of the house that had once been home. Glancing at a wilted bouquet of wildflowers, Shannon said brightly:

"Kerry must have picked those."

"She did. I don't know where she is. She ought to be back soon, though. Here—let me take your suitcase into the bedroom."

As she watched him, Shannon was ashamed of the thought that seized her. She couldn't wait to leave Koonwarra. Shuddering as if a cold wind had hit her, she reached for the memory of beauty and luxury that would one day be hers as a plant reaches for the sun.

"By the way, Dad, one of the things I have to do while I'm here is get a copy of my birth certificate. As soon as I get back to Sydney I'll have to apply for a passport. Lady Fortesque is going to help speed things along, as I haven't all that much time."

81

Brendan's face darkened. "Birth certificate? I wouldn't know where it is."

"Of course you do. It's in the deed box where you keep all your papers. You must have one. Didn't you need it for registering me in school when we came to Koonwarra?"

"I'll have a look, but I don't think it's there. With one thing and another, things get misplaced," he said absently.

"But Dad—you've got to have it. I can't get a passport without a birth certificate," she said urgently.

"There's no use getting worked up. If it isn't there, it isn't there."

"Dad, you don't understand," she said as panic rose in her. "If I don't get a passport in time, then I can't go to England. I'll have to contact the registrar's office in Brisbane and get a copy, then go there in person to save time."

The awful prospect of not sailing to England with Jonquil hit her with full force. The thought of missing the greatest opportunity she would ever have filled her with terror. It couldn't happen—not now, when she was so close.

Sensing her desperation, Brendan shifted uncomfortably. "You should have told me before, that's all. Now calm down."

"I know, I know—I should have. But Dad—please—go and have a look right now. Otherwise I'll have to leave for Brisbane first thing tomorrow morning. I just can't take the chance that they might not send it in time."

Brendan turned resignedly. "All right," he muttered. "I'll have a look."

Her heart pounded in anxiety as she heard him drag the deed box from beneath his bed. Her ears strained for every sound as she heard the lock opening and paper being shuffled. When Brendan finally appeared in the doorway with a piece of paper in his hand, Shannon felt relief flood through every inch of her body.

"See? I told you, didn't I? It was there all the time. What a lot of fuss for nothing," she said with a laugh.

He handed her the certificate, his face strangely grave. "I think you better have a good look at it."

"What do you mean?" Shannon glanced down at the document she had never seen before, scanning the familiar information: Brendan Faloon, born in Limerick, Ireland. Mother: Françoise Paillard, born Nouméa, New Caledonia. Then she read her own name: "Shannon Françoise Paillard, born in Brisbane May 25, 1957."

"Dad, why doesn't it say Shannon Faloon? It says Paillard. That was Mother's maiden name."

Brendan didn't reply but met her eyes with difficulty.

Suddenly it dawned on her, and she gasped. "I see," she began haltingly. "That's why you pretended it was lost. You didn't want to show it to me, did you? It's because you didn't marry Mother, isn't it?" Tears sprang to her eyes as she regarded her father's face, tortured with guilt. His eyes cast down in shame, he couldn't bring himself to look at her. "Why didn't you marry her? Wasn't she good enough for you? Wasn't a half-caste grand enough for a Faloon? You and your big ideas. What do you think you were, anyway? You were nothing but a bastard yourself," she spat out bitterly. In a quavering voice she continued, "You told me often enough how much you loved her, how much you missed her after she died. Or was that a lie, too? For God's sake, Dad, why didn't you tell me the truth?" she cried, her eyes blazing with accusation.

"Shut up, Shannon," Brendan retorted angrily. "You don't have any idea what it was like back then, what people thought about half-castes and still do. . . ."

"Oh, yes, I do know. I know what it makes me," she retorted. Through her father's pathetic attempt at self-justification, Shannon saw the truth. His facile charm, his paternal manner fell away, revealing a weakness in him that hurt her so deeply she couldn't bear to think about it. How would she ever be able to tell Jonquil? There was no way she could hide the fact that her real name was Paillard. Her ticket had already been purchased in the name of Faloon, and Jonquil would undoubtedly consider her an imposter whose integrity would be suspect from then on. Being born illegitimate was bad enough, even in a place like Koonwarra, but her shame would be multiplied a thousandfold in the circles she longed to be a part of. A cry of desperation escaped her as she regarded Brendan through a blur of tears, wishing desperately that she had never come back.

Unable to bear her misery a moment longer, Brendan turned away. "Think what you want and go to hell," he snarled, slamming the screen door behind him.

She watched him stride down the path, knowing that he would be blind drunk within the hour. For an instant she wanted to run after him, but stubborn pride in the face of his betrayal of her mother held her back. All her hopes for the future spiraled down into a black pit. Folding the birth certificate, she put it in her bag, thinking of Jonquil, who had turned her own dubious beginnings to her advantage. Would she prove sympathetic to Shannon's start in life—a legacy even more blighted than her own? A great tremor of determination passed through Shannon as she struggled to shake off the despair that had overtaken her. Whatever the outcome, this unexpected catastrophe meant she would have to polish her image to such a blinding sheen that it would more than compensate for the stigma of being born a bastard.

The blind flapped in the dry, hot breeze churned up by a table fan as Shannon shifted restlessly on the bed, half listening to a fly circling the room. She knew she wouldn't be able to relax even for an instant until she had arrived back in Sydney and told Jonquil about her past. Every time she heard a sound beyond the bungalow, she thought it would be Kerry. She dreaded breaking the news to her that she would have to leave early the next morning.

Her eyes strayed to Kerry's bulletin board, now a mass of blue-and-red rosettes that she had won at gymkhanas all around the countryside. On a shelf nearby were several silver cups and a presentation riding crop proudly displayed by a collage of photographs of horses. These symbols of Kerry's success reassured Shannon that she would be all right where she was for the time being. Her passion for riding gave a meaning to her life at Koonwarra that Shannon had never experienced, and though Kerry yearned to leave the Outback, Shannon felt sure she would find city life intolerable. All she had to do to be in another world was to mount a horse. At last Shannon heard Kerry running up the steps of the bungalow, and she bounded excitedly out of bed.

"Shannon! Shannon! Are you there?" shouted Kerry, her voice resounding through the house. Dashing into the bedroom, she let out a squeal of delight and rushed to fling her arms around her.

"Wow, just look at you!" she enthused. "I can't believe it. I don't know what to say," she said, breaking off with an inarticulate gasp. "Look at your long fingernails—and your hair—you're unbelievably glamorous. Just look at me—I'm a mess," she said with a laugh, running her fingers through her tousled hair. Her shirt and jeans were caked with dust, her hands rough and sunburned. Admiration and envy slashed at her self-esteem as she drank in Shannon's polished elegance.

"Oh, Kerry, I'm so glad to see you, honestly," Shannon

said, hugging her once more. "You don't know how much I've missed you." As her sister regarded her with dazed admiration, she wished she, too, could slip into a pair of comfortable old jeans and a T-shirt.

Pouncing excitedly on the contents of Shannon's suitcase, Kerry exclaimed, "Just look at all this stuff! It's gorgeous. You must be making a fortune now." Reverentially she ran her fingers over the gold monogram of Shannon's suitcase.

"Not that much, really. And anyway, I seem to end up spending everything I earn," she replied with a disparaging smile.

"Look at your underwear. Is it real silk?" she whispered in amazement.

Shannon nodded. "I pick up things for next to nothing at Elena's.

"Here—let me show what I brought you," she said, changing the subject. She unfolded a beautifully made blue dress with a famous label and held it up to Kerry's shoulders.

"You don't mean to say it's really for me? It must have cost a packet. Oh, thanks a million, Shannon," she gushed, darting to the mirror. Imagining herself in it, she tilted her head to one side. "It's an absolute dream. Of course I'll have to get some shoes to do it justice. Oh, thanks a mil," she cried, rushing to hug Shannon.

"Wait—here's a bracelet and necklace to go with it."

"They're really beautiful. You've got such good taste."

As Kerry preened in front of the mirror, Shannon watched her quietly, realizing that in her own way her sister had changed as much as she had. Kerry's provocative allure had bloomed precociously since they'd last seen each other, ripening lusciously, like a peach in the hot sun. Her little sister had left childhood behind her forever, and the knowledge made Shannon feel nostalgic and a little sad.

"Just wait until you see me when I get all dressed up," Kerry bubbled. "You wouldn't know me. How was Dad when he met you?"

"Oh, just fine. I thought he looked well," she said evasively.

"He'll be on his best behavior," Kerry replied cynically. Preoccupied, she didn't notice Shannon's troubled expression. "I'm going to wear my new dress to Mattie's tomorrow. Did Dad tell you? She's having a party especially for you. Charlie's supposed to come up from Canberra just to see you.

85

What are you going to wear? Try everything on for me, and let's decide," she said excitedly.

Shannon took a deep breath. "Look, Kerry, I don't know how to break the news, but I can't stay. I'm going back to Sydney tomorrow morning."

Kerry whirled around and regarded her in stunned silence. "What? You can't mean it. You said in your letter you were going to stay a week at least. You can't go back. There's the party and everything. Why do you have to?" she cried.

"Lady Fortesque needs me," Shannon replied weakly.

"Lady Fortesque?" Kerry exploded. "What kind of monster is she, anyway, to let you stay only one day? Why did you come at all, then?" The hurt in her voice conveyed her crushing disappointment.

Shannon sighed and slumped on the bed. "I suppose you might as well know. I found out half an hour ago that I'm illegitimate. Here—have a look at my birth certificate. I had to ask Dad for it to get a passport, and he couldn't hide the truth any longer. We had an argument when he gave it to me. Go on—read it. You'll see that Dad never married my mother."

Kerry snatched it from her hand. "So what? Who cares? If you don't tell anyone, who's to know?"

"Kerry, you don't understand. I'll have to explain to Lady Fortesque why I'm changing the name on my ticket, and when she finds out she might change her mind about taking me back to London. I can still call myself Shannon Faloon, but she'll have to be told the truth."

"She's not going to give you the boot for such a silly little thing. You're still the same person, aren't you?"

"That sort of thing may mean nothing here, but it means a lot in Sydney or London, believe me. That—and the fact that I'm what some people consider a half-caste."

"When a woman is as beautiful as you are, all that doesn't matter," said Kerry blithely. She paused for a moment, her face set with determination. "I wasn't going to tell you straight away, but I'm coming with you. I've been thinking—I could come to Sydney, take over your old room, even your job, until I can join you in London. . . ."

"Don't be absurd," said Shannon irritably. "Stop all this daydreaming. It isn't going anywhere."

"Just a minute, Shannon. You don't understand. All these rosettes and cups—every gymkhana I enter I earn prize money. Today I won twenty-five dollars, see?" she cried,

86

digging into her pocket. "I've saved it all up, every penny. I have almost enough for a one-way airfare to England. I even sent away to Qantas for a timetable."

Shannon looked away gloomily, unable to cope with Kerry's irrepressible enthusiasm. "We've been all through this before, Kerry. You have to finish school, for a start," she said flatly.

"I don't want to finish school. It's a waste of time. I can pass for eighteen any day."

"I've given up my room already. And as for Elena's— what can I say?" she said exasperatedly. "Kerry, surely you can see it's hopeless. You have no idea how tough it is."

"Then I'll find another room, a job. You did it, didn't you? Anyway, it won't be for long. I'll be in London in no time."

"And just where do you think you're going to live when you get there?" retorted Shannon, unable to repress her sarcasm.

"At Lady Fortesque's, of course. I'm sure I could be useful. You wrote me what a huge house she has in London. Surely there's room for me. You can't say no, Shannon—not anymore. I'm coming with you."

Shannon gave a dry laugh. "Just a minute, Kerry. This is *my* opportunity. I can't bring all my relatives with me."

Kerry's eyes flashed. "*All* your relatives? You mean the only one, your sister. You write long letters about Lady Fortesque's generosity, but if I ask for a crumb from your table, you turn on me."

"Let's drop it, all right? You've said enough," said Shannon tartly. "The fact is, you have a ridiculous idea of what life in a city is like. You'd hate it. What makes you think you'd be happy cooped up in an office or a shop? Be realistic, Kerry, and quit daydreaming."

"Don't tell me what I want, Shannon. And don't tell me about dreams. You're not the only one who has dreams. It's all right for you, isn't it? Your dream is coming true. You've come back to say good-bye like some fairy princess visiting all us poor earthlings. Well, you're nothing but a selfish bitch, Shannon Faloon, or Paillard, or whatever your name is," she cried.

Shannon turned on her angrily. "Just watch what you say, I'm warning you. Yes—I do like pretty clothes. And what's wrong with that? I earned the money to buy them by working damn hard. You have no idea what it's like to arrive in a big city all on your own. I was lonely, scared, miserable.

I didn't dwell on that part in my letters, but I should have. Maybe it would have helped you grow up. It's hell out there."

Regarding her glamorous sister, Kerry gave a scoffing laugh. "Oh, really? Tell me all about it."

"No, I wouldn't bother telling you anything. But I wonder if you would be willing to start at the bottom like I did, I really do. And how would you feel if you were about to sink back into the mire again because you're a bastard? I can't pull your weight, too. It's all I can do to get myself out of here," she cried desperately.

Kerry regarded Shannon with wild-eyed fury. Grabbing the dress she had given her, she tore the trimming violently from the sleeve. "Here's what I think of your bloody bribe, your charity. Take it back. I don't need handouts." Throwing it in Shannon's face, she whirled to kick her sister's suitcase with her boot, causing it to tumble to the floor.

"Why, you ungrateful little wretch," Shannon spat out. She slapped her across the face so hard Kerry reeled back. "I worked hard to buy that dress and all these things that you seem to despise because you can't have what you want. I wouldn't take you with me now for all the tea in China."

Kerry regarded her hatefully, pressing her hand to her cheek. "I'll pay you back one day for that, I swear. I don't care if I never see you as long as I live. Get out and good riddance." With that she stormed out of the bungalow.

When she had gone, their bitter words hung in the air like the echo of a sudden avalanche that had descended, taking love with it. As tears scalded her cheeks, Shannon struggled with a sense of suffocating isolation. But there was no time to turn back, no time to even think of trying to heal the breach between her and Kerry and Brendan. The only thing Shannon could think of was the P&O *Oriana* disappearing over the horizon, leaving her on the quay in Sydney.

With frenzied haste she began to gather up her precious finery spilled so carelessly on the floor. As her hands touched the lace and satin, she could almost hear the metallic clatter of the train pulsating in her imagination, promising freedom with every mile.

Three weeks later Shannon cast a glance around the room she had rented for almost two years in Paddington, pausing for a moment. She had always been indifferent to the shabbiness—the worn linoleum, the chip in the basin in the corner—regarding her surroundings as temporary. Standing by the window in a shaft of afternoon sunlight as she waited for the car to fetch her, she drew back the lace curtain and looked down the line of terraced houses decorated with wrought-iron balconies that sloped on the choppy blue waters of Sydney Harbor.

A warm breeze licked her face as she recalled the tumultuous events of the past few weeks that had led to this moment—to the pinnacle of expectation upon which she blanced so precariously. Stop, she told herself sternly. Looking back is dangerous; memories are like anchors tugging at your coattails.

Suddenly she heard footsteps pounding up the stairs, then a fist hammered on the door.

"Hey, Shannon, the big car is here for you."

She opened the door to admit Nico, the Cypriot owner of the house, who had rented her a room when she'd first arrived in the city. He grabbed her suitcases and trundled downstairs with them. Scooping up her hand luggage and coat, Shannon followed without looking back.

A huge black Daimler was parked at the curb, sparkling in the brilliant sunshine. When the uniformed chauffeur saw her, he opened the door.

"Hey, Shannon, here's something for you," called one of Nico's little sons, handing her a box of chocolates.

As she embraced him warmly, her name was echoed by several well-wishers who had come to say good-bye, most of them Greeks and Italians she had made friends with in the neighborhood.

"Good-bye, Nico," she said, hugging him, then his wife and children in turn.

"Don't forget us, remember," he said, tears in his eyes.

"How could I?" she said fondly, feeling the painful tug of departure.

In this ethnic heart of Sydney, Shannon had always felt at home. She glanced around for the last time at the pretty little terraced houses of Paddington, with their wrought-iron balconies, her refuge from the cold inner core of an indifferent metropolis. The part of her that had always felt a foreigner in the wide brown land of Australia had found a temporary home amongst Greeks, Italians, and Eastern bloc refugees. She had adored their smiles and friendliness as much as the aroma of their Mediterranean cooking. Leaving it all now was much more difficult than she had imagined.

She paused to wave, and when the chauffeur shut the

door of the Daimler, enclosing her in the comfort of the substantial limousine, Shannon knew another fragment of her past had faded away.

After picking up Jonquil at Double Bay, they drove straight to the harbor, and Shannon would never forget her first sight of the P&O *Oriana*. The vast multitiered liner dominated the quay like a floating city in miniature, its great funnels painted against the brilliant blue sky. Following in Jonquil's energetic wake, Shannon looked at her fellow travelers with a sense of delicious promise at the prospect of discovering their identities. The moment her feet left Australian soil she was filled with a sense of adventure. When the steward led them to their first-class cabins, she felt that they had left the humdrum routine of life on shore and were now ruled by the ship's timetable, a miracle of scheduling that crowded amusing events into every possible moment, from lectures to handicrafts, to movies, to shuffleboard, with endless meals, cocktails, and dancing sandwiched in between.

They were ushered onto the upper deck into the plush, paneled stateroom, already packed with flowers, baskets of fruit, and champagne sent by Jonquil's friends, who would be arriving at any moment for a send-off party. Then Shannon was shown to her own quarters, a small but very comfortable cabin with a bath adjoining Jonquil's suite. As she regarded the spectacular waterfront of Sydney through the porthole, Shannon grasped for the first time the meaning of her departure. She had no time to wallow in daydreams, however, for within minutes Jonquil's stateroom was filled with laughing, chatting visitors who had come for a *bon voyage* party.

Shannon moved among them, filling glasses, emptying ashtrays, exchanging conversation with people who remembered her from the luncheon at Witterings. She moved cautiously, feeling her way in that twilight area between servant and acquaintance; but a sweet smile from Jonquil and the twinkle in her eyes reassured Shannon that her employer was as pleased as ever that she was coming along for the voyage.

When she had refilled his glass, Colonel Jenkins, a huge man with a handlebar mustache, said warmly, "You're such a pretty creature, and we hear so capable, too. We're all relying on you to take care of our Jonquil."

"Yes, my dear," echoed his wife, a birdlike little woman, "the darling needs such a lot of looking after," thus perpetuating the charming myth that Jonquil was as helpless as a kitten.

By now the cabin was so full of people it was impossible to move, and from the shrieks of laughter and the din of conversation, it seemed that none of them would budge before midnight.

"Why don't we all go along to Antibes in September, Jonquil? It would be such fun. . . ."

When Shannon caught this snippet of conversation, her heart skipped a beat, and it took her a moment to remember why. It was Zan's description of the port on the Côte d'Azur, still as vivid to her as the reality. She tried to shrug off the surge of vulnerability she experienced at the thought of him, but it was hopeless: even the simple mention of a faraway place was enough to trigger a charged memory of Zan that made her stomach contract.

At last the ship's deep horn vibrated through the cabin, alerting visitors that it was time to depart. After noisy and affectionate good-byes, the crowd trickled out onto the deck, calling out promises to write. Jonquil dabbed at her eyes with a handkerchief as she embraced each one of them.

Those loving good-byes among old friends touched a raw nerve of loneliness in Shannon, and she felt a lump rising in her throat. Not a soul would notice her own departure. She was about to slip quietly and unobtrusively, however grandly, from the only world she had ever known.

"Feeling a bit teary?" Jonquil asked when the crowd had gone. She regarded Shannon sympathetically, sensing the poignant importance of the moment, then took her hand and squeezed it as if she were a bewildered child. "It will be a bit of a wrench at first. It always is, but the journey is so enthralling that I'm sure you'll soon forget your homesickness."

"I'm fine, really I am," said Shannon.

"You're much too young to look back. Why, even at my age I try not to do it."

"I think that's your secret, Jonquil," Shannon said thoughtfully.

"I'll tell you what—let's go on deck. Leaving Sydney Harbor is one of the grandest sights in the world, and we shouldn't miss a minute."

When they had posted themselves at the railings, the *Oriana* started to glide regally through the sapphire water, lending the thrilling sensation of a titan on the move. The atmosphere was reminiscent of New Year's Eve, with an orchestra on shore playing "Auld Lang Syne" and people on deck throwing colored streamers. Gazing at the panorama of

91

Sydney, Shannon felt she was being lifted and carried away by some giant unseen hand. In a mantle of apricot evening light, towering buildings rose in tiers through green, hilly vistas, and the jigsaw of islands and coves at the city's feet, washed by a glassy sea, held the enchantment of a mirage. The invisible bond between Shannon and this bold, beautiful city began to tug at her self-possession as the distance length-ened between boat and shore. Australia had been home, no matter how vast and indifferent, and she was letting it go as if it had never meant anything. She had jumped aboard the *Oriana* with Jonquil as a child leaps on a carousel horse, and where it would take her was anybody's guess.

A chilly salt breeze sprang up as the last tug departed, hooting farewell, and the *Oriana* passed through the magnifi-cent harbor toward the open sea, where the sky now melted orange and lemon on the horizon.

Jonquil shook herself from her reverie and blew a kiss to Australia. "Good-bye—*a la prochaine fois!*" she called gaily.

Shannon waved her hand, and waved to no one.

"And now the fun is going to begin. Let us amuse ourselves for three glorious weeks," said Jonquil triumphantly.

When Jonquil went to the captain's cabin for cocktails, Shannon was left to the pleasure of unpacking. With the appreciative instinct of someone who cherished beautiful things, she carefully hung the two dozen evening dresses in the closet, folded piles of downy-soft lingerie away in the draw-ers, then unpacked the lilac ostrich-skin dressing case with Jonquil's monogram on it, arranging each silver-topped bottle on the dressing table. As a last touch she unfolded the bed and laid a crêpe de chine nightdress on the satin coverlet, knowing somehow without being told what was expected of her. The ritual of it all satisfied her natural instinct for order and beauty, and she glanced with pleasure at every detail in the glowing stateroom.

Ceremoniously, she poured herself a glass of champagne and proceeded to her own cabin to dress for dinner with Jonquil at the captain's table. Opening her handbag, Shannon came across her passport. For the hundredth time she relived the shock of discovering she was the bastard daughter of Brendan Faloon and Françoise Paillard. This last imbroglio before leaving Sydney, one that Jonquil had had to pull strings to sort out, had profoundly shaken her carefully culti-vated self-confidence. To her relief and amazement, the in-trepid Jonquil had passed over her humiliation as if it meant nothing, but still Shannon was tortured with a feeling of shame. She read her name again: Shannon Françoise Paillard.

Now, however, from a first-class stateroom on the *Oriana*, she reached for splendor. Raising her glass to her reflection in the mirror, she said resolutely:

"Here's to us, Shannon Faloon—happy landings, girl."

Chapter IV

London, England, 1977

When the Jaguar swept into Chester Square on the last day of February, Jonquil could hardly contain her impatience to be home and had opened the car door herself before the chauffeur could leap out.

"Never mind, Bagley," she chirped, springing from the soft leather seat.

Shivering at the chill wind that had been biting into her bones from the moment the liner had crossed the oyster-gray water of the English Channel, Shannon followed. Rain clouds as solid as mountains had weighed down on them all the way through London's straggling suburbs, and Belgravia was the first promise of glamour she had seen since they'd docked. A hundred chandeliers sparkling from the townhouses glinted through the leafless trees lining the square, and even though it was only five o'clock, it was as dark as midnight. The travelers were met at the door by the housekeeper, whom Jonquil enfolded in a warm embrace.

"Irma, dear—and Buggles!" she shrieked joyfully at the dog prancing at her feet.

Though London was wrapped in sleet and mist, the interior of Jonquil's house was gleaming with light and warmth. A fire blazed in the drawing room hearth, waiting to welcome them, and Shannon had the impression that this sumptuous home only needed laughter and conversation to enliven it. Irma took their coats, while Bagley carried the luggage upstairs. Not quite knowing what to do with herself while Jonquil fluttered from place to place with Buggles in her arms, inspecting the mail and calling out orders to the housekeeper, Shannon looked around at this new frontier of grandeur,

93

feeling like a cricket in a cage who was expected to sing for its supper. Fulfilling the role of lady's maid on the *Oriana* was one thing, but here in Chester Square every detail of the grand house seemed to be regulated by caring hands, from the polished brass fireguard to the Meissen figures in a marquetry cabinet. Fascinated by the overblown luxury of chintz rose curtains, plush furniture, shaggy carpeting, and fussy antiques, Shannon wondered how to make herself indispensable as quickly as possible, anything but adverse to being cosseted in this heart of the English establishment. Recalling the dreary succession of poor neighborhoods she had noticed on the way there, she realized once again just how lucky she was. She was studying the portrait above the fireplace when Jonquil bustled in with Buggles in her arms, followed by Irma carrying a tea tray.

"Darling baby boy, yes, Mummy's home at last," she crooned in the dog's ear.

"I love that painting," said Shannon.

"Oh, that's me by Augustus John. Freddie commissioned it the summer we were married."

The artist had captured all Jonquil's dimpled blond beauty in full bloom against a backdrop of sequined green light in a summery English glade.

"Can you believe it's ever like that in England?" said Jonquil, pouring tea from a silver pot, then whisking off a napkin to reveal a pile of hot crumpets. When she saw Shannon looking at a collection of silver-framed photographs on a table, she said, "Oh, that's Freddie's goddaughter just before her wedding. And the picture to the right is her with her dear little baby girl, already six months old now. And that's me and Freddie with the Churchills at Chequers. Wasn't I thin, though? Oh, to be that thin again," she lamented.

But Shannon's eyes were still resting on the image of the regal woman in a gown of white satin. Shiningly blond and unsmiling, she stared directly into the camera. In the other photograph, cradling a baby swaddled in lace, her eyes had that same unswerving directness. Shannon perceived at a glance that, whoever she might be, she lived in another world, a safe world for those who belonged.

By the end of March Shannon could see the first green buds beginning to sprout from the trees outside her room at the top of the house in Chester Square. A blustery wind pushed at the windows of her own little enclave under the eaves, cozily furnished with a brass bed and comfortable chairs.

She had just finished a long, descriptive letter to Kerry, which she now signed "Love, Shannon" with a flourish. Shannon had been the first to swallow her pride after their quarrel, aware that as the elder sister it was up to her to heal the rift; besides, at a distance it seemed easier to be generously forgiving. But she had written half a dozen newsy letters to Kerry before she had finally received a grudging reply. It had upset Shannon when, reading between the lines, she sensed Kerry's misery, and now whenever she wrote a letter she was careful to tone down her enthusiasm for London, to underplay her joy at being there. It wouldn't be long, she knew, before Kerry's longing to join her would begin to creep into their correspondence, and for the present she was simply unable to pay her way. London had proved to be full of delicious temptations that were far beyond her means, even though Jonquil paid her a generous weekly allowance. She seemed unable to even walk into Harrods or Harvey Nichols without spending money.

Shannon looked around her room, wondering what to do next. Jonquil liked to have her around the house the way she liked to see Buggles dancing at her feet. Over breakfast in her room they would natter about the party she had been to the night before. Jonquil seemed delighted with her young companion and sought her advice on everything from clothes and accessories to flower arrangements. But her day was packed with engagements, which left Shannon with nothing to do after breakfast. At first she had been content to explore the delights of London from Hyde Park to Hampton Court, but as spring progressed she felt a growing restlessness to meet people, to become involved. What she needed was a life of her own, she thought. Grabbing her coat and her letter to Kerry, she flew from her gilded cage in Chester Square out into the world.

Strolling past a news agent's kiosk in King's Road, she caught sight of a card on a notice board. It was an advertisement for an artist's model; the remuneration was good, the hours were flexible, and the card itself had been beautifully lettered in an old-fashioned handwriting that intrigued her. There was no description of what kind of girl the artist was looking for, but imagining *la vie bohème* in a Chelsea garret, Shannon's curiosity was aroused.

By now she knew Chelsea well enough to find Rossetti

Studios in Flood Street, which at this time of year was lined with cherry trees in bloom. Entering the redbrick Victorian building, she walked through the old carriage way to a courtyard and down a long corridor lit by skylights, searching for the name of the artist on the brown varnished doors of the studios. She felt a tingling sense of history with every step, as her feet touched the same ground trod by pre-Raphaelite artists and poets. Finally she found the number given on the notice and knocked at the door.

"Yes? What is it?" boomed a voice from behind the door.

"I've come about your advertisement," she called.

When the door burst open Shannon was startled to see a huge bearded man, his face cast in shadow.

"What in heaven's name do you want?" he asked gruffly.

She swallowed nervously. "I've come about the advertisement at the news agent's. This is number three Rossetti Studios, isn't it?"

"It is. Can't you see the number on the door?"

"Well, do you want an artist's model or not?" she shot back. An indignant anger rose in her to combat the timidity this fierce man aroused.

"Why didn't you say so in the first place?" he said. "Come in." He brushed his hands through his unkempt gray hair with a touch of awkwardness, as if suddenly aware of his tattered paint-splashed smock.

Shannon walked into the huge chilly studio filled with vast canvases of bold nudes. At first impression, the artist's work was as overpowering as his personality.

"Come over here. I'm glad you came, really. I've been painting nonstop since this morning, without a break." He filled a dingy glass and thrust it at her. "Have a glass of wine."

Under his bristling eyebrows were a pair of pale, piercing eyes that bored into her critically. She felt as if she were being judged as no one had ever judged her.

"Well, what about the job?" she ventured when she had suffered from his stare long enough.

"Don't know if you'll do yet. Go and take your clothes off and we'll see."

"Take my clothes off?" she said, aghast.

"Yes. What do you take me for? I'm a painter of female pulchritude, not of sweaters and skirts. Over there in the corner—there's a door. You can leave your things in there. Go on, now. I haven't got all day."

Shannon considered it for a split second. She was damned if she was going to let this rude, pompous painter make a meal of her. Rushing to undress before she could have time to reconsider, she tore off all her clothes and stalked back into the frigid studio, edging toward a shaft of sunlight falling from the glass above. Her arms folded self-consciously, she looked wildly around—anywhere to avoid those penetrating eyes.

She was a study of shadow and light with her glossy black hair and tawny skin. His eyes followed the definition of her collarbones; nervousness beat at the hollows in her throat. The splash of embarrassment on her cheeks was the only smudge of color on a body that was already a canvas in the painter's eye. The natural grace of her unclothed body moved him to stalk restlessly in front of her as he considered the dynamic possibilities of painting her. Her small, high breasts, her hipbones flaring from a deeply carved waist were an artist's dream, and her perfect head, held proudly above her fine shoulders, caused a thoughtful frown to darken his face. Shannon took it for disapproval, not realizing it was his habitual expression when consumed with a craving to paint the image before him.

"You'll do," he said curtly ."When can you start?"

"You haven't told me yet how much you'll pay me," she retorted, sorry now that they hadn't settled it before she had revealed herself to him stark naked.

"Two pounds. I pay the best, and I expect the best. I'll need you about ten hours a week. It's long, hard, cold, and boring work, but there'll be no absences once we start, no slacking off."

A quick calculation told Shannon that the money would be more than enough to cover her little extravagances, and maybe enough to send for Kerry someday.

"All right—I agree," she replied with far less cowardice than she felt.

"Fine," he growled. "You'll start tomorrow. By the way, my name's Hawke Sutherland. What's yours?"

"Shannon," she replied, amazed at her own courage. "Shannon Faloon. I'll start the day after tomorrow."

He scowled but nodded. "Fine. I'll see you day after tomorrow, Shannon Faloon."

With a sense of exhilaration, Shannon left Rossetti Studios. Her embarrassment at standing in the nude was quickly forgotten. She was now employed—she was an artist's model in Chelsea.

As the tall, broad-shouldered gentleman in a pin-striped suit strode through the old-fashioned door of Asprey's in Bond Street, the uniformed doorman tipped his hat.

"Good morning, m'lord," he said deferentially.

"Morning," Zan replied with a congenial smile.

Once within the glittering inner sanctum of jewelers and silversmiths to the queen, his eyes roamed around the display of precious objects sparkling in display cases.

"Good morning, Lord Fitzherbert," said the dark-suited salesman. "May I help you?"

"Good morning, Mr. Cecil. Yes, I think you might. I'm looking for something rather special." Scanning an array of rings and earrings spread on velvet, he considered the possibilities.

"May I ask the occasion, sir?"

"It's our wedding anniversary. I'd like to look at some sapphire and diamond earrings, I think. You know the sort of thing."

"What about these, sir?" The salesman removed a tray of earrings from the case. "These run at just over six hundred guineas."

"Yes, these will do nicely. They're exactly what I wanted," Zan said after a moment. "I'll take them with me. Just put them on my account."

"Very good, sir."

Emerging from the subdued lighting of Asprey's, Zan paused and glanced at his watch, realizing he had a quarter of an hour to spare before meeting Noel Villiers at White's. This would allow him the unexpected luxury of a stroll along the crowded pavement of London's richest emporium of shops, an all too infrequent pleasure since he had begun his career in property development in the City.

The sunshine of late May was tempered by a fresh breeze that rustled the skirts of women meandering past the elegant boutiques. The spring colors they wore with such flair had all the freshness and brilliance of the tulips and crocuses that proliferated in Hyde Park.

Passing Agnew's Fine Art Gallery, Zan stopped in his tracks and turned to stare. Dominating the huge display window was a picture that sent a shock of recognition through him. The life-size nude of a girl was a breathtaking masterpiece

98

in sepia and glossy browns executed with the strength and perception of genius. The artist had captured all the alluring delicacy of a young woman's body, but it was the exquisite face that jarred his memory. A few brush strokes portrayed a mouth melting with sensual promise, but it was the eyes— the same proud regard that had haunted him ever since his stay in Australia—that now pinned Zan to the street with such power that he felt his heart ripping through his chest.

Slightly intoxicated from the shock, Zan rushed into the gallery. The last thing in the world he had expected to see that pleasant afternoon in Bond Street was Shannon Faloon's unforgettable image, and he was thrown into confusion as he asked himself what she was doing there.

"May I help you, sir?" said a young man.

"I—I don't know if you can. I mean, it's about that portrait in the window," he stuttered, feeling foolish.

His eyes darted about the gallery, where he was surprised to see pictures of Shannon multiplying in a variety of guises. There she was lying dreamily on a divan; then again, wrapped in a green paisley shawl. Without doubt it was the same beautiful girl he remembered.

"You will find there are half a dozen of the same subject by Hawke Sutherland in his exhibition, but I'm afraid they are all sold. . . ."

"Where can I get in touch with the artist?" Zan asked abruptly.

"I'm very sorry, sir, but we don't divulge our artists' addresses. But as we represent him, we could deliver any message you might have."

"That's not good enough," Zan snapped irritably. "I want to speak with him in person. Oh, very well," he added impatiently, grabbing a catalog and storming into the gallery for a last look at the pictures.

The images leapt off the wall at him. Shannon's arresting face, her perfect body, swirled around in a taunting vortex of eyes, lips, and flesh. Somehow he knew that the artist had been as enamored of her as he was. Then, like a demented man, Zan tore from the gallery and hurried to his club. Taking the steps of White's two at a time, he passed the doorman without acknowledgment and raced to the leather-bound telephone books.

"Sotherby, Sothern, Sutherland . . ." he murmured, his finger following the long column until he found Hawke's

99

name. He scribbled the address on a piece of paper and curled it up in his pocket, then headed into the bar.

For once, the air of civilized calm that pervaded London's most exclusive men's club mocked his turbulent mood. He pulled himself together, trying to look normal when he spotted Noel.

"Where have you been, old man? You look in a bit of a state. What's happened?"

Noel, whom Zan had known since he was at Eton and who had been best man at his wedding, regarded him curiously. An evasion sprang immediately to Zan's lips.

"I was just at Asprey's to pick up an anniversary present for Rosemary. I was in a complete flap, as I thought I'd lost it. But in fact I had absentmindedly tucked it into my back pocket after all."

Noel laughed sympathetically. "That was lucky. Rosemary would never have let you get away with that. You'd have had to go back and buy the same thing again."

"Yes, that would have been a damned nuisance," he agreed, forcing a smile.

Taking their drinks with them, the two men went upstairs to the packed dining room, its crimson walls hung with dark portraits. They helped themselves to the buffet hors d'oeuvres, and when they were seated, Noel studied the wine list.

"Let's have some of the seventy-two hock, Felix," he said, and the hovering sommelier nodded approvingly and moved away.

Zan listened to what now seemed like mindless chatter regarding their forthcoming polo match at Lord Vestey's country retreat in Gloucestershire. All the time his mind throbbed with the shock of his discovery. Shannon. She must be in England. There was no one else in the world who looked like her—richly mysterious, darkly beautiful, haunting Shannon. He had relived their encounter in the stables at Koonwarra a thousand times since then, and at the suggestion his brain churned up a half-forgotten desire that destroyed his appetite and swayed his reason.

An hour later he was hailing a taxi in St. James's, now firmly in the grip of obsession.

"Thanks, guv," said the taxi driver as he hurriedly overtipped him the fare outside Rossetti Studios.

He walked quickly into the shadowy hall, his footsteps echoing, and knocked at Hawke Sutherland's door.

"What do you want?" demanded the artist, flinging open the door.

Zan caught a glimpse of a nude woman pulling a wrap around her as he charged into the studio. The sloe-eyed blonde looked at him haughtily from a divan below a half-finished canvas.

"It's all right, Miranda," called Hawke. "I'll be with you as soon as I've ejected this intruder. Now, get the hell out of here, whoever you are."

"Just a minute. You don't understand," blundered Zan inarticulately. "It's that girl—the one in your pictures at the Agnew's. I must find out who she is—I mean, where she is. She's somebody I know."

"So that's it. I suppose you think you can get a discount by barging in here. Well, you're mistaken," he flared angrily.

"No, no, that's not it. I'm a friend of hers, and we've lost touch. I just want her address, her phone number."

"I'm an artist, not a pimp. You've got a bloody cheek. Now get out." Threateningly, he moved toward Zan.

"Please just tell me this—she is Shannon Faloon, isn't she? At least then I'll know."

"I'm not in the habit of divulging the identity of my models, not even to the aristocracy," Sutherland replied imperiously.

Zan numbly came to the realization that he had reached a dead end. "I'm sorry to have troubled you," he said, retreating to the door. He walked dejectedly down the corridor, fumbling with hope like a bright talisman.

When the door was closed and bolted to make sure the intruder didn't lay siege to his studio again, Hawke turned with a chuckle to the model, who slipped the wrap from her shoulders.

"That's genius for you. This isn't the first time my nudes have caused young men to tear their hair and run wild in the streets," he said, pleased in spite of himself.

"That was extremely gallant of you to shield your protégée like that."

"Not at all. I'm taking her out myself. Why should I share her with that bastard?"

She laughed. "Do me a big favor, Hawke. If anyone as handsome as that one beats down the door for my name and number—give it to him."

As Kerry glanced up at the hard china-blue sky that mocked the chilly air, she sensed that winter had arrived. Dark-edged clouds streamed over the hills around Koonwarra, masking the sun, and she made a wish that summer would come again soon, even though there was nothing to look forward to now that Shannon had left Australia for good. For weeks after her departure a storm had hung over Kerry, robbing her of her usual pleasure in working with the horses on the station, until Shannon's persistence had established a truce between them. Kerry was still capable of bouts of hateful resentment, but she kept them to herself, and a letter from her sister was enough to stir up all her old restlessness. As she walked toward the paddock, her mind was swamped with images of London recounted in the pages she had read moments ago.

Shannon—an artist's model. Kerry had a mental image of her perched on top of a marble pedestal swathed in gauze. Though Shannon had complained of the tedium and the cold in the artist's studio, Kerry could sense that underneath she was giddy with excitement at her latest turn of fortune.

Kerry had practically memorized every word of her letters, hungrily consuming the scraps of news about Shannon's eventful life in Chester Square where the dog Buggles ate minced steak from a china plate and Lady Fortesque's linen sheets were changed every day. She was so absorbed now in her daydream that she started in surprise when a deep voice called her name. She turned to see a shearer named Toby watching her from the doorway of one of the horse boxes.

"Oh, it's you," she said languidly.

"What about it? You coming with me into Wishbone for the dance tonight?"

"I might," she said, toying with her crop. "I don't know if I'm in the mood, really. I've got a lot on my mind."

"Come on—you said you would. I've been counting on it all week."

"I'll let you know later," she said casually, walking on.

"Don't think I'm going to take no for an answer. I'll be over at your place about six-thirty."

She gave him a wisp of a smile, briefly resting her clear green eyes on him long enough to reassure herself that the intensity in his own eyes contradicted the casual tone of his conversation. She couldn't help but smile inwardly, knowing

102

perfectly well that as she walked away Toby was greedily consuming every inch of her retreating figure.

Since Dan Roper had garnered her virginity, Kerry had made enormous strides in the game of love. She had learned that men were basically fools, and that they could be played like fish. Almost overnight she had established herself as the prettiest, most popular girl for miles around, a position she had maintained by never going with a man long enough to let him get tired of her. Leaving them hungry for more, she moved on, juggling her string of admirers like a stable of ponies, roping them in if they strayed too far, yet feeding them with the sugar of her teasing manner. They fell for it every time. Once in a while, if she were in the mood, she let them have what they wanted, but it was rare she went that far, preferring the power over men that unconsummated love gave her. What had begun as defiant rebellion had now progressed to an amusement that filled her time whenever she wasn't attending local meets with Splendor, still her first and only love.

Teasing men no longer held the same challenge it had once provided, however, since Brendan had relinquished the battle of wills to control her. His resistance to her seemed to have collapsed the day Shannon left, robbing Kerry of the triumphant rebellion she had come to expect and almost to enjoy. Since then she had done exactly as she pleased, but her new freedom wasn't as sweet as she had expected.

Passing by Mattie's office on her way to check the mail table, Kerry paused to overhear a conversation that drifted through the open window.

". . . this is a working station, Mat, not a flophouse. If I let Brendan get away with a three-day drunk every week, what will the other men say? I take your point about Kerry, but I'm at the end of my tether. He hasn't even poked his head through the shed door this morning. I'll give him one more chance, and if he blows it, he's through. As for the girl, she can stay here, sure. We can find a place to put her until she finishes school. It's an act of charity and the least we can do."

"Lord knows, Bob, you're right," said Mattie with a sigh. "That girl is running wild, and he's taken no notice of her since Shannon left. I'm getting worried about her. One thing for sure, if she's landed on us, she'll be a handful. . . ."

Kerry turned on her heel abruptly, coloring with indignation as fear ripped through her. The words "landed" and "charity" jangled in her mind, and suddenly the confident

103

young beauty in tight jeans crumpled to a frightened child. What would she do if Brendan were thrown off the station? She knew one thing—she would never stay at Koonwarra to be bossed around by Mattie and Bob Fremont. If she had to, she would run away to Sydney like Shannon. Knowing full well what she would find, and distracted by Mattie and Bob's discussion, she mounted the steps of the bungalow. If Brendan hadn't shown up at the shed that morning, he must be somewhere in the house, lying in a drunken stupor. She opened the screen door and looked around the living room warily, but he was nowhere to be seen.

"Dad?" she called. His room was empty. Then she heard a sound coming from her own room and ran to investigate.

There was Brendan, kneeling on the floor by her bed. "What are you doing in here?" she shouted angrily. "What have you got? Here, give me that!" she screamed, tearing the paper from his hands.

"My little girl—she's gone. She's never coming back," he sputtered, doubling over.

"How dare you—those are my letters! You have no right coming into my room and breaking into my private things. You've been doing it all along, haven't you? Answer me— haven't you?" she shrieked, snatching the pile of letters scattered on the floor.

"I should have gone after her when she went to Sydney, brought her back," he mumbled drunkenly, breaking into a fresh bout of tears and self-pitying incoherence.

"You are disgusting," she said. He lay in a crumpled heap at her feet, and the sight of him revolted her. "And now you're going to lose your job. I heard Bob say it. You'll be thrown off Koonwarra, and then what'll become of me?" Her shrill voice resounded in the little room.

Brendan's bleary eyes focused on Kerry. His unshaven face, stained with tears, was suddenly ravaged by loathing.

"Why couldn't you have gone instead of her?"

Pain stabbed through her. It was the first time he had ever said it, but somehow she had always known.

"That's right—she's gone. And she's never coming back. No wonder—she left this godforsaken hole to get away from you, you drunken slob. And I will, too—just as soon as I'm able, and I'll never see the back of you again as long as I live. . . ."

* * *

A week later, in London, when the bell rang at Chester Square, Shannon masquerading as Scheherazade rushed to the door to find a sultan in a mirrored waistcoat and gold turban. His blue eyes contrasted incongruously with his skin, darkened by burnt cork, and a beard disguised the fact that he was really Hawke Sutherland.

"You look absolutely delicious," he declared when he saw Shannon. "A Turkish delight."

"Thank you. You look quite magnificent yourself," she replied. Resplendent in turquoise harem pants and an embroidered bolero, a veil suspended from a jeweled cap, she curtsied for him. Since Hawke had invited her to a summer costume ball at the fabled Chelsea Arts Club, she had thought of nothing else. After ushering him into the drawing room, she dashed upstairs and tapped at Jonquil's door.

Lady Fortesque was in bed, wrapped in a maribou bedjacket and propped up by a pile of cushions. With one hand she stroked the snoozing Buggles; with the other, she was rather unceremoniously blowing her nose.

"You make a ravishing odalisque, my dear," she croaked when Shannon came through the door. "Didn't I tell you you'd find exactly what you wanted at Berman's? It's where all of London fill their historical fantasies. Do have the most wonderful time." She gestured. "Don't come near me with this wretched cold I've got."

"Promise me you'll stay in bed all weekend and pamper yourself," Shannon admonished. "You'll be fine on Monday if you do."

"I do hope so. If this turns into the flu, I might miss Ascot. What a tragedy! I do so look forward to it every year."

Moments later, Shannon and Hawke were chugging along toward Chelsea in Hawke's old Volkswagen. In Eaton Square, the trees formed a dome of blossoms against the salmon-colored sky. They sped down the King's Road, where trendy boutiques were lit like jewel boxes and people spilled from the pubs onto the pavements. Tonight the street had a carnival air.

When Hawke beamed broadly at her, Shannon returned his smile. She had discovered that underneath his gruff exterior was a wicked sense of fun, and she sensed tonight would be her reward for two months of grueling work in his uncomfortable studio. Hawke's concentration and capacity for work were prodigious, and she had been exhausted when it was over.

At the time they'd begun, she had had no idea that he was a painter of world renown. The exhibition at the Agnew Gallery had electrified the art world, and the half dozen studies of her he had exhibited had been snapped up by collectors from Paris to Tokyo. She had chosen to stay away from the opening itself but had slipped down alone one afternoon to the gallery to see his one-man show. It came as a shock to see her own naked image displayed in a huge window on a busy street, and she felt an embarrassment as profound as if she had disrobed in public. Unable to bring herself to enter the gallery in case she were recognized, she had turned away. But beneath her sensitivity to this public display of her body was pride at having played a tiny part in the history of art. Hawke Sutherland was now in his prime, and his work was being compared to Bonnard and Picasso. She was flattered at having been chosen as his inspiration.

She had worried what Jonquil would say if she found out her secret but soon realized that Jonquil's interests lay as far away as possible from serious cultural pursuits. Though Shannon was proud of her achievement, she felt reluctant to share it with anyone.

When he had parked the car in front of the club, Hawke helped her out with a flourish.

"It's true what they say, that a woman is much more provocative with her clothes on," he remarked, making her laugh. "By the way, I'd forgotten to tell you about an amusing little incident. A demented young man rushed into my studio the other day, demanding to know your name and address."

"You're joking. I certainly hope you didn't give it to him."

"Of course not, but I couldn't get rid of the man. Practically had to shove him out of the door, he was in such a blaze of passion."

They shared a laugh. Absurd as the idea was, she couldn't help but feel that the little incident was another feather in her cap—and a fitting tribute to their joint triumph.

"And to think it all began when I took a walk to post a letter. Imagine—I might have applied for a job baby-sitting instead."

Slipping into the Regency house through an unimposing little door, they found themselves in another world. In an Aladdin's cave sparkling with lights disguised as rubies and emeralds, characters from the four corners of the Middle East had gathered in jeweled and turbaned splendor.

"Oh, Hawke, it's wonderful!" she exclaimed above the din.

Towering over most of the crowd, the magnificent Hawke swept through the multitude with Shannon on his arm. They passed a bevy of Circassian slaves in transparent gauze, swarthy desert nomads in burnooses who looked as if they had left their camels outside. The smoky room rocked with belly dancers in jangling bracelets, leering pirates in bandanas and gold earrings, and soothsayers and fortune-tellers fresh from the souks of Cairo. Carried along by the throng, they spilled onto the terrace, where a Persian garden had materialized on a patch of English lawn. A hundred flares wavered up into the midnight-blue sky, illuminating a grove of trees hung with gilded fruit. Through arches of marbled paper they viewed a singing fountain floating with rose petals. They wandered among the cream of London's pleasure-loving artists and writers, who were disguised as conjurors with wild eyes and outrageous tricks up embroidered sleeves, sleek acrobats from the corps de ballet, who tossed balls in the air. The star of the evening was a voluptuous odalisque who shimmied to the music of reed pipes and a tambourine on a brass tabletop. Shannon gazed in astonishment when an admirer leapt up beside her and stuffed a banknote into her sequined halter. A moment later the unsuspecting Hawke was nearly knocked off his feet when a shepherd herded three bleating goats through the crowd, an intrusion everyone found hilariously funny.

"Let's head for the bar—perhaps it's safer there," Hawke bellowed, elbowing aside a tipsy carpet merchant.

The oasis proved to be a striped tent on the far edge of the lawn. To the popping of champagne corks, punctuated by shrieks of laughter, slaves in loincloths were offering drinks. Eyes darkened with kohl, they lent further credence to the fantasy that a little square of London was careening madly into the night on a flying carpet.

Hawke handed Shannon a glass of champagne. "Here's to you, dark muse," he said with a devilish smile.

"And here's to a genius." She raised her goblet. "Thank you for bringing me. I'm having the time of my life."

"There's an aura of the East about you that lends further enchantment tonight." His voice was playful, yet serious. "You're one of a rare breed, Shannon. There's an intriguing sense of destiny about you. I noticed it the moment you walked into my studio. That quality is what raises a mortal

107

from the mundane to the sublime. Remember that, and don't settle for anything less. There's where you belong, there's where your destiny lies," he said, gesturing to the sky, "among the stars."

"That's what I used to tell myself back home." She looked up at the blaze of bright stars and the silver fulcrum of moon on which they seemed to turn. She lowered her gaze to find Hawke's eyes boring into her. In all their months of working closely together, she realized, rarely had they had so intimate a conversation.

"Ride the wild horse of destiny fearlessly," he said passionately.

"The wild horse of destiny," she repeated. "You're such a romantic. You know, I think I've done it. Hawke, by coming to your studio. But you frightened me to death, you know. You were such an ogre. I don't know why I didn't bolt when I saw you."

"An ogre?" he said, pretending to be offended. "You stayed because you wanted to. Because I wanted you to. But more important, because it was kismet." He sighed. "How I wish I were twenty years younger."

Seeing the nostalgia in Hawke's eyes, Shannon wished for a moment that he were, too.

They were interrupted by a tall, striking man in a flowing white caftan who was approaching like a ship in full sail. His noble head, topped by a red fez, was dominated by a hawk nose and a magnificent silver mustache that swept halfway up his cheeks.

"My dear Parks," exclaimed Hawke. "Let me introduce you to my muse."

"The lady in the paintings," he pronounced, and taking Shannon's hand, raised it to his lips. "*Enchanté, ma mystérieuse*. We meet at last. May I say you have illuminated Bond Street like a torch in a dark bazaar, and tonight you even outshine your own image."

At this outrageous flattery Shannon blushed furiously, reminded that the nude of her was still hanging prominently in the window of the Agnew Gallery. Hawke excused himself to fetch more champagne, leaving Parks to stare unabashedly at Shannon.

"Do I detect that you were born under the Southern Cross?" he inquired when they had chatted a moment.

"Yes, I'm from Australia," she admitted. The way the stranger's eyes roamed over her reminded her uncomfortably of her first meeting with Hawke. There was that same consuming thirst, as if he were trying to memorize her face.

"Are you still at school?"

She laughed. "Oh, no—I left years ago."

"As you are here tonight, I assume you might be immersed in the arts. Let me guess—a painter? a writer? a musician?"

"No, though I wish I were. In fact, I am what is known as a lady's companion."

He was delighted with her lack of guile. "A lady's companion? Does such a thing still exist? And if so, aren't such creatures little brown mice who sit in the corner knitting? Whose company do you keep, then?"

"I'm companion and secretary to Lady Jonquil Fortesque."

"Good heavens—so you are the handmaiden of the delicious Jonquil?"

"Don't tell me you know her?"

"Known her for donkey's years."

Shannon sought for a new topic. "And what do you do?"

"I'm a photographer. And before the great Mr. Sutherland comes back and accuses me of poaching on his terrain, would you be interested in modeling?"

"I would never pose nude for a photographer," she said, feeling ridiculously prudish but adamant.

"My dear, when I say modeling I mean fashion. High fashion. *Harper's Bazaar*, *Vogue*, that sort of thing. You needn't answer right away. I'll be in touch." He winked conspiratorially as Hawke approached.

Later that week Shannon met Irma leaving Jonquil's room with a tea tray. Looking pale and weak, Jonquil was tucked up in bed, surrounded by cushions, tissues, and books.

"What did the doctor say?" asked Shannon.

"It's too maddening," she complained. "If only I had stayed put yesterday, I would have been fine, but he says if I want to be in any condition at all for the ball on Saturday, I'll have to stay in bed till then, and that means missing Ladies' Day at Ascot. I'm simply furious with myself."

"What a terrible shame. Is there anything I can do for you?"

"You know, I was just thinking—why don't you take my ticket and go? After all, it would be a grand opportunity to see one of the most exciting events of the London season. You'll love it," Jonquil insisted. "You'll be shoulder to shoul-

109

der with royalty in the royal enclosure. Letitia Somerville—you remember her—she's arranging a picnic. I'm sure you can join them. Your red shantung suit would be perfect, and you can fish out any hat you want from my cupboard."

"Well, if you're absolutely sure," said Shannon, not wanting to appear too eager, though she was exultant at the prospect of going to Ascot. It was an event that had shone in her imagination for years—the high point of the summer season.

"Hand me the telephone right now, and my address book. I'll call Letitia this minute," announced Jonquil.

On Ladies' Day the village of Ascot was invaded by an armada of Rolls-Royces, Daimlers, Bentleys, and Jaguars. It had rained earlier in the morning, but the sun was beginning to shine through, and a jolly fairground atmosphere prevailed as people of all descriptions flocked to the racetrack that had made the town a household name. Men in tophats and morning coats squired elegantly dressed women, many of whom used the occasion as license to exhibit their originality, with outlandish hats dripping with feathers, flowers, and lace. At Ascot, excess and elegance mingled comfortably.

"Twenty to one on Gofair, long shot on Darling Boy!" shouted a punter in a brown derby on a street corner. "Read all about it in *Sporting Life*. . . ."

Shannon glanced at Giles Slingsby, who had turned up in a Rolls-Royce Silver Cloud as her escort for the day with Letitia and Rupert Somerville. Her head was already light from the champagne they had drunk with their picnic. It had seemed wonderfully absurd to see women dressed to the nines and men in tophats produce elegant spreads from the boots of their big expensive cars, complete with garden furniture, silver, and crystal, in the middle of a paddock turned car park.

"I've got a tip on Tender Folly in the two o'clock," Giles confided to Shannon as he twiddled the red carnation in his buttonhole.

On his arm, she felt unutterably elegant in her red shantung suit and Jonquil's hat—an eleborate black-veiled affair trimmed with a ring of flaming poinsettias. It didn't matter that she had nothing in common with Giles Slingsby, or that the conversation that morning had revolved around people and places she had only read about in gossip columns. Shannon was out to have a fabulous time and had begun to enjoy the frankly admiring glances that men cast in her direction.

Even the most nondescript Englishman had been transformed by the glamour of a morning coat and striped trousers, and the women were glorious to behold in dresses of every color of the rainbow. Elegance jostled with extravagance as they came into the royal enclosure, and Shannon was amazed to see one woman bearing a replica of a garden gnome on her head and another sporting a miniature Eiffel Tower. The photographers in the press box above leaned forward to catch the most outrageously dressed women as they paraded into view, anxious to capture their outfits for the front pages of the *Times* and the *Daily Mail*.

"Are you enjoying yourself?" Giles asked solicitously as they watched the procession of royal carriages from the upper terrace. Standing on tiptoe, Shannon managed to catch a glimpse of the Queen and Prince Philip as they alighted.

"I'm having a grand time, thank you," she replied with sparkling eyes. "The queen is much tinier than I expected."

They positioned themselves to watch the first race as the line of horses strained behind the rope.

"Dash it, I wish I'd put a last minute bet on Rose of Tralee," said Giles under his breath.

"They're away!" boomed the announcer, and jockeys in rainbow silks streaked by on glossy thoroughbreds across the green turf, leaving a blur of color in their wake. The crowd roared the names of their favorites, their voices mounting to a frenzy. When the race finished moments later, there was a great surge all around them as a mass of people rushed downstairs to collect their winnings and place bets.

"Well, I can kiss good-bye to a tun," commented Giles with a sigh. "Laughing Gas seems to have been placed next to last. Oh, well, we're meeting Letitia at Brigadier Gerard's Bar. Let's go and console ourselves."

"What's a tun?" asked Shannon.

"A hundred quid."

She swallowed hard. A hundred pounds would have helped to bring Kerry over right away. Combined with what she had already saved.

"Not to worry, however," he said with a devil-may-care smile. "It's all good fun. I'll bet Letitia and Rupert will wonder what's become of us."

They threaded their way through the throng of people to

a terrace set with tables and chairs, where they found Rupert and Letitia surrounded by a group of friends.

"Guess what—Rupert's won fifty pounds on Gofair, the clever boy!" Letitia exclaimed. Every time she moved, a mass of turquoise egret feathers quivered on her hat.

Rupert winked at Shannon and handed her a glass of champagne. As she was sipping it, she turned to scan the crowd in the inner sanctum of Ascot, the royal enclosure.

". . . anybody can get in," Rupert was explaining. "All they have to do is to apply."

"And be sponsored," added Letitia.

Shannon only half heard this last exchange. She suddenly found herself staring at a very particular profile. As her heart lurched wildly, she turned abruptly away, thankful for the veil and the low brim of the hat which shielded her face. Her throat was so constricted with panic that she couldn't speak. There seemed no place to turn as she grappled with a sense of crushing suffocation. But as she heard the unmistakable voice not far away, she realized that something she had told herself could never happen in a million years was about to occur, and nothing she could do would prevent it.

"Letitia, darling, how lovely you look."

"Zan, darling, hello. You know Giles, of course. And this is Shannon Faloon. She's a friend of Jonquil's. Shannon, may I introduce Zan Fitzherbert."

Shannon felt herself turning as if by remote control. Wrestling with her sudden loss of poise, she faced him.

"How do you do, Shannon Faloon," he said, slowly extending his hand.

"How do you do," she murmured, eyes cast down.

Their hands met in a polite handshake, but Zan gave himself away for a moment when his fingers squeezed hers tightly, and Shannon looked up at him in response.

His eyes met hers with the power of a hammer shattering glass. The blurred handsome image she had carried of him, resolving to forget, came into focus with pulsating clarity, breathing life into the emotion she had tried to kill. Verdant memories of Koonwarra passed before her eyes behind the veil, and when she saw the tremor in Zan's smile Shannon wondered what he was thinking. In a moment, when everyone had turned away, he whispered urgently.

"Where can I get in touch with you?"

"I'm staying with Lady Jonquil Fortesque. You see—I'm wearing her badge. I came in her place today."

"My God, I don't believe it," was Zan's shocked return as he stared disbelievingly at her name tag. "You—at Jonquil's, all this time . . ."

They were interrupted by a striking blond woman whose face seemed familiar. She dismissed Shannon with one glance.

"Zan, darling, would you run down and put twenty-five pounds on Spring Fever for me? The odds are twenty to one, and Rupert tells me he's bound to come up in the fourth race."

"Oh, Rosemary, there you are," said Zan absently.

"Do hurry—there's very little time left."

"Of course. I'll go right now," he replied.

Zan dashed off without a word, and Rosemary melted into the crowd. Shannon stood numbly at Giles's side, oblivious to the mindless chatter swirling around her. Who Rosemary was was not clear, but she had called Zan "darling," and her manner had been unmistakably familiar, even intimate.

The rest of the afternoon was dead for Shannon—the people, the gay ambiance, the champagne and laughter, even the excitement of the races, everything faded to nothing. At every opportunity she looked around for Zan, but both he and the mysterious Rosemary seemed to have disappeared.

That evening, when Shannon let herself into the house, she went straight upstairs to Jonquil's room. She found her still propped up in bed, but the color had come back to her cheeks and she smiled brightly when she saw Shannon at the door.

"Come and sit over here and tell me all about it. I'll ring Irma and have her bring tea up. Now, I want to hear everything. What they were all wearing, who you saw, every last detail. Did you manage to see the queen? I do hope you won something," she said breathlessly.

"I was going to ask Giles for a tip, until he lost a hundred pounds, but I did win five pounds on the fourth race," Shannon said, taking off her hat.

When Irma had brought the tea and Shannon had exhausted every detail she could think of to entertain Jonquil, she took a deep breath, preparing herself to bring up the subject that had tormented her all afternoon.

"Oh, by the way," she began casually, "I met someone called Zan Fitzherbert who said he knew you."

"Did you really? They must have come back from Antibes. I must call them tomorrow. You know Rosemary?

113

Freddie's goddaughter? Zan is her husband. Their little daughter is such a dear. Now, where did I put my diary? I'm going to call them and fix a date for dinner next week," said Jonquil, placing her glasses on the end of her nose.

Shannon leapt up and pretended to look for Jonquil's calendar, turning away to hide the shock and hurt on her face.

"Here it is—yes, I think I could manage next Thursday," said Jonquil, scanning the pages of her diary.

Fighting her tears, Shannon made up her mind that whatever happened, when Lord and Lady Fitzherbert came to Chester Square, she wouldn't be there.

Early the following morning Irma called Shannon to the phone, and she knew who it would be even before she heard the voice at the other end of the line.

"Hello, Shannon? This is Zan."

She paused before replying. "Oh, hello, Zan. I'm afraid Jonquil is asleep. Can I get her to call you?" she said, her pulse quickening at the sound of his voice.

"Well, actually, I was calling you. I was wondering if you might like to have lunch with me today."

She thought for a moment, feeling torn. "I don't think that's a very good idea, quite honestly, Zan."

"Why not? It was such an incredible surprise to see you at Ascot. I mean, you, at Jonquil's, of all people. By the way, I had a letter from Charlie Fremont not long ago. Did you know he got married last month to Heather McNabe—you remember her."

"Yes, of course. No, I hadn't heard."

There was a silence. "Well, what about it? Let's meet at Alvaro's on the King's Road about one o'clock."

Shannon said in a controlled voice, "No, really, I don't think so. You're married now, and I think it would be better if we don't meet privately. I'm sorry, but I've got to go now. Good-bye, Zan."

She put the phone down, not trusting herself to speak further. Zan's call had shaken her more than she might have expected. She rebelled against the disquietude that he injected into her blissful new life. Everything had been going so smoothly up until now. More unattainable than ever, Zan was anchored solidly in the center of Jonquil's circle, and she would have to cope with his disturbing proximity whether she liked it or not.

114

Rushing upstairs, Shannon grabbed her bag and raced out of the house, making sure that Zan had no chance to put a wedge between her and her conscience before she had firmly shored up her own feelings, once and for all. As she closed the door behind her, she heard the phone begin to ring.

One brilliant Sunday morning in late July, Shannon and Jonquil were being driven in the Jaguar through Windsor Great Park. Towering lime and beech trees dressed in the full splendor of summer cast a lacy shade on the rolling green lawns that dipped down to the edge of a pond alive with ducks and teal.

As they crossed a bridge Shannon looked serenely out the window, her calm expression hiding her inner turmoil. Since Ascot she had successfully avoided a confrontation with Zan. Her days had been long and full, and she had filled her spare time with elocution, French lessons, and a correspondence course in typing and shorthand, all of which left her no time to brood. Whenever Zan was expected at Jonquil's she made sure she was out, but now, finally, she had run out of flimsy excuses, even to herself. When Jonquil had invited Shannon to accompany her to watch Zan play polo at Smith's Lawn, she had accepted, tired of playing hopscotch with her own feelings. The time had come to face him again. Only then could she be sure that Zan Fitzherbert meant nothing to her. By confronting him, she would once and for all banish the ghost of their past at Koonwarra.

When Bagley had parked on a stretch of lawn before the wide polo field, they got out of the car, and Shannon, cool in a splashy cotton print, followed Jonquil, who had put up a parasol against the sun. By now she was completely accustomed to Jonquil's running commentary about the people who passed, and it was easy to disguise her own nervousness. Shannon looked toward the field, where players of various teams were already practicing, racing to and fro after the ball, but they were too far away for her to make out if Zan was among them.

"I don't see anybody here yet. We're a bit early, so let's take a stroll." She gestured toward the royal box above the stands. "Philip is playing, and Charles will be here, too. I imagine the queen will come to see them."

They passed by the glass-fronted clubhouse, where members were already at the bar. The crowd that frequented Smith's Lawn was the same group of pleasure-seeking aristocrats who had been at Ascot, and who would be at Cowes in August, before grouse shooting in Scotland. Shannon had become well schooled in the role of lady-in-waiting to Jonquil, and she now moved confidently among the charmed circle that included her friends. The two of them meandered past the ponies and grooms near the elaborate loose boxes hauled to the park for the match, but there was still no sign of Zan.

"Let's go back to the car now," said Jonquil. "I'm simply dying for a G and T." On the way she stopped at the railing. "I wonder, isn't that Zan?" she said, raising her fieldglasses. "My, but he does look magnificent on that horse. Yes, that's him on Zanzibar all right. Zanzibar—isn't that the perfect name for a horse belonging to Zan? Rosemary gave him the mare as a wedding present. Here, take the glasses and have a look."

It was indeed a riveting sight. What could be more magnificent, she asked herself, than a bronzed, handsome man streaking across the green turf on a coal-black thoroughbred?

"See him?"

Shannon nodded.

"He rides like a dream. Always did."

Shannon lowered the glasses, wondering what Jonquil would think if she knew how often the two of them had ridden together.

They arrived back at the Jaguar to find that Bagley had opened the trunk and laid out drinks on a table surrounded with chairs in the square of shade at the side.

"Oh, look—Rosemary and Daphne are already here. Yoo-hoo!"

Jonquil rushed forward to greet the two women, and they all exchanged warm hugs and kisses as Shannon stood to one side.

"I think you met Rosemary at Ascot, didn't you, Shannon?"

"Yes, I did. Hello," she said with a nod.

Shannon felt herself smarting with discomfort at Rosemary's dismissive coldness. She had met her type before. Rosemary undoubtedly viewed the world as a social pyramid, with herself and a few close intimates at the top, and she had instantly summed up Shannon as unworthy of her notice. Shannon watched her in uncomfortable silence. Fashionably thin, she dressed with an understated elegance that made Shannon feel painfully inadequate as she listened to her easy

116

conversation about people and subjects she had never heard of. Her restrained laughter, the way she tossed her glossy blond hair, bit deeply into Shannon's self-confidence. So this was Zan's world and Zan's woman, she thought, observing Rosemary's cool, sophisticated beauty. She wished desperately that she hadn't come. At least at Jonquil's she was happy, she was secure and made to feel as if she belonged. But though she was daunted by Rosemary and the rich, well-bred circle she represented, Shannon had no desire to be like her. Finally Rosemary seemed to become aware of Shannon's presence, throwing a remark in her direction.

"You're Australian, aren't you?"

"Yes, I am," Shannon replied, caught off guard.

"I was completely fooled at first. You have barely a trace of an accent. You're from Sydney, I suppose?"

"No. From New South Wales originally, though I worked in Sydney before I came here."

"New South Wales? Zan was there, ages ago. In a place called Chicken Bone, or something like that. Extraordinary name."

Shannon resisted coming to Rosemary's aid as she struggled to recall the name of Wishbone.

"Oh, look, here's my favorite girl," chirped Jonquil, holding out her arms. "Come to Auntie Jonquie, you adorable creature."

The first sight of Zan's little girl threw Shannon into confusion. Golden-haired Saffron was accompanied by her uniformed nanny. Entranced, Shannon watched as the child toddled forward, then fell into the grass with a bemused smile. Getting up with a giggle, she ran toward Jonquil, her dimpled arms held wide. While Daphne and Rosemary looked on, Jonquil smothered her in kisses.

Real or imagined, Shannon couldn't help but find a strong resemblance to Zan in his daughter, and when Jonquil suddenly passed the child to her she found herself being hugged with a delicious warmth she could not resist. No one seemed to notice how tightly she clasped Saffron to her except Jonquil, who remarked:

"Look at that. She seems to have taken to you right away."

Saffron touched her fingers in fascination to Shannon's glossy, blunt-cut hair.

"Here's our hero now," called Daphne. "I say, who is that with Zan?" she said, with a glance at Rosemary.

117

Zan strode into the circle, accompanied by a player from his team. In a green polo shirt and jodhpurs, his muscular arms and bronzed face were glossy with sweat.

Zan's surprised glance rested on Shannon, and she was struck with how much he looked like the Zan she remembered, his fair hair tousled, his face gleaming with exhilaration from being on a horse. Swooping up a delighted Saffron in his arms, he masked his astonishment at Shannon's sudden reappearance and proceeded to introduce the powerfully built Ramon Alvarez, who immediately placed himself next to Shannon. They were soon joined by two other players. Darkly suntanned and muscular, they injected a welcome male tension into the female gathering. Even the cool-headed Rosemary and her sensible friend, Daphne, were rendered frivolous in the presence of this virile clutch of polo players. The conversation became markedly more flirtatious with these handsome warriors in their midst, like an orchestra shifting to a quicker tempo.

As Ramon talked attentively to Shannon, she was acutely conscious of Zan's presence and didn't dare look at him. Bagley passed drinks and sandwiches, and suddenly the group mushroomed into a party that included friends from nearby cars. Just before the first chukka started, Ramon rose to go.

"May I perhaps invite you to dinner next week? I'll get your number from Zan. We could go to Annabel's."

"Oh—thank you. I'd love to," she replied uneasily, feeling Zan's eyes on her.

When Ramon had left, Zan strolled over and took the seat beside her. "You two seemed to have a lot in common," he remarked casually.

"Yes, he's asked me to dinner. He seems very nice."

"He's got quite a reputation, you know."

"Good—I like a challenge. Anyway, I think it's about time I spread my wings, don't you?" As she spoke, she was surprised to see his eyes narrow with jealousy.

"Well, I suppose it's entirely up to you," he said with pretended indifference.

Feeling Rosemary watching them, Shannon returned her cool gaze with an innocent smile.

A few days later Irma called her to the telephone with a whispered remark.

"It's a man."

Half expecting Ramon Alvarez, Shannon was startled to hear a rich voice that she couldn't place.

"Is that the breathtaking Shannon Faloon, born under the Southern Cross?"

Feeling somewhat foolish, she replied, "Yes, it is."

"You may not remember our meeting in the perfumed garden of Arabia in June, or my mention of modeling. This is Norman Parkinson. Since we last spoke I have been given an assignment that brought your inimitable face and form immediately to mind. In short, dear lady, would you care to be one of my models? Before you say yes, let me warn you it will involve an expedition across Africa that would have given Livingstone second thoughts."

"Mr. Parkinson!" she exclaimed in surprise.

Since Shannon's social debut the night of the costume ball, she had discovered to her chagrin that Hawke's friend "Parks" was none other than the renowned fashion photographer, Norman Parkinson. She had expected never to hear from him again.

Two days later Shannon found herself in the unexpected grip of destiny when she signed with London's top modeling agency, Model's One, and had been booked by Parkinson for a three-page spread for *Vogue*, to be shot in the Mountains of the Moon, one of the most remote corners of Africa. She would have only two weeks before flying to Uganda, and her schedule was already filled with introductory "go-sees" to photographers to present herself as a new face on the London fashion scene. Parkinson's offer was like a burst of cannon fire that could launch her to the top at once. Already she heard herself spoken about in extravagant terms as the agency sought to define her image: dark and dangerous, smoldering, with a cheetahlike grace. She was defined as an unbroken thoroughbred, as a romantic hybrid of East and West, as darkly enigmatic. The last word made her smile as she recalled Zan's remark years ago. Perhaps there was a glimmer of truth in it after all.

Jonquil was thrilled speechless that the protégée she had harbored under her roof had been plucked for stardom by the famous Parkinson, and she gracefully relinquished Shannon to follow her dream.

"You'll always have a home with me, my dear, wherever you are. Of course, I always knew something great would happen to you and that you wouldn't be with me forever,"

119

she said, embracing her affectionately. "And Irma, Bagley, Buggles, and I will always be here should you ever need us."

The moment Kerry received Shannon's letter full of news about her budding career, she dashed off a reply that rekindled all her old dreams of living with her sister, blithely assuming that Shannon would be able to afford to bring her to England at last.

Shannon was dismayed at Kerry's reaction and at a loss as to how to handle it. She had only herself to blame, she reflected somberly, for brandishing her own success so blatantly. And even if she did have the means one day soon to bring Kerry to London, would it be a good idea? After all, she told herself, Kerry's misery at Koonwarra was probably just a passing phase; and if not, she would have her chance one day. But now now. Kerry had always been a handful, and now, at fifteen, she was undoubtedly more headstrong than ever. There just wasn't room in Shannon's life for a teenager who needed care and supervision when she had to be free to fly off at a moment's notice for an assignment.

These were all rationalizations, of course, fueled by Shannon's understandable impatience to live her own life. She was on the brink of the greatest adventure she would ever know, and her impulse was to to live it to the full. And what was wrong with that? she asked herself defiantly, keeping her guilt at bay.

On a warm September day one week before she was to leave for east Africa, Shannon left the modeling agency with the beginnings of her portfolio under her arm. Pausing to look into the window of a boutique on the King's Road, she caught a glimpse of her own reflection. It was still impossible to believe that she was making as much in an hour as most girls made in a week, just for posing in front of a camera. In addition to her dramatic test shots, including Parkinson's, she already had half a dozen photo sessions to her credit and found that she was much less shy under the scrutiny of a lens than that of a pair of human eyes. The camera was impersonal, and she was an object.

Seeing a free seat on the pavement at the Picasso Café, Shannon put down her portfolio and ordered a coffee, content to grab a rare moment of idleness to watch the world go by. The King's Road was packed with leggy young women in miniskirts and teased hairdos. Suddenly a voice brought her out of her daydream.

"Shannon?"

She looked up, startled. "Zan—what are you doing here?"

"I was going to ask you the same thing," he said, sliding into a chair beside her.

They hadn't seen each other since the polo match. There was no fluttering of her heart, no tension. She smiled at him, confident that this was no more than a meeting of two old acquaintances.

"Well? What are you doing here?" she asked mischievously.

"I'm just looking over a house in Oakley Gardens. I'm in property now, you know. I've got my own agency. I've never had the chance to tell you. What have you been doing? Shopping?"

"No, in fact. I've just come from a modeling agency. Model's One. They represent me."

"Modeling? What? You? You mean fashion?" he said, surprised.

"Yes. This is my portfolio, if you want to have a look."

She handed him the volume, and he thumbed through the glamour shots, glancing up at her as if he were uncertain she was the remote and glamorously dressed woman he saw in the photographs.

"When did all this happen? Jonquil didn't mention it."

"Very recently. I'm leaving for my first assignment abroad with Norman Parkinson in a week's time." Try as she would, Shannon couldn't restrain a certain note of triumph in her voice, even though she was amazed every time she saw herself transformed by the camera lens.

"Well, this is a big surprise," Zan said, shaking his head. "Congratulations, Shannon. I'm pleased for you. These photographs of you are nothing short of marvelous. But they don't really do you justice," he added with a wry smile.

Shannon suddenly felt a twinge of regret that she had ventured to appear smug about her own success. She resisted interpreting the look of admiration in his eyes, but it touched something disturbingly familiar within her, a part of herself that she thought was well out of Zan's reach by now.

"Come on—this calls for a celebration," he said suddenly. "Something much more festive than a cup of coffee." He took her firmly by the hand and tugged her up.

She couldn't help but laugh at his burst of enthusiasm, and to skitter away like a frightened mouse seemed foolish. They strolled down the street toward Margaretta Terrace, a

121

street lined with pretty houses, with flowers tumbling from terraces and window boxes. Zan chose a pub with tables set in a secluded garden, and before they sat down he ordered a bottle of champagne. The moment came when they faced each other in silence across the table. Shannon was unprepared for the expression of hurt reflected in Zan's eyes.

"Why did you leave me like that, Shannon?" he said, reaching for her hand. "You disappeared from Koonwarra without a trace, and when I got to Sydney I walked around like a zombie looking for you. I was absolutely frantic. . . ."

"How can you say that?" she said, astonished. "I saw your picture in the *Morning Herald*. You looked perfectly happy to me. And anyway, why didn't you contact me? You got my letter. You knew where I was." It was not possible to hide the bitterness in her voice.

"What are you talking about? What letter?"

"Do you mean to say that you didn't get the letter I sent? I wrote a few days later—as soon as I had a place to stay in Paddington. I hardly moved from there, waiting to hear from you."

He shook his head sadly. "Shannon, I never got a letter."

They faced each other across a chasm of time and circumstance. All barriers between them came crashing down at the realization of their tragic mischance.

"I can't believe that you thought I wouldn't contact you once I was in Sydney. How could you think that—how?" His desperation turned to anger. "I suppose you thought I simply seduced you, that you were a summer fling or something, didn't you?"

"What else could I think? Oh, Zan, when I saw your picture that day it came home to me that we are from two different worlds. I was so hopelessly naive then. Now it's too late. You're married, with a child."

Like a man possessed, Zan hurtled in, brushing aside her protests. "All summer long I've been obsessed by you, tried to pursue you, just to talk as we're doing now, but you wouldn't give me the chance. When I saw that portrait of you in Bond Street, it drove me mad knowing you were probably somewhere in London and that I couldn't find you. I even went to the egotistical bastard Sutherland, but he wouldn't tell me a thing."

"So it was you," she murmured, smiling faintly at the idea.

"I'd almost given up, and suddenly, there you were at

Ascot. I simply turned my head and you were standing there. I felt struck by lightning. Couldn't you see the effect you had on me? But what to say, what to do, to convey to you how desperate I was? And then, when you refused to talk to me, the whole summer became a nightmare. I was wild with jealousy when Ramon asked you out. Did you go out with him?"

Zan's face went dark, but he stopped short of prying into the details about Ramon, trying to read her eyes. Shannon felt no need to admit that she had been momentarily carried away by the South American playboy, or that now, looking at Zan, Ramon meant nothing to her whatsoever. Explanations and excuses seemed useless.

Anguished, she retorted, "What right do you have to ask me this?"

Zan reached out for her hand and clasped it tightly, conveying a tremor of passionate desperation. "To touch you like this, to speak to you at last, Shannon. What are we going to do?"

"Nothing. What can we do? It's too late."

"There's never been anyone but you. I went through with my marriage like a sleepwalker. I've never been able to get you out of my mind."

"Don't. Please don't."

"I may never have another chance again, now that you're going away. Don't stop me from saying what I've longed to say. Please, Shannon, let me have that."

Zan's eyes were a turbulent microcosm of the passion their breach of destiny had summoned forth, and she could bear it no longer. She rose, but his hand gripped her arm.

"Shannon, you can't go. I love you. Come with me now. A friend of mine has a studio nearby, where we could be alone."

"This is crazy. What are you doing to me?" she whispered. The temptation to reenact their night together—a night that still lingered strongly in her memory—was almost too strong to resist. "No, I won't," she cried. She pulled free from his grasp, fled through the gate of the pub, and was gone.

Helplessly Zan watched her go. With a defeated gesture, he turned the bottle upside down, emptying it into the ice bucket. For a long while he sat there, absently watching yellow leaves spiral down from the chestnut trees overhead, to land at his feet.

Chapter V

Like dark sentinels crows wheeled over the hills of Koonwarra, painted against a field of mottled blue sky. It was spring, and the first flush of vivid green had begun to spread over the dead landscape.

Mattie glanced at the horizon and the gathering storm, calculating that there would be just enough time for the graveside service before it unleashed its fury across the plain. A great spoke of lightning shot up from the plumed clouds, followed by a roll of far-off thunder, a fitting farewell as dramatic as cannon fire for the funeral cortege of Brendan Faloon.

His was the first death at Koonwarra in nearly twenty years. All the employees of the station had turned out, along with their wives and children. As they followed the pallbearers who bore the pine coffin from the church, stifled sobs could be heard from some of the women. The men, Brendan's friends, and occasional enemies, looked ahead with solemn, set faces, turning their hats awkwardly in their hands.

At Mattie's side, Bob shuffled with an uneasy gait as they approached the graveyard surrounded by an iron fence. The gloom ever attendant upon death was further deepened by an underlying sense of guilt. None of those who had come to pay their respects had ever suspected Brendan's despair would end in suicide, and now they all shared a portion of the guilt. But the greater burden was borne by Bob, who had given Brendan his notice a few days before. His strict code of values made him blame himself for what had happened.

It was Bluey who had found Brendan's body not far from Bramble Cottage, with half his head blown off. He had heard the shot echo through the grove of trees not far from the clearing and had gone out to investigate. He had found Brendan's body at once, his blue eyes staring up at the clouds above the bloody remains of his face.

Just ahead of Mattie and Bob, Kerry led the procession in a plain navy-blue dress, a scarf around her head. She followed the priest through the narrow gate to the grave, a little square of earth that was in the shadow of a golden midas tree. Kerry looked at its brilliant flowers, thankful for one small thing to cling to. The splash of color distracted her from the sight of the bare coffin at the graveside. But she could no longer avoid the dark trench when the priest began to read from Corinthians, and she stared at it blankly.

" 'What you sow does not come to life unless it dies. . . . There is one glory of the sun, and another glory of the moon, and another of the stars; for star differs from star in glory. We shall not all sleep, but we shall all be changed in the twinkling of an eye, at the last trumpet. . . .' "

When the priest had closed his Bible, the coffin was lowered into the grave by ropes, and all of the funeral party filed by, each taking a trowel of earth, which they cast into the pit. When Kerry's turn came, she tossed with the earth a small bunch of blue cornflowers she had gathered, tied with a red ribbon that Shannon had once worn in her hair.

A few people lingered, some of them murmuring inarticulate words of condolence, but Kerry set herself aside from anyone who might try to comfort her. Mattie hovered nearby, and when Kerry made no move to leave, she went up to her and took her hand gently.

"When you're ready, come up to the house. A few people will be calling in."

Without turning her head, Kerry nodded, relieved to be left alone. Dark clouds now obscured the sun, casting the graveyard into cold shadow. A biting little breeze bent the brown grass, and she hugged her arms against her chest to ward off a shiver. Sunk in the dark hole, the coffin seemed insignificant. Glancing at it, she felt no emotion she could put a name to, only emptiness. Kerry's last heated argument with Brendan echoed in her mind and heart, filling the void created by his indifference and disregard. His cruel retort would always haunt her: "Why wasn't it you that left instead of her?"

Some avenging angel had denied Brendan the last favor he would have wished. Shannon, the daughter he had loved, had not been able to come home to mourn him. Kerry knew that Shannon had never needed to win their father's love, therefore she could never comprehend the tortured wheel that had turned deep within him.

Like lightning playing across the sky, thoughts singed the dry, aching void within Kerry, setting her emotions alight.

125

Brendan *had* loved her, Kerry was sure. The love between them had often burned like hatred, tormenting them both, but she understood it now. It was a violent, proud love that had no room for tenderness or indulgence. They shared the same Irish blood tie that bound them more closely than habit or even preference, and that's what united people in the end. They had both given as good as they got, had fought their way into each other's hearts, snarled and torn at each other like beasts. This realization was outlined clearly against the murkiness of the past, and Kerry drew strength from it. Brendan's love reached to her from the grave, numbing her guilt. He had had to die before she could understand him.

"Bye, Dad," she murmured, her eyes still dry. She walked away from the grave and closed the gate behind her, never to return.

Later that night, looking around the guest room of the big house where she had moved the day Brendan had died, Kerry thought how ironic it was that she would once have done anything to spend the night in the big four-poster bed where Shannon had recovered from her fall. Now, however, on the eve of Brendan's funeral, the comfort of the pretty room had no effect whatsoever on her. Tucked up under the covers, her eyes kept straying toward the big suitcase Mattie had bought her for her things. It was packed and ready to be put in the Land Rover at dawn, when Bob would drive her to the airstrip at Wishbone.

When Brendan had died, the first thing Mattie had done was to get his brother, Jack, on the telephone in America. In retrospect, Kerry wondered if both she and Bob would have insisted on paying her passage to the States if they hadn't been bowed by guilt. Unlike Shannon, Kerry had never warmed to Mattie's earthy manner, seeing it simply as a ruse to mask the power she wielded over the two of them, who were no more than glorified—if privileged—servants in the household. Whisking her up to the big house when Brendan died didn't disguise the fact that Mattie would be glad to get rid of her, Kerry thought. The Fremonts obviously felt their debt to her was canceled by the purchase of a one-way ticket to the Green Spring Valley in Maryland.

The moment she heard Jack's familiar Irish voice crackling over the wire, Kerry had nearly unleashed all the tears she had been holding back. Shannon was abroad on a shoot, somewhere in Africa, and it seemed to Kerry that Jack was the only person in the world who cared about her. When he heard what had happened he immediately suggested that her rightful place was with him, and his warmth had crossed continents to comfort her. When Mattie and Bob offered to pay the fare, the decision was made, and she accepted their charity with an indifference that they interpreted as shock and grief.

Kerry's head rested on the same pillow where Shannon's had once lain, but she wasn't thinking of her sister now. With a restless sigh she turned off the light and nestled into the unfamiliar bed. By the time Kerry drifted to sleep, the pillow was soaked with tears she had waited until she was alone to shed.

Putting the Jaguar into fifth gear as the lights of Heathrow Airport disappeared behind them, Bagley glanced at Shannon in the rearview mirror.

"I hardly recognized you when you came through the barrier, Miss Shannon. May I say you're looking very smart?"

"Thank you, Bagley. I was let loose on the Via Condotti in Rome for a day on the way back. You can guess from the pile of packages you loaded into the trunk that I went mad in the shops. Rome took my breath away," she said, settling back into the seat. Even now the deep chords of church bells reverberated in her ears, and she could almost smell the fragrance of espresso drifting from the sidewalk cafes.

"Lady Fortesque is waiting for you at Chester Square."

"I'll have so much to tell her, I won't know where to begin."

"Sunny Rome, the Dark Continent—I guess it must be quite a change from London with this drizzle and all. It hasn't stopped raining since you left." Bagley met Shannon's eyes in the rearview mirror, aware that she didn't have a clue of the sad news awaiting her. He chatted to her as they sped along, pleased to lend the illusion that all was right with the world for a while longer.

"It took us two days to get to the Mountains of the Moon over the roughest terrain I've ever seen. Makes Australia look like a landscaped garden."

"Did it, now?"

She settled back in the seat, her mind still full of Africa.

The trip to the location Parkinson had chosen had been a major expedition in Land Rovers over dizzying mountains and through jungles and valleys, confirming that the great man was an adventurer at heart as well as a photographer. It wasn't until the crew arrived at this remote corner of the earth that Shannon understood why they had come so far simply to take photographs. The breathtaking landscape of high green mountains materializing through wispy clouds, peculiar vegetation that belonged to the realm of science fiction—it was the perfect foil for this globe-trotting genius. The clothes Shannon modeled were as outrageous as the setting, but her limited experience with stylists and photographers in the closed atmosphere of a studio in London was useless in the middle of a wilderness, where everything was inclined to go wrong. There had been moments when she'd wanted to scream from the tedium, the heat, and the stylists who, armed with tongs, combs, and makeup brushes, buzzed around her like flies, while the assistant poured her into dresses that were more like works of art being draped on a statue than clothes for a living woman. Modeling in the jungle had proved to be anything but glamorous. She had no choice but to put her trust in the unflappable "Parks," though sometimes she was convinced it would all end in disaster, shattering her fledgling career before it had begun. Only the sight of Parks busily snapping away, his bristling eyebrows below the embroidered cap that had become his trademark, reassured her. The power of concentration in his blue eyes was as sharp as the focus of his battery of lenses. With that faraway look on his face that marks a genius, Shannon observed creation at work as he strove to marry the ultimate in fashion with the wild, savage beauty of the Mountains of the Moon.

The crew had left Uganda exhausted but triumphant. They had achieved a great coup that would rock the world of haute couture. Parkinson's parting remark as he patted his satchel full of undeveloped film, was: "What I have in this bag will change your life overnight. You do realize that from now on the world is going to be your oyster, don't you?"

Now, as the car sped into rain-soaked London, Shannon was still riding high on a breaker of exhilaration that would take her to where she was sure she wanted to be—the top.

When Bagley rang the bell of the house, she was already up the steps with an armful of packages stamped with the trademarks of Gucci and Ferragamo.

"Look at you, then. You've become a real fashion plate," remarked Irma, embracing Shannon.

She rushed into the sitting room, to find Jonquil waiting for her by the fire. "I'm back!" she cried with a little fanfare, dropping her packages to embrace Jonquil.

"Oh, my dear, you look quite sensational. What a transformation! Why, you've had the time of your life, haven't you?"

When Shannon released Jonquil from a breathless hug, she saw her face was stamped with an unusually serious expression.

"Come and sit down. I'm afraid there's something I have to tell you before I hear all your news."

"What is it?"

"A telegram came for you, and I took the liberty of opening it, knowing it must be urgent. I can't bear to shatter your happiness. I've been dreading this moment. My dear, I'm so sorry."

Taking the telegram from her, Shannon read the short message informing her of Brendan's death.

"Here's a letter that came for you yesterday from Australia, which I'm sure must elaborate on the details. And now, I know you'd like to be alone for a moment. I'll be upstairs if you need me. I'll ask Irma to bring you a brandy," she added, seeing Shannon tremble.

When she had gone, Shannon sank numbly into the wing chair by the fire and read Mattie's letter. Brendan's death hadn't been an accident. Suicide. She repeated the word aloud, but it couldn't make the horror real. She tried to remember where she had been at the exact moment her father died. She had probably been sleeping soundly in a tent under the stars when a gun went off on the other side of the world, ending his life. She was tormented with questions she would never be able to answer. The gloom that had shadowed her father all his life had finally overtaken him, putting an end to any hope she'd had that they would one day be reconciled. No amount of happiness seemed strong enough to counterbalance this sudden tragedy—not money, nor sudden fame, nor travel, not even discovering that Kerry was now safely in America with Uncle Jack. For an instant life exploded in her face, scattering the fragments of meaning beyond reach. The fragile unit of what had once passed for a family at Koonwarra existed no longer; she and Kerry were now prey to the wolves of fortune. She forgot all the harsh words they had exchanged in the past, remembering instead Kerry's vulnerable little face as she looked up at her the morning she

129

had left the Outback for Sydney. Had she looked like that, Shannon wondered, as she stood at Brendan's grave? Yet Shannon's first reaction to the news that Kerry was with Jack had been a rush of relief, which now left her feeling guilty. If it hadn't been for Jack, she would have had to send for Kerry at once, a move that would have curtailed her own independence. Shamed at her want of feeling, Shannon focused instead on what she might give Kerry to make up for everything. It was the least she could do. Now that her earnings potential was nearly unlimited, Kerry would have the best clothes that money could buy and plenty of spending money. It gave Shannon's own ambition a sharper edge to dream of fighting for them both. That way, Kerry would be obligated to no one and want for nothing, a kind of security Shannon herself had rarely known.

Suddenly she was seized by an animal restlessness as she looked around the comfortable surroundings that seemed to mock her burgeoning grief. The security of Jonquil's lovely home suffocated her, and she had the overpowering need to discard all this rich superfluity. Grabbing her coat, she ran out the front door and into the wet darkness. The moment she was plunged into the elements, tears began to flow down her face. The wind that flailed mercilessly against her as she walked along the storm-drenched pavement became a symbol of despair too wild to tame, too awesome to understand, a tempestuous return to the primeval source of her own beginnings. Sobbing her heart out, Shannon walked the rain-swept streets of Belgravia, where golden reflections ran into the gutter. Memories surfaced . . . reminiscences of the earliest days of her childhood, when her father had told her stories and whittled her toys, when Doreen had died and they had comforted each other. Now she was an orphan. She had no one. If only she had gone back, maybe she and Brendan could have forgiven each other. But now she realized she had been waiting for her own mountain of selfish pride to melt. The memory of Brendan's raging love bore down on her in awful retribution, reminding her he might have behaved differently all those years ago. He might have abandoned her and Kerry, but instead, in his own pathetic way, he had tried to stumble on as best he could. Yet she had abandoned him, and now he lay in the graveyard at Koonwarra, in a small plot carved out of the wilderness that was nothing compared to the devastation that laid waste to her own heart.

Chapter VI

The Meadows, Maryland, November

As they neared home, Kerry gave Troika his head, letting the chestnut gelding gallop wantonly down the leaf-strewn bridle path. She bent her head low over his neck to duck an overhanging branch, feeling the power of the animal surging beneath her. The rolling hills of Maryland were covered with the first light snow, masking the seemingly eternal green of the valley, and the thick wall of trees that secluded the big house of The Meadows Stud were now bare. Even now after two months she still felt a thrill at the sight of the rambling colonial mansion now set in the gloom of a late November afternoon.

Twice as big as Koonwarra, it suggested a cottage constructed on a grand scale. The clean colonial lines of the clapboard house had a misleading simplicity that gave no clue to the luxury within or to its renown as one of Maryland's most respected stud farms. Whenever Kerry approached the house after exercising one of the horses, she indulged herself in the fantasy that it was her own home. It was easy to conjure up such a dream as she glanced down for the hundredth time at her own immaculate riding costume, bought in Glyndon with a check Shannon had sent. What she had always wanted was now hers, and she had bought the entire outfit just as it was displayed in the shop window, from the waisted black jacket and dun-colored trousers to the stock tied at her throat. Her hair caught in a black net under her black bowler, Kerry perfectly emulated the show jumpers she so fiercely admired in the copies of *Equus* she read avidly. But it was the boots that had sent her heart racing when she saw them. Wildly expensive, and of the finest leather, they were far superior to the pair she had coveted in Wishbone.

Kerry trotted into the cobbled stable yard, waving to one of the grooms who was leading a blanketed thoroughbred into its box. Today was Thanksgiving, and she and Jack had been invited with all the other employees on the stud to the big house for a grand dinner, an event she had anticipated eagerly all week long. The entire Van Buren clan would be gathered for the occasion, and she had never laid eyes on any of them, though she felt as if she knew them already, having heard so much about them from Jack and the other employees.

When she had brushed Troika down, she hoisted the saddle over her shoulder and went to the tack room, where she saw a young man putting a saddle back on a hook. She knew instantly who he must be.

"Hello—you're Mark Van Buren, aren't you?" she said brightly, extending her hand.

"Hi there. You must be Jack Faloon's niece. I heard you'd arrived."

There was no denying Mark Van Buren was a disappointment. At twenty there was something unfinished about him; he still had the gangling appearance of a high school boy even though he was in his last year at Harvard. The second son, he had become heir to the estate when his elder brother Lindy IV, had been killed in Vietnam two years before. Lindy had been handsome, talented, and adored by everyone. Even now, his legend lived on at The Meadows. Lindy had been everything Mark wasn't. Sensing a distinct shyness in his manner, Kerry gave him an encouraging smile.

"Your uncle sure knows horses," he said after an awkward pause.

"Right on. He cut his teeth on a horseshoe, as he always says."

Mark laughed, and Kerry knew she had broken the ice.

"I certainly hope you like the United States. It must be quite a change after Australia."

"It sure is. We're just going into summer at home. You know, I'd never seen snow until this week."

"Is that right?"

"I couldn't believe my eyes when I woke up and looked out the window."

"Don't you have snow in Australia?"

"Yes, but it's down south in Victoria. That's hundreds of miles from where I'm from in New South Wales."

By the time Kerry and Mark left the tack room, an easy rapport had been established between them.

"How long are you planning to stay?" said Mark, his eyes catching Kerry's with growing interest.

"Permanently. I'm here for good," she replied breezily.

"I really like your Australian accent. It's cute. I've never heard one before—in person, that is."

"Do you really? Uncle Jack tells me I'm losing it the longer I'm here," she replied, not revealing the pains she had taken to soften her twang. "Of course the Faloons are originally Irish from way back. It's one of the oldest and most aristocratic names in Limerick."

She looked up at him, her heart-shaped freckled face shaded by the brim of her bowler, aware her skintight jodhpurs showed her ripe figure to advantage.

"You're coming up to the house for Thanksgiving dinner, aren't you?"

"I certainly am, and I'm really looking forward to it. Uncle Jack tells me that a Thanskgiving dinner in America is really something to behold."

"Well, in that case I guess I'll see you then."

Kerry watched him go, then turned with a confident air, knowing she had established herself in the good graces of at least one Van Buren. There were only two more to go that counted, Mark's father, Lindy III, and Carter, his sister. Kerry couldn't imagine why anyone would call a girl Carter. She leapt up the steps of the flat she shared with Jack above the garage that had been home since she came to The Meadows. Hearing her come in, Jack turned from his desk at the window.

"There you are. You've been out on Troika for a long time. I was beginning to wonder if you'd forgotten Thanksgiving dinner. Once you get on a horse, young lady, you seem to forget the time," he said with an affectionate smile.

"Not very likely, today," she retorted, her eyes shining. Peeling off her gloves, she smiled at him.

There was little of her uncle that reminded her of Brendan. Small and compact, he had a terrierlike quickness, and he'd inherited the ginger hair and freckled complexion of his mother. There was an open quality about hs boyish face that made him look much younger than he was, and the copper glint of his eyes, like pennies thrown in green water, could flash with temper as readily as Brendan's had. But there was an air of self-assurance and quiet strength that commanded the respect of both men and thoroughbreds. Unlike his older brother, who had swaggered so belligerently, so willfully through life, Jack had chosen instead to follow the steady course of a realist who augmented his knack for scenting fortune with hard work.

As he regarded Kerry now, in full riding regalia, he was reminded of the beautiful young Kathleen, his mother, who

133

had never let convention stand in the way of her passions. The mother of two bastard sons by a lord, and herself a laundry maid, she'd been scorned by the Anglo-Irish aristocracy when she rode to hounds. Supported in modest style by her lover, she had nonetheless held her head high, and there was no doubt that young Kerry had inherited her spark. Small-boned and curvaceous, her froth of coppery hair was much like her grandmother's, as was the provocative expression on her foxy face. She had an infallible instinct for handling horses, and the dashing figure she cut on the thoroughbreds she exercised was a distinct source of pride to Jack, though he sometimes wondered what other talents she had perfected since he had set her on her first orange crate as a child to learn the ABCs of dressage.

He asked himself if the time hadn't come to hint to the girl that her full riding habit was inappropriate. But when she had received the windfall from Shannon, she had insisted on purchasing the entire outfit, which would have better suited a well-heeled member of the hunting establishment than the niece of the head stable lad. But in the light of all Kerry had gone through, Jack had resisted being too honest with her, knowing there would be plenty of time for her to learn to appreciate the subtle social distinctions of the neighborhood's ruling gentry. The Meadows was a feudal estate in microcosm, and Kerry would find her proper place in it soon enough.

Late that afternoon the two of them crossed the frozen stable yard toward the big house for Thanksgiving dinner. In a dress of purple crushed velveteen, Kerry clutched her arms tightly to her, hoping Jack wouldn't scold her for not wearing a coat. She didn't own one that was nice enough. She gazed expectantly toward the mansion, its endless windows blazing with amber light, and beyond to its fiefdom of undulating hills, thickly wooded with bare trees pressed against the blazing orange horizon.

"What did I tell you? It's folly to go even a hundred yards without a coat. You must be freezing to death," chided Jack. In a tweed jacket and twill trousers, he had the uncomfortable look of a man unused to wearing a tie.

Changing the subject, she said, "How many rooms do you think The Meadows has?"

"I imagine it must have thirty at least. It's a fine house, built for a squire, to be sure."

"It's a lot bigger than Koonwarra."

"That it is," he agreed, his thoughts now on the prospect of a lavish dinner.

Kerry told herself she wasn't shivering because of the cold, but from excitement at the idea of dining in the grand mansion. They walked up wide steps flanked by tall white pillars that skirted a deep circular veranda. Jack rang the brass bell beside a door wide enough to admit a carriage, and it was opened by a uniformed black maid.

"Evening, Cora," said Jack with a nod.

"Hello, Mr. Jack, Miss Kerry. Everybody is in the living room. Come on in."

They paused in the entrance hall just long enough for Kerry to gather her composure at the sight of such splendor. They stood on an oval of gleaming parquet that led to a curving staircase in rosewood, overlooked by a huge sash window. She followed Jack into a huge room of an elegance she hadn't even imagined. It was filled with people, only a few of whom were familiar to her. Most were strangers distinguished not only by their expensive, conservative clothes, but also by their rather aloof air as they chatted with one another. Kerry took a sherry from a silver tray being circulated by one of the maids, and Jack helped himself to a whiskey. Looking around the room, Kerry realized uncomfortably that she was overdressed. All the other women seemed to be wearing muted colors, and the only jewelry they wore was an occasional string of pearls or a gold bracelet. She had somehow expected friends and relations of the Van Burens to radiate an aura of wealth and glamour, and now she felt her cheeks burning with self-consciousness at her own gaucheness.

Kerry immediately spotted the illustrious head of the Van Buren clan, who had been absent from the farm since her arrival. He had been running his empire by telex and telephone while he bought horses in Europe and played polo at Palm Beach, and now that he had come home, he dominated the room like a bronzed titan. As Lindy Van Buren turned to survey the gathering, Kerry found she couldn't take her eyes off him. She experienced an attack of nerves when he walked toward her and Jack.

"Good evening, Jack. Glad to see you."

"Good evening, Mr. Van Buren. You haven't met my niece yet. This is Kerry Faloon."

"Welcome to The Meadows, Kerry," he said affably.

She extended her hand, aware that in one lightning glance he had taken her in, but through her hammering nervousness she was taken aback to detect a spark of provocative interest in those shrewd eyes.

"I've had some very positive answers from Dublin this afternoon, Jack, but I'll tell you about it tomorrow. Let's meet in my office at nine. How's Talisman, by the way?"

"I looked in on him just before we came, sir. That problem with his fetlock has completely cleared up."

"Good, good." With the briefest of nods, Van Buren moved away.

As Jack chatted with one of the grooms, Kerry edged toward the crackling fire. Sipping her sherry self-consciously, she singled out a girl who could only be Lindy's daughter, Carter, home for the holiday from boarding school. Everything she had heard about the sixteen-year-old Carter had made Kerry yearn to know her—from her room, which was reportedly furnished with white Empire furniture, to her closet, which was rumored to be as large as an ordinary bedroom. Seeing her studying Carter, Jack took Kerry by the elbow.

"Come on—let me introduce you," he said, and Kerry followed him reluctantly. "Carter, this is my niece, Kerry, who has come to live with me, as you've probably heard." He smiled at the girl by her side. "I suppose the two of you have just come from Foxcroft together?"

"Yes, how do you do? I'm Abigail Gilmour," she said, curious brown eyes on Kerry.

Shrugging off her shyness, Kerry anxiously filled the gap in the conversation when Jack had left them. "I've heard so much about you, Carter. Uncle Jack told me how well you ride—"

"Did he really?" There was a glacial edge to her thin smile as she cut Kerry off in midsentence. Turning to Abigail, she continued, "As I was saying, Melanie's parents have stopped her allowance and aren't going to let her come skiing in Aspen. I told her I'd telephone later in case there's any change of heart, but I can't bear it without her. . . ."

As Abigail and Carter resumed their intimate huddle, Kerry felt herself being smoothly ostracized. The slight had been so practiced, so subtle, that all she could do was stand there, marooned, in the middle of the room. Smarting with humiliation, she edged away. Kerry had come up against the same impenetrable social barrier before, as solid as plate glass, and her reaction was to cast a hateful glance in the direction of the two bitches with piano legs and flat chests.

Every detail about the two of them spelled money, from their pale cashmere sweaters and skirts to their smoothly coiffed hair and scrubbed faces. There was polished and asexual blandness about the two girls that spelled careful conservatism. Kerry tried to console herself with this thought, but it didn't lessen the hurt of their insult.

"Hi, Kerry."

At the sound of a familiar voice, she turned to find Mark at her side. His hesitant manner was a complete contrast to his sister's.

"Oh, hi. I was looking for you."

"Were you? I like your dress," he said shyly.

"Do you really?" she said, pleasantly surprised. "Thanks."

"Yes, it suits you. That color looks great with your hair."

Sensing that compliments didn't come easily to him, she tilted her head in coquettish appreciation.

"What are you going to do for the holidays? I suppose it's just one long party when you're home, isn't it?"

"Is that what you think?" he said with a laugh. "As a matter of fact, I usually spend most of my evenings at home alone, reading or doing schoolwork. You probably know by now that life at The Meadows revolves entirely around horses, and if you don't live and breathe them, you're the odd man out. I'm more like my mother than my father. She never got on a horse if she could help it."

"Is your mother here tonight?"

"No. My parents have been divorced for years. She lives in New York, and I usually spend the holidays with her. Dad's between wives at the moment."

Catching sight of Lindy Van Buren, who even at a distance dominated the room, Kerry mentally compared the dynamic, virile father with the son, who showed no sign of his strength of character or his good looks. The bitter little smile on Mark's face told her that the mountains of wealth and tradition that surrounded him, symbolized by the grand room where the clan had gathered, served only to disguise his pathetic inner loneliness and dissatisfaction. A few moments later, when Lindy spoke a few cold words to Mark, distaste in his eyes, Kerry felt his disdain for his own son somehow compensated for Carter's behavior toward her. His daughter might not think much of her, but in his son and heir she sensed she already had an ally.

Later, when she went down the hall to look for the bathroom, she saw that the double doors to the dining room

137

had now been opened. She paused, transfixed by the sight of the long table covered in lace and set for dinner. Two huge candelabra blazed above the china and silver adorned with a bank of pink poinsettias. With gloved hands, the butler was just setting a domed silver dish on the polished sideboard. The burgundy walls, the curtains falling from huge windows, lent an aura of old colonial magnificence to the dining room used by generations of Van Burens, whose portraits gazed down on the scene as if they were still enjoying the splendor that lingered there. Kerry watched in fascination as a maid came through the door bearing a huge soup tureen, and as she counted the crystal glasses and silver cutlery, she felt both awe and excitement at the prospect of dining in an atmosphere of such luxury. She forgot all about her hurt and embarrassment.

"Excuse me," she called to the maid. "Where's the bathroom, please?"

"It's under the staircase, down the passageway."

"Thanks," said Kerry, thinking to herself that there was probably just enough time before dinner to wipe off some of her makeup. As she was about to push open the door, she heard Carter's voice from within.

"Have you ever seen such a common-looking tramp as that niece of Jack Faloon? I was so taken aback when she came up to us, I didn't know what to say. Daddy *will* insist on inviting everyone."

"You could cut that accent with a knife," said Abigail. "Do you suppose she dyes her hair?"

"Of course she does. But wait till you see her in her riding gear. You won't believe your eyes. I saw her this afternoon. She puts the two of us in the shade," said Carter with a giggle. "Really, it's so embarrassing. Somebody ought to drop her a hint. . . ."

"Do you you mean to say she has full riding gear? Where does she get the money?"

"Your guess is as good as mine. Personally, I wouldn't want to speculate."

Before their conversation ended, Kerry rushed blindly down the passage. The outfit she had waited years to own had been dismissed in one flippant remark by two smug girls from Foxcroft. She didn't know how she was ever going to face them at dinner. When she came into the hallway, the group had already begun filing into the dining room. Jack came up and touched her arm.

138

"There you are, honey. Come on. We're going in this direction."

"What do you mean?"

He led the dazed, bewildered Kerry to a room at the end of the passage, the servants' dining room. Nobody had told her. A buffet had been laid on the sideboard, and the long table had been decorated with bright paper streamers and a cardboard turkey. Laughing and talking, all the employees of The Meadows, from the youngest groom to the senior housekeeper, were lining up to help themselves to turkey and cranberry sauce. Everyone was there except the black servants, who she supposed must be having their own dinner elsewhere.

It was as if a dark cloth had been cast over the brilliance of The Meadows. They were the servants, and she was one of them. They had been conveniently tucked out of sight, far from the grand room where the Van Burens entertained themselves in great style, and to Kerry's disbelief most of them seemed to be enjoying themselves royally, as if they were unaware of the slight. Their bland, happy faces, their jollity as they tucked away the plain food served on thick white china, made tears of rage spring to her eyes. All of them had been charmed by a great powerful snake into accepting their place in this social Siberia, and she revolted at the injustice of it. So this was the land of the free and the home of the brave, she told herself bitterly.

"Come on, honey, keep the line moving," said Jack impatiently behind her.

As Kerry numbly forked a slice of turkey onto her plate, she made up her mind that never again would she eat Thanksgiving dinner in the servants' hall. Someday, if she should still happen to be at The Meadows, she would be dining alongside the Van Burens, eating off real china with sterling silver, drinking champagne and Burgundy instead of cheap Chianti from a thick glass. Already the idea was forming in her mind of exactly how she would get there.

April 1978

When spring came to The Meadows, Kerry knew how the Green Spring Valley had gotten its name. Riding Troika down the stallion run of the farm one fine morning, she headed for the paths that wound through the acres and acres

139

of woods, a bolt of happiness shooting through her at the prospect of being alive on such a beautiful day. The shimmering green light filtering through the leaves overhead was almost painful to her eyes and cast a diamond brilliance on the wet grass growing thickly between the trees. Coming upon a clearing, she had a sweeping view of the richest grassland in America, as emerald as Ireland ever was, according to Jack—a lushness that nourished the delicate nerve and bone structure of fine thoroughbreds.

There had been a cloudburst, and a great rainbow arced in the blue distance over a landscape of almost absurd perfection. The order and symmetry of the fences crisscrossing the distance, the distant mansions tucked in clefts of green, were symbols of the concentrated wealth and power that governed every priceless acre the eye could behold. After the dusty, limitless expanse of the Australian Outback, this was a green paradise, and Kerry reveled in the power of Troika beneath her. A precious hour was hers, and she headed for a distant jumping paddock to put him through his paces in preparation for the Glyndon Horse Show, her shining goal throughout the long winter.

Since November and her first painful initiation, Kerry had shot through a number of awkward hoops, many of them embarrassing to recall. Carter's scathing comment at Thanksgiving had prompted her to fold away her treasured riding habit until she had earned her first rosettes in competition. Then the hunt would be more than pleased to have her follow their hounds. All that lay in the future, however. For the moment she had to be satisfied with modest ambition, until she had a horse of her own. Even Shannon's generosity wouldn't extend that far, and she had to be content with Troika, who she realized had little chance of competing successfully against horses she had seen at shows all winter.

She had to start somewhere, however. Kerry had begun her assault on the equestrian world by beating down the door of the famous Colonel Bryce Paget, a doughty English ex–cavalry officer who had established himself as a superb trainer for local riders whose ambitions centered on the prestigious show rings in Harrisburg, Washington, and Madison Square Garden. She had sought him out in mid-December, riding to his stables on a bicycle from The Meadows. She had known immediately who he was when she saw him silhouetted on a dashing Anglo-Arab as he demonstrated a point to a pupil in a drenched paddock on a misty winter afternoon. He had the ramrod carriage of a born horseman, and when he strode through the gate, his sharply chiseled face told her everything about him. His withering expression cut Kerry down to size in one glance, and as his eyes stared insolently at her from beneath his riding hat, she felt desperately unsure of herself.

As they walked toward the stables he said, "And where, may I ask, do you hail from, young lady? Surely not from around here with that accent."

She felt herself flush. "My uncle, Jack Faloon, is the head lad at The Meadows," she said, proudly tossing her head. "I work out the horses there."

He regarded her critically with an arched eyebrow, seemingly unimpressed, but her cocky self-assured manner had piqued his curiosity. "You've a damn cheek coming over here without an appointment, but as long as you're here let's see what you can do," he said gruffly, his eyes narrowing with skepticism. "Where's your horse?"

"I don't have one, yet," she blurted out, an excuse on her lips. Her last shred of self-confidence vanished as she endured Paget's fierce scrutiny.

"In that case I'll put you on Intrepid to see if you're as good as you think you are. I must say, you don't look up to much," Paget said, reminding Kerry that dressage and show jumping were nearly the exclusive preserves of men.

Intrepid turned out to be a gray gelding with a rather suspicious gleam in his eye, and when Kerry was in the saddle she discovered the horse was one of the most uncomfortable mounts she had ever been astride, a sign that Colonel Paget wanted to discourage her quickly. She had only a few moments to compose herself before heading for the jumping paddock.

Her first few jumps were disastrous. Intrepid certainly did not suit his name. Rather than jumping free, he had the nasty habit of fly-bucking at every fence. After a few rounds Kerry loosened up a bit, but she felt she was making no impression whatsoever in front of Colonel Paget. How she was supposed to exhibit her talent on a horse that didn't like to jump was a mystery. When, after repeating at least twenty jumps, he called a halt to her performance, she trotted up to him, now in full mastery of Intrepid as well as herself, yet sure she had failed miserably. She gave the colonel a tentative smile as he barked at her sharply.

"You ride abominably, just like a cowhand. I can tell you're Australian by your seat, legs forward, too far back in the saddle."

141

In one swoop he decimated all the illusions she had about herself.

"There are, however, the makings of a horsewoman in you. I can take you on under certain conditions," he announced, slapping his crop across his palm. "You'll have to work yourself to the bone if you want to work with me. You'll have less than eight months until next autumn. I don't accept excuses about school work and boyfriends. I demand the best from every rider, and believe me, I get it. Another thing—you'll have to start from the beginning. Learn the ABCs of dressage my way, and correctly."

She had opened her mouth to point out that she had been doing nothing else for the last five years, but something in his steely eyes stopped her.

"Yes, sir," she replied meekly. It was the first time she had been prompted to call anyone "sir" in her life.

"And another thing. You'll have to come up with a good horse. We can help you out here for a few months, but you'll need a mount of your own if you're going to get anywhere next autumn."

Kerry left the riding academy sensing just how a wild mustang felt when it was lassoed and broken by a master horseman, but she was dazed with happiness that he had accepted her. During the dark months of winter, Colonel Paget threw Kerry mercilessly into the training ring, where he stamped out all the bad habits she had acquired in Australia, molding her gift for form and movement on horseback into the consistent sure grace that distinguishes a champion. Rising at dawn, she doggedly mucked out the stables at The Meadows and from there went to school, impatiently waiting out the hours until she could go on to the riding academy. There she spent two grueling but glorious hours training with the colonel, which she paid for with checks from Shannon. Sometimes she was so tired she could hardly speak at the end of the day.

Now, as she rode out on that long-awaited day in spring, her mind kept going back to the parcel she had received in the mail that morning from Paris. When she had unrolled the magazine she was astonished to find Shannon's picture on the April cover of *Vogue*, and though she knew all about the layout that Shannon had done in the fall, her off-hand mention of it in her letters had disguised the importance of her stunning debut into the fashion world. Only then did Kerry realize with biting envy just how far their lives had diverged.

142

The glamorous, unfathomable woman in dramatic clothes, photographed against a wild backdrop in Africa, bore no resemblance to the girl who had fled Koonwarra early one morning, toting a battered suitcase. Shannon's recent generosity to her now seemed like a crust tossed to the dogs from the high table. Trotting toward the jumping paddock on the narrow green lane, Kerry struggled with her jealousy, more determined than ever to succeed in the world she had chosen. Shannon's beauty had once again effortlessly accomplished what her own talent would need a savage dedication to achieve, and her spirit leapt to the challenge. She rode up to the white-fenced paddock, determined to try something she had never dared do before.

Troika pricked up his ears as Kerry leapt off to open the gate. The course of jumps in the paddock had been carefully laid out for Lindy IV and his prize Anglo-Arab jumper to practice on, but it had rarely been used since his death. Kerry wanted more than anything to mount one of these fine hunters and jumpers, but she had never dared to ask Jack if she might, knowing he would laugh in her face. Troika was a fine gelding and a good jumper, but he would never be a champion. The time had come for her to have a horse of her own, but a top jumper was out of the question, costing well into five figures. She couldn't help dreaming at every horse show, though, every meet that she visited with Jack.

Taking Troika into the paddock, she strode across the glistening grass to set her jumps at over four feet, an ambitious height for her experiment. Then she went back to the horse, removed his saddle, and took a white handkerchief from her pocket. Mounting the horse from the fence, she led him to the middle of the field and positioned herself in front of the long line of twenty jumps, each with a distance of thirty-five feet in between. Then she blindfolded herself. She and Troika were so attuned to each other that the slightest pressure from her knees urged him forward into a trot that soon turned into a gallop. As they sped forward, Kerry gave herself to Troika completely, like a lover, sensing every nuance of motion as he carried her toward the jumps.

She was unaware that her feat was being witnessed from the edge of the paddock by Lindy Van Buren, out on a morning ride around his domain. He reined in his horse when he caught sight of her. From her flaming hair, he instantly identified her even from a distance. Riveted by the drama, he watched as she took jump after jump with Troika,

143

a horse that he remarked to himself was no match for its rider. Gripping the reins of his horse, he waited for Kerry to tumble into the soft turf at any moment, but she never faltered. He smiled sardonically to himself, remarking how rare it was for a rider of her age and background to have the courage to take such a course blindfolded and bareback. His own daughter, Carter, would never have done it. Mark—Mark would have broken out in a cold sweat at the suggestion. But Lindy had done it himself often enough when he was just a kid.

When Kerry had taken the last jump she ripped off the blindfold and fell forward with her arms exuberantly gripping Troika's neck, conveying even at a distance her sensual link with her horse as she stroked her fingers through his mane while whispering approval in his ear. It was a strangely disturbing sight to witness the private moment between this impressive young rider and her mount, and he turned instinctively as if he had been caught in the act of spying. But he couldn't take his eyes off Kerry's curved torso as Troika shivered beneath her. She had all the arrogant pride of a passionate woman as her thighs gripped the broad flanks of the sweating horse.

As if sensing she was being observed, Kerry turned with a startled look on her face. They regarded each other at a distance for a moment before Lindy urged his horse away.

"Rainmaker . . . I wonder, . . ." he muttered thoughtfully to himself as he trotted down the bridle path.

That evening Kerry went up to the big house in response to a summons from Lindy. The yard was lost in the gloaming, heavy with the smell of mown grass, horses, and the cooing of pigeons. But Kerry was oblivious to everything as she prepared her defense, knowing full well why she had been ordered to see Mr. Van Buren. No doubt he was furious that she had been using the paddock without his permission, and she wondered what he might do to punish her.

Rolling up the sleeves of a clean starched shirt, Kerry confronted the house, her courage leaving her for a moment as she recalled the Draconian power that the lord of The Meadows wielded over his employees. The butler grimly ushered her through the huge, dimly lit sitting room, its windows thrown open to admit the fragrant air. When the door to Van Buren's study was opened, he was sitting in the leather chair behind his desk.

144

"Good evening, Mr. Van Buren. You wanted to see me?" Her voice was small and insignificant, and she was instantly ashamed of it.

"Come in and sit down, Kerry," he said casually, gesturing to the chair on the other side of the desk.

She did as she was told, taking in at a glance this impressive room of The Meadows that she had never been in before. The walls were paneled in bleached oak mellowed by time, housing row after row of shelves lined with leather-bound books. This was a man's room, smelling faintly of tobacco and exuding an aura of moneyed seclusion. From the leather-topped desk Lindy Van Buren commanded an empire of thoroughbreds that had made his name renowned in breeding circles around the world, and the wall behind him was devoted to rosettes, photographs, and trophies of his triumphs, awesome symbols of his exalted status.

It was all Kerry could do to meet those rather cruel, shrewd eyes as she sat across from him, fear throbbing in her throat. He toyed with a pencil, apparently in no hurry to let her know why he had summoned her.

"I hear from your uncle that you're taking lessons with Bryce Paget." Before Kerry could answer, he continued, "I've had a word with him, and from what the colonel tells me, the only thing standing between you and the top is the right horse."

"Yes," she replied. All her fears fell away, to be replaced by breathless anticipation.

"You've probably heard of my son Lindy. That's him in those photographs," he said, turning to the silver-framed pictures behind his desk. Picking one up, he handed it to her. "This is the last picture of him in the show ring, accepting first prize at the Piazza de Siena in Rome."

Kerry looked at the handsome young man about whom she had heard so much since her arrival. So here was the heir of the emperor of The Meadows, who had been cut down so tragically before his time. A more refined and slender version of his father, Lindy IV stood beside one of the most beautiful horses she had ever seen—a gelding, its glossy black flanks gleaming like patent leather. They were photographed against a line of Roman pines, Lindy proudly holding a silver cup.

"Here's another one of him jumping with Rainmaker."

Fascinated, Kerry reached for the stunning image of this pair of champions. Rainmaker had been captured in full gleaming stretch as he hurtled a wall that was easily six and a half

145

feet. His noble head thrust forward, his splendid quarters were aligned in a perfect soaring leap across an impossible distance. Kerry looked up to find Van Buren studying her, sprawled back like a lion in his chair. The penetrating glint in his eye reduced her to confusion as she sensed the coiled power that lay behind that bold stare. With a wave of his hand he could raise her to the heights or reduce her to obscurity, depending on his whim. Suddenly, in spite of the differences in age and status, a glimmer of understanding passed between them.

"He's absolutely beautiful," she whispered. But her glowing appreciation did nothing to melt the steel in his eyes.

"How would you like the chance to ride Rainmaker on the show circuit, starting with Upperville, Virginia, this June?"

Her breath seemed trapped in her throat. "You can't mean it."

"He's been stabled at the Ludwick Estate since my son's death. He's been ridden off and on, even won a few prizes. But I'm thinking of bringing him home—where he belongs. And I want you to ride him. I saw you today, taking those jumps blindfolded, and I admit I was impressed. You'll never go far on Troika. You need a thoroughbred like Rainmaker. He's an Anglo-Arab hunter, going on fourteen, and he was a champion like his rider. He can be again, if given the chance."

Nothing could have prepared Kerry for this moment. Van Buren's breathtaking offer was the very last thing she had ever expected of him. Here at last was someone who believed in her. The firm set of his broad suntanned face relayed that he meant business, and only her stubborn pride kept her from rushing behind the huge desk and throwing her arms around his neck. Instead, she bowed her head for a moment, biting back the raw happiness that coursed through her at this miraculous gift of fortune. At that moment she passionately loved Lindy Van Buren with all her heart.

All Kerry's defenses were down as she looked up at him with tear-filled eyes. "Mr. Van Buren—I'm honored, I'm privileged. It's like an answer to my prayer, really. And I want to thank you from the bottom of my heart. I just hope I never disappoint you—sir," she added, the words tumbling out.

All the hard work of the last ten years of her life merged as her spirits soared. It was a moment that could only be eclipsed in the show ring when she won her first trophy. She

146

could hear the applause already as she pranced on the magnificent Rainmaker into the blinding spotlights of the arena.

"I've already asked your uncle to go on over to Ludwick to have a look at him. I told him today that we're bringing him home."

"Where he belongs," she echoed.

Van Buren smiled for the first time, rising from his chair. "I think that this occasion calls for a drink, even though you are under age." From a crystal decanter on the butler's tray, he poured two balloons of cognac, handing her one.

"Here's to Madison Square Garden in two years' time," he said.

Raising her glass to his, Kerry tilted her head back and took a gulp of the cognac, which she had never tasted before. Though it scalded her throat all the way down, she showed no sign of it.

The day Rainmaker came home to The Meadows, the apple blossoms had just come into bloom. Kerry was awake long before dawn to see the first light filter through the leafy treetops beyond her bedroom window. Each time she had closed her eyes during the night, she had been awakened by a jolt of anticipation, and when she heard Jack slam the front door, she got out of bed excitedly and pulled on her jeans, realizing he was on his way to Ludwick Estate to fetch Rainmaker.

Without pausing for breakfast, she was out the door and down the stairs of the apartment over the garages. Walking to the yard, she paused to savor the beauty of the day. Doves cooed from somewhere in the verdant chestnut trees that climbed high against the pure blue sky of the May morning. The Meadows seemed to vibrate with the droning of insects, with birdsong, and there rose a rich smell from the soil of the farm that promised a new season of growth. Kerry walked to the stables with an awareness of the perfection of life in a universe that seemed to revolve around the momentous fulfillment of her dream—to have a thoroughbred of her own.

She paused for a moment to look proudly at Rainmaker's name engraved on a brass plaque above the door of his box. It had once been taken down, but it was back again and polished to a gleam appropriate for the return of a prodigal son, a prince reinstated to favor. In the box everything was in perfect order, since she had spent all the previous evening

147

there before going to bed. As she stepped in, Willie, one of the black grooms, passed by.

"You're up early. You've got more than an hour yet before they get back from Ludwick," he chided her.

"Oh, I know. I just want to put a few finishing touches on things before he gets here. You don't think they'll take too long, do you?" she said anxiously, taking up the broom to sweep the brick floor yet again.

"Shouldn't think so. I never thought I'd live to see this day," he said, shaking his head in amazement. "I'll never forget that afternoon when Mr. Van Buren got that telegram from Washington. We didn't see him for three days. He locked hisself in his office. Wouldn't even answer the phone. I always thought he'd sell that horse. Could'a got a packet for him, too. He just couldn't take the sight of that horse no more after Mr. Lindy."

"Tell me again what Rainmaker looks like, Willie," she said, even though she had heard him talk of nothing else since the gelding's homecoming was announced.

"I never seen a horse that was finer than Rainmaker. Why, you could see your face in his flanks. They shine just like polished boots. . . ."

"Tell me about his eyes," she said, leaning on the broom handle.

"I never did forget them eyes, no, sir. They be as bright as burnin' coals. Just lookin' at him, why, you can see that horse thinks like he was a person. And the way he looks at you—it's like he's measuring you up, knows what you're thinkin'."

"Willie, I think I'm going to die if he doesn't get here right away," she said dramatically.

"But don' you make no mistake. He be hot-blooded. He ain't easy to control," the stable boy said, looking skeptically at Kerry. "He's in his prime still. Nearly sixteen hands, and packed with power." He gave an amused laugh. "You should'a seen Mr. Lindy on that horse. Rainmaker sure knew who was master."

Without meaning to, perhaps, Willie had suddenly sown seeds of doubt within her. Was she a match for this magnificent thoroughbred? Tomorrow she would have to prove it, and everyone would turn out to watch and see if she was going to make a fool of herself. Even Willie, who knew how superbly she rode, seemed to doubt her. Kerry turned to the groom, her eyes blazing with determination.

148

"You just wait and see, Willie. We're going to be champions together, just like him and Lindy."

"Why, I never said no different," he replied with a laugh.

"Are you going to be here when they come?"

"You kiddin'? I wouldn't miss seeing that horse for nothin', but the thing I reckon we'll all be watching is the expression on Mr. Van Buren's face."

When Kerry didn't reply, he said, "Well, I got work to do. See you in 'bout an hour's time."

"Okay, Willie," she called absently. She paused to let her eyes roam over the most magnificent box in the stables. The paneled walls met a sloping, beamed ceiling that gave the quarters a dark, cool aspect during the hot summer and a cozy warmth in winter. Rainmaker had his own trough with running water, and the lattice window looked onto a private, white-fenced paddock partly shaded by a huge oak tree. In comparison to Splendor's box at Koonwarra, Rainmaker's private apartment was like a gentleman's country retreat. Sighing impatiently, Kerry wandered from stall to stall. She had nothing more to do, and her stomach churned with excitement as she passed the tedious minutes. She was like a Hindu princess awaiting her unknown betrothed, her lord, or an untried ballerina waiting to dance a pas de deux with Nureyev.

When at last she heard the distant sound of the horse van coming up the long drive, she raced from the box, her heart hammering. The sound had already alerted others to Jack's arrival with Rainmaker.

"Mr. Jack," called Willie with a wave as the stud's horse van—navy blue with The Meadows logo scrolled in silver on the side—cruised slowly into the cobbled yard.

Suddenly people materialized from nowhere. Even some of the house staff came down to the stables to see this momentous event, causing Kerry to hang back on the sidelines.

When Jack got out of the car and waved to Kerry, Willie said teasingly:

"Where you all been, anyway? Miss Kerry thought you was never comin'."

"I came as quick as I could. Kept the speedometer at twenty all the way. This is precious cargo, you know," replied Jack, beaming triumphantly. "Somebody run to the house and tell Mr. Van Buren we're here."

Lindy strode into the yard just as Jack was opening the

149

bolt at the back of the van. Kerry watched, paralyzed with expectation. She glanced at Van Buren, impatient and rather distant, then quickly looked away again. Perhaps he had begun to regret his decision to let her ride Rainmaker.

"Well? What are we waiting for?" snapped Van Buren when Jack turned to him.

The bolt shot back, and the doors were flung open to reveal Rainmaker's shadowy hindquarters.

"Easy, boy, easy," Jack crooned as the groom pulled out the ramp below. There was tension in the air when the groom eased his way into the van to loosen the tethered horse, highstrung like all his breed; but though Rainmaker was twitching nervously, he allowed himself to be eased slowly backward without balking. When he was on firm ground, Jack reached up and pulled off the monogrammed blanket across his back, unveiling the horse for all to see as though he were a work of art.

Kerry's eyes darted to Van Buren, who was staring at Rainmaker, his face a mask. Only the tightening of his jaw and his white, clenched knuckles betrayed what this moment must have meant to him. If she had felt in awe of Lindy Van Buren that summer evening when he had fulfilled her wish, Kerry worshiped him now.

"Yes, he's a beauty. A beauty he is," pronounced Jack, taking the reins and parading Rainmaker in a circle for them to behold.

It was love at first sight as Kerry took in every magnificent detail of this fine animal, as rich and dark as molasses, and he carried himself in a proud, mischievous fashion as if aware of his admiring audience. He was the classic example of the pure, rangy thoroughbred with a small velvety muzzle and a bold, arched neck, a short back, and legs as delicate as musical notes, yet crafted of steel. He looked at them with dark eyes that held an ancient intelligence, and Kerry wanted to laugh out loud with happiness as she perceived the energy, the personality, the iron will coiled in this member of the finest of all the equine races. The twitching of his ears told her he was striving to identify every sound his long memory associated with The Meadows. He was home again. Kerry had never seen a horse as fine as Rainmaker, and her imagination took flight, her mind's eye seeing them together in the deserts of Arabia, she in the robes of a prince, streaking across the sands in the burning sun. She could hardly wait to be astride him, to feel his

150

power beneath her. Together there was nothing they couldn't conquer.

"Here, girlie, I think it's your turn now. Why don't you take him into his box?" said Jack, giving her the reins.

Reaching into her pocket, she brought out a few choice carrots she had brought for him. Rainmaker tossed his head for a moment before deigning to lower his velvety muzzle to her hand. The first contact against her flesh sent a tingle along the hollow of her arm.

She proudly led him to his box, feeling that now he was hers alone. As she passed by Van Buren, they exchanged a look.

"I'll be in the ring tomorrow morning when you mount him for the first time. Give him a rest today, then we'll see how the two of you get on."

"Yes, sir," she called over her shoulder.

The moment he entered the stable, Kerry felt Rainmaker shudder, and pausing to look up at him, she could tell by the expression in his eyes that he knew exactly where he was. When she had stroked him and talked to him, she removed his lead rein and opened the door to the paddock, then watched him bolt free. With a whinny of delight, he frisked and shied joyfully. His grace of motion was a marvel to behold. The muscles of his glossy quarters rippled as he gamboled across the grass in the brilliant sunshine, and the promise of riding this dark, sculptured beauty was almost too incredible to comprehend. Feeling tears springing to her eyes, Kerry turned her back to the stable door where Jack and the groom were watching. When Rainmaker had vented his energy, he stopped, turning his full regard on her. Tossing his head high, he communicated his proud sense of repossession of the turf that had once been his.

"Yes, my beauty, you're home," she whispered, voicing the words that everyone had left unspoken in Van Buren's imperious presence. The words unleashed a torrent of feeling inside her. It was as close as she had ever come to adoration. No man had yet touched the secret part of her that yearned to care passionately, to belong, to give, to hope, to dream. All the complex emotions of full-grown love sprang to life as she regarded the proud horse that would carry her toward her future.

The next morning Kerry allowed herself plenty of time to round up Rainmaker from the paddock and saddle him.

151

She had put on a pair of bisque-colored jodhpurs, boots, a black velvet riding hat, and a checked shirt rolled up at the sleeves. She had been up at dawn to feed and water him, and Rainmaker came to her playfully after she had tempted him with several lumps of sugar. When she had slipped the bit into his mouth, she carefully placed the exquisite English riding saddle onto his back. Once owned by Lindy IV, it had hung unused in the tack room since his death. She had polished it painstakingly until the neglected leather shone like new.

"There, boy, easy," she whispered, smoothing his flanks.

When she had adjusted the stirrups to her satisfaction, she led him to the yard, where she saw Willie heading for the stable.

"They all waitin' over at the ring, Mr. Jack and everybody. Mr. Van Buren'll be along any minute. You going to get on him now, Miss Kerry? Or take him there?"

They exchanged a glance, and Kerry could see Willie still had his reservations about the ability of a girl her size to control the magnificent Rainmaker. But it wasn't her muscles or her strength that she relied on to master a horse, but the silver thread of confidence that ran through her nature, the command of a born rider that conveyed itself to a horse—any horse—the moment she was in the saddle.

When they got to the training ring, a huge barnlike structure, Jack and several of the stable lads were already hanging on the railing. The sawdust that covered the practice arena had been raked smooth, and the cavallettis and practice jumps were already in place.

"Good luck, girlie," said Jack with a wink when he saw Lindy come through the doors.

Coolly, Kerry led Rainmaker through the gate, then she swung into the saddle without hesitation. It was like mounting a volcano that might erupt at any moment. She could almost feel the adrenaline surge through the horse as he took her weight, and she leaned forward to stroke his neck, praising him softly all the while. Then, giving him no time to reflect, she moved him into the center of the ring. The observers on the sidelines, including Van Buren, blurred into the background as she gathered her concentration. Never had Kerry felt such a smooth, elegant stride in a horse, and as she trotted him 'round the course, they moved as one, fulfilling the ideal of the art of dressage that had its roots in Arabia, its purpose to allow a mounted animal to exhibit the same unfettered stride as an unsaddled colt flying across the desert. Now in perfect command, Kerry took Rainmaker through his paces on the cavallettis. In front of Van Buren, Jack, and the others, she put all her skill into play, letting Rainmaker find his own rhythm as he approached the barriers. Horse and rider soared over the jumps as if they had been teamed together for years instead of moments. As a finale, Kerry took the first set of practice jumps in a stride, sailing over each one as if she were flying.

"That's enough for today," she whispered affectionately in Rainmaker's ear. Flushed with success, she cantered to the fence to a little burst of applause. She grinned triumphantly at Willie and the grooms, aware of Jack's pride as she reined in the prancing Rainmaker, who already seemed eager to have another go. Finally her eyes sought Van Buren. He stood back from the rest of them as he watched her performance. The look in his eyes told her that he didn't trust himself to speak, inspiring her to say:

"Mr. Van Buren, I know why you called him Rainmaker. I felt like I was riding a cloud pulled by the wind."

Chapter VII

Paris, July 1979

Chaos reigned in the dressing rooms off the salon of the Palais des Invalides moments before the countdown to the Chloë Winter collection. Forty models in various stages of undress dashed from one corner of the dressing room to the other for makeup, clothes, and accessories. The assistants, drab little stooped women a race apart from the statuesque mannequins, stitched hems, fumbled with zips and buttons as they cursed under their breath in French. The overwhelming feminine aromas of perfume, sweat, and the scent of new clothes filled the air of the crowded room, which was rapidly becoming a pressure cooker in the heat of mid-July in Paris. Tempers frayed to the breaking point when zippers caught on tender skin or heels snagged the delicate fabric of a dress.

Ready except for the final details, Shannon presented herself for accessories to a harassed little woman who miraculously produced the right pair of shoes for each ensemble. Hers were of pearl-gray kid that perfectly matched her pale gray ruffled tunic of wool as fine as gauze.

With only minutes to spare, Shannon rushed to makeup to have her face dusted with powder as she kept her eyes on the clock: it was nearing eleven much too quickly. First in the lineup, she presented herself before Karl Lagerfeld, presiding at the exit. Handsomely lean, and with the distinctive blond ponytail that was his trademark, he scrutinized every detail of Shannon's ensemble in one expert glance.

"Bring me that scarf," he commanded above the din, snapping his fingers. "Who told you to wear pearls?" he growled at Shannon in French, not expecting an answer. Irritably he wound a diaphanous length of printed chiffon around her neck, then smoothed a tendril of glossy hair that had escaped from her curled chignon before giving her a curt nod of approval.

As Shannon collected herself in the shadow of the entrance. The murmur of the crowd reached her. Like an actress in the wings, she slipped into character as she waited to begin the voyage down the long zigzag catwalk before hundreds of spectators. The instant Lagerfeld gave her her cue, she slipped into the mannequin's languid saunter, her eyes focused as if on a distant shore.

As she entered the huge gilt-paneled salon, her appearance ignited a wave of excitement in the expectant audience beneath the glittering chandeliers. The music swelled to a crescendo, and flashbulbs began to pop in every direction, but she hardly saw the photographers leaning toward her; elegantly she moved forward, catching only a blurred glimpse of the Eiffel Tower framed in the giant window. A roar of applause broke out in the front row as Shannon gazed unseeingly across the sea of faces above the gilt chairs. Lagerfeld had declared an age of femininity, and the audience was eager to show its appreciation for his inspired flowing lines, his palette of pastel colors. With long, smooth strides, Shannon reached the end of the catwalk and with perfect aplomb turned on one toe, then paused and dipped elegantly before strolling back to the beat of the music. For a few seconds she hesitated like a pale bird, raising her gossamer wings, fingertips touching. A veil of concentration over her beautiful eyes, Shannon saw nothing, certainly not the man in the front row who was appraising her.

She returned again and again as the show progressed.

Her last ensemble was a black sequined sheath, and as she floated down the catwalk, her dress shimmering like moonlight on dark water, a crescendo of applause filled the salon. A cannonade of flashbulbs erupted madly, and there were calls of "bravo!" proclaiming the dress to be a triumph. Shannon suppressed a smile at the ecstatic response and lowered her eyes as she posed at the end of the catwalk, an air of powerful mystery playing across her face. The man in the front row unfolded his crossed arms as interest flickered on his hawklike face.

Amadeo Benguela narrowed his eyes as if he were trying to pierce the glamorous façade contrived by fashion, to see the real woman. As Shannon disappeared to prolonged applause, her gown trailing light, he withdrew a notepad from his pocket and began to scribble on a card engraved with his name. He paused, wondering whether he should write in French, Italian, or English.

At his side, Doña Inés Oliviera smiled knowingly to herself when she noticed what Amadeo was doing. The chicly dressed blond wife of the Argentinian ambassador knew perfectly well what her old friend was up to. She had always been able to spot his type at a glance, a useful talent since there were many women who caught his fancy, brunettes, blondes, and redheads.

"That dress would look divine on Angelina. Why not surprise her?" she leaned over to whisper mischievously.

Catching the sly smile on her face, he replied, "You know me far too well, Inés. I can keep no secrets."

She threw back her head and laughed appreciatively, pushing up the sleeves of her crimson linen suit.

Later, when the show was over and before the crowds had begun pouring from the Palais des Invalides, Shannon hed down the steps of the building into the brilliant sun- .me to the busy square, where people were already hailing taxis to rush to another show.

"Are you going to Cardin by any chance?" she called to a woman about to enter a taxi.

"Yes, come on—hurry," she shouted.

"Wait for me!" called another model through the window before they could close the door. "I'm going to Cardin, too."

As she collapsed on the backseat of the Citroën, Shannon sighed with relief, then exchanged a smile with the other two women, who were caught up in the same frantic rush. The week of the Paris collections was always like this. Balancing her tote bag on her lap, Shannon realized she was still clutching a card that the directrice of the couture house had pressed into her hand as she'd dashed out. Glancing at it, she scanned the familiar name, then slipped it into her bag.

That evening, as a deep blue dusk settled over the city of Paris, Shannon emerged from a taxi on the corner of the rue de la Seine, then walked toward the striped awning of the Épicerie Provençal.

"*Bon soir, monsieur,*" she called to the *patron*. She tossed a few items into the shopping basket, including a baguette, several fragrant white peaches, and a slice of ripe melting Brie. Leaving the shop, she stopped at the *tabac* for a *Herald Tribune* before making her way toward her apartment in the rue Bonaparte.

Letting herself into the high porte cochere, she felt a delicious rush of cool air from the interior courtyard. It had been a sizzling day, and she had hardly paused for breath. Now, as she climbed the winding staircase to the third floor, balancing her groceries, she was grateful she didn't live any higher in the building.

Turning the key in the lock, she called, "Jackie—I'm home," but there was no answer from the American model staying with her for the collections. Kicking off her shoes in the hall, Shannon stooped to pick up the mail the concierge had slipped under the door. She put her groceries in the kitchen and went to the bedroom in the old-fashioned flat overlooking the Ecole des Beaux Arts. The first thing she did was to fling open the double windows and gaze out at the gray rooftops of Paris pressed against the pink horizon, a sight she had never tired of in the year and a half she had lived in the city.

When she had showered and changed into her dressing gown, she curled in the deep chair by the fireplace. The uneven parquet floors, the shabby but elegant furniture, the frayed carpets, all of it made the flat a welcoming place to come home to after her frequent trips abroad to Milan, London, or Rome, or even as far as the Séychelles, Thailand, or Goa. Setting aside the bills, cards to openings, and invitations, she found a letter from Kerry, which she opened first.

In the last two years, their lives had veered in opposite directions at such speed that the two sisters had never managed to arrange a reunion. Shannon had been in New York only once, but it had coincided with the Devon Horse Show in Pennsylvania, which Kerry couldn't miss. They had only been able to talk on the phone, something they tried to do at least once a month. Kerry, it seemed, was even busier than Shannon was now that riding Rainmaker took up all her spare time. Still, she managed to write brief, newsy letters, which Shannon often failed to answer. Since her climb to the top, however, Shannon had never neglected to send Kerry a generous monthly allowance, a gesture that reassured her that Kerry had everything she could possibly need. The prize money that she and Rainmaker won traditionally went to The Meadows, and though Van Buren paid for everything, it gave Shannon satisfaction to know that Kerry was perfectly outfitted for every event and that she could afford to buy clothes for the parties that inevitably followed the competitions she entered.

Smiling, Shannon read the latest news of Rainmaker, who had bruised a tendon, a near catastrophe that Kerry had underlined and embellished with punctuation marks, breathlessly following with the news that she had applied to enter Braemar Junior College outside Boston the following September.

When Shannon had finished the letter she pondered for a moment. Sending Kerry an allowance was one thing, but putting her through college seemed like an awesome undertaking. She was living within her income at the moment, but there was little to spare. Never inclined to save money, Shannon had indulged herself in many of the luxuries that her newfound independence offered, including the rental of a two-bedroom apartment in one of the most chic quarters of Paris. Obviously Kerry was blithely assuming that Shannon could pay all of her college expenses, even though they had never discussed it. Shannon's mind ranged over her projected income for the coming year. She would be doing a layout for *Officiel* in September to be shot in Morocco, the Italian couture collection that autumn, and she had several bookings within a day's reach of Paris before Christmas. Calculating all the work she had, and knowing there would be more, she decided she could manage to pay the first installment on Kerry's tuition if she were careful. Just then she heard the key turn in the door.

"Is that you, Jackie?" she called.

"Boy—am I bushed!" the model groaned, staggering into the living room. The tall brunette slumped into a chair across from her and moaned, "I've got to get into that shower. If I

157

don't, I'll never make it. I told Eileen I'd meet everybody at Castel's at nine, but I don't know how. If it wasn't Friday, I swear I'd kill myself."

"I don't think I'm coming tonight. Could you tell Eileen I might join everybody for lunch tomorrow?"

"What? You're not coming? Well, I guess Castel's and Jimmy's are old hat to you. You can do it anytime. But I have to live it up in Paris while I have the chance. You sure you won't feel better after you've relaxed a while?" Jackie asked, not bothering to stifle a yawn.

"Nope. I'm going riding tomorrow at the crack of dawn in the Bois de Boulogne."

"I hope to be riding myself at the crack of dawn—a certain Giorgio I met on Monday."

Shannon laughed. "Speaking of Giorgio, that reminds me. Here's another one who might interest you."

"Who?"

"The directrice slipped me this card when I left Chloë today. Let's see. . . . Oh, yes. Amadeo Benguela. Argentinian, I think. They're all the same. Paris is full of them at this time of year. And if you miss them this time around, don't worry— they'll pounce on you in Milan. They make you feel you're the only girl in the world—for twenty-four hours."

"Terrific—I don't care if I'm a statistic. I'm not waiting for Mr. Right like some people. Wait a minute—Benguela. Isn't he some South American tycoon? I saw his picture in *Jours de France* with—"

"What difference does it make?" Shannon interrupted, tossing the card into the wastebasket. "If you spend three months in Milan or Paris, you'll feel exactly the same way, believe me. Jackie—I want to ask you something. Do you think it's really important for a girl in America to go to college?"

"And how. You can't even find a job selling shoes without a degree. Not to mention finding a husband—"

"Thanks. That answers my question. I guess that settles that," she said half to herself, slipping Kerry's letter into the pocket of her robe. Braemar she wants, Braemar she'll get."

The landscape of Touraine was wreathed in mist late one Friday afternoon in October as Fabrice Pomfret drove his Renault through an ancient stone village. By his side sat Shannon wrapped up in a gray fox coat.

158

"What luck it was that I remembered you not only ride, but hunt as well. Clever girl that you are," Fabrice said with a sideways smile.

"Hold on—I've only hunted once, and that was in Fontainebleau," Shannon teasingly reminded him. "And French hunting etiquette, like the French themselves, will always remain a mystery."

Shannon had known the Anglo-French art dealer casually for months. Amusing and witty, he was a pet of Parisian society, and no soirée or spectacle was complete without Fabrice. Always a natty dresser, he now wore a camel-colored coat with a beaver collar and a red bowtie. Knowing that anything he suggested was bound to be fun, Shannon had accepted his last minute invitation that very afternoon when she'd flown into Paris from the Italian collections; normally she would have declared herself too exhausted to go.

"Wait until you see Les Tourelles—The Towers—my darling." He gestured. "It has the fatal enchantment of the seventeenth century, with the plumbing of the twentieth. You can hunt for both of us. I never get up before noon. I prefer to see the autumn leaves from the window of my room in my dressing gown as I sip my *chocolat*. The idea of tearing around in mad pursuit of the scent of a stag they've dragged across the fields is anathema to me."

"You're joking. Do they really do that?"

"Of course I'm joking. Believe me, at Les Tourelles they would never stoop to that. Our host is a perfectionist."

As she looked out at the mysterious undulating landscape in the golden grip of autumn, Shannon began to relish the thought of escape from Paris, where winter had already closed in like a gray clamp, shutting out its famous blue skies for days at a time.

"And the chef—his *soufflé aux cèpes* is incomparable. And he's not bad-looking into the bargain."

"Oh, no, Fabrice. It's not going to be one of *those* weekends, is it?"

"Certainly not—*hélas!*" he answered, and they shared a laugh. "I promise I'll be on my best behavior."

Shannon knew that Fabrice dipped into the seamier *boîtes* of Montmartre with the same ease that he frequented the most sophisticated salons of the Faubourg. He had already shown her this racy side of Paris, which would normally have been closed to her. Certain people speculated about their relationship when he walked into a reception or a ball with Shannon on his arm. But she considered him the perfect escort, and his cosmopolitan air and dry sense of humor set him apart from the ordinary upper-crust Frenchman. Shannon had discovered long ago that Paris could be the loneliest city in the world. The French lived up to their reputation for closing their doors to outsiders.

By now Shannon was used to everyone's assumption that she was dangling dozens of men in her wake; however, while her life had a certain surface glitter, closer examination revealed a different story. Modeling had been her passport to life at the top, but from the beginning she had decided that it was her beauty she was selling and not her soul. She preferred to keep her professional life separate from her private life, choosing the company of many-faceted characters like Fabrice to the photographers and playboys who hung on the coattails of models. Five more years, she kept telling herself, five more years. Then she would do what she wanted. By then Kerry would be out of school, and she would have saved money. She would find a desert island somewhere, paint, write, anything as long as it didn't involve dashing from one booking to another, posing for tedious hours in bizarre clothes against absurd settings that had nothing to do with real life. Nevertheless, she was becoming addicted to the fringe benefits that she now enjoyed. After all, here she was with Fabrice, driving through the heart of Touraine to the château that was suddenly outlined in the distance like a phantom, its golden windows piercing the mist. It was a long way from Koonwarra. The car sped down the long, treeless drive toward the house, set in a wide clearing against a dark backdrop of copper beeches.

"Didn't you say our host was Baron Rothmere?"

"Oh, no," replied Fabrice. "Rothmere *used* to own it. He sold it a few years ago to Amadeo Benguela."

"Fabrice—you are a fiend!" she exclaimed, unable to decide whether to be amused of annoyed by his complicity. "And after what I told you."

"Exactly. I remember your mentioning that you'd given him the brush-off once. Naturally I knew you wouldn't come if I told you. Don't be angry. He's forgotten all about it, I'm sure. He won't have a clue who you are."

The imposing sixteenth-century château of dressed stone the color of pale honey was flanked by round towers, their steep pitched roofs covered in slate. The spare lines of Les Tourelles, uncluttered by flowerbeds or shrubbery, gave an overwhelming impression of masculine solidity and power. As they sped down the long graveled approach through clipped lawns, the great house loomed larger and larger against a bank of towering chestnut and beech trees. Fabrice pulled up in front of the massive double doors and alighted from the car to ring the bell. While the houseman collected their bags, Shannon turned for one last look at the orange sun sinking into the deep forest behind the château. Through the mist that curled from the grass she could make out the motionless silhouettes of deer grazing in the immense park that sealed off Les Tourelles from the surrounding countryside.

The moment she entered the hall Shannon realized that the stark grandeur of the façade of the château gave no clue as to the rich charm of the interior. Fine tapestried chairs in gilt wood, a marble-topped console table set with an enormous bouquet of hothouse flowers, and the Savonnerie carpet on the ancient flagstones suggested the luxurious taste of their host. A huge cubist abstract commanded the spiral stone staircase, a provocative switchback from one century to another.

"Robert Delaunay," remarked Fabrice when he saw Shannon looking at the picture. "Benguela has one of the finest collections of twentieth-century art in France."

Abstract art seemed surprisingly at home in this ancient setting. Shannon turned to observe another spectacular painting in hot colors, like a splash of sun-fired water.

"Where is everybody?" she asked, her voice echoing in the stairwell as they followed the footman upstairs.

"We're probably the first. Everybody else, including Amadeo, is probably speeding here on the *autoroute* at this very moment." They walked down a carpeted hallway hung with Flemish tapestries.

"Don't think this is any ordinary château," Fabrice continued. "Amadeo has spared no expense to house his collection. The place is centrally heated for a start, so you don't have to wear long johns under your evening gown. And the plumbing is as good as at a Hilton. It looks like this is your room—see you later," he called.

When the footman had deposited the luggage, he asked, "Would madame care to take tea in her room?"

"Yes, thank you, that would be lovely."

"Aperitifs will be in the salon from eight, and dinner will be served at nine," said the footman, retiring with a bow.

Shannon removed her fur and inspected the sumptuous

161

bedroom, deeply impressed in spite of herself. Above the pale blue wainscotting was an old Chinese wallpaper patterned with birds and flowers; and the delicate Louis XVI furniture upholstered in silk and the Aubusson carpet evoked the femininity of Pompadour and Marie Antoinette. Every detail, from the Watteau engravings to the inner shutters on the windows, to the boxes of Limoges porcelain on the dressing table, reflected such attention to detail that Shannon's thoughts turned to the man who commanded all this splendor, wondering what he would be like. There was a knock at the door, and the maid entered bearing a tray which she set by the fire.

"I'll return in a moment to unpack madame's case," she said. "When madame wishes her bath poured, would she please ring?"

"Thank you," said Shannon as the girl disappeared. Almost struck dumb by this unaccustomed luxury, Shannon decided she wanted nothing more than the time to enjoy every precious second of her stay at the château. Feeling the most pampered creature alive, she curled up by the fire to sip her tea and inspect the pile of books and magazines in several languages set out on the table, secretly grateful Fabrice had tricked her into coming.

Night had fallen when a silver-gray Mercedes pulled up sharply to the entrance of the château. With a sixth sense born of long service to his master, Amadeo's valet had already stationed himself at the door within seconds of the crunch of gravel on the drive.

"*Que tal*, Miguel," said Amadeo, charging up the steps. With a quick gesture he flung off the camel coat he wore over a dark suit. He spoke an abrupt Spanish to his valet, distilled to a shorthand over the years. Running his hand through his silvered dark hair, combed severely back from his high, bronzed forehead, Amadeo glanced around the entrance hall as if pacing himself to the slower tempo of life away from the clamor of Paris.

"Has everyone arrived?"

"*Sí, señor*. All the guests have come. His Excellency the ambassador and Doña Oliviera came only moments ago, and I've just shown them to their room. The Comte de Vauchamps came only just before them. The Comtesse came separately."

Amadeo scanned the list Miguel handed to him. "Ah, good. I see Monsieur Fabrice was able to come after all with Sabine. . . ." He smiled, thinking the pretty redheaded vendeuse from Dior would add a certain sparkle to the party.

162

"No, señor. Apparently Mademoiselle Sabine was unable to come at the last moment, but Monsieur Fabrice brought someone else along instead. A Mademoiselle Faloon."

The name seemed familiar, but Amadeo dismissed it when he was unable to connect it to a face. A frown of annoyance creased his forehead. "How inconvenient," he commented. "But no matter. Have the guests been installed comfortably?"

"Yes, señor. Everything has been attended to. There was a problem when the Comtesse misplaced her dressing case, but it was quickly found."

Impatiently, Amadeo cut him short. "How many of us will be hunting tomorrow?" he said, mentally counting. "I make it ten from here, so that we will be nearly forty including the parties from Bellepoire and Guise."

"No, señor. There will be eleven from Les Tourelles. Apparently Mademoiselle Faloon will be hunting."

Amadeo raised an eyebrow, mollified that Sabine's replacement would at least prove to be an addition to the hunt.

"Come to the kitchen, Miguel. Then I must hurry upstairs before the guests start to descend."

With restless energy and an air of preoccupation, Amadeo moved through the doors that led to the interior of the château, striding over the flagstones. His grasp of every aspect concerning his prize showpiece, Château Les Tourelles, was prodigious, and all his servants knew that nothing escaped his attention.

"*Bon soir*, Albert," he greeted the chef as he swung through the doors of the kitchen, a whitewashed chamber with arched ceilings lined with copper saucepans, aspic molds, and cooking utensils of every description. The chef in the tall white toque was presiding at the stove, assisted by two apprentices. The huge room was filled with the succulent aromas of that evening's dinner.

"*Bon soir*, Monsieur Benguela," the chef acknowledged, then produced the weekend's menus. For several moments, the two men consulted over the seven-course dinner for that evening.

"Miguel, remember to take care the Meursault is properly chilled."

"Yes, señor."

With an approving nod to Albert, Amadeo left the kitchen. Glancing at his watch, he calculated he would have just enough time for a quick sauna before dressing for dinner.

Moments after eight Fabrice tapped at Shannon's door, straightening his bowtie and smoothing the lapels of his dinner jacket.

"*Comme elle est ravissante,*" he declared when she appeared. "Givenchy, isn't it?"

"It is. What a memory you have, Fabrice," she said, brushing the gown of midnight-blue silk georgette, its sloping neckline embroidered with sequins. Her eyes dramatically made up, Shannon had pulled her hair into a tight chignon at the nape of her neck, and she wore the slenderest black satin shoes with pencil-slim heels.

"I think I just might be able to clinch the deal for that Miró I offered Amadeo when he sees you. He adores beautiful women and fine paintings. And his eye for both is infallible," Fabrice whispered confidentially as they swept down the long corridor.

Shannon felt a knot of anticipation tighten within her at the idea of meeting the legendary Benguela. She had almost forgotten his cavalier approach three months before, and it was amusing to speculate whether he would even remember the model he had briefly seen on the catwalk. Thinking how ironic it was that they should meet so soon by coincidence, she wondered if he would be cool to her—if he should recall her face.

They arrived at the high double doors of the salon, before a sweep of shining parquet that ended in the deep borders of a fine Chinese carpet, and paused to locate their host. Shannon stood on the threshold of one of the most magnificent rooms she had ever beheld. The entire room had been painted with a mural by Poussin of the French countryside in deep, dark colors pierced with haunting glints of golden sunlight. The imaginary vistas gave the room the romantic nostalgia of another more mellow century, where shepherdesses and lute players lingered in dark glades beneath pale skies. In the huge marble fireplace a fire blazed, casting a rich glow on the priceless French furniture. Beyond a modern coffee table displaying a Benin bronze head stood Amadeo, who immediately left the group of guests to welcome them.

"Fabrice!" he called exuberantly.

As Amadeo approached, Shannon was struck by the field of energy that surrounded him. He strode across the room and shook Fabrice's hand with an almost peasant warmth, using both of his hands, and his welcoming smile slashed

164

through an otherwise stern face, hawklike in its aspect and set with gleaming dark eyes. As their fingers touched, a sort of current seemed to dart from him, and as he raised her hand to his lips, Shannon decided he had the countenance of a gypsy, a rogue. He could have been the reincarnation of a nobleman who had plundered the countryside in centuries past.

"*Enchanté*," he murmured to Shannon with no sign that he recognized her. Releasing her hand, he brought them into the gathering. After she had been introduced to several of the guests, Shannon stood back to consider her first impressions. How often she had been exposed to counterfeit glamour during the last two years, but here she was fascinated to encounter the real thing, and it surpassed all her expectations. Amadeo had collected a diverse and interesting group of people that reflected his cosmopolitan preference for intelligent company, ranging from a vigorously dark Italian film producer to a handful of Parisian socialites, men and women distinguished by generations of fine-boned breeding. Each of the guests was like a well-cut gem with its own special depth and glimmer, and all of them adorned the crown of Amadeo's social prestige, though he was reputed to be a man who came from nothing.

At her side, Fabrice proved a fund of gossip and anecdotes about the various guests, so that in moments she knew why the vivacious Comtesse de Vauchamps's eyes kept wandering toward a certain footman, and that the stunning Doña Oliviera, one of Argentina's greatest beauties, had once been in love with their host. Shannon found herself wondering which of the dozen or so stunning women, each ravishingly different from the other, was Amadeo's current mistress, and she watched as he made the rounds. He had the charm of a true Latin, his eyes gleaming with pleasure as he talked and flirted with each of them equally.

"He's really the *grand seigneur* holding court, isn't he?" whispered Fabrice as the conversation swirled about them in several languages. "Aren't you glad you came?" he said—a question that needed no answer.

As the evening progressed, it seemed as if they were floating on a barge of idle luxury, surrounded by the haunting antique vistas of Poussin, images from another time. The firelight cast a patina on the faces of the men and women, who suddenly seemed like characters abducted from a period play.

Amadeo came to Shannon's side with the remark, "I hear you're hunting with us tomorrow." There was a hint of challenge in his voice. "Have you ever ridden to hounds in France?"

"Once, ages ago, for a morning in Fontainebleau. I try to go for a canter in the Bois de Boulogne when I'm home at weekends, but I realize it's a far cry from the hunting field." When she saw the skeptical look on his face, she added, "But I did grow up on a horse. Even so, I hope I won't disgrace myself." She felt herself flush at his close scrutiny.

"Come with me for a moment. There's something I want to show you," he said abruptly.

Realizing he had hardly heard what she said, Shannon was startled to find herself being guided into the adjacent salon, where the walls were covered with spectacular paintings chosen from every phase of the twentieth century—from the Impressionists to the Fauvists to the Cubists. Shannon's appreciation of art had begun with Hawke Sutherland, and she gazed at this dazzling private gallery of treasures with a feeling of awe as she recognized the inimitable styles of de Chirico, Matisse, Kokoschka, and de Staël.

Amadeo inclined his head toward the picture above the fireplace, illuminated by a picture light. It was one of the portraits Hawke had done of her.

"It is you, isn't it?"

"Yes, it is," she admitted, her mouth dry from the shock of recognition.

"I've coveted this painting since I first saw it at Agnew's in London. It had already been sold, but I always kept tabs on it through my dealer there, and when it came on the market about six months ago, I bought it at once."

Though he spoke with courtesy, his eyes were free to roam with the private knowledge of a lover over the canvas that revealed the intimate details of her body.

"What attracted me to this picture was the innocent pride, the sense of defiance translated into the lovely form of the young woman."

She looked at her own powerfully seductive image as if seeing it for the first time, as he considered her in the abstract.

"Do you know, Hawke frightened me to death. But I wasn't going to let him know it. Perhaps that's why I seem defiant," she mused.

"I respect Sutherland as perhaps one of the five most important painters of his generation. You can imagine how surprised I was that day at the Lagerfeld show, Miss Faloon. It took me some time to recall whom you reminded me of, and it wasn't until the following weekend when I saw the picture again that I knew for certain it was you. And now, here you are—the clay of reality from which he created his work of art. You've changed since then, I think. You've won a few battles. You were a little David in those days, challenging some imaginary Goliath, but not anymore. You have confidence now. You are more reflective yet less afraid of life, though still athirst for it, I think."

How could he know so much about her? In a few words Amadeo had lifted the veil of mystery she put between herself and the world. Some ancient force bound them for a moment as she met his dark eyes, which glimmered like jewels in the shadows.

"Come, I think we ought to rejoin my guests." With a light touch on her elbow, he led her past the rich harvest of Mirós, Kandinskys, Marquets. Their fascination paled against the revelation of her own inner self as held up to her by Amadeo, and she wondered if any of the guests would suspect she was the model for the portrait. A glance at his wide shoulders suggested he was built like a bullfighter, and she looked away sharply when he caught her staring at him as they crossed the threshold of the room. The unfathomable but rapacious glint in his eyes passed through her body like a knife from head to foot, and she shivered involuntarily. Feeling distant ripples of passion about to take hold of her, Shannon resisted. Amadeo Benguela was not going to gather her in his net, dip her in gold, and place her like a prize piece of Sèvres on his mantelpiece. He had bought her image, and that would have to be enough.

At nine the next morning, dressed in skintight riding breeches, a black coat, and a bowler, Shannon was downstairs to join the hunt assembling on the graveled forecourt. She was slightly apprehensive as she found herself amidst the chaos of eighty restless hounds skirting several dozen mounted riders, many of them in the deep plum coats of the Chatillon Hunt. Several women in chic black habits riding sidesaddle reined in their impatient horses, whose hot breath frosted on the sharp, misty air. A silver huntsman's horn around the shoulder of the hunt master caught the first point of sun rising beyond the blur of trees. Footmen in tailcoats and white gloves were passing the traditional stirrup cup to the mounted hunters and the villagers who would follow on foot. Already the mulled wine had lifted the spirits of ruddy-faced farmers in boots and tweed coats. Shannon was joined in the forecourt by the flirtatious Comte de Vauchamps, and as they exchanged greetings her mind flew to the night before and the memory of Amadeo at the head of the glittering table. She had unconsciously collected every detail about him since he had shown her the portrait of herself, and she was irritated with herself for automatically seeking him out. Easily identifiable in the heart of the horsemen, he was mounted on a magnificent gray stallion. His body erect, Amadeo created a formidable impression of power and virility astride the fine dappled thoroughbred. His plum coat and riding breeches seemed molded to his body, and he flashed a flirtatious smile at the dowager Duchesse de Crècy, seventy if she was a day, mounted sidesaddle with the carriage of an eighteen-year-old girl. In the traditional long black skirt and veiled top hat, with an ivory horn around her neck, she was a creature of another age.

Catching sight of Shannon, Amadeo led his horse to her. "*Bonjour*, Miss Faloon," he said with a smile that held only the warmth of a solicitous host, yet somehow his glance gave the casual greeting intimacy.

Her heart gave a lurch at the sight of his dark eyes beneath the velvet hat, and she tried to mask her weakness with a friendly air.

"Good morning. What a grand day for the hunt."

"I've told the groom to bring your mount around now. You'll be riding a French-Arab gelding called Oceansong fifteen hands high. He's well trained and knows the countryside. I used to ride him quite often. Give him his head at the fences, and he'll jump anything."

At the sight of the glossy chestnut gelding, Shannon smiled in pleased surprise. She reached out to stroke his small, beautifully proportioned head, intersected by a white blaze, and exclaimed, "What a beauty he is! I've never ridden such a fine horse. I'll take good care of him, I assure you."

"*Es suyo*," Amadeo said gallantly.

She gave an embarrassed laugh at this remark as the groom helped her to mount.

"*Es suyo*—it's yours."

"Thank you very much," she replied, knowing this to be

168

a symbolic gesture of Latin hospitality. From the intensity of Amadeo's eyes, however, he might have been serious. When he had left her side, she felt the grip of tension slowly leave her, and turning, she looked directly into the eyes of Doña Inés Oliviera, who had been watching them. She was regarding Shannon with what seemed to be a kind of nostalgic envy, but in a moment she had turned her head and cast a provocative remark to the man next to her—who Shannon guessed must be her current favorite.

Shannon leaned down to accept a stirrup cup, and as the scent of cinnamon and cloves teased her nose, she glanced up to see Fabrice fling open a window above. Still in his brocade dressing gown, he waved gaily at her.

"What a lovely sight you make, darling, especially from this comfortable vantage point. You're mad, every one of you. I'm going to retire again—I must gather my strength for tonight's ball. *Bonjour, Amadeo—ça va, chère Duchesse, vous êtes ravissante ce matin. . . .*"

At that moment the muted sound of the bugle alerted the riders that the hunt was about to begin. The most eager and experienced huntsmen and women urged their horses to the forefront of the yard, where the whipper-in was trying to contain the foxhounds, which were barking excitedly. Shannon steeled herself for the start of the hunt, feeling Oceansong straining beneath her as she caught sight of the flushed faces of the women, the rugged countenances of the men alive with expectation for a mad chase around the French countryside on this brilliant morning.

"*Allons-y!*" came the cry, and they surged forward.

Hundreds of hooves pummeled the gravel, then thundered across the park to a copse of trees. In tandem, dozens of riders pursued the hounds down a narrow path, where the French autumn lingered, throwing up the scent of moss and mushrooms. Woodsmoke rose from the chimneys of neighboring cottages to mingle here with the scent of rich, wet loam and the smell of sweating horses. Racing beneath the avenue of bare trees, Shannon was swept up by the pulse of the chase.

The throaty cries of the huntsmen, evoking images of warriors centuries past, rose above the rich music of bugles and horns, echoing through the misty reaches of the forest. Suddenly came the signal that the hounds had caught the scent of a stag. The drumming of horses' hooves commanded Shannon's own heartbeat as she hurtled forward with the others. Transformed by blood lust and the thrill of the chase, the huntsmen avidly traversed the very same fields where their aristocratic forebears may once have sported with the kings of France, driven then—as now—to taste the elixir of danger and lust for the pleasures of the hunt.

Emerging from the woods, they came to an open field, following the baying hounds. To the fore Shannon could make out Amadeo as he effortlessly took a stone wall. One at a time, she saw the glossy hindquarters of the horses hurtle over the barrier ahead, and when it was her turn she remembered to let Oceansong have his head. They sailed over smoothly, and as they landed she noticed two riders had been unhorsed and were brushing themselves off. From the edge of the clearing she caught sight of Amadeo regarding her performance, and it gave her a triumphant sense of satisfaction that he had seen her perfect jump.

For several hours the hunt strayed over miles and miles of Touraine, over hills and flatlands, as the sun rose through the pale autumn sky. Long after noon, the last traces of mist had lifted from the trees, revealing the muted colors of the countryside. Wet grass caught the light like spun gold, and black rooks wheeled above leafless trees hung with balls of mistletoe. The hazy light of late autumn mined the land, unearthing a palette of metallic ocher, copper, and gold. Like the embers of a dying fire, this would be the last glorious blaze of color before thick snow and clouds rendered the land barren during the long winter.

Near midafternoon Shannon began to tire. Even Oceansong seemed to have lost his taste for the chase as the sun began to sink on the horizon. Finally she turned the horse in the direction of home as the indefatigable regulars of the hunt disappeared ahead. No one could predict if the stag would tire and be cornered by the hounds, but this was a moment that Shannon preferred not to see. She had noticed the long knife sheath dangling from the hip of one of the huntsmen, and she knew it was meant for the throat of the roebuck or stag that had become their quarry.

Cantering through a darkening glade, her eye caught a movement among the trees. Two of the hunters, a man and a woman, had tethered their horses to a tree and she wondered fleetingly if there had been an accident. But she instantly recognized the fragile young Comtesse de Vauchamps, locked in the embrace of a uniformed footman, who was impatiently unfastening the front of her jacket. Their private laughter

170

echoed through the forest, and they seemed oblivious of her as she passed by. Shannon couldn't keep herself from glancing back, to see them tumble into a pile of leaves. She felt a tremor of envy at their abandoned moment, remembering the sensual thrill of flesh on flesh which she hadn't experienced for months. Only one man aroused that shiver of yearning in her, and she pushed his image resolutely from her mind. But as she cantered home alone, the wood seemed haunted by the passionate whispers of the Valois kings and their court, who had pursued the spoils of the chase and those of love with equal relish.

On the eve of the grandest hunt ball of the season at Les Tourelles, a thousand torch lanterns flickered along the approach to the château. Chandeliers blazing from the windows of the façade cast spears of light onto the graveled forecourt, where cars were already beginning to deposit the guests at the entrance met by footmen in gray livery and powdered wigs. Besides *le tout* Paris and the nobility of the great houses of the region, the three hundred guests in full evening dress included some who had come from as far as Madrid, Acapulco, and Athens. Among the limousines, the Citroëns and Mercedeses, was a closed landau drawn by four horses belonging to the eccentric young Baron de Ganet, who for years had adopted the manner of the eighteenth century. His château was illuminated only by candlelight, and he was known to bathe in a copper tub before a fire. Now, he alighted from his coach in silk knee breeches, frock coat, and a powdered wig, with a lorgnette in his hand, leaving the scent of attar of roses in his wake.

Just after eight, Shannon swept down the hall on Fabrice's arm, resplendent in a floor-length gown of topaz paper silk whose fan-shaped bodice, caught at the waist with a crimson sash, artfully suggested her honeyed shoulders rose from a tiger lily. Borrowed at the last minute from Dior, this fantasy of a dress was hers for a few rich hours.

"You're looking very distinguished this evening, Fabrice. Wherever did you get that little bauble on your lapel?"

He stood proudly for a moment, straightening his white tie at the bottom of the stairs.

"Bauble? Do you mind? This is the personal decoration of Prince Horlinger von Swartzenburg." He dusted off the sunburst of semiprecious jewels surrounding a cross of pink enamel.

171

"In recognition for what?"

"For my services in the restoration of the family schloss."

"You won't get a medal if you get schlossed tonight," she quipped caustically, causing him to throw back his head and bray with laughter.

As they descended the stairs, guests were pouring into the Poussin salon. The far doors had been flung open to reveal the long gallery, where dancing had already begun. As they threaded their way through the crowd, Shannon remarked that never had she seen so many spectacularly dressed women in a single room, and she speculated that the *haute couturier* houses of Paris must have been stripped bare of all their finery to create this swirl of color. Even the coffers of the jewelers on the Faubourg St. Honoré must have been emptied, and bank vaults stripped of their treasures to adorn the throats and arms of the women of the *haute monde*. The men, handsome in the stark, black and white of formal evening dress, sported their own brand of finery—medals, decorations, and colored sashes.

The music of Offenbach drew Shannon toward the ballroom, where dancers were swirling beneath the crystal chandeliers. Turning to Fabrice, she saw he was staring transfixed toward a corner of the room.

"Look!" he gasped, his eyes blinking in disbelief. "What a dream, a mirage. *Quelle beauté!*"

"Who do you mean?"

The crowd parted, and she saw the Baron de Ganet posing with all the shy wiles of a young maiden waiting to be discovered. He lowered his eyes demurely when he saw Fabrice staring starstruck at him.

"Do forgive me, Chérie, but you will excuse me, won't you?" her escort murmured. "Destiny calls."

"Of course." In any other circumstances she would have been annoyed to be abandoned, but she couldn't help but be amused as she watched Fabrice approach the waiting baron and heard him say, *"Enchanté, monsieur."*

Within moments a lean young man with arresting blue eyes and a full sensuous mouth presented himself before Shannon, bowing at the waist. Recognizing the dueling scar on his left cheek and the Germanic flavor of his French, Shannon remembered that this was the son of an American film star and a German prince, whom she had met the spring before at Monte Carlo after he had narrowly brushed death at the Grand Prix.

172

"May I have the honor of this next dance, mademoiselle?"

"I'd adore to," she said with her most ravishing smile.

They made a startling couple, the handsome racing driver who thrived on danger and this beauty whose striking image had caused whispers of inquisitive comment at the ball. She had appeared on the covers of all the major European fashion magazines, from *Vogue* to *Marie-Claire*, and since her discovery by Norman Parkinson she had become one of half a dozen faces that had defined the style of a generation.

The mirrored ballroom eclipsed even Versailles in splendor that evening as the dancers swirled to the music of a string orchestra mounted on a dais. The countless tall windows of the ballroom overlooked the floodlit garden of the château, where carved hedges swirled around an oval basin crowned with a fountain surmounted by Perseus and Andromeda.

As Shannon danced in the young German's arms, she couldn't help but recall that two years before one look from him would have sent her heart racing. Then she would have capitulated to his charm without protest, but now she found his classic good looks left her unmoved.

"You're the most beautiful woman here tonight," he declared. "But you have blended your beauty with intelligence and charm. The moment I saw you I was drawn to your side as if by some magnetic force. . . ."

"Thank you," she said inadequately.

"Do you live in Paris now?"

"Yes, on the Left Bank. I have a little apartment between a *boulangerie* and an art gallery."

"You're the toast of Paris. I thought surely you'd be living on the avenue Foch."

"Oh, no, not me." She was in no mood to explain why she preferred the earthy simplicity of life on the rue Bonaparte to the cold grandeur of the Right Bank.

"You're a paradox of a creature, aren't you? I like that in a woman. Yes, I like that," he declared, as if making up his mind.

When the waltz came to an end, Amadeo relinquished the Marquise de la Coudraye, frivolously swathed in ruffles of cerise taffeta. With a gallant smile he looked around for a convenient parking place for the marquise now that he had discharged his duty as host to an entire clutch of nobility.

"Ah, Fabrice—may I present the Marquise de la Cou-

173

draye," he said, delivering his charge to the bewildered art dealer, who was looking around for the fickle baron.

Amadeo threaded his way toward Shannon but saw to his annoyance that she was still being monopolized. Catching the sleeve of a footman, he whispered a message, and within minutes the servant interrupted Shannon and her attentive partner as they were poised to begin another waltz.

"Monsieur, there is an urgent call for you. You can take it in the library."

Startled, he excused himself from Shannon with a polite bow. The next moment she felt a strong hand close around her wrist. Turning, she found Amadeo's eyes upon her. Without a word he claimed her, slipping his arm around her waist, and swept her into the dance. The moment she felt herself in his arms, the crowded room fell away, and she realized she had been waiting for him to come to her side. The power of his body next to hers through the crush of silk was so intoxicating that she closed her eyes. An inner voice whispered that she should resist this imaginary bubble of enchantment, before emotions more overwhelming than she had ever known rooted themselves in her being; but as she reveled in a sensation of weightlessness, she knew it was too late. As he consumed her with his eyes, she knew she had already been branded with desire for Amadeo Benguela.

Crushing her closer he said, "You were the only woman who existed for me from the first moment I saw you." Brushing her cheek with his lips, he set off a ripple of unfathomable longing. Though she was sure he must have repeated the same words to a thousand other women in his lifetime, she let herself believe him. When the music faded, they stood for a few seconds, hand in hand. The slightest pressure of his fingers on hers was enough to seal the bond between them. The mood was broken only when the string orchestra was replaced by a wild troupe of gypsy violinists, who serenaded the guests as they went in to a supper of oysters, caviar, and champagne.

The next morning Shannon was awakened when the maid set her breakfast tray on the table and drew the curtains, then kindled a fire on the hearth. From the luxurious warmth beneath the satin eiderdown, she could see that the château was cloaked in a fine mist.

"*Notre petit déjeuner est servi, madame,*" announced the maid, and softly departed.

174

As Shannon drank a steaming cup of *café au lait* by the fire, wrapped in her dressing gown, her thoughts irresistibly returned to last night's ball. After supper she had danced with Amadeo again and again until nearly six in the morning, when the party finally broke up. His eyes had never left her, and the powerful but almost formal way he had held her next to him was a warning of what lay ahead. Once the dam had broken between them, once she allowed him into her life, there would be no turning back. None of the casual and light-hearted affairs she had had in the past to help her get over Zan had prepared her for a man like Amadeo, but the compulsion to unlock the mystery that surrounded him was intensified by the seductive atmosphere of great luxury in which she now found herself. Cosseted in the tranquillity of the ancient château, she knew she wanted it all, regardless of the cost—every ounce of excitement, pleasure, and riches. For one hour she spun her silken illusions. Later joined the dozen other guests who had gathered in the library for drinks before luncheon. Pale sunlight filtered through the tall double windows of the room hung with tapestries, its vaulted ceiling and carpets in mellow colors. For a moment, unobserved, she regarded Amadeo. His hair, streaked with gray, was combed back severely, and he was wearing a business suit as he chatted to the Argentinian ambassador. The moment he saw Shannon, however, he crossed the room to meet her, but to her surprise he took her by the shoulders and looked somberly into her eyes.

"I'm so distressed—I've just heard that I must leave for Athens in only a few moments. It's unforgivable for a host to leave before his guests, but I'm afraid there is nothing I can do."

His apology seemed to be for her alone, and that softened her disappointment somewhat, but the intensity of his manner in front of the other guests made her feel selfconscious.

"What a great shame. You must be very put out," she replied, flustered, as he led her to the group.

After a few moments he said, "I'm afraid I must go now," as he glanced at his watch. "Please say good-bye to Fabrice, Shannon. Tell him I'll telephone him as soon as I return to Paris." He paused to kiss the hands of Doña Inés, and the Comtesse de Vauchamps. Shannon's hand he kissed last.

When he had gone there was an emptiness in the room. Not even the witty remarks of Fabrice when he joined her could enliven what had become an anticlimax of the momentous weekend. The grand house that lacked no comfort or luxury had lost its spirit, and Shannon passed the rest of the afternoon in the company of glamorous strangers, whose conversation never once seemed to travel beyond the superficial, the polite, the banal. It was then she realized how brightly Amadeo's flame burned in comparison to all the brief candles that surrounded him. The stamp of his original and arresting personality, forged by the conflicting winds of destiny, was on every detail of the château, from the Flemish tapestries to the collection of rare musk deer that wandered in the park beyond the windows. But all was diminished without its owner's magnetism.

Later that afternoon, Shannon and Fabrice drove away from Les Tourelles, and as it was swallowed into the mist behind them they fell silent for a long time.

"What do you think of Amadeo?" said Shannon at last.

"I was wondering when you were going to ask me that," said Fabrice with a wry smile. "If you want my blessing, you have it. Go ahead and have a wonderful time. He'll open every door for you, he'll spoil you to death, but just remember to keep your heart intact. It won't last. It never does with him. As I told you, he is as much a connoisseur of beautiful women as he is of paintings. You'll be his prized possession for one brief hour, but don't let him hang you on his wall. That's not where you belong."

Shannon laughed richly at this remark, remembering that in one sense Amadeo had already done just that.

Amadeo looked impatiently out the window of his Citroën at the heavy traffic ahead. It would cause him even further delay as they approached Orly Airport. Trying to contain his restlessness, he forced himself to lean back into the leather seat and use the time productively. The crisis that had exploded with his insurance brokers when the tanker *Medusa* had caught fire off the coast of Cyprus had roused him to battle, and the stormy expression on his face as he allowed his mind to play on several different levels was one few of his weekend guests would have recognized. At that moment his fighting instincts sprang back to their source, to the days when he had been a street urchin in Buenos Aires, fighting for survival. During the time it had taken to reach the outskirts of Paris, Amadeo's mind had been brooding over the labyrinthine puzzle of the tanker and the solution to the complex problem that now threatened a substantial part of his

176

fortune. He would need all his wits about him to ensure that the syndicate compensated his loss, and as the pieces fell into place he picked up the radiophone and dialed New York, setting the wheels in motion. By this time the word was out, and his enemies would be sharpening their knives against him.

As Miguel drove the car onto the tarmac of the airport, he remembered one last thing he had to do and dialed the number of his secretary.

"Monique? I want some flowers delivered this evening."

"*Oui, monsieur.*"

"The biggest and most expensive, sent to Mademoiselle Faloon, Number Nine, rue Bonaparte. And book my usual table at Maxim's for Friday evening." He dictated a message to accompany the bouquet.

"*D'accord, monsieur, et bon voyage.*"

Hanging up the phone, Amadeo looked ahead to the row of golden discs shining in the distance, the windows of his waiting Gulfstream jet that was ready to take off for Athens.

Shannon let herself in through the *port cochere* and walked through the cobbled courtyard. To her surprise, the *concierge* was hovering near the stairs. Gesturing, the small woman in black spoke almost too rapidly for Shannon to comprehend.

"*Mademoiselle Faloon—il y a quelque chose pour vous. Je l'ai mit devant la porte, mais c'est enorme. . . .*"

"*Merci beaucoup,*" she said, puzzled.

Shannon guessed what "*quelque chose*" was even before she had climbed the last steps to her floor. Before she could see them, she could smell the enormous bouquet of flowers placed before her door. She dropped her suitcase and leaned down to bury her face in the mass of blossoms of every description that cast up the fragrance of a garden at the height of summer. By what miracle had they appeared on a Sunday night? she wondered. Tearing open the envelope attached to the bouquet, she read: "Please dine with me on Friday—Amadeo."

That Friday evening at eight Shannon paced the room nervously as she waited for Amadeo to call for her at her apartment. His secretary had phoned during the week to say they would be dining at Maxim's, and Shannon had chosen to wear a spectacular model she had obtained from Valentino, a

177

fluid tube of persimmon crêpe de chine, trimmed in black. She had swept her hair up simply into a chignon and wore no jewelry except a pair of huge jet earrings.

Throughout the week she had been anticipating this evening, even though her schedule had left her little time to think about it. All during sessions at the *Vogue* studios in the Place de Bourgogne, on a shoot for *Elle* at Malmaison, the image of Amadeo had hovered at the back of her mind. Now as the hands of the clock neared eight, she felt so agitated she wished she had never agreed to go.

Staring at her own flushed face in the mirror, she realized how little she had changed in the four years since she had arrived in Sydney from the Outback. She had lived an entire lifetime since then, but now it all seemed immaterial as she felt the underpinnings of her own poise collapse. She reminded herself a man like Amadeo was bound to be disappointed when he discovered the impostor behind her façade. What did she have to say to a man who was twenty years older and worlds more sophisticated than she was? An international businessman who jetted from one continent to the next and spoke half a dozen languages fluently? A man who had a priceless art collection and who could buy anything his heart desired on a whim? At the last moment she had rushed to the Louvre to bone up a little, and as she trotted down the steps, her head spinning with facts and dates, she realized the absurdity of trying to impress a man who had a lifetime's knowledge of the subject. Her stomach contracted as she heard Amadeo come bounding up the stairs, two at a time.

Her heart hammering in response to his knock, she opened the door, but the words of welcome were forgotten. The undisguised elation on his face when he saw her banished every fear. She had forgotten the virile warmth that radiated from his dark eyes, and his easy spontaneity dissolved all her nervousness at once.

They descended the stairs in a whoosh of gaiety, Shannon's feet hardly touching the carpet. When they were speeding along the quay, Paris was a chain of brilliant lights adorning the Seine. The dome of the Petit Palais shimmered like a balloon beyond the floodlit winged statues soaring above the Pont-Neuf. This was a private heaven created for monarchs, and its monuments were constellations. The Arc de Triomphe glimmered in the distance as they passed, casting a spoke of unbroken light down the Champs Élysées that ended at the gushing, floodlit waters of the fountain at the Place de la Concorde, not far from their destination.

When the car stopped at the distinctive red awning of Maxim's, Shannon was exposed for the first time to the slavish welcome that immense wealth and power could command, from the deferential stance of the doorman to the fluttering attendance of the maître d' in the dining room. She was aware of curious eyes on her as they were ushered to the best banquette in the plush art deco dining room, decorated with murals of nymphs, mahogany woodwork, and mirrors.

"I've always wanted to come here," she exclaimed, when they were seated. "And it's far more beautiful than I imagined."

"Do you mean to say you've never been here?" Amadeo replied delightedly. "I was trying to think of someplace original, someplace amusing for you."

Considering the huge menu in front of her, Shannon realized she had no appetite whatsoever, aware that he was studying her intently.

"What are you thinking?" he asked.

"I'm thinking that I've never met anyone like you in my entire life," she replied, and they both laughed.

"Do you know that I used to dream about coming here when I was a boy in Buenos Aires? There are many restaurants where the food is better or where the decor is prettier, perhaps, but for me this is a symbol. Spain is my cultural home, but like all of my countrymen, France is where my spirit resides."

The revelation of this sentimental streak running through the steel of his nature surprised her. How often she had felt like that—first in Sydney when she dreamed of entering Elena's, and much later in London.

"I felt exactly like that the first time I went to Ascot."

"People like you and I thrive on dreams. What is your dream, Shannon?" he asked, his lustrous dark eyes searching hers.

"I don't know, now that you ask me. It's something I don't think anyone has asked me before."

"You're honest—I like that," he said.

The waiter was hovering attentively, and without consulting Shannon, Amadeo swiftly ordered, in French, *quenelles de brochet* to start, followed by *canard à l'orange*.

"Bring us a Montrachet sixty-four with the *quenelles*, and a Romanée-Conti fifty-eight to follow," he commanded.

There was something excitingly reassuring in the way he

179

had taken charge of the entire menu without consulting her, as if he assumed they both wanted to share the very same thing at that moment.

"Now, Shanita—that's what I'm going to call you. I want to know everything about you from the beginning. I intend to find out how you came to be on the catwalk at the Palais des Invalides."

"I'm warning you—it's a very long story."

"We have all the time you need."

She sketched her background in Australia, skirting the blacker aspects of her childhood and avoiding any mention of Zan, the two influences that had so shaped her life. When she had ended her tale, he said unexpectedly:

"Perhaps when I know you better you will tell me the important things—the things you left out. I think that it would interest me far more than your miraculous climb to where I found you. Was it a man who drove you so far so fast?"

"Of course not," she denied hotly. She felt herself blushing at the raw truth these words evoked. Though still dazed by the glamour that emanated from him, she couldn't help but feel a twinge of uneasiness that his judgment struck home every time, like a series of well-aimed arrows.

"Now, it's your turn to tell me about yourself."

"It's a very similar story, really. I was born a poor boy in Rosario, far up the Rio Parana, but I ran away to Buenos Aires when I was twelve. That's where I began my training as an international businessman, when I began to shine shoes."

"That seems an unlikely beginning. I've come to believe that if you start at the bottom, you'll probably stay there."

"Oh, no—you're wrong. I learned to size up a man by his shoes, and it became a tool of survival to sum up how long I should spend polishing and cleaning, whether a man would tip well or whether he would try to cheat me. But while I worked I began to listen to men talking about tankers, grain, meat, and leather, as I fought for a place outside one of the best hotels in Buenos Aires."

As he talked, Shannon could envisage the wiry, dark little urchin going quickly about his work as he soaked up all he heard, and she perceived that the man before her was fired with the kind of ambition that only poverty could breed, something she understood well. If you stopped, you were lost, crushed beneath the grinding wheel of a great city that was built on the backs of the poor.

"I learned to look at the world from the ground up. It's the only way to understand it. Not from the top down. I still make it my business to know everything about the people I'm dealing with. That's the secret of any success I may have had. It's strange that our life stories resemble each other. We have more in common than you think."

Her eyes flickered with private irony at this remark when she remembered that Zan had spoken nearly the same words one day at Koonwarra. And yet, Amadeo was as unlike Zan as a gypsy was to a prince, a pirate to a king. There was an earthy possessiveness about Amadeo that couldn't have been more different from Zan's cultivated, refined nature. His veneer of civilized charm couldn't disguise the raw, almost primeval force of will that emanated from him. Zan's breeding had endowed him with the natural self-confidence of the aristocrat, in such contrast to Amadeo's thrusting egotism that both fascinated and repelled her. As the images of the two men clashed in her mind, she realized that to her Zan was still the measure for all other men. Though she might never see him again, his image would always be a constant and unchanging star. When they had finished their meal Amadeo said: "Little Shanita—you're so serious all of a sudden."

"I couldn't help but speculate if it was a girl in Rosario who drove *you* so far so fast."

He laughed. "A woman? No, it wasn't a woman who drove me. You forget that a man is different from a woman. He fights in the arena with the bull, he battles to survive, to dominate. It is a woman's destiny to be the reason for that battle, to be adored, to be loved. Isn't that enough?"

Without replying, she sipped the golden Sauternes the waiter had just poured to accompany the dessert.

"Do you realize that perhaps hundreds of thousands of years ago our ancestors may have been lovers in the South Pacific?"

"What on earth inspired you to say that?" she said with an incredulous smile. The delicious perfumed wine seemed to have gone to her head as she regarded his candlelit image. "Anyway, I am sure your ancestors were conquistadors."

"Some of them, but I have Indian blood in my veins, too. And the Indians came across the Pacific to colonize South America. Can't you see them?" He gestured broadly. "Our great-great—who knows how many 'great' grandmothers and grandfathers, on the silver sands of Polynesia, the

181

moon shining down on their entwined silhouettes as the waves gently lap the shore beneath the palm trees. . . ."

"How do you know who I am? Where I come from?" she murmured. He had wrested another secret from her. She couldn't remember telling him anything about her mother, but he had guessed her origins with uncanny accuracy.

"Imagine—to the rhythm of drums they fell into each other's arms," he continued. "Think of their hunger for each other in the reflection of the firelight. Do you know, you and I, we could recreate the same scene at my apartment near the Bois," he said with a wicked smile.

She laughed abandonedly at the unexpected end to his romantic imagery, aware their mating dance had begun on an utterly original note.

"No, I think not," she replied with an enigmatic smile.

Catching the faint edge of surrender in her voice, he said softly, "You and I, Shanita, will share an adventure which will unfold like some wonderful and glamorous journey on the silk route to far-off Samarkand."

All the fabled city's gilded domes beckoned in the pink dawn as Amadeo's hand entwined possessively around hers.

Chapter VIII

The Meadows, November

As Mark Van Buren drove his Mustang down the dark country road not far from The Meadows, the headlights made a tunnel of yellow light down the avenue of leafless oak and aspen trees. At his side Kerry leaned back languidly and listened to the crooning of Neil Diamond.

"Why don't we turn off a little farther down the road and look at the moon coming through the trees?" she suggested.

"Sure—anything you say."

From the eager tone in Mark's voice, Kerry knew he was waiting for some sign from her that she wanted exactly the same thing he did, that all he needed was encouragement. Reaching out, she rested her hand lightly on his shoulder. Tonight she was gathering the fruit of all her persistence since his father had put Rainmaker at her disposal, an event that had proved the perfect excuse that summer to send Mark long newsy letters full of the details of her progress. Mark had been with his mother in Long Island for the summer, and Kerry was much too busy to think about anything but garnering her first rosettes at horse shows, until that autumn.

The first day he had come back from the Hamptons, Mark had asked her to go out with him. It had taken him two years to build up his courage. She was in the paddock working out on Rainmaker as usual, and he regarded her from a distance as if she were a goddess on horseback. Later in the tack room he had asked her to the movies, and when he leaned down to kiss her cheek at the end of the evening, she had put her arms around his neck and pushed her tongue in his mouth. Terrified that she would discover the erection that had sprung to life the moment she pressed against him, he trembled with astonishment when he felt Kerry's hand tracing the line of his hard penis. Her half-closed eyes bore a look of pleasure as she said huskily:

"Thank you for a wonderful evening, Mark."

All during the term at Harvard Business School Mark had fantasized that she would repeat their encounter when he returned for Thanksgiving vacation. The breezy confidence of college girls from Smith, Vassar, and Wellesley had always struck terror in him, and he had shied away from them at dances. He thought their giggles were aimed at him, suspecting that they were comparing him to his brother, who had made such an impression on their older sisters. The world in which Mark moved was too small for both of them, even though the handsome Lindy IV was dead.

Now, Kerry lay an arm's length away from him, contemplating the evening they had just spent together in Baltimore. At her suggestion, they had gone for a drink at the renowned Belvedere Hotel, a place Kerry knew was frequented by the very best people. As she'd entered the lobby on Mark Van Buren's arm, she was too elated to care that the Belvedere had the same low-keyed ambiance, the same lack of tangible glamour, that she found so puzzling in exclusive establishments. Marconi's, too, the townhouse in old Baltimore where they dined, had proved to be quietly understated, almost Spartan, though the food had been superb. It was hard to believe that the men in sober suits and quiet women in plain dresses were a clutch of the richest, most distinguished people in the city.

Mark turned off the motor as he swung the car directly into view of the moon flooding through the trees.

" 'Fly Me to the Moon'—that's appropriate," remarked Kerry with a little laugh as the radio played softly.

Mark sighed and swallowed nervously as he moved toward her.

"Kerry—I don't know what to say—I've wanted so much to . . . I can't get you out of my mind."

"Don't talk," she murmured, drawing him to her.

His first touch was hesitant, but the moment she put her soft, giving mouth on his, he was in a ferment of desire.

"Kerry, oh, Kerry," he moaned.

"I've missed you so much, Mark," she said, breaking away. Throwing back her head, she looked up into his face. "I was so thrilled when you asked me out tonight. I couldn't believe it."

"Do you really mean it?" he exclaimed joyfully. "You're so different from any other girl I've ever met."

"Am I? Why?" she said softly.

"I don't know. I just can't explain it. You're so much nicer, more feminine. You're so honest—so real," he whispered, choked with longing.

Her hand was roaming treacherously near his upper thigh as she spoke. "And you, Mark—you're nice, too. I enjoyed tonight so much. I really did. You're such a gentleman. You know how exactly to treat a girl. The equestrian world is a man's world; and it feels so good to be treated like a woman."

She was working her fingers delicately toward the clasp on his trousers, and when she had released his belt buckle she slowly, very slowly, began to pull the zipper down. With tender pressure she reached inside his fly and withdrew his hard penis, eliciting from Mark a suffocated gasp of desire. At the touch of her fingers he lurched with passion and came instantly in a halting spasm.

"Oh, God, Kerry, I'm sorry," he said with a sob of embarrassment. He fell back with his hands covering his eyes in shame. "Forgive me, Kerry. I just couldn't help it."

"Mark—hush. You mustn't be ashamed of what is perfectly natural. You're manly, virile. You're just wonderful," she cried, hugging him.

His response was to crush her to him with trembling joy.

"It's going to be so good between us, I know," she

184

continued soothingly. "I always knew that, even from the very beginning. . . ."

He looked down at her in disbelief. "Do you mean. . . ?"

"Yes, Mark. I want to give myself to you, yes," she said happily. "What's the matter?" she asked with a little laugh when he didn't reply.

"It's just that I can't believe that you want me." He pulled her to him and devoured her mouth in a kiss that was almost painful in its intensity.

"When can we . . . when do you want to . . . ?" he breathed. "Tomorrow?"

"Tomorrow's Thanksgiving. Have you forgotten?"

"That's right. And you won't be there, but maybe later—"

"But I could be there, couldn't I?" she interrupted him.

Kerry held her breath as Mark paused to think, sensing the turmoil in his mind. Less than twenty-four hours before the Van Buren clan gathered for dinner, he would have to approach Lindy for permission to invite her, and she had no idea whether he would approve or disapprove of this last minute addition. She had calculated that even if he refused, the burning promise of her body would inspire Mark to stand up to his father. Last year Kerry had pretended to be sick rather than eat in the servants hall.

"Yes, I could invite you. Would you like to come?" he asked.

"Yes, I would. I'd like it very much."

"All right—I'll ask Dad when I go home tonight. He'll be working late in his study. And I was thinking—we could sneak away to the Lazy Boy Motel when everybody else is recovering from Thanksgiving, couldn't we?"

"Is that a threat or a promise?" she said, reaching over to give him a little peck on the cheek.

"It's a promise. Oh, Kerry . . ."

As she crossed the stable yard the next evening, Kerry looked at the sky, thinking it was the same burnt orange as last year. Nothing had changed, yet everything had. And this time, Jack's mood was sullen.

"I don't have to tell you again, but I really don't like this messing around with Mark, young lady. Believe me, one lesson you'd better learn for sure is to keep your distance. We're not their sort, and you're asking for trouble."

"Really, Uncle Jack, I don't know what you're going on about. If Mr. Van Buren thinks I'm good enough to win blue ribbons on Rainmaker, surely I'm good enough to sit at the same table with the family." For the first time in speaking to Jack her voice had a cool and confident edge that irked him further.

"You shouldn't have accepted Mark. I would have thought you'd have understood by now. Your riding Rainmaker has nothing to do with it."

"What was I supposed to do, refuse him?"

Jack had no reply to this, but he gave Kerry a long, hard glance as if seeing her for the first time.

"The Faloons are as good as anyone," she continued, undaunted. "We go back to long before the Van Burens were even heard of. We had a castle, and we were nobility."

"You're talking like your father now, girlie, and it won't get you anywhere except into trouble." Ringing the doorbell, Jack gave her one last glare of disapproval. She had crossed the invisible line, and he could hardly contain his anger.

Kerry smoothed her hair with one hand as she looked up at the fan of illuminated glass above the large front door. The beauty of it prompted her to live in the future for a fleeting moment, to when her show-jumping career would be over, to the day when she would no longer have to ring the bell to gain admittance. As they heard the maid's footsteps on the parquet, she said provocatively:

"If I were mistress of The Meadows one day, you'd sure change your tune."

"You get those ideas right out of your head," was all Jack had time to say before the door swung open.

The moment they walked in, Kerry confidently took off her loden cape to reveal a tailored dress of burgundy wool. A year ago, she wouldn't have looked at such a dress. Everything about her tonight was in perfect taste, from her pumps to her subtle makeup, but she radiated a vivacity that set her firmly apart from the women and girls mingling among the conservatively dressed men. Without pausing a moment, she walked into the glowing room and headed straight for Lindy Van Buren. He had been away buying horses in Lexington, and she hadn't seen much of him that autumn, though she knew he was monitoring her progress carefully.

"Good evening, Mr. Van Buren."

"Kerry—how are you?" She had caught him by surprise, and his eyes reflected a mixture of hearty amusement and reserve.

"Thank you very much for inviting me to have Thanksgiving dinner with the family. It was so kind."

"Why, it's entirely my pleasure, my dear. I was delighted that Mark thought of it," he replied. Accustomed to seeing her in a riding habit or hacking jacket, he thought there was nothing about her now that suggested the stable. In a dress, with her bright hair tumbling down, Kerry looked more like a lithe little jockey than a sturdy girl who excelled at show jumping.

"We've just got the pictures back from Devon," Van Buren said. "There's a good one of you accepting second place next to the all-round winner. . . ." There was mockery in his voice, but before Kerry could make a sarcastic retort, the sort that he seemed to enjoy immensely, he added: "Which is damn good for a girl who's only been on the circuit for such a short time."

She beamed at his praise. "I haven't forgotten our toast that night. Next year it's going to be first at Madison Square Garden and Harrisburg. Just you wait."

"I'm counting on it," he said, and she knew he meant it.

Kerry helped herself to a drink, and as she sipped it she masked a flutter of relief at having crossed the hurdle with Lindy. She had learned long ago that there was no point in hovering shyly on the fringes of power, and she was well aware that this occasion marked the consolidation of her position within the family circle. Glancing around, she realized that many of the friends and family gathered there recognized her, whereas the year before they hadn't even known her name. She had distinguished herself as the gifted young rider Lindy had hand-picked to replace his son on Rainmaker, and now she was about to take her first step into the heart of the family circle as Mark's girl.

When he saw that his father was engrossed in another conversation, Mark came to Kerry's side.

"Hi—how are you?" she whispered sweetly to him, conveying in her smile the secret they shared.

"You look sensational," he whispered in admiration.

"Thank you. You're sweet to say so."

Mark looked away to hide his embarrassment. For twenty-four hours he had been obsessed with what would follow Thanksgiving dinner, in the Lazy Boy Motel.

As they talked, Lindy was watching them from a distance, remarking to himself that at last his son was sowing some wild oats. "Carter," he said, approaching his daughter.

"Yes, Daddy?"

187

Clutching her elbow, he led her toward Kerry and Mark. "You remember Kerry, don't you?"

Caught by surprise, Carter couldn't hide the angry contempt on her face as she glared at Kerry. Ever since early summer, when he had broken the news about Rainmaker, Carter had maintained a stubborn coolness toward her father. She had reacted with almost hysterical outrage to his heretical decision to put the abrasive upstart from Australia on the finest jumper ever seen at The Meadows, thereby desecrating the memory of the brother she had loved. But not even the laurels that Kerry was beginning to gather for the stud could heal Carter's wounded pride, and now, as she confronted Kerry, she seethed at the intruder's latest attempt to weasel her way further into the family. Nobody, least of all Carter, could be fooled by the way Kerry was toying with the hopelessly naive Mark, who was obviously besotted with her.

"Carter, how nice to see you again," Kerry purred. "I don't think we've met since just before you went to Europe last summer, remember? You must have had the most wonderful time. How I envy you. I'd love to hear all about it."

Carter was forced to make small talk with the two of them.

After a few moments Mark said impatiently, "Carter, I want to introduce Kerry to Aunt Lilian. She's been asking to meet the girl who's riding Rainmaker," he added with a proud smile.

They walked toward the matriarch of the Van Buren clan, Lindy's older sister, Lilian.

"So you're the girl who's gathering blue ribbons on Rainmaker. I'm delighted to meet you at last, my dear. Where do you go to school?" said Lilian when Mark had performed the introductions.

"I'm going to high school locally at the moment, as I have to be nearby, but next fall I'll be entering Braemar outside Boston," she announced in quiet triumph.

"Braemar? Are you indeed. How very nice," she replied approvingly.

Half an hour later an elated Kerry walked toward the dining hall at Mark's side.

"See you later, Uncle Jack," she said quietly to him as he passed by.

His reply was a curt nod in her direction.

There were over twenty of them sitting down to dinner in the burgundy dining room. The tall silver candelabra

188

glimmered even more brilliantly than Kerry remembered as she recalled all the sumptuous details. She reflected how the murmur of gentle laughter and civilized conversation contrasted with the vulgar humor in the servants' dining room. She took in the muted richness of the Chinese carpet and the brocade curtains closed against the falling night.

Mark escorted Kerry to the chair next to his near the center of the table, and she glowed when she saw her name in scrolled black letters on the place card: Miss Kerry Faloon. Her name jumped out amidst the daunting array of dragon-patterned china, the cut-crystal glasses, and heavy silver spread out from her plate on the lace tablecloth. It wasn't until that moment that she knew for sure she was really there, where she wanted to be. When everyone was seated she stole a look around the gathering of bankers, gentlemen farmers, and society matrons, feeling momentarily uneasy. When it was her turn, she carefully helped herself from the huge soup tureen presented by a maid. She was only half a beat behind Carter, across a bank of poinsettias, as she picked up the right spoon to sip the game consommé. Throughout dinner she was careful to mimic the actions of the Van Burens, wary not to do anything that would distinguish her as an outsider. But as glass after glass of wine was poured and the atmosphere mellowed, the little spring wound tightly inside her began to relax. She made a great fuss over Mark's elderly Uncle Prescott at her left, finding his droning conversation gave her time to enjoy the beautiful spectacle of the table. When she turned her sparkling eyes on Mark, who ate little but drank freely, she tried to ignore his nervousness, which was beginning to irritate her. She wasn't giving a thought to the Lazy Boy Motel, but to here and now. Every detail about her suggested a newfound poise, a transformation that didn't escape Lindy's notice as he observed her from the head of the table. Her eyes caught the light of the candles, and her hair seemed tipped with gold. She had never looked prettier, he thought. When she turned her head, his eyes glanced off hers immediately, but she sensed that he had been studying her.

By the end of the meal Kerry had gathered confidence around her like a sable coat, so that even meeting Carter's hostile gaze couldn't disturb her. As the last remains of mince and pumpkin pie lay untouched on the plates, Lindy tapped his glass with a knife.

"Here's to the next generation of bluebloods sired at The

Meadows—and a happy Thanksgiving to all, family and friends alike."

Kerry raised her glass with a serene smile, privately extending the reference to the next generation of bluebloods to include herself, then turned to meet Mark's eyes.

The dinner was finally over near seven, when the guests began to drift away from the table.

"We could probably sneak away now," said Mark under his breath as they left the dining room together.

Kerry was amused at Mark's self-conscious behavior as they pretended to loiter in the hallway. No one even seemed to notice them; Carter had gone directly upstairs, and Lindy had disappeared into his study.

"I feel like a breath of fresh air. Why don't we go for a drive?" she suggested playfully.

This remark, loud enough for everyone to hear, caused Mark to look around uneasily.

"Sure—good idea," he said casually. "We could go into Glyndon and catch a movie."

Moments later they were driving down the tree-lined road, Kerry's head on Mark's shoulder.

"Don't be nervous. I've heard that people do this all the time," she said reassuringly. "Kids at school say they don't ask any questions at the Lazy Boy."

Mark turned off at the flashing neon sign and drove up to the office.

"I'll wait in the car," she said.

As she watched him go, Kerry felt impatient with his adolescent behavior, and she couldn't help but compare him with the frank and lusty boys she had taken for granted at Koonwarra. It suddenly dawned on her that Mark must be a virgin, and if so, she knew it would be even easier than she'd anticipated.

"It's all right," he said with a relieved smile when he got back into the car. "The guy hardly looked at me. I just paid thirty dollars in advance, and he handed me the key."

"What did I tell you?" she said with a giggle.

He unlocked the door of the cabin tucked away in the trees and turned on the light to reveal a small plain room almost entirely filled by a bed.

When Kerry had taken off her coat she said demurely, "I'll just go into the bathroom for a minute."

She stayed there long enough to give Mark time to settle down. When she came out shyly in her bra and slip, he was

190

huddled under the covers, and she noticed he had put his handkerchief over the harsh bedside lamp. She looked at him doubtfully.

"I hope you don't think I'm easy or anything," she said in an emotional whisper. "It's my first time."

"It's mine, too," he said. As she slipped into bed beside him, he emitted a shudder of desire. Nestling next to him, she felt his already rampant penis.

"Turn off the light," she murmured, then slipped off her underwear.

They began to kiss passionately, and when in a moment she felt Mark reaching the point of no return she broke away and said with a worried little sigh:

"Oh, Mark, what if I get into trouble?"

"It's all right. I brought something," he replied.

"I knew I could depend on you," she replied sweetly. "I feel so safe."

He fumbled with the condom, and when he returned to her side she sensed he was on the brink of a climax. As she lay back he burrowed directly into her, and she let out the whimper of pain expected of her. Before he had fully penetrated, he came in a great shuddering sigh of ecstasy that left him out of breath. He lay heaving on top of her for a few moments, but when he rolled off he muttered apologetically:

"I'm sorry, Kerry—I hurt you, didn't I? I couldn't help myself."

"Please don't say that. It didn't hurt half as much as I expected, I guess because I wanted you so much." She stroked his hair gently.

"Did you really? I can't tell you what it means to me to hear you say that. Kerry—I think I love you," he said, hugging her to him.

"I never thought I'd hear you say those things to me. I'm the luckiest girl in the world that it was you for the first time. You were so gentle, yet so strong."

As they lay together Kerry struggled to hide her disdain for Mark's gratitude. She hadn't wanted that. She liked a man to make passionate love to her, with no excuses or remorse. She wanted a man to be masterful in his ardor, to arouse some elusive passion in her that no one had ever touched but that she knew existed. It was a wave that threatened to break but didn't, a dream from which she always awoke before the moment of truth. Though their lovemaking hadn't

191

even come close to arousing a response in her, she buried her own need where it wouldn't get in the way of the girl she was determined to be for Mark.

Mürren, Swiss Alps, December

When the pilot turned off the sign, signaling that the Gulfstream had reached twenty-five thousand feet, Shannon detached her seat belt. Turning to look at the thick clouds below, she caught sight of Amadeo in the rear of the aircraft, his face intense with concentration as he talked on the radiophone in Spanish. He had taken off his jacket and loosened his tie as he worked feverishly with his secretary on the papers before him. Feeling her gaze on him, he glanced up for a second to cast her a warm smile that broke through his preoccupation. The line of his strong shoulders, the play of muscles beneath his shirt of fine cotton, reminded her of the implications of their sudden journey. She would be spending the entire week of Christmas alone with Amadeo in a remote village in the Swiss Alps. Glancing around the luxurious gray-and-fawn leather interior of the most prestigious jet money could buy, Shannon reflected on what had led up to this impetuous fling.

The week after their dinner at Maxim's, Amadeo had called her from Hong Kong—a business trip, he'd explained, that might keep him away from Paris for several months, at least until December. As if sensing that the cord of romantic tension between them might slacken as a result, he'd called her almost daily and regularly sent huge bouquets of fragrant flowers. When he had telephoned one Sunday morning in December to announce he was back in Paris, inviting her to lunch at a restaurant in the Bois de Boulogne, she'd realized he had whittled away all her resistance with his attentiveness, and she'd gone to lunch on a crest of anticipation. Amadeo had seemed unable to disguise his own happiness at seeing her at last, and as the mood had mellowed over lunch, Shannon was startled when Miguel had interrupted them to say that it was time to leave for the airport to fly to Zurich. Only Amadeo's good-bye, full of tender regret, had soothed her disappointment at his abrupt departure the moment she had made up her mind she would allow herself to be seduced. Then she'd been surprised yet again when he telephoned only days later asking her to spend the Christmas holidays with him.

"I'm afraid I've accepted an invitation to go down to Grandchamps for Christmas," she had replied when he'd phoned her.

"Then why don't you cancel it? Tell them you have an urgent summons to come to Mürren—one you can't refuse."

"All right," she'd said simply, knowing full well that had been her intention all along. She'd hung up feeling her feeble resistance hadn't fooled him for a moment.

An hour after landing at Berne they were wending their way up the snow-covered slope in the little train, toward Mürren. Wrapped snugly in a fox coat and hat, Shannon sat by Amadeo's side, and as the train chugged along the crest of a great chasm that overlooked the distant Eiger and Jungfrau, tinted rose by the setting sun, caught her first glimpse of the remote village nestled in a valley blanketed in deep snow. Behind them was Miguel, who was to come as far as the chalet to see to the luggage and the basket of gifts and provisions they had brought along, among which was Shannon's present to Amadeo, a small still life that Fabrice had helped her choose at the last moment for the man who had everything.

"Well? What do you think of it?" asked Amadeo when they had alighted from the train.

"It's almost ridiculously quaint," she remarked. "Like something out of the Brothers Grimm."

"There are no cars here. We have to walk to the house. It's not far up the slope, and Miguel will put all the bags on a sleigh. We can ski down to the lifts, cariña," he said, catching her gloved hand in his as their feet crunched on the snow-packed path.

"You can ski," she said laughingly. "Don't forget, I'm just a beginner."

"You'll be skiing down the piste like an expert in no time. Unless, that is, you prefer to lounge by the fire and do nothing at all."

A strange tingling sensation shot through her at the thought of the two of them alone by a blazing fire, and she avoided his eyes.

They climbed up the hill past wooden chalets like gingerbread houses, with delicately traced balconies banked with snow. Above the white rooftops, smoke curled from the chimneys into the iridescent blue sky as late evening fell over the

193

Bernese Oberland. Dark pines, their branches weighted with snow, looked silently down on them as they passed. They had entered another world, where the only sound was that of feet crunching on the ice and church bells echoing across the valley through the pure, clear air.

"This is it—we've arrived," said Amadeo, stopping in front of a chalet set in a cul-de-sac far from any other.

She regarded the enchanting three-story house, icicles hanging from its carved eaves. Coming from a nearby barn was the wonderful earthy smell of cows and hay, a living warmth that seemed to melt the crisp air. The moment they crossed the threshold Shannon felt an atmosphere of rare calm take hold. One huge window overlooked the range of distant alps across the valley, and beneath the high-pitched beams ran a balcony skirting the living room, dominated by a vast stone fireplace complete with blazing fire to welcome them.

"Ah, good, I see Helga has just been here," said Amadeo, rubbing his hands with satisfaction. "She and her husband look after things. Come—take off your coat and stand before the fire. You must be frozen."

She could tell by the way he talked, the way he moved around the huge room, how content Amadeo was to be there. He appeared to have shed all his cares as he looked around the chalet, allowing her time to gather first impressions.

Whereas Les Tourelles was a tribute to European sophistication and elegance, the chalet was a return to a simple, warm way of life that Shannon sensed Amadeo Benguela found much more satisfying. It was here he had chosen to hang old bridles and gaucho bandoliers encrusted with silver, as well as a collection of South American guns and rifles and personal mementoes. This was the retreat of a caballero, a chieftain, unlike the grand château that was a prestigious showcase for the international businessman. The priceless antiques that Amadeo stored at Les Tourelles were the spoils of his battle to the top, but here in the heart of the Alps, Shannon sensed she was meeting the real man for the first time. Glancing at the Aztec and Inca pottery on a shelf, she knew that Amadeo was offering her a glimpse of the most guarded and precious part of his life, and something that she had been holding back began to unfold in her.

When Miguel had come and gone, Shannon slipped onto the sofa in front of the fire, watching Amadeo as he piled on more logs.

"Helga is the perfect housekeeper, but she never puts enough wood on the fire to keep it going. The Swiss are very thrifty."

"I guess they have to be, they're so cut off from the world in these valleys," she said, noting that there was nothing thrifty about the chalet. No expense had been spared to make it comfortable, from the low leather chairs and sofas to the fur rugs strewn on the floorboards. As the flames flared high, they cast a bronzed light on Amadeo's strong features. Dressed in faded jeans and a sweater, the energy flowing from him had a newfound strength and a solid simplicity, dimensions that surfaced in this environment. She stopped short of wondering how many other women he had brought here in the past, remembering Fabrice's words before she'd left Paris: "It's a fairy tale that will end happily as long as you close the book when it's over."

Looking up, Amadeo reached out and brushed her cheek. "What are you thinking?"

"I was thinking that simplicity is the key to your strength, your success."

"You're wise as well as beautiful," he murmured, his eyes full of appreciation. He went to the bar and came back with two glasses of clear liquid.

"It's Poire Williams," she said, smelling the distilled essence of ripe pears that always poignantly recalled summer's end. "Just think, all the pear trees are under ten feet of snow."

Sitting beside her, he raised his glass to hers. "Here's to spring. To blossoms that turn into ripe fruit." Bending over, he kissed her ardently on the lips.

She leaned back in the soft couch, suddenly light-headed.

He took her hand. "Do you know, I used to have a chalet in Gstaad once owned by the king of Albania, and before that I used to stay at the palace there. But I discovered Gstaad was just an extension of Paris. Here in Mürren it isn't chic. No one knows me, no one invites me. I'm happy. I can do what I like—eat with my fingers, nap in the afternoon. There's no telephone or radio. I bring very few people here," he added.

"How ironic it is that you've spent your whole life striving to rise above the common herd, but now that you've achieved it all you want is anonymity—and simplicity."

"No—that's not all I want," he said. With a gentle tug at her wrist, he drew her to him. As she lay back in his arms he

195

stroked her cheek. "I was afraid you might change your mind at the last minute. I sensed a wariness in you that I feared would hold you back. But you didn't disappoint me—you came. You followed your instincts, *cariña*." His tender words ignited sparks of feeling that would be ablaze within the hour, and he leaned to place his mouth on hers in a hungry kiss.

"Today, and tomorrow, and tomorrow are for us alone. I'm too selfish to share you with anyone. I've waited for the moment to be with you as a man and woman are meant to be—one spirit, one flesh. That's why I brought you here, so you can know me as the simple man you see, Shanita," he murmured. Slipping his hand to the nape of her neck, he said, "Wear your hair down for me. I want you wild and untamed tonight."

Later, Shannon climbed the wooden staircase to the bedroom under the eaves, a room that gave an impression of alpine coziness reminiscent of a *Heidi* storybook. Beneath the low pine beams was a painted Swiss bed covered with a huge fluffy eiderdown, and there was an enormous bearskin in front of an old tiled stove that warmed the room.

She was glad there was no maid to unpack the simple clothes she had brought with her. Later, when she had showered, she changed into a long sage-colored dress of cashmere and shook out her hair, letting it curl and tangle wherever it wanted to go. Regarding her own changed image in the little glass on the dressing table, Shannon's eyes grew distant as she remembered how Amadeo's words had touched off a nerve of passionate abandon in her: "I want you wild and untamed tonight."

When he heard her footsteps on the stairs, Amadeo turned from the fire, where he was standing reflectively with his arms crossed. He had put on a South American record, and sensual appreciation flickered in his eyes as he watched her feet touch each step in counterpoint to the music. He came toward her with arms wide, and they began to sway to the earthy beat of a tango sung in a rich Spanish voice. With a devilish smile he brushed Shannon back and forth across his chest, then let her fall back dramatically in his arms, her hair touching the floor. Their dance ended in breathless laughter, which subsided into a deep kiss as they stood before the fire.

He poured her a glass of champagne, then clinked her glass with his.

"Merry Christmas, *cariña*," he said with a kiss.

"Merry Christmas," she replied. "It's the loveliest one I think I've ever spent. I'm glad I'm not in Grandchamps."

"If you had gone, I would have followed you there."

He bade her sit before the fire, then brought in a tray laden with a fondue pan, dishes of sauce, and a basket piled high with coarse peasant bread.

"Don't tell me you cook, too," she marveled as she watched him spread out the feast on the table before them.

"It's one of my favorite pastimes, but I wouldn't dare compete with Albert at Les Tourelles. I have a housekeeper in Paris, too, who cooks for me, but here I love to do it myself. The meat is from Argentina—the best in the world. I have it flown from Buenos Aires," he said, lighting the spirit lamp beneath the copper fondue pan.

"I can't believe how hungry I am. I'm ravenous."

"It's the mountain air. You won't have to watch your model's figure here. You're much too thin, you know," he admonished, breaking off a chunk of bread and handing it to her.

The act of eating before a fire created a mood of languid sensuality. Amadeo insisted on feeding her tidbits of meat cooked to perfection and dipped in his favorite sauces. As they laughed and ate and quenched their thirst with a bottle of full-bodied Argentinian wine, the last barriers between them slipped away. Here in this valley high in the Alps, locked above the world, their raw appetite symbolized the hunger for life itself. Every time Shannon looked at Amadeo's strong face, streaked with firelight, she felt desire twist within her. Even after the meal had ended, they lingered over the wine for a long while, chatting, reflecting over the year that had just passed. Finally there was a long silence, when neither of them seemed to have anything more to say. When he drew her to him she surrendered instantly to the sensation of his tongue exploring her mouth, her body arching toward him involuntarily in a taut bow of longing.

"Shanita—my beautiful, passionate Shanita. You are made for love," he whispered.

He slipped her dress from her body in a slow-moving ritual, holding her gaze all the while, and then swiftly removed his own clothes. They tumbled onto the rug in the warm glow of the firelight, where he took her in his arms, pressing fully against her. The first touch of his maleness between her thighs made her gasp with arousal. Weeks of pent-up longing exploded at the first impact of their nude bodies as they reveled in the silken sensation of skin on skin.

197

With his gentle hands he conveyed his desperate need to know the proud curve of her small, perfect breasts, her slender waist beneath his palm, discoveries that aroused him to a tempest of desire. When he gently stroked her sex, he murmured as if it were some wild part of her waiting to be tamed, and her fingers reached out instinctively in response, to discover his phallus throbbing with the power of compressed steel. Like a pirate claiming a princess whose kingdom had fallen, he entered her in one thrust, and she gave herself up to him desperately. The heady aroma that came from Amadeo, of linen, leather, and sweat, was like a mystic unguent that she had known forever. Drawing himself above her, she watched him through half-closed eyes as he reveled in the sight of her hair tangled on the fur like a dark cloud. Her hips flaring voluptuously beneath him, he plummeted and rose like a wave breaking relentlessly on a wine-dark sea, until she was dragged achingly, throbbingly, and thrown on the shore of a shattering climax.

As they lay entwined together, Shannon came slowly back to reality. Pressing him to her, burying her face in the cleft of his shoulder, she breathed, close to tears, "It's never happened to me before like this, never." An aftershock of ecstasy came over her and she embraced him passionately.

To her surprise, he said nothing; but at this searchingly honest admission of tenderness from her, he withdrew and turned toward the fire so she couldn't see his face.

"Amadeo?" she whispered, pulling herself to her knees and resting her hands on his shoulders. She needed him to hold her in his arms.

When he faced her she saw his mood had changed from one of passion to solemnity. After their shattering encounter she'd expected some words of tenderness, if not love, and she was hurt that he could drift away from her so abruptly, so unfeelingly.

"Excuse me, Shanita. I'm going upstairs. Don't catch cold here. You had better dress, as the fire has burned down."

Her body still trembling with its sensual awakening, she reluctantly rose and began to dress, feeling bewildered.

Upstairs in the bathroom, Amadeo turned on the lights that ringed the mirror and gazed down at himself narrowly, brushing back his hair with both hands. Then, resolutely, he began to splash cold water on his face as he thought of what had happened between him and Shannon. His seduction of her had veered totally from his control for a few moments, robbing him of his self-possession. To his chagrin, she had taken something from him that he'd had no intention of giving anyone, a treasure he guarded more closely than anything else he owned—the command of his own emotions. Until he'd felt her moving beneath him, he hadn't known how much he'd wanted Shannon Faloon. Glancing down at himself, he realized angrily that he wanted her again, that very moment. With a great effort he resisted the temptation to return to her side. Instead, he stepped into the shower, then rubbed himself down vigorously to allow himself time to cool this unexpected volcanic passion that threatened his island of independence.

The next morning Shannon was awakened by a tap at the door, and, turning her head, she saw Amadeo open his eyes next to her beneath the eiderdown.

"It's only Helga. She's left the breakfast tray at the door." He slipped from the bed and went to look out of the window.

"Look—it's snowing," he announced with a smile.

She reluctantly turned her gaze from the sight of his nude body to the windowpane, where fat white flakes floated by.

Fetching the tray, he came to her bedside, and as she gazed up at him she felt desire stir strongly with her once again. She had drifted off to sleep the night before wondering why Amadeo had left her side so cruelly that evening. In the light of a new day Shannon was grateful that he had made it easy for her to resist falling in love with him. Now, at least, she was assured that he could never touch that still secluded part of her that lay in waiting for someone who could love her passionately the way she wanted to love in return.

"Merry Christmas, *cariña*," he said, placing the tray on the bedside table as she propped herself up on the pillows.

"What's this?" she said, seeing a gold package tied with a blue velvet ribbon nestled in the basket of croissants.

"It's for you—open it."

Excitedly she tore it open to discover a blue enamel and gold egg; she hesitated before opening it, glancing first at Amadeo. His face was suffused with an almost childlike pleasure at her surprise.

"You're like some adorable little boy presenting a girl with a rose," she couldn't resist saying, reaching over to kiss

199

him. Inside the egg was coiled a platinum watch with a face of lapis lazuli set in diamonds. "It's beautiful!" she gasped.

She had expected him to give her something lovely, but not this wildly extravagant gift. The jeweled watch was something she would never dream of buying for herself, even if she had money to burn; it was so outrageous. As she began to set the watch, Amadeo reached out, closing his hand on hers.

"No—don't wind it. Let time stand still for us while we are here."

Taking the watch from her hand, he put it aside and came to her beneath the covers.

Chapter IX

Paris, May 1980

Climbing the stairs to her apartment, Shannon put the key in the front door as she balanced a baguette, a carton of milk, and the newspaper in one hand. When she walked into the kitchen, her instinct was to look at the clock to make sure it wasn't yet nine o'clock. On this glorious day in mid-May, when all the chestnut trees were unfurled against a sky of burnished blue, Shannon had risen early; now her ears were alert for the ring of the telephone as she made a cup of coffee, though she kept telling herself it was still far too early for the call she had awaited impatiently all week.

When she had arranged her breakfast on a tray, she sat in a chair by the open window, which admitted the echo of traffic winding down the narrow rue Bonaparte. Distractedly sipping her coffee, she realized she had read an entire column of the paper without comprehending it, and she wondered with a sigh how she would be able to spend another day waiting by the telephone when all Paris was lingering at sidewalk cafes in the brilliant sunshine beneath blossoming chestnut trees.

For an entire month, since she had been notified she was a prospective candidate to become the face that would launch the new look of the house of Valentin, Shannon had lived in a maelstrom of suspense. The coveted five-year contract would guarantee the lucky girl one million dollars, a sum that even now Shannon found incalculable. That kind of money would mean the fulfillment of her most cherished ambitions. There would be no more collections, no more catwalks, no more rushing around. As the exclusive Valentin girl, she would lead a more leisured existence, involving personal promotion tours and photo sessions with top photographers, all structured around her alone. She could stop hustling for catalog and editorial work to keep her name on the books of the agency. Her fortune would be made, and when the five years were over she would be able to leave modeling forever, an independent, wealthy, famous woman who had her whole life ahead of her. All this would be hers if she drew the right straw. If not, she would go back to the same interminable grind of the model's life until she could afford to quit—which, with Kerry's schooling and expensive hobby to pay for, not to mention her own taste for extravagance, now looked like never.

Shannon had just about made up her mind that the house of Valentin must have surely chosen another model when the phone rang. Answering it breathlessly, her heart lurched when she heard the familiar voice of one of the bookers at the agency.

"Shannon? You've got it," she cried ecstatically. "I've just heard."

She let out a little shriek. "I don't believe it!"

It was as simple as that, almost anticlimactic after waiting for so long. When she had hung up, Shannon danced around the room in a private little waltz of joy. Exalted with happiness, she went to the window and looked out over the gray rooftops painted against the vibrant blue sky. Hearing the cries and laughter from the students coming out of the École des Beaux Arts below, the honking of taxis, she felt a sudden rush of sentiment for the city that had brought her everything. Her first impulse was to telephone Amadeo. He had rung the evening before from Milan, where he was on business, to see if she had heard anything, but now she put the telephone down, deciding she would much rather wait until she saw him that weekend in Cannes. She could imagine how pleased he would be that she had won the Valentin contract against such tremendous odds. All the girls vying for it had been stunning beauties, tops in their field, and up until now Amadeo's attitude toward her prospects had been understandably cautious. She realized that he hadn't wanted her to get her hopes built up for a crashing disappointment.

Her first act as a woman of means was to write a check to the bursar at Braemar, accompanied by an ecstatic letter to Kerry, who would be in Pennsylvania, that weekend for one of the most important events of the show-jumping season. Shannon had already sent her a good-luck telegram, and this wonderful news, which ensured both their futures, would add luster to the laurels she was tipped to win on Rainmaker.

Dashing from the apartment to mail her letter, Shannon looked into the same art gallery she passed every day, pausing to glance at a painting in the window that she had been admiring for several weeks, a pastoral landscape of Provence in riotous colors. Suddenly, riding a wave of unbridled optimism, she charged through the doors and approached the girl behind the desk.

"That painting in the window—I'd like to buy it."

The girl looked up in surprise. "Why, certainly, madame. Would you like it delivered, or will you take it with you?"

Shannon left the gallery with the painting under her arm exhilarated at having given in to such unbridled extravagance without thinking twice, an impetuous act that turned all the tension of the past weeks into euphoria.

The next day Shannon took an afternoon flight to Nice, and as the plane began its descent over the sea, she had a sweeping view of purple hills bordered by the snow-capped Alpes-Maritimes, its Fauvist palette recalling the landscape she had purchased the day before. As a hilltop village flashed into view, its red-tiled roofs conjured up the dream she had harbored ever since she'd lived in France: to buy a cottage of her own in one of these picturesque hamlets. Now, however, it need no longer be a dream, she mused; perhaps on their way back from their week-long cruise to Sardinia, she and Amadeo could take a leisurely drive along one of the little winding roads that cut through the hills thick with thyme and lavender.

That evening Shannon and Amadeo were driving along the light-spangled Croisette of Cannes, lined with palms tossing in the breeze from the sea. Yachts crowded the harbor, trailing lights on the dark water below purple hills smudged against the burnt orange sky. Amadeo had arrived at Nice Airport from Milan just in time to dash to the *Karisma*, moored off Cannes, and change for the reception at the Palais des Festivals.

"You've never looked lovelier," he said to Shannon, by his side in the back of the chauffeured car. He leaned over to kiss her on the cheek. "Undoubtedly Vittorio Conti will try to sign you up with a movie contract," he said teasingly.

Brushing his cheek with her hand in a tender gesture, she laughed, thinking that she was already under contract. Tempted to burst out then and there with the news that she was now the Valentin girl, she checked herself. From the minute she had thrown her arms around Amadeo's neck at the top of the gangway of the *Karisma*, she had hardly been able to contain her elation, but in moments they would be swept up by the excitement of the premiere of Conti's latest film, which Amadeo had backed heavily.

"I have a little surprise for you later on," she couldn't resist saying, thinking of the little Chinese sculpture of rose quartz that she had bought him during her wave of extravagance.

"And I have one for you as well," he replied mysteriously.

"You do?" she said, surprised.

But there was no time to speculate. The car was cruising slowly through the throng of cheering fans surging behind the police barriers. When it drew up alongside the curb, Amadeo helped her alight from the car onto the red-carpeted walkway, amidst a blaze of flashbulbs. Shannon was glad to see that he was taking the burst of publicity with good humor; she knew he detested the paparazzi. They made a striking couple, he bronzed and distinguished in evening clothes, she in a fluid gown of black crêpe slit from the neck to the waist. The photographers jostled aggressively forward to catch Amadeo Benguela, one of the world's richest and most glamorous men, escorting Shannon Faloon, famous cover girl, rising star of the house of Valentin. They made their way through the glass doors of the Palais just as the crowd roared out the name of Belmondo, whose arrival had followed theirs.

Later that evening, when they had had a token glass of champagne at the reception, they escaped the mad crush in Cannes and slipped back to the *Karisma*, a streak of white sparkling with lights that lay anchored far out in the harbor. Over eighty feet long, and second to none in luxury, it was an impressive sight.

When Shannon came onto the upper deck, she leaned her elbows on the railing and regarded the lights of Cannes in the distance. She had spent a weekend on the *Karisma* in February and had adored it, but now she savored the prospect of having an uninterrupted week to enjoy its fabled comfort. Turning, she saw Amadeo watching her from the illuminated saloon, his face lost in the shadows. She smiled at him, and he came toward her with outstretched arms to lead her to the dining table, elegantly set with snowy-white damask, napkins edged in navy, and gold-rimmed china stamped with the logo of *Karisma*.

"You're cold," he whispered. "I'll tell the steward to go below and fetch your shawl."

"Please—tell me—what's this surprise you mentioned in the car?" she said, impatient to deliver her own news at last.

"No—you tell me first."

"All right." She glanced at the sculpture she had wrapped and placed by his plate. Seeing a sudden look of bemusement in Amadeo's eyes, she felt a stab of uncertainty, wondering if he would be as pleased for her as she had anticipated.

"Come, let us sit down. I know you're as hungry as I am." When he had pulled out her chair he wrapped her shawl around her shoulders, hugging her for a moment.

"Now—begin," he said, unfolding his napkin as the steward poured the wine. "What's this?" he said, seeing the package for the first time.

She beamed as she watched him open it.

"*Cariña*—it's exquisite," he marveled when he had unwrapped the statue. He examined the carved prism of transparent pink stone in the light. "It's lovely, an absolutely beautiful piece. Thank you, my darling." When he set it down he leaned back to interpret the look on her face.

Shannon took a deep breath. "I've got it—I've got the Valentin job," she burst out, unable to contain her joy any longer. "Isn't that the most exciting, wonderful thing you've ever heard? It's the most marvelous thing that's ever happened to me."

"Congratulations, Shanita," he said with a broad smile, reaching out to draw her wrist to his lips. "I never doubted for a moment that you would get the contract."

"Didn't you? Oh, but I did. They didn't call me until late yesterday morning, and by that time I'd nearly given up. I can't imagine how I was able to keep it all to myself this evening. I was dying to tell you the moment I saw you, but I wanted to wait until now—when we were alone." The water sequined with light, and the waves gently rocking the *Karisma* to and fro on its moorings cast a mesmeric spell. She knew she would never forget this moment.

"And now it's my turn. I have a surprise for you." He paused for a suspenseful moment, holding her eyes across the table as he hovered on the brink of what would change both their lives. As he looked at Shannon, Amadeo was no closer than ever to understanding how she had insinuated herself into the very core of his being. Unlike his other affairs, their liaison hadn't ended after the habitual few weeks, and he found himself obsessed with her image when he should have been concentrating on business in Hong Kong or Rio. Although he wouldn't stoop to jealousy, this driving passion for Shannon had brought him to the reluctant decision that he must secure her for his own.

Taking a little velvet box from his pocket, he handed it to her without a word.

When she opened it she was staggered by the size of the heart-shaped diamond ring it contained.

"Amadeo—I don't know what to say."

He interrupted her. "Shanita, we have known each other for only a short time. You're so much younger than any woman I've ever cared for, but that doesn't matter. You know how I think of you when I'm away. And I've given this much thought, believe me. It's not a proposal I make lightly. I want you to be with me all the time from now on—to travel with me, to share my life, whether here or in Paris or Les Tourelles, or anywhere I am." He gestured, pausing to let the importance of his words sink in.

"Amadeo—are you asking me to marry you?" she whispered incredulously. Though she had never considered the idea, she suddenly realized that it was what she wanted, too, with all her heart. She gave him a dazed smile, thinking how wrong Fabrice had been. He had sworn Benguelo would never marry, and Amadeo himself had hinted the same thing before.

"No." He waved his hand impatiently. "Not marriage. That's not what I'm saying, Shanita. I want you to live with me, to enjoy a life of ease and luxury which I can offer you. But I don't want your work to interfere with us. I want you to be free, free to roam the world with me. Free to go to Acapulco one day, London the next. Which brings me to your contract with Valentin. In a way, I was hoping you wouldn't get it. That would have made things much easier. But no matter. You've told me how you wanted the Valentin

205

contract to get off the treadmill of collections, catalogs, and if you are with me, you will never want for anything. . . ."

"Wait a minute—are you saying that you want me to break my contract?" She looked at him blankly.

"Yes, of course," he continued, unaware of her amazement. "But don't worry. I'll call Henri Dufaur of Valentin myself. I know him, and I'll explain. He'll understand. Of course, be assured that I'll make it up to you financially. You will have a private income, the security you need and deserve—"

"I can't believe you're saying this to me," she interrupted him.

"What do you mean? It's a perfectly practical solution to our being together, *cariña*. . . ."

"You're asking me to be your mistress and give up everything I've worked for, and you think I'll toss it out the window, just like that?" Her voice dropped to a whisper of stunned indignation.

"Shanita," he said with an indulgent smile, "don't you understand? We'll be together."

"I understand perfectly," she replied, choked with anger as she rose from the table, slapping down her napkin. "You ask me to be your paid whore, and you expect me to be thrilled at the prospect?"

"How can you speak like that?" Eyes flashing, Amadeo's anger blazed up to counter hers. "How dare you use such a base word for the proposition I'm offering you? Have you gone mad?"

"Yes—proposition. Like a business merger, a company deal. But never once have you mentioned love. You think you can buy me? Well, go and buy somebody else. Find yourself another whore, a tramp who wants your money. Fabrice warned me about you, and I should have listened. Here—keep your damned ring and everything it represents."

Her fury boiling over, she grabbed the rose quartz statue and flung it with all her might on the deck, shattering it into a hundred pieces.

"How dare you, you little bitch—destroy that statue? It was not yours to destroy."

"That's typical of you. Money and objects mean everything to you, don't they? Well, they mean nothing to me, and there's the proof," she said scornfully, regarding the fragments that lay at their feet.

She stormed from the deck and ran downstairs, through

206

the narrow passageway to their stateroom. Flinging open the doors of the closet where all her things had been carefully put away, she began throwing them at random in a suitcase, her hands trembling with rage. Hearing the door fly open, she pivoted to confront Amadeo, his face dark with anger.

"I want the tender to take me back to shore immediately," she said with an imperious tone she had never used to anyone.

"I give the orders on this yacht," he replied. "Who are you to insult Amadeo Benguela?" Lunging toward her, he grabbed her by the wrist, spun her around, and pinned her to the wall. His face was a merciless mask as he shoved her roughly into the bed, tearing at her clothes. Suddenly he had become the street fighter, the ruthless cutthroat who would stop at nothing to get what he wanted. Shannon was paralyzed with disbelief, long enough for him to overpower her with superhuman strength fueled by passionate outrage. Like a lion with a spear through his heart he bore down on her dropping his trousers.

"You think I treated you as a whore? Very well—this is how a whore is treated in my country—*puta*," he spat out in Spanish. He crushed his mouth against hers in a brutal kiss. Entering her in one violent thrust, he slammed against her again and again with demonic rage. He drove deeply, rapaciously, as if he would annihilate every shred of will from her. Her resistance as she struggled beneath him seemed only to further inflame his vindictive lust. The violent explosion of his climax ripped the anger from his countenance, changing it to horror. As he moved away, Shannon heard a moan of shame escape from deep within him.

"I hate you—despise you," she emitted in a flat voice full of coiled venom. Shaking, she looked down on him as he buried his face in his hands.

He didn't look at her as she finished gathering her things and stuffed them into a bag. All she could think of was to escape. Rushing from the stateroom, she entered the nearest cabin and locked the door behind her. It was far too late now to leave the *Karisma*. The entire crew would be asleep, and she had no energy to rouse them or cause a scene.

Shannon slipped into the bunk fully clothed. Turning off the light, she lay dry-eyed and numb as she kept vigil over her own emotions. Like the lone survivor of a shipwreck, she felt utterly abandoned when the first pale rays of dawn came through the porthole. Within minutes she left the cabin, closing the door quietly behind her. Climbing to the upper deck, she saw that the lights of the Croisette were still shining, far across the harbor, like lingering stars in the pink dawn.

"Steward," she called, recognizing the officer in a white jacket as he came out of a cabin. "*Je m'en vais, toute de suite,*" adding, "if you don't take me I'll swim ashore."

In moments she was being ferried across the glassy water in the tender, the clean wind whipping through her hair. She spotted a taxi driver asleep in his cab at the quayside and lugged her suitcase in his direction.

"*Aeroport de Nice,*" she said as the driver looked up at her through half-closed eyes.

All the way to the airport Shannon stared out the window, too lost in thought to see the stony beaches of the Côte d'Azur washed with pink, foaming breakers. As they passed through the coastal villages of Juan-les-Pins, Antibes, Cagnes-sur-Mer, she tried to clear her mind. When she saw the grove of palm trees that marked Nice Airport, something prompted her to lean forward and say:

"*J'ai changé d'avis—Hotel Negresco, s'il vous plait.*"

"*Mais bien sûr, madame,*" replied the driver with a prosaic shrug, as if he were accustomed to mad foreigners.

The Negresco was the first hotel that had come into Shannon's mind. As she entered the rococo gilt lobby, nearly empty at that hour, she realized she could have chosen no better sanctuary. Approaching the reception desk, she said calmly:

"I would like a room with a bath for a few days, please."

The correct little concierge gave her a penetrating glance, noticing that her hair was disheveled, that she wore no makeup; but he noted approvingly her expensive clothes, her Louis Vuitton suitcase.

"But of course, madame. Your name?" he said with an ingratiating smile.

"Françoise Paillard," she replied automatically.

When Shannon had closed the door of the room behind her, she climbed into bed and fell into a healing sleep until evening. After eating supper from room service, she turned out the light and returned once more to a deep sleep.

The following morning, sipping coffee, she stared out the open double windows of her room and watched the brilliant Mediterranean sunlight reflect off the Baie des Anges.

Regarding the smoking ruins of her love affair with Amadeo from a distance, she was grateful now that she had never allowed her emotions to grow out of control. How close she had come to disaster, she reflected. She had been ready and willing to marry him yesterday, when in fact marriage had never been his intention. A wave of sadness came over her when she recalled that unguarded moment when his ruthless instincts had shattered his cultivated façade. It would have been better if their affair had ended the way she had always imagined, like a civilized minuet, prompting them to change partners and dance away from each other. Now, she would always be plagued with the base image of the face she had once found so handsome, contorted with crushing possessiveness. She never wanted to see him again as long as she lived.

She decided that with ten empty days stretching ahead of her, there was no point in returning to her flat on the rue Bonaparte. All her friends expected her to be away. Why not take a holiday as planned? Nothing had changed, after all, she consoled herself. She was still the Valentin girl, still on top of the world. She could hire a car if she felt like it, drive up into the hills.

That afternoon she left the cool, dark lobby of the hotel and strode confidently into the brilliant sunshine. Heat seemed to rise in waves from the sidewalk as she strolled down the tourist-packed Promenade des Anglais. Now and then she found herself looking uneasily over her shoulder, wondering if Amadeo might try to track her down. Suddenly she was ravenously hungry. Stopping at the first sidewalk cafe she passed, she sat down under a red umbrella and ordered a bottle of rosé from a smiling waiter with a carnation in his buttonhole. As she sipped it, life seemed once again to flow through her veins. The *salade niçoise* with olives, sweet tomatoes, and anchovies tasted like ambrosia, and the crusty bread was the most delicious thing she had ever eaten. Seduced by the pink brilliance of oleander, the fragrant sea breeze from the bay, she lingered a long time, simply enjoying the parade of people passing by.

After lunch Shannon meandered contentedly down the boulevard, pausing to browse in the shop windows. Seeing a sign that read *Agence Immobilière*, she stopped to look at a fascinating display of photos of farmhouses and villas for sale in the hills behind Nice. She became so deeply absorbed in studying them that she failed to notice the reflection in the window of a man standing behind her. When his hand clenched her shoulder, she whirled around in shock, startled to find herself looking into a pair of familiar blue eyes.

"Shannon—what are you doing here?"

"Zan!"

BOOK II

Chapter I

Seillans, France, May 1980

"Just wait until you see the house," Zan said as he drove the Peugeot convertible along the winding road through the hills behind Nice later that afternoon. "Seillans is completely unspoilt. I know you'll love it."

"Do you know, I had no idea you were involved in business on the Côte d'Azur," replied Shannon, casting him a glance. "That shows you how out of touch I've been. I've been meaning to write Jonquil for ages. She always fills me in on all the news."

"We've had an office down here for nearly two years, but it wasn't until lately that things began to move. You know, I just can't get over our bumping into each other like this. If I'd known you were looking for a house on the Côte, I would have done the groundwork before you came. You're in luck, though, I think. This house I want to show you is a find. It's only been on the market a week and hasn't even been shown yet. Anyway, Shannon, what are you doing in this neck of the woods?"

She had already prepared herself for this question. "I thought that buying my dream house would be the perfect way to celebrate an amazing stroke of fortune I just had a few days ago. Do you know the name Valentin? It's a cosmetics company."

"Yes, I do."

"Well, they've chosen me as their exclusive model for a five-year contract. It's the break that every model dreams of."

"That's fantastic, Shannon," he said in amazed admiration. "I suppose that means you'll make a fortune into the bargain."

"As a matter of fact, I will," she said laughingly. "And I'll only be working about three months a year, so now I'll have time to find out what I'm really good at—something I've never had time for before, and I need a place where I can put down roots—a home. I love France, and who knows, when I get my dream cottage perhaps I'll discover I'm really a painter

213

at heart, or that I want to write the great Australian novel, or even turn into a business tycoon," she said elatedly. When Zan didn't reply she asked, "Well? What do you think about it all?"

"I'm thrilled for you. It's wonderful—marvelous. The thing is," he said wryly, "that I'm trying to swallow the hat I've just chewed up."

"What hat?"

"Don't you remember that day at Koonwarra when I was so skeptical about your coming to London? I recall giving you wise fatherly advice about the fate of Australian girls in Earls Court. But before I eat my hat I suppose I should take it off to you."

She smiled. "No, you were right to tell me what you did. I could easily have been one of those girls if it weren't for luck."

"Shannon, believe me, it's more than luck, though who could have known it at the time?" Zan reached out and squeezed her hand. "Lord, but it's good to see you."

As quickly as his hand had touched hers, he moved it away. An inexplicable ebullience came over her as she looked at him, his fair hair blowing in the wind, against the backdrop of a cloudless sky. She was intoxicated by the heady aroma of lavender and thyme as she caught a glimpse of the ice-spangled Alps beyond the blue hills framing the road.

She resisted the warmth that shot through her at Zan's touch; the familiar feeling contradicted the idea that this was just the meeting of two old friends and nothing more. From the moment they had walked together along the Promenade des Anglais Zan had put her at ease. Neither of them had mentioned their last disturbing meeting in a London pub, and now, looking at Zan beside her, suntanned, handsome, self-confident, Shannon sensed a new maturity in him. Or was it in herself? she reflected, adjusting her sunglasses in the brilliant light that poured down on them. Every time she looked at Zan's profile she felt a twinge of disbelief that they had run into each other; but she had already learned that life was full of unexpected turnings.

"What are you thinking?" he asked.

"I still can't get over the fact that we met."

"I know, it's incredible—but in a funny way it seems perfectly natural," he replied, with the quick smile that had always made her feel absurdly happy. For a moment he was the same Zan she had known in Australia all those years ago,

214

before their lives had become so complicated. "I would have known you anywhere," he continued. "I don't know what it is—your walk, the angle of your shoulders. And when I was sure it was you, I followed you for several moments, not knowing quite how to approach you. I felt like a shy school-boy, and to be honest I didn't know if you'd be glad to see me."

"How can you say that? It was a wonderful surprise. I can't tell you how delightful it was to run into a friend—" She broke off, afraid her voice would betray the genuine rush of emotion she felt at seeing him; she wondered if Zan had sensed the fear in her when she'd whirled around to face him. She had never felt so safe as by his side when they'd climbed through the hills, leaving the ugly drama aboard the *Karisma* far behind. Amadeo—if he was looking for her—would never find her now.

"You're looking wonderful, Shannon. Success becomes you, you know. Whenever I go to dinner at Jonquil's she brings out the latest clippings of you, and when I pass a newsstand I find myself sneaking a look at the covers of *Vogue* and all those magazines. There you are, staring out at me, and I say to myself—I know that girl."

The edge of respect in Zan's voice reminded Shannon of how dramatically things had changed since that day she'd regarded his unreachable image in the *Sydney Herald*. With his shirt-sleeves rolled up to reveal his well-developed fore-arms, and his hair flecked with golden light, he had never seemed more handsome. He still had the same easy grace, the same laconic regard in his blue eyes, that natural air of self-confidence that had always impressed her. She couldn't help but compare his shining balanced nature with Amadeo's driving complexity. It occurred to her that Amadeo's thirst for life had drained her of her own vitality with its incessant demands. Even the way Zan casually shifted the gears of the car contrasted with Amadeo, who would have been pushing the accelerator to the floor by now, his mind fixed on the important calls he had to make. Amadeo always lived one step ahead as he strove to push his life's frontiers forward. Neither she nor Zan had even paused to ask what the next moment would hold, and the contrast was exhilarating.

"How's Saffron, by the way?"

"She's marvelous. She's grown up a lot since you last saw her. She's so spirited—knows exactly what she wants," he said proudly. "She's started nursery school this year, and

215

loves it. I bought her a Shetland pony for her birthday, which we keep at Kilgarin. We spend a lot of time there. Father is still mad as a hatter and, I'm afraid, not in very good health."

"Is he still racing whippets in the ballroom?"

Zan laughed. "Do you remember that?"

Without thinking, she said, "I remember everything you ever told me."

Zan gently glossed over this remark. "Business has suffered because of all the problems with the Kilgarin estate. But let's not talk about all that. It's much too boring on such a lovely day."

"And Rosemary? How's she?"

"Oh, fine, fine. She's been a brick about everything. It's been a difficult time for her, really. She's one of the few people who know how to handle Father. I'm very grateful to her for it."

Picturing his wife, Shannon said, "I must admit I was awfully intimidated by Rosemary when I first met her. She was so poised, so in control, and so beautiful in that classic English way of hers that it made me feel awkward to be around her. To me she seemed hopelessly glamorous," she added, remembering with perfect clarity Rosemary's condescending smile, the faint amusement in her eyes that made her feel so gauche.

"You? You felt awkward with Rosemary? But you're one of the most glamorous women I've ever known. Even in Australia in a pair of blue jeans with your hair flying in the wind as you raced to Koonwarra on horseback ahead of me, you had an indisputable aura of glamour, believe me. No one could ever touch you."

"Oh, come on," she said disparagingly.

"And as for poise and control . . . well, you always managed to keep me at arm's length."

Not always, she thought to herself, but she said, "That's not the same thing, and you know it."

Glancing at her, he noticed that a fascinating new sensuality had blossomed about her dark beauty since they had last seen each other.

"You've changed, though. For the better. You're much more sure of yourself. Do you remember how you used to tell me you were going to conquer Australia and then Europe? Well, you've done it, in a way. You've got continents at your feet now that you're one of the top cover girls in the world."

216

She was struck by his tone of nostalgic admiration. How different things were now from what they had been, yet how much the same, she thought, looking toward Seillans nestled in the lush hills. She felt closer to Zan than ever before.

"You've changed, too."

"Have I? How?"

"You seem much more settled in yourself than you were before."

"Settled?" He grimaced, eyes on the winding road. "I suppose. Organizing the new office down here has been a tremendous challenge for me," he said elusively.

"That's not exactly what I meant."

"I know," he admitted.

They arrived at the village and parked the car near a small square shaded by a huge old tree. As they climbed the cobbled streets past the line of houses of worn white stone, Shannon was once again touched by a feeling of peace and calm. Crimson geraniums tumbled from window boxes, and cats dozed in the sun. Drinking it all in, she felt an inexplicable sense of belonging. With its red-tiled roofs, its blue-and-green shutters, Seillans looked like the village of her dreams.

"Here we are—this is it," said Zan, pausing at the hewn wooden door of a two-storied house tucked away at the end of a street.

Shannon touched the knocker, a tarnished brass hand clutching a ball.

"That's the hand of Fatima—it's an ancient sign of good luck," said Zan.

"I think I've had my share already," she said with a smile.

Zan led the way into the cool tiled hall. "The bedrooms are upstairs," he said, flinging open the windows and shutters. "The house has been modernized, but all of its original features have been kept, like the old fireplace, the beams . . . Look at them." He gestured as light flooded through double windows that led to a terrace.

"That sounds suspiciously like a sales pitch," she remarked with a mischievous glimmer in her eyes.

He laughed, delighting in her pleasure. "Well, if that doesn't convince you, come and look at the view," he said, leading the way to the terrace.

Beyond the wrought-iron balcony stretched the endless landscape of Provence. Shannon stood for several moments regarding the sweeping vista, which evoked the palette of

217

Bonnard and Cézanne with its burnt umbers, ochers, and terra-cottas, colors fired by a life-giving sun that glazed the sky a pure cerulean blue. Pulsating crickets invaded the hush of all she surveyed in this new kingdom, where the smell of jasmine and geraniums ruled the senses. "Oh, Zan," she breathed.

"Well? What do you think?" he said, seeing the rapt expression on her face.

"I have to have it—I simply have to. It's *the* house, Zan. The house I've always dreamed of." The thrill of possessing this tiny bit of France swept over her. "Do you think it's possible? I'll sign the contract here and now."

"Why not? You're the first to see it."

It would take nearly all her savings and then some, but with her Valentin contract coming through in the next few weeks, it didn't matter.

Shannon leaned forward to take another look at the breathtaking panorama, and when she turned she found Zan studying her, inches away. She felt her knees go weak, and as she looked into his eyes she was unable to disguise the effect his nearness had on her. It was all he was waiting for, and as he reached out for her she opened her lips instinctively to meet his. Feeling his body against hers, she plummeted to the depths of remembered emotion, resurrecting the sleeping passion that had always tied her to him. He was her first love, her only love, and she yielded to him as a tree bends in the hot, strong sirocco that blows across the Mediterranean from Africa.

"Shannon, Shannon, my darling," he whispered into her hair. "How long I've dreamed of this moment. I love you, Shannon. I've loved you all these years. I've never stopped, not for a moment, my darling."

Drawing back, she caught her breath, looking at him incredulously. "I've loved you, too. I always have."

"God, what it means to me to hear you say that," he murmured, crushing her to him. "I didn't know what I had. To think I ever let you go, Shannon."

Her spirit rushed headlong to meet what seemed to be destined. She had struggled against it, but she could fight no longer. Theirs was a passion that sprang from the embers of first love; something that, once shared, could never be forgotten.

* * *

Later, when long, violet shadows had fallen across the hills and the blue of the sky had deepened on the horizon, presaging rain, they drove in silence toward the eye of the storm. When Zan slowed down the car to turn a corner, they had an awesome view of the snowcapped Alpes-Maritimes, blushed rose by the setting sun. He reached out to clasp her hand tightly, and glancing at his profile, she saw his jaw tighten with emotion.

"There's a wonderful hotel in Saint-Paul-de-Vence called the Colombe d'Or. I know the patron very well. I think we could stay there tonight. How does that sound?"

"It sounds wonderful," she murmured.

"We'll stop on the way and pick up what we need for the night."

As they shared a glance potent with meaning, Shannon felt her pulse quicken at the thought of what was about to occur. The moment they had crossed the threshold of the house in Seillans, she realized they had unwittingly crossed another threshold in their lives.

They arrived in Saint-Paul-de-Vence just as the sun was sinking into the distant sea, gilding the ramparts of the village set on a hilltop. In a square bordered with chestnut trees they passed a group of men playing boules not far from the vine-covered hotel, its shutters flung back.

"They have a fabulous collection of modern paintings in the dining room," he said, taking her hand in his.

"Why don't we give them a miss?" she said as they exchanged a smile.

Zan booked them in at the reception desk while Shannon listened to him bantering back and forth with the patron. Once in their room, Zan pulled the shutters together just as a distant roll of thunder resounded. Time raced with poignant suddenness as they faced each other, and she trembled as he reached to unzip her dress. The fragrance of summer lingered on their flesh, in their hair, as they shared the first caresses of arousal. Letting the world slip away, they charted their own course in a passionate reaffirmation of life, growing closer with every intoxicating sensation. With whispers and kisses they unlocked what was most precious in their hearts. The sweet living smell of sweat, of hair, and of skin carried them to the molten heart of their existence as Zan entered the velvet softness of the woman who ached to receive him. Concave, convex, their bodies met like peaks and plains in the raw power of rediscovery—he glorying in the dark shadow

219

of her being, she drinking in his fair Englishness. All the heavens' opposites clashed and merged.

"Zan, Zan, I love you, Zan," Shannon whispered rapturously.

"And I love you, Shannon—always, forever."

In one great wave their crescendo of desire hurled them into the mysterious chasm that was their union, until they lay breathless in each other's arms. As the tremor that had overtaken them died away, they stared at each other like two dreamers who had just awakened, then gradually fell into a profound and untroubled sleep to the saraband of a summer deluge upon the eaves.

Later that evening, as they sat at a table on the terrace of the hotel, Shannon entwined her fingers around Zan's and gazed through the vine-covered arches at the glimmering chain of lights that marked the houses set among the hills. Both were content to drift in the blissful aftermath of their lovemaking.

"Shannon?" said Zan.

"Yes, my love."

"I don't want to think more than a moment ahead, but what are we going to do?"

"I don't know. What are we going to do?" The troubled expression on his face reminded her that beyond their sanctuary of dreams, the real world still existed. Soon they would have to cope with it. "I only know that we can't let each other go again this time. Do you feel the same?"

"Of course I do. But I know you must be thinking about Rosemary," she said, reluctant to break the spell.

Leaning back, Zan brushed his hand through his hair and sighed. "Oh, Lord, I don't know. It all seems so complicated now. I just didn't realize how much you meant to me until I saw you that day in England. I was devastated when you left and furious with myself. I sat there in the pub for the longest time, thinking. One look at you yesterday in Nice proved to me that the kind of love we have for each other can't die. I know that now, and I must do something about it. I want you for all time, for all my days, Shannon. We have so much time to make up, you and I. I never knew how lonely life could be when you're married to somebody you don't love. . . ."

"Zan, please don't say these things unless you mean them."

"I do mean them. I realize now I've never really loved Rosemary the way I'm capable of loving you. Rosemary and I set the wheels in motion for marriage without even thinking, because both our families were all for it. I was confused when I came back from Australia. When I went out to Koonwarra Rosemary and I had a kind of understanding, but coming back, my reason was clouded by losing you, by not recognizing what I really wanted out of life."

"And Rosemary? How does she feel about you?"

"It's difficult to say, really. She never expresses her feelings. I suppose she's come to terms with our life together, but I can't help believing that she's in the same limbo I am, emotionally."

"But does she love you, Zan? That's what I want to know."

"Would it make any difference if she did?"

"I don't know, quite honestly. There's Saffron to think of, too."

"I don't think Rosemary is really capable of love as you and I understand it, Shannon. She's never responded to my affection in the way I need as a man, the way you and I care for each other."

Another veil fell away from Shannon's past. It had never occurred to her during those days in London that Zan had been lonely. She had always been tormented by the idea that he and Rosemary shared the same passion the two of them had once known. His confession brought on a rush of tenderness for him.

"I imagined things were completely different between you," she said.

"Now you know. And what about you? Is there anyone in your life? It's hard to believe there isn't."

How much should she tell him? Indeed, was there anything to tell? At that moment, her past seemed insignificant compared to what they now shared.

"I won't deny that there have been men in my life. I've had a few affairs—some of them casual, some I took seriously at the time, but I always ran away from pain, from involvement. Looking back, I think I couldn't face really caring for someone after what had happened between us."

"My God, did I hurt you that much?" he murmured. "Darling, I promise I'll make it up to you." Drawing her hand to his lips, he said, "I'm going to ask Rosemary for a divorce the minute I get back to London."

"Oh, Zan, be absolutely sure," she urged.

"I've never been more sure of anything in my life."

Five days later, as Shannon's taxi drove through the rain-spattered streets back to the rue Bonaparte, she could still feel the warmth of the sun of the Midi on her. Scenes from five glorious days with Zan flowed through her mind. She glanced indifferently at the stacked chairs of the Café Deux Magots dripping with rain and the blackened façade of the church of Saint Germain des Prés. In one short week her entire life had changed course. She had begun her journey south triumphantly with the contract of a lifetime in her pocket and as the toy of a millionaire on a yacht in the Mediterranean. Today she was returning as Zan Fitzherbert's beloved.

Letting herself into the flat, she saw the painting of Provence hanging over the fireplace, and its vibrant colors reminded her of the village house that was the embodiment of the picture.

Thumbing through her letters and messages, she was both surprised and relieved that there was nothing from Amadeo. The thought of him evoked comparisons that she had tried desperately to avoid, but she still couldn't help contrasting his passionate earthiness with Zan's almost reverential touch. For a moment she wondered how she had allowed herself to be dominated by a man as egotistical as Amadeo, or to believe that their common roots in early hardships had bound them together. Now that she was a grown woman she realized that the disparities between her and Zan, which had once seemed insurmountable, were rendered insignificant by the love they shared.

Looking around the flat, she was reminded of the million things she had to do before Zan rejoined her in only a few weeks. The plan was that when he had worked out a separation, he would come to Paris for a few months while she worked for Valentin, and there they would begin their life together. In a gesture that seemed to heal the wound Amadeo had inflicted, Shannon emptied a vase of dead flowers she had forgotten to remove before her departure. The withered lilacs were all that remained of the last extravagant bouquet he had sent her, and she stuffed them deeply into a garbage bag and dropped it down the chute outside the kitchen door.

* * *

The carriage clock on the mantelpiece was just chiming the quarter hour when Zan strode into the drawing room of his house in Pelham Crescent in London. The fashionable drawing room papered in yellow curved out to a wide bay framed by gray curtains, overlooking the square. The family portraits, the Queen Anne tallboy, the gilt mirrors, and porcelain and silver bibelots all reflected Rosemary's expensive but conservative taste.

Zan lit a cigarette, and for an instant, as he struck the match, he stood in a cameo of light. Slipping on his dressing gown, he had left Rosemary sleeping soundly in the big canopied bed upstairs. Noting that he had a few minutes before midnight, when he usually called Shannon, he went to the book-lined study and opened the window. It was a warm evening in late July, and all London lay quiet beneath the pink dome of sky.

Slipping into the chair before his desk, he avoided turning on the lamp. Darkness made it easier to consider the things weighing on his mind. That day marked the beginning of the week, after which there would be no turning back. The three of them were scheduled to go to Kilgarin Castle for the month of August, and Zan knew that tomorrow at lunchtime he would have to break the cruel news to Rosemary. Picking up the phone, he dialed Shannon's number.

"Darling, it's you—hello," she said happily when she heard his voice on the line. "I was hoping you'd call tonight."

"What are you doing?"

"Oh, it's been baking hot here. It's too hot even to sleep, and I'm just reading in bed."

"What are you reading?"

"I'd better confess. I picked up a stack of travel brochures today. I had the sudden inspiration that if we could get away at Christmas, we might go to the Caribbean."

"Sounds wonderful. Listen, Shannon, why don't you go on down to Seillans now that you're free for the whole month? I'll join you there as soon as I can. Wouldn't that be better than waiting for me?"

"Why? Has something happened? You are coming, aren't you?"

"Yes, yes, of course. It's just that some complications have come up. I've been discussing everything with Noel Villiers this week, and I'm getting things sorted out as quickly as I can, but I might be stuck here another week."

223

"But you are coming, aren't you, darling?" She couldn't disguise the note of anxiety in her voice.

"Yes, of course I am," he replied, injecting a bright note into his own voice. "I can't wait."

"Have you told her yet?" Somehow, she couldn't say Rosemary's name.

"No, I haven't. I'm going to do it tomorrow. I've put it off until the last possible moment, I know."

"Oh, Zan, why haven't you done it as you promised? You said you would tell her earlier in the week," said Shannon with a sigh. "It won't be any easier, will it?" she added tenderly.

"I know, I know. All I want is for us to be together again."

"I know how much harder it is for you than for me, darling. I'm trying to be patient, but sometimes I miss you so."

He said in a gently teasing tone, "You'd better make damn sure that I'm what you want, because once I get my hands on you I won't let you get away. I want to be tangled up with you for the rest of my life, you gorgeous creature. Sleep tight, my darling. I'll try to call you tomorrow night when it's all over. But whatever, I'll be with you by the weekend, and from then we'll have our entire lives to spend together."

"Of course we will. I'll be thinking of you every moment, darling. Remember that."

"Good night, my treasure, my angel face," he whispered, quietly putting down the telephone.

Upstairs in the bedroom in Pelham Crescent, Rosemary uncupped her hand from the receiver of the bedside telephone when she heard a click on the line and carefully replaced the receiver before sliding back under the covers. When Zan came into the bedroom she pretended to be sleeping. Within moments of slipping into bed beside her, she heard him fall into an uneven, restless sleep while she lay wide awake, staring into the darkness, her mind racing back to years ago—to Ascot, to Windsor Great Park, and to images of Shannon Faloon.

When Shannon had put down the telephone she lay in bed thinking for a long time. Though it was too hot in the city to sleep, that was only part of the reason why she lay wide awake. She was pregnant. She had kept it to herself for days as she waited anxiously to hear from Zan, but when he had finally called, something had kept her from telling him, and now she was glad she hadn't given in to the impulse. Soon they would be together in Seillans. There, when the moment was right, she would break the news. By that time Zen would have walked out on his empty marriage, and until he crossed that bridge she would hold back. She wanted him strong, free, and unfettered, as he had been that first night they'd spent together at Saint Paul-de-Vence.

Gazing at the little glass chandelier on her bedroom ceiling, Shannon touched her stomach, feeling momentary happiness at the thought of the child she was carrying. That unpremeditated night they had spent together in Nice was the only time in her adult life that she had thrown caution to the winds, not stopping to consider that she was unprepared. There had been no time to think about precautions. When she'd first learned she was pregnant, she had been numb with shock, but gradually, as she felt the first stirrings of motherhood, she knew the baby would be a great consolation for the contract with Valentin that she would be forced to give up. All her joy at winning it now seemed shallow and misplaced compared to what she was feeling now. This was happiness, or at least the promise of it, when she and Zan would be together, awaiting their child.

Rosemary and Jonquil were lunching on Jonquil's terrace, overgrown with roses and honeysuckle. They sat opposite one another, across the glass-topped table under a yellow-striped awning.

Jonquil tossed the salad with deft movements and handed Rosemary a plate. "Just smell those white petunias. Aren't they glorious? Rosemary? You haven't heard a word I said. What's the matter, dear? I sensed the moment you walked in that something was on your mind."

Rosemary put down her fork. "I was supposed to have lunch with Zan today in the City, but after what I found out last night I had to talk to you. You're the only person I can confide in," she said with a gush of emotion that made Jonquil look at her in concern.

"Darling, you know you can tell me anything."

"Well, Zan has been behaving very strangely lately. I don't know if you've noticed how absentminded he's become since he went down to the south of France. I kept telling myself it was because he was so preoccupied with business, but last night when I heard him phoning downstairs I picked up the telephone in the bedroom. It's not the first time I've heard him calling someone late at night. I'm not in the habit of eavesdropping. Jonquil, it's much worse than I thought. It crossed my mind he might be having some sort of fling, and it may not have been the first time, but I never dreamed he could be serious." She broke off. Two sharp lines bit into her forehead and her mouth was twisted.

Jonquil blinked at her in surprise. "I don't know what to say. Who is it? Do you have any idea?"

"Yes. I know exactly who it is. It's Shannon Faloon, that girl you had here who became a model," she announced coldly.

"Shannon?" gasped Jonquil. "Oh, you must be mistaken, Rosemary. It couldn't be."

"There's no mistake. Beneath those well-modulated vowels I can still hear that Australian accent of hers, no matter how hard she tries to disguise it. Besides, I heard Zan call her Shannon."

"I'm simply flabbergasted," exclaimed Jonquil, falling back limply into her chair. Her face was a study in confusion— her eyes those of a child who has just had her favorite toy broken.

"He's apparently already discussed the details of the separation with Noel, and he's planning to leave me and Saffron high and dry this weekend instead of going with us to Kilgarin. That's probably what he was going to tell me over lunch. So civilized, isn't it?" Rosemary said with bitter sarcasm. "It threw him completely off balance when I told him I couldn't make it."

"Oh, my dear, what can we do?"

"Jonquil, I need your help. I'm relying on you. Will you help me?"

"Why, you know I will. My dear, this is an outrage. I simply can't believe it," she muttered.

"It's just that I know you were very close to Shannon at one time, and frankly, I didn't quite know how to break the news to you."

"You know perfectly well where my loyalties lie, Rosemary. They're with you—Freddie's goddaughter and my own dearest godchild. To think of Shannon behaving with such ingratitude when I took her into my home, introduced her to my friends, treated her like one of the family. I'm hurt, I'm

226

angry that she could take advantage of all of us like this. How long has it been going on, I wonder?"

"I really have no idea, but one thing is certain. We must be very careful. One wrong move could send Zan flying in her direction. Do you know where she lives?"

"Yes, of course. I've been corresponding with her off and on ever since she left London. To think of the treachery! I'm going to fly over to see that girl at once," Jonquil said, slapping down her napkin. "Irma!" she called. "I want you to go upstairs and pack my overnight bag." Turning to Rosemary, her eyes melted with concern. "At all costs we must keep him from confessing to you this evening. Once he does that, it might be too late. What I'll do is summon him here—to confront him, this evening after he has finished work. I'll pretend I found out on my own; then I'll go straight to Shannon. What you should do is get a group of friends together this evening—go out somewhere, so you won't be alone."

"I think I can manage to stave off a confession," said Rosemary, her manner suffused with a new calm. "I knew I could count on your loyalty, Jonquil."

"After all, what is family for? Blood runs thicker than water, Rosemary—don't ever forget it."

When Jonquil descended the stairs of her home that evening, all the windows had been thrown open to admit the song of blackbirds coming from the cool, darkening garden. Irma was turning on the lamps in the sitting room, casting a warm glow. An enormous bouquet of yellow roses had been arranged in a Chinese bowl before a gilt mirror in the hallway, where Jonquil paused to fluff up a blond curl and rearrange the ruffles of her dotted swiss blouse, her mind distracted by Zan's impending visit. When the bell rang a few moments later, she darted to the door.

"Zan, darling! Come in," she said brightly.

"It's lovely to see you," he said, bending to embrace her warmly.

"Do come and sit down, and let me get you a drink. Would you like a kir?" she said, fluttering to the butler's tray as Zan stood before the fireplace, his hands deep in his pockets.

"I'd love one, thanks."

As she poured the white wine, adding a dollop of cassis, he gazed around at the familiar room, and the thought crossed his mind that from now on he might not be as welcome here as he had been in the past. He was accustomed to Jonquil seeking his advice on business matters, but tonight he was in no mood to linger. His plans to break the news to Rosemary had been postponed until evening. He glanced at his watch impatiently.

"Should we sit here or in the garden?" asked Jonquil, handing him a goblet.

"Here is fine. I really can't stay long, I'm afraid. Now, what can I do for you, my dear?"

Jonquil settled herself into a chair by the fireplace, nervously toying with the large sunburst of diamonds on her finger. He caught the wind of seriousness in the air and shifted uncomfortably in his chair.

"I suppose I may as well get straight to the point, since you're in such a hurry."

"You know I have all the time in the world for you," he replied guardedly.

The shrewdness that Jonquil concealed under layers of frivolity suddenly took command. "I asked you here to talk about you and Shannon."

"What?"

"Please don't bother to deny it, Zan. I know everything." Seeing his confusion, she added, "Don't worry. Rosemary doesn't know, and I have no intention of telling her."

After a long pause he managed to say, "How did you find out?"

"Zan, darling, you can't carry on an affair in the world we live in and keep it a secret for long. Anyway, that doesn't really matter. What concerns me is Rosemary and, of course, Saffron. And you. Not to mention Shannon. You know how fond I am of her. I feel a certain responsibility toward her. After all, I brought her into the family circle. She's a grown woman now, but I'm sure she's still very vulnerable. She could be deeply hurt by a casual love affair." Her wide blue eyes radiated sadness and concern.

"Jonquil, you've got it all wrong—believe me. It's much more serious than you think. I'm in love with Shannon. I want to marry her."

"I see," she said, her face a mask of mock surprise.

"In fact, I'm on the point of asking Rosemary for a divorce. I was going to do it today, but she canceled our luncheon appointment. But tonight I'm going to lay everything before her—tell her exactly how things stand. I'm tired of concealing, hiding, lying. . . ."

"Zan, this is terrible news. I'm absolutely stunned. Dear Lord, to think I'm the cause of it all by bringing Shannon here to London in the first place."

"Jonquil—just a minute! I can't let you blame yourself for what happened. This may come as a complete surprise to you, but Shannon and I knew each other a long time before we met by chance at Ascot that day. I never told you this, but I met her in Australia when I went out to Wishbone to stay with Charlie Fremont."

"Do you mean to say you've been involved with each other all this time?" She recoiled in genuine horror at the thought. "Which means that Shannon wanted to come here just to be with you. Extremely clever of her," she observed tartly.

"No, no. We simply had a summer romance when I was in Australia. Then we lost touch until we met through you. You can imagine how bowled over I was by the coincidence that the two of you had met. Shannon refused to have anything to do with me when she arrived here. Wouldn't even speak to me when she found I had married Rosemary and that we had a daughter. We had no more than a few moments alone the entire time she stayed with you. But two and a half months ago we ran into each other in Nice and the whole thing started up again. During our week together we came to the conclusion that we couldn't be apart any longer. Since I came back to London I've been getting things in order so I could ask Rosemary for a divorce. I intend to live with Shannon in Paris for a while until I get things organized. She's doing very well, you know. She's just landed an amazing modeling contract."

"Zan, you can't possibly be serious. Do you really mean to say you're intending to throw away *everything*? Your marriage, your position, your future? For a teenage romance that happened to turn into an affair that lasted a week?"

"Of course, I know what it must seem like to you. . . ."

"But Zan, you haven't given it any time at all. Have you thought what this will do to Rosemary and Saffron?"

"Of course I have. I never stop thinking of it. But there's no other way." Zan's brow knitted in worry.

"Darling, have another drink," Jonquil said, bustling to the bar table. "Now," she said, handing him the glass, careful to keep any note of condemnation from her voice, "let's be completely practical about all this. First of all, what are you two going to live on? I mean, honestly, Zan, I know you're not earning enough yet without Rosemary's support to live in the manner you're used to. Is Shannon prepared to subsidize you?"

"Of course not, and I wouldn't dream of asking her. But the property market is looking up in the south of France, and my prospects are excellent."

She looked at him doubtfully. "But what about Kilgarin? To put it bluntly, Kilgarin needs Rosemary's fortune to survive. You have a title, position, standards to uphold. Does all of it mean nothing to you? And you will destroy Rosemary if you leave her, you know."

He looked at her blankly. "I've thought of it all, believe me. But as things stand now, my life would be empty without Shannon. I can't go on without her, and I don't want to."

"All right, then, let's look at what you can offer her. Has it occurred to you that you'd be a lord without a castle or a fortune to go with it? Not to say that she isn't in love with you, but surely the idea of security represents something in her mind. She wouldn't be normal if it didn't. Have you told her what you stand to lose if you leave Rosemary? Does she know the truth?" Jonquil saw by the look on Zan's face that she had hit a raw nerve.

"No, she doesn't know it," he admitted. "But it wouldn't matter to her a bit if I had to sell Kilgarin. She's not like that. That's what I love about her."

"Zan, I hadn't meant to bring this up," she said, reaching for her ace card, a copy of *Paris Match* that she had saved, "but Shannon's name has been linked to one of the world's richest men."

"She doesn't have anyone in her life. She would have told me."

"Look—here she is at the Cannes Film Festival with Amadeo Benguela. Read what it says. Their names are linked romantically in the story by the picture. Why, according to this the two of them were about to leave for a holiday on his yacht in Sardinia. The point is, Zan, Shannon is no longer the little homespun girl from the Outback. She moves with the international jet set. Are you so certain that she doesn't expect to live at Kilgarin as a countess?"

She fell silent, allowing him to draw his own conclusions from the photograph. When he looked up, she could see by his eyes that he was no longer as sure of himself as when he came in.

"Zan, I hope you understand my motives for interfering in your personal life like this. You know I want the best for all of you, Shannon included. I love life's lighter side, and no one's less of a snob than me, but I am a realist. I know that underneath it's the foundation on which life is built that counts. Family and fortune—that's what it all boils down to in the end, Zan, believe me."

"I don't know what to say," said Zan at last. "Perhaps I'd better not say anything at this point." Deeply disturbed, he rose to go.

"Please promise me one thing—one very small thing," she pleaded. "Give yourself more time. Life is long, and once you've made such a decision there's no turning back. Go to Kilgarin as planned. Get to know Rosemary again. Go back to everything you once held dear, and think what life would be like if you threw it all away."

"I can't promise anything, Jonquil, but thank you for your concern. I do appreciate it, believe me. Good-bye."

They embraced in the hallway, and she watched him as he walked down the steps.

Irma came into the hallway. "Bagley said he'd be here at six-thirty to drive you to Heathrow. How long will you be staying in Paris, madam?"

"Not long, Irma. I have some unfinished business to attend to that shouldn't take more than a day."

When Zan left Jonquil's he walked with a preoccupied air past the cream-colored houses of Belgravia, their windows overflowing with bright flowers. The slate roofs pressed against the pale evening sky, the seductive smell of summer, the polished brass doorknobs and letter boxes, all served to remind him of who he was. Jonquil's words had brought him back to London with a crash, back from France, where he had planned to be in only a few days' time, and he began to realize that for the past few weeks he had been living life in the future tense. His thoughts suddenly traveled to Kilgarin Castle, set in the heart of County Limerick. Its gardens would be thick with the fallen petals of summer roses and peonies. He could see its lawns clipped as closely as green velvet, rolling down to the lake bordered by beeches and weeping willow trees, the hush of evening broken by birdsong. At one time he had had so many dreams of how things would

231

be when he was the earl. Where had they all gone? When he tried to focus on Shannon, he found it too painful to contemplate as he confronted all that Jonquil had said. Trivial as it was, what had hurt him most was the photograph of Shannon with Amadeo Benguela. By his reckoning, she was with him the same week they had met in Nice, and he wondered why she hadn't mentioned it. He knew he would be too proud to ask.

When he arrived at the glossy black front door of the three-storied house in Pelham Crescent, he paused before opening it.

"Darling, I was worried about you," said Rosemary with a welcoming smile, standing in the hallway lit by picture lights over the portraits that covered the walls. She brushed his forehead with her hand and kissed him tenderly.

"Vanessa has asked if we'd like to join them at the Orangerie tonight. I know you must be exhausted, but it's so warm I thought you might like to go out."

"Daddy!" cried Saffron, rushing up to him in her nightgown.

Rosemary smiled as Zan reached down to hug her. "I let her stay up because I knew she wouldn't fall asleep with all the excitement."

"Excitement? What excitement?" asked Zan, mustering a smile.

"Ireland, Daddy. Have you forgotten? Only three more days until we leave for Kilgarin. And do you know what? Mummy says when we get there I can ride Mr. Sandman all by myself, alone."

"Did she, now?"

"Come on, darling. Off to bed with you. Nanny's waiting upstairs."

When she had gone, Rosemary regarded Zan sympathetically.

"You do look tired, darling. The heat must have exhausted you. Why don't you go upstairs and have a shower while I get you a drink?"

Zan hesitated just an instant before taking her in his arms. Hugging her tightly, he whispered, "Thank you, Rosemary."

The following afternoon Shannon walked through the revolving doors of L'Hotel, discreetly tucked away on a side street not far from the rue Bonaparte. She had always thought there was something charmingly overblown about L'Hotel, which seemed the perfect little hideaway for clandestine rendezvous, tinged with the decadent glamour of Oscar Wilde and the memory of Mistinguette. She had been taken by surprise when Jonquil had phoned her that morning, asking her to lunch. Pleasant as the prospect of seeing her was, the timing was all wrong, and she walked through the doors feeling like a hypocrite, wondering if this would be the last time she and Jonquil would ever see each other. When she stepped out of the elevator, they fell into each other's arms.

"What a wonderful surprise!" said Shannon, swept up in her ruffled, jasmine-scented embrace.

"Shannon, dearest!" she cried, kissing the air near her cheek. "You're looking simply marvelous. As lovely as ever!" she declared, regarding her at arm's length. Not one detail of Shannon's dark exotic beauty, now refined to the ultimate degree, escaped Jonquil. But it was her radiance—undeniably that of a woman in love—which caught her attention.

"You haven't changed a bit," said Shannon as they moved toward the dining room. "You're still as youthful as ever." As she spoke, she couldn't help wondering if Jonquil would be so glad to see her if she knew she was carrying Zan's child.

"My secret is a little nip and tuck behind the ears every now and then. It does wonders for the self-esteem. And of course I always pay attention to the window dressing," she said, patting her hair. When the waiter had ceremoniously ushered them to a table, she said, "Speaking of window dressing, I must tell you I saw Elena on my last visit to Australia."

"Did you? How is she?"

"Simply marvelous. Quite frankly, I've been avoiding her all these years after what happened—you remember. But I decided to bury the hatchet. Well, the truth is, I needed a dress desperately. . . ."

"Oh, Jonquil," said Shannon, laughing. "That's just like you!"

"Anyway, we're just as thick as ever, now. She wanted to hear all about you. She's even kept a little scrapbook of cuttings of your pictures. Practically takes full credit for your success, between you and me."

Shannon smiled. "I really must drop her a line one of these days. I do owe her a lot." Glancing at the fountain surrounded by greenery, where caged birds twittered, she said, "I was surprised you were staying here. I thought you always stayed at the Ritz?"

"My dear, Freddie brought me here on the first night of our honeymoon, before we went on to Monte Carlo. It suits me somehow."

As the waiter poured the wine, Shannon said, "What on earth brings you to Paris in August? You usually go to Scotland or Antibes this time of year."

"I came here specially to see you, Shannon."

A warning went off like a gun in Shannon's head. "But why?"

"Shannon, this is very, very difficult for me." She chose her words carefully, disguising her anger with a soothing warmth. "I've come to see you about Zan."

"Oh, no, please, Jonquil," she murmured, shock on her face.

"I beg you not to interrupt me. First I must tell you I've already spoken to Zan. He knows I'm here. In fact, he's asked me to talk to you."

"How did you find out about us? Did he tell you? Did Rosemary tell you?" she said, thrown into confusion.

"Let's not go into that. It's unimportant. It wasn't Rosemary. She doesn't know. I'm only grateful that I found out in time to plead with you to consider what you're doing. It hurts me more than anything in the world to say these things, loving you both as I do. Shannon—do you realize that without Rosemary's money Zan will be penniless? That he will lose Kilgarin after his father dies? But that's only part of it. Rosemary loves Zan deeply and always has since they were children. Their destinies have been intertwined from the beginning. What Zan is undergoing now has nothing to do with reality. Believe me, every marriage experiences difficulties, temptations. And though I have no doubt Zan is very fond of you and you of him, if you really love him, don't do anything rash. I feel you've both jumped into this without even thinking."

"How did you find out?"

"It was quite by chance, and when I confronted him with it he had to confess. It was obvious to me that he was in a state of deep distress and confusion, and though I hesitated a long while before interfering, I felt I was the only person who knows everyone well enough to make you two see reason."

It was the first time Shannon had seen Jonquil stripped of all her eccentric frivolity. Beneath all the glitter and furbe-

234

lows that Jonquil used to disguise her true nature, Shannon perceived the woman who had climbed from London's impoverished East End to its most exalted quarters. It was that formidable woman, nobody's fool, who bargained with her now. Suddenly she felt sickened, as if she were falling helplessly from a great height. She couldn't deny to herself that it had taken more than two months for Zan to accomplish what he had promised to do in a week, and a knife of pain went through Shannon's heart when she recalled that he hadn't phoned her the night before, as he had promised. Stoically, she listened in silence as Jonquil continued.

"Shannon, Zan has always loved Rosemary, though it may be different from what he feels for you. If he leaves her, he will come to you as a man filled with remorse and regret. A bitter man, who has chosen to turn his back on his own destiny. You are stronger than he is. Only you can keep him from making this horrendous sacrifice. I beg you to give him up, for both your sakes. Zan is leaving things in your hands and has said he'll abide by your decision."

Ice ran through her veins. She was unable to speak, to argue, as she saw the integrity of their love impaired by things she had never considered until now. She and Zan had allowed themselves to be carried away by a balloon of fantasy, thinking they existed exclusively for themselves. A sadness greater than any she had ever known weighed down on her. With shattering clarity, the same emotions she had experienced the day she had seen Zan's picture in the Sydney newspapers came back to her, magnified a thousand times. To him, she was nothing more than a wild card in a life charted by convention.

"I'm sorry, Jonquil, but under the circumstances I think there's nothing more to say," she said stiffly, rising abruptly. "Please forgive me for rushing off."

"I understand, my dear," she replied, presenting her cheek for Shannon to kiss.

Shannon rushed from the hotel into the bright sunshine, carrying the memory of Jonquil's anguished blue eyes. By the time she arrived back at her apartment, she had calmed down enough to reassure herself that all was not yet lost. Zan still cared, she was sure. Her pulse began to race with a mixture of impotence and anger. Why didn't he speak for himself? Had he sent Jonquil to let her down gently? Surely he had more courage than that, she told herself. One telephone call

235

from him could change everything, and she clung to that hope like a bright talisman lost in the dust.

That evening, when Jonquil forged through the door of her house, she didn't even pause to pick up Buggles dancing at her feet.

"Irma!" she called anxiously.

"Madam!" the maid replied from the landing. "We weren't expecting you so soon. Bagley is waiting. . . ."

"Never mind, Irma," she said, a powerhouse of energy as she charged into the sitting room and headed for the telephone. Dialing Zan's office number, she prayed he hadn't yet phoned Shannon. She could just catch him if she was lucky.

"Zan?" she said urgently when she heard his voice on the line.

"Jonquil," he echoed in surprise.

A few words of conversation told her that the door was still open, and she stifled a sigh of relief.

"Zan, I've just come back from Paris, where I saw Shannon."

"You what?" There was confusion in his voice, but no condemnation.

"Before you speak, let me explain. After you left yesterday my intuition told me that Shannon was probably in the same state of turmoil that you were. So I took it upon myself to go and see her. I wasn't at all surprised to discover that she has had a lot of time to reflect about things these last weeks and that she is beginning to feel that the two of you have been overhasty. I told her exactly what I told you, and it made her think, I could see. I don't believe she was aware of how much was at stake."

"Yes," he interrupted anxiously, "but what is the outcome of all this? What did she say?"

"Quite frankly, it took no persuasion at all on my part for her to see the wisdom of you going off to Kilgarin as planned, to think things out more clearly. She realized that your relationship has little chance of surviving if you start out on the wrong foot. And she's got her whole life, her career ahead of her, Zan."

After a long pause Zan replied, "I see."

Jonquil took a deep breath before delivering the biggest lie that had ever passed her lips. "I don't know how to break this to you. It seems terribly cruel, but she thought it might be a good idea if the two of you didn't contact each other for a while. A few weeks, or perhaps even a few months, until you sort yourself out. She seemed relieved when I said I thought it was sensible. Quite honestly, the poor girl has an awful lot on her plate at the moment. She expects to be very busy with this new contract of hers. My heart went out to her." When he didn't reply she said, "Zan? Are you there? What do you think about what I've said?"

"I suppose it's the best thing for the time being, under the circumstances." His voice was empty and defeated.

"I was hoping that was what you'd say," she replied, keeping a note of triumph from her voice.

"I've got a lot to do here at the office before I go to Kilgarin, Jonquil. I'll be in touch as soon as we get back. I'm sorry you've been caught up in the middle of our affairs."

"Don't be silly. That's what I'm here for, darling. Give my love to Rosemary and kiss Saffron. Try to put things to one side while you're there, if you can."

"I'll try," he said flatly.

The moment she had hung up, Jonquil telephoned Rosemary.

"Everything is all right, darling," she gushed, giving her a quick summary of what had transpired.

"Thank you, Jonquil. I knew I could count on you. Believe me, by the time we get back from Kilgarin I'll have him well in hand," was Rosemary's parting comment.

Chapter II

Sweet Willows, Maryland, June

At the edge of the dance floor erected in the garden under a marquee, Kerry let out a peal of laughter as the boy who had cut in on Mark swung her around at the end of a fast foxtrot. When the music ended she slipped her arms from the tall young man from Harvard, whom she had decided was irresistibly handsome. It was nearly midnight, and Cynthia Frobisher's coming-out party was in full swing.

"Why haven't I ever met you before?" he said flirtatiously.

"I don't know. Why haven't you?"

"That's what I'm wondering. You're the prettiest girl here tonight."

She laughed with pleasure at this compliment, knowing it was perfectly true. The way she smiled as she tilted her head seemed to fascinate him, and she knew she had never looked more stunning, with her pretty shoulders shown to advantage in the simple long dress of blue-green silk made from a length of cloth Shannon had sent her from Bangkok. From the moment she and Mark had arrived at Sweet Willows, the fabulous colonial house of the Frobisher family a few miles from The Meadows, Kerry had moved with confidence. Her curvaceous figure was in provocative contrast to the tall, big-boned girls from patrician Maryland families, whose expensive evening gowns did nothing to enhance their athletic brand of femininity. Among the hundred girls there, Kerry stood out like a brilliant firefly among drab moths. Watching her in sullen rage from the edge of the dance floor was Carter Van Buren with Lindy, who had motored over from The Meadows with Lindy.

Though Kerry was treated as an equal by members of the national horse fraternity as the up-and-coming junior champion who rode Rainmaker, this was the first time she had mingled with the local gentry with a sense of her own worth. Much as she enjoyed the big celebrations following equestrian events all over the countryside, the select Frobisher party had an added cachet that she recognized immediately.

"Where are you going to college next fall?" asked her partner, taking her hand as the music struck up again.

"Braemar," she said nonchalantly as he pressed his cheek against hers.

"I'll be at Cape Cod all summer, but I'll give you a buzz in the fall."

"Sure—do that," she replied, keeping her response cool. She was aware of Mark's eyes following them anxiously as they danced. Finally, when he could stand it no longer, he made his way through the throng of dancers and cut in.

"I thought I'd never get rid of him," she whispered, pretending relief.

He gave a laugh of disbelief. "I didn't know whether I should spoil your fun. The two of you seemed to be having such a good time."

"He was so boring, I can't tell you."

"Are you kidding? Boring? Him?"

"Quite frankly, I found him really slow going."

238

"Do you know who he is? Randolph Hunnewell is Porcellian Club and editor of the *Lampoon*. He's one of the smartest, most popular guys around. He has to beat the girls off."

"Well, he won't have to beat me off." A little smile crossed Kerry's face as she savored this coup. "What did you say his name was?"

"Randolph Hunnewell."

"Well, I thought he was totally predictable and b-o-r-i-n-g. Conceited to boot. I can't stand a guy who is so full of himself."

She could almost feel Mark's heart swelling with pride as he pressed her closely to him. Randolph was a possibility she tucked away at the back of her mind for the future. Perhaps in two years at Braemar Junior College she might be able to catch such a prize, but for the time being she preferred to keep Mark securely in her pocket.

"Do you realize that I'm going to Europe in only a couple of days, Kerry?" He gave an exasperated sigh. "I wish I could get out of it. I'm going to miss you so much," he murmured in her ear.

Kerry suppressed a spasm of naked envy that Mark was going to Europe. It was exactly how she wanted to spend the summer. If it hadn't been for her intensive schedule of training on Rainmaker for the autumn events, she would have asked Shannon for the money to take a long trip to Italy, France, and Spain.

"Once you're there you'll forget all about me. Wait until you see those cute French girls and ravishing Italian brunettes who look like Sophia Loren."

"You know that's not true," he said in a wounded tone. "I'll write you every day."

"Don't make any promises you can't keep," she said. As she gazed up at him with a smitten expression, she was unaware that Lindy was staring at her from a distance. In beautifully cut evening clothes, he stood at the bar thoughtfully sipping a whiskey, until the spirit moved him to slam his glass down and make his way toward Mark and Kerry. With a sharp jab, he tapped his son on the shoulder.

"Oh, hi," said Mark, astonished to see his father cutting in.

"May I take over?" It was a command, not a request.

"Why, of course," said Kerry, feeling a thrill of expectation. Only moments ago he had been waltzing around the floor with Mrs. Frobisher, one of the foremost society women in the Green Spring Valley, and now he had singled her out.

She was struck by the contrast between Mark's hesitant grip and the way Lindy masterfully scooped his arm around her waist. He had just returned from Palm Beach, and his blue eyes were set off by his deeply bronzed face. She was astonished when she discovered his hands were exploring her back beneath her thin evening dress, making her heart pound violently. With a fixed smile he gazed down at her, appraising her with the same calculating study that he would a thoroughbred he wanted to add to his stud.

Up until now Lindy had seemed only vaguely aware of the progress of her equestrian career. Her Uncle Jack, Bryce Paget, and the grooms at The Meadows saw to it her entrance fees were paid, drove the van to the meets, supervised her training. Lindy was like the chairman of the board, who caused a flutter of nervousness when he occasionally appeared. Even so, Kerry always felt extraordinarily proud whenever he watched her working out on Rainmaker. The Meadows was only part of Lindy's rich and varied life, which included polo in Florida, part share of a stud farm in Ireland, and business interests around the world. Kerry had heard rumors that the women he preferred were rich divorcées, and that he was known as a womanizer.

"What the hell do you see in that son of mine, anyway?"

"What do you mean, Mr. Van Buren?" she replied, unnerved. From the slur in his voice Kerry realized that he had had too much to drink, and she sensed they were on dangerous ground. His mocking smile cut through her poise.

"Don't give me that bullshit. You know the difference between a man and a boy," he said, clutching her tighter.

His remark was both exciting and disturbing. Swallowing nervously, she said piously, "Mark is nice, very sensitive. You ought to take the time to get to know him better."

He threw back his head and laughed. "That's rich. You telling me to get to know my own son. Mark's not for you, and you know it as well as I do, so don't try and pretend."

"No, I mean it. You never give Mark a chance."

"Balls," he interrupted. "He's had every chance in the world to prove himself. He's weak. He takes after his mother's side of the family, not mine."

"I don't want to argue with you over him, please," she said with an air of hurt innocence, which he brushed aside. She changed the subject awkwardly. "You know, I hope I do better this year at the Hampton Classic than I did last year. With another year's experience behind me, Colonel Paget thinks I have a good chance at the Worthington Cup. Did he tell you? The purse is a thousand dollars—"

"Don't talk shop. You're a girl who needs long odds, Kerry. Not a sure thing."

"What makes you so sure of that, Mr. Van Buren?" she said coldly, her temper breaking through.

"Because you like a challenge. That's why I put you on my horse. That's why I'm dancing with you now."

"Would you excuse me?" she said, trying to release herself from his grip.

"The dance hasn't ended yet. Stay where you are," he commanded gruffly.

When the music finally stopped, she broke away from Van Buren before he could speak.

As she pushed her way through the crowd, Kerry felt his eyes boring into her. She was glad to escape into the living room, where a few couples locked in conversation seemed to take no notice of her. Her dance with Lindy had disturbed her carefully cultivated social façade, leaving her feeling unkempt and disheveled. She tossed her head, indignant that their relationship as owner and rider made Lindy believe he could treat her as he pleased. He didn't seem aware, she told herself as she climbed the big oak staircase, that she was there in her own right, invited by Mark. Drawing herself up confidently, she went toward the bedroom where she had seen the other girls go to powder their noses. There was a cluster of them in fussy evening dresses, sitting on the white four-poster bed and gathered around the mirror of the dressing table. She felt her stomach lurch when the conversation dropped as she entered.

"Hi," she said with a smile in the direction of a clutch of Cynthia Frobisher's friends, among whom she immediately recognized Carter and her friend Abigail.

Silence prevailed until she had gone to the bathroom and locked the door, when she heard muffled laughter break out. When she left the bathroom she steeled herself for another distinct silence, which ended as soon as she left the bedroom. Stung with humiliation, she heard echoes of hysterical laughter as she stood on the landing, staring down at the sweep of stairs and marble entry hall. If only Carter or one of the others had had the courage to speak their minds, she could have defended herself. It was the undercurrent of whispering innuendo that had always tormented her.

She had been delighted and relieved to discover that the horse fraternity was robustly egalitarian, and that even though it was a tightly knit world, the poorest competitor was welcome at the grandest party following the events she had attended in Washington, Virginia, and Pennsylvania. There, people were more interested in Rainmaker's lineage than in hers. But here, it was different. Sweet Willows was a glasshouse of Baltimore society that would be forever sealed off from her. When she and Mark had driven up the long, floodlit drive, she had been naive enough to suppose that things would be different. Now, her throat dry, her knees weak, she left the house by the front door and went around to the garden. The hem of her dress dragging through the dew-soaked lawn, she headed toward a wrought-iron gazebo, close to tears, when she heard Mark call her name.

"Kerry, Kerry." Catching up breathlessly, he said, "I've been waiting for you to come down. Where are you going?"

"I don't know—anywhere. I don't care."

"What's wrong?"

She kept on walking.

"Please tell me what's the matter," he pleaded.

They entered the gazebo, fragrant with the scent of roses. Slow-moving fireflies blinked in the surrounding shrubbery, but Kerry didn't see them. She gave a long, quivering sigh.

"You know, Mark, I realized tonight I've been kidding myself. I thought if I rode Rainmaker, if I won enough blue ribbons and trophies, that I'd fit in, that some of the Van Buren luster might rub off on me."

"What are you saying?" He moved closer to her on the bench.

"I'm not good enough for any of you. Not for your father, or your stuck-up sister. All of you look down on me." She sat rigidly, staring toward the distant marquee filled with dancers. Her desire to play on Mark's sympathy was jumbled up with the truth.

"You know I'm not like that."

"You don't know what it's like, Mark. Carter's friends stare at me as if I don't exist. Maybe if I win the Grand Prix, or if I make it to the Olympic team, things might be different. But by then I'll be too disillusioned to care."

242

"What did Carter say to you? I want to know," he said urgently.

"She didn't say anything. They all use the subtle technique. It's much more effective. The whole little clique from Foxcroft, Madeira—they stick together like a bunch of maggots on a stick."

Mark's mouth was set firmly. "I'll have a word with her. You can count on that."

"What's the point? She's your sister." Kerry moved away from his comforting embrace. "I've decided to go away. To California. To someplace where I can fit in and be me. There's no room for me in The Green Spring Valley or at The Meadows."

"But you can't do that. What about Rainmaker? And what about me?"

"What about you? If your father told you to quit seeing me, you would—come on, admit it. Wouldn't you?"

"That's stupid. My father would never ask me to do that. And if he did, I'd refuse. Oh, Kerry, don't you see? I'm just like you. I've thought about it so much. The reason why we get on so well is that both of us are on the outside looking in, but for different reasons. Me, because I always compare myself to my brother, Lindy, and you because you popped out of a foreign country into a strange environment. Do you know what that means, Kerry, to find that sort of thing in common with somebody? It means everything, and you're the only girl I've ever felt that way about."

Pausing at Mark's sudden eloquence, she said, "Do you really mean it?"

"Yes, I do, Kerry."

"Sometimes I think you only like me because I slept with you. That's why I said no at Easter."

"Is that why?" he said exultantly. "I thought it was because you didn't want me anymore. I thought you'd changed your mind about the whole thing after Christmas. I used to lie awake at night worrying about it."

Her reply was to tilt back her chin for him to kiss her. Her anger had simmered down to emptiness. As they clung to each other she said, "But it's true. No matter how much we care for each other I'll always be on the outside. You're one of them."

"You wouldn't be if we were married."

"What do you mean?"

Mark stared at her intently. "If you were Mrs. Mark Van

243

Buren, my wife, everybody would accept you. You'd be one of us."

"Mark—I don't know what to say." His impetuous proposal was the last thing she'd expected, and for once in her life she was dumbfounded.

"Think about it, Kerry. I'm afraid of losing you, I admit. But I love you. We could be secretly engaged. We could get married now, if you want, and keep it a secret. I know how much you want to keep on riding and go to college," he said excitedly as the idea gained momentum.

"But what about your father? What would he say?"

"He probably won't approve at first, but he'll come around. In two years' time we can lay our plans about how we'll break it to him."

"I hope you're right. He might cut you off financially. And you can't get through Harvard Business School without his help."

"He'd never do that, believe me. He wouldn't have given you Rainmaker if he didn't like and respect you. And it just might be the biggest surprise he's ever had if he discovers we're married." There was a gleam of defiant pride in his eyes that Kerry had never seen before.

"I hope so," she said uneasily. "I wouldn't want you to be deprived because of me." She kissed him again with mixed emotions, wondering what Mark Van Buren would be like without the money to go with him. Her mind leapt frantically ahead to her glorious career, to Braemar, where there were new fields to conquer. As Randolph Hunnewell's face flashed into her mind, she weighed up her chances. It was the oldest rule of the game—don't wait for Boardwalk or Park Avenue. Buy Baltic Avenue, pass go, and collect two hundred dollars.

"Say you will, Kerry. Say yes."

"Yes, I will," she whispered.

The moment she spoke, Kerry experienced a sinking sensation. It was as if she had lost her grip on an imaginary ladder that she had been climbing all her life.

"You're really just a kid, aren't you?" he whispered gently. "You've made me the happiest man in the world, knowing you need me."

"Have I?" she said in a small voice, wondering what would happen if Mark had to pit himself against the unpredictable sleeping giant, his father.

Later, the two of them slipped unobtrusively onto the

dance floor as the party was coming to an end. Lindy, who had been dancing with Mrs. Frobisher, gazed over her platinum hair and freckled shoulders when he saw Kerry's coppery mane flash by. Snuggled up to Mark, she looked right through him. The movement of her hips beneath her dress snared Lindy's attention long enough for desire to quicken in him, the way it had that day he'd watched her riding Troika blindfolded. He reflected that he would like to feel her astride him with the same reckless abandon.

The next morning Mark was in his room packing his suitcase with a dreamy, preoccupied air. Looking out at the sun-drenched treetops, he sighed restlessly. Then his eyes fell on the pile of starched shirts on top of the mahogany highboy, his tennis and swimming gear, his blazer hanging ready to be packed alongside his dinner jacket. Only yesterday he had been picturing himself in Portofino, Rome, Paris, and Eden Roc on Cap d'Antibes. But the prospect of his first trip to Europe as a grown man had lost its luster since the night before, when he'd realized just how deeply he was in love with Kerry. He would be counting the hours until they were together again. They had more or less decided that they would slip away to Connecticut to get married before she went to Braemar. The first thing he would do in Paris would be to buy her an engagement ring at one of the jewelry shops in the Place Vendôme, near the Ritz.

Hearing the door open, Mark turned to see Carter sidle in in her dressing gown, balancing a cup of coffee.

"All ready for the Grand Tour?" she said with a note of sarcasm that irritated him.

"I guess so."

"Be sure and take a box of corn pads. You'll be standing hours in Gucci and Cartier. Mother will want to hit every boutique between London and Rome."

"I don't mind," he said noncommittally.

"You're quiet this morning. Didn't you enjoy the party last night?" Curling up in a chair, Carter gave him an appraising glance. "I ought to tell you that Cynthia was really pissed off that you brought that little mick with you last night. You were supposed to be part of the stag line."

"Don't you dare call her that," he flared, wheeling around.

"Oh, excuse me. I'm terribly sorry. Wouldn't she let you kiss her good night?"

He looked at his sister fiercely, controlling his voice with

245

an effort. "I want you to lay off while I'm away, Carter. I mean it."

"My, we are touchy," she said with a laugh. "You're so pathetic, so naive. You looked like some big, slobbering dog hanging over her when you were dancing. I suppose you seriously think she's interested in you just because you're so handsome. Do you think she'd even look at you if it weren't for all this?" She gestured. "Somebody ought to clue you in. Why do you suppose she's going to Braemar? To find a rich husband, that's why. Randolph was telling me the boys are already getting in line, because she's got a reputation for being an easy lay."

Mark lunged for Carter and clenched her arm violently, causing her to cry out in pain.

"Hey—stop that! Let go, you're hurting me."

"Good—maybe then you'll get the message. From now on, Carter, hold your tongue about Kerry, do you hear?"

"It makes me sick the way she rides Rainmaker. He was Lindy's horse. And the way she fawns over Daddy. Can't you see what she is?"

"I'm warning you." There was a contorted rage in his face that Carter had never seen before.

"You're pathetic, you really are," she spat out.

"Kerry and I are going to be married as soon as I come back," he blurted out. "So just cut it."

"What?" she shrieked. "Married? I don't believe it."

"Well, it's true. I proposed to her last night, and she accepted." He glared at his sister with hatred, instantly feeling a stab of regret at his confession when he saw the look of sly triumph in her eyes.

"Accepted? Well, I'm not surprised. Of course she's accepted."

"Don't you dare breathe a word to a soul. If you do, so help me, I'll kill you. I didn't mean to tell you. You dragged it out of me."

She slipped from the chair. "Pardon me for breathing. It's your life. Do what you want with it."

"Thanks a lot—I will," he retorted, slightly mollified, but his eyes followed her uneasily. He had never been able to trust her. She had always told on him whenever she'd had the chance.

"Remember—don't breathe a word."

"I won't," she said blithely. "Who cares, anyway?"

Sailing from the room, she slammed the bedroom door, a triumphant smile on her face.

The day that Carter knew Mark had safely embarked for Europe, she came downstairs to join Lindy for an early supper on the terrace. The following morning she was going off to Nantucket for the summer, and this would be her last chance to see her father alone before he departed for the Hamptons. She had seen Kerry only once since her conversation with Mark, riding Rainmaker, a sight that so enraged her that she had called Abigail immediately. Carter reflected that she was lucky to have such a wise, clever friend as Abigail, who coolly pointed out the far-reaching consequences of Mark's marriage to Kerry. Shock after shock had rolled over her as. Abigail outlined what it would mean in real terms. Now, seeing her father's familiar outline on the terrace bordering the floodlit garden, she felt her mouth go dry at the prospect of delivering a blatant lie under the scrutiny of his steely blue eyes.

"Hi, Daddy," she said sweetly, kissing him on the cheek, then slipping into the chair opposite him at the glass table set for dinner.

"I told Cora to serve supper right away. I'll going out as soon as we finish," he said, not looking up from the copy of *The New Yorker* in front of him.

"Oh," she replied, swallowing nervously. "That's too bad, because there's something I wanted to talk over with you."

"What is it, sweetie?" he said absently.

When Cora set the plates of crab salad and corn on the cob in front of them, Carter began.

"Daddy—I don't quite know how to say this."

"Yes?" He looked up from his plate.

"I really don't know how to begin, but there's something I've got to tell you. Mark's secretly engaged."

"Engaged? Mark? What do you mean?" Van Buren said, as if it were unthinkable. He gave a snort of laughter. "Who's he engaged to?"

She took a deep breath. "To Kerry Faloon."

"Kerry?" A dark look of skepticism crossed his face.

"It all happened at Frobishers' party. I could see her trying to make him jealous by dancing with Randolph Hunnewell. That's how it all started. Later when she came upstairs where some of us girls were combing our hair, I could see she had a look of triumph on her face. Out of the blue she started in on me. I was so shocked that I didn't know what to say—I mean, she shocked me by saying Mark had just proposed and that she had said yes, that they were going to get married as soon as he comes back from Europe. It was awful—she said she could twist him, and even you, around her little finger if she wanted." Carter paused for a sigh of distress. "She said that one day, when she was mistress here, she'd make sure I was never allowed to set foot on The Meadows." Her voice broke, and tears sprang to her eyes. She'd almost forgotten she was lying, so compelling was her story. "I didn't know what to say. Daddy, you've got to do something about it. I don't know what she has against me. I know I wasn't very nice to her at the beginning, but that was ages ago. Mark and I have never been close, but I can't stand to see her ruin him. And it's true what she said—she does have him wrapped around her little finger."

All during Carter's monologue Lindy had said nothing, but he seemed to be weighing her every word with that frighteningly impassive expression she knew so well, like a Roman general receiving bad news from a distant front.

"I confronted Mark with the whole thing the day before he left, but he wouldn't believe me when I told him what she'd said." Carter dropped her fork, an anguished expression in her eyes.

She said nothing more, and they finished their meal in silence. Finally he laid his napkin on the table and stood up. "We won't say another word about what you've just told me. I'll handle it, don't worry."

The next evening Kerry went up to the house in answer to a summons from Lindy. Walking through the garden alive with fireflies and crickets, she thought of him with mixed emotions, remembering their last encounter at the Frobisher party. So much had happened since then, particularly her promise to marry Mark, that she had conveniently pushed Lindy to the back of her mind, rationalizing that his behavior toward her that evening had been due to nothing more than too much alcohol. Sometimes, however, the memory of his strong hands around her returned with unwanted clarity, and she couldn't forget his eyes, branded with the kind of potent male desire that she had all but forgotten existed. As she approached the house her instincts told her to be careful. So much was at stake, and she couldn't afford to get on the wrong side of him. This would be the last time they would see each other, perhaps for months, and she hoped it would amount to nothing more than a polite good-bye, with good-luck wishes for her first meets of the season at Washington, D.C., and Harrisburg. She rang the bell nervously, telling herself she had more important things on her mind, like going to Braemar and shopping for her school wardrobe with the money Shannon had promised to send her, not to mention her secret wedding to Mark as soon as he returned. Glancing up at the big fanlight over the door, Kerry reflected with a private smile that her impetuous boast last year to Jack had come true. Here she was, about to reach out and grasp the brass ring that she had always known lay within her reach.

When Cora let her into the house, she walked to Lindy's study through the living room. She was unable to resist noting the changes she would make at The Meadows someday when she was mistress. She would get a decorator to advise her. The house would become the envy of everyone in The Green Spring Valley. Knocking on the heavy door, she heard Lindy's familiar gruff voice answer.

"Good evening, Mr. Van Buren." There was no trace of flirtation in her manner as she slipped into the chair across from him, but the moment she saw the pugnacious set of his jaw, she was on guard.

"I guess you'll be going off tomorrow. I want you to know that while you're away I'll be working out on Rainmaker every day. And I'm determined that school won't interfere with my riding. . . ."

He held up his hand to silence her. "I understand that you and Mark have become engaged."

There was no time to think. She blushed in surprise. "I thought Mark wanted to keep it a secret."

"I'm afraid the secret is out," he said with a cryptic glint in his eyes.

"I don't know what to say. We weren't planning to tell anyone right away," she replied, flustered.

"Why is that? In our family we usually make an engagement a big occasion."

Thrown into total confusion, Kerry desperately tried to gauge his mood. "It was Mark's idea. I couldn't really tell you why he wanted to keep it a secret. I guess that he probably thought everyone might think we were too young, no matter how much in love we were—"

249

He cut her off impatiently. "The real reason could be that Mark was afraid I might cut him off financially and stop paying his tuition and expenses at Harvard. Or perhaps even cut off his inheritance. In fact, he was quite right. That's exactly what I intend to do. The two of you better start looking for a gas station to run somewhere."

She went cold at these words, delivered in an imperious voice devoid of emotion. The giant had awakened, and his coiled wrath came down on her with all the latent power she had once feared.

"I want you out of here by the end of August. As for Rainmaker, he's going back to Ludwick next week. I don't want you on him ever again. My decision is final, as I'm sure you realize. Letting you ride him in the first place was my mistake. As for Mark, if you have anything to do with him, that's your affair. But you'd better be aware of the consequences. You'll never set foot in The Meadows again, you can be sure of that."

She jumped to her feet, tears in her eyes. "Please, Mr. Van Buren," she pleaded, "what did I do? I haven't done anything wrong."

"I don't wish to discuss the matter further. Now, get out," he said, glaring at her distastefully.

The loss of Rainmaker was so shattering that she felt a great bolt of pain shake her from head to foot. She reacted to Lindy's monstrous injustice in the only way she knew. Quivering with venomous hatred, she faced him across the wide desk.

"You bastard, you!" she spat out. "You're just eaten through with envy that your son has something you lust after yourself. I felt sorry for Mark, but he's ten times the man you'll ever be. You're nothing but a dirty old lecher."

She whirled around and ran from his office, blinded by tears.

When she had gone, Lindy stood with his fists clenched, his face red with fury. He had been so enraged at the naked truth of Kerry's sudden attack that had she stayed another moment he would have struck her violently across her provocative little face, to wipe off the sneer of contempt that had pierced his self-esteem. No one had ever challenged him with such brutal accuracy, and his anger splayed like lightning seeking to ground itself. He poured himself a whiskey and stared blackly into the night.

250

"The little bitch," he growled to himself, his voice like thunder.

Kerry broke into a run toward the stables, driven by the wild idea that she would saddle Rainmaker and ride him off into the night. But the moment she saw him lying on his side and slumbering comfortably in the hay in his box, she knew she couldn't do it. The tears she had been too proud to shed in front of Lindy now began to fall; she rushed to Rainmaker and collapsed beside him sobbing, her face buried in his flank. He whinnied and nuzzled at her face as if he sensed the depth of her misery but had no means to convey it.

Looking into his dark eyes, Kerry whispered haltingly, "Oh, Rainmaker, I wouldn't ever do anything to hurt you. My darling boy—I can't bear to be without you. Oh, God," she wailed into his velvety muzzle.

Losing him was the most devastating thing that had ever happened in a lifetime full of miseries insignificant by comparison. She alone understood every nuance of this beautiful creature. Only she knew exactly how he liked his rubdown after an event, his favorite treats. Only she knew just how to calm him when he was nervous before a show; she understood his limits and his triumphs. The idea of a stranger riding him was intolerable. He would be banished from the home he loved and sent back to Ludwick because of her. Her regret was unfathomable. She had allowed herself to be persuaded by Mark, who was weaker than she was, into an act that had resulted in her own downfall. And Lindy—she had fallen into his carefully laid snare like a rabbit into a trap. As she sobbed on Rainmaker's neck, she remembered the day Brendan had died. All Faloons seemed cursed by some strange fate that kept them from harvesting their heart's desire. Their destiny was to wander aimlessly across the earth like the remnants of some despised tribe that had broken a sacred covenant.

Exhausted from crying, Kerry finally fell asleep next to Rainmaker, lulled by his warmth, his comforting, horsey smell.

When a taxi dropped Shannon in Neuilly one day in mid-August, she walked down the tree-lined street seeking her destination. Only a brass plate on the door told her that the old-fashioned apartment house with wrought-iron balconies was the Clinique Lefevre. The sound of children playing

251

in the park nearby struck a strangely discordant note, and she couldn't keep herself from stopping to watch a game of hopscotch.

The nurse who opened the glass paneled doors might easily have been a maid admitting a visitor.

"*Entrez, madame*," she said, ushering Shannon to the reception desk. She filled in Shannon's card in the comfortable room, silent except for the tick of the clock and the scratch of the pen on paper.

"We have put you on the second floor—a quiet room with a nice view and a bath. Shall we go upstairs now?"

They took a rattling birdcage elevator, then walked along a strip of carpet. The high metal hospital bed seemed out of place in the light, spacious room with elaborate moldings on the ceiling. Her closest friend at the agency, another model, had recommended the discreet Clinique Lefevre, where Parisian society women came for abortions.

"I'll leave madame to unpack her things, and then I'll come back. You'll find a dressing gown in the cupboard. Your operation is scheduled for this afternoon."

Shannon stood motionless, staring toward the open double windows through which came sounds from the playground below. A breeze catching the net curtains seemed to hypnotize her for a moment.

She would never know what had made her change her mind, but some unnamed instinct dictated her behavior. Opening the door quietly, she looked to see that there was no one in the hallway before creeping out, suitcase in hand. She didn't wait for the noisy elevator, but descended the staircase, and when she saw the ground floor was empty, she walked to the front door and closed it behind her, feeling an involuntary shudder of relief.

All the way back home in a taxi, she stared at sidewalk cafes, shops, and tree-lined streets without a single conscious thought. At the rue Bonaparte, she climbed the steps slowly, then closed the door of her apartment firmly behind her and locked it. The first thing she did was to close the living room shutters halfway. It was going to be a scorchingly hot day in Paris, she told herself.

Her actions still dictated by an unconscious force, she picked up the telephone and dialed the agency.

"Hello, Yvonne? This is Shannon." Her voice was rational, calm. "I'm phoning to ask you to call Valentin to tell them I've decided to back out of the contract. I can't explain now, but it's for personal reasons. . . ."

Shannon hung up, Yvonne's screeches of protest ringing in her ears. Moments later, when the telephone began to ring, she didn't answer it, knowing it was bound to be the agency. When it stopped, she took the phone off the hook and placed it under a cushion. More than a week had passed since she had seen Jonquil. Zan hadn't phoned, and he was never going to. Trembling involuntarily, she stumbled to the bedroom and slid under the covers fully clothed. All she wanted was sleep, mindless sleep.

Dumping the breakfast dishes into the sink, Kerry turned her back on Jack, who rose from the kitchen table without saying a word. She was becoming used to his long, frigid silences and his monosyllabic replies to her attempts at conversation since her downfall. She reminded herself cynically that like any other employee at The Meadows, her uncle knew that his loyalties were to Lindy Van Buren, a revelation that came as no surprise to Kerry once she considered it. From now on, she reminded herself, she had only herself to rely on.

Wiping her hands on a towel, she turned to glance at the calendar on the wall featuring American thoroughbreds, knowing Jack was counting the days to her departure for Braemar as impatiently as she was. When she heard him slam the front door she rushed to the phone and anxiously dialed Shannon's number in Paris, an act she must have repeated dozens of times.. This morning her stomach churned again when she heard the rapid French on the end of the line—"n'est plus abonné"—that she now knew meant the number had been disconnected. Slamming down the phone, she buried her face in her hands.

She had frantically telephoned Shannon after her showdown with Lindy to break the terrible news about Rainmaker, and when she couldn't get through Kerry had imagined with a sinking heart that Shannon must have jetted off on an August holiday without telling her. Now, as each day passed and the check that Shannon had promised her ages ago for her initial expenses at Braemar failed to arrive, Kerry was close to panic. She had even tried calling Shannon's modeling agency in Paris and the Vogue studios, but no one seemed to know where her sister could be.

Going into her bedroom, Kerry looked at the photograph

of Shannon with Amadeo in Cannes in the People section of a May issue of *Time*. Bitterly she imagined the two of them blissfully sunning themselves on that huge yacht somewhere in the Mediterranean, without a care in the world as far as she was concerned. What was she supposed to do? Get money out of Jack? Kerry shrugged despondently. He would probably sneer and suggest she get a job mucking out a stable somewhere.

Unable to bear the claustrophobic apartment any longer, Kerry clattered down the stairs and walked toward the paddocks. For the last weeks she had been serving the remainder of her sentence like a sleepwalker, cleaning brushes, polishing saddles, exercising horses, hating every moment of it. Everyone seemed to avoid her, and everything reminded her unbearably of Rainmaker, who might have been as far away as China rather than only a few heartbreaking miles.

Leaping over the white fence, she sank into the deep rich clover, but the buzzing of insects and the warm sunshine, the rich damp smell of earth, failed to comfort her. Staring up at the sky, she considered her options. She had immediately rejected the idea of trying to get a job at another stable. She had already tasted the cream of the show-jumping world, and starting at the bottom again was unthinkable. She had come too far, climbed too high for that.

Combing her fingers through the clover, she consoled herself that at least she wasn't pregnant. Her period had been an agonizing week late after sleeping with Mark the night of the Frobisher party, and when it had finally come she had been filled with relief. She'd stopped wondering why she hadn't heard from Mark, knowing perfectly well that Lindy must have delivered an ultimatum. Like everyone else, Mark had abandoned her. Suddenly a thought crystallized in her mind. How would Lindy Van Buren like it if he thought she were pregnant? she asked herself. She calculated just how much it would be worth to him to conceal the fact that she was carrying Mark's child. Everyone would think that was why he had taken Rainmaker from her, and that he had turned his back on her because she was pregnant. Surely even the most hard-hearted members of the establishment would find Lindy's behavior incredibly callous. He would probably be relieved to pay for an abortion and to buy her silence for a sum in cash.

Sitting upright in excitement, Kerry decided she would confront him the moment he got back from the Hamptons.

She would lay all her chips on one number, and if it didn't come up, she would take a bus to California.

The following week Jack conveniently went into Glyndon one evening, and the minute he was gone Kerry went into high gear, emerging from her bedroom to look at herself in the full-length mirror of the coat closet. Tonight her looks, which she had always underplayed on horseback, would be her trump card. Her hair fell like a bolt of burnished copper around her shoulders, and she wore her most becoming dress of champagne silk with an insert of lace at the cleavage. Gold and ivory jewelry, beige kid pumps, and subtle makeup completed the look of provocative but discreet sexuality that she wanted to achieve. Tonight she was the girl who had been turning men's heads since she grew up at Koonwarra, drawing on the capital she had seldom used since she had come to The Meadows. Blowing her nails dry, she began to look forward to one last confrontation with Lindy Van Buren.

When Cora answered the door, Kerry didn't hesitate but strolled in casually, glancing around the hallway.

"Miss Kerry, what are you doin' here?" said the maid in surprise.

"I have an appointment with Mr. Van Buren."

"Why, he didn't say nothin' to me 'bout it," Cora called anxiously after her as Kerry nonchalantly crossed the huge living room.

Seeing the study door ajar, Kerry pushed it open. Looking tanned and relaxed after a month in the Hamptons, Lindy's eyebrows shot up when he saw her. He was sitting at his desk as usual, the sleeves of his blue cotton shirt rolled up.

"What are you doing here?"

She closed the door behind her and leaned against it. "There's something that you and I have to discuss."

"We have nothing to discuss," Lindy said coldly, looking at his papers.

"I'm afraid there's quite a lot to discuss." Slipping into the chair across from him, she said coolly, "I'm pregnant with Mark's child."

After a glacial pause he said, "I see. And just what do you expect me to do about it?"

"I thought you ought to be told, that's all, before everybody else finds out about it. Your sister, Lilian, for example, would be very interested to know. And when word gets around the Valley, everybody will realize why you took me off Rainmaker."

"Is this blackmail?" he said, unmoved.

"Not at all. I just thought we could talk things out in a civilized fashion before Mark gets back from Europe."

"What do you want? Just tell me—quit fishing."

"I want enough money for an abortion. It will cost at least a thousand dollars. And I want another four thousand for some other expenses."

She met his gaze unflinchingly as he considered her demands. He rose abruptly, and her heart lurched when he went to the safe in the corner and opened it. Extracting a pile of notes, he slammed the safe closed, then laid the money on the desk. She was stunned that it had all gone so smoothly and was about to reach out for the money when Lindy crossed the room and locked the door, removing the key. She whirled around, fear registering on her face when she saw he was unbuckling his belt.

In a mocking voice he said, "You want money? You can have it. But I never give anything away for nothing." Towering over her, he reached for her shoulders and pulled her up roughly. "This should come as no surprise to you, since you so accurately pointed out my true feelings the other night."

Before she could protest he scooped her up and hauled her to the leather sofa, where he deposited her roughly. In one gesture he ripped the front of her dress to the waist, exposing her breasts. She cried out as his mouth closed hard on hers in a rapacious kiss.

He hadn't meant to kiss her, but seeing her lying beneath him, her eyes wild with outrage, his anger gave way to passion. He kissed her again, this time hungrily. As she felt Lindy's voracious mouth on hers, at some confused moment Kerry's shocked resistance dissolved, and she was sucked into the whirlpool of her own involuntary response, crushing every sensation from her except desire for his savage lovemaking. She pulled him to her and thrust her tongue in his mouth. He drew away in surprise, and it was like a fist in his loins when he recognized the flush of longing that illuminated her face.

"I've wanted to fuck you ever since I first saw you," he muttered, surveying her half-exposed body beneath him.

They consumed each other with deep kisses as his hands raked over her creamy exposed flesh. Impatiently he pushed up her dress and put his hand between her thighs, eliciting a moan of pleasure from her. Her hand urgently sought his thick penis, rampant with a virility that he hadn't known for a dozen years.

"I want you, I want you," she moaned.

As she parted her legs, he fulfilled the obsession that had pursued him and hitched her forward, cupping her to him in frenzied lust. Drinking in her youth, her skin, the curve of her throat, he was maddened by her beauty. As he thrust into her she let out a cry, and welding her gasping mouth to his, he entered her fully, linking them violently together. He rode her with sharp thrusts, and she gave herself up to his forceful rhythm. Falling back, he pulled her onto him and let her buck wildly as his hands held her firm. Her eyes closed in ecstasy, she eclipsed his every fantasy as she brought him to a shattering climax, filling his mouth with her tongue, drowning him in the mane of her coppery hair. Convulsed with a jet of pleasure, he clutched her in a crushing embrace. Rocking her back and forth, he whispered obscene incoherencies, draining his desire.

For a long moment Kerry languished over him, heaving with exhaustion. When finally she moved away, her knees seemed too weak to sustain the weight of her body. She straightened her torn dress, her hair, in a trance, unable to bring herself to look at him or to speak. He lay motionless on the sofa, and the rustle of the bills as she gathered them and thrust them into her purse made him turn his face away. Words rose and died in his throat as he heard her unlock the door, and when she had gone he pulled himself up in a daze and arranged his clothes, then sank into his chair, incredulous that Kerry had coaxed forth his life's force like sap from a dwindling tree, rescuing him from perpetual winter's exile.

Kerry crept from the house unnoticed and hurried back to the apartment, where she slumped against the door in relief, like the survivor of a great cataclysm. Not allowing herself a moment to analyze her shattered emotions, she went to her room and tore off her ruined dress and underwear. Stuffing them into a bag, she threw it in the trash can, then pulled down her suitcase from the closet and began to pack feverishly. Finally she sank into bed exhausted, ready to bolt at dawn to catch the first bus to downtown Baltimore, where she could get a Greyhound bus for New York City. She thought about leaving a note for Jack telling him where to send the rest of her things, but she decided against it. When the sun came up tomorrow she would start a new life, and she wanted nothing from the past to tarnish her bright new image.

Chapter III

Paris, September

The garden of the Tuileries was nearly empty of tourists and children now that it was mid-September. Shannon walked slowly toward an empty bench facing the fountain of the Grande Ronde and sank down tiredly, wrapping her trench coat around her as she absently watched a workman sweeping the path. She looked at the chestnut trees against the overcast sky, tinged as they were with yellow, and felt the cool breeze on her face. Vaguely she registered that autumn was coming, but it didn't seem to matter.

She had completely lost track of the time after staying in her apartment for weeks, except for going shopping now and then; and this morning, in a departure from her dull routine, she was exhausted after walking around the Pont de Carrousel. Feeling nauseated, she sat on a bench, trying to gather the strength to go back home, and stared at people passing to and fro. Lately she had lost the ability to measure time, retreating further and further into a world of her own. Just getting through each day seemed a great effort.

In the beginning Shannon had been a woman bereaved at the loss of a great love, but as the weeks passed without any word from Zan, her grief turned to apathy. Always, though, she clung to the idea that he might suddenly turn up and the nightmare would end. The city of Paris seemed to have faded like a photograph left too long in the sun. Her only escape was in sleep behind the closed shutters of her apartment, and the only reality that strung the days together was the child she was expecting, which often threatened to become just another specter of her imagination.

In this cocoon of listless waiting, she had to remind herself to eat, though the smell of food made her sick even now late in the fourth month of her pregnancy. She had to force herself to get out of bed in the morning, to tidy the flat in a daze, to go up and down the impossible stairs to the *épicerie*. Recently there had been entire days when she had stayed in bed, too lethargic to move. The phone had been cut off because she hadn't paid the bill, and she'd stuffed all the mail the concierge had slid under the door into a drawer without even opening it. Now and then she'd remembered that she hadn't seen a doctor since the early days of her pregnancy, but she'd pushed it from her mind, telling herself she would eventually. Sometimes the awful thought that her mind had snapped swept over her, but she was too weak to care.

Shannon didn't bother to turn her head as a man walked briskly past the bench where she was seated. It was Fabrice, on his way from the Louvre.

"*Merde*," he cursed, glancing at his watch. He would be late for his luncheon engagement with Amadeo at the Meurice if he didn't hurry. Sporting a red-dotted bowtie that complemented his double-breasted suit of gray flannel, he looked as if he ought to be wearing spats instead of brogues, and he had the air of a gentleman carrying an imaginary walking stick. His attention was caught by the figure of a pregnant woman seated on the bench, a composition that had the dramatic quality of a Whistler. Alone, deep in thought, wrapped in a plain coat, her hair was unkempt and her face gaunt, but it seemed to Fabrice that she might once have been extraordinary looking. As she stared solemnly at her hands, Fabrice found himself wondering about the story behind her suffering. He sighed to himself, wishing that he could paint what he saw, from the curled green bench to the mottled chestnut trees, to the nanny pushing a pram near a boy chasing a ball, all of which created a timeless capsule of Parisian life.

He was just skipping up the steps leading to the Rue de Rivoli when he came to a halt and emitted a gasp that caused people to turn their heads.

"Good Lord! It couldn't have been Shannon—it couldn't have been!" Turning, he descended the stairs and quickly retraced his steps, but he could see from a distance the bench was empty.

Wiping his forehead with his handkerchief, Fabrice stared at the spot where he had seen the apparition, trying to match it with his glowing memory of the girl he hadn't seen since early summer.

Seated across from Amadeo in the paneled dining room of the Hotel Meurice, Fabrice smiled at the waiter who had just served him grouse flown in from Scotland, then glanced at his friend. All through the foie gras he had fenced with Amadeo over the price of the little Chagall of the Champs de Mars until they had reached an agreement. Now, out of the blue, Fabrice said:

"Do you know, I haven't seen Shannon for months. I must get in touch with her." He watched Amadeo's face for a clue, having no idea what had happened between them.

"The reason I mentioned it is because the strangest thing occurred on the way here. I was passing through the Tuileries when a young woman drew my attention. She was pregnant and had an aura of tragedy about her. I got rather carried away and imagined she was a young Italian war widow who had just lost her husband. She was a bit like Violetta in *La Traviata*—you know—beauty shattered by suffering. It wasn't until I was nearly here that I was aware of her striking resemblance to Shannon. I was so certain it was she that I rushed back, only to find she had vanished."

Fabrice was interrupted as a waiter wheeled a trolley of desserts past their table. "I'll never be able to resist those profiteroles," he said with a little sigh. Leaning over to inspect them, he missed the expression on Amadeo's face.

The moment Fabrice finished his grouse, Amadeo stood up abruptly. "I'm very sorry, Fabrice. I just remembered there's an important call I must make. You'll have to forgive me for leaving before you've finished. I'll settle the bill on my way out."

Fabrice stared after him in annoyance. They had been at lunch barely an hour, and looking at his watch, he remarked to himself that there was no point in making a fortune if you couldn't find the time to enjoy it. Still, he had sold the Chagall. . . . He shrugged.

Once in the lobby of the hotel, Amadeo headed for the telephones and dialed Shannon's number. The recorded message that it was disconnected sent adrenaline shooting through him. Propelled by anxiety, he rushed to the foyer to get a taxi, too impatient to wait for Miguel, who wasn't due to fetch him for another half hour.

Speeding through the Place de la Concorde, Amadeo's face was a mask of concern. From an early age he had learned never to ignore his hunches, and Fabrice's casual mention of the incident in the Tuileries sparked off an urgent premonition that Shannon needed him.

Since May he had waged a ceaseless campaign within himself to annihilate Shannon from his mind. His savage attempt at exorcism had driven him to make love to a dozen other women. He had deliberately sought Shannon's antithesis by pursuing women who bore no resemblance to her, but he was left with an emptiness that enraged him. He found himself making love to a shadow of what he remembered, an act that further wounded his self-esteem. Until now, he had begun to believe he had built an impenetrable barrier between him and Shannon, so that should they meet at a reception in Paris or at the races at Longchamps, he would be able to greet her without a trace of emotion. But imagining her alone, helpless and pregnant, stirred a deeply buried protective urge within him. His pride, his anger were nothing, and he crushed them underfoot as a stampeding bull tramples the dry pampas grass when he charges to protect his own.

Alighting from the taxi on the rue Bonaparte, he looked up at the tightly closed shutters of Shannon's apartment. Ringing the concierge's bell, he almost expected to be told Shannon was in Bali or the Seychelles.

"Mademoiselle Faloon? Elle est en haut, comme d'habitude, monsieur," said the concierge, recognizing the rich gentleman who used to call for Shannon in his chauffeur-driven car.

It seemed an ominous thing to say, Amadeo thought, racing up the stairs, that she was there—"as usual." He pounded his fist on the door several times, but there was no reply. Swiftly he descended the stairs to alert the concierge.

Grudgingly she fetched the keys, then climbed ahead of him with maddening slowness to open the door.

"Allez-y, monsieur," she mumbled irritably, turning the key.

He didn't wait but pushed his way ahead of her. "Monsieur," she called after him.

In the gray light filtering through the shutters, Amadeo could see the room was in disarray, unlike the well-ordered feminine flat he remembered. On the desk were unwashed coffee cups. Envelopes spilled from an open drawer. It was as if no one had been living in the flat for months, and the rooms were permeated with the stale odor of apathy.

"Shannon!" he called, going to the bedroom.

She was sitting on the edge of the bed, clutching her

dressing gown to her, having been roused by the pounding on the door.

"Shannon," he whispered in disbelief at what he saw. Her large, dark eyes looked at him blankly from a face of shocking pallor surrounded by a snarl of uncombed hair. Her dry lips opened, forming his name.

"Amadeo . . ."

"Shanita," he murmured, sinking down beside her. Folding his arms around her, he realized her body had wasted away in proportion to her swollen breasts and abdomen. This waif of a creature bore little resemblance to the enchanting woman with mysterious eyes who had stalked his imagination for so long, but at first recognition, all his resistance to loving her was melted by the strangest, most unexpected tenderness he had ever known.

"Why? Why didn't you tell me?" he muttered fiercely. His heart pounded as if it would burst, to think she had been too proud to come to him, that she had carried his child all these months alone, without his care. He was eaten with remorse, remembering their violent scene aboard the *Karisma* and the aftermath, when he had been completely absorbed in soothing his own feelings.

As he held her to him, Shannon began to shake with silent sobs, her tears fed by a deep well of trapped despair that miraculously rained on his own starved spirit. Pressing a gentle hand to her curving belly, he closed his eyes, unspeakably moved by the significance. His mouth went dry when he thought how much was already at risk due to neglect, but this time, unlike once so long ago, he vowed that his child would survive, even if it cost him everything he owned.

Later that afternoon Amadeo descended the stairs with Shannon in his arms, wrapped in a blanket, to his car waiting in the courtyard. The concierge stood by the open gates, gaping incredulously as Amadeo eased her onto the backseat, then leapt in beside her. When Miguel had slammed the door behind them, he said,

"We're going to Les Tourelles at once."

Night was beginning to close in on the château as Amadeo paced the floor before the fire in the library, glancing irritably at the clock that marked the long wait he was forced to endure. Hearing a tap on the door, he pivoted expectantly, but it was only the maid.

"Oh, it's you, Annette. Come in."

"I've come to draw the curtains, monsieur," she said, bustling to the window, her eyes darting with curiosity toward Amadeo.

His arrival that evening with a woman wrapped in a blanket had caused whispers to echo through the corridors of the château as the servants speculated who she could be. It was totally out of character for the exalted Monsieur Benguela to arrive in such a fashion, virtually unannounced, and the fact that he himself had carried the woman with no baggage up the stairs had caused consternation in the well-ordered Benguela household.

"Monsieur Albert has asked me to inquire how many there will be for dinner."

"I don't know," he snapped, glancing at her sharply.

"Of course, monsieur," she said, retreating before his famous temper rose.

Moments later Amadeo turned when he heard a discreet cough at the door. The doctor had come down at last.

"You've been such a long time I was becoming concerned. Is anything wrong, Doctor Fabert?"

"She will tell me very little, but it's clear she has been in a state of deep melancholy for some time."

"But she's all right?" he asked urgently.

"Yes, although she is exhausted, which in her condition is always delicate. She must stay in bed for at least a fortnight, and afterward, until the *accouchement*, she must take life very easy—plenty of rest, the right food, exercise."

"And the child? Will the child be all right?"

"The girl is four months pregnant."

"Yes, I know," said Amadeo.

"I've ascertained that the heartbeat is completely normal. She's young and will soon recover her strength. The birth should be without complications, sometime in February."

Amadeo's face was a study in relief and joy. "Forgive me—won't you have a drink with me? Whiskey, isn't it, Doctor?" Handing him a glass, he said, "To the birth of my child."

The doctor looked startled for a moment, and as their glasses clinked he said, "Congratulations, Monsieur Benguela." When he had taken a sip he added tactfully, "I suspected as much, of course, though she told me nothing." He studied

263

Amadeo, whom he had known for years. "You seem very pleased. You have no children. Isn't that correct?"

Amadeo changed the subject abruptly. "May I see her this evening?"

"Yes, but just remember—she's had a hard few months. She needs total tranquillity to recover. Don't say anything that might upset her."

The doctor regarded Amadeo, probing for an answer to the riddle, and could only conclude that the Argentinian magnate had seduced the girl, abandoned her, and had then changed his mind. Remembering his pleasure when he spoke of the birth, it was obvious that this frailly beautiful young woman had captured his heart.

"It's remarkable what tender care can achieve in the way of healing," was the doctor's parting comment.

Amadeo went to the wing of the château where Shannon had been installed, in the same room she had occupied during her first visit. At the sight of her propped up against the pillows, her hair combed softly around her shoulders, he approached with all the shyness of a young lover. There was a stillness, a serenity about her, that had escaped him until now. It was as if all her outward beauty had been pared away, revealing the spiritual loveliness within that had brought him to love her. The hollows of her cheeks, the impenetrable shadows under her eyes summoned a pure feeling within him that was like a treasure, its whereabouts forgotten until now. Pulling up a chair by the bed, he took her hand gently and kissed it.

"Thank you, Amadeo," she whispered, her eyes half-closed in sleep.

"No, it is I who owe a debt of gratitude to you. You have made me so happy."

She smiled vaguely, the meaning of his words eluding her. For now, she was content to float in this heaven of comfort and tranquillity while others made the decisions for her. Why and how she came to be here seemed unimportant as she let sweet, restful sleep overtake her.

Leaning over, he kissed her forehead, then sat for a long time absorbing every detail of the picture she made against the pillows, this waif who had been returned to him by some miracle. Once, long ago, the jaws of fate had devoured everything that had been precious to him. In the last twenty-four hours the lesson of humility that life had been so long in teaching him had taken hold. Amadeo was seized with a reverence for the totem force of destiny, as he realized how slender was the thread on which happiness hung.

"*Bonne nuit*, Shanita," he whispered, awaiting the moment when he could confess his love at last.

One afternoon in late September a black Lincoln limousine drove through the rolling suburb of Chestnut Hill outside Boston, past huge Victorian houses set among trees ablaze with autumn color. Kerry gazed indifferently through the tinted glass, as one grand house after the other flew by. During the entire drive from the train station she hadn't spoken a word to the uniformed chauffeur she had hired to pick her up.

Absently opening her Hermès handbag, she fished out her cigarette case. Lighting up, she leaned back in the deeply cushioned seat as if limousine service were an everyday feature of her existence.

The girl who had left The Meadows a month ago in blue jeans with a suitcase in her hand had altered completely. With scrupulous attention to detail, she had transformed herself into a carbon copy of all the rich girls she had ever known. Her clothes were quietly discreet and of the very best, from her white cashmere turtleneck and gray flannel skirt to the camel-hair coat flung negligently across the seat, its satin lining and designer label turned outward. She glanced at the label, recalling the day she had cut it from a coat in the changing room at Saks, to stitch it into the bargain coat she had bought at Klein's. This little inspiration had prompted her to brazenly snip labels from more clothes in the fitting rooms of Bergdorf's and Bendel's to sew in the designer clothes she had bought at discount houses when she got back to her cheap hotel on the West Side in New York City. All her accessories were the real thing, however, and had cost the earth, but looking down at her Italian boots and handbag, she knew they were worth it. She would arrive at Braemar with the best of everything, including a matching set of Vuitton luggage monogrammed with her initials. Vowing never to look poverty in the face again, she had left her sleazy hotel in New York City, pausing only to mail a letter to Shannon—a carefully composed parting sally that would leave no doubt in her sister's mind as to what she thought of her. In another much grander and more positive gesture, she had given twenty dollars to the old man who acted as porter in the hotel, asking him to mail one of the stamped addressed envelopes to her every week.

Her heart pounded furiously when the limousine passed through the high gates emblazoned with the august name of Braemar. For the last three weeks she had been rehearsing for the performance of her life, and now that it was actually about to begin, she suddenly wanted to tell the chauffeur to turn back, in a twanging Australian accent that she had so expertly replaced with a slight English intonation. If she had felt alone a month ago when she'd headed for New York from The Meadows, she felt even more so now. The sound of the hissing brakes of the Greyhound had spelled change of terrifying proportions the day she'd blotted out Jack, Rainmaker, Shannon, Mark, and Lindy for good. From now on she would be somebody else, she told herself, taking a deep breath as the chauffeur opened her door.

A number of big luxurious cars were already depositing girls and their luggage in front of the dorm, where a crowd of well-dressed mothers and fathers were gathered with girls who greeted each other with squeals of delight. The hazy autumn air was full of the buzz of a new academic year, and Kerry knew eyes were turning in her direction as the chauffeur carried her luggage into the foyer. She returned curious stares with an aloof, practiced smile before going to sign the register with a flourish as the Honorable Kerry Faloon.

Her roommate arrived, dragging her bags into the room, just as Kerry was hanging up a black evening dress. She turned to appraise the short plump girl whose face wore an earnest, happy expression.

"Hi—you must be my roommate," she said breathlessly. "I'm Betsy Belmont."

Seeing that Kerry had already chosen the best bed and desk by the window, Betsy dragged her suitcase uncomplainingly across the room. As the two of them unpacked in silence, Betsy stole a glance in Kerry's suitcase at the piles of neatly folded shirts done up with pins and monogrammed nightgowns wrapped in tissue paper, indicating that a maid had packed for her with meticulous care.

"Where are you from?" asked Betsy, unable to contain her curiosity any longer.

"I was born in Ireland, but I grew up partly in Australia," Kerry said. "I've been living with some family friends for the last three years, in Maryland. I'm an orphan," she added, embroidering her story with details she had rehearsed dozens of times, so that it would dovetail neatly in case she met anyone who remembered her from her show-jumping days. "My father was killed in a riding accident in Australia when we were on our ranch there. I went to Europe again for a while to stay with my Uncle Desmond, the Earl of Shannon. He inherited Daddy's title when he died. He's my guardian until I'm of age."

Awestruck, Betsy stared at Kerry, the living embodiment of a romantic heroine, whose life was full of glamour tinged with tragedy.

"What about you?" said Kerry politely.

"Oh, me? Well, I grew up in Philadelphia. I went to Emma Willard before I came here. I was glad I got in because my college boards weren't very good—that's why I didn't go to Europe this summer. Math and science are my downfall, and I had to study instead. It's awful, because I've got two brainy brothers, one at Princeton, one at Harvard," Betsy chirped. "It wasn't too bad, though—about Europe, I mean. I went to Maine instead, where we have a summer house."

Betsy glanced at Kerry, already on the verge of asking her to spend the holidays with her if she had nowhere to go. Seeing her new roommate hang up a superb riding habit, she exclaimed, "Oh, do you ride?"

I hunt with my uncle when I'm in Ireland, but I'm not that keen on blood sports. I did some show jumping here in the States, but unfortunately I had a rather bad fall so I'm taking it very easy for a while." Turning her cool green eyes on Betsy, she confided, "I was so nervous when I arrived this afternoon. I was the only girl who came in a chauffeured car without her parents. But now that we've met I feel so much better. I have a feeling we're going to get along very well."

Betsy felt a rush of gratitude at Kerry's friendliness. Impulsively about to drop a hint about Thanksgiving and Christmas, she was interrupted when a girl charged through the door bearing a huge bouquet of yellow roses.

"Are you the Honorable Kerry Faloon?"

"Yes, I am," she replied.

"These are you for, apparently."

"Thank you." She placed the flowers on her desk and opened the attached card that she had written herself at a florist's on the way to Braemar.

"Who are they from?" asked Betsy, consumed with curiosity.

"Uncle Desmond—wasn't it sweet of him?" Kerry injected her voice with wistfulness.

"He's your uncle—the earl? And you're called "the Honorable'?"

"Yes—that's right. In England a lord is sometimes an earl, but an earl is always a lord. It's so confusing. Daughters and sons of lords and earls are called 'honorables' or 'ladies.' "

"Where does your uncle live?"

"At Castle Shannon in Ireland. The Faloons have lived there for over nine hundred years."

"Nine hundred years?" echoed Betsy. She was bursting to know more about Kerry's intriguing Uncle Desmond and Castle Shannon, but something about the girl's manner discouraged questions, as if she were nurturing some deeply buried hurt in her past that was painful to talk about.

A month after Amadeo first carried Shannon over the threshold of Les Tourelles, she was standing at a window of the château overlooking the park enveloped in autumn mist, sipping a cup of tea and listening to Chopin as she awaited Amadeo's arrival. On the table near a comfortable chair by a blazing fire was a copy of George Eliot's *Middlemarch*, a reminder of the gentle, sustaining pleasures she had pursued without interruption that had contributed to her recovery. For the last three weeks she had been on her own at the château while Amadeo traveled extensively in the Far East and South America, but the weekends had been enlivened by Fabrice, who joined her for long walks beside the river lined with tall poplars shedding their leaves. Weekdays passed uneventfully, with exquisite meals prepared by Albert and an occasional visit by Doctor Fabert to mark the time. Shannon had begun to return to the world around her. Now, feeling her health and vitality fully restored, she told herself it was time to face reality again. She had left so many threads of her life tangled up in Paris that if she didn't start to unravel them now, she would never put things right. There was a pile of unpaid bills, her apartment to attend to, her future to think of, and Kerry as well, who would now be forced to rely on Jack. Knowing how fond he was of Kerry, she was sure Jack wouldn't mind, but nevertheless Kerry was one of the most important reasons for Shannon to stand on her feet again. Before that, however, she knew she must confront Amadeo.

Sinking into the chair by the fire, she tried to recall for the hundredth time his exact words to her the night he had brought her there. Had he actually declared she had brought him happiness? Had she dreamed that he referred to the child she carried as theirs? During the few days they'd spent together, he hadn't mentioned it again, but the uneasy suspicion had begun to creep over her that his sudden sense of obligation came from his misapprehension that she was pregnant with his child.

She was waiting for him in the entrance hall when he arrived.

"Shanita," he called when he saw her, moving swiftly toward her with open arms to fold her in a warm embrace. "It's wonderful to see you, wonderful."

He gazed down at her with a vibrant joy that was contagious, injecting her quiet existence with a vivacity that she had missed.

As tea was served in the library, Amadeo brought in a pile of gifts, which he demanded she open on the spot.

"Well, what do you think of it? Like it?" he said, unfurling an embroidered silk dressing gown from China. "Now open this one," he insisted.

She threw back her head and laughed in delight when she saw the brightly colored mittens and booties from Peru that were tiny enough for a doll.

"Go on—open the other one."

"Oh, they're beautiful," she gasped when she saw half a dozen exquisitely embroidered baby nightgowns from Brazil.

"So, you like the baby clothes?" he said, his face illuminated by a smile.

"Like them? I love them." Tears came to her eyes as she looked at him. It was the first time she comprehended the reality of the baby as a living child with hands and feet, ears and eyes.

"The stores and markets of the world are full of baby clothes. I never realized it before. I had a wonderful time picking them out," he said, reaching for another package.

"What's this?" she exclaimed, unwrapping a rattle of beaten silver set with turquoise beads.

"I got it in Colombia."

"Thank you for everything, Amadeo," she said, gathering up the brightly colored paper at her feet.

"Ah—I'm so glad to be back," he said, stretching before the fire, pushing his fingers through his hair. As he turned, his eyes met hers for an instant, but he was careful to keep his feelings in harness, content to enjoy the simple emotions

269

that were flowing between them. Slipping his hand in his pocket, he touched the small box that contained a cluster of diamonds pierced with a large Colombian emerald. Sometime that weekend he would find the right moment to present it to Shannon and ask her to be his wife.

The next afternoon they were wandering in the park. As they skirted the lake beyond the vine-covered château, blurred by mist as golden as wine, it was easy for Shannon to believe that she hadn't a care in the world. She followed Amadeo toward the herd of red deer that were regarding them inquisitively.

"Amadeo," she began, "there's something I must discuss with you. I think the time has come for me to go back to Paris. Thanks to you, I'm feeling so much stronger now, and perfectly able to cope with life. I've got to sell that house I bought in Seillans and start tidying up my affairs. . . ."

"*Cariña*—what are you saying?" He reached for her shoulders, his face full of confusion.

"You've been more than kind, and I thank you from the bottom of my heart, but I can manage on my own, really I can."

"What you are really too polite to say, Shannon, is that you still can't forgive me. I was wrong not to bring it up before now and I apologize. The truth is, I've been tormented by my behavior to you that night aboard the *Karisma*."

She regarded him with shock. "Is that what you think? Oh, no, Amadeo, I can't let you believe that. I've forgotten all about it. So much has happened since then, it doesn't seem to matter anymore."

"But it does matter. It matters a great deal to me. If it's not that, then what is it?" A storm of protest broke in his eyes as he sensed everything that he wanted slipping away from him. The declaration of love that had been building died on his lips. "What about our child, then, *cariña*? Surely you must know that I want to care for you. It's my right as a father, whatever you may feel about me."

She closed her eyes in horror. What she had suspected was true. "Amadeo—the baby isn't yours." All the emotion in his eyes was extinguished as she went on. "The father is someone I've known ever since Australia. We spent a week together in Nice after I left you. I've never told you about him before as I thought I would never see him again, but then we met by chance. I suppose I still love him in spite of everything that has happened. And so you see," she continued as they walked, "it wouldn't be right. I can't accept your generosity any longer."

Acid gnawed at Amadeo's guts as he listened to her sweet, soft voice. His hurt boiled over to a violent jealousy that threatened to choke the life from him. Finally he spoke, his voice full of condemnation.

"Where is this man now? Why isn't he looking after you?"

"He's married, Amadeo. I didn't even tell him I was pregnant."

"Why haven't you told him?" he retorted furiously. "You mean to say that he wouldn't want you if he knew? Shannon—don't be a fool to love such a man."

"No—you don't understand at all," she protested. "I still believe and hope that one day we will be together. But at the moment it's impossible."

"Where does he live?" he demanded.

She sighed. "In England. He's English."

He gave a contemptuous laugh. "I might have known. What is he, a poet? Or some sort of artist with his head in the clouds? Why do you protect him?"

"Amadeo, you must never speak of him like that—never. I've told you how I feel, and I'll never change my mind."

"All right," he said, throwing up his hands. A bitter envy washed over him at such fierce loyalty that he himself could not command. Hope was an emotion he had always despised, but he suddenly found himself its victim. His voice gruff with feeling, he said, "In that case, I will take no argument. You will stay here with me, under my protection, until your child is born. It's settled."

She thought it over for a moment, feeling stranded by her own pride. It hurt to admit that she had canceled her modeling contract of her own accord when she had refused to do so for Amadeo's sake, and that now she was accepting his charity.

"I really do want to stay," she said quietly. "I don't know how to thank you. It will be lovely to remain here until the baby is born." She was unaware that he was crushing the little box in his pocket, which now seemed to weigh like lead.

Chapter IV

Braemar, Boston, Massachusetts, October

Darkness had already begun to fall one late October evening as Kerry stared out her dormitory window. Sitting at her desk in her robe, she shifted restlessly, trying to keep her mind on the Romantic poets. When Betsy bit noisily into an apple behind her, she said irritably without looking up from her notes, "Would you mind terribly not making so much noise? I'm trying to concentrate."

"I'm sorry," Betsy replied guiltily, quietly turning a page of her book in order not to aggravate Kerry, who had been moody and depressed all week. "Listen—don't worry about Randolph Hunnewell. He'll call," she said sympathetically.

"Randolph? Oh, I don't care," Kerry replied distractedly.

Randolph, whom she had fought off in the backseat of his car three weeks ago, was the furthest thing from her mind.

"The Lady of Shalott" was forgotten as she stared at the dark window, her mind obsessed with money.

Time had galloped by with appalling speed since school had started. Already she had received the bursar's note that next term's tuition, room, and board would soon be due. She had been so anxious to get to Braemar that she had deceived herself into thinking that once she was installed at the college, she would find a way to continue or, if not, at least find a husband. It was a notion that now seemed terribly naive. What she hadn't realized was that countless girls' colleges revolved around Harvard and MIT like constellations, and that they were full of rich, well-connected coeds whose ambition was to capture a husband in law, medicine, or business. At open houses given by the prestigious Porcellian and A.D. clubs at Harvard, Kerry had been astonished at the fierce competition from Radcliffe and Wellesley girls, who looked down on Braemar as a school for dumbbells. With such disadvantages, she could only hope to storm the walls with money to keep up her image, but the sum that had seemed so huge when she'd gotten it from Lindy was almost gone, and there seemed no hope of ever getting any more.

Kerry sighed and rubbed her eyes. She was tired—tired of living a lie, of keeping watch over every detail of her own behavior, of being the Honorable Kerry Faloon. The bright crest of ambition that had brought her to Braemar had turned to fool's gold. Lately, when everyone else lay sleeping in the dorm, she found herself paralyzed with terror at the moving ice floe beneath her. She had begun to regret writing that scathing letter to Shannon, but her pride wouldn't let her go down on her knees; and after what she had said she doubted if it would do any good. Even Shannon had her pride, and the fact that she hadn't replied told Kerry her sister was glad to be rid of her. Money, she concluded, was the only thing in the world that would guarantee her the purring contentment of security, and without it she may as well take that bus to California while she still had the fare. Releasing her hair from a ponytail, she let it fall in a cascade down her back.

Betsy stared enviously at Kerry's shimmering copper mane. "God, I'd give anything to have hair like yours."

"Anything? Would you really? Well, you can have it."

"It's not fair, you know," Betsy said with a sigh, picking up the apple. "You have everything to go with it, too. Face, figure, and personality, and even a title."

Kerry said nothing but felt her irritation rising at Betsy's slavish devotion. Just then the door opened.

"Hey, you two. Want to make up a foursome at bridge?"

"Sure, why not?" replied Kerry, relieved to be distracted by Alison who roomed down the hall.

"Any excuse to give up French grammar," agreed Betsy.

"Who's for pizza?" asked Alison.

"I'm on a diet," said Kerry. Playing bridge meant that she would have to give up dinner in the cafeteria, and pizza was an extravagance she would have to do without.

Later, seated on the bed in the room next door, her feet tucked beneath her, Kerry tried to ignore the appetizing aroma of pizza as Alison's roommate, Stephanie, opened the box. Smoke from four cigarettes curled through a tole lamp toward the collection of Braque and Picasso posters stuck on the walls along with pictures of John Travolta and Robert de Niro.

Kerry hardly heard the vapid conversation about the upcoming Harvard-Yale game, the color of nail polish and wonder diets. Reaching out for her cards, she looked critically at Stephanie and Alison, who had baby pillows and teddy bears on their beds, proving their veneer of sophistication was only skin deep. There was a smugness about their attitude to life—acquired, no doubt, from sucking on a silver spoon. The harrowing problems of real life had never cast a frown on their smooth foreheads.

"Spades are trumps," announced Betsy.

Kerry glanced at her cards distractedly, trying to concentrate, but watching the three of them consume huge chunks of steaming pizza made her dizzy with hunger.

"I don't know why you're watching your weight, Kerry," said Stephanie. "You're the thinnest one here."

"Remember anorexia nervosa," remarked Alison.

"Come on, Kerry. Have some of mine. I don't want it all," said Besty.

"No thanks," she replied, shaking her head.

"You'll never guess what I heard last night," said Alison breathlessly, causing them all to look up.

"What?" begged Betsy.

"Well, you know the Statler Hotel. They have all those conventions from out of town. I heard from a very reliable source that there's a ring of girls from Maple Hill who are providing exclusive room service for some of the male guests." She paused to let her meaning sink in.

"Room service? You mean they're working as waitresses?" said Betsy.

"For God's sake," shrieked Stephanie. "Room service— what do you think they're doing, dummy?"

"They're call girls," said Alison. "Isn't that unbelievable?"

"I can just see them wheeling in a trolley with a domed platter—tah-dah. They take off the lid, and there's a blonde from Maple Hill covered in parsley."

They all laughed uproariously, even Kerry.

"I'm sorry, but I find it impossible to believe," she said. "I mean, why would a girl from a school like Maple Hill do a thing like that?"

"Because they're all sluts, that's why. Not pure as the driven snow like we are," said Stephanie.

"What do you suppose the men are like?" Kerry speculated, glancing at her cards. "I pass."

"I guess some of them aren't bad. Guys with kids who are let out of their cages for one weekend a year. But even so. . ."

"Ugh—I can't imagine doing it with someone for money, can you?" said Betsy. "It makes it so *dirty*."

"Oh, I don't know. If the price is right," said Alison with

274

a toss of her head. "But I think I'm worth at least five hundred dollars."

"Oh, yeah? You're really a knockout in those curlers," said Stephanie, causing more giggles. "Personally, I think I'm worth at least eight hundred. You know what they say— gentlemen prefer blondes, and I'm the real thing."

"What about you, Kerry? What do you think you're worth with your figure, and red hair—and a title. Wow!"

"Me? Oh, I'm the thousand-dollar blue plate special. They'd roll me in with pastry dabbed on in all the right places, like *filet mignon en croute*," she said with cool sarcasm that made them roar with amusement.

The following Saturday Kerry waited until Betsy had gone to the library to study before taking a leisurely bath and applying her makeup with elaborate care. From her wardrobe she chose her most sophisticated dress, a black jersey wraparound with a plunging neckline, which she had bought in New York, imagining herself in it having dinner in Boston with Randolph Hunnewell. She was struck by the irony that the first time she wore it would be for a man who was willing to pay for the body underneath. Splashing perfume generously at her wrists and neck, she clipped on a pair of rhinestone and pearl earrings, then grabbed her mohair coat, ready to go downstairs to meet the taxi she had ordered for six-thirty. She was about to leave the room when Betsy charged in unexpectedly.

"You look gorgeous," she gasped. "Randolph called, didn't he? Why didn't you tell me?" she gushed in a torrent of vicarious excitement. "He'll be bowled over when he sees you. Where are you going?"

Kerry's eyes strayed to her desk and the stack of cream envelopes conspicuously tied with a blue ribbon, addressed to The Honorable Kerry Faloon. The porter in New York had kept his promise to mail one every week, and she had explained the postmark by saying they had been sent by courier from Ireland to her uncle's office in New York. "No, it's not Randolph. Uncle Desmond called from Boston just now and asked me to come for dinner. He's in town just for tonight."

"Oh," said Betsy, deflated. "That sounds like fun. Have a good time."

Alighting from the taxi at the Statler Hotel, Kerry entered the lobby and headed straight for an empty chair in a

275

corner, where she coolly crossed her legs and lit up a cigarette. Glancing at her watch, she pretended to comb passersby for someone she knew. Tonight she would go home richer, if rumors were true. She had decided that two hundred was a good figure when it popped into her head. Two hundred—it had a nice ring to it and didn't seem wildly expensive. Her heart pounding, her mouth dry as paper, she wondered how to let a man know she was for sale. None of them passing by gave her more than an admiring appraisal, and as she dragged languidly on the cigarette, she avoided their eyes. Surveying the lobby, Kerry could see no one who might be a girl from Maple Hill, a discovery that brought on a wave of misgiving.

After she had waited nearly half an hour, her nerves in shreds, she was alarmed to notice two clerks at the reception desk looking in her direction, but she told herself she was only imagining things. She was on the verge of bolting when, glancing at the carpet, she saw a pair of shiny brown shoes in front of her. There before her stood a balding man in his forties with a thin mustache and glasses. He might have passed by a dozen times, but she wouldn't have remembered him, he was so nondescript.

Moistening his lips nervously, he said, "Hi—can I buy you a drink?"

"Maybe," she said, trying to appear cool. "The bar here is a bit depressing."

"What about coming up to my room, then?" he ventured.

"Sure—why not?" she said abruptly. Nervously she stood and scooped up her bag and coat, then followed him to the elevator, her heart pounding as if it would burst. When the door closed behind them he gave her a tight little smile.

"What's your name?"

"Sandra." She stared straight ahead, dreading the moment when they would reach his floor.

"My name's Art Shanklin. I'm from Racine. This way—I'm in room six ten," he said casually when the doors had opened. She followed him down the long, carpeted hallway, which seemed to grow darker with every step.

"After you," he said, flinging open the door of his room.

He strode in and turned on the lights, then loosened his tie and took off his jacket as Kerry numbly surveyed the room.

"Is a hundred bucks okay with you? I know you girls like to settle everything in advance. You know, for a few minutes

276

I wasn't sure if you were on the game. I mean, you would have made one hell of a scene if I had been mistaken," he said, injecting a note of humor that she didn't appreciate.

In a cold voice that didn't seem to belong to her, she said, "I usually get two hundred. If you're not interested, I'll go back downstairs," she said, turning.

"Two hundred? That's pretty steep, even for Boston. Are you worth it, Sandy?" A leer stole across his face as his eyes traveled over her.

Kerry felt a wave of nausea. All she could do was to stare at him with forced indifference. Her heart seemed to stop when she saw he was unbuttoning his shirt.

"The silent type, are you? Okay, it's a deal if you stay all night. I like them cool and sophisticated, anyway. For the extra hundred I'll just lie back and enjoy myself." taking off his cufflinks, he tossed them on the dresser.

"What about a bourbon on the rocks, Sandy? I like to take things nice and easy. Put your coat over there and I'll fix us a drink." He went to the little refrigerator and mixed them a drink.

"*Campai*," he said, clinking his plastic cup to hers. "That's Japanese for bottoms up."

He turned on the television, and Kerry pretended to check her makeup in the mirror. The room behind her seemed to darken like a theater, and her own face stared back at her as if in a spotlight. The dialogue from the television seemed to come from a faraway room.

"Excuse me, honey. I'm just going to the john. Make yourself comfortable, won't you?" He brushed her bottom suggestively as he passed by. When he had gone she felt a shudder of disgust. She stood helplessly imprisoned in her own terror until the sound of him urinating in the toilet broke through the thin membrane of her subconscious. There was something intolerably intimate about the sound that sent a current of repulsion through her, and grabbing her coat and purse, she was out the door in an instant, flying down the hallway past the elevators to the stairs.

Her knees nearly gave way in relief when she caught a taxi at the floodlit entrance to the Statler, looking over her shoulder for Art Shanklin.

"Some hooker you make," she whispered to herself as the taxi sped down Newbury Street in central Boston. Why had she lost her nerve? Why couldn't she go through with it? Next time she would go into the bar and have a stiff drink

277

first. But the thought of offering herself to another Art Shanklin, even for a thousand dollars, made her skin crawl. She had done it before, she reminded herself. Why not now? What was the difference between making love with Lindy Van Buren for five thousand dollars and with a stranger for two hundred? The barrier she had constructed between herself and the past gave way to tendrils of sensual memory that wound around her, summoning forth the raw lust of her encounter with Lindy. She had ruthlessly exiled him from her consciousness ever since that encounter in his library, recognizing that he had mined a vein of desire over which she had no control. The awesome power of such shameless, abandoned lovemaking, experienced for the first time that night, came back to haunt her with unexpected force.

One night the following week, when Betsy had gone down the hall to play bridge, Kerry turned from her desk, where she had been pretending to study, her eyes falling on Betsy's handbag on the bed. It was the end of the month, and Kerry knew Betsy had been to the bank that day to draw her monthly allowance. Rising from her chair with a pounding heart, she picked up the purse and took out the wallet. It was packed with crisp notes. Betsy would never miss a twenty or two right away, Kerry told herself, and by the time it was discovered she would be far away. In the split second she was making up her mind how much to take, she heard footsteps outside the door. In a panic she threw the bag on the bed, grabbed a brush, and darted to the mirror.

"Kerry, you're wanted on the phone," said Alison.

"Who is it?" she asked, turning with a blank expression on her face.

"I don't know. Margo took it. I think it's a man."

Kerry walked down the hall, thinking that if it was someone asking her for a date, they would have to drive across country to pick her up, because she would soon be in California.

"Hello," she said flatly.

"Hello, Kerry This is Lindy Van Buren."

The sound of his low voice struck her dumb for an instant.

"Kerry? Are you there?"

"Yes—I'm here. What is it?" A strange cocktail of emotions coursed through her, leaving her weak and afraid, and at the same time exultant.

"I'm in Boston for a couple of days, staying at the Ritz. I was wondering if you're free tonight."

"Free? Yes, why?" Suspicion crept into her voice.

"I thought maybe you'd like to come in and have dinner with me. I'll send a car for you. Seven-thirty all right?"

All her poise suddenly rushed back as she replied coolly, "I think that will be all right."

"Good. Come up to my room first. We'll have a drink. I'll see you then."

She hung up, the unmistakable catch of desire in Lindy's voice exploding like a gun in her ear.

"Well, I'll be damned," she murmured to herself.

Later that evening Kerry was speeding into Boston in the backseat of a luxurious limousine similar to the one that had brought her to Braemar. Pulling her mohair coat around her, she recalled with pleasure the amazed expression on the faces of her friends when the chauffeur had come to fetch her. Betsy had instantly carried the news to every corner of the dorm that the Earl of Shannon had arrived in Boston and had sent for his niece in style.

As the lights of outer Boston flew by, a bolt of anticipation released itself inside Kerry. Lindy hadn't been able to get her out of his mind, and for a few seconds she allowed herself to admit that he exercised the same magnetic power over her. But hatred still ruled a part of her that Lindy would never conquer, born the night she had lost Rainmaker. No savage lust could erase the pain she felt whenever she saw a Braemar girl canter by on the sandy bridle paths that crisscrossed the campus, or whenever she knew the college equestrian team had departed for an event somewhere in Pennsylvania, Washington, or Rhode Island. If she happened to catch sight of a girl in a black velvet riding hat, a hacking jacket, and jodhpurs, she was consumed with bitterness; and one day when she had seen a display of the Braemar equestrian team's blue ribbons and trophies, she'd felt as if she were viewing her own stolen goods, brazenly displayed to taunt her. Now she made up her mind Lindy wasn't going to have her just for the asking, this time or any other, and she considered how to make him pay the debt he owed her.

She'd even had the wild idea of demanding Rainmaker back, but she had read in the sports section of the *Boston Globe* that The Meadows had sold him to Ludwick. The news shattered her heart all over again. But it was just like Lindy.

In his cruel, vindictive way he had made sure she would never ride Rainmaker again—just as he had promised.

When the limousine pulled up in front of the Ritz on Boston Common, a smart uniformed doorman dashed to open the car door for her, then ushered her toward the revolving door. She couldn't help but contrast this cermonious reception with her furtive arrival at the Statler only a few evenings before. The lobby of the Ritz glittered like a jewel box, its chandeliers casting a rich golden light into mirrors that reflected lavish bouquets of flowers and women passing by in sable and mink. The very air was perfumed with luxury.

Kerry held her head high as she sauntered confidently to the reception counter, where she said in a well modulated voice:

"My name is Kerry Faloon. Mr. Lindy Van Buren is expecting me."

"Yes, Miss Faloon—I'll announce your arrival. He's in suite five seventy-three."

As she crossed the lobby, Kerry was aware of admiring glances cast in her direction. She knew she had never looked more stunning, although she was wearing the same black dress, the same coat she had worn to the Statler. But tonight the image she projected was one of refined elegance rather than brittle seduction. Hungrily, she took in every detail of this old-fashioned luxurious hotel patronized by the cream of the Boston establishment, feeling that this was where she belonged.

When she knocked at the door of Lindy's suite, she brushed her hand through her hair, trying to ward off the nervousness that beat like wings in the hollow of her throat. When he opened the door, she strolled past him. Throwing her bag on a chair, she took off her gloves and swung 'round to look at him with a challenging little smile.

"Well, well. What brings you to Boston?" Slipping off her coat, she dropped it on a chair like a heroine in the movies.

Not waiting for him to answer, she walked around the room pretending to examine the details, aware his eyes were following her every move. As she touched the mantelpiece above the blazing fire, she saw in the mirror that he was approaching her. Feeling his hand on her shoulder, she removed it delicately and turned to him in mock surprise.

He acknowledged her theatrical coyness with an amused smile.

"Would you like a drink? I'm having a whiskey, but I thought you might like some champagne," he said, nodding toward the bottle cradled in a bucket.

"Thank you—that would be lovely."

She watched intently the movement of his shoulders beneath his jacket as he worked the cork free. Handing her a glass, he said:

"I'm glad you could come, Kerry."

As she sipped the champagne, she perceived a mixture of curiosity, respect, and desire in his face that even his iron will couldn't crush, a realization that aroused a shiver of triumph at her own power. For a moment the urge to toy with his raw need for her slackened as she felt desire take hold, a change in mood that wasn't lost on Lindy. Taking her glass from her hand, he pulled her to him and kissed her impatiently. As they embraced her whole body was convulsed with a need that she struggled to keep at bay for just a moment longer.

"What's the matter?" he said gruffly when she pulled away. "Don't pretend you don't want me. We've been through all that." He gazed down hungrily at her face, flushed with a woman's arousal, the same look that had often disturbed his sleep at night.

"You might be right," she said, freeing herself from his arms. "But last time you seemed quite happy to pay for it."

"So that's the way it is, is it?" He gave an ironic little laugh, then took a gulp of whiskey. "In fact, you didn't give me time. I was going to suggest that we come to some sort of arrangement. I wouldn't want it any other way. How does five hundred dollars sound to you, every time I see you?"

All her quivering defiance evaporated. "That would be all right," she murmured.

"I usually get to Boston about every six weeks. Sometimes more often. What do you say?"

"Agreed," she replied, quickly calculating that she could just manage to survive the rest of the year if he meant what he said. She would have to make sure she was good enough for him to want to come back more often, and as her hunger for him moved her, she sensed that that wouldn't be difficult. It added hugely to her pleasure to think that Lindy was paying for her.

"Now, let's get down to what we're here for," he murmured, following the line of her chin to her throat, her breasts.

281

The time before he had been in a rush to conquer her, driven by an angry sort of lust; but this time he allowed himself the tantalizing prospect of her slow surrender. At first touch passion ripped through him, driven by the winds of memory. He removed her dress, her slip, revealing her nakedness slowly, like the petals protecting the heart of a flower. She stood proudly before him, glorying in the appreciation in his eyes, as he moved his hands over every finely carved inch of her body, the color of rich cream. His lips started at her shoulders, dropped to her breasts, then he tasted the hollows of her belly. When he parted her legs with impatient hands and nudged his tongue against her sex, a current shot through her, and she arched in a bow of utter abandon. With impatient hands she reached to unbuckle his belt. Her hands stroked his swollen stem with a coaxing lasciviousness that ignited an explosive impatience within him. Drawing her up powerfully, he hitched her to him. She clasped her legs around him with possessive urgency as he carried her to the bed, where he unfurled her away from him like a bolt of pale satin shot with gold.

"God, I've wanted nothing but you since that day in the library, you gorgeous little bitch. Kerry, Kerry," he moaned.

Hearing her name chanted with such fervor opened gate after gate in her subconscious. His handsome, rugged face was suffused with an untamed desire that churned up a rhythmic movement of her being. Feeling her perfect young body move with pleasure beneath him, hearing her cries, Lindy gorged on a golden cornucopia of pleasure more intense than anything he had ever known. She tossed rapturously, meeting him to the hilt as she emitted cries of release that carried with it all her ecstasy, all her need, in the shimmering dome of their erotic union.

"Lindy, oh, Lindy," she begged half-consciously as he brought her to yet another peak of exquisite pleasure. As her yearning retreated he began again, propelled by the energy she had engendered in him, then impaled her with a final thrust that seemed to rise from the depths of his being.

For a long time he lay beside her, his flesh welded to hers, feeling all the redoubled strength of a wave that had the power of the sea at its beck and call. He kissed the source, her soft, giving mouth, drinking with it the youth that had coaxed his root to life again.

His head buried in the curve of her shoulder, he whispered, "What have you done to me, Kerry? . . ."

She, too, had felt the force of the emotions that had rocked their lives apart for the last moments, and she moved toward him in a supple gesture of total surrender.

Chapter V

Les Tourelles, France, December

One afternoon in early December Shannon sat at a satinwood escritoire in a corner of the château library, watching the deer wandering in the snow-covered park as night closed in beyond the forest. Casually dressed in an Egyptian caftan of dove-gray wool, her hair twirled into a chignon, she felt a welcome sense of coziness, heightened by the crackling of the fire. Sorting through the pile of mail Amadeo had brought with him from her apartment, she turned to glance at him. Even though he had just returned from an exhausting trip to Brazil and Colombia, he was busily at work, catching up on correspondence he could never seem to escape.

"Do you know, some of these letters you brought were posted way back in July. I must have been in a very weak state of mind to shove them away in a drawer, thinking they'd take care of themselves."

"Don't worry about those in the envelope, Shanita—those are only bills that I've had Delphine take care of," he remarked.

She cast a thoughtful look at him. "Just the same, I'll keep a careful record of what I owe you. I will pay you back someday, you know, every penny."

"Of course. But for the moment, what does it matter?"

As she concentrated, she was unaware that Amadeo was studying her. The nape of her bowed neck was a perfect curve that sloped to the line of her shoulders and the tracery of her full breasts above the swell of her abdomen. Every time Amadeo's eyes fell on the evidence of her womanly fullness, his possessive instincts rebelled against the truth. Even now, after all these weeks of living with the knowledge that Shannon was pregnant with another man's child, his Latin heritage compelled him to prove the paternity his own.

With a new patience that he was learning to exercise one day at a time, he kept his thoughts to himself, sensing how many wounds had to heal within Shannon before she could want him again. For the time being he avoided any intimate gestures that might give him away, contenting himself with her presence in the room, her laughter, her smiles. But he knew she had come to depend on him far more than she realized.

"Is this all the mail there was?" Shannon asked casually when she had sorted through the pile. She had noted with dull disappointment that there was nothing from England.

"Everything is there." He suppressed the annoyance he felt, knowing she was still expecting a letter from her lover in England. He had already checked the letters himself. If there had been a letter, he wondered, would he have given it to her?

He glanced up sharply when Shannon cried out.

"What is it? What's wrong?" he said, rising in alarm.

"It's just the baby. She never seems to sleep." She gazed down at her abdomen, which she had cupped with her hand. "Look—there she goes again, kicking up a storm."

"She?" he teased, raising an eyebrow. "I'm sure it's going to be a boy. The kicking—that's a sign."

"Nonsense—it's going to be a girl. Obviously she's going to be a great dancer. She's practicing already."

He leaned toward her with a mischievous smile. "On the contrary. *He* will be a great polo player—for my team, the Vaqueros. Can't you see he is trying out his stroke?"

Laughing, they shared what had become a private joke between them. Glancing up at Amadeo's strong face, softened now by a wide smile, Shannon felt tempted to say just how much she had missed him all these weeks. Her illness and pregnancy had brought out a side of him she had never suspected—a tender, gentle, and touching aspect of his nature that he had concealed until now.

Shannon returned to her letters, taking the one from Kerry first. The time had come to tell Kerry that she couldn't hope to meet the expenses of a college education under the circumstances. Shannon half hoped Jack would offer to pay Kerry's way until she had sold the house in Seillans; but that could take time, and she wanted him to offer without being asked. Now, as Shannon scanned Kerry's letter, full of terse, angry outpourings, her face flushed with shock.

"What is it?" said Amadeo, hearing her shift restlessly.

"It's a letter from Kerry. I can't believe what she's saying—my own sister."

"Here—let me see it," he said, taking it from her.

"I've been such a fool. I assumed that Jack would be taking care of everything, at least until I was able. I feel so guilty. So much time has slipped by, and I've done nothing. I've been so absorbed in my own problems. Apparently, Lindy Van Buren took her off Rainmaker. And she was desperate for money to start school. But to lash out like this . . ."

Amadeo's face contorted with anger as he read the letter, until at last he exploded. "What kind of language is this to use to a sister, I ask you, Shanita? She calls you a bitch," he fumed, waving the letter. "And me—she calls me a gigolo. The girl needs to be horsewhipped. Who does this child think she is anyway?"

Shannon sighed. "I owe her an explanation, at least, I suppose. I paid her first term's tuition plus room and board, but she needed money for clothes, books, and lots of things."

"You owe her nothing," he said emphatically, pounding his fist on the desk. "You are her older sister and you are the one with problems. Is she concerned about you? No—she selfishly assumes that you are amusing yourself. If she needed money, why didn't she get a job? Did you complain when you had no money? No—you went out and got a job modeling for Sutherland in his freezing cold studio." He gave an impatient growl. "I have no pity for people who think the world owes them a living. I never asked anybody for anything," he said, stabbing the letter with an accusing finger. The more he thought about it, the angrier he became. "Can you imagine how spoiled she would be if you had fulfilled your contract? Then you could have bought her a villa and a racehorse."

"No, Amadeo. You don't understand Kerry. She's not really like that, deep down inside. I can't believe she means what she wrote. She's enormously talented and has worked so hard. The poor kid—everything seems to have fallen in on her at once." Loyalty had made her rally to Kerry's defense in front of Amadeo, but inwardly she was still smarting from the language in her sister's letter. What was the truth behind Lindy Van Buren's high-handed behavior, and why hadn't Jack come to Kerry's aid?

Seeing Shannon's distress, Amadeo's manner softened.

"I suppose she is your sister," he said reluctantly. "Let me arrange to send her some money."

"That's generous of you, Amadeo. But she's very proud. She's just like my father in that way."

"We'll see if she's so proud," he remarked skeptically.

"I'd rather help her in a way that salvages her pride. She doesn't want charity, really. And by the tone of this letter she never wants to see me again. To her, my life seems impossibly glamorous, I suppose. I seem to be the one who had all the breaks. In a way, the money will just cause more bitterness between us," she said doubtfully.

"Well, something must be done at once, if only to set your mind at rest. I'll pay her fees, give her some sort of allowance anonymously. That way, she won't know whether the bitch or her gigolo is responsible—both of whom she hates so much!"

Betsy charged through the door, her coat and hair glistening with melting snowflakes.

"Kerry—you wouldn't believe it. We're supposed to be snowed in. Logan Airport is already closed, and the road to Boston is blocked." Shaking the snow from her hair, she hung her coat by the radiator.

Kerry rose from her desk and stared stoically into the blizzard beyond the window.

"Oh, no," said Betsy. "Your Uncle Desmond—he won't be able to make it, will he? You never know. Maybe it will lift," she said, trying to be hopeful. "I'm so sorry, Kerry. I know how much you've been looking forward to having a birthday celebration in town with him."

"I'm going out for a walk," said Kerry abruptly, grabbing her coat. She couldn't bear even to look at Betsy for fear of bursting into tears.

Kerry rushed out into the storm, trudging through the drifting snow that had already buried the benches under the trees and obscured the road. The tears that ran down her cheeks froze in the biting wind as she gave way to the misery bottled up inside her. Everything in her life depended on Lindy's visit that night. He had had no idea it was her birthday when he'd called earlier in the week to say he would be spending the night at the Ritz, and she had taken it as a good omen. This would have made his third visit—three times lucky, totaling fifteen hundred dollars. He had been in a very mellow mood the last time, and now, so close to

Christmas, she was counting on his generosity. By the time he came again it would probably be January, and then it would be too late. The bursar had already told her that she would have to settle her account by the holidays or drop out of school. She had refused Betsy's invitation to join the Belmonts in Sugar Bush, with the excuse that her uncle expected her at Castle Shannon for Christmas, and now she began to compose the letter she would send Betsy, announcing her whirlwind romance and engagement to Lord Desborough, her childhood sweetheart. She tried to console herself that her sudden marriage to a peer of the realm would be a glorious and blazing retreat from all the sordid realities of Braemar, and nobody would ever be the wiser.

After a long walk on the snowbound campus, Kerry returned to the dormitory, half-frozen and still unable to shake her feeling of desolation.

"So long, Honorable Kerry Faloon," she whispered to herself, close to tears as she saw a pink slip of paper with her name on it wedged in above her mail slot.

Her heart sank when she saw it was a message from the bursar, requesting her to come to his office immediately. But though it came as no shock that the guillotine was finally about to fall, it astonished her to find an envelope bearing a Paris postmark inside her mail chute. A balloon of hope rose and fell when she saw it was a birthday card from Shannon, with a short, scrawled message. Typical Shannon, she thought sourly. This was her idea of an olive branch—written months after receiving her own angry letter, and with no reference to Kerry's troubles. Tossing it into the rubbish basket, Kerry put Shannon out of her mind and marched back out the dorm to the administration building.

When the bursar's secretary announced her arrival, she breezed in, half inclined to tell the truth. One glance at his long New England countenance and coldly pompous expression gave her a devilish urge to spill the whole shocking story. It would wipe that smug, critical expression off his face when she revealed that she would have to default on her tuition because her john didn't show up for his fuck that weekend, due to inclement weather. She would like to ram it down his establishment throat that the roll of bills tucked away in a shoebox in her closet had been earned by offering her body to a horny old goat who was a pillar of respectability himself, and end with the titillating news that her whole

287

façade was a sham. She was nothing but a stray dingo from the Australian Outback, who had fooled all of them.

"Ah, Kerry, there you are. I asked you to come over right away because I thought you'd like to know that everything has been taken care of."

She stared at the bursar blankly.

"The order came this morning from Manufacturers Hanover Trust in New York, covering your tuition and board and room, plus instructions for you to draw five hundred dollars every month through this office. I imagine you've already heard from your uncle, however."

"My uncle?" she said, aghast.

"I assume your uncle made the arrangement."

"Yes, of course," she said hurriedly.

"There is a further instruction to the effect that future tuition and expenses will be met in the same manner. I'm glad everything is in order now, and that your uncle has seen to it that you will have no more worries in this regard."

"Yes, so am I," she replied with a startled smile, noting the sudden warmth in the bursar's manner. He saw her out the door with jolly remarks about the blizzard and hopes for a white Christmas.

Kerry rushed into the snowstorm, driven by a gust of dazed euphoria, a feeling that hadn't come her way since the day Lindy Van Buren had promised Rainmaker to her. She bounded across the snow-covered quadrangle, laughing incredulously, and a great coil of energy that had been winding up inside her released itself, sending her in a mad whirl. Suddenly all things were made possible by Lindy, who had once again taken on the proportions of a god in her mind. At that moment she could have kissed the ground he walked on. He was a big, soft-hearted sugar daddy underneath the sinews of steel, and his magnificent gesture, worthy of a great gentleman, made her realize that he cared more deeply than she had ever imagined. It was undoubtedly an act of atonement for what he had done to her. But why hadn't he told her? Still, if he wanted it to be anonymous, it was all right with her. She would find other ways to thank him when they met again.

She made her way back to the dormitory, glowing with the inner security that only money could buy. She felt a gush of affection for the Braemar campus, and her mind was jumping with plans now that she was going to stay. She thought of the presents she would buy for Betsy and her family when they went skiing in Vermont—Scottish cashmere sweaters for Betsy's two brothers, Irish Waterford crystal for Mrs. Belmont, a briarwood pipe for Mr. Belmont. And tonight it would be pizza and Chianti for her birthday celebration. From now on, the Honorable Kerry Faloon would be known for her generosity. Taking the stairs two at a time, she shouted, "Betsy, Betsy, I'm coming to Sugar Bush for Christmas after all!"

When she burst through the door of her room, she was greeted by cheers.

"Surprise! Surprise!" shouted a roomful of girls, following with a rowdy chorus of "Happy Birthday."

Betsy came forward triumphantly, bearing an enormous cake lit with eighteen candles, and there were balloons and streamers everywhere. Kerry looked 'round the circle of girls squealing with delight, tears in her eyes. Now that she had truly become one of them, she began to sob with a profound joy and relief that none of them would ever understand.

Betsy hugged her affectionately. "Isn't she sweet? Crying like a baby, she was so surprised. Come on and open your presents!"

"What you need is a good stiff drink," announced Stephanie, handing her a glass of wine.

Wiping her tears, Kerry managed to say, "This is the best birthday I've ever had in my life. Thank you, everyone."

At two in the morning on Christmas Eve, the headlights of the Mercedes picked out the fields of Touraine, covered with hoarfrost, as Amadeo and Shannon drove back to Les Tourelles.

Shannon snuggled down into her velvet cloak, next to Amadeo at the wheel. "What a lovely party. The baron and his wife are such wonderful hosts, and their château is fabulous. But I'm afraid the baby is going to have a hangover in the morning."

Amadeo cast her an indulgent smile. "Henri and Simone both told me how much they liked you and how they would love to see us soon. They're two of my favorite people in the region."

"What did you tell them about me? They must have thought it very peculiar for you to turn up with a strange woman huge with child. I know how curious the French are."

"I told them I found you wandering in the streets of Paris on a donkey, looking for a stable."

She threw back her head and laughed at this; but on her lips was an unspoken speech of gratitude for his finesse in handling a delicate situation. Though they had never mentioned it, she knew that Amadeo must have given up a whirl of glamorous parties to be with her at Christmas now that she was so heavily pregnant; and she guessed it had always been a tradition with him to take his girlfriend of the moment to his chalet in Mürren.

"Let's go into the drawing room for a nightcap," suggested Amadeo when they entered the hall, where the grand staircase was hung with holly and branches of pine.

In the Poussin room stood a tall fir tree dressed with gold and silver, which had been cut in the park.

"A glass of champagne to drink the baby's health?"

"All right. But just one," she said, taking off her cloak and slipping into a chair by the fire.

When he had poured the drinks, Amadeo withdrew a gold filigree coffer from the heap of presents at the foot of the tree.

"As you know, it is the custom in France to present gifts on *Réveillon*. This is for you." His formality puzzled her.

Opening the coffer, Shannon expected to find a piece of jewelry, hoping it wouldn't be something too extravagant. But there, nestled in pale blue velvet, was the most exquisite bottle she had ever seen, of washed opal. "How beautiful!" she exclaimed. "Is it Lalique, by any chance?" He nodded. "I've always longed to have a piece of glass made by him." Seeing Amadeo's face alive with mystery, she guessed that this pretty bottle represented something more than its face value.

"It was rather difficult to know how to package such a thing."

"The coffer was a lovely idea. It's as beautiful as the bottle."

"That's not what I meant. It takes a lot of paper and ribbon to wrap a company."

"A company? What are you taking about?"

"Figuratively speaking. Have you ever heard of Galant?"

"Let me think—isn't it something to do with soap or perfume?"

"Yes, that's right. Perhaps you've heard of *Chanson de Mer*. It was a great favorite in the twenties and thirties."

"Oh, yes—I've heard of it. And didn't they do a perfume in the early sixties called *Peut-Être*?"

"That was the beginning of their decline, in fact."

"If it's the one I'm thinking of, it was awful."

"That perfume cheapened their image. Apparently it was a brainstorm of the marketing people, made to appeal to the masses, but ultimately it proved to be a failure. Marcel Galant, who had been the creative genius behind the family business and the youngest of the three brothers, withdrew his involvement. He was the one responsible for such successes as *White Jade* in the early fifties, and after he left, everything at Galant went downhill."

Cradling her chin in her hand, Shannon looked at Amadeo with curiosity. "I'm intrigued to know why you're telling me all this at three in the morning on Christmas Day, and what it has to do with the bottle."

"Because I've just bought Galant," he said with a triumphant edge to his voice. "And your future, Shannon, is in that bottle."

"My future?"

"I don't have time for another business. I want you to fill that bottle. To invent a perfume that will revive Galant and bring it back into prominence along with names like Guerlain, Lanvin, Chanel, Molyneux . . ."

She gave a peal of incredulous laughter. "Me? Look at me. I'm nearly eight months pregnant! And anyway, I don't know a thing about business. It would be a tall order for anyone, let alone me."

"I know you, Shannon," Amadeo said with a sweeping gesture. "Your life isn't going to end with the birth of your child. It will begin again and take a new direction. It's clear to me that you don't wish to be dependent on anybody, that you have ambitions and perhaps talents that you haven't dreamed of. . . ."

"I must say, I'm overwhelmed, and surprised."

"Surprised? At what?"

"I've done you a great injustice, Amadeo. Sometimes I've had the outlandish notion that you rather liked the idea of me, of any woman, being dependent. That you thought a woman's natural place was at home with her children. You've always pointed out to me what strong traditions Argentina has on that score," she said with a mischievous smile.

"I've changed a lot, Shanita. Perhaps it's you who have changed me."

"Amadeo—I have to ask you this. You're not just being kind, are you? Because if you are, it won't work. . . ."

"Kind? Why should I be kind? I need someone I can

291

trust, someone I know. It couldn't be more perfect. You have the image, the contacts in the fashion industry, and you have brains. Does that convince you?"

"Do you really have that much faith in me, then? I'm flattered and amazed," she remarked, gazing down at the cool oval of glass resting in her hand.

"I do. Will you accept the position of managing director of Galant?"

She thought for a moment. "Without capital, there's nothing I can do with a flagging company. Galant is only a shell, from what you tell me. And there's the matter of my salary package to discuss."

A look of amusement crossed his face. "All right. Let's talk over the whole thing. I'm pleased to see you're not afraid to ask questions."

For half an hour she sparred with him concerning the financing of the company, and he treated her like any other business partner.

"Well? What do you say? Do you want to take charge of Galant, in spite of what I've told you?"

"Well, it's certainly a challenge, and an enormously exciting one. But if it wasn't, it wouldn't be worth doing. I accept," she said with a smile, astonished at herself.

"Shanita—we're partners now. Let's shake hands."

As they concluded their deal with this little formality, something made her draw him close to her, brushing her lips against his cheek. The nearness of her, the smell of her skin, her touch, sent a wave of nostalgic desire through him, and he suppressed a bolt of longing to crush her passionately to him. He turned abruptly to stir up the dying embers of the fire.

"I'm pleased we've agreed, Shanita. I needed someone I can trust—a friend."

Paris, February, 1981

Shannon's baby was born at the American Hospital in Neuilly on St. Valentine's Day at eight o'clock in the evening. When the nurse brought in a tiny bundle wrapped in a soft woolen shawl, she lay in a state of serene exhaustion, yet she couldn't sleep until she had seen her baby and held him in her arms.

"Voilà, votre petit fils," announced the sister. *"Quel beau garçon,"* she added approvingly, stroking his shock of black hair.

292

"Please let me see him," she whispered, holding out her arms. "I can't wait another moment."

When Shannon peered into his tiny squinched-up face for the first time, she felt a throb of adoration. Watching his kittenlike gestures as he pressed his almost transparent pink fingers to his eyes, she felt her son was the most endearing creature on earth. She kissed his small perfect head and whispered a private little conversation that seemed to have been waiting in her heart all these months.

She was feeding him for the first time when there was a tap at the door. It was Amadeo, and he entered the room with a shy, almost hesitant expression, bearing red roses and champagne.

"I got here as soon as I could. Miguel told me the news as soon as I landed at Charles de Gaulle, and he drove all the way like the wind. If I had known, I would have postponed my trip to Milan today. Shanita—are you all right?"

"I'm fine, but he was a week early, the little devil."

She was still so preoccupied with the child suckling at her breast that she didn't see the look of proud exultation on Amadeo's face as he observed the serene image of mother and child.

"Please—may I hold him?" he asked when she had drawn the baby away from her breast.

If anyone had the right to share this moment with her it was Amadeo, and she smiled at the exaggerated care with which he picked up the infant. With instinctive tenderness he pressed him to the crook of his shoulder, brushing his cheek against the tiny head. For several moments he clasped the baby to him with a look of pure enjoyment on his face that seemed to transcend mere pride in her miraculous achievement. He was too overwhelmed to speak, and his dark eyes showered her with a kind of speechless adoration.

"He was born at eight. Just in time for dinner. Isn't he a civilized baby?"

He laughed. "But of course, and on Saint Valentine's Day, too. Do you know, he looks just like his *maman*." Returning the baby to her arms, Amadeo stooped to kiss her forehead affectionately.

"Do you really think so?" A picture of Zan came to her mind, and as she looked at the baby she realized it was true. There was no trace of his fair good looks in her child, though she must have subconsciously looked for a resemblance the minute she saw him.

Sensing he had touched a sensitive point, Amadeo changed the subject. His private moment of recognition of his child was over, and he could only suppose that Shannon was probably wishing that her Englishman was standing there in his place. His heart, bursting with pride, had no room for petty jealousy, only a determined possessiveness. Shannon's child, his child, was a product of their love, however tempestuous, and already in his mind he had set the wheels in motion to prove it.

"So what is the young gentleman's name to be? Have you decided?"

"Patrick Brendan Faloon. Patrick, because it's both French and Irish, and Brendan after my father."

"It's a good name," Amadeo agreed, brushing the baby's dark hair with his fingers while he inwardly voiced to himself that one day his child would carry his father's own name.

When he had gone, Shannon was suddenly hit by a wave of sadness. As tears came to her eyes she tried to tell herself it was just a bout of postnatal blues; but she knew the real reason was Zan's absence. Would he be with her now, she wondered, if he knew the truth? The helpless little creature sleeping soundly in her arms was the most powerful weapon she could wish to bind Zan to her, but it was one she would never use. Patrick Brendan Faloon was the natural son of the future Earl of Kilgarin—and his possible heir, should Rosemary fail to give him one.

How attitudes had changed since her father had told her that she was illegitimate! At the time she had expected the stigma of her birth to pursue her forever, but the cosmopolitan society in which she moved admitted human foibles with a nonchalance that was a far cry from the small-town narrow-mindedness of her youth. Independent women all over the world were unashamed to give their babies their own name, and she was one of them. Patrick Faloon would be loved and adored, and there would be no dark secret waiting to taint his life. When the time came she would be proud to reveal the identity of his father, and to tell him he was conceived in love. As her depression lifted, Shannon saw the clear path to a bright new future. Almost immediately she could feel vitality begin to pulse through her at the thought. In the glimmer of the most blissful sleep she had ever known, it seemed that she had almost everything: an exciting new career ahead of her, a fiercely loyal friend in Amadeo, and now the most beautiful boy that God had ever breathed life into. She had no right to ask for anything more.

Chapter VI

Fayence, France, May

Shannon shifted into second gear as the Renault climbed the last hill to Fayence, its ramparts gleaming against a sky of unclouded blue. During the trip from Paris to Nice and the ride into the hills, she had had time to reflect on the last three months, the most eventful of her entire life.

Her first act upon leaving the hospital had been to locate a new apartment on the fashionable Île Saint-Louis, signaling a change in style from the Bohemian to the chic. As a model, her life away from the camera had been her own, but now that she was constantly on display as managing director of Galant, she knew she would have to abandon jeans and boots for the sleek image expected of her in status-conscious Paris, and that meant dressing for the part in St. Laurent suits and Maud Frizon shoes.

In the meantime she had tracked down the perfect English nanny, who Shannon was satisfied would be as devoted to Patrick as his mother was. During the first weeks of breastfeeding she had juggled the baby in one hand and a book in the other as she studied the fascinating field of perfume, a strange marriage of art, high finance, and chemistry. After an exhaustive study of the history of the house of Galant, she had come to the conclusion that the key to the whole enterprise was Marcel Galant himself, the youngest of the three brothers who had carried the family banner into the fourth generation. An acknowledged genius of perfumery, he had been in his twenties when he'd created *Chanson de Mer* and then the renowned *White Jade*. But the war years had interrupted his meteoric career and the fortunes of the house of Galant, and when the two elder brothers had decided that the new postwar social order demanded cheaper perfumes for the masses now that the price of real essences had soared,

Marcel Galant had opposed them. There was no substitute for the purest jasmine from Grasse, picked by hand in the cool air of dawn, nothing to replace attar of roses from Bulgaria or the finest musk pods from Tibet, frankincense from the Persian Gulf. Like planets in collision, the three brothers had clashed in the midfifties. Marcel had left the company in a blaze of anger to retire in Fayence, reputedly taking all his formulas with him, including one for an unnamed perfume that legend now whispered would have been the greatest fragrance of a generation had it ever been produced. That it must be produced, by him, under the umbrella of the new management at Galant, had become Shannon's obsession.

Parking in the village square beneath a ragged chestnut tree, Shannon felt a welcome warmth beat down on her even though it was only mid-May. Asking directions at the cafe, she walked to her destination down a narrow street, aware that her whole future hung in the balance. She felt the weight of her precious cargo, the touchstone of good luck in her shopping bag. The small bottle of perfume, her gift to Galant, was the result of a month's detective work that had begun with a stroke of pure inspiration one afternoon while reading an old biography.

While gathering all the information she could on Galant himself, she had stumbled across the story of his passionate and tragic love affair with Princess Xenia of Serbia. Like star-crossed lovers in literature, Galant and the princess had fallen in love in spite of the opposition of the Serbian royal family. Their affair had smoldered until the eve of World War II, when Xenia defied her family's wishes, promising to marry the young Galant. She flew to join him in Switzerland, where they were to begin their life together, and tragedy struck as he awaited her in a chalet on the shores of Lake Geneva. All on board were killed when her plane went down in a storm over the Alps.

From the photographs in the old book, Shannon was intrigued by Xenia's proud and haunting Slavic beauty. In one snapshot of her standing beside Galant, taken in Cannes, it was easy to see from their posture, their loving smiles, that they radiated an aura of intense private passion. Moved by the love story of the man she had yet to meet, Shannon had noted that the princess's favorite scent was reputed to be a perfume called *Love in Idleness*, which had been discontinued for thirty-five years, and she was seized by the idea of sending Galant a bottle as a tribute—if she could find one.

When she had almost given up hope of ever locating a bottle, one had turned up in an old-fashioned pharmacy in Passy. Guessing that nothing had the power to unlock memory like scent, she was sure her gift would be a bold move that would either alienate Galant on the spot or capture the imagination of this reclusive genius.

Shannon hoped the letter she had sent from Paris a month ago would have already paved the way for the meeting she sought. Arriving at Galant's house of rough-hewn stone, its windows hung with faded green shutters, she rang the bell. Hearing footsteps echoing inside, she waited in suspense.

"*Oui?*" said the old woman in black who opened the wooden door. There was no welcoming smile on her face as she looked at Shannon suspiciously.

In precise, polite French Shannon explained that she had written some time ago asking for an appointment.

"Monsieur Galant said nothing to me about an appointment." With arms folded, the solidly built peasant woman blocked the entrance to the house like a bulldog. It took all of Shannon's persuasion to get her to relay a message to the master of the house.

Slamming the door in Shannon's face, the old woman left her standing there for at least ten minutes, and when she returned her face was set stubbornly.

"No, mademoiselle. It was as I thought. He will not see you."

When the door slammed a second time Shannon stood piqued and bewildered for several moments, wondering how to scale the heights of Marcel Galant's bastion of privacy. Short of catapulting over the high stone wall or breaking a window, there seemed nothing she could do. But she had come too far and there was too much at stake to be daunted by a first refusal. Taking out her card, she jotted a message on it:

> Chèr Monsieur Galant: Please accept this small present as a token of my esteem. Should you perhaps change your mind, I will be waiting in the cafè on the square until one o'clock.
>
> Regards,
> Shannon Faloon

Taking a deep breath, she rang the bell again. This time the housekeeper threw open the door in exasperation.

"Yes? What do you want this time? I've already told you that Monsieur Galant doesn't wish to be disturbed."

"Please, could you give this gift to him? That's all. Thank you very much, madame."

She turned and walked resolutely toward the village square, where she seated herself at a cafe table dappled with shade. With three hours to wait for Marcel Galant, she settled down to read a volume entitled *The Essential Oils*, in preparation for her visit to Grasse for the rose harvest later that week. As the sun rose and gathered strength overhead, Shannon found herself distracted by passing villagers carrying baskets full of summer produce over their arms—scarlet tomatoes, scored green courgettes, bunches of garlic and onions. Setting down her book, she gave in to daydreaming, and her mind leapt ahead to the following day, when she planned to visit her house in Seillans, with the intention of putting it on the market. Feeling vaguely upset at the thought, she pushed it out of her mind and turned to look inside the cafè, where men in berets and caps were drinking their noontime aperitifs at the bar.

When at last the hands of the clock reached one, she began to gather up her things and stuff them in her bag in preparation for an ignominious retreat, deeply disappointed that her siege had failed. She smiled mockingly at her own impetuous naiveté. She must have been mad to believe that womanly wiles would gain her admission to a wizard's cave; it was wildly romantic of her to assume Galant would open doors closed to the world for more than twenty years just on account of an old bottle of perfume. When she had thought of it she had been so sure of herself, but now she was certain Monsieur Galant must be thinking she was an ignorant fool; no doubt he considered her gift an outrageous impertinence.

Hitching her bag over her shoulder and adjusting her sunglasses, she was just about to leave the table when she heard the patron call out:

"*Bonjour, Monsieur Galant. Ça va?*"

She turned to see the great man himself regarding her with wry amusement. He was the opposite of what she had expected. Unlike the suave and elegant character she had pictured, a boulevardier with the air of an intellectual, he was exactly like any other villager who played *boules* in the square. Short and stockily built, he was of the ancient Gallic race that seemed close to the earth. He wore a beret on his white cropped head, and his blue shirt matched shrewd eyes set deeply in a weathered face. He's a peasant, she told herself, but she was surprised when he spoke French with a cultured Parisian accent.

"Excuse me, mademoiselle, but I am rather late. Would you like to take lunch at my house?"

"Why, thank you, monsieur. I'd be delighted."

They returned to his house, followed by a little spotted *ratier* called Coco.

"I believe you've already met Angélique." He nodded when the housekeeper met them in the hall.

She was all smiles now that her master had given his approval. He ushered Shannon through a cool hallway laid with ancient uneven tiles to an enclosed sunlit garden.

It took Shannon's breath away when she saw the banks of roses climbing the stone walls, blue-and-mauve delphiniums, scarlet poppies, and a host of flowers of every color, many she couldn't name.

"Does my garden please you, mademoiselle?"

"I've never seen anything like it. It's remarkable. It's like a painting by Monet."

"My garden is one of my greatest hobbies. It's at its best now, in May," he said, bending to pluck a few dead blooms. "So you see, I'm not so far removed from the world of perfume as it may seem."

She breathed deeply of the fragrant waves that seemed to surround her. Silently he led her to a small table under a vine-covered pergola near a basin floating with water lilies. The housekeeper emerged from the house bearing a basket of coarse peasant bread and a jug of wine.

"Angélique loves having guests, but she is cross with me that I gave her so little notice," said Galant with a smile as he poured Shannon a glass of rosé wine the color of crushed raspberries. Encapsuled in this world alive with droning bees, Shannon felt a dazed enchantment take hold of her. Slowly, as Galant talked, she adjusted her preconceptions of him to conform to an undeniable reality: she had been so obsessed with the idea that he was the answer to all her problems that she hadn't considered he might have sunk permanently into this simple peasant existence.

"The rosé we are drinking comes from my own vineyard," he was saying. "I grow it only for myself and my friends. I take great pride in the pruning of the vines, the pressing of the grapes, the blending and bottling, just the way I used to with perfume in my laboratory in Paris."

"It's delicious," she said, taking a sip.

Just then Angélique came to the table bearing a platter of stuffed courgette flowers.

"Bravo," said Galant approvingly.

"If only monsieur had given me more notice," she scolded him.

"Now, what can I do for you, Mademoiselle Faloon?" he said as they ate.

She had waited for this moment for weeks, but here in this blissful garden, the idea that she had the power to disturb the rhythm of Galant's tranquil life seemed absurd. What could she, an intruder, offer a man who seemed to have filled his life with the simple pleasures that brought him contentment? Neither money nor fame appealed to him. He had already tasted those and rejected them.

"I have a proposition to make to you, monsieur. First, I must tell you that you have become my obsession during the last three months. I have thought of nothing else, night and day."

"Really? You flatter me, mademoiselle," he said gravely, but there was an amused twinkle in his eye.

Suddenly she was flushed with the wine, the sun, with determination as she met his eyes, so full of wisdom.

"You know from my letter that I am the new director of Galant. But, monsieur, only you can bring the house founded by your family back to its former glory. Only your prestige and genius can achieve what I have in mind. At the moment the great perfumes you created, and those of your grandfather before you, are only a memory. What I want to do is bring the legend to life again." She finished breathlessly and waited for him to reply. Finally he said:

"I'm trying to remember all the details of your letter. I didn't expect a woman as young as you, or a foreigner, for that matter. I expected you to be one of those ageless Parisian creatures whose velvet exterior is threaded on a will of steel—like Chanel. You know the type."

"Monsieur, I can be one of those businesswomen when required. Make no mistake. Don't be fooled by appearances, or by my youth. You'll find I am determined to make a success of Galant, and I have great motivation. Perhaps you recall my contacts in the fashion industry from my letter, but besides all this I have a very substantial budget to accomplish my goal."

"How did you come to this position, may I ask?"

"It's a very long, complicated story, one I would love to tell you one day."

Bending to cast Coco a morsel from his plate, Galant looked up at her with amusement. "Just what makes you think you can succeed in this ruthlessly competitive business? In your letter you admitted you knew nothing of the industry."

"I have only the burning ambition to succeed," she said simply. "But that's why I need your genius."

"You have much more than that, mademoiselle. This morning you reminded me that even the strongest resolution can be conquered by the senses."

She acknowledged this unexpected compliment with a startled smile.

" 'Perfume is the alchemy of love's possession,' " he said reflectively. "I wrote that in my memoirs, which I will publish one day. This morning when I opened the bottle of perfume you sent, I began to live a memory. Do you realize, mademoiselle, that memory is stronger than experience itself?"

"I've never thought of it."

"Of course, you're still young. But it's true. The moments we truly live to the full are few and fleeting, even in the richest of lives. But the impressions events make on us last a lifetime, whether good or bad. Perfume is the golden key that turns perfectly in the lock of memory, opening wide a window into a treasured past. Its nuances paint colors, sounds, touch, more than any of the other senses. Imagine—when I opened that bottle in my study this morning, I was suddenly in the year 1936. A young man in white flannels was ushered onto the terrace of a house with a garden rambling down to the sea on Cap Ferrat. He had met his hostess the night before at the gaming tables of Monte Carlo, and he arrived to discover he was the first guest at the luncheon party. When the butler led him to the sunny terrace, he found her alone. She was wearing a white halter-necked dress and a turban that covered her dark hair, and her eyes were shielded by sunglasses. Like a statue dipped in gold, she held out her slender brown hand for him to kiss, and as he bowed his head he caught the powerful scent of *Love in Idleness*. The young man had no idea that the recollection of that beguiling moment would have to last a lifetime, or that it

301

would spring forth instantly, fully formed, forty-odd years later when he opened an unmarked bottle a young stranger had sent him. The young man, now grown very old, was so intrigued that he decided he had to meet this young woman to find out what she wanted."

Up until that moment Shannon had been spellbound by the slow unfolding of his recollection of Princess Xenia. As the vision died she said urgently:

"Monsieur Galant, I want your formula—the one that you were developing when you left Galant. The one everyone said was going to be a perfume greater than *Chanel Number Five*, or *Mitsouko*."

"Ah, so you know about my formulas, too, do you?" he said, meeting her eyes, alight with enthusiasm.

"There's nothing that's been written about you that I haven't read. I left nothing unresearched to discover the source of your inspiration. And I'm here to offer you all the resources at my disposal, the capital you need, your own laboratory—at Grasse."

"I've been approached with an open checkbook before, but never by someone who intrigued me as much as you do, I admit."

As Angélique placed a platter of cheeses and a bowl of cherries and peaches before them, he poured Shannon's glass full of wine.

"Are you as much of a romantic as you seem? Are you romantic enough to take the chance I'm offering you?" she said provocatively.

He chuckled. "What makes you think you'll like this formula of mine, the one you seem to think I have?"

"I don't know how or why, but I feel as if it's already familiar. I've read so much about your style of perfume."

"It has a high percentage of jasmine, you know. The price of French jasmine has become nearly prohibitive, and I wouldn't use anything but the best."

"I know, but it's not beyond reach. And if there's a market for your perfume, and I'm convinced there is, there are people who will be willing to pay for it." Seeing him weaken, she reached for her briefcase, fired with excitement. "I have here the launching study outlining from day one to two years later, when I hope the perfume will be on the market. Perhaps this will convince you how serious I am."

"Have you given any thought to the name? That could take a long time, to find one and research it." His tone was doubtful, but already she could see his mind was leaping ahead.

"Did you ever name your formula?"

"No, that's for the experts. Any name appropriate twenty years ago might no longer be marketable."

With a burst of enthusiasm she said, "I thought of a name and I've already researched it. My legal consultant in Paris is waiting for the word to patent it in forty-five countries, Monsieur Galant."

"What is it?"

"*Samarkand.*"

He considered it as he gazed at a dragonfly swooping in a trail of color near the basin. Shannon could almost see the images flickering in his eyes of the quest for frankincense and myrrh. Dark domes against the pale evening sky, the call of the muezzin. All the things that suggested Samarkand belonged to him as well as her, passed down through the ages ever since Marco Polo had brought the riches of the East along the silk route to the West. The name had sprung from Shannon's subconscious one day, and she had latched on to it immediately as fresh, provocative, and unforgettable.

"Yes, I like it," he admitted. "And it's not inappropriate. The perfume created is animal, exalting, with overtones of sandalwood, attar of roses, jasmine, among a hundred other things."

"You don't have to give me your answer now. I'm here to study the preparation of floral essences at Grasse in time for the rose harvest. I want to learn every aspect of the business from the bottom up. If you like, I could come back in a week or two."

"No, I'd better give you my answer now."

Her heart lurched.

"I will set you a little task. If you can bring me a parcel of the finest Tibetan musk, which I will need to prepare the first samples—within two weeks—my answer will be yes."

He was setting her a daunting challenge, as a wise king sets hurdles for a prince seeking his daughter's hand. But musk, she thought with dismay. It was the most wildly expensive ingredient in the world. She would have to advance in the region of twenty thousand dollars, with no promise of success.

"This will prove your intentions to me. It will assure me that *Samarkand* will be a rare and exquisite perfume, and that you and your backers have no intention of cutting corners. That's why I retired, and I don't want it to happen again."

"Agreed, Monsieur Galant," she replied, suddenly terrified at her own largesse.

After the espresso, Shannon sensed that it was time to go. Rising, she extended her hand.

"À bientôt," she said, her imagination already galloping ahead. She was impatient to rush back to Nice so that she could set the wheels in motion to obtain the musk. Looking into Galant's kind blue eyes, set in a sun-creased face, she felt a soaring elation. Her mind reeled with the publicity implications of drawing the legendary Marcel out of retirement, armed with his formula.

Pausing at the entrance to the house, she stole one last look at the garden and at Galant's rugged silhouette against the delicate tracery of a thousand flowers as he stooped to pick up a handful of rose petals. How strange it seemed that the most decisive meeting of the whole venture had taken place against this backdrop of utter tranquillity, rather than in a boardroom. It was a reminder that without creative inspiration, all the facts and figures on her balance sheets would be meaningless.

When they were at the door she said, "By the way, I have a house in Seillans, which I bought last year."

"Do you? That's most appropriate. We'll almost be neighbors. It's not all that far to Grasse."

"I'm intending to sell it, however, and look for something else."

"In Seillans?"

"No, somewhere else, I think," she hastened to say. "Au revoir, monsieur."

"Au revoir, mademoiselle," he replied with a formal nod.

As Shannon disappeared down the street, Marcel reached to pat Coco at his feet, reflecting that yesterday he had been a retired gentleman with the quiet occupation of tending flowers and vines. But there was life within him that still burned to spend itself. He had briefly scented the paradise of his youth when he'd opened the bottle of Love in Idleness. The beautiful young stranger had christened what would be his tribute to Xenia. Samarkand. A word that conjured up the Eastern stamp of her dark eyes, his youthful discovery of the meaning of life itself. Samarkand. It would be his legacy to a passion that had never died.

A week later, driving to Seillans, Shannon recalled her tour of the Grasse perfume industry. Swirling around her head like invisible silk was the powerful aroma of rose santiflora, the modest ragged little bloom of deep magenta harvested by the bushel for distillation into the powerful essence that gave character to a multitude of perfumes. She had observed, too, the gathering of the narcissus to create a concentrate so powerful that it had given her a headache. Heliotrope, mimosa, oakmoss, jasmine, vetiver, tuberose, citriadora, bergamot, ylang-ylang, and ambergris—all clashed wildly as she struggled to keep them in order in her head, feeling a layman's daunting confusion. Would she ever achieve a fluency in this strange new language spoken in the industry that supplied the hundreds of vital components of scent?

She had called Amadeo immediately following her meeting with Galant, to tell him the news.

"Bravo, Shannon," he had exulted. "I knew you would do it."

He had immediately offered his influence to ensure she received the musk in time, and she hung up feeling yet another phase in the production of *Samarkand* had come to fruition with his help. Lately she had assessed the battles ahead, aware of the power of envy marshaled against anyone like herself, who seemed to have a wildly unfair advantage. To her detractors it must surely seem as if she had skipped from one bright stone to the other, when in fact her life had had its full share of disasters and disappointments, all of which had served to prepare her for the setbacks she was encountering. A sudden frost or a laborers' strike could cause precious jasmine to jump in price, and she already anticipated patent difficulties, to name a few problems. There must be an easier way to make a living, she told herself wryly. But at the heart of her struggle lay a simple desire to prove herself in the high-powered world that considered her nothing but a pretty face. The complex web of responsibility that seemed to be weaving itself around her felt like a kind of protective armor? it made her feel strong—even strong enough now to visit the house in Seillans.

Shannon armed herself against the power of suggestion as every familiar landmark came into view, reminding her of the first day she and Zan had driven there together. Parking her car in the village, she walked up the hill and when she stood before the shuttered house realized with a start that it was exactly a year that week since she and Zan had stood in the same spot. As she opened the door a cool rush of stale air hit her face. The rooms seemed full of ghosts, and she flung open the windows and shutters to admit the light. Even the fragrant morning air, the sunshine, the twittering of birds couldn't animate the charm she remembered as the memory of Zan's voice echoed in her mind.

"I love you, Shannon—always and forever."

She wouldn't be able to leave the house soon enough and moved to the dining room to pack the set of pottery she had bought in Vallauris during their meanderings down the coast.

Just as she was closing up the house, she heard the scuff of steps in the hallway.

"Who's there?"

A long shadow fell across the threshold of the room. Whoever it was seemed to hesitate.

"Shannon?"

Zan's voice broke across all the months of misery.

"Shannon?"

As he came from the shadows she was too startled to speak. Two extremes of emotion clashed within her—the pain of abandonment and joy at seeing him again. He paused just long enough to gauge the look on her face before enfolding her in his arms, and as he held her tightly to him, layers and layers of accumulated loneliness seemed to dissolve miraculously. Neither of them could speak for several moments.

"Why are you here?" she managed to say finally.

"I told you I'd be here this year, no matter what happened. I came hours ago but when I saw the house closed up I waited at the cafe for you to pass. I had this absurd hope that you'd come, but when I saw you it was half an hour before I could bring myself to come to the house."

She closed her eyes in disbelief that he, too, whether by chance or design, had kept the vow they had made. What mattered was that they had both come to Seillans, driven by the same unconscious need for each other. Even if they parted at that moment, Shannon now knew that Zan's love was as strong as hers. The tenderness she had always felt for him was as strangely untouched as it had been twelve months before. Looking into his face, she realized his eyes were filled with a misery that surpassed her own, and when he murmured, "God, how I've missed you, Shannon," those simple

306

words held more emotion than either of them would ever be able to express.

Later that evening they lay in each other's arms, spent with exhaustion after making passionate love. There was a rare bittersweet quality about their every forbidden moment together that made the outside world seem insipid. They began to talk about everything, except what mattered most to Shannon—Patrick—and she wondered how to break the news to Zan that they had a son. Resting her head on his shoulder, she searched for the words she knew would thrust them from the eye of the storm into the troubled world again. All her anxieties, past and future, would then become his, but as Zan began to confide the tangled web of his own problems, her reluctance to tell the truth increased. She felt her heart go cold when he said:

"The truth is, I can't leave Rosemary now. The situation is worse than ever, with Father so ill in Ireland. And I'm sure you're aware of the collapse of the property market. If it weren't for Rosemary, I would have gone under, quite frankly. I've really gone out of my mind with worry about money this past year."

She was almost relieved when her instincts told her to postpone the announcement that would divide his loyalties. She found herself responding to Zan's dilemma with more strength and sympathy than she'd ever thought she possessed. What really mattered was that he hadn't stopped loving her.

"Zan—do you have any idea how long it will be before we can be together?"

"Another year, darling. Maybe two at the most. But this year it will be different. Last year I couldn't face it, and tried to forget. Now, you'll always be in my thoughts until we're together."

Stroking his hair, she felt warmth radiating from him like a second sun. Love was never easy, she told herself. A year ago she had wanted Zan Fitzherbert strong, unfettered, and free, and now their love had withstood incredible forces that had tried to tear them apart.

That evening they dined on the terrace of the village cafe, intoxicated by the sublime atmosphere of this far-off corner of the world, so remote from Paris or London. The conversation wandered to Jonquil's high-handed intervention, which Shannon reflected had only strengthened the bond between her and Zan.

"Tell me more about Valentin—why you didn't sign the contract? I was so surprised when you mentioned it earlier," he said, entwining his hand in hers across the table.

She had already prepared an answer. "Being the Valentin girl seemed like child's play compared with taking on Galant. I've discovered I have a taste for jousting with windmills. I realized that I wanted to get out of modeling entirely, and working for only three months a year was a recipe for dissatisfaction. I knew I would probably blow the money and fritter the time away, so when this chance came up, well, I thought it over carefully. I changed my mind about Valentin at the last minute. Of course it means I have to work ten times as hard for less money, but if I make it, I'll have carved out an empire of my own."

"How did you come to be offered the job?"

"Oh, through somebody I've known for ages, ever since I started modeling. I'm just in a sort of showcase position at the moment, until I prove myself. A front," she said with a self-deprecating smile that hid her own duplicity. It wasn't really a lie, only a convenient deception to underplay her real position and to avoid any awkward mention of Amadeo.

Too starved of her company to probe deeply into the details, Zan seemed to accept her explanation.

"I'll try to come over to Paris in a week or two, and maybe we could steal a weekend together. Can you manage that? Where are you living now—the same apartment?"

"No, I moved. I found a much better place." As she spoke she wished fleetingly that she had confessed everything to Zan. Once he came to Paris he would discover the truth, further complicated by the fact that they were no longer the anonymous young lovers they had been in Australia. The idea of concealment, sneaking around back streets to avoid the press and friends, tainted the nature of their relationship, and she wanted no part in it.

"Do you think it's such a wise idea, Zan, with so much at stake? You said Rosemary would divorce you if she found out about us. And my new job involves a lot of traveling at the moment."

"Are you content with that?"

"No, but we'll find a way to see each other soon. And if we have to wait, it won't matter, darling. You and I have come to terms with the fact that miracles don't happen in a month, or even a year."

"Shannon, my love," he whispered, kissing her hand. "You can't imagine how much strength it gives me that you're so strong, so determined. When I came to Seillans today, hoping to find you if you were here, I didn't really dream that we would be starting all over again."

"What did you think would happen?"

"I just hoped that if you had remembered our promise to come back, I could see you for an instant. But to feel your love and support as strong as ever . . . well, it's more than any man deserves. You're so brave, so fine. You never cease to surprise and delight me. How can I live up to it?"

She smiled to herself. If only he knew the source of her strength had been to travel to the abyss of her own dark emotions, then to return again to bring Patrick into the world. His birth symbolized the renewal of her own life. For a moment she was tempted to take out Patrick's first baby picture, which she carried in her bag, and show Zan the source of her strength.

A week later, when Zan had gone back to London, Shannon waited at Nice Airport for Amadeo's Gulfstream to arrive, bearing the precious parcel of musk. Unlike their last parting, this time she had the launch of *Samarkand* to think about, an enormous distraction that made it possible to contemplate the long period of waiting that lay ahead.

She drove as fast as she dared to Fayence and walked hurriedly to Galant's house, where she rang the bell excitedly.

"*Bonjour*, Angélique," she exclaimed when the door opened. "Please tell Monsieur Galant I am here."

He was in the garden, trowel in hand, wearing a blue smock and a straw hat. Shannon raced outside, bearing a parcel no larger than a shoebox, wrapped in brown paper, tied with string, and secured by seals. It seemed the proudest moment of her life when she handed it to him, her face wreathed in smiles.

He shook his head in amazement, unable to contain his pleasure. Shannon watched nervously as he opened the package laboriously, snipping each string and cracking the seals. He opened the lid of the aluminium box to reveal a row of musk pods that looked like ovals of chocolate.

"What a strange thing to hold such treasure in my hands after all these years," he said, examining them. "They seem magnificent, of the first quality."

"Oh, I'm so glad," she said, feeling indescribable relief.

"So now, mademoiselle—it would seem we're ready to take the road to Samarkand."

In his office on the fifth floor of a modern block on the rue Wagram, Amadeo leaned back in his chair and flipped the intercom.

"Get me Frank Bevan in London, Delphine."

He drummed his fingers impatiently on the top of the vast modern desk, uncluttered apart from five telephones. The de Kooning abstract on the opposite wall contrasted with the stark tone of the huge room, which overlooked the slate rooftops of Paris through smoked glass windows that reached to the floor. Amadeo took out a file marked "Cornwell Security Limited in Red Lion Square, London," which outlined the life and habits of one Lord Fitzherbert. The dossier forwarded by the agency proved conclusively that he had been Shannon's lover, and Amadeo know he was the man she believed to be the father of her child.

He scanned the familiar details once more: Lord Alexander Henry James Fitzherbert, Eton, Oxford, Coldstream Guards, married to Rosemary Felicity Baring, one daughter, Saffron Jane, living in South Kensington, director in the City of Azure International. Clubs: White's, Annabel's, RAC, member of the Red Lancers polo team. There followed a rundown of his routine, and Amadeo noted that Zan traveled frequently to Cannes on business, and to Kilgarin, Ireland.

When the phone rang he picked it up and heard Frank Bevan's Cockney-accented English. "Good morning, Mr. Benguela. What can I do for you? I hope you've received my report."

Amadeo said brusquely, "That's why I'm calling. I want to take it one step further. It's important for me to know the subject's blood group as soon as possible. You can easily do it through his insurance company, or better still via the doctor who treats the Red Lancers. I want it by tomorrow morning—shall we say nine o'clock Paris time?"

"Don't worry, sir. We have these things in hand and I can get the information to you with no problem."

When Amadeo had hung up he flipped the intercom. "Tell Miguel to bring the car to the front of the office, Delphine."

In a quarter of an hour he was climbing the curving staircase of Shannon's apartment house on the Île Saint-

Louis. Brushing his fingers restlessly through his hair, he rang the bell.

"Oh—good morning, Mr. Benguela." Shannon's young English nanny, Fiona, fluttered the moment she opened the door to him. "Please come in." The plump Scotswoman led the way into the light salon papered in almond green and comfortably furnished with feminine elegance in creams and pale apricot.

"Could I get you a cup of coffee?"

"No, thank you, Fiona."

She looked at him with veiled curiosity. She was used to Amadeo's presence, as he often dropped in in the evening to see Patrick and Shannon, but his arrival at ten in the morning while Shannon was away surprised her.

"Patrick is in his room. He's just had his bath and his juice. I was going to take him out for a little walk, but it's starting to drizzle. I'll go and fetch him." She came back, proudly bearing the fat, rosy-cheeked baby smelling of talcum. "He's very disappointed not to go for his walkies, isn't he?" she cooed.

"Come to *Tío*," said Amadeo, beaming at Patrick with outstretched arms.

Patrick gave him a grin of recognition.

"I'd like to take him out for a little while—to see some friends of mine. They're in town overnight, and it will do him good to get some fresh air."

"Oh, do you think that's wise?" Fiona worried. "You see, he has his lunch by twelve. There's not really time."

"Don't worry. I'll have him back in an hour or so, I promise, Fiona. My friends don't live far from here. Let me just take his shawl," he said, tucking it around him.

Before the nanny could protest, he was walking out the door in an authoritative manner. "Are you sure you don't want me to accompany you, Mr. Benguela—just in case he starts fussing?"

"That won't be necessary. I'm used to babies."

"He must be back before twelve for his lunch. I'm sorry to insist, but I am responsible and we must keep to his routine."

With anxious concern she watched him go down the stairs.

When the Mercedes drew up before an office building in the Trocadero, Miguel leapt out to open the door and Amadeo

311

slid from the backseat, cradling Patrick in his arms. Passersby turned their heads at the incongruous picture of an impeccably dressed man of fortune swaddling an infant in a shawl as the smart uniformed chauffeur pressed a button at the entrance. Amadeo strode through the plate-glass doors, smiling indulgently at the bundle in his arms.

"You like going out with Papa, don't you?" he whispered in Patrick's ear. Approaching the receptionist, he said, "I'm here to see Dr. Darlan, the phlebologist."

Within the space of half an hour the doctor had placed a vial of blood in the rack on the instrument trolley. Patrick was still wailing indignantly as Amadeo rocked him to and fro.

"All I need now is the other blood type. We have yours, the mother's, and now the baby's. As soon as I have his, I'll let you know. Come and sit down in my office." He gestured toward the adjacent room.

Clasping the whimpering Patrick, Amadeo sat down across the desk.

"Your blood type is AB and the mother's is A, so that any child resulting from you and the mother will have to be an AB combination. If the alleged father who is in dispute is also A or B, I'm afraid there will be no way to confirm your paternity. There's tissue typing, but even that's not conclusive. However, should his blood group be outside AB, at least we can rule out the possibility of his paternity, though as I've said, it cannot confirm yours."

"How soon will I know?"

"I should have the child's blood test back by tomorrow morning, so that if you then know the other party's blood type, we can at least solve part of the riddle."

The next morning Amadeo was in his office earlier than usual, waiting for Bevan's nine o'clock call. It had been the longest twenty-four hours he had spent in years, and he had been brooding ceaselessly over what he would do if he should discover that Patrick was really Zan's child after all these months of feeling so sure of himself. Yesterday, when he had touched the fine dark hair on Patrick's head, he had been sure that it was impossible for a fair, blue-eyed Englishman to be this child's father, and no proof seemed stronger than his own love, which had burned fiercely when Patrick had clasped his tiny hand around his outstretched finger.

Now, as the clock neared nine, Amadeo almost regretted his own dogged persistence, telling himself that it would have been better to go on believing that Patrick was his without putting it to the test. He had tied Shannon to him by the silken thread of Galant, and it was only a matter of time before he could reel her in back to his side where she belonged. But it was his nature to seek the truth, to get to the bottom of things, whether in business or private life. He had to know the why and how and who of any question that affected his affairs, and his tenacity made it impossible for him to exist in a state of blissful ignorance. Should Lord Fitzherbert prove indisputably to be Patrick's father, all his dreams would have to be realigned with his lifelong conviction that fate would restore to him what it had stolen one night in Rosario.

It could have been yesterday, it was so clear in his mind, but it was more than twenty years ago that he had returned to the two-room apartment he shared with his wife, Consuela, in the suburbs of the city, to discover that the baby she was carrying had arrived a month ahead of time and that she had been rushed to the hospital. Nothing the doctor could say had consoled him when he broke the news that both his wife and child were dead. Had he not prolonged his business in the north, he might have arrived in time to ensure she had been taken to the best clinic, but his absence had meant the loss of valuable hours.

From that moment on, Amadeo had set himself a ruthless course, determined to forge a towering international business empire that absorbed all his thought and energy, and until that day he had successfully avoided the painful repetition of any emotion that involved loss and despair.

The sharp shrill of the phone brought him back from the past.

"*C'est Monsieur Bevan à l'appareil, monsieur,*" said his secretary.

"Put him through."

"Good morning, Mr. Benguela," said Bevan cheerily. "I have the information you asked for yesterday. It seems that the party in question has the blood type O."

He felt his heart pound. "Are you absolutely sure of that?"

"There's no doubt about it, sir. We obtained it from the files of the Red Lancers' doctor as you suggested, and just to be sure I cross-checked it with his health insurance file."

Hanging up, Amadeo paused for only a second before dialing Darlan. "It's Benguela here," he said, trying to sound calm. "I got the blood type I've been waiting for this morning."

"Just a moment. Let me get my notes. The child's test just came in."

Amadeo felt a hammer of suspense beating at his temples as he waited for the doctor.

"The child's blood type is AB."

"The party in question has a blood type O," he said tersely.

"Then that settles the matter. He certainly cannot be the father of this child. By process of elimination, from what you tell me, there's no doubt that you are the father."

When he had hung up, Amadeo sat in his chair for a long moment as a broad smile spread across his face. Falling back in his seat, he raised his clenched fists in the air and gave a lusty laugh, venting his uncontained joy. Jubilantly he strode to the bar concealed in a cabinet and took out a bottle of champagne, then flipped the intercom.

"Delphine—come in here at once."

When his secretary entered she was startled to see Amadeo's face and the champagne bottle in his hand at that hour of the morning. Benguela was an exacting man to work for, and his attention to business at all hours was obsessive.

"Don't look so surprised, Delphine. I have something momentous to celebrate," he said, popping the cork. With a ceremonious gesture he filled two glasses to the brim.

"Is there something I should be aware of?" she queried.

"Yes—I've just concluded the coup of a lifetime. Let us drink to it," he announced triumphantly.

"It's all very mysterious," she replied in confusion.

"For the moment it's top secret." Raising his glass to hers, he said with a devilish smile, "À le vôtre," as he toasted Patrick Benguela, his son.

When Delphine returned to her desk, Amadeo settled in his chair, his mind racing ahead. Now that he was certain he was Patrick's father, his life was entirely different, but so was Shannon's. Since that day at Les Tourelles they had never discussed Patrick's father, and by now he hoped she had come to terms with the fact that her affair with the Englishman was over. Surely, Amadeo told himself, if she was confronted with the astonishing news that he was the father of her child, they would be united at once. Patrick was the product of that stormy scene between them on the *Karisma*, and an indissoluble parental bond had been born of their conflict. It was now his duty to tell Shannon the truth—and to win her back.

Moments later, when he telephoned the Negresco in Nice, he was surprised to discover that Shannon had checked out two days before, only a day after he had last spoken to her about the meeting with Galant.

"Get the factory in Grasse for me, Delphine," he said impatiently. "They'll know where she is. Better still, put me through to the director there."

When he came on the line Amadeo greeted him expansively, feeling well disposed toward the human race and even more impatient to tell Shannon he would be coming to Nice that evening.

"I'm trying urgently to contact Mademoiselle Faloon. I thought perhaps she might be at the factory today or tomorrow, or that perhaps you know where she is staying."

"I'm afraid I have no idea, monsieur," he replied in an ingratiating tone that indicated he recognized the illustrious name of Benguela.

"Have you any idea where I might get in touch with her? It's most urgent."

"I'm afraid not. When I last saw her she was with a colleague of hers."

"You mean Monsieur Galant?"

"No, an English gentleman. She took him 'round the factory. I recall his name was Lord Fitzherbert. Before they left she told me she would be out of touch for a few days and that she would call in here before she left. May I take a message?"

"*Non, merci*," he said tersely. Replacing the receiver, Amadeo felt his heart slacken like a flag that had lost the breeze.

Chapter VII

Bending to pick up a piece of driftwood, Kerry paused for a moment to watch the sun dropping into the iridescent water, where a few sailboats still played in the evening breeze. It was Labor Day weekend, and already some trees bordering the rocky beach had begun to change color. Closing her eyes, she breathed in the fragrant sea air, feeling vibrantly alive after spending an entire summer at North Haven, Maine, with the Belmonts, and she dreaded the idea that it was about to end.

"All right, let's get moving. We need that wood for the bonfire," called a voice.

With a smile on her face she turned to see Betsy's older brother, Hal.

"And what are you doing, may I ask? Supervising?" she retorted with a laugh.

"I'm exhausted from opening beer cans," he replied, looking appreciatively at Kerry's suntanned legs. Her coppery hair, tousled by the breeze, was tipped with gold from being in the sun all summer. She pulled her powder-pink shetland over her cutoffs and smiled up at him sweetly.

"Here, Mr. Universe. You can take this," she said, scooping up a pile of wood and thrusting it into his arms.

The two of them walked back to the cove along the rocky shoreline, toward the noisy group of people gathered for a clambake. Among them were a clutch of Lamonts, Gardiners, Cabots, and Cushings who represented the comfortable old fortunes of Boston and New York. These large, boisterous families migrated seasonally to North Haven, where they played at a deceptively simple seaside existence.

The competitive outdoor existence of rich New Englanders at play had appealed at once to Kerry, who had thrown herself vigorously into the swimming, sailing, and tennis that filled the hours from dawn until dusk. The solid, down-to-earth Mr. and Mrs. Belmont had immediately taken her under their wing, pleased that their daughter had befriended such a well-mannered, attractive, and enthusiastic young woman. With the dauntless spirit of a natural champion, Kerry had distinguished herself as just the "right" kind of girl—athletic, competitive, and full of pert enthusiasm. She was alwasy eager to put up the colorful spinnaker of the Belmont sailboat, thrilled to see it billowing up against the blue sky as they cruised the choppy dark Atlantic. She was always fresh and smiling when the sun rose, ready for tennis or swimming, or even clearing up the breakfast dishes on the screened porch of the house overlooking the sea.

The arresting edge of Kerry's personality made her popular with the boys home for the summer. Their eyes followed her curvaceous little behind in tight cutoffs, her high, firm breasts as she lunged for a tennis ball or trimmed a sail. But though no one ever made her feel excluded, she had become aware of the network of family ties that bound this seemingly casual crowd together. Their open friendliness almost made her believe she was one of them, but she sensed the first tugs of common interest that would unite families of solid wealth and position beginning to assert themselves in the form of summer romances between boys and girls who had been friends since childhood. Kerry ached to join them. This effortless belonging, this acceptance without question, was what she desperately wanted from life.

Kerry looked at Hal, destined to be a lawyer in his father's firm. Maybe he would be the one, she thought, and then, maybe he wouldn't. She reminded herself she still had another year to narrow the field down to a husband.

They joined the crowd gathered around the bonfire blazing up into the pale evening sky, where seagulls wheeled noisily. Mr. Belmont and the other men, in Bermuda shorts and sneakers, were seeing to the truck that had delivered big caldrons of mussels, clams, and lobsters steamed on beds of seaweed, while their wives set out corn on the cob, Boston baked beans, and garlic bread. Tom Belmont was just pulling the top off a can of beer to hand one to Kerry when she happened to glance across the crowd. She felt as if ice water were sliding down her back when she saw Betsy talking to Mark Van Buren.

"Here, Kerry, have a beer," said Tom, thrusting one into her hand.

"Thanks," she murmured numbly.

Mark turned with a look of pleased surprise on his face and gave her a little wave. Paralyzed with dread, Kerry could

317

almost read Betsy's lips as she asked Mark how they knew each other, and she waited for the existence she had so carefully built over the last year to come crashing down on her. In a moment Betsy came rushing toward her, with Mark in tow.

"Why the hell didn't you tell me you knew Mark? We've known each other for ages. His aunt's house is only half a mile away from ours."

Kerry looked at him blankly, waiting for him to expose her.

"Hi, Kerry. I think we met at a dance last summer, didn't we?"

A moment later, when Betsy moved away, he said, "You're looking very well, Kerry."

"And so are you. It's been a long time, hasn't it?"

The lopsided, rather shy smile she remembered so well cut through the barrier that protected her most sheltered emotions. Mark had matured to young manhood in the last year, losing that unfinished look, and the bruised expression she remembered in his eyes had given way to a quiet self-confidence. To her surprise she found his modest demeanor appealing.

"Come and get it, everybody—the clambake is ready," called Mrs. Belmont.

Mark and Kerry got in line, and when they had heaped their plates with food he said, "Why don't we go sit on that log over there?"

When they were seated Kerry stared at the lobster and the corn on the cob. Moments ago the salty sea air had made her ravenous, but now her appetite was gone.

"Why did you do that? Why did you pretend that we had met at a dance?" she challenged him.

"Well, didn't we? Have you forgotten the Frobishers?" As he spoke he blushed, reminding her of the old Mark. She sensed that he was thinking of all the painful events that had followed that party.

"But what was your real reason for lying?"

"I guess it was because I saw the fear in your eyes. And anyway, Betsy had been telling me all about you before you saw me, filling in all the gaps about the person you had obviously become. I've never forgotten that conversation we had that night on the lawn—you remember, about feeling on the outside looking in. Congratulations," he said sincerely.

318

"I'm really glad to see that you made it. You seem very happy."

His sincerity was almost painful to her. "Anyway, thanks a lot for not giving me away," she said contritely. "All those things I told Betsy are partly true in a way. I hope you don't think I'm awful for telling a few fibs."

"You don't have to explain. I understand," he said sympathetically. "Kerry—I want you to know I'm not proud of what happened last year. I let my father walk all over me."

"Let's not talk about it," she murmured, wondering what lies Lindy had told him about her—but knowing Mark, she supposed his father's fierce ultimatum had been enough.

"I'll always hate my father for the way he treated you, for taking Rainmaker away. I know what that horse meant to you, and I'm aware that your career was ruined—all because of me. I was a fool, Kerry, and I want you to know how sorry I am. I've wanted to look you up so often."

"Please—let's just forget all about it. It's over now, and done with," she said with a tired sigh.

"All right. But let me say this. You taught me one thing—that somehow I'll have to stand on my own two feet if I want to keep my self-respect. I'm not doing too badly, either," he said proudly. "I've got only one more year left at Harvard, and I'm in the top third of my class."

"That's great, Mark. I knew you'd do it. But still—you'll always be a Van Buren."

"And you'll always be the Honorable Kerry Faloon."

"Touché," she said with a laugh.

As darkness set in beyond the ring of firelight, singing broke out in the crowd, churning up a rare homesickness in Kerry. These campfire evenings always reminded her of home—of Koonwarra. The summer was turning to embers as fast as the wood on the fire. For one golden season she had been cocooned like a child, she had been Kerry the carefree sophomore from Braemar with the sea breeze in her hair, rather Kerry the woman of the world, who seemed to have all the answers.

The mesmeric atmosphere of the cove was suddenly dimmed for her by the memory of black silk underwear, of champagne in an ice bucket, of powerful hands roaming over her body, of obscene whispers in her ear as she and Lindy hungrily made love together. What would they think, all these uncomplicated and nice people, she wondered, if they knew she had an addiction that both excited and shamed her?

319

To the summer vacationers at North Haven, sex was probably something awkward and hurried done in a warm double bed in the middle of the night, with no sighs, no whispers. And what would Mark say if he knew? She couldn't help wondering as she glanced at his innocent face glowing in the firelight. How would he react if he could see her writhing passionately beneath his father?

"You're daydreaming, Kerry. What about?"

She glanced up to find Mark studying her.

"Nothing. I'm just sorry to see the summer end, that's all."

"Would you mind if I called you at Braemar when you get back?"

"Sure. It would be fun," she said without thinking.

The day school started, Mrs. Belmont drove Betsy and Kerry through the campus in the family station wagon. Kerry looked at the familiar landmarks of the idyllic campus, now diffused with a golden autumn haze. She felt an inexpressible joy well up inside her at being back at Braemar again. Exchanging warm hugs and kisses with Mrs. Belmont and showering her with effusive thanks, she and Betsy lugged their suitcases into the ivy-covered dorm, now echoing with the squeals of excitement that indicated a new term had begun.

"Go on ahead upstairs. I'll check the mail," Kerry called to Betsy.

She was pleased to see messages from two boys she had met that summer in her slot, confirming that her blaze of social success would continue in the new term; but the first envelope she opened was her bank statement. Scanning it quickly, she felt a nervous tension subside in her that she had kept at bay all summer. Every time she bought a hotdog or a soda she had felt a stab of insecurity; but now, seeing that Lindy's monthly installments had been as regular as clockwork, she was inexpressibly relieved. Still, she knew she wouldn't relax completely until he called her in October as he had promised he would.

A week later, when Mark rang, Kerry thumbed through her diary.

"Mark, it's terrible, but I can't fit you in for at least two weeks," she sighed, conveying that the days when he was the only boy in her life were over.

"Are you ever popular," he said with a dry laugh that didn't conceal his disappointment. "Let's make a date for that Friday for the movies and dinner somewhere. I'd better book you now for the Yale-Harvard game. What do you say?"

It was typical of Mark to pin her down for one of the most exciting events of the autumn, and she felt cornered. It was maddening to be committed so early, when someone better would almost certainly ask her.

"Sure, okay," she replied frostily.

When she had hung up she was sorry she hadn't lied. Why had she said yes? Mark still provoked a feeling of pity and guilt that she felt for no one else. Though Lindy had never once mentioned his son, Kerry felt an ominous discomfort that they were dating again and reminded herself that she would have to be careful he didn't find out.

A week before the Harvard-Yale game, Kerry was called to the phone.

"Kerry—this is Lindy," came a low, familiar drawl.

"Hi," she said, her heart pounding. For an entire month she had been worried out of her mind that he had forgotten all about her, throwing her right back to where she had been a year ago. "I've been wondering about you. You said you'd phone in late October," she said, careful to keep her voice coyly playful.

"I decided to fly over to Paris for the Arc at the last moment, and then I went over to Ireland for a couple of weeks to look at some new thoroughbreds. Wait until you hear about the beauty I've picked up."

At the mention of one of the highlights of the international racing season, the Arc de Triomphe, Kerry felt eaten through with jealousy, and his casual mention of horses seemed deliberately cruel. But she took care to inject just the right note of suggestive compliance into her voice to rekindle his appetite for her.

"Lucky you," she said with a throaty little laugh. "Anyway, glad you're finally back in town." She would taste revenge when she went to the Harvard-Yale game with Mark.

"Kerry—the reason I called is that I'm coming up for the Harvard-Yale game. . . ."

"You are?" she said, feeling a stab of apprehension.

"I'll go to the game, and then I'll be dining with friends in the evening, but I want to see you after that."

"I'm going to the game, too, and there are lots of parties afterward," she blurted out resentfully.

He cut across her protest. "I'll be expecting you at the Ritz-Carlton when I get back about eleven. Just ask for the key."

There was no point in arguing. She was Lindy Van Buren's mistress, and he owned her time as surely as if he held a deed of title.

"Right—I'll be there. Can't wait," she whispered.

On the morning of the Harvard-Yale game, the stairwell echoed with shrill conversation when Kerry dashed downstairs, bundled up in her camel-hair coat and a long scarf of crimson and white, the Harvard colors. There was a contagious enthusiasm in the air as boys from Harvard cruised their cars up to the dorm to pick up the lucky girls who had landed a date for the game. Catching sight of Mark in the hallway, in a tweed overcoat and scarf around his neck, Kerry called out, then felt a grudging affection for him as she watched his face light up at the sight of her. Even Alison and Stephanie, who were terrible snobs, had been impressed when she'd told them casually she had hit it off with Mark Van Buren that summer, and it began to dawn on her he wasn't nearly as bad as she had supposed.

They began the day with brunch in Harvard Square, then drove over to Soldier's Field for the game. It was bitterly cold, and the sky threatened snow as they walked to the stadium, Kerry's arm looped through his, her eyes glowing with the excitement of it all. Swept along with the crowd, they made their way to the bleachers, where the pennants, the pompoms, and the roaring cheers of thousands of Yale and Harvard fans thrilled her. As she and Mark huddled together on the cold bench, it started to snow big fat flakes that melted on her eyelashes, and Kerry was suddenly consumed with the carefree joy of being a college girl for the first time since she had been at Braemar. She gave Mark her most ravishing smile, and he hugged her happily. When he passed her his hip flask she took a slug of brandy to ward off the cold, laughing out loud when Yale supporters trailing blue-and-white scarves charged onto the field with their mascot, a large, surly bulldog, chanting, "Bull dog, bull dog, bow, wow, wow! . . ." She screamed at the top of her lungs when the Harvard team jogged onto the field with a rolling, powerful gait, weighed down with helmets and shoulder pads like modern-day gladiators. Cuddled closely together, she and Mark cheered throughout the entire game, and it didn't matter that Harvard lost two to seven. When the game was over they went to a bar in the square with a high-spirited crowd of Mark's friends from the business school, including the dark, good-looking Buff Coolidge, who flirted with her outrageously. Her cheeks pink from the cold and the brandy, snowflakes sparkling in her coppery hair, she laughed vivaciously at him and pretended not to notice. But she noted the name Coolidge.

"You're the prettiest girl here," Mark whispered in her ear, basking in the admiration she had elicited. It didn't occur to him to be jealous.

"I'm having such a great time. It's the most fun I've had since I came to Braemar," she exclaimed.

"Are you really? Me, too," Mark confided. "But we're not finished yet. Buff wants us to come back to a big party he's having at his apartment, and before that we're going out for dinner. What do you say to that?"

"It sounds wonderful," she replied distractedly. Looking at her watch, Kerry was reminded that the magical hours were slipping by, bringing her nearer to her appointment with Lindy.

From then on the evening seemed to lose its sparkle. As they left the restaurant Mark slipped his arm around her and whispered:

"What's the matter, Kerry? Is something bothering you?"

"No, nothing," she said, shaking her head with a strained smile.

"You looked so pretty there in the restaurant. I wanted to reach over and . . ." His voice was mellowed by happiness.

"And what?" she replied. They had paused in a dark doorway as the others strode on ahead, their laughter echoing in the night, now bright with stars.

"And kiss you." He reached out to embrace her awkwardly through their winter coats, his lips finding hers in the darkness.

"Kerry," he gasped as he hugged her to him. "I still love you. I always will. Is there a chance for us again, in spite of everything?"

The look of pure devotion on his face was unbearable.

"Why don't you pursue me and find out," she called, dancing down the street ahead of him. As he caught up with her, reality tugged her back to earth. How would he feel if he could see her near midnight?

"There's something I have to say, Mark," she began haltingly. "I hope you don't expect us to pick up where we left off. I mean, sleeping together."

"Of course not," he said sincerely. "I don't blame you, not after what happened. Let's start all over, right from the very beginning—pretend that we just met and take it from there."

The party at Buff's was in full swing by ten-thirty, with guests littering every inch of the floor in the smoke-filled apartment. A Rolling Stones record blasted from the stereo, drowning out shrieks and laughter, and bottles and beer cans littered the tables. Glancing furtively at her watch, Kerry realized it was time to go. She picked her way across the living room, passing the kitchen, where a couple were necking furiously, and went to retrieve her coat from a pile on the bed. Mark was nowhere to be seen when she looked over her shoulder at the door in the hall. She was already dreading his frantic telephone call tomorrow, when she would tell him she had drunk too much, was sick and too embarrassed to ask him to take her home.

She went out into the cold, silent street, past apartment houses where parties were just getting started, feeling like Cinderella leaving the ball. Beneath her skirt and sweater she wore the black underwear that Lindy loved to see against her creamy skin, and in her bag was a bottle of his favorite perfume. In the space of a taxi ride she numbly felt herself metamorphosing from a freshly scrubbed Braemar girl into a sultry whore.

Near midnight, when Lindy's mouth closed on hers in a rapacious kiss as they lay on the rumpled sheets of his bed, all the simple pastimes of a college weekend were shorn away. As their passionate rhythm gained momentum, she soared above the mundane earth on powerful adult wings, far from bright pennants and nonsense rhymes, and innocent hugs in dark doorways. She had been gladly and willingly corrupted by Lindy's profane lust, which fed an inferno of passion that raged in the center of her being.

The minute Shannon arrived at the door of her apartment she slipped out of her patent heels with relief. Dropping her briefcase, she slipped off her suit jacket, calling, "Fiona, I'm home."

The nanny came through the door that led to the bed-rooms, closing it quietly behind her.

"I tried to keep him up until you got home," she whis-pered, "but he just couldn't keep his eyes open."

"The little sweetheart," said Shannon with a disappointed smile. "I'll just tiptoe in to have a peek at him." When she came out of the nursery, Fiona said:

"You look shattered. Let me get you a drink."

"Thanks. That would be wonderful," Shannon said with a sigh, sinking into a chair by the fireplace, where Fiona had lit a fire to welcome her.

Handing her a gin and tonic, Fiona asked, "Are you staying in tonight? I've put a shepherd's pie in the oven."

"Wonderful—can't think of anything I'd like better. I've got to leave the house by eight tomorrow, so I'd better have an early night. Only two more days—then I can drop every-thing for Christmas. I haven't even had time to shop yet."

"Shannon—I've been thinking. Are you sure you don't mind me going to Aberdeen for Christmas? You know, as far as I'm concerned, Patrick comes first. You've got a pile of invitations for the holidays, and you won't have anybody to look after him if you want to go out."

"That's awfully sweet of you, Fi, and I'm grateful, but there's nothing I want more than to stay here for a week, with Patrick. I'm dreaming about it already. Bathing him, feeding him, playing with him all day. When he's having his nap I'll have one, too. You know, if somebody had told me years ago that I would refuse invitations to balls and soirées in Paris to stay home with a baby, I wouldn't have believed it, but it's true."

On a table nearby was a picture of the infant who had looked like an Eskimo when he was born. Now he was a dark-eyed little boy of almost eleven months, just about to walk. He was growing up so fast. Shannon's day was com-pletely absorbed by her work, and even on weekends she pored over business papers to prepare for the launch of *Samarkand*. All too frequently her evenings were taken up with entertaining a host of important new clients who had become part of her life, from the staff at Galant to a galaxy of publicity and manufacturing agents who were involved in the birth of her treasured brainchild. But this Christmas, she promised herself, would be just for her and Patrick. She had turned down invitations to innumerable parties, and not even the chance to spend Christmas in Marrakesh or St. Moritz had tempted her. Nothing was more appealing than spending an entire week alone with her baby in the flat she had had so little time to enjoy.

Shannon had just stepped out of the shower when she heard the doorbell ring. Wondering who it could be, she slipped into her terry-cloth robe and pulled her hair up into a ponytail.

"It's Amadeo," called Fiona.

Shannon gave him a welcoming smile when she saw him standing by the fire. In a beautifully cut navy suit, he looked undeniably distinguished and handsome, exuding the aura of charismatic power that had always attracted her. She greeted him with a kiss on the cheek.

"I hope I'm not disturbing you. I just got in from Charles de Gaulle and had the impulse to drop by and ask you for dinner."

"I'm delighted you came by. It's been ages since I've seen you," she replied warmly. "Would you like to stay and have supper with us? If you don't mind eating shepherd's pie, that is."

"There's nothing that I'd like better."

She poured him a drink. "Your secretary said you weren't coming back until the end of the week. How were the Emirates?"

"Hot," he replied with a humorous glint in his eye as she handed him a glass. "And moderately profitable."

She curled up in a chair across from him, thinking she had never seen him looking better.

"Is Patrick in bed already?"

"Yes, but you can tiptoe in and have a look at him."

Since Shannon's trip to Grasse in May she had seen little of Amadeo. Their paths seemed to have crossed much less frequently than before, and Shannon sometimes wished he would drop in to see Patrick more often when he knew she'd be there. They had had dinner once in October to discuss business, and occasionally he had come to the flat in evening dress on his way to a soirée. Rumors of his new conquests had reached her, and she had seen his name and photograph in the gossip columns. She could always spot his type—socially prominent, polished women who added a certain luster to his already glamorous image. They made Shannon feel she had never belonged in his gallery of famous beauties. Her friendship with Amadeo seemed to have reached

326

a comfortable plateau, but she was always careful not to pry into his private life, and he treated her with the same consideration. Not once had he brought up Patrick's father, but Shannon sometimes felt by a look or a gesture that he was aware they were in touch. When she'd returned from that glorious week in Seillans, she had been tempted to confide in Amadeo, to prove to him that Zan's love was constant and that her faith in him was not misplaced. But pride had held her back. As a Latin male, Amadeo would never be able to fathom such a strange relationship. How could he understand that she and Zan found it less painful to love each other at a distance for the time being, that they were willing to make a sacrifice now for the harvest they would eventually reap? Amadeo would only heap scorn on her with dark accusing eyes, she knew.

"Now, tell me what's happening at Galant."

"I've got the prototype of the bottle—wait until you see it," she said, leaping up to fetch her briefcase. From a pouch of cream suede she brought out a dome-shaped bottle of amethyst glass adorned with silver filigree.

"This is very fine, lovely," he pronounced. "A perfect package for *Samarkand*. They've done an excellent job."

"Don't you think it conjures up the domes of the East? And here's a drawing of the presentation box. I just got them this week. Marcel was delighted, and I've given my approval to go ahead. For the launch in Paris and New York we're doing a thousand in real silver."

"Excellent," he commented.

In a private but informal board meeting they discussed the trademark registration, the manufacturing schedule, the advertising campaign, and the budget, all timed with precision for the upcoming months.

"It looks like the price of jasmine is going up again after the late frost, so I'll have to readjust the cost projections. I could have used your advice lately. I've simply had to ride on my intuition for a lot of things."

"You seem perfectly capable of handling all the decisions by yourself. I had confidence in you all along."

Their eyes met for a long moment. "I hadn't realized how lonely things can be at the top. Now I've had a good dose of it," she said with a deprecating smile.

"Yes, but when praise is being handed out later on, you'll be the one to receive it. That will be your reward," he said encouragingly.

327

Later, the three of them gathered around the kitchen table to have supper in relaxed informality. Amadeo had removed his jacket and rolled up his shirt-sleeves as he talked animatedly. He drank the inexpensive claret with the same zest as that with which he enjoyed vintage wine from his own fabled cellar, and he complimented Fiona lavishly on the shepherd's pie. Recalling the night they first went to Maxim's, Shannon realized how incongruous it would have seemed then that the two of them could enjoy themselves just as much eating simply on a checkered tablecloth, she in her robe, the nanny in an old sweater, Patrick's bottles in the sink. Amadeo gestured expansively as he related an afternoon he had spent with a Saudi prince falconing in the desert.

"This is a remarkable change from yesterday," he was saying. "We lunched in the prince's tent in the middle of the desert. It was furnished with priceless carpets, and his retinue of servants came in bearing huge silver trays of mutton and rice that we ate with our fingers. They offered me the sheep's testicles and eyes."

"Oh, no," said Fiona, throwing up her hands in disgust. "You didn't eat them?"

"Of course. It was a very great honor," he said with a wink, causing them to laugh.

After dinner, as he and Shannon sat by the fire, Amadeo said, "By the way, what are you doing for Christmas?"

"I'm staying here with Patrick. Fiona's going home for the holidays. Are you going to Mürren?" As she said it her mind went back to the Christmas they had spent together. Now she calmly imagined someone else in her place.

"I really don't have the time this year. I was wondering if you might not like to come to Les Tourelles with Patrick."

"That's very kind of you," she began hesitantly. "But I've planned to do nothing at all. I really need some peace and quiet."

"But that's just what I want. I haven't invited anyone else, and only the staff knows I'm coming. Please say you'll come, Shannon."

The thought crossed her mind that his woman of the moment had let him down, or that he had capriciously changed his mind. The picture of the huge Christmas tree at the château invaded her mind, and the idea of the three of them spending evenings by the fire. Christmas was for children, after all. Did she really want to be alone while Zan was with Rosemary and Saffron in Ireland?

"I think it sounds wonderful. I'd love to come," she said warmly.

On Christmas night, when Patrick had been tucked into bed, Shannon and Amadeo were sipping calvados by the fire. In the formal atmosphere of the château, Shannon always liked to change for dinner, and tonight she had worn elaborately worked evening pantaloons with an embroidered peasant blouse.

"Thank you again for all your marvelous presents. This is the most beautiful cashmere shawl in the world, and the Bedouin jewelry is so lovely. I'll always treasure it," she said, touching the silver necklace and soft shawl he had given her that morning.

"My greatest happiness is to see the pleasure my gifts have given you," he said expansively.

"And you've been so generous to Patrick, Amadeo. I'll never forget the look on his face when he saw the Shetland pony and cart. I thought he would burst," she said with a laugh, recalling his small arms gesturing with excitement as they led him through the park.

Shannon had begun to suspect from the discreet but elaborate Christmas preparations at the château that Amadeo had planned all along for them to be together. Every now and then she caught him looking at her with what seemed to be nostalgic affection, causing her throat to tighten with nervousness. It was Les Tourelles, she told herself. The château was haunted by the dangerous memories of their powerful first encounter that weekend she had come to hunt with Fabrice.

A clock chiming on a commode seemed to ring in a new era as the year drew to a close almost the way it had begun, with the two of them by the fire. When Amadeo put on a record, the sweet nostalgic notes of a French ballad, Shannon sank into a reflective mood. Approaching her chair, he reached for her hand.

"Let us dance once before we retire, Shanita."

Her heart beat faster when he held her. She was taken by surprise to find herself in his arms again, but she gave herself up to the music and gazed dreamily at the reflected shadows through half-closed eyes, searching the corners of the magnificent room. But each note of the music seemed to coax forth a yearning for warmth and tenderness after all the bleak, lonely months since May, and she had to steel herself against the seductive power of Amadeo's nearness. He, too, seemed to be holding back, she sensed, making her suddenly want him all the more. When she felt his lips brush her cheek, a desire so potently irresistible overtook her that it crushed any last resistance. The parquet was suddenly as dangerous as black ice, and they skated across it in tandem, locked in a rhythmic revival of a passion she had thought was dead. Shannon felt her arms wind around him, involuntarily searching the tautness of his back and shoulders. He still seemed to hold himself aloof, as if exerting his will to tempt her to the edge of a breaking wave, where he would lure her further still. It wasn't too late to change her mind even then, she told herself. But part of her had gone too far, like a number placed on the table when the wheel of destiny was already in motion. When she felt him hard against her, her longing uncoiled within her and spun madly out of control. The music came to an end, and they confronted each other like harlequins, their faces half in shadow cast by the fire. As he kissed her passionately, tremblingly, they clung to the precipice of desire, neither daring to speak. When Amadeo swooped her up powerfully and carried her toward the staircase, she let out not a murmur of protest but clung to his neck, burying her face in the cleft of his shoulder.

The following morning Amadeo awoke at dawn with Shannon sleeping beside him in his high carved walnut bed. Staring up at the ceiling frescoed with nymphs and naiads cavorting on banks of soft clouds, he considered the turbulent emotions stirred up by last night's passionate and unpremeditated encounter, which had brought the woman he loved back to his bed.

The rapturous fervor of her response had astonished him, and his loins still seemed to retain the impression of her pressing against him. He had reciprocated with an unprecedented ardor, keeping nothing of himself back. But now, by the light of morning, he perceived that Shannon had withheld the vital spark without which lovemaking was incomplete, just as he had once done himself. Would she regret what had happened when she awoke? The thought was as intolerable as the long months of starvation for her love, and he slipped from bed and went to his dressing room before she awakened.

Half an hour later, dressed for riding in a tweed jacket, jodhpurs, and polished brown boots, he crossed the frozen park toward the stables, where his saddled dappled-gray mare awaited him. He felt her shy as he mounted, but swinging himself into the saddle, he took command of the horse. Leaving the cobbled yard, he urged the mare toward a copse of trees set against the silvery sky. As he rode he was haunted by the thought of Shannon's eyes, darkened with regret, as she awoke.

Riding hard across the frozen ground, he reflected on all the lonely months since May, starting from the day he had found and lost his son. His joy at the confirmation that he was Patrick's father had been instantly diminished by the discovery that Shannon was with Zan in the south of France. He had observed her numbly all these months at a distance, as if through a wall of crystal, locked away but temptingly near. The discovery that she was still in love with the Englishman had savaged his pride and churned up a tortured jealousy, even though he was almost certain she hadn't seen Zan again since May. Gradually he had come to admit the futility of hoping to bind her to him with gratitude, which he had assumed would turn to love. Now he realized that if he foisted the truth about Patrick on her, she might even begin to hate him for shattering her dreams. Returning to the château, he was pursued by the impassioned night in her arms.

When Shannon awoke in Amadeo's room it took her a moment to recall where she was. It had been a long time since she had observed the frescoed ceiling in the mellow light of a winter morning. Her first thought was of Patrick, but she remembered Annette had promised to get him up and feed him. Then, turning, she realized the bed was empty. Her body still alive and tingling from lovemaking, she suppressed disappointment that Amadeo wasn't there to take her in his arms; yet she felt a sense of relief as the memory of the night before returned to her. As she lay there, her body warred with her conscience after so many loveless months. The impulsive act had cleaved her, body and soul, and she asked herself how she could respond to Amadeo as she had, when she knew she was in love with Zan.

Rising from the bed, she surveyed the debris of the night before, her clothes crushed in a careless heap on the carpet, her stockings and underwear flung on a chair, her satin shoes kicked off in a corner. The silken, lacy chaos suggested some violent abduction, but the only struggle had been her own impatience to discard her clothes, so anxious had she been for Amadeo's strong, virile body. She wrapped herself in a dressing gown and went to draw the heavy brocade curtains, suppressing a shiver. How had she allowed herself to be carried away by a burst of momentary passion—how? She had behaved no better than a bitch in heat, yet she was the mother of a child by a man she loved, a man who would be hers one day. A circle of self-condemnation closed around her as she looked into a mirror at the reflection of a woman who was still an enigma. Zan's face came painfully to mind. He had never missed a chance to tell her that he adored her, though his life was a treadmill, a struggle to free himself from the great dynastic weight that bore down on him. His gentle, unassuming love had conquered her where Amadeo's driving passion had failed. He had slipped thoughtlessly from bed at dawn after slaking his thirst for her. Zan, she knew, would have been there beside her to awaken her with gentle kisses.

Boston, February, 1982

While Lindy was taking a shower, Kerry went to his open suitcase in the corner of the room and pulled out his silk paisley dressing gown. Rolling up the sleeves, she plopped languidly into a chair and picked up the phone to dial room service for a club sandwich. She was starving after jumping into bed with Lindy the moment she walked through the door of his suite that February evening. Propping her bare feet on a table, she swept up her hair, smiling wickedly to herself as she thought of their lovemaking. They hadn't seen each other for over a month, long enough to provoke her appetite for him, but not so long that she was tempted to sleep with any of the boys she was dating. It was all very well if you were a Belmont, a Pratt, or a Cabot with a fortune to back you up, but Kerry was scrupulously careful of her reputation. Besides, she told herself, her standards for a lover had become dauntingly high.

Kerry picked up a copy of *Vogue* she had bought at the newsstand in the lobby. Funny, she thought, how she hadn't seen Shannon's picture in any of the magazines for ages. There was an ad for Valentin, but Shannon wasn't the model. Kerry could only imagine that she had become tired of working and had opted for the easy way out as some millionaire's pampered mistress. Maybe at that very moment she, too, was in a luxurious hotel suite on the other side of the world, her bills being paid by some aging Casanova. The more she thought about it, the more amusing it seemed. She fantasized the fabulous Faloon sisters swathed in furs, meeting by chance in some grand hotel—the Dorchester in London, perhaps, or the Gritti Palace in Venice, squired by their sugar daddies. Would they cut each other dead or fall into one another's arms?

As she flicked over the pages of *Vogue* she came across an advertisement telling her that diamonds were forever. It totally ruined her mood. Engagement rings had been popping up at Braemar like spring crocuses in the weeks since Christmas. Stephanie was already engaged, and Alison was on the brink. Even Betsy had someone in tow. Diamonds might be forever, but Kerry felt far from possessing one.

When Mark had proposed before Christmas, she hadn't said yes, she hadn't said no, but she was beginning to get seriously worried now that she had no other real contender. But Mark continued to be her adoring slave, even though she constantly broke dates with him at the last moment for something better, and in spite of the fact she wouldn't let him make love to her no matter how hard he pleaded.

She looked up when Lindy came out of the bathroom, a towel wrapped around his waist, casting him a private little sensual smile that prompted him to approach her chair and slip his hand inside the dressing gown. His fingers toyed with her nipple, touching off a lurch of desire that was never far away when they were together. She tilted her chin enticingly, and he bent down to kiss her. When he went to the mirror to comb his hair, she watched the muscles play across his broad brown shoulders.

"Incidentally, Kerry . . ."

"Hmmm?" she murmured, wondering if they would have time to make love again before he had to go out to a meeting.

"I hope you're not seeing Mark again."

His dangerous monotone jolted her from her little dream.

"What made you say that?" she said warily, heart pounding as she wondered how much he knew.

"It happened to cross my mind, that's all, and I thought I ought to mention it."

Underlying her fear, Kerry felt an angry rebellion at the commanding arrogance in Lindy's voice.

"Well, I did happen to run into him at a clambake in Maine when I stayed with Betsy last summer, if you must know," she said tersely.

"Why didn't you tell me?"

"Why should I? There's nothing to say."

"I see. And you haven't seen him since?"

"I think I saw him at the Harvard-Yale game, as a matter of fact," she said cautiously. "I can't avoid him, you know."

Lindy slipped on his shirt, then buttoned it in front of the mirror without turning to look at her. "I just want to make one thing clear. My feelings haven't changed about you and my son. Do you understand, Kerry? I don't want you to see each other under any circumstances. Don't get it into your head you can defy me."

"Believe me, Mark is the furthest thing from my mind." Her voice was coolly defiant, and he didn't see the sparks of anger flashing from her eyes.

Before Lindy left, he kissed her long and sensuously, reminding her of what was to come when he returned. But once he had gone, his words seemed to linger in the room like the scent of his cologne. She threw the magazine angrily on the floor and slumped in the chair, seething with outrage.

What did Lindy think was in store for her, she wondered, when her two years at Braemar were up? Did he suppose he had paid for her to mark time at school so she could wind up being his kept woman in an apartment in Boston or New York? She usually avoided thinking too far in the future, but as she stared her life in the face, she sensed that the winds of fate were shifting. Even the rich and powerful Lindy Van Buren couldn't manipulate the lives of everyone to his satisfaction. Then and there she made up her mind to become Mrs. Mark Van Buren as soon as it suited her.

Five weeks later Kerry left a gynecologist's office in central Boston on a dull spring day brightened by a flower seller's barrow packed with tulips and daffodils. Wrapping her coat around her, she crossed the street toward Boston Common, where a blustery wind chased kites high into the air. As she walked toward the restaurant where she was meeting Mark for lunch, the doctor's words rang in her ears.

"I'm afraid there's no doubt about it. You're pregnant," he said, glancing at her card to note that she was registered as "Miss" Faloon.

"It's all right—I'm engaged to be married at Easter," she blurted out.

As she walked on determinedly, she felt no emotion she could name, only a vague satisfaction that was dulled by the shock of the doctor's revelation. There would be a little Van Buren heir before anyone thought, she told herself, and he would be born prematurely seven and a half months after a Bermuda wedding. And he—for he had to be a boy—would be conceived that night in Mark's studio apartment.

BOOK III

Chapter I

On a late September afternoon Kerry pushed the baby stroller down Fifth Avenue. Only one more block to go, she told herself, dodging the crowds of shoppers who came at her in a solid wave. A dirty wind blew her hair in her face as she arrived at the entrance of Bergdorf Goodman.

"Hush," she said to Lindy, who had started to whimper. "Mommy won't be long—and when I'm finished I'll buy you a present."

Once in the store, she had to fight her way through the blocked aisles to the elevators. Glancing at the clock, she saw to her horror that it was nearly four o'clock, but her face was set firm. She had resolved to buy the dress she wanted, no matter what. Nothing would stop her. Not a cranky two-year-old, not the baby-sitter canceling at the last moment, not even the fight through the crowds with a stroller would throw her off course. Her entire life depended on having that black dress by tonight, and none other would do.

When she had arrived at the carpeted inner sanctum of the designer department, there were new obstacles to conquer. She adopted her best Mrs. Mark Van Buren manner as she faced the battalion of disapproving saleswomen, none of whom appreciated harassed young housewives invading their territory with pushchairs and drooling toddlers.

"Look—look, light, Mommy," said Lindy, gluing his sticky fingers to a glass display case as Kerry paused.

Ignoring a reproachful glance from a sales clerk, she said with a slight English intonation, "There was a black Halston advertised in last Sunday's *Times*. I'd like to see it in size eight, please."

As she followed after the girl, Lindy pouted.

"Mommy will buy you a new car if you're good."

"Car, car," he crowed excitedly.

When the saleslady brought the Halston she stared at it in rapture. It was a pure fluid drop of black silk jersey with a back scooped to the waist, and it made her heart melt with longing. It was priced at five hundred dollars, but she would buy it if it cost a thousand. She had wasted the entire morning trying on cheap copies but here was proof that nothing could have the impact of the real thing. Parking the apple-cheeked Lindy near the saleslady, she went to try it on.

When she exited from the changing room, she announced, "I'll take it." The dress fitted as if it had been made for her. She dashed off a check with a defiant cachet, telling herself that when he found out, Mark would sulk in that hangdog way of his because she had been so extravagant. But she hadn't become Mrs. Mark Van Buren to wear polyester, particularly when their entire future depended on it. That night, she was determined to shine in the eyes of the president of Wyndham and Hanbury Trust.

With the dress box tucked under arm, she went from the designer department to the shoe salon, where at least people seemed friendlier.

"Isn't he a cute little toughie," said one of the sales-ladies, tickling the gurgling, good-natured Lindy under the chin. "I'll bet you're a real little devil, aren't you? Yes, you are," she cooed. "And just look at those blue eyes. He's a real towhead, isn't he?"

Taking advantage of the kindly woman, Kerry picked out three pairs of black evening shoes to try on, none of them under a hundred dollars. There was nothing like expensive shoes, she told herself, deciding on a pair of sling-back pumps with heels studded with rhinestones. She wrote another check with a vindictive flourish and wheeled Lindy to the elevator, laden with her packages. On the way down she didn't dare look to the right or left in the packed elevator when she detected the smell of a dirty diaper emanating from Lindy, who was looking up at her innocently.

"You would, wouldn't you?" she whispered with a frown.

As Kerry made her way out of the store, she noticed a wonderful perfume scent wafting by. A beautifully groomed woman was offering a complimentary spray of the new perfume on promotion.

"Madam, would you like to sample *Samarkand*?" she asked silkily, holding up a beautiful amethyst glass bottle encased in silver filigree.

"Yes, thank you," Kerry replied, offering her wrist.

Samarkand, she thought to herself, drinking in the exquisite new scent. For a moment she remembered a small house in Australia that she hadn't thought of in years. It was almost as if she could hear Shannon's voice as she read aloud the adventures of Marco Polo on the silk route to the East. For both of them *Samarkand* had represented all the glamour of travel, magic, and escape. For a strange second or two she could hear the wailing of the wind, taste the dust, feel the heat pierced by a young girl's image of Samarkand. She heard the woman say:

"Sixty dollars half an ounce—that's the smallest size."

"I'll take a bottle," said Kerry, plunging into her wallet for her grocery money.

When she was on the pavement outside she was glad that Lindy's attention was diverted from F.A.O. Schwarz's toy store across the street to a horse and carriage in front of the Plaza.

"Horsey!" he cried, pointing excitedly.

"That's right," she said, giving him a quick kiss on the forehead, feeling guilty that there was no time to buy him the car she had promised.

"To hell with the bus," she said to herself, exhilarated by her spending spree. She was out on a dare, and there was no point in cutting corners now.

"Taxi!" she shouted at a passing yellow cab. Balancing Lindy, stroller, and packages with the proficiency of a juggler, she deposited them all on the backseat, then collapsed beside Lindy.

"Two fifty East Seventy-seventh Street," she said with a sigh of relief. She would have half an hour to transform herself from Kerry Van Buren, exhausted mother of a toddler, into the sleekly sophisticated young wife of a rising merchant banker.

At six-thirty, when they were waiting in the lobby of their apartment building for a taxi, Kerry brushed Mark's hands aside as he twiddled with his black bowtie. She straightened it for him, then turned to take one last look at herself in the mirror. She was fully satisfied that the afternoon's spending spree had been a wise investment.

"You're getting a bit carried away, Kerry," said Mark, resuming the argument that had begun in the elevator. "I haven't been with the bank long enough yet for them to send me to London."

"Mark, when are you going to learn that you've got to put yourself forward in life? You told me last month that you thought you might have a chance for the job, so why are you backing down now?" she said impatiently.

"I wish I'd never mentioned it. You've got to promise me you won't say anything to Mr. Hanbury about it."

"What do you think I am, stupid? I certainly know better than to be pushy or talk business, but I'm not going to let a chance like this go by. I'm tired of living like we do, of struggling the way we have been, when I see London like a golden apple on the tree."

"Tired? You think I'm not tired of it?" he replied weakly. "If you'd only listened to me about moving to Long Island instead of paying half of what I earn for a two-room apartment, we'd have a lot more money to spend on the things you want—like that dress."

Her defiant glare stopped him from going any further.

"A good address is like money in the bank, and so are clothes on an occasion like this. If we were living on Long Island, we'd arrive looking all hot and frazzled. This way we'll make our entrance cool, calm, and collected."

"Honey," he began gently when they were speeding along in a taxi, "be patient, please. We'll have everything you want someday." He reached out and squeezed her hand. "I know how tough these last two and a half years have been on you."

"You seem to forget, Mark, that you're a Van Buren and that we're entitled to have everything now."

Kerry was reminded of their hurried wedding in Bermuda the Easter before her graduation from Braemar, when it had rained nonstop, and when she had suffered every day with morning sickness. Instead of heralding her arrival into the world to which she had always aspired, their marriage had been the beginning of hardship, which until now showed no sign of ending.

There seemed to have been some sort of strange conspiracy to rob her of her triumph in marrying Mark. Despite the announcement sent to The Meadows, Mr. and Mrs. Mark Van Buren received no messages of congratulations from the family of the groom, no crystal pitchers or silver candlesticks. There had been no lavish reception with banks of flowers and champagne as befitted a Van Buren, nor the honeymoon in Europe she had always dreamed of.

After they had returned to New York, they'd begun their married life in a tiny apartment. Mark's salary had proved to be inadequate to set up a household and all it contained.

Kerry would never know how she got through that first steaming summer being pregnant, or the following nightmarish months when Lindy was an infant. Cut off from the entire world, the only thing she had to cling to was the future, as she waited for Lindy Van Buren to relent and provide her and Mark with all the things they deserved; but for nearly two years her letters and photographs had been returned unopened. Little Lindy's growing resemblance to his father made her determined to find a way to breach the wall he had thrown up between himself and the flesh and blood he didn't yet know was his.

When they walked into the elegant lobby of the Pierre Hotel, Kerry forgot all her grievances. Linking her arm through Mark's, she reveled in the sensation of being beautifully and expensively dressed for the first time in years. As they approached the room reserved for the Wyndham and Hanbury reception, she gave Mark's arm a reassuring squeeze to allay his nervousness. Head held high, a confident smile on her face, she was calm and unflustered as they entered the brightly lit room. When they had helped themselves to drinks from a tray, Kerry compared herself favorably to the other women there, reassuring herself that she had every reason to feel pleased with her appearance. She could easily spot the wives who had come into the city on the train, probably rushing all day to get there.

As Mark chatted to one of his colleagues, Kerry moved to a conspicuous position not far from the company top brass— Judson Walker, Mark's boss, and Henry Hanbury, the big man himself, with the director of the London branch, Trevor Hodge. Within moments she was talking to Mrs. Hanbury.

The look of approval in the eyes of the chic, platinum-haired Mrs. Hanbury told her that she had made the right impression.

"Lovely Halston," she remarked, establishing an instant familiarity between them.

Months ago Kerry had mentally filed away the information that Mrs. Hanbury was a keen horsewoman, and she adroitly turned the conversation to the Van Buren stud, modestly underplaying her own show-jumping laurels.

"Van Buren? Do you mean to tell me that you're Lindy's daughter-in-law? No wonder you're so knowledgeable. Henry," she called to her husband. In an aside to Kerry she whispered, "Let's go and break up that huddle. Henry—I didn't

343

know that Kerry is Lindy Van Buren's daughter-in-law? You remember him. We met him at Palm Beach Club last year."

"So you're Mark's wife. I can certainly see why he's been hiding you all this time," said Hanbury warmly, clasping her hand. "It's high time we met, young lady." His shrewd eyes passed over her.

"Imagine, I had no idea Mark was one of those Van Burens," Mrs. Hanbury was saying.

The moment Kerry had been waiting for came when Hanbury introduced her to Trevor Hodge and his wife. Ever since Mark had mentioned the chance of a London posting, Kerry had devoured all aspects of English social life and politics. It was a stroke of luck that she happened to mention Cowes Week to Hodge, setting him off on an enthusiastic tangent about yachting to which she listened attentively. When she caught Mark's eye, she gave him an affectionate private smile.

"Mr. Hodge—would you mind if I called my husband over? He'd be so fascinated to hear this," she interrupted politely just as he was waxing lyrical about shearing the waves of the Solent in the race for the Admiral's Cup.

Once Mark and Hodge were locked in conversation, she excused herself to go to the ladies' room, overjoyed that everything was going even better than she could have hoped.

Walking down a carpeted corridor, Kerry paused before an announcement of a press reception being held at that moment for *Samarkand* by the house of Galant, and she couldn't resist having a look, her curiosity piqued by the coincidence. In a way, she thought, buying that bottle of perfume had capped her luck for the evening. It was like putting down your last few dollars on a number at Monte Carlo, hoping it would come up.

There were hundreds of screamingly glamorous people milling about in the ornate French ballroom, and Kerry saw at a glance that the extravaganza was streaks ahead of the Wyndham and Hanbury party. Within moments of fascinated observation she had caught sight of the inimitable profile of Diana Vreeland and identified the genial smile of George Plimpton. The high-powered party was too tempting to pass up, and telling herself she wouldn't be missed for a moment, she helped herself to a glass of champagne to toast her own triumph that evening. She was awestruck at the conversation whirling around her. Just as Brooke Shields broke into a peal of laughter, Kerry's attention was riveted by a dark beauty with sparkling eyes, her stunning face framed by a ruff of silver lamé. There was Shannon—no more than a few feet away in the middle of a little clique of people who seemed to be hanging on her every word.

The confrontation was so unexpected that Kerry stood immobilized in devastated silence as she traced and retraced every detail about the woman to make sure it was really Shannon, but it was her voice carrying across the crowd that sealed Kerry's recognition. Her eyes traveled in disbelief to the man by her side. Vibrantly attractive and undeniably Latin, she knew instantly he could be no one but Amadeo Benguela, who was even more handsome in reality than in his photographs. Kerry felt a surge of repulsion overtake her at the sight of him. He was too sleekly dressed, too suntanned, too high-powered. A dark, festering anger welled up in her as she recalled that if Shannon hadn't met him, her whole life would have been different, and hers, too, in consequence. It was easy to see Shannon had been seduced by his wealth and magnetism.

What were the two of them doing here? Why did they seem to be the center of attention? she wondered. Suddenly a photographer thrust a bottle into Shannon's hand: it was *Samarkand*, the perfume she had bought that afternoon. As his flashbulbs popped someone fired a question at Shannon that made her smile broadly. None of it made any sense at all until Kerry edged up to a table draped with a silver cloth and piled with lavishly designed brochures announcing the launch of *Samarkand* and illustrated with pictures of Shannon at Grasse, in the laboratory, with the creator of *Samarkand*, Marcel Galant. The entire legend unfurled in one slick paragraph, describing how former top model Shannon Faloon was now at the helm of an international enterprise that had produced a perfume destined to capture the spirit of a generation.

"Isn't she stunning?" Kerry heard someone say as applause broke out. "So serene. You wouldn't know the whole thing rested on her shoulders," said a willowy young man with plucked eyebrows.

"You'd look lovely and serene, too, if you had the Benguela millions behind you," replied his laconic companion, a bearded man in a shocking-pink evening shirt.

Kerry clumsily knocked over her glass on the table and turned away from the gathering, too choked to speak. Her entire life came toppling down as she fought her way out of the room. The sister she hadn't seen for so many years seemed to be towering over her as she looked up from her own position of crouching insignificance. The crowd that had flocked to celebrate *Samarkand* represented the glitterati of international society, and Shannon blazed like a star among them. There could be no greater accolade than their applause, or their envy. At that dizzying height you could go no further, and Kerry was sickened with the irony that while she had been groveling to get Hanbury and Hodge to notice her, Shannon had, as usual, been skating on rainbows.

As traumatized as if she had been knocked down by a taxi on Fifth Avenue, Kerry somehow made her way to the ladies' room, struggling to pull herself together before she was missed at the company party. She regarded her own face, drained of color, and dabbed lipstick on thoughtlessly. Snapping her purse closed, she ventured forth, hurrying past the corridor where the *Samarkand* reception was being held. She shuddered involuntarily, as if hit by a blast of arctic air.

What was wrong with her? What was wrong with Shannon? How had their paths diverged so wildly since that last bitter confrontation at Koonwarra? Strange, Kerry thought numbly, how she hadn't the slightest desire to approach Shannon or to know her. The only thing she wanted was to put her sister out of her mind for the rest of her life.

When she rejoined the party, Mark immediately came up to her.

"Honey, I've been looking for you," he said anxiously, taking her elbow. "Are you all right? You look a bit pale."

"Just a little tired," she said. "It's all the excitement."

"Wait till I tell you what's happened. The Hanburys have invited us to lunch on Sunday at their apartment on Park Avenue. What do you think of that? It's just us and the Hodges and a few other people. It's all because of you, darling. I'm so proud of you," he whispered. "Mr. Hanbury took me aside and said what a great asset you were, then he started talking about London. I know it's a sure thing. I can feel it."

When they left the hotel Kerry impulsively stopped at the reception desk to ask if Shannon were staying there. When it was confirmed that she was, she turned abruptly and joined Mark at the door, not knowing what she would do with this meaningless bit of information.

"Just checking to see if Betsy and her mother are going

to be in town. They usually come by the end of September," she murmured hurriedly to her husband.

As they left the Pierre and came out into the clear night echoing with traffic, Kerry noticed a few strikingly dressed women who had obviously been at the *Samarkand* party. The coveted invitation to lunch with the Hanburys on Park Avenue withered in the bright flash of Shannon's meteoric rise to international success.

By eleven o'clock the ballroom of the Pierre was deserted except for Shannon and Amadeo, who had just bade good night to the entourage of promotional people and Galant representatives.

"I guess the ball is over," said Shannon with a tired but triumphant sigh as the waiters moved in to clear up the debris. She saw her own reflection mirrored beside a giant spray of black tulips and white lilacs.

"Exhausted, Shanita?" asked Amadeo.

"Shattered," she admitted, closing her eyes for a moment. The past twenty-four hours of the launch were a crazy jigsaw in her head, following on the heels of her whistle-stop tour of fifteen American cities, which had been crowded with press conferences and radio and television broadcasts. Hundreds of impressions, names, places, and faces had clamored for space in her memory; and everything had had to appear sharp and responsive that evening as she'd answered the questions fired at her from the press: "Do you wear *Samarkand* to bed?" "What does the phrase 'Eastern promise' suggest to the modern woman?" "Do you think Marco Polo brought perfume from the Orient for his mistress?"

"Come up to my room and see the tape of the *Johnny Carson Show*," she suggested. "You may not have a chance to see it for a while if you're away when I get back to Paris."

He hesitated. "Are you sure you're not too tired?"

"I'm too excited to sleep. Please come up."

"All right," he said. "I'll come for a little while. Then I should catch a taxi back to the hotel."

It was like him, she thought, not to stay at the Pierre while she was staying there, though it was the hotel he preferred in New York. It was her unspoken wish to avoid having her name linked unnecessarily with his; and to his credit, Amadeo seemed to know without having to be told that her image would be tarnished by gossip if it leaked out that she was nothing but the mistress of a rich man who had given her an expensive toy to play with, particularly since she was trying to establish her credibility in a serious enterprise. Always under the relentless scrutiny of the gutter press, Amadeo had continued to lead a separate, visible life, often in the company of glamorous women. Suddenly Shannon discovered that she, too, had become the subject of gossip on a new and disturbing scale. She had all the necessary ingredients to feed the paparazzi's hunger for new faces—beauty, a rather mysterious and closely guarded private life, and business connections with one of the world's richest men. Her greatest concern was that Patrick's future might be threatened if the discovery of his illegitimacy should come out. Though such a revelation no longer had the power it once did, Shannon was afraid the news would spark off endless gossip about the identity of his father. Several lurid reports had already been published on the Continent, where Amadeo was well known.

When they went up to her sumptuous suite, Shannon ordered scrambled eggs and smoked salmon and together they laughed over the videotape. She had kicked off her shoes and curled up in a chair, and Amadeo had made himself at home by removing his tie and jacket.

"I'll bet you haven't eaten all day," Amadeo chided her.

"No—I went to the Russian Tea Room for an interview with *Women's Wear Daily*, but I was talking so much they whipped my blinis away before I could finish them."

She leaned back in the chair, sipping her Perrier. The last frenetic weeks leading up to the American sales campaign, thrown like confetti in the air, had settled to earth, leaving the two of them regarding each other by candlelight.

"Are you happy, Shanita?"

"Of course. Who wouldn't be? I'm the luckiest girl in the world. All thanks to you."

"I think it's fair to say you've succeeded beyond your wildest dreams. You have my admiration and approval, for what it's worth."

"It's worth everything. You know that," she said affectionately. "Do you know, I hadn't realized until lately what it means to succeed. It's not like a book that has a beginning, a middle, and an end. It's a mountain you climb, and find there's another one just a bit higher that attracts your attention. I've discovered I've got a taste for climbing those mountains."

"So tell me, what mountain are you going to climb now?"

"*Dressage*, that's my next mountain."

"You've definitely decided to go ahead with the men's cologne, then?"

"Yes, Marcel and I can't wait. He was so excited by the sales figures—imagine: Bloomingdale's, to name only one outlet, has sold three thousand bottles of Samarkand in a week, and stores on the West Coast like Magnin's aren't far behind. We've decided on a spring launch."

"I think that's a wise decision. Capitalize on the phenomenal success of *Samarkand* while it's still in people's minds. By the way, I had a splendid idea the other day. We're planning to take the Vaqueros to England in April. Galant could sponsor a cup for a match. We could put up a marquee in your colors. I think the connection with horses would prove to be invaluable for marketing and all the resulting publicity."

"It's a brilliant idea," she said hesitantly. "The thing is, I wonder if there's actually time."

"Of course there is. I'll make sure. You see? Now you've got me climbing mountains," he said with a laugh.

"Great—I'm thrilled," Injecting enthusiasm into her voice, she pushed aside her own misgivings. She had always avoided involving herself with the promotion in England because of Zan, but she knew that eventually it would be unavoidable. And anyway, she told herself, there was a chance that by next spring she and Zan would be together. So much had happened in these last two and a half years. His father's death meant he had his destiny in his own hands for the first time, and now her business was well established.

"Shanita—I think it's time for me to say good night," said Amadeo abruptly, rising to get his coat.

"So soon? Don't go. Stay a while longer, please."

"No. You're exhausted, and I have an early meeting tomorrow."

She said nothing but suppressed a twinge of disappointment that smacked dangerously of territorial jealousy. It was an emotion that had no place in the polite minuet they had danced for the last few years, but she couldn't help herself. She had been looking forward to unwinding slowly with him as she used to, talking about a hundred subjects they hadn't yet touched on after a separation of over two months. Suddenly she recalled seeing Amadeo locked in conversation earlier that evening with a raven-haired Portuguese enchantress who was a well-known sculptress. There was a lithe voluptuousness about her that suggested a Goya, and Shannon was sure Amadeo couldn't resist adding such a jewel to his collection. How well she knew all his seductive little mannerisms that signaled the beginning of an affair, from the tilt of his head as he laughed to the concentration on his face as he looked at the object of his desire. She felt an unreasonable hurt at his abrupt departure on this particular night—her night—and she couldn't keep a certain aloofness from her voice as she led him to the door, where they kissed politely.

"Good night, Shanita," he said, brushing her chin with his fingertips.

"Good night," she whispered.

When he had gone she walked restlessly toward the window to survey the lights beyond Central Park, feeling robbed of her victory. Tiredly she recalled the hoopla of the reception, the thousand faces she would never see again, the popping of flashbulbs, the absurd but exhilarating illusion that for a few moments she was the center of the universe. Now, all of it was over.

She undressed slowly, layer by layer, then went to the shower and regarded her naked image before the mirror, clasping her slender arms tightly to herself. There had been times in the last two years when Amadeo had uncannily gauged her mood. Since that Christmas at Les Tourelles, they had made love perhaps half a dozen times. Amadeo had never imposed himself on her but only answered the sensual invitation in her eyes. It had happened at unexpected moments: twice aboard the *Karisma* during the summer, again at Les Tourelles, once in Amadeo's apartment on the avenue Foch. Each time was an exception in her mind, and tonight would have been one of those exceptions.

After her shower Shannon spent several moments jotting down notes about the evening, then glanced through her engagement diary for the following day, where she had penciled in a little note to try to call Kerry. Earlier in the week she had impulsively phoned Jack, and though they'd had no contact for the last few years, he was so coldly indifferent when she'd inquired about Kerry that it had discouraged further conversation. Shannon supposed that after the incident over Rainmaker, their rift had never healed. In response to her question, Jack had replied he had no idea where Kerry was, but that he'd heard she now had a baby. When Shannon had hung up she'd made a note to contact Braemar, thinking she could obtain her sister's address through the alumni association. When she got back to Paris she would send her a baby present. It was time, she thought, that the two of them made up their quarrel.

Slipping between the smooth, cool sheets, Shannon stared at the pattern of light on the closed curtains, then turned restlessly. Here she was, in a fabulous suite of one of the best hotels in the world, in the city she had annexed to her empire, yet she could not overcome a feeling of emptiness. She chided herself that she was behaving like a spoiled girl at her birthday party, a girl who had been given every present except the one she wanted most.

In the darkness she saw the shadow of the huge bouquet of roses Zan had sent her with a quote attached:

Each morn a thousand roses brings, you say;
Yes, but where leaves the Rose of Yesterday?
And this first summer month that brings the Rose
Shall take thee, my love, and me away.

I love you,
Zan

This, she was sure, was his romantic way of telling her that when summer came they would be together at last. So much had happened since that spring in Seillans, yet on the surface so little. Zan's own problems in unraveling the tangled affairs of Kilgarin wove through the demands of her own life. The calendar year seemed to swing from one May until the next, when, like two pilgrims, they revitalized their hopes for the future at the source of their love, the house in Seillans, in a sojourn so passionate, so intense, that it lingered throughout the seasons. The house in France had become the aerie of two far-ranging eagles whose territory was the wide world.

Shannon had been too involved with *Samarkand* to fall prey to doubt. Zan telephoned her faithfully, and just the sound of his voice touched a resonant chord within her. He had never forgotten a birthday, never failed to congratulate her on her small successes. What had begun as a grand passion had evolved into a union as durable as any marriage; but looking back, Shannon realized Jonquil had been right. Had Zan left Rosemary in the beginning, their own relationship would not have survived that first burst of sexual pas-

351

sion. Now they had proved themselves, they still had the greatest chapter of their lives to look forward to, when she, Zan, and Patrick would become a family. Nothing could stop it now— not Rosemary's money or her tenacity, not even Shannon's recurring attraction for Amadeo.

She had drifted asleep when she was awakaned by the telephone.

"Hello?" she said sleepily, fumbling for the light. It was just after one.

There was no answer. "Hello? Who is it?" When there was still no reply she listened for a moment, then hung up, imagining she had heard a baby in the background, before someone slammed down the receiver.

Now fully awake, she suddenly remembered something she'd wanted to ask Amadeo, something that couldn't wait. He would probably be getting into bed just about now. When the reception at his hotel put her through to his room, she let it ring for a long time before she hung up, realizing she had been right about the sculptress. She turned off the light and lay wide awake, unable to sleep, until the phone rang again. She reached for it warily.

"Shannon?"

"Zan!" she exclaimed. "Did you try to call me a few moments ago?"

"No. Why?"

"Oh, nothing. It must have been a wrong number."

"Tell me, darling, how did everything go tonight? I've been thinking of you all day."

"It was a smash success," she said, giving him a rundown of the evening. "Thank you for the beautiful roses. And the poem you sent. Does it mean what it says?"

"Yes, my darling. It means I love you and that I want to be with you."

"Oh, Zan—" Her voice died as she began sobbing into the telephone. She had never before let go like this, but suddenly the emotion was too much to restrain.

"What's the matter, Shannon? Please don't cry."

"I'm sorry. It's just that I wish you were here—to hold me. Tonight was supposed to be one of the happiest nights of my life, but somehow it's empty."

"Shannon, where's my good, strong girl?" he cajoled. "You make me feel so helpless. There's nothing I can do over the phone, my darling, though I'd give anything if I could be with you—you know that."

She sighed. "I'm sorry. I'm just tired, Zan. Exhausted. I've been living on my nerves for so long."

"What you need is a holiday. Is there any chance we could grab a weekend together between now and Christmas?"

"We could try. Where could we go, though?"

"How about Nagaland? It's east of the sun, west of the moon. No one will know us there."

She laughed, and so did he. "You are silly. Oh, Zan, it's so good to hear your voice." She felt a deep sense of release at the sound, as if a cellar of trapped demons inside her had escaped.

"Believe me, we're getting much closer to having what we want. I won't say more, but I'm keeping my fingers crossed. It won't be long, darling. That's what the poem was meant to say. I love you. Feeling better now?"

"Much better. Ring me in Paris on Thursday. Good night, darling."

Chapter II

"Come on, sweetheart, up, up," said Kerry to encourage Lindy as he climbed the front steps of the Plaza Hotel. When they were in the lobby she snapped open the stroller, then unbuttoned Lindy's new baseball jacket that matched his blue eyes. That week she had bought him an entire outfit, from sneakers to corduroy dungarees. Fluffing his platinum hair, she wheeled him past the Palm Court, where people were beginning to arrive for afternoon tea. As she headed for the reception desk she felt every inch the wife of the newly promoted junior partner of Wyndham and Hanbury, in a new fall suit of lavender-blue tweed and a gray cashmere wrap that would be perfect for London. Her coppery hair was swept away from her face with tortoiseshell combs, and the big, smart burgundy bag over her shoulder contained all the disposable diapers and teething biscuits and toys she would need for a vigil that might go on until well after the cocktail hour, when Lindy Van Buren showed up to collect his key.

The minute Mark had departed for London the week at the end of September, leaving her to tie up all the loose ends in Manhattan, Kerry had telephoned the Plaza in New York and the Ritz-Carlton in Boston to find out when Lindy was expected. She was prepared to go as far as The Meadows, if necessary, to lay siege to him. This would be her last chance for a long time to accomplish what she wanted, and she had no intention of putting three thousand miles of ocean between her and the Van Buren millions—especially now that Carter had married a Dupont and would soon be producing grandchildren.

Inquiring at the reception desk, Kerry wasn't surprised to find that Lindy hadn't returned, so she settled into a chair that gave her a view of the front desk.

She didn't have long to wait. In less than half an hour Lindy came through the side entrance of the hotel with his familiar stride, heading toward reception, and her heart lurched at the sight of him. Dressed in a dark suit, he had obviously just come from a business meeting.

"Lindy, darling," she called across the lobby just as he was asking for his key.

He wheeled around to face her with a startled expression. Kerry swept up to him and kissed his cheek.

"Just what the hell do you mean by this?" he snarled under his breath.

"Tea in your room? Why, I'd love to. Would you mind taking little Lindy for me?" she said, thrusting the astonished toddler into his arms. The resemblance between them was unmistakable, even comical. The adorable, chunky little boy was a miniature version of his father. He reached out a dimpled fist to grab Lindy's pocket handkerchief.

"Yes, that's Grandpa," Kerry cooed. "Just a minute while I get the stroller," she said to Lindy, smiling sweetly.

Lindy was left like a trussed bull, helplessly holding the baby. She forged ahead of him to the elevator.

He didn't say a word until the doors had snapped closed.

"Now, what the hell do you want?" he said angrily.

"Please don't talk to me in that tone of voice in front of little Lindy," she said sweetly.

"Don't you bandy with me, you little bitch."

"Wouldn't it be better to discuss this in private?"

When he had opened the door of his room he slammed it behind him and set Lindy down.

"What's all this about? I want you out of here—now."

"You haven't answered my letters, haven't acknowledged the pictures of Lindy that I sent you." Turning to face him,

354

Kerry felt no fear, only a ruthless determination to even the score between them.

"You and my son and your child are of no interest to me whatsoever. I thought I made that abundantly clear quite some time ago. Now, I don't know what you expect to achieve by this brazen approach, but you leave me no choice but to have you thrown out of here."

She paced thoughtfully toward the fireplace. "You may not be aware that Mark has just been promoted to the London branch of Wyndham and Hanbury. In fact he's there now, and I'm joining him in two weeks."

"Well, that is good news. Good riddance to both of you."

"Actually, that's not the reason I came. The real reason I'm here is that I thought you might like to see your son before he goes to England."

Lindy received the news in dead silence. His only reaction was a deceptive narrowing of the eyes. She continued in a quiet tone:

"Everyone is under the impression that Lindy was premature, but the truth is there's no such thing as a premature baby weighing eight pounds six ounces. Lindy was born full term at the end of November, nine months after he was conceived in February at the Ritz in Boston the last time I saw you."

He let out a sarcastic laugh. "You're something else, Kerry. But you know, you're not as smart as I thought you were, if you expect me to believe that little speech. It's all very convenient, isn't it? Especially knowing what a little gold digger you are."

Observing him carefully, Kerry knew her devastating revelation had found a chink in his impenetrable façade. The flicker of an eyelid, the slight pause before he spoke told her she had hit home, and she was quick to take advantage.

"Just take a good look at him," she said, scooping up the baby. Her voice was gentle, pleading. Lindy stood motionless, his back to her as he stared out at the autumn leaves falling in Central Park. "If you don't believe what I said, you can contact Dr. Sydney Bamber in Boston. He knows the whole story. Look at him—look at those blue eyes. They're your eyes, Lindy. Look at his hair, his hands. Everything about him is as much an image of you as your son Lindy was." She brushed the baby's hair affectionately as she spoke, and her serenity seemed to make him content to rest in her arms.

355

"When I began to sleep with you there was no one else, not even Mark until just before we got married—but by then I knew I was pregnant. You're probably wondering why I didn't have an abortion. Why? I didn't really know at the time. It didn't even enter my head. But I know now. I wanted your child, Lindy. But I had no illusions about my place in your life. Oh, no, I was your part-time hooker, and when you got tired of me that would have been it. Of course you would have paid for an abortion. You'd done that once already. I married Mark because I needed a father for my child—our child. I knew Mark loved me. I'm a good wife to him, Lindy. He's in London now because I fought for it, because I pushed him forward. I'm not here to blackmail you. As far as I'm concerned, no matter what you say, this conversation will never go any further than this room. That might hurt little Lindy someday, and I wouldn't want that. I'm here to ensure our son inherits what's his and so we can all be a family again. Think about it—you once lost the boy you loved. That wasn't your fault. But if you lose your son this time, you'll have no one to blame but yourself."

Lindy stood with his back to her for a long time, giving no sign that he had been moved by her speech.

Resignedly Kerry began to gather up her handbag, the stroller, and Lindy. She had a feeling of *déjà vu* that took her back to the library at The Meadows, when she had gathered the pile of hundred-dollar bills from his desk that day. But this time she wasn't running away. Now, if anyone was running away, it was Lindy.

"Go bye-bye now?" said little Lindy. "Bye-bye," he called, casting a wave.

Taking his tiny hand in hers, Kerry led him toward the door. As she turned the knob she heard Lindy speak in an almost inaudible voice.

"Kerry—don't go. Wait a minute."

When Kerry left the Plaza, drained of emotion, she went back to the apartment to drop off the baby and change, glad she had had the foresight to book a sitter earlier in the week. She met Lindy for dinner and by the time the bill had come they had talked about everything except what mattered most—little Lindy, and themselves. As they fell silent Lindy's eyes met hers, and he reached for her hand across the table.

"Come back to my room for a nightcap?"

His touch, his words sent a familiar current throbbing through her, and the simple gesture of his hand closing on hers sent them back in time, with all the unspoken implications that had been building up throughout dinner.

Would it be the same? she asked herself, leaning back in the taxi on the way to the hotel, listening to Lindy's deep voice as he talked. For two and a half years she had lived in a sexual wasteland, indifferent to Mark's lovemaking; now, as Lindy explored the palm of her hand with his fingers, desire raged through her.

The moment he had closed the door of the hotel room behind them, Lindy locked her in a voracious embrace, kissing her as if he would devour her. Impatiently he unzipped her dress and carried her to the bed, where she lay breathless, her full breasts rising and falling, her eyes glistening with sensuality. The curving line of her body was carved in erotic invitation against the sheets, her hair a froth of fire. When she saw Lindy's erection rising hard and high against his sinewy torso, she opened her thighs in waiting. As he moved toward the bed, his eyes searched every part of her, sending ripples of impatience down her spine.

"Lindy—oh, Lindy," she cried when he was in her arms. The gathering force of their passion ruptured and overflowed like rain across furrows of parched earth. Seeds of renewal quickened in the warmth they shared, and the seasons turned full circle, to where they had begun.

As they lay in each other's arms, shattered by their passion, Kerry perceived a truce in Lindy's eyes. He smoked a cigarette thoughtfully, and she knew he was thinking of their child. For the first time they were equals. The strange empathy of souls hewn from the same wood now bound them irrevocably. With the regal carnality of a young queen who had granted the aging monarch a bid for immortality, a gift beyond price, Kerry regarded her lover.

"When Lindy's old enough I want him to come back to The Meadows in the summer. I want him to grow up on horses. And in England he should have a pony of his own."

"What more natural thing than for a boy to spend as much time as possible with his grandfather?" she purred, tracing the line of his jaw.

"And I'm concerned that you and Mark set yourselves up properly in England. I don't know how much he is earning, but I'll ensure you have enough money to make life comfortable. London society can be a tough nut to crack, but if you've got the right connections, you're accepted immediately. They like Americans, particularly the right kind. I've got a lot of friends there—the Vesteys, the Barkers, the Sangsters. They're all people who breed and race horses. In fact, there's a very dear old friend of mine, whom I've known for years. She can provide all the introductions. I'll call her this week and ask her to arrange a dinner for you and Mark as soon as you get there. That would be a good start."

"Thank you, Lindy. It sounds wonderful." Kerry snuggled up to him like a sleepy kitten, supremely contented that she was home free, where her every dream would be gloriously fulfilled.

"And another thing," he said after a pause, stroking her hair. "I want to make Rainmaker up to you."

Of all his astonishing promises, this last sent the most powerful jolt of surprise through her. Just the sound of his name could still do that, even after all these years. At Lindy's mention of the subject that had become the fulcrum on which their lives had turned, victory had never seemed so sweet.

"I want you to have the finest hunter you can find. Start looking around when you get there. I'll put you in touch with some people in Newbury who can help you. I'll pay for it and stable it."

"I don't know how to thank you," she whispered.

"Don't you?" he said sarcastically. Cupping her chin in his hand, he playfully nibbled her lip.

"And another thing," he murmured as Kerry threw her arms around his neck and arched ardently toward him. "First thing tomorrow I'm going to take you to Tiffany. I want to buy the mother of my son a going-away present. . . ."

She had the presence of mind to say:

"I'd rather have a letter of introduction to the master of the Alderly Hunt, if there's one going."

He laughed. "Why not have both?"

Dropping her parcels on the doorstep, Kerry let herself into the house in Markham Square, making a mental note to tell Mrs. O'Brien that the brass door knocker should be polished to such a sheen that she could see her face reflected in it. Entering the hallway, fragrant with beeswax and hothouse flowers, she felt that lilt of pleasure that had yet to pall since Mark drove her up to their white four-storied townhouse in London the day she and little Lindy had arrived from New York.

"I'm home, Theresa," she called toward the stairwell to the Filipino au pair girl. "Any messages?"

"Yes," she said from the landing. "Mr. Van Buren called and asked you to pick up his dinner jacket from the cleaners."

"I've already done it," she replied, dropping her shopping in the kitchen. Then she walked into the spacious drawing room which she had already begun to decorate in her own taste with antiques from the King's Road: a Victorian rosewood sewing table and an Edwardian glass-fronted bookcase. On a table lay a pile of sample swatches in elegant and expensive fabrics, and she picked them up, pondering for the hundredth time whether she preferred Sanderson Liberty, or Osborne and Little for the new curtains and chairs. There had been nothing worth bringing with them from New York that suited a Regency house in Chelsea, and Kerry wanted every detail to be right, from cut-crystal decanters on the butler's tray to embossed writing paper and engraved visiting cards that had been delivered from the printers only yesterday. Now she took them from the desk drawer, unable to resist looking at them one more time: "Mrs. Mark Van Buren, 57 Markham Square, London S.W.3." She enjoyed the significance of that simple name and address. As she ran a finger across the lettering, she reflected that it had taken a lifetime to achieve. There was no one she would rather be at that moment.

Glancing at her watch, she saw she had half an hour before Lindy woke from his nap. She seated herself at her desk by the window overlooking the pretty walled garden and dialed the upholsterer, to make sure the sofa would be ready for the cocktail party she was giving before Christmas. Her next call was to a caterer recommended by someone at an American embassy reception the week before. She dashed off a thank-you note for a dinner party, then opened her Liberty's diary. Of all the engagements whose impressive invitation cards had begun to fill the mantelpiece, tonight's dinner at Les Ambassadeurs was the most crucial. She and Mark were to be the guests of honor at a dinner party arranged by Lady Jonquil Fortesque, signaling their entry into the very heart of English society. And it had all been made possible by one transatlantic telephone call from Lindy. Of all Lindy's generous gifts to her and Mark since their reconciliation, that little gesture, she knew, would have an even greater impact on their lives than carte blanche to establish themselves in a fashionable home. No amount of money could buy the prestige commanded by the Van Buren name.

Settling into a wing chair with a cup of black coffee, Kerry surveyed her domain, which was taking on the semblance of the perfect English household. Picking up the latest issue of *Harper's and Queen*, she turned to "Jennifer's Diary," full of pictures of receptions and balls accompanied by a long, gossipy exposé of the social calendar. This time next year she and Mark might be invited to weddings like the one in the picture, with a reception at St. James's Palace attended by the queen and the Queen Mother.

Her arrival in England had seemed like the homecoming of an exile, harking back to the earliest days of her childhood in Australia when everything English had been held up as the epitome of sophistication. Though she and Mark had been there only a month, America already seemed like a distant interlude. She adored every detail about London, from the red double-decker buses and the friendly postman tipping his cap, to the butcher in a blue-striped apron and straw boater. She was fascinated by the corridors of power, money, and position represented by the narrow streets of Mayfair, the grandeur of Westminster, the illuminated mansions of Belgravia. She adored the shops tucked away in corners of Chelsea and Knightsbridge, which supplied every luxury from custom-made nosegays and monogrammed table linen to fresh plover's eggs. Lindy's generous allowance, in addition to Mark's salary and fringe benefits, meant that for the first time in her life Kerry had no money worries. In fact, she told herself with a happy sigh, she had no worries at all. Turning the pages of the magazine, she came to a full-page advertisement for *Samarkand*, featuring purple domes set against a pale evening sky with the message "*Samarkand*—the discovery of a dream, the promise of a legend." Kerry closed the magazine, but not before the image had recalled another, more haunting specter . . . of Shannon that night at the Pierre. Strange, she thought. They had approached each other blindly, like two meteors narrowly avoiding collision, from opposite ends of the earth. Now, with only the English Channel between them, they had never existed in such close proximity. When Kerry had called Shannon's room that night following the party at the Pierre, her only motive had been to hear her sister's voice one last time before she'd assigned her permanently to the past; it had been a symbolic act that would forever free her of Shannon's domination. Since that night, fortune had smiled on Kerry to such an extent that she could afford not to care. Now her own star was rising fast.

She reached for a copy of *Horse and Hound* to skim over the coming horse sales, indulging in a flight of fancy about the hunter she was going to buy. She had put choosing a horse off on the advice of Lady Fortesque.

"Don't do anything, darling," she had chided. "Not until you come to dinner at Les 'A.' The whole table will be knee deep in stalwarts of the racing fraternity. So much relies on word of mouth. They'll be delighted to advise you."

That evening, as Mark was struggling with his tie in front of the mirror, Kerry opened a drawer and withdrew a velvet box from Tiffany's that contained a pair of diamond bow earrings with emerald drops, recalling that on the day Lindy had taken her to choose them, he had remarked they were just the color of her eyes. Sweeping her hair away from her neck, she clipped them on and leaned back to admire the effect they made with her Halston. Mark came up behind her and brushed her neck with his lips.

"You look great, honey. A knockout. I thought you were going to get something new for tonight."

"I decided that this was my lucky dress. Look what happened the last time I wore it. You got the job." Tossing her head, she appraised her face in the mirror, glowing with excitement, the diamond-and-emerald earrings like fiery exclamation points.

"I hope we come back early tonight. I'm kinda in the mood," he murmured in her ear.

"You are silly, Mark," she said with an embarrassed laugh. She slipped from the stool and went to her wardrobe to take out her red fox coat. As she slipped it around her shoulders, Mark regarded her with a sheepish, adoring smile.

"I just can't get over how sensational you look."

"You don't look so bad yourself," she said, pecking him on the cheek as they left the bedroom. But her mind was miles away, on the party that would launch the young Van Burens into society.

Before going downstairs, Mark slipped into the nursery to have a look at Lindy. The cozy room, furnished with a crib and chest of drawers painted with balloons and clowns, smelled comfortingly of talcum powder, and a paper mobile turned slowly in the dim light. Lindy was sleeping soundly, one plump arm curled around his stuffed panda. Mark resisted brushing his round cheek, his heart suddenly swelling with pride at the sight of his son. He left the room and closed the door quietly behind him.

"Come on—we'll be late," Kerry called to him from the bottom of the stairs.

The moment she saw the look on his face, she guessed he had been in to see Lindy. "Mark, you could have woken him up. You know how hard it is to get him to bed at night."

"What he needs is a little brother or sister to play with all day," he remarked.

Kerry pretended to ignore him, sweeping out the door, leaving a trail of perfume behind her.

As they drove through Chelsea toward Mayfair, Mark knew by Kerry's silence that he had annoyed her with his mention of another baby, a subject he had tried to bring up several times before. Since they had come to London, his wife seemed to be absorbed by so many things that didn't include him, from decorating the house to pursuing her ambition to hunt, that he was afraid of losing her, and never more so than on nights like tonight when she looked unapproachably glamorous.

The moment he felt resentment he checked it, conscious of the debt he owed her. If he had looked up to Kerry before, he worshiped her now. With the tact of a diplomat she had healed the rift between him and his father, when he had been resigned to the likelihood that they would never speak again. Naming the baby after Lindy, Sanford Lindhurst Van Buren V, had been a stroke of genius, and Mark guessed it had gone a long way toward softening his father's heart. If it hadn't been for Kerry, he wouldn't have been posted to London, which she had brilliantly used as an opportunity to unite the Van Buren family. Proof of his father's change of heart was his generosity to the two of them. It was hard to imagine, Mark thought, that Lindy had ever opposed his marriage to Kerry. Before going permanently to London, he had flown back to New York, where Kerry had greeted him with the news of the reconciliation. That evening they'd had dinner with Lindy at the Knickerbocker Club, and the affection he had shown to Kerry that night had made Mark warm to his father as never before. As he'd glowed in Lindy's approval, Mark had recognized the mellowing effect of Kerry's charm on his father's intransigence. Suddenly he couldn't seem to do enough for them, now that there was a grandchild who carried his name. Mark allowed himself the private satisfaction that at least he had been the one to recognize her extraordinary qualities the first day he'd met her at The Meadows.

"Isn't London beautiful by night, honey?"

"Mmm," she replied distractedly. "Mark—Lady Fortesque told me there's someone coming tonight who's very knowledgeable about property. Be sure and bring up the subject. People like that are on the inside track, and if something comes up, they'll let us know. I've almost decided definitely on Gloucestershire."

"But honey, you haven't even been there."

"That's got nothing to do with it. Everybody I've spoken to says it's the place to be. That's where Princess Diana and Charles live—in Tetbury. They all have their estates down there."

"Estates? Kerry, we can't afford an estate."

"A cottage. Not an estate. A cottage on an estate."

"I don't know, Kerry. I haven't really had time to think about it. I doubt if we could afford to run two homes."

"Don't be silly. Your father has as much as said he'd like us to buy something in the country. He insists that I hunt because it will bring us in touch with all the right people. And he'll get the benefit, too. He'll be coming to stay."

Mark didn't dare protest when he saw the determined angle of Kerry's chin.

Kerry had retreated for a moment into her most private thoughts. Ever since she had crushed underfoot the dream of being a champion equestrienne, she'd kept her misery to herself. She had never confided to anyone, even Mark, what it was like to have her heart broken. And now she felt like a cripple who had been told she would walk again, like a blind man who had been cured by a miracle: soon she would once more experience the almost mystical union between rider and horse. It was more than a passport to social success—it was her gift, her birthright, a spiritual necessity that she could no longer live without. The longing to ride again had seized her passionately one day when she'd seen a woman mounted on a beautifully groomed thoroughbred in Rotten Row in Hyde Park. Now her entire life was falling neatly into place: she was going after what she wanted, with or without Mark's approval.

They arrived at Les Ambassadeurs, once a fine mansion on Park Lane and now one of the most luxurious private clubs

363

in London. A uniformed doorman tipped his hat and opened the door for them to enter.

As Mark checked her coat, Kerry took in the sumptuous hall, where an iron staircase curved against paneled walls hung with paintings, suggesting an elegance that lived up to its reputation.

"This way, please, sir," said a woman. "Lady Fortesque and her party are waiting for you in the adjacent room."

"My dears!" cried Jonquil, her arms open wide the moment she saw Kerry and Mark. She fluttered toward them, trailing a yellow chiffon gown painted with butterflies. "We're not quite all here yet. My, but you look stunning," she whispered to Kerry as she kissed her cheek.

Looking over Jonquil's shoulder, the first person Kerry saw was a man whose face seemed instantly familiar. The sight of him sent a shiver of apprehension through her. After all these years, could she possibly be about to confront Zan Fitzherbert again?

"Come along, and let me introduce everyone," said Jonquil, shepherding them to the waiting circle.

"Let me present Kerry and Mark Van Buren. Now, I know you won't remember everybody's name, but that doesn't matter—Vanessa and Julian Davenport, Hugo Delamain and his wife, Nicole, Anthony Bonham . . ."

Kerry didn't register any of the introductions until she heard Jonquil say, "And this is Rosemary and Zan Kilgarin." The syllables fell like glass shattering at her feet. She raised her eyes to meet Zan's in a prolonged study crowded with past associations, dominated by the terror that he would recognize her. Then, woodenly, she reached out to shake the hand he offered, feeling drained of all sensation. The moment passed, and the group began to mingle with friendly chatter.

They moved on to the main dining room, sparkling with crystal chandeliers and alive with the buzz of conversation. The muted tinkle of china and silver echoed discreetly in the elegant room that suggested the sumptuous ambiance of the belle époque. A three-piece group was playing romantic Cole Porter tunes, and as Kerry caught Mark's admiring glance across the long table, she smiled at him in a daze of apprehension.

"Kerry, I've put you between Zan and Noel Villiers," chirped Jonquil. "Between the two of them, they know everything there is to know about horses. Now, Zan," she chided as he held Kerry's chair for her, "I've told Lindy Van Buren that we'd see Kerry is well advised about the purchase of a hunter. She's held off buying one just because I told her there would be sporting gentlemen here."

"I'm very flattered," he said as he seated himself next to her.

Kerry took a sip of wine and glanced down the long table, marveling at the impressive group Jonquil had assembled with a wave of her hand to welcome her and Mark. Of all the men, Zan was without doubt the best-looking. The years had enhanced his irresistible good looks and added a sophisticated luster to his personality. She felt compelled to take a long glance at Rosemary, whose striking blond beauty had a certain brittle edge that surprised Kerry. She had always imagined Zan ending up with a woman of a softer, more tender nature—someone more like Shannon. Instead, she found a certain languid cynicism in Rosemary's blue eyes, a quality that she might once have mistaken for mere sophistication. Her attention reverted to Zan. He was so suave that she'd been unable to detect any hint of recognition in his acknowledgment of her when they'd shaken hands. Was he just pretending, or would he remember who she was as the evening wore on? If he did, she decided with a thumping heart, she would deny everything.

As Zan talked about the forthcoming thoroughbred sales at Newmarket and in Ireland, Kerry's mind reeled back to that dreadful night at Koonwarra when Brendan had humiliated her on the dance floor in front of hundreds of people. The entire table was engrossed in animated conversation when she gathered the courage to look at him directly. As she took a bite of smoked salmon, Zan put down his fork.

"You know," he said, "you're completely different from any other American girl I've ever met."

"Am I?" she replied coolly.

"Yes—most American girls are very gregarious. You seem rather reserved."

He gazed down at her heart-shaped face, set in a blaze of coppery hair, jewels sparkling at her ears, captivated by an unexpected aloofness that contradicted her fiery beauty. He watched her as she considered his remark critically, aware that his easy way with women seemed to have little effect on her. Her face seemed familiar, then he dismissed the idea.

"And you're different from most Englishmen I've met.

I've found they're very reluctant to make a snap judgment after they've known someone only ten minutes."

Zan threw back his head and laughed. Turning, she met his gaze. There was still nothing in his handsome face to convey any suggestion that he had recognized her, but she was unnerved. Would he recall in an hour, a week, who she was? Would he connect the thirteen-year-old in pigtails and a flannel shirt, who rode like the wind in the Outback, with the grown woman sitting beside him at Les Ambassadeurs?

She switched the subject to horses. "I understand you know a lot about Irish bloodstock," she remarked.

"Well, the finest horses are still bred in Ireland. If you like, I'll make a few inquiries about a suitable hunter for you. You seem to know exactly what you want, and if anything comes up, I'll let you know. Perhaps you and your husband would like to join us one weekend at Kilgarin. We're right in the middle of Limerick, where you'll find some of the finest studs in the country."

"Why, thank you very much. That's very kind of you," replied Kerry, taken aback at this magnanimous offer of hospitality and startled to imagine herself at Kilgarin.

Only a week later Kerry was driving the car she had hired at Shannon Airport through the heart of County Limerick, she gazed in rapt fascination at the landscape that unfolded with every passing mile. She was so thrilled to be on Irish soil that she had been oblivious to the modern details of the airport itself or to the town of Limerick, which she had just passed through. But now she was in the country, the real Ireland.

If she'd ever thought she had beheld the true color green, she'd been mistaken. This Emerald Isle was the truest, purest form of green on earth. Its hills and meadows captured the lush verdure of moss, the brilliance of parrots' wings, the heart of a cut emerald, and the splendor of new grass, distilling all into a shimmering essence that spread in every direction as far as she could see. Brendan had often tried to describe it to her when she was a little girl, but in the barren waste of the Outback she'd been unable to fathom the deep, rich hue that was Ireland. Who said dreams didn't come true? she asked herself, content with every mundane detail—from farmers' thatched cottages, smoke rising from their chimneys, to the darkly boiling clouds on the horizon.

When Zan had rung her up that week to tell her of a superb hunter that had come up for sale at a stud not far from

Kilgarin, she had jumped at the chance to see it. He had generously put Kilgarin Castle at her and Mark's disposal, though he and Rosemary wouldn't be there, and when Mark had suggested she go on her own, her decision had been sealed. Zan's absence meant freedom from the nagging worry he might recognize her, and now that Mark wasn't there to tag along after her, she could do as she pleased.

It was a novel sensation, coming to the place where her roots lay buried. Every signboard brought her closer to where the Faloons had flourished. The names of the towns seemed so familiar, as if springing up from some unconscious source: Adare, Rathkeele, Croom, Ballingarry; and the sight of a sign that marked Killarney, in her namesake, County Kerry, gave her an unexpected thrill.

Content to daydream she slowed down for a flock of sheep moving along the road in a curly mass. It was the dead of winter now, but nothing could kill the blazing green that thrived all around her. As the shepherd, followed by his dog, nudged the flock aside for her to pass, she drove by, waving cheerfully. Her heart thudded involuntarily at the sight of the man's finely chiseled countenance as he smiled and tipped his hat. The men of Ireland—again and again she was to see those devastatingly handsome faces as she passed farms and villages. Their disturbing deep blue eyes rimmed in black projected a Celtic magnetism undimmed by poverty or shabbiness; reflecting a dark, brooding spirit fed by a wild pagan strain that was barely held in check by Christianity. They were universally misunderstood by the Anglo-Saxon race, whose own dry nature lacked their passion and fire. Here were people like herself, Kerry thought, spotting one after the other with coloring the same as hers. She found herself slowing to a crawl so as not to miss anything and was content to follow for miles behind a wobbling hay cart drawn by a horse.

The landscape was littered with ruins—gateposts and walls, crumbling towers and the shells of houses, all suggesting Ireland's noble past. Her first stop would be Castle Shannon, which she had located on a detailed map. Her curiosity to see it had become intense over the years, ever since Zan had planted the seed by suggesting to her and Shannon that it was a real place and not just one of Brendan's exaggerations.

A gentle rain had begun to fall when she reached a village called Dooley, a few miles from Kilgarin, and she stopped at a thatched pub called The Swan and Shamrock to ask directions. When she found the muddy lane corresponding to the description given by the tavernkeeper's wife, she drove slowly toward a hill shrouded with bushes. When she could go no farther she stopped the car on the verge and tugged on her Wellington boots. Wrapping her raincoat tightly around her, she disregarded the rain, eager to reach that magic hill. After a gradual climb up the track, she came to a crumbling arch that marked the entrance to Castle Shannon. She shivered involuntarily as she walked beneath that arch, and the sight of the decaying ruin took her breath away. Over fifty years of abandonment had stripped its savage beauty to a bare skeleton outlined against the darkening sky. Vines like arteries climbed the walls and threaded through the empty stone window frames. It was so quiet that Kerry could hear her own heartbeat against the strumming rain as she regarded this forgotten hill where Faloons had once lived in splendor. Here, alone with the past, she gathered all the half-remembered legends about her, paying homage to Brendan and the vanished people whose blood still rang strong and true in her. Here was no fantasy, but a cornerstone of substance that infused her dispossessed life with meaning. Something stopped her from entering the house, a sense of wishing to leave her discovery of this wild and peaceful place undisturbed. For the moment it was enough just to know it was really there. She turned and walked back the way she had come, leaving the rain-filled dusk to close in on Castle Shannon just as it had done for hundreds of years.

Later, when she drove through the high gates of Castle Kilgarin and the great house came into view, she was astonished at its size and imposing grandeur—acutely aware of the contrast between Castle Shannon and this fortress, which fortune had never allowed to decline. Kilgarin seemed a castle out of a storybook, inhabited by a princess and a wicked king; and it could easily have been the place she had so often described to Betsy Belmont as belonging to her mythical Uncle Desmond. Stepping from the car, she was struck by a kind of beauty emanating from its forbidding solidarity. She stood proudly for a moment, recalling that she, Kerry Faloon Van Buren, had come at the invitation of its owner, the Earl of Kilgarin. This unsurpassed moment blotted out many petty injustices she had endured in the past. She had made it, she had arrived, she told herself elatedly.

Moments later, when the housekeeper, Mrs. Flaherty, was leading her up a grand wooden staircase to her room, droning on in a melodious voice, Kerry's thoughts were of Zan. She would never be able to regard him in the same light now that she had seen the splendor of Kilgarin.

"I hope you'll be comfortable here, madam" said the housekeeper, ushering her into a magnificent round tower room dominated by a four-poster bed.

"Indeed, I'm sure I will," replied Kerry.

Stoking the fire in the cast-iron grate, the Irishwoman remarked, "When the fire goes down just put another piece of peat on it from this basket. That'll make it blaze bright enough. You must be wanting tea after your journey. I'll send Bridie up right away. And I expect you'd like some scones, too."

"Thanks very much."

"Look at your mackintosh. It's soaking wet. Let me take it downstairs to dry," scolded the housekeeper, bustling around the room. Before departing, she said with a cheerful smile, "I'll be serving your dinner in the green room. It'll be more to your liking on your own. Lady Kilgarin said if there's anything at all you need, just ask."

When the housekeeper had gone, Kerry walked to the leaded window of the room, which commanded a sweeping view of Limerick. Looking out, she recalled her first meeting with Zan at Koonwarra. It seemed like another existence, seen through time's distorting lens. If she'd had any idea of the style of Zan's background, she and Shannon would have been too awestruck to speak, let alone throw themselves at him. How dull, how backward and uninteresting Koonwarra must have seemed to him, and how their gaucheness must have amused him: the two Faloon sisters, who lived on horses like tomboys and who seemed more comfortable barefoot than in shoes. Their lack of sophistication must have seemed appalling to him, their idea of glamour quaintly homespun. Pity poor Shannon. Her self-image hopelessly inflated by a teenage flirtation with a man way beyond her reach, she had left for Sydney under the sad illusion that Zan Fitzherbert was in love with her. How things had changed. She, Kerry, had waited long years for her reward, and it had been worth waiting for. The staff at Kilgarin Castle treated her like visiting royalty, and tomorrow she was going to buy her own thoroughbred, a horse that would be every bit as splendid as Rainmaker . . . and probably twice as expensive. The acquisition would undoubtedly cement her entrée into the circle of society to which she had always aspired. She need no longer feel envious of Shannon's life-style, ephemeral and full of such shallow glamour, now that she had embraced the real thing. For a change she was destiny's darling, Kerry thought triumphantly as the maid knocked and entered bearing a tray laid sumptuously for tea.

Urging her horse to a rolling canter, Kerry gave him his head as he took the hedgerow, landing in the lush, wet grass on the other side. Trailing at the end of the Alderley Hunt, she caught sight of the head huntsman's pink coat ahead of her as he disappeared over the brow of a hill after the pack of hounds. She had been careful to keep a respectful distance the entire day, so as not to appear pushy, even though Criterion, her chestnut gelding, was more than ready to bolt to the fore. Hearing hooves pummeling the turf behind her, she turned to observe the elegant Lady Penwarren pass. It wasn't until Kerry saw her black habit disappear toward the hill that she gave Criterion his head. Now, for the first time that day, she could disregard etiquette, and she let him fly at full gallop across the sweeping plowed fields of Gloucestershire, under a lowering winter sky, exhausted but exhilarated after five hours in the saddle.

When Kerry had sailed joyously over the last fence, she slowed to a trot and made her way back to Dearborne Hall, Noel Villier's Georgian mansion that crowned the hilltop in the distance. She was surprised to see Zan just ahead of her. He seemed to be waiting and looked over his shoulder in her direction.

"So—how was the first hunt on the noble Criterion?" he called as she rode up beside him.

"Sublime," she called back with uninhibited enthusiasm. Beneath her superbly cut black jacket and silken stock she was drenched with perspiration, and her face glowed from being out of doors in the bracing winter air. Her bisque jodhpurs were flecked with mud from leaping down to close gates, and her hair was beginning to escape from the net under her black riding hat.

"I must admit I had my reservations about Criterion when I saw him—I thought he might be a bit too much for you."

"Did you?" she said, casting him a wry smile as they rode side by side. "The minute I saw him I knew I wanted him. He reminds me of a horse I used to have," she said with private irony, thinking of Rainmaker. It wasn't Criterion's color or grace of movement, but his challenging, volcanic nature that had appealed to her. Touching her gloved hand to his glossy neck, she felt a shiver of memory that thrilled and haunted her, though she would never feel the same about any other horse as she had about Rainmaker.

"How does this compare with hunting in the States?"

"Oh, you know what it's like, don't you?" she said evasively.

"No, I don't. I've never hunted there."

"I see. I assumed you knew all about it," she said, not glancing in his direction.

"I've been to Maryland and Kentucky, but I've never hunted there. I met your father-in-law once, years ago, at Jonquil's."

"Then I suppose he would have told you everything, wouldn't he?"

"Do you always answer a question with another question?"

"I suppose, when I think someone already knows the answer."

He gave an amused laugh at her rudeness, which made her blush in confusion. She felt as if she knew him far better than she wanted to since staying that night at Kilgarin Castle, and she couldn't rid herself of the paranoia that he was setting her up, ready to pounce, to reveal that he had known her identity all along.

The invitation to spend the New Year weekend hunting at Dearborne Hall had been extended to her and Mark following her successful cocktail party two weeks after she had gone to Kilgarin. She had discovered that Zan and Noel Villiers were close friends. Since they had arrived at the house the day before, she felt Zan had been seeking her out. It seemed a cruel irony that perhaps the most attractive man she had ever met was the one she had to avoid.

Feeling his eyes on her again, she couldn't wait to reach the stables and the safety of the house. When they clattered into the courtyard Kerry dismounted quickly and tossed the reins to a waiting groom. They had been the last to come home, and she was obliged to walk with him, aware that pointed rudeness might provoke him even more; after his hospitality at Kilgarin and the trouble he had taken to find Criterion for her, she couldn't afford to offend him.

They approached the back of Dearborne Hall, now outlined against dark, scudding clouds, and entered the boot room, its walls lined with mackintoshes, Wellingtons, and riding gear. Kerry took the boot jack and began to tug at her boots.

"Allow me," said Zan.

"Thanks. I can do it."

"Why do you insist on being so damned independent?" he said, taking the jack from her hand.

She leaned against the wall as he cupped her muddy boot in his hand, forcing her to look at him. As they observed one another, an unexpectedly potent charge passed between them. Her first crush on Zan at Koonwarra—so long ago! —had wounded her so deeply that even now she could recall the pain of it. The rugged worldliness of his demeanor made her wonder how he had filled in the years. Did he know what it was like to be driven by all-consuming ambition and deep-seated yearnings to possess, to do, to belong? She was taken aback to see Zan regarding her with the same intensity that in her imagination he had once reserved for Shannon.

"Do you know," he began thoughtfully, "it finally dawned on me who you remind me of."

She froze in terror at these words, struggling to maintain an indifferent expression. "Oh? Who?" she said casually.

"A girl I knew in Australia years ago. Oddly enough her name was Kerry, too, and she had red hair."

"Oh, really? Well, they say that everyone has a double in this world," she replied with a shrug. "But it is odd just the same."

The moment he put down her boots, she flung off her hat and hung it on a peg, murmuring her thanks, then walked down the passage in her stockinged feet, shaking inwardly.

"Going into the drawing room for tea or something stronger?" he called after her.

"No, I'm tired. I'm going upstairs for a hot bath, or I'll never make it to the ball tonight," she said, not wanting to sound too frosty.

Ignoring her remark, he said, "You know, Kerry, you remind me of the fox diving for cover, with that red hair of yours trailing after you."

As Mark drove the car past the gatekeeper's lodge at Ravensbury Park that night, his headlights picked out the high rhododendrons by the side of the road that cut through the park blurred by mist. During the winding drive from Dearborne Hall Kerry had fallen silent as she contemplated

372

how ironic it was that she should find herself arriving at a grand ball given by the duke and duchess of Roxleigh. Following the taillights of a long line of other cars, they approached the huge mansion, its domes and porticoes rising disjointedly out of the fog. As they passed through the high postillions into the graveled courtyard, Mark said:

"Just think—a year ago who would have thought we'd be here for New Year's. Remember? We had to stay home because we couldn't get a sitter, and we missed Nancy and Ralph's party. Think of the look on her face if she could see us now. This is quite a pile. It makes The Meadows look like a shack," he remarked, parking the car.

Getting out of the car, Kerry wrapped her long cloak securely around herself against the cold, then listened as the laughter of guests echoed against the well of dark mist that had closed in on the countryside.

As they walked toward the house Mark chattered excitedly, and she could tell by the way he cleared his throat that he was more nervous than she. It mystified her that he should feel so ill at ease in these grand surroundings; he belonged to this world, while she, a fraud and an interloper, felt only a voracious excitement. She was about to mention how well he looked in his white tie and tails, knowing it would boost his morale, then was distracted as she searched for Zan and Rosemary, who had come in another car. In the space of one afternoon her fear of meeting Zan had turned into intense anticipation.

When she had gone upstairs to her room at Dearborne Hall, she'd lain quietly on the bed, gazing into the fire on the hearth. She had come to the conclusion that if Zan hadn't identified her in the boot room—in a riding habit and with no makeup on her face—he never would.

As she and Mark approached the floodlit portico of Ravensbury Park, she suddenly felt free. Here she was, Kerry Faloon Van Buren, mingling among Pembrokes, Vesteys, Tennants, and Roxleighs, some of the foremost names in England. Peals of laughter and conversation filled the great hall as they entered. Observing the throng of guests from high on the paneled walls was a full complement of Roxleigh ancestors in ruffs, velvet, and lace. The present duke and duchess had paused at the bottom of a curving staircase decked with holly and pine, the duchess in a froufrou of green organdy, her bony shoulders protruding above her gown, the duke tiny and bent, with a balding pate and a monocle screwed into one eye. Kerry fought off a mad fit of the giggles when she saw them. Their eccentric appearance was so much more thrilling than if they had resembled chocolate-box Gainsboroughs, and they set a bizarre and unexpected tone to her first plunge into the heart of the English aristocracy.

The huge ballroom packed with people was painted in Wedgwood blue with white moldings, its Venetian chandeliers twinkling with light. Debutantes with creamy bosoms overflowing from décolleté necklines mingled with hearty hunting types and old dowagers in velvet and lace. The swarm of men of all ages were either in white tie or hunting pink, and the entire crowd swirled together in a mad carnival that was more like a costume ball than the correct and elegant upper-class world of Kerry's imagination. She felt glamorous almost to the point of absurdity in her ruby-red ball gown of grosgrain silk. It had cost a small fortune, and she had combed the shops for days for the right dress; yet here were women in street shoes and fussy gowns that had been out of fashion for years. Mark was the height of distinction compared to the duke himself, whose yellow argyle stockings peeked above his evening pumps. Kerry had been worried about her own modest jewelry, the earrings Lindy had given her as well as a double string of pearls with a jeweled clasp, but some of the women seemed to have thrown on anything that came to hand, from dowdy garnets to plastic bracelets.

"May I have this dance?" She turned with a shiver of excitement to see Zan awaiting a reply. Nodding to Mark, he swept her away.

He whisked her onto the gleaming floor packed with couples, crushing her to him as they weaved in and out.

"Who's that man whose red braces are peeking out from behind his jacket? He looks familiar," said Kerry laughingly.

"That's Mr. Mellors, the gamekeeper," Zan retorted.

"You've got to be kidding. I suppose Lady Chatterley is here, too?"

"I wouldn't be surprised," he replied, holding her back in his arms as he gazed at the portrait of her titian hair tumbling onto china-smooth shoulders, the dash of scarlet at her lips, her billowing dress cut low to show off her high breasts.

In Zan's arms for the first time, Kerry gave in to the sensation of being a beautiful woman flirting with the handsomest man in the room. The past had ceased to pursue her, like a hound that had tired from the chase, and her life seemed to be charging ahead, carrying her buoyantly along.

"There's so much I have to learn about England," she said.

"I'd like to teach you."

She responded with a vivacious laugh of disbelief.

"At last I've got you alone. The thing is, how can we get rid of all these people?" His eyes danced, but suddenly he was serious. "Why have you been avoiding me? Don't deny it. You know you have, ever since we met at Les Ambassadeurs. Today, for example, when you bolted straight up to your room."

"Me? Avoid you?" she said in mock horror.

"I had the distinct feeling that you had taken a dislike to me, and I found it most upsetting. I couldn't imagine what crime I had committed. I think you owe me an explanation."

"Well, I suppose the truth is that you scared me half to death."

"Come on—you're not afraid of anything."

She smiled enigmatically.

Later, when Noel Villiers had whisked Kerry off to dance, Zan regarded the melee from the edge of the floor, a glass of champagne in his hand. It was a quarter of an hour to midnight, and already guests were appearing in gaudy paper hats, blowing horns. This was the first moment Zan had had alone all evening, as he observed the familiar faces passing by. He had known most of these people for years, yet how many could he count as real friends? he wondered. For a few seconds he drifted on an island of self-imposed isolation at the edge of the bacchanalia, his thoughts reverting to Shannon. She would have already seen the New Year in an hour ago, at the house party she said she was attending somewhere in the Touraine with a group of Parisians and French country gentry. It seemed sadly ironic that this New Year, as in the past, she was celebrating in a château with glamorous companions, and he was partying in one of England's grandest houses; yet both of them could not have been more alone. He watched the frank, refreshing little beauty waltz by, the redheaded American Kerry, her head thrown back as she talked vivaciously to Noel. Was she happy? he wondered, catching sight of her tall, lanky, and likable husband. From the laughter in her eyes Kerry obviously believed that this year would prove better than last, just as he had believed it on the brink of

1985. Yet for him, things were just the same. Every year started with a bang, then ended with a whimper.

He and Shannon had tried to meet in Paris before Christmas, but her many commitments had made it impossible. She was so convinced of their love, so strong and true, that it was easy to make promises, many of which sounded hollow when he thought of them later. It worried him incessantly that he was falling deeper and deeper into debt to Rosemary after paying off the death duties of Kilgarin, and she seemed unable to stop her from striding ahead with refurbishing the castle, where she was determined to entertain as countess. Nothing great enough had materialized in his business to counterbalance the morass of debt that threatened to overwhelm him. Yet here he was in evening clothes, the new earl of Kilgarin, with a fixed look of enjoyment on his face as if he were the happiest man in the world—a man who had everything.

"Darling, you look like a little lost boy," he heard a voice say.

It was Rosemary. When she looped her arm through his for a moment, he looked down at her. In a blaze of gold lamé, her smooth blond hair framing her face, she was one of the most attractive women at the ball, and they made a striking couple.

"Isn't this the most marvelous party?" she said, scanning the room.

Before he could think of a reply, she had been swept off to dance. He watched her go with tired irony. At times it seemed to him Rosemary had the power to unmask his most private thoughts. There was that trace of mockery in her voice he knew so well. She was rich, beautiful, and envied, she had his loyalty, even his admiration, but not his love. Guilt had begun to twist his uncomplicated nature, withering his self-respect; only Shannon could give meaning to his life. He made a silent resolution that this year he would free himself of the burdens that weighed him down, in an effort to end this hopeless stalemate. Though only the English Channel separated him from Shannon, it might as well have been the Pacific Ocean.

Minutes before midnight, Kerry approached him. He found the sight of her pretty upturned face distracting, and the lightness of her laugh had the power to lift the dark dome pressing over him.

"Let's dance the New Year in," he said, sweeping her up

376

impetuously in his arms, whirling her madly around the grand ballroom, where old loves and new brushed shoulders, where age and beauty roamed freely together, where yesterday and tomorrow seemed to merge.

At midnight the orchestra stopped abruptly, and over the loudspeakers came the voice of the BBC announcer. The entire room regrouped itself into a serpentine as people linked hands to the first deep resounding notes of Big Ben striking the hour in London, and hundreds of voices broke into "Auld Lang Syne" as the lights dimmed. Balloons came cascading down from a net on the ceiling, and streamers engulfed Kerry and Zan. He swept her in his arms, and feeling her soft mouth yield to his, he forgot everything as a ritual New Year's Eve kiss exploded into private, unexpected passion.

Taken by surprise, Kerry felt herself floating weightlessly in Zan's arms, consummating a dream that she knew she had always harbored, returning his kiss ardently. They clung in a still epicenter as the mad pinwheel of gaiety spun around them. Oblivious to everything, they drew back and regarded each other in shocked silence.

The party didn't break up until after three, and Zan and Kerry had long since drifted in opposite directions. Kerry and Mark drove along the darkened road back to Dearborne Hall with another couple, and as Mark chatted to them, Kerry pretended to doze. Her mind kept leaping back to that unforgettable kiss at midnight that had changed her life, and she knew without doubt that she wasn't the same person who had come to Ravensbury Park earlier in the evening. She was drowning, she was flying, both at once. It wasn't the carnal desire she had experienced with Lindy, it was far removed from her fledgling crush on Zan all those years ago, and it was nothing like the uncomplicated intimacy she had shared with Mark—yet it was all of those.

So this was what it was like to be in love, she thought.

At one o'clock on New Year's Eve in Paris, Shannon glanced at her watch, noting that in England it would be midnight. A chorus of "Auld Lang Syne" would be breaking out at Ravensbury Park, where she knew Zan was spending the New Year, and she tried to imagine what it must be like. She picked up her glass and sipped a silent toast to the two of them, sure that at that very moment Zan was thinking of her, too. "I'll be thinking of you at midnight, darling," he had said when he called earlier in the week. She came back to reality and looked around the dark, smoky Spanish nightclub in Montmartre, Los Banditos. Amadeo had persuaded her to accompany him when a sudden change in his plans had forced his early return from Les Tourelles, where they had spent the traditional Christmas holidays with Patrick and a few close friends.

The guitarist was just warming up in one corner of the tiny stage, where a spotlight curled with smoke, and Shannon glanced down at the long table filled with raucous Greeks and South Americans, a dozen or more of whom Amadeo had insisted be his guests after they had seen the New Year in at Castel's. The men were a collection of rich international pirates with tough, rough-hewn faces; all had amassed fortunes in shipping, oil, trade, and real estate—like Amadeo himself. They had glamorous women in tow, wives or mistresses, each outdoing the other in bejeweled Parisian splendor. Like priceless statues, the women regarded the scene with aloof amusement while the men rocked with uninhibited laughter, gesturing like peasants in the marketplace. Amadeo wiped his mouth and shirt with a napkin after displaying his skill at drinking red wine from a vessel held high above his head. He laughed and reached over to clasp Shannon's hand when he saw she, too, was laughing at his exhibition.

"Not bad, eh, Shanita? I'm out of practice. I used to be able to drink half a liter without stopping."

"It was worth coming here just to see that," she said, shaking her head as she regarded Amadeo's animated face, flushed with wine and the pleasure of being with his most intimate cronies. She had seen Amadeo like this all too seldom over the years, and it was a contradictory aspect of his complex nature that fascinated her. This was the Amadeo she had once loved—the warm-hearted, generous, uninhibited man with feet of clay.

A hush fell over the table as the tempo of the guitar increased, and clapping broke out in the dark little club. Into the spotlight leapt a Spanish gypsy girl announced as "La Joya," her arms arched above her head as she regarded the audience dramatically with dark, flashing eyes. Her mouth a gash of red, her breasts heaving passionately, her glossy hair pulled back severely, she stood tall and proud, a voluptuously beautiful animal. With a disdainful gesture she kicked back her fishtail of yellow and black ruffles, then, dragging

378

her train in the dust, she began to click her heels in counter-point to the plaintive wail of Flamenco music, sung by the guitarist. The heartbeat of the music strummed to a cre-scendo as her fingers curled sinuously around the castanets, her face a mask of contempt. The spotlight veered toward Amadeo's table as the hypnotic beat increased and the singer lamented in a minor key. The gypsy's heels struck the floor inches away from Amadeo as she stared at him hypnotically. The sweat was pouring from her face and running down her arms as she vibrated with increasing intensity.

Glancing at Amadeo, Shannon felt annoyance pass through her at the way he was leaning back in such rapt enjoyment, his eyes caressing the quivering dancer, who returned his regard with a seductive stare, singling him out. Swiveling her hips, she cocked her head sharply over her shoulder as, arms held high, she twisted like a rope to the relentless guitar.

When the music came to an abrupt halt, the audience erupted in wild cheers and applause. After a sweeping bow, "La Joya" left the stage in a trail of black and yellow.

Watching her go, Shannon couldn't keep her face from burning with indignation at what she regarded as an insulting and cheap display. She felt the same outrage she would have experienced if Amadeo had stopped the car and picked up a whore in the Place Pigalle on the way home with her beside him. Oblivious to her pique, he laughed and exchanged what she sensed were crude remarks about the gypsy with an Argentinian next to him. When he finally turned his attention on her, she glared at him with icy reserve, trying to disguise her fury. He grabbed her hand and attempted playfully to kiss it, but she yanked it away.

"More wine!" he called to the waiter. "Drink up, every-one. Shanita—Happy New Year to you!" he said exultantly, raising his glass.

Annoyed by his drunken sentimentality, she stared at the stage and the guitar player, smarting under his amused scrutiny: she had had enough of this vulgar, low dive, she fumed to herself. Such an atmosphere brought out the most primitive instincts in Amadeo, who, after all, was nothing but a peasant for all his surface sophistication, his yacht, château, private plane, and art collection.

His behavior suddenly became intolerable as she watched him talking and gesturing to his table companions. She guessed that before they left he would send a note to "La Joya," making some sort of assignation, and she didn't want to be there to witness it.

"Having fun, Shanita?" he asked.

"I'd like to go home now," she replied frostily, reaching for her purse.

He smiled broadly and patted her cold hand. "Soon—soon," he said expansively.

She didn't notice the narrow prisms of satisfaction in his eyes as he cannily interpreted the dark look of jealousy on her solemn face. He smiled ironically to himself as he reflected that all his subtle attempts to provoke Shannon's jealousy by allowing his name to be linked with a number of glamorous women had failed, and yet now he had innocently ignited a raw possessiveness in her that thrilled him.

One evening in April Mark entered the house, and dropping his briefcase in the hall, he called, "Kerry, honey, I'm home."

"Mark—where have you been?" she asked, coming down the stairs in her dressing gown. "You've only got twenty minutes to shower and change before we have to leave for the Villierses'." She kept her irritation under control.

"Look," he began hesitantly, "isn't there any way we can get out of it?"

"At this hour? Don't be silly. It would be extremely rude."

"I know. But we've seen an awful lot of those people lately, and it's just a cocktail party. Nobody would miss us. I'm tired, Kerry. You seem to forget I work a nine-hour day," he said, trying to smile pleasantly, "and with Hanbury coming next week my workload is—"

She cut across his protest. "Don't be ridiculous. You're no different from anyone else. There's no way I would cancel it at this hour. Now, come on upstairs and change."

He sighed in exasperation and trudged upstairs, pausing to peek in the doorway of the nursery. Lindy was playing with a truck on the floor in his pajamas, and Mark scooped him up in his arms.

"Hi there, big boy," he whispered.

"Come on," he heard Kerry call impatiently. "You haven't got time for that."

Moments later, when Mark was tying his tie in front of the highboy mirror, Kerry could sense by his silence that he was annoyed. She came up behind him and rested her arm affectionately on his shoulder. "I know how hard it is on you, but if we want to take advantage of all the opportunities that have come our way these past few months, we have to put ourselves out." She brushed the big collar of her sage-green linen dress. "Like my dress?"

"Mmm. . . . Listen, Kerry. Don't count on me for anything this weekend—including Smith's Lawn. I've got work to do and I'll probably have to stay home."

"Mark, what's come over you?" she exploded. "First you want to cancel tonight, and now you tell me you won't be at the polo match on Sunday. Do you realize that I've been looking forward to this for weeks?"

"What's come over me?" he repeated. "I was wondering the same thing about you. Honey, you've changed during these last few months." He put his hands on her shoulders, but she avoided his eyes. "You seem to be so caught up in the social whirl and riding that we're hardly ever alone anymore."

She tore away from him. "Don't you see, Mark? I'm having fun for the first time in my life. How can you be so selfish—why should I bury myself in purdah while the whole world is having a good time? The season has just begun. There's Ascot, all those spring balls, Henley, Glyndebourne—I want to enjoy all of them to the hilt." Snatching up her handbag, she said, "And I want to start eventing in the fall, too, as well as join the Alderley Hunt."

He looked at her resignedly. "Yes, I guess I am being selfish to want you all to myself."

When they arrived at the Villierses' townhouse in Old Church Street, Chelsea, they passed through the pretty sitting room to the walled garden blooming with fragrant cherry trees and forsythia, tulips and bluebells. It was one of those unseasonably warm spring evenings, a false summer full of birdsong. Kerry and Mark were welcomed into the circle gathered on the flagstone patio. As Kerry sipped a gin and tonic, Mark's words came back to her: "What's come over you, Kerry?"

Since New Year's Eve she had been moving carefully within a fragile web of unexamined emotions, not daring to pause for a moment's introspection. Glancing everywhere but toward the door, where she expected to see Zan at any moment, she was seized by that same weak-kneed feeling that had plagued her for so long, the same blind panic; with a mixture of hope and dread, she waited for him. As light faded, she found herself instinctively aware of his presence before turning to see him as he stood, his hands in his pockets, on the steps leading to the garden. He acknowledged her with a smile that seemed for her alone, a fleeting, ironic glance that confirmed for her that he, too, was consumed by the same fierce attraction.

"Hi," he said, coming to her side.

"Hi," she replied, feeling self-conscious and foolish.

They joined the conversation, which centered on the polo match at Smith's Lawn between the Vaqueros and Zan's team, the Red Lancers. Kerry listened without hearing: ". . . Ramirez is handicap eight, Delmas is only six, Oliviera six, and Benguela five. The Vaqueros haven't been beaten once, and they're in top form. If you ask me, the Lancers don't have a chance, with all due respect, Zan."

He gave a rueful smile but didn't reply.

"Oh, I don't know," said Mandy Villiers. "It's the Lancers' home territory, after all, and the Vaqueros might have become too big for their breeches. I'll put my money on the Lancers any day."

"Thanks for your undying loyalty, Mandy," he replied with a nod.

"Zan, darling, where's Rosemary? Don't tell me she's still down with the flu?"

"I'm afraid so. She can't seem to shake it off. She thought if she stayed in bed all week, she'd be all right by Sunday."

When the conversation had veered in another direction, Zan turned to Kerry.

"How have you been?"

"Fine. Very busy, really."

"How's Criterion?"

"In great form. I still manage to get to Sunningdale nearly every day to take him for a workout."

They made polite conversation for several moments.

"Is Mark here? I haven't seen him yet," asked Zan quietly.

"Yes, but he'll probably go home early. He said he was tired."

When their tête-à-tête was interrupted, Kerry left Zan's side feeling she had been too eager to mention Mark's departure. For the next half hour she made her way 'round the circle of people, keeping up a stream of mindless chatter but aware of Zan's nearness at every turn.

All her social ambitions, as Mark called them, had crystallized into the singular desire to be where Zan was. To achieve it, Kerry had thrown herself into a round of entertaining people on the periphery of Zan and Rosemary's circle, and now she was becoming known as the vivacious, lovely American, the wife of the up-and-coming merchant banker, son of Lindy Van Buren.

When Zan still hadn't called her a week after New Year's Eve, she contacted him on the pretext of asking advice about the purchase of a country cottage in the Cotswolds; this, in turn, gave him an excuse to call her about properties for sale. Once he had driven her down to the country to see a house himself, and their conversation had been about everything but themselves. Although he didn't say so, Kerry sensed Zan was lonely. She had already heard that he was marking time in his marriage to Rosemary. All winter she had waited for him to declare what he had conveyed to her with his eyes every time they'd met on the hunting field, at parties or balls. All Kerry's experience with men to date seemed useless. She felt green, vulnerable, and confused. Love was hope, she had begun to realize, the overriding conviction that something was about to unfold that would give meaning to life. Her marriage to Mark almost ceased to matter, and only little Lindy grounded her to the daily routine.

Seeing Mark approach her, Kerry sipped her drink, fighting her irritation at the sight of him.

"Honey, I've got to get an early start if I'm going to make it to the office by nine tomorrow, and I've got some papers to look over. I think we ought to go."

"If you don't mind, I'll stay on. I can get a ride home, or call a taxi."

"Sure—if you want," he said, masking his disapproval. "I guess I'll see you later, then."

Moments later Zan approached her. "Where's Mark?"

"He's gone. He wanted an early night."

On impulse he said, "Would you be averse to having a little light supper somewhere? After all, just because the two of us have been abandoned is no reason to go to bed hungry."

She smiled. "I think that's a wonderful idea. I'd love it."

When the party had broken up, they drove to a little Indian restaurant off Flood Street, decorated like the interior of a tent in red and gold, with braziers hanging over the tables.

As they talked about horses, about polo, hunt meets, and

383

Ireland, Kerry stared hypnotically at Zan. She hardly heard what he was saying as she looked into his eyes, where there seemed to be a world waiting. Suddenly she was tired of talking about things that didn't really matter. They had done it for so long, and it was like going in circles, leaving unexplored the heart of what drew them to each other. She had thought endlessly how she would say it. A woman wasn't supposed to declare her love. All she could do was suggest her availability.

"Zan—do you realize that the two of us have been dancing sideways since New Year's Eve?" she said thoughtfully.

He registered a look of surprise, then gave a laugh. "Well, what do you think we should do about it?"

"We could have an affair," she said, stirring her coffee methodically, her heart pounding. She had never been so bold—never had to or wanted to.

"Do you think that's wise?" he said, taken aback by her frankness.

"It has been known to happen when two people find each other irresistible."

Resting his elbows on the table, he regarded her, flattered by her approach. There was no irritating coquetry or coyness about Kerry, and any resolutions he might have had left him as he regarded her eyes reflecting the flames of the candlelight, her hair like burnished copper.

"I must admit the thought has crossed my mind. But it's always more complicated than that."

"What do you usually do in a situation like this?"

"What do you mean?" he said. His mind flew guiltily to Shannon, and he remembered they would be seeing each other again in only a few days when the Lancers met the Vaqueros.

"Are you and Rosemary happy?"

"What's happiness?" he said with a shrug. "We're like any other married couple, I suppose, who are used to each other."

"That didn't answer my question."

"You said 'usually.' I suppose that implies you think I have experience." He reached out to toy with her fingertips.

"Well, haven't you?"

"If I said yes, you might think I was trying to impress you, and if I said no, you probably wouldn't believe me."

She laughed, entwining her fingers in his.

"Kerry," he began, "you've been honest with me, and now I'll be honest with you. I suppose you've wondered why

384

I haven't pursued things any further," he said reflectively. "I was captivated the first time I saw you, and even that night I went home thinking how much I'd like to go to bed with you. I was intrigued by your provocative manner—you were different. But then, when I felt the passion in you on New Year's, I realized that if we started, we'd never be able to stop."

"You make me sound overwhelming."

"No, not that. Vulnerable. And I didn't want to hurt you," he said, though his instinct told him Kerry was a ravishing and confident young woman who knew exactly what she wanted.

"Aren't you vulnerable, too?"

"A lot goes on inside that head of yours, doesn't it? There's so much I don't know about you, so much."

The irony of this remark made her smile. "There's only one way to find out, isn't there?"

Later Zan drove her home, and when they were outside her house he said, "Are you coming to Smith's Lawn on Sunday to watch the polo?"

"Yes, I'm coming. On my own," she added.

"I'll see you then," he whispered.

Taking her in his arms, he kissed her, leaving her no wiser than before, but aware that her longing for him was more acute than ever.

Watching Kerry let herself into the house, Zan drove under the streetlights of Chelsea toward home, disquieted by the turn of events. It had been foolish of him to invite Kerry to dinner, he told himself, tempting as she was to him. In a few days he would see Shannon; then, at the end of May, they would spend a blissful sojourn in Seillans before she disappeared again for another year, like the *princesse lointaine*.

There was something exciting about the new blood Kerry had injected into his circle of lifelong intimates. Her personality was a fascinating kaleidoscope of emotions that had triggered off in him a desire to pursue her out of curiosity. Examining his feelings, he couldn't deceive himself that it was anything resembling his enduring love for Shannon; but too much wine and the late hour had mellowed his resistance.

Chapter III

Smith's Lawn, Windsor Great Park, England, May 1985

It might have been a day in ancient Persia, where polo originated, Shannon thought as she alighted from the chauffeured Mercedes that had brought her to Smith's Lawn in the heart of Windsor Great Park. She felt a surge of pride at the sight of the purple-and-silver-striped Galant tent flanked with silver banners now unfurled against the brilliant May sky.

"It looks really grand, and so do you," remarked Susie, the young bilingual American who had become her personal assistant at Galant.

"This is my garden party number," she said with an ebullient laugh. She had chosen a dress of fine navy wool with padded shoulders and a white collar, and every detail of her appearance was consummately French, from her hair swept back with ivory combs to her spectator shoes and navy bag.

On the way to the tent her eyes scanned the wide green field. It was much too early for Zan to be there, but her heart fluttered in anticipation of spending a few hours together the following day. It was all they could arrange, but it was better than nothing. She, Susie, Amadeo, and some of the other players from the Vaqueros had flown over from Paris the day before and were staying at Claridge's. That morning Amadeo had left his suite ahead of time to attend to his string of polo ponies, which had come over by train earlier in the week.

The catering van was parked outside the marquee, and white-coated waiters were already putting champagne on ice and carrying in huge silver platters and tureens for the luncheon that would be served before the match. Shannon approached the entrance to the tent she had commissioned, leaving a P.R. company to organize the entire project from London. The moment she entered she realized that the colored drawing she had kept on her desk for months couldn't do justice to the reality.

It might have looked awful, but the impact was truly

wonderful, Shannon thought with relief. Before her was a perfect replica of a desert tent, with Persian carpets scattered on the floor. Bolts of rainbow-colored silk had been unfurled from the central tent pillars, creating pinwheels of color, and an elaborately carved ivory-and-sandalwood screen had been erected behind a long buffet banked with camellias, bleeding hearts, and roses. The round tables were covered in silver-gray damask and set with exquisite china and silver, while a fountain in one corner and orange trees in tubs gave the illusion of a garden. All of it had been erected for one day, to honor the launch of *Dressage* and celebrate the success of *Samarkand.*

"It's sensational, isn't it?" Susie commented.

"Not bad," replied Shannon, smiling at the understatement. It had cost a fortune, but it was worth it.

The marquee was already buzzing with public relations people, and Shannon scanned the guest list while Susie went to unpack the special promotional bottles of the two Galant scents: for the women, amethyst glass and silver filigree vials of *Samarkand*; for the gentlemen, flacons of *Dressage* handsomely packaged in burgundy and white, the Vaqueros' colors.

Shannon double-checked the seating arrangements. For two months she and Susie had been occupied with the complicated protocol of seating such luminaries as the Rajmata of Jaipur, the Aga Khan and his wife, and Prince and Princess Michael of Kent. Shannon surveyed the place cards engraved with names that read like the pages of the *Almanac de Gotha*, *Burke's Peerage*, and the *Social Register* combined. Taking out the notes she had made that morning at breakfast, she was suddenly overcome by an attack of nerves when she realized that the chairs for the high table hadn't arrived yet. Keep calm, she told herself; don't panic. Wishing she could practice her curtsey one more time, she regarded the waiters scurrying to and fro. Her first brush with royalty was a nerve-racking occasion. Remember the Aga Khan is Your Highness—not Your Royal, she reminded herself. There were the security men to think of—she should see to it that they have some lunch, she thought. Were the centerpieces on the tables too big? Too late to do anything about it now. And the carpets—some of the edges might catch on the ladies' heels. Better ask someone to tack them down, quickly. Her eye was drawn to the samples Susie was arranging on a special table next to the big silver Galant trophy waiting to be engraved with the name of the winner of the match. At the last moment she had tucked in an extra box of samples, on the advice of a shrewd friend who had warned her that some people, no matter how rich, might brazenly ask for extras.

She glanced out at the field, reminded of Zan. Amadeo had told her the results of the playoffs only two weeks ago, when he dropped by to see her one evening. She had looked straight into his eyes, giving no indication whatever of the turmoil this unexpected news aroused in her. No one had expected the Lancers to win, and when a devilish smile of satisfaction lingered on his face, she'd said casually, "You seem extraordinarily pleased with the results of the playoffs. Do the Lancers have a low handicap?"

"On the contrary, they have a fairly high one. But I'm looking forward to this match. It may prove one of the most challenging of the season."

She had immediately called Zan, to relay the news. And now that the day had come she found it much easier to cope with the strain of organizing this great occasion, knowing that they would spend time together tomorrow.

Finally, the hour approached when the guests were expected; and somehow everything had miraculously fallen into place. Standing alone for a moment, Shannon suddenly realized what it all meant. What would people like Mattie Fremont say if she could see her now, in command of a battalion of waiters ready to lavish hospitality on some of the most glittering names in Europe? Shannon Faloon, a mongrel from the Outback, ruler of a business empire that spanned the globe as far as Sydney and Melbourne. Picking up a place card at random stamped with the *Samarkand* logo, she read the illustrious name, Count Alexander Benckendorff, recalling Mattie Fremont's party at Koonwarra for Charlie and Henry and how awed she had been by it all. Where were they now, and what would they think if they could see her? The dress of cheap chiffon she had worn that night had seemed so glamorous. And yet, she reflected, nothing had changed. She was as nervous and unsure of herself this glorious morning as she had ever been, but she'd learned over the years how to conceal it with a veneer of self-composure that had become her trademark. Today, instead of dancing with roughnecks from the Outback, she would be curtseying to royalty. She thought of Kerry in that ridiculous green dress of

388

hers and wondered where her sister was at that moment and whether her life had changed as dramatically as her own. Braemar had never answered her letter requesting Kerry's address, but she would locate her one day. Last of all she thought of Brendan—her dad. If he strode into the tent at that moment, she imagined he would look around and shake his head in mock disgust. She could just see him sniffing *Samarkand* with a grimace on his face, saying, "This stuff stinks to high heaven." Or passing judgment on the food: "Salmon mousse, prosciutto and melon, lobster salad—that's food for poofters. Who's this bunch of pommie bastards you've got coming, anyway?" Underneath the swaggering disapproval and scowling bravado lurked his deep Irish insecurity. His pugnacious attitude to life had been his protection against class snobbery. Shannon's response had been to storm the high walls and enter the world that had been closed to her; but underneath, part of her would always be unsure. As the first Rolls-Royce drew up beyond the tent, Shannon felt a bittersweet emotion from the past color the moment. She could see Brendan's weather-beaten face as he winked at her affectionately.

"Good luck, girlie," she could imagine him saying. "I'm proud of you."

On the far side of the polo pitch, Amadeo ran his fingers through his hair and squinted up at the sun. Tethered near his private horse box, painted in the burgundy and white of the Vaqueros, were six of his best polo ponies.

"Hey, Juan," he called to the horsemaster. "I'm not going to use Blackjack until the second chukka. I'm going to start play on Rioja," he said, running his hand over the flanks of a roan Carillo. "He looks feisty today, but Blackjack is better," he remarked with a laugh as he caught the sharp eye of his most volcanic gelding.

Today, in cream jodhpurs that enhanced his leanness, a Polo-shirt that exposed his strong brown forearms, and brown boots polished to an immaculate sheen, Amadeo looked every inch the conquering general of an athletic army. His eyes traveled incessantly up and down the lines of the ponies. He knew all their quirks, and each one had been chosen for stamina. He plotted his attack. Should he come out, all guns blazing? Or should he save his stronger ammunition for the later chukkas, and take his opponents off guard?

Amadeo had felt the thrill of a warrior called to battle when he'd heard that Zan Fitzherbert's team would play the Vaqueros. From the morning when Shannon had sent shards of ice into his heart by telling him she was irrevocably in love with the man she believed to be the father of her child, Zan Fitzherbert had become his mortal enemy; now fate had decreed they would be locked in ritual combat. Though they had never met, the very sound of Zan's name sent arrows of venom through Amadeo's veins. Lord Kilgarin, the product of decadent Anglo-Irish nobility, represented everything he despised. He knew Zan's face well from photographs, and he guessed his aristocratic façade disguised a feeble sense of purpose and an indecisive and prevaricating nature. Fitzherbert was a man who owed everything in life to an accident of birth and was unaccustomed to hardship or challenge. All these years of gnawing love for Shannon now gathered force as Amadeo gazed across the lush polo field, as yet unmarked by the clashing of horses and their riders. Had Zan won Shannon honorably, hard as it might have been to accept, he would have conceded. But as time went by and Zan failed to do the decent thing by Shannon, yet continued to enjoy the security provided by his wealthy wife, Amadeo's sense of injustice increased, and with it his taste for vengeance. He had once contemplated trying to sabotage Zan's business, but his pride craved a more direct and violent confrontation. Zan was nothing more than a thief who had robbed him of precious years with his son and the love of the only woman he wanted to make his wife. When he told Shannon that the Lancers would compete for the *Samarkand* trophy, she'd shown no sign of emotion, accustomed for years to concealing the truth. Did she have any idea, he wondered, that he would be fighting symbolically for her favors? His role was that of the unnamed black knight, who wore his lady's colors hidden between his heart and his armor.

"Have another gin and tonic, Kerry," said Noel, reaching for her glass.

"Thanks, but just a little one," she replied with a giggle. "Otherwise I'll be on my ear before the match starts." Tilting her sunglasses back, she trained her eyes on he field, where already two of the Vaqueros were taking practice shots.

"What luck we were here early enough to find a space right in front of the rails," said Mandy. "Otherwise we wouldn't be able to see a thing."

The grassy parking area reserved for members of the club and their guests was now packed with Range Rovers and Rolls-Royces, their backs flung open to dispense lavish picnics set out on portable tables surrounded with folding chairs, and bright tartan rugs were thrown on the grass in the shade of the cars. Kerry had motored from London with another couple, and already their party had begun to merge with others as people, roamed, drinks in hand, shrieking enthusiastic greetings to each other. She wandered to the rails and looked down the line, catching sight of the silver-and-purple-striped marquee next to the viewing stands.

"Is this your first polo match?" asked Noel, joining her at the rails.

"Yes, and I'm so excited," she said, raising her fieldglasses to view the players riding at full tilt as they practiced. There was still no sign of Zan.

"We've got a superb day for it—it's not always like this in May."

"So I gather." Kerry's mood was buoyed by her first English spring. The drive past the estates of Ascot and through sun-dappled Windsor Great Park, where the first azaleas and rhododendrons were in bloom, was a prelude to what she was sure would be the most glorious summer of her life. Today at Smith's Lawn she was beginning to sense the rhythm of the English social year, now that the lowering skies of winter had cleared and hunting had come to an end. There was the season to look forward to, with Ascot, Henley, Wimbledon, and Cowes. Her diary was already beginning to fill up with balls, weekends in the country, and invitations to house parties in Devon and in Tuscany.

"Pity Mark couldn't make it today," remarked Noel.

"Yes, it is a shame. I can't tell you how disappointed he was," she replied, disguising her irritation. They had been invited as a couple, and she was determined he wouldn't make a habit of working on weekends. Without a husband in tow, she'd quickly be dropped from invitation lists—hostesses didn't like the numbers of their parties upset at the last moment.

"Is Rosemary Fitzherbert any better? I haven't seen her today," she said, not wanting to seem curious.

"Apparently she's still weak from the flu and decided to stay at home. Poor Zan will need extra moral support," he replied humorously.

Kerry's heart thumped at this surprise. She hadn't seen or spoken to Zan since their dinner together. Now she scanned the field for him once more.

"Will Zan be joining us before the match?"

"I'm sure he'll come along afterward. I heard the team has been invited for drinks beforehand at that marquee over there."

"Oh, I see," she said, disappointed. "What's it for, anyway? I haven't had a chance to get a program yet."

"Some French firm promoting their products. Rolex and Rothman's do the same thing. Kouros sponsors a trophy, too."

Lowering her glasses, she looked at Noel, and remembering he was Zan's best friend, she gave him her most fetching smile.

"Tell me more about the game. For somebody who's supposed to know about horses, I'm ashamed of my ignorance," she lied, having already read a book on the subject. "I always think there's something so sexy about a man on a polo pony. Why don't you play?"

Noel smiled at her saucy allusion. "You have to be a much better horseman than I am to last out six chukkas. They're only seven minutes long, but the ponies are changed after each chukka. I've always said they ought to change the rider as well," he said, making her laugh.

At that moment the Bentley carrying Prince and Princess Michael of Kent swept past the parking lot toward the Galant tent, where a battery of photographers awaited their arrival. The blond Austrian princess alighted first, smiling graciously as the cameras clicked. She projected a shining glamour in a cream wool dress, a rope of pearls draped around her neck, her flaxen hair swept up in Edwardian style. Her shy, bearded husband walked by her side.

Inside the tent a flurry of conversation rippled through the gathering. The guests of honor had arrived. Shannon was waiting at the entrance to greet them, having collected herself the way she once had before proceeding down the catwalk. Projecting a warm and welcoming persona, she waited for this remarkable moment. The prince came forward, and Shannon reached out to take his extended hand, curtseying gracefully first to him and then to the princess as the cameras clicked. She led them into the tent, where a small select group waited to greet the royal visitors.

392

"How imaginative," remarked the princess, glancing up admiringly at the exotic tent. "What a work of art. And the orange trees and a fountain are a delightful touch."

Hands behind his back, the prince remarked to Shannon, "What a pity it's only here for one afternoon. I suppose that like the Bedouin, you'll soon be folding your tent and quietly stealing away," he quipped wittily.

"Yes, we will," she replied with an amused smile, pleased and relieved at the prince's affable manner.

When the introductions were over, a waiter passed the traditional stirrup cup of champagne, and at that moment Shannon felt her tension ebb away. Everything had been building up to this exalted moment, and now that it had passed without incident she felt a tremendous sense of relief. Not long afterward Amadeo came into the tent with the other members of the Vaqueros to join the party. She couldn't suppress a broad smile when he gave her a signal of Latin-American approval by tugging his ear.

As she was chatting to one of the guests, Shannon caught sight of the red-and-yellow Polo-shirts of the Red Lancers, Zan's team, as they strode into the tent radiating a magnetically virile aura. Lean and suntanned to a man, they were all somewhat taller than the dark Vaqueros, and their sun-bleached hair was tousled from wearing helmets during practice. When Shannon caught sight of Zan she felt her tension mount again, but there had been no way to avoid the meeting without appearing conspicuous. It now seemed an extraordinary irony that the last time she had been at Smith's Lawn was that day she had come to watch Zan play, with Jonquil as her companion, but now here she was, hosting the cream of international society in the atmosphere of unparalleled glamour. She was only half listening to the Aga Khan as he talked of his latest racing triumph when she saw Amadeo approaching Zan through the crowd. She felt a sickening apprehension that the two men who had determined the course of her life were about to meet, and she couldn't resist edging closer to overhear them. Amadeo clutched Zan's shoulder, causing him to whirl around in surprise.

"At last we meet. Lord Kilgarin, I'm Amadeo Benguela," he said in a staccato voice, his manner coldly formal as he offered his hand.

"How do you do?" Zan replied solemnly with a polite nod as he beheld the Argentinian magnate who had introduced himself so suddenly. That he had once been Shannon's lover registered in the back of his mind.

To Shannon's dismay, she saw Amadeo guide Zan in her direction with the words, "Come—you must meet our hostess. The arrangements were entirely her doing."

The day was suddenly charged with a dark undercurrent as she watched the two approach.

"Shanita," called Amadeo, his smile twisted, his eyes glinting dangerously.

Hearing him use her private nickname, Shannon blushed involuntarily. His possessive manner had no place at the Galant reception, and she refused to meet his eyes.

"Have you met Lord Kilgarin yet? He's one of my opponents today," said Amadeo with false joviality, ignoring her coldness.

"Yes, Lord Kilgarin and I have met," she said, barely glancing at Zan as they shook hands. She was overcome with confusion. Had Amadeo remembered who he was? And if he had, why was he behaving in such a fashion?

"I'm sorry, I hadn't realized the two of you were already acquainted," said Amadeo smoothly.

"It's nice to have seen you again, Miss Faloon. Would you please excuse me?" said Zan. "There's someone I must speak to."

"Of course," Shannon murmured.

When Zan had turned away, Amadeo paused only to glint narrowly at her before striding off.

Throughout the luncheon Shannon couldn't regain the ebullient mood she had enjoyed earlier in the day. Though she had Prince Michael on her right and the Aga Khan on her left, the crowning achievement of her life had been robbed of its glory. She had been cleaved into two people—the high-powered director of Galant, who was being showered with kudos and compliments, and the woman inside, trapped by emotional conflict. The rivalry that had ignited between Zan and Amadeo left her perplexed, but she had no time to think about it now.

As the guests began to leave the luncheon table for the chairs set in front of the tent, Amadeo and the other players rose to go, and Shannon was unable to avoid him.

"Wish me luck," he said to her.

"Good luck," she replied sharply. His eyes betrayed a smoldering rage—jealousy—that suddenly filled her with apprehension as she went to take her place among the guests.

Signaling the match was about to begin, the four hel-meted players of each team cantered up to the referee as they restrained their ponies in front of the stands and the royal box. When the bell rang shrilly, the referee tossed the ball into the air, and there was a confused scuffle as the players strained powerfully in their saddles and struggled to gain control of the ball with their mallets. The Lancers broke away with the ball, and the two teams raced pell-mell toward the Lancers' goal.

From the front row of chairs placed near the railings for the guests of honor, Shannon watched tensely as glossy po-nies hurtled across the field. Excitement gathered as it be-came apparent that this was going to be a thrilling contest. In the first chukka the teams raced from one end of the field to the other, the *thwack!* of their mallets striking the ball accom-panied by hooves pounding the earth. Poised on the edge of her seat, Shannon was gripped by the most powerful sus-pense she had ever known. Though the speed and distance of the game made it hard to distinguish one player from an-other, she sensed that Zan and Amadeo were locked in per-sonal combat. They seemed on a collision course, tearing madly down the field, swiping their mallets far too close to each other. At one point the announcer's voice rose in excite-ment as they converged at a dangerous speed over the pocked turf toward the goal, wheeling apart at the last second as Amadeo narrowly missed, which caused a roar of excitement from the stands.

"Benguela's missed it!" she heard someone behind her cry as she searched the field.

When the bell ended the first chukka, Shannon felt as if she had been dropped to earth from a great height. The picture of decorum masking her inner turmoil, she turned to chat with Prince Michael, then with the Begum Aga Khan. The lull lasted only moments before the Vaqueros and the Lancers returned to the field amid cheers and applause.

Mounted on fresh ponies, the players began the second chukka with even more unbridled vigor than the first. Within moments the Vaqueros had scored a goal, causing a roar of approval from the stands. As the ponies raced pell-mell to-ward the opposite end of the field, Shannon saw Amadeo charge toward Zan as if he were out for blood. He sliced his mallet savagely, their two ponies neck-and-neck as they warred over the ball in violent combat. The ball shot free, and Zan raced after it at full gallop, swinging wide as he rode. In swift pursuit, Amadeo raced off, and suddenly events crowded in in quick succession. Taking advantage of a momentary lead, Amadeo urged his horse in the line of Zan's pony as he struck out viciously for the ball; Zan's horse reeled violently. There was a crush of riders, horses, and mallets as people leapt to their feet. Through the legs of the horses Shannon saw a body falling as if in slow motion, while horses and riders veered away from the vortex. There was a gasp of horror from the crowd.

"Someone's been unhorsed!" came the cry.

A riderless horse bolted free and galloped toward the boxes.

"Did you see that?" someone commented. "He cut him deliberately."

"Who was it?"

"Don't know. One of the Lancers, I think. There'll be a foul called, wait and see."

The announcer's voice boomed over the loudspeaker. "Number two of the Red Lancers has been unhorsed at the end of the second chukka, ladies and gentlemen. Lord Kilgarin. It is not known yet whether he has been injured. It seems a foul will be called against the Vaqueros. Play will be resumed as soon as possible, but in the interval would you please go to the field and tread in the divots. Thank you."

At the mention of Zan's injury Shannon rose abruptly and left the front rank of her guests without even pausing to think. Fleeing from the Galant tent, she ran as fast as she could to the first-aid post, driven by the fear that Zan might have been crippled for life—and by the stark realization that Amadeo had most likely been the cause of the accident. Through some twisted sense of possession, he had tried to avenge his wounded Latin pride in the only way he knew how, through an act of violence, with a ruthlessness he hadn't displayed since that night aboard the *Karisma*. He must have known all along about her and Zan, and now he was exerting a crude assertion of his ownership over her as if she were his chattel. Amadeo never gave anything for nothing, and now Shannon knew all his generosity was of a shallow, material kind. His raw power had seduced her into believing he had an almost paternal regard for her and her child, when all this time he had been planning to crush the thing she held most dear. As she caught sight of the first-aid tent, Shannon came to the

396

instant decision that she would resign from Galant as soon as possible.

Every thought left her as she rushed into the tent, and her knees seemed to buckle with relief when she saw Zan lying on a cot, conscious and speaking softly to the doctor who was attending him.

"Zan! Are you all right?" she cried, rushing to his side. "Zan, darling . . ."

Pale from shock, he smiled. "Don't worry, I'm all right. The doctor says it's just my cartilage." Managing a smile, he reached out for her hand. "Darling, you shouldn't be here. Don't worry about me."

"You can't imagine what went through my mind when I saw you fall," she whispered, close to tears.

"I suppose all our carefully laid plans for tomorrow have gone awry, haven't they?"

"Don't worry," she said soothingly. "We'll be in Seillans in just under three weeks. I'm leaving for the Far East tomorrow afternoon, and I've decided to fly via Rome on the way back and go straight to Nice, so I'll be waiting for you at Seillans on the twenty-seventh."

"That sounds wonderful." Kissing her hand, he said in a low voice, "I wanted so badly to hold you when I saw you there in the marquee. It's agony to meet you like that, and not even be able to touch you. I suppose you'd better get back to your guests. . . ."

Shannon and Zan were so absorbed in each other that they didn't notice they were being observed from the entrance to the tent. Stunned, Kerry watched them clinging together, two people who were, and always had been, lovers. Before they became aware of her, she turned and fled in a state of dazed bewilderment.

Shaking from head to foot, she wandered aimlessly down the road through the afternoon shadows, oblivious of the cars or the crowd as she struggled to understand what she had just witnessed. This was the cruelest blow fate had ever inflicted on her, but when she considered it with numb clarity, it wasn't at all surprising to her.

Shannon, her own sister, was Zan's lover—had been for years, probably since Koonwarra. Obviously that was why Shannon had never married. It was why Zan hadn't followed up their attraction. It had nothing to do with integrity or caution, as she had imagined, but because Shannon—that

397

selfish, possessive bitch—had bewitched him with that sweet, soft voice of hers, that come-hither beauty, that exotic smokescreen of mystery that concealed her devious nature. It wasn't enough that Shannon had Amadeo Benguela, one of the world's richest men. No—she had to have Zan, too, the only man Kerry had ever loved.

Her unshed tears turned to self-ridicule for allowing Shannon to make a fool of her once again. How was she ever going to face Zan after throwing herself at him the other night? And that embarrassing, vulgar remark: "We could have an affair"? It would haunt her forever. She had learned nothing about life since she'd fallen for Zan a decade ago. Like a gauche teenager she had been seduced by one passionate kiss, spinning a pathetic fantasy for herself. Painfully, she relived the same intense jealousy she had experienced that day she had intercepted and destroyed the letter from Shannon to Zan. All these years it had niggled at her conscience, but now she was glad she'd done it. If the chance came her way to do it again, she would. Had she burst into the tent and confronted them when she had the chance moments ago, she knew they would have regarded her from a plateau of indifference. The self-confidence that had taken years to build was swept away by the realization that she was nothing to either of them.

Trying to pull herself together, she walked past the clubhouse overlooking the polo field. Play had resumed. She stopped at the railings to regard the match that had so thrilled her moments ago. Mortified, she realized that if her hatred for Shannon was stronger than ever, so was her love for Zan. But what could she do about it? Was their relationship so permanent, so stable? Society was a glass coach that traveled in view of the rest of the world, yet surely the ménage à trois of Rosemary, Zan, and Shannon was a secret, or she would have heard about it.

She strode into the clubhouse, sparking with defiant belligerence, and ordered a double gin and tonic at the bar. When it came she took a deep gulp, then, feeling somewhat better, looked down the bar lined with men chatting volubly. She was wondering what to do next when she happened to glance at two men next to her, one of whom seemed familiar. He was flamboyantly dressed in a blazer and a yellow paisley tie, and he sported a gaudy waistcoat. Seeing her staring at him, he cast her a curious, inviting smile as his companion turned to leave.

"I'm going down to the Galant tent for a bit of freeloading and to see if I can sniff out a story. You coming on?"

"In a minute. I'll see you later."

When his friend had gone he moved toward Kerry. "I say, that was a bit of foul play earlier on, wasn't it? The whole club is still in a state of outrage," he remarked by way of conversation. "These hot-blooded Latins don't know when to stop."

"I really didn't notice," she said distractedly. Looking at the man's name tag, she put the name to the face. He was Graham Gilston, London's most notorious gossip columnist. The fancy vest was his trademark, she recalled, and everyone in London, including her, consumed his daily column with toast and marmalade for breakfast. Gilston's name struck fear in the heart of anyone in the public eye with something to conceal, and he had made a career of tracking the lives of the international jet set, splashing their indiscretions across his column.

"Could I offer you a drink?"

"Yes, thank you. A double gin and tonic."

"That's a bit strong for a sunny afternoon, isn't it?" he chided amiably. "Waiter—one double gin and tonic, please, and a whiskey."

"I noticed when you came in that you looked a bit perturbed," he continued.

"I've got a good reason."

"Kilgarin was pretty lucky to escape that clash with no more than a few bruises, wasn't he?"

"You could say that."

"Why? Do you know him?"

"Yes, I know him quite well," she said as the gin suddenly took effect.

"You know the Villierses and all those people, do you?"

"Yes. I'm with their picnic in the car park."

"Are you? I say, you don't happen to know Shannon Faloon, do you? That gorgeous model who is heading Galant? Someone said she rushed out of the tent when Fitzherbert was injured."

Kerry looked him directly in the eye. "Funny you should ask. I happened to know her years ago. She grew up in Australia. She's the illegitimate daughter of a sheep shearer and a half-caste."

"She's Australian? I didn't know that," replied Gilston, his mind ticking over.

"Oh, yes. She may be at the top of the pile now, but she had very humble beginnings. Pretty sleazy, in fact."

"And what about this Benguela fellow? Do you know if it's true that she's his mistress? The story has circulated for years."

"Not only is she *his* mistress, she's been Lord Kilgarin's mistress since she was seventeen in Australia." When Gilston looked incredulous she added, "If you don't believe me, you can check it out. He stayed one summer at a ranch called Koonwarra in New South Wales, with a family called the Fremonts. That's where it all started."

Gilston's face registered no emotion. "Mind if I just jot that name down—Koonwarra and the Fremonts?"

"Please, be my guest."

"Thank you so much. You've been very helpful. Do you suppose I might have your name and telephone number to get more details if necessary?" He was straining to get away to find his photographer and check the validity of this juicy scoop.

"No, I'd rather remain anonymous," she said hastily. "I don't want my name mentioned."

"Naturally. I wouldn't dream of it. This is strictly confidential," he said reassuringly. "Let me buy you another drink before I go."

When Gilston had gone, Kerry felt a stab of desolation. Despite his vicious reputation, he had been the opposite of what she had expected—easygoing, understanding, and sympathetic. But when it dawned on her what she had done, she felt uneasy. Not because of Zan and Shannon—she would tell everything a thousand times over to anyone who would listen—but because she had broken a cardinal rule of society in feeding a gossip columnist with confidential dynamite. The only thing she cared about was that no one ever discover the story came from her. But after three double gin and tonics she decided she didn't give a damn about anything.

The following morning Kerry was propped up in bed with tea and toast and the freshly delivered morning papers. She had complained to Mark that she wasn't feeling well, intending to ride out the storm in the place she felt most secure, her pretty bedroom decorated with Sheraton furniture and pastel floral prints. She glanced down at Lindy, who was playing quietly on the floor with his blocks. Everything seemed so normal, yet her life was in tatters. Her son toddled to his feet, and she absently handed him a piece of toast while she turned nervously to Gilston's column. It came as a shock to see a picture of Shannon in dark glasses as she hurried from the Galant marquee on Sunday, with the caption "The Silk Route to Fortune." Kerry read the story with compulsive anxiety.

Having taken the Silk Route to Fortune, with the assistance of tycoon Amadeo Benguela, to launch the perfume Samarkand, followed by *Dressage* aftershave, ex-model Shannon Faloon seemed none too pleased when her own Marco Polo took a tumble at Smith's Lawn on Sunday. A foul was called against Benguela for unsportsmanlike behaviour, but all was not lost—his team, the Vaqueros, won the trophy from the Red Lancers. This is rumoured to be his consolation prize while Miss Faloon was playing Florence Nightingale in the first-aid tent, where Lord Kilgarin lay injured. Question is: Will Benguela chukka?

Kerry lay back on the pillows, relieved and disappointed that the article was so tame. Moments later Mandy Villiers called.

"Hi," said Kerry, trying to sound herself. "I was just going to call you and thank you so much for including me yesterday. I had a marvelous time. . . ."

"You're entirely welcome. Listen, Kerry—have you seen Gilston's column?"

"No. Why?" she replied, on her guard.

"Rosemary is absolutely livid. But of course if you haven't read the column, you don't know yet."

"Just a minute. I've got the papers here. I'll have a look." Pausing, she pretended to read the article. "I don't understand it at all. What do they mean by Marco Polo?"

"Zan, silly. He's the one who fell off his horse."

"Oh, how stupid of me. Of course. The whole story is probably a lot of lies, anyway."

"Oh, no, Gilston is much too clever for that. You can be sure he's checked it very carefully and that there's a grain of truth there. The thing is, I've been trying to piece this together. You don't know who Shannon Faloon is, do you? I mean, she's a model, but how on earth do you suppose she knows Zan?"

Kerry was suddenly beset by panic. She had to get rid of Mandy before she gave herself away. "Oh—Lindy, stop that this minute! I'm sorry, Mandy, but I've got to go. Lindy's just knocked my coffee over."

She put down the phone, her hand trembling.

The moment she had hung up she jumped from the bed and got dressed to go to Sunningdale and take Criterion out for the day. When she came back in the evening, exhausted and feeling better, her heart lunged with dread when she saw Theresa had noted down several phone calls from friends of Mandy's and Rosemary's. Was she being paranoid? Would they have called anyway? Or had someone guessed she was having a flirtation with Zan and decided to implicate her in the scandal exposed by Gilston? Perhaps someone had seen her going to the tent at Smith's Lawn, or at the Indian restaurant with Zan. Perhaps Gilston had used the information she had given him to uncover the fact that she was Shannon's sister, and she would be next on his list. The implications were shattering to contemplate. Her life was still strung on the same delicate skein as Shannon's own, like it or not. She had been a fool. When she thought of all the dirt people could dig up about her, she shuddered. Everything she had fought so hard to win was in peril because of her rash behavior, and the only thing she could do was to wait for the storm to blow over.

On Monday ten days later when Kerry turned to Gilston's column she was aghast to realize that he had worked very fast and that the scandal had taken on a bizarre new twist. Splashed across the column was the lead story featuring Shannon, revealing more about her life than even Kerry had dreamed of. There was a picture of Amadeo carrying a little boy, with Shannon at his side as he tried to fend off photographers. According to the caption, the candid photo was taken the previous summer, and when Kerry read the accompanying story she numbly began to comprehend the cataclysmic forces she had set in motion. Gilston had skated a hairsbreadth from libel but had subtly implied that the child called Patrick, the boy that the French gossip columns had tried for years to prove was Amadeo's and Shannon's love child, could prove instead to be the son of the current earl of Kilgarin. Gilston

402

went on to intimate that Shannon and Zan had been meeting for years at their love nest in southern France, where they had conveniently placed businesses, and that Shannon herself was illegitimate and of mixed blood.

White with shock, Kerry let the paper fall from her hands. Several lives, including her own, had been blown up in one succinct paragraph.

The following evening Rosemary and Zan closed the drawing room doors behind them at Pelham Crescent and confronted each other with undisguised hostility. Gilston's lurid exposé lay between them on the desk, and the argument it had sparked had been raging furiously between them since Rosemary first opened the paper over breakfast.

"You make me sick. I suppose this is what is so quaintly referred to as a 'meaningful relationship.' And you expect me to believe that all these years you didn't even know she had a *baby*?" Rosemary fumed. Her slender frame vibrated with outrage, and her blue eyes were glacial, signaling a new ice age between them.

"Don't keep ranting on about that. It's not true," replied Zan, his voice deadly calm. "This is as much of a shock to me as to you, even though you might find it hard to believe." His shoulders slouched; he sighed tiredly. The picture of Shannon with Patrick and Amadeo was branded into his brain, yet he couldn't keep himself from staring at it once more.

"How could you make such a fool of me—how?" Rosemary exploded. "Do you realize that I'll have to face everybody's pity for the rest of my life? I want you to sue the paper, I tell you, to exonerate our name. . . ."

"Now you're being absurd. A moment ago you said you couldn't believe the child was mine, and now you're saying I should sue to prove it isn't. You're being totally unreasonable."

"Well, is it or isn't it?"

"No!" he shouted violently, slamming his fist on the desk. "For the hundredth time, Rosemary, that child isn't mine."

"All right, then, sue them," she replied coolly.

"On what grounds? That column is so cleverly worded, I'd never get anywhere. The only winners would be the solicitors. I've admitted the truth about me and Shannon. For God's sake, leave me alone. This whole thing will die down in time. What's done is done."

"Oh, yes, it will blow over—after everyone has finished amusing themselves at my expense. I'll never be able to hold my head up again, and neither will you. I should have chucked you out years ago when I had the chance. I shouldn't have listened to Jonquil, shouldn't have given you a second chance. I was an idiot."

"What are you talking about?"

"Do you think I didn't guess what was going on four years ago?" she said scathingly. "Those secret late night phone calls you used to make to her in Paris? Zan, you were stupid, sneaking downstairs when you thought I was asleep. Jonquil flew to Paris hours after seeing you that evening, to talk that woman out of the whole thing. And now I wish she hadn't. You went on seeing her anyway, not thinking of anyone but yourself. Oh, I've been a fool."

It was as clear as crystal what had happened, Zan realized, remembering the chain of events that had led to his breakup with Shannon. How much did Jonquil and Rosemary have to do with it? He would never know now, and he no longer cared. "I suppose this means that you want a divorce," he said defeatedly.

"What?" She whirled around. "So that you and your trollop can escape to a desert island and leave me to pick up the pieces?"

"Think what you like. I've told you it's over."

Venomously spitting out the words, she went on: "I've been paying the bills all this time, and I'll call the tune, if you please. You and I will present a united front until this whole thing blows over, and we will salvage what remains of our reputation. We'll go to Kilgarin for the summer, until the autumn, when I hope and pray people will have forgotten about it. We'll go ahead with the plans for opening the castle as if nothing has happened." When he tried to interrupt, she said in a dangerous monotone, "I'm giving you an ultimatum, Zan. There will be no divorce—not now, or under any circumstances."

"But my work—I can't just drop everything like that," he cried.

"I think they can manage without you at the office," she replied frostily. "You can take a leave of absence and putter about on the estate. I'm sure you'll find lots of things to keep you busy. I'll continue to pay the lion's share of the expenses, as I always have, and," she added with venomous finality, "you will write to your mistress and inform her that you wish never to see her again, that it's all over—finished and done with between the two of you."

Zan turned his back on her. "I'm tired, Rosemary. We can talk about the details later," he said wearily.

"I'm going to bed," she announced tersely. Pausing at the door, she said, "I want that letter to be in tomorrow's post, Zan. You can't deceive yourself or me a moment longer. If you weaken, I'll ruin you. I'll make sure you have nothing but an empty title to your name."

When she had slammed the doors behind her, Zan collapsed into a chair, on the brink of despair. His face was unshaven and his eyes bloodshot from drinking. He surveyed the bleak ruins of his life, not knowing which stone to pick up to begin the long, agonizing process of rebuilding; it all seemed so hopeless.

His eyes fell once more on the picture of Shannon and her child. It was inconceivable that their relationship, which had thrived for years on the purest form of trust, had been based on vile duplicity. He would never know what had gone on between the people in the photograph, but the scope of Shannon's betrayal had wounded him immeasurably. Even now it was like a physical blow to regard her blurred image, knowing that to her he had represented nothing more than a romantic interlude. No matter how hard he tried to find an explanation, he was forced back to the same conclusions as any observer looking at the picture. Her baby by Benguela was the reason she never wanted him to come to Paris. Shannon was afraid he would discover she was Benguela's mistress—a relationship that had been going on long before their own affair had begun. Now he understood the Argentinian magnate's vicious attack on him at Smith's Lawn. Shannon was Benguela's, and he didn't intend to give her up. Benguela had bought Shannon's affection with his millions, and now he would be able to give her all the things Zan knew he could never provide, things that meant so much more to her than their pathetic little dream, the empty fantasy that had come to such a sordid end. If ever he was going to express the hurt in his heart, he knew he had to do it now. Something within him seemed to wither and die as he picked up his pen and wrote, "Dear Shannon . . ."

*   *   *

405

As the plane made its final approach over the Baie des Anges, Shannon looked out contentedly at the familiar sweep of the deep blue Mediterranean, set with jewel-like clarity against the city of Nice rising against the background of the Alpes-Maritimes.

Less than three hours ago she'd been in the center of Rome. Now, as she left the airport, she breathed deeply of the air unique to the Côte d'Azur, an intoxicating blend of sun-baked earth, bright, blooming flowers, and a battery of herbs and spices, seasoned with the crisp suggestion of pure air from the lavender fields high in the hills. If she could bottle the fragrance, label it, and market it, Shannon thought, the air of the Côte d'Azur would make a sensational perfume. Though perhaps, like rosé de Provence, the delicate wine of the coast, it wouldn't travel well. It had to be savored here beneath unclouded skies, she decided, putting her bags into the hired car. Pressing down on the accelerator, she drove past palm trees tossing in the wind.

Out of habit she left the coastal road at Cagnes-sur-Mer and headed toward Grasse. The winding drive to Seillans made her forget her exhaustion after two weeks in the oppressive heat of the Orient. She had metaphorically locked all her business problems in her briefcase, where she was determined they would stay for the entire week that she and Zan would be together. They hadn't spoken since she'd left him in the first-aid tent at Smith's Lawn, and in the interim she had had time to think about the climactic end of the Galant launch.

That day, as she'd watched Amadeo accept the Galant trophy from Princess Michael of Kent, she had been forced to contain her simmering anger. Later, when a team of assistants had come to pack up her Oriental fantasy as quickly as they had assembled it, she'd felt the irrepressible urge to retire her own ambitions along with the marquee. When Amadeo had walked in unexpectedly, a little speech of resignation had risen to her lips, but he had given her no chance to speak.

"Shannon—I've come to apologize, to tell you how deeply sorry I am that I spoiled your day," he'd said abruptly. "I had no right to behave as I did. It was unforgivable."

Cheated of her outrage, she'd been taken completely by surprise at this unexpected mellowing of his swaggering egotism, and she'd let him walk away without a murmur. The naked remorse in Amadeo's eyes was so unusual, so incomprehensible that she had been unable to speak her mind; and during her long trip to the Far East, she'd had time to think about her impetuous decision to leave Galant. So many people depended on her now, and she had come to realize that she could ill afford the self-indulgence of false pride. Her resignation at this point might jeopardize Zan's leaving Rosemary, and with no income of her own she would be back in the same position as when she'd been penniless and pregnant. Whatever decision she came to concerning Galant, she was determined to reach it calmly and rationally, with Zan's advice. For the moment, as a gentle breeze blew through the car carrying welcome waves of perfumed heat, she felt she hadn't a care in the world. The only thing that weighed on her mind was the information relayed by her assistant that a story full of innuendo about her and Zan had appeared in an English paper following the polo match. At first she had been aghast at the news, but after she had calmed down she realized that it might prove to be a blessing in disguise. At worst Zan might be forced to leave Rosemary sooner than he had expected, a prospect that filled her with joy.

Arriving at Seillans, she parked the car in the square and walked up to the house she had come to regard unreservedly as home. Carlo, the housekeeper's husband, would see to her luggage. Among the piles of clothes neatly laundered at the Peninsula Hotel in Hong Kong were a number of presents for Zan—a lizard-skin belt, a gold lighter, and a little laughing Buddha in old ivory.

She let herself into the house, noting that Carlo had whitewashed the exterior and given the blue shutters a fresh coat of paint and that the scarlet geraniums in the window boxes had been expertly coaxed into a mass of blooms. As usual the shutters of the sitting room had been closed, and flinging them open, Shannon saw that Aurore had arranged everything in immaculate order, even remembering to put a jug of marigolds on the table.

Over the years Shannon had transformed the little house from a simple holiday retreat into a comfortable home. She and Zan had combed the antique shops together in the hillside villages for old Provençal furniture, pewter, and pottery. Her favorite room was the bedroom, and as she opened the shutters to admit the warm, fragrant air, patches of sun fell on the worn tiles. She smiled contentedly at the painted blue wooden bed covered with a patchwork quilt and made up with crisp monogrammed linen sheets. Aurore had even re-membered to lay bags of lavender under the lace-trimmed pillows.

In the big sunny kitchen, copper caldrons Shannon had collected gleamed above the huge old fireplace set with blue and white tiles. She took a grape from the bowl of fruit on the big wooden table surrounded with straw-bottom chairs. To-night she and Zan would have dinner at home, as they always did their first evening together. In the refrigerator was a colorful salad of mesclun, a plump chicken larded with rose-mary, and a wheel of chalky-white *chèvre*, along with several bottles of rosé from a local vineyard. Shannon gaily hummed a tune as she broke off a chunk of a fresh baguette, then popped an olive into her mouth, beginning the sublime ritual to which she looked forward the whole year long. She would take a long bath and change into her jeans, then putter about the house to her heart's content until Zan came through the door. The nights were still cool, and before he arrived she would make a fire to welcome him, filling the house with the fragrance of burning olive wood. Hearing a tap at the front door, she looked into the hallway to see Carlo.

"*Bonjour, Carlo,*" she said, happily extending her hand. "*Ça va?*"

"*Bonjour, Madame Faloon.*" He always called her "Ma-dame," a sign of respect. "*Oui, tout va bien. Soyez la bienvenue.*"

When they had exchanged all the news about his family and the house, he said, "I'll bring your bags up from the car now, if you wish. By the way, there's a letter that arrived for you earlier in the week. I put it on the refrigerator."

"Thank you," she called after him. Taking the letter, she went to the terrace off the sitting room and plopped down in a chair near pots blooming with geraniums and oleander. Over the years bougainvillea had been trained up the side of the house and was now growing as far as the red-roof tiles. She breathed deeply, listening to the hum of cicadas. She never tired of the view of sweeping hills and plains painted with the clear, dramatic light of southern France.

Holding up the letter, she looked at it curiously, won-dering whom it could be from. Few people knew of her retreat in Seillans. Her name had been typed, and the enve-lope bore no return address. As she opened it and removed the single sheet of paper, a newspaper clipping fell out, and

408

when she unfolded it she was stunned to see a photograph of herself, Patrick, and Amadeo that had been published in an Italian magazine the year before, an intrusion into her privacy that had upset her deeply at the time. Then with dismay she saw another news photo, one taken of her by Parkinson for *Vogue* in her modeling days, next to yet another of Rosemary and Zan at the Badminton Horse Trials earlier that spring. Her heart began to pound as she read the article and its headline. This couldn't be the story her assistant had warned her about. No, this was yet another one, and its implications were shattering. By Shannon's reckoning it had appeared within the last few days when she had been out of touch with Paris. In a state of shock she opened the letter accompanying it, seeing instantly that it was from Zan.

Dear Shannon,

Of course you must already be aware of my reason for writing this letter, and I'm sure it will come as no surprise that I won't be joining you in Seillans. Should you decide not to come after what has happened, there is an identical letter to this one waiting for you in Paris. I enclose the photograph of you with Benguela and your child, which speaks for itself. I think it will come as a relief to both of us to end this ridiculous charade.

Zan

Moments later Shannon was running from the house, down the street to the village phone box, where she dialed Zan's number in London. There might still be time to catch him before he left the office, she thought frantically.

"Hello—I'd like to speak to Lord Kilgarin, please."

"I'm sorry, but he's on extended leave until fall. May I relay a message?"

"Extended leave?" she replied, aghast. "But he can't be. Do you know where he's gone? I'm a personal friend of his, and it's very urgent."

There was a pause. "He's on holiday with his family in Ireland."

"Could you give me the number there, please?" Shannon shot back.

"May I ask who's calling?" said the secretary, aggravated by her persistence.

"Shannon Faloon is my name."

There was a dead silence on the line for a moment. "I see. I'm afraid I'm not authorized to give Lord Kilgarin's number in Ireland to anyone."

When Shannon had hung up she walked from the shadows into the blinding sun, quaking with shock. She shouldn't have given her name, she thought numbly. Then she might have gotten through to Zan to untangle this nightmare. Now he was out of touch for the whole summer.

When she got back to the house she forced herself to read the letter once more, and as she interpreted each word of the cruel message, she comprehended that Zan had closed the door irrevocably in her face and that there was no point in pursuing him any further. He was using this hideous piece of slander as a pretext to back out of an entanglement that had begun to pall. At the first sign of turbulence he had bailed out, giving her no chance to defend herself.

She lay on the bed and stared out at the square of perfect blue sky captured by the long window. The brutal finality of Zan's words stemmed the tears that threatened to fall. A will to survive this awful blow began to gather strength within her. Surely, she told herself, their relationship wouldn't have survived a week if a breath of scandal could knock it sideways. If she was indeed as precious to Zan as she had imagined, he should at least have had the courage to face her in person. Instead, he had gone sulking off to Kilgarin with Rosemary, his ice maiden of a wife. His cold-blooded attempt at a reconciliation with Rosemary sickened her.

Through Shannon's maelstrom of emotions surfaced one poignant regret: if she had told Zan about Patrick, would things have been different? No, she decided. That way she might never have discovered his true nature. She might have wasted long years in a hopeless relationship before she realized the truth.

She felt herself sinking into a lifeless torpor and tried to rally her spirits, fumbling blindly to reknit the fabric of her torn life. Forcing herself from the bed, she walked down the stairs and into the kitchen. She would go to the phone box, telephone Fiona, and tell her to come down to Seillans with Patrick on the first plane. She would spend her holiday as planned while she was piecing her life back together. She still had Patrick and her work—nothing could ever take them away from her.

Zan stood at the threshold of the great hall of Kilgarin Castle, an overnight bag at his feet, his raincoat flung over his arm. After being cloistered for a month at the castle with Rosemary, he had been looking forward to a trip to London on business, but the mounting tension of the last weeks, coupled with the parting argument he had had with Rosemary that morning, had made him tense and irritable. At the bottom of it lay her unyielding obsession to refurbish the castle to its former glory. All Rosemary's thwarted energy had been diverted from the usual social season in London to asserting herself as countess at Kilgarin, and she countered his criticism of her plans with angry sarcasm. She was feverishly marshaling servants, decorators, and caterers in preparation for an autumn ball at the castle, which she calculated would make people forget the recent scandal and reestablish them socially. Hearing footsteps, Zan turned to see Rosemary descending the oak staircase in a heather-colored sweater and skirt, her bag flung over her shoulder.

"Oh, Rosemary—I'm afraid I'm going to have to take your car to the airport. I've just telephoned the garage and they said the Aston-Martin won't be ready until tomorrow. Shaughnessy can drive the car back as soon as he's dropped me off. . . ."

"I'm afraid that won't be possible," she interrupted, glancing at him coolly. "I need the car this morning to go into the village."

"Couldn't you just drop me there on the way?" he said, reining his impatience.

"No, I couldn't. It's entirely out of my way. I've got a million and one things to do and I have to be back by noon. Julian's coming with the tassels for the dining room curtains. I want them hung by tonight. Anyway," she said, tossing her head, "it looks like this gives you the perfect excuse to stay for the party tonight with the Conolleys."

He sighed irritably. "We've been all through that, Rosemary. I've got to be at that meeting. Now, please give me your keys or else drive me there yourself." He extended his hand, his face flushed with repressed anger at her imperturbability.

Jingling the keys provocatively, she regarded him with narrowed eyes. "You're determined to embarrass me at any cost, aren't you? Of course you realize what everyone is going

411

to say if you go back to London during Ascot week on your own, don't you?" she said venomously, her voice echoing in the hall.

"That's absurd, and you know it. I'll be back in twenty-four hours. Now for God's sake, Rosemary, keep your voice down. I don't want Saffron and the servants to hear us quarreling."

"How marvelously considerate you are of other people all of a sudden," she retorted. "Don't think that I don't know what you're up to. Twenty-four hours is quite enough for what you have in mind." She strode past him and out the door to the forecourt, where her white Alfa Romeo was parked.

Fuming, Zan grabbed his suitcase and charged after her. As she opened the door of the car he caught up with her.

"For God's sake, Rosemary, don't be so damned unreasonable. I'm going to miss my flight."

She turned to him, utterly calm, with disdain in her voice. "You're the one who's unreasonable, Zan. You've spoiled my first dinner party at the castle."

"Oh, very well," he said angrily. "I'll get Shaughnessy to take me in his car. I don't know why the hell I even bothered to ask you, anyway."

"I'm afraid I sent him into Bantry early this morning to collect the lobsters for tonight. So you see, Zan, you're stuck. That makes a change, doesn't it?" she said, taking obvious pleasure in his helplessness.

The cold amusement in her blue eyes as she twisted the knife triggered an insane rage in Zan, shattering his self-control. He grabbed her arm violently, trying to wrest the keys from her. "Give me those!"

"Don't you dare touch me," she gasped, drawing back.

For an instant the mask dropped, and a look of naked hatred he had never seen before contorted her face, shocking him to his senses. Repulsed, he stumbled back. Rosemary leapt in the car. With a dry laugh she called out the window, "I'm afraid you're caught, you poor fool."

Just then, Zan turned to see the carpenter's van coming through the gates.

"Oh, no I'm not," he said triumphantly, a smile spreading across his face. Turning his back, he ran across the courtyard to hail the van. "Dermot!" he called urgently, breaking into a run.

When he had hopped inside next to the driver and

412

slammed the door, Rosemary brought her car to a screeching halt in front of the van.

"Go to hell!" she screamed. As she accelerated sharply, the wheels bit deep, spraying the van with gravel. In seconds she had disappeared down the drive.

Embarrassed by Rosemary's breach of good behavior in front of the carpenter, Zan mumbled, "Lady Kilgarin is running terribly late this morning."

"She'd best slow down, sir. I noticed on the way here that they're cutting the hedges on the road into town."

When Zan opened the door of the house in Pelham Crescent, the first thing he did was turn on all the lights in the drawing room to chase away the gloom. Flinging open the window of his study, he looked out onto the dark garden, where summer evening had faded to violet beyond the darkening trees. He was hot and tired, yet now that he was alone he could still find no peace. He was pursued by a demonic restlessness that made him crave company, but who to phone? There were few people whom he wished to see at this moment, and they would all be engaged, anyway. Just as he had decided to go out somewhere for dinner by himself, the phone rang. He was tempted not to answer it, knowing it had to be Rosemary. Hardly anyone else knew he was there.

"Hello," he said brusquely.

"M'lord? This is Shaughnessy, calling from Kilgarin."

"Yes, Shaughnessy?" he replied curtly to his estate manager, irritably wondering what he wanted. His obligations seemed to pursue him no matter where he went. "Listen, couldn't it wait? I'm on my way out."

"I'm afraid not, m'lord, and I'm sorry to be disturbing you, I'm sure. It's fallen to me to deliver the unhappy news."

He realized then that Shaughnessy's voice was strained. "What news?" he said sharply.

"You'd better sit down and prepare yourself, sir. I'm afraid it's the countess. There was an accident, m'lord. She was killed most tragically this afternoon in her motor car—" Shaughnessy broke off for a moment, his voice quavering. "Please, sir—are you all right? I'm sorry to be the one to tell you, but someone had to do it."

"Oh, dear God, it can't be true," murmured Zan, his voice strangled with shock. The room began to spin as he let the phone slip. After he had collected himself, he said gruffly, "Just give me a minute, will you?"

413

"Take your time, m'lord. About Miss Saffron—she's with Mrs. Flaherty. We thought it best to leave you to tell her about her mother."

"Yes, of course. Thank you, Shaughnessy. That was wise. Please—I'm in control now. Just tell me how it happened."

As Shaughnessy struggled inarticulately to relate the details of the accident, Zan was seized by a cold premonition of what he was going to say. In her angry impatience, Rosemary had hurtled down the narrow lane, disregarding the danger. She'd taken the sharp corner too fast to see the hedge cutter, and as she'd braked violently the tires had skidded on the rain-drenched road and the car had careened out of control and smashed into the ancient rock wall. Moments later, a farmer had found Rosemary dead in the twisted wreckage of the Alfa-Romeo.

"May I offer my deepest condolence, m'lord? Everybody on the estate is heartbroken."

"Thank you, Shaughnessy. Let me think. No, I can't make it back tonight. It's already too late. I'll be on the first flight tomorrow. Please just hold on until I get there."

A week after Rosemary's funeral in Ireland, Kerry stood nervously on the doorstep of the house in Pelham Crescent. She and Mark had returned the day before from a two-week holiday in Tuscany, which seemed to have restored her composure. But within hours of coming back she was thrown into turmoil again when she heard the terrible news about Rosemary, a discovery that caused a great wave of guilt to wash over her. Though no one would ever know what part she had played in the tortuous turn of events, she couldn't keep from blaming herself for what had happened, and she had been unable to sleep the whole night. She was conscience-stricken as she prepared to face Zan. She knew his hasty retreat to Kilgarin with Rosemary at the height of the London season had made tongues wag. Obviously they had gone into seclusion until the scandal had blown over, and Kerry could imagine the atmosphere of accusations and recriminations between them. Who could say whether Rosemary's mind had snapped from the tension? People had even begun to suggest that her death wasn't an accident, but suicide caused by grief and depression following her discovery of Zan's infidelity. Kerry had faced up to the shattering realization that if she hadn't told Graham Gilston about Zan and Shannon, life would have continued as normal, and that she would have had only her own hurt to cope with. Now someone had died because of her actions. In spite of the hatred and vindictiveness she felt toward Shannon, she had never meant this to happen—not to Rosemary, not to anyone. She rang the doorbell more than once before Zan finally opened it. He looked at her blankly, his face drained of color, shadows under his eyes.

"Kerry—what are you doing here?"

"Zan—I came as soon as I heard the news. I've been away. Oh, Zan, I'm so sorry," she said compassionately. Suddenly she felt strangely awkward, wondering if she should have come. But she had been compelled to atone in some way, any way she could.

"Please come in—forgive me," he said at last. "I'm afraid I'm still not myself. Everything is in such a chaotic state. I just came back from Ireland a few hours ago. I've got so many things to attend to here."

He ushered her into the drawing room. "Would you like a drink? A glass of wine? Or is it too early?" Running his hands through his hair, he looked at her in confusion.

"No, thank you," she replied, shaking her head. They regarded each other silently, and tears came to Kerry's eyes. "Zan, I'm so sad, so sorry. When I heard about what happened, I was miserable for you, and now—" She broke off as she began to sob uncontrollably.

"Kerry, please don't cry," he said kindly, putting his arms around her. "It's so thoughtful of you to come, and I'm grateful you did. I'm so alone at the moment. Everyone has been very considerate, but at the end of the day I'm always alone."

"Zan, I know this may not be the time or place," she said haltingly as she wiped her tears, "but you know how much I care for you, for your well-being. I just want you to know that if I can help you in any way, do anything for you, take care of your daughter or anything, please tell me. . . ."

"Dear Lord, you are sweet," he said, deeply moved by her unashamed display of emotion, which contrasted markedly with the shallow condolences of some people he had known for a lifetime.

How she wanted to tell him everything, beginning with Koonwarra and ending with her role in Rosemary's death. But she couldn't—not yet. One day she would have to do it, Kerry knew. Feeling his arms around her, she buried her face in his shirt and sobbed. Zan held her close, and as she unburdened herself she became aware that she had triggered a sense of release in him.

"I can't tell you what it's like to hold somebody after all these weeks. To feel the warmth and closeness of another person. To know someone cares, understands. Kerry, you're so good, so sweet . . . so innocent," he whispered.

A fresh wave of guilt overcame her at these words. Maybe one day she would be all those things. As Zan held her she had the illusion it might be possible.

Early the next morning Kerry awoke with Zan in her arms. All through the night he had clung to her like a child, and now, as she lay with him sleeping on her breast, the first light of day filtering through the curtains, she reflected on the metamorphosis that had taken place within her in the space of a few hours.

Last night, guided by the ardent desire for human closeness, she and Zan had revealed their true selves to each other for the first time. Kerry's willpower and determination, which she always used to control events, seemed impotent against the great force that had come into play now that they were lovers. By some miracle Zan had unlocked a treasure in her that she had no idea she possessed, a quality of inestimable worth without which life was meaningless—the capacity to love without asking anything in return. She lay contemplating the passionate renewal of life, the moment when two people who needed each other were fused closer together than she had imagined was possible; and as morning came she drifted in a sea of utter tranquillity, as though becalmed after a storm that had raged a lifetime. With daylight would come terrible obstacles, she knew, and she and Zan would perhaps never spend a night together as important as this one. The union of their bodies had been an act of profound redemption for both of them, an acknowledgment of complete trust. It had healed all past wounds—and it promised that tomorrow would be different. As she studied the line of Zan's strong shoulders, the curve of his bare arms, feeling his weight against her, she knew that she had stumbled upon her destiny. No matter what happened, she would never let him go.

Later that morning, when Kerry returned home, Mark was waiting for her in the sitting room. Dropping her bag in the hall, she went in to face him, feeling a strange sense of courage.

"Where have you been?" he asked flatly. "All I had was a message from Theresa that you weren't coming home last night." His face was strained from lack of sleep; she had never seen him so angry. "I was ready to call the police. I couldn't imagine what might have happened to you. God, Kerry, how could you do this to me?"

"I'm sorry to have worried you, really I am, Mark," she said with passive resignation. "I was with Zan."

"All night?" he demanded.

"Yes, all night." She had come home vowing not to lie, but as she faced Mark she discovered she couldn't hurt him with the truth. "Yesterday when I dropped by to offer my condolences I found he was in an awful state about Rosemary, and I felt I couldn't leave him. We talked and talked until the early hours of the morning, and eventually I fell asleep on a sofa."

Taken aback by Kerry's calm, he muttered, "Well, the least you could have done was to tell me what was going on."

"I know I should have. But when you're trying to comfort someone in a state like that, you don't always think of everything."

"I really don't understand the whole thing," said Mark, flaring up again. "We're not that close to either one of them."

"That's true. But sometimes a relative stranger can be of more comfort than a close friend. Zan needed someone to talk to, and I'm just glad I was there, that's all."

He looked at her uncomprehendingly. Normally if he were this aggressive, she would have responded with an angry retort. Her composure unnerved him more than her temper. Shifting uncomfortably, he said, "Well, I'm going to work. I'm late as it is." Striding to the doorway, he turned to look at her. "Are you going to see him again?"

"I don't know. Maybe I will."

Looking at his watch, Mark said, "I'm going to have to stay late at the office to make up for the time I've lost this morning. I don't know what time I'll be home."

"I'll see you later. If for any reason I'm not here, I'll leave you a note."

At this remark Mark gave her a searching glance, that told Kerry he knew he had lost her.

* * *

Shannon's hairdresser at Carita on the Faubourg Saint Honoré was just working a handful of mousse through her wet hair as she thumbed through an old copy of *Paris Match*, featuring pictures of the English royal family at Ladies' Day at Ascot in June.

"*Je ne comprends pas les anglais*," said Didier, snatching a comb from the pocket of his white smock. "Look at those hats—*ridicule*! Except for the Princess Diana they are all in extremely bad taste. So vulgar—how is it possible? They have no taste whatsoever."

Shannon laughed at his little outburst as she regarded her reflection in the huge mirror of the busy salon.

"Don't be such a hypocrite. I know you wear a Burberry, have marmalade on your *petit pain*. And what about *le cocktail* and *le weekend*? All the French adore the English, despite what they say to the contrary."

Didier gave her a pouting shrug as he began to blow-dry her thick dark hair, now worn in a wedge style cut bluntly below the ears.

Flipping through the magazine, she came across pictures of sun-splashed beaches that reminded her the month of August was fast approaching. Amadeo had suggested she join him with Patrick and Fiona for a cruise on the *Karisma* up the Dalmatian coast, and thinking it over, she was tempted. After avoiding each other for weeks since May, there had been an unexpected thaw between them. The first time he had arrived with a bouquet of roses, eager to see Patrick, she knew her anger with him couldn't last forever. Once her two weeks in Seillans with Patrick and Fiona were over, she had hurled herself into her work; and on her return to Paris she had accepted every invitation that came her way, determined to keep herself too busy to think. But no matter how hard she tried, the loss of Zan had made her suffer at unexpected moments. She would be reminded of him when walking down a leafy street in Paris, when glancing at her own reflection in a shop window, when the telephone rang late at night or she heard a certain love song; and if she saw a couple kissing in the street, she had to resist an aching depression that plunged her into momentary darkness. But with every passing day she had begun to feel stronger.

As Didier began to dry her hair, Shannon found herself looking at the stark black-and-white photographs of a ghastly car accident. The twisted wreckage of an Alfa Romeo was photographed against a stone wall, and on the opposite page there was a picture that struck an instant chord of horror in Shannon: it was the formal wedding portrait of Rosemary that she had seen on a table in Jonquil's sitting room. She lurched forward, clutching her throat in disbelief.

"*Qu'est-ce qu'il y a?*" asked the hairdresser, regarding her in surprise.

The macabre details exposed in the accompanying story dramatically recounted the violent end of a glamorous young Irish countess, leaving her husband, the earl of Kilgarin, and their small daughter grief-stricken.

"Didier—I must go. I've just read some terrible news," she cried, leaping up and tearing off her smock.

"But Shannon, I haven't even begun," he protested with injured pride.

Without another word she ran from the salon and into the street, where she hailed a taxi. Arriving at the apartment on the Île Saint-Louis, she dashed upstairs and let herself in. It was a brilliant Saturday morning, and Fiona was out with Patrick in the Jardins des Luxembourg. Picking up the telephone, she thought for a moment. If he were in London, he would be at home, not in the office. Without even pausing to consider what she would say, she was conscious only of a yearning to reach out to him. She felt her love rushing back, affirming that no matter how badly he had hurt her, she had to extend her sympathy and support. Her heart pounding with anxiety, she couldn't suppress the hope that Rosemary's shocking death meant Zan was now free. Shannon was completely unprepared to hear the voice of a young woman on the line.

"May I speak with Lord Kilgarin, please?"

"Lord Kilgarin? I'm afraid he's not here," came the well-modulated mid-Atlantic voice.

"I see. Do you expect him back soon?"

"Yes, at any moment, as we're going away for the weekend. Is there something I can do for you?"

The confident edge to the woman's voice left no doubt in Shannon's mind that she was meant to understand she was more than a friend.

"Thank you very much. I'll call again some other time," she replied abruptly, then hung up.

A gasp of outrage escaped Shannon at this unexpected discovery, instantly dissolving all her pain. Zan hadn't wasted any time in finding someone to take Rosemary's place, and she marveled at her own naïveté. When was she ever going to learn her lesson? Moments ago she had been burning with that same childish faith in Zan that had motivated her for ten years. If anyone had told her that he would be involved with another woman within a month of Rosemary's death, she would never have believed it. Perhaps he had been involved with her all along, and the proud winner of his affections was the one who had gotten there first. Glad it hadn't been she, Shannon unhesitatingly dialed Amadeo's number.

"Amadeo? Good morning. Hi, it's Shannon. I'm very well, thank you. And you? The reason I called is that I'm wondering if that offer of the cruise in August is still open. Yes, I'd love to go," she said with a lilt in her voice that reflected the sudden sense of freedom blowing through her life. "Dinner tonight? Yes, I'm free. That would be lovely."

Her heart pounding guiltily as she put down the phone, Kerry turned to see Zan enter the drawing room with a pitcher of sangria, on his way to the garden.

"What a magnificent lunch you brought. I'm absolutely famished. Who was that on the phone?"

"Oh—she didn't give her name. It was a journalist fishing for information. I just told her you were away."

"What would I do without you?" he said, coming to kiss her on the cheek.

"I don't know. What would you?" she replied with a teasing smile. But the voice she was sure was Shannon's was still ringing in her ears. Why, Kerry wondered, had she called Zan out of the blue like that? Just the sound of her soft, insinuating voice struck terror in Kerry's heart, and the white lie had sprung instantly to her mind in case Shannon had any ideas about regaining her former place in Zan's life.

They went to the doorway leading to the garden, where Saffron was playing with Lindy in a paddling pool, shrieking with laughter as he threw a bucket of water over her.

"Look at those two," he said, putting his arm around Kerry. "They could be brother and sister, their coloring is so alike."

"They're adorable together, and Saffron is so good with Lindy," she replied, yielding to his soft kiss. She slipped her arm around his back and hugged him tightly for an instant, knowing that from that moment on she would live in fear of Shannon.

Chapter IV

On a day in late September Shannon left Galignani's bookshop on the rue de Rivoli with a big bag of books. She had gone a bit mad, she told herself, buying practically everything in sight. She had been unable to resist several recent novels and biographies, as well as a volume of interior decorating she had been coveting; and for Patrick she had picked up some Babar and Dr. Seuss books that he would adore. At the last minute she had spotted the perfect present for Amadeo, a book on Chinese porcelain that would be her gift to thank him for the holiday in August. Already she was composing the dedication in her mind: "Dearest Amadeo: Just a token to thank you for the most wonderful holiday I've ever spent. . . ." Recalling the new closeness that had sprung up between them on the voyage, she would sign it "all my love, Shannon." The days they had spent together had been unexpectedly blissful as they'd cruised in along the jagged coast, its shores carved by the clear, whispering waters of the Adriatic.

Amadeo had invited only a handful of his friends, all of whom she knew well and felt comfortable with, including Fabrice. They had passed the long, sultry days meandering up the coast, anchoring wherever their fancy took them, buying fish from local fishermen, which they grilled on the deserted, pine-covered beaches. They had stopped at little villages and churches, gone ashore sight-seeing when they were in the mood for a change of scene. Amadeo had taught Patrick to swim, and she had called encouragement from the deck as he'd poised himself on the edge of the small boat, his compact little body bronzed from the sun, while Amadeo waited in the water for him to jump.

"Come on, come on, jump to *Tío*," Amadeo would shout, a broad smile on his face as he'd held out his strong arms. Patrick would leap bravely in the air and surface like a seal, his hair glistening with water as he spluttered and shouted happily at his own courage.

The days had often ended with herself and Amadeo

alone on deck late at night, listening to the waves lapping gently against the yacht, talking endlessly, and getting to know each other all over again. One night toward the end of the voyage, as she'd gazed at his profile outlined in the darkness a yearning to be physically close to him had taken her unawares. At that moment it had seemed the most natural thing in the world that they should pass the rest of the night in his stateroom, locked in each other's arms. She had wanted him more than ever and sensed he was only waiting for her to make some gesture, some sign. But for the first time in years she'd felt a painful vulnerability to the fatal attraction he had always exercised over her. Without Zan's love to shield her, she was as defenseless as a newborn baby. She'd resisted those passionate stirrings that night, telling herself she could never be the only woman in Amadeo's life.

Shannon was just turning the corner to walk up toward the Place Vendôme and back to her office off the Faubourg Saint Honoré when she came face to face with Jonquil Fortesque.

"Jonquil! Hello," cried Shannon. Her instinctive reaction at meeting her after all these years was one of unabashed pleasure.

"My darling Shannon—fancy running into you like this," exclaimed Jonquil, radiant with delight. "My dearest girl, how are you?"

"What are you doing in Paris?" asked Shannon after they had embraced warmly.

"I'm over just for a few days, to do a bit of shopping. I'm staying at the Ritz, and in fact I was just on my way back there now."

"Lovely—I'll walk with you. I'm on my way back to my office, not far from here. I was just buying a few books on my lunch hour."

"You're looking simply sensational, I must say," remarked Jonquil, eyeing Shannon's belted suit of rust and petrel blue. "I've never even had a chance to congratulate you on your phenomenal success with Galant. I'm so thrilled for you. I can't tell you how often I've thought of you, how many times I meant to write—" She broke off with embarrassment as she recollected what had led to the breach in their friendship.

"Thanks so much, Jonquil. I want you to know that I'll never forget the debt I owe you."

As they walked through the arcaded street lined with boutiques, Shannon thought to herself that although Jonquil had aged slightly and her figure was a bit plumper, she was as flamboyantly turned out as ever in a crocheted suit of fire-engine red woven with navy ribbons; she trotted along lightly on the slenderest of red pumps, and her hair, as always, was whipped up into a froth of tinsel-colored curls.

When they reached the street corner there was an awkward pause between them. Feeling it was up to her to make the first move, Jonquil gushed, "Couldn't you come to the hotel for tea or something? Lunch, even, if you've the time. There's so much we have to catch up on."

Shannon hesitated a moment, but seeing the expectant look on Jonquil's face, all the old affection for her came flooding back. Whatever Jonquil had done, she hadn't done it out of malice; besides, that was all in the past.

"I know, better still, why don't you come to my apartment for dinner tonight? Just the two of us," Shannon suggested.

"Splendid—I'd adore to. I was supposed to dine with la Duchesse de Brax and I'd love to get out of it," she said gleefully.

"Here's my card. I live on the Île Saint-Louis now. Come 'round about eight, won't you?"

"Oh, wonderful. My dear, wait until I tell you about Elena. You simply won't believe it. She's married some sort of Balinese prince twenty years younger than herself, and she's living on the proverbial desert island with him. They're made for each other."

Shannon gave a peal of laughter. "I've really missed you, Jonquil," she said, kissing her on the cheek.

"What a lovely natter we'll have," she replied, blowing Shannon a kiss as she trotted down the street. "See you this evening," she trilled.

As Shannon walked back to the office she thought with curiosity of Zan. She was surprised that Jonquil hadn't mentioned him after the tragedy of Rosemary's death. What had happened to him? she wondered. And did she really want to know?

That evening she and Jonquil were having a drink in the sitting room when Fiona brought Patrick in to say good night. He was four and a half now, and his captivating looks caused people to stop in the street and comment on his extraordinary coloring, his large, dark eyes.

"Come in, darling. Don't be shy," she said, holding out her hand. "I want you to meet a very dear old friend of mine from London. Jonquil, this is my son, Patrick," she announced proudly.

The look of astonishment on Jonquil's face as she kissed Patrick's cheek was amusing to behold, and Shannon couldn't help but smile.

"What an adorable child! Those eyes—they're as bright as buttons. And just look at his thick dark hair," she exclaimed, kissing Patrick on the cheek. "Why, he's the very image of you, Shannon." Looking from mother to son, Jonquil was consumed with curiosity. Had there been any truth behind Gilston's column in May that Patrick was Zan's child? Rosemary had cautiously kept her own counsel following the scandal, and the last time Jonquil had seen her was prior to her departure for Ireland.

When Fiona had taken Patrick off to bed, Shannon leaned back and regarded Jonquil intently, almost as if divining her thoughts. It dawned on her that there was no longer any point in concealing the truth, and she made the impulsive decision to confide in the one person who had played such a dramatic role in the chain of events that had led to this moment.

"You're right—he doesn't look a bit like his father, does he? Zan is so fair and Patrick takes after me. . . ."

"So, it is true," Jonquil breathed, aghast.

"Well, I suppose I may as well tell you, Jonquil," Shannon began. "It's all water under the bridge now. So much has happened since then. Do you remember that time you flew over to Paris to see me about Zan? Well, I was pregnant then—with this child. . . ."

And she began to unfold the story that had remained a secret for such a long time, starting at the beginning, at Koonwarra.

Later that night Jonquil put through an urgent call to London from her suite at the Ritz. As she heard the long-distance ring, she was acutely conscious of having interfered once before in the lives of Zan and Shannon when she ought to have minded her own business; now, however, perhaps she could make amends.

"Zan? Thank goodness I've caught you before you left for Kilgarin. I want you to prepare yourself for some news—wonderful news—that is going to come as quite a shock to you."

At seven-thirty the following evening, when the doorbell rang. Fiona answered it.

"Who is it?" Shannon called as she swept into the sitting room in a black ball gown of moiré silk, buckling a diamond bracelet on her wrist. Smoothing her hair in the mirror, she glanced over her shoulder, wondering if Amadeo could have returned from New York earlier than expected.

"Shannon, there's someone to see you," said Fiona, ushering in the visitor.

"Zan! " Shannon gasped, whirling around when she saw his reflection in the mirror.

He stopped at the threshold of the room, transfixed by the aura of glamour emanating from her. All the way to Paris he had imagined the Shannon he knew in Seillans, in jeans and a T-shirt with windblown hair; but now, seeing her robed in such regal sophistication, glinting with jewels, he was awestruck. She appeared completely unattainable, out of reach, and the errand that had propelled him to her side seemed futile.

"Shannon—how lovely you look. You're exquisite," he whispered.

"Why are you here?" she demanded unsteadily.

"Surely you must know. Jonquil called me last night and told me everything. Darling Shannon, why didn't you tell me?" he pleaded, his voice gruff with emotion. "Why did you do this to us?"

She felt herself flush. "Believe me, Zan, I didn't confide in Jonquil so you'd come rushing over here. And anyway, it's too late for explanations," she said sadly, determined to cling to her own convictions. Experience had proved to her that Zan was weak, unworthy of her devotion, but the sight of the man she had loved so deeply, his face haunted by all he had recently been through, made her weaken. She sank into a chair by the fireplace, and they looked at each other for several moments without speaking.

"Shannon—please, may I see Patrick?" said Zan hesitatingly.

She had imagined this moment so many times, anticipating the thrill of bringing forth her son to meet his father. She had always pictured herself in Seillans, waiting at the door with him as Zan came up the hill. It was a silly, romanticized drama, straight out of a novel, set in high summer in southern France against the backdrop of flowers, cicadas, and a clear blue sky. How absurd she had been, and what a dreamer. The reality couldn't have been more different, she reflected wryly as she and Zan faced each other across a chasm of strangeness caused by hurt piled on hurt. Then, as she observed the anguished expression in his eyes, the line of tension around his mouth, she wondered whether she had the right to hold him in suspense even one moment longer. She began to comprehend the harrowing intensity of Zan's mission, the search for a son he had never seen, and she doubted the wisdom of the decision she had made years ago.

"Let me go and get him," she whispered, her gown rustling as she left the room.

Moments later she returned with Patrick. In his pajamas, his dark hair tousled, he rubbed his eyes sleepily.

"Patrick, I want you to meet Zan."

"*Bonjour,*" he said, glancing up at his mother in confusion as he extended a suspicious hand toward Zan.

"You can speak English, darling," she said gently to Patrick.

"Hello, Patrick," said Zan, bending down. His eyes luminous with feeling, he seemed too moved to speak.

Patrick pulled his hand away politely, sensing a strange undercurrent in the air. He tried unsuccessfully to interpret the look on his mother's face, a look he had never seen before; nor could he comprehend the familiarity radiating from this stranger.

"Kiss Zan good night now," she whispered. "And then off to bed with you. Maybe you'll see him in the morning."

Patrick obeyed, turning both cheeks as Zan leaned down to kiss him with a tenderness he knew he must conceal until he had earned his son's affection.

When Shannon had taken him back to bed, she returned to the drawing room and closed the double doors behind her, leaning against them, her hands clenched on the doorknobs. She tried to collect herself but realized it was impossible and gave a helpless little laugh as tears welled up in her eyes.

Zan was standing with his hands uncomfortably in his pockets, more unsure of himself than when he had arrived.

"He's a fine boy. So well mannered, so handsome," he began.

"He was a bit shy tonight, but normally he's very friendly. Children are so sensitive, aren't they? They seem to know when adults are in turmoil."

"Yes, they do."

"How is Saffron? Has she gotten over Rosemary's death?"

"No, not really, and I don't suppose she ever will. But she's trying hard, and the loss of Rosemary has brought us much closer together."

"She was such a lovely child. I always liked her—" Shannon broke off inarticulately. The conversation seemed to dry up as they regarded each other like strangers.

"I don't want to keep you any longer. You're obviously dressed to go out, and I've come at an inconvenient moment." The fusillade of passion that had driven Zan from London had now left him marooned on an unfamiliar shore, where his future seemed to depend on every word he uttered.

"I couldn't go out now. Please stay awhile, if you like."

"Shannon," Zan began, "maybe I was too hasty in coming. Maybe I should have telephoned first, but I felt I had to come, the moment I heard the news. Do you wish I hadn't?"

"I don't know what I feel at this moment, quite honestly. But no, I'm not sorry you came." She thought of Jonquil and wondered if she had subconsciously confided the secret of Patrick because she still harbored hope for her relationship with Zan. It hurt to think that he believed her story now, when he had been so quick to condemn her following the scurrilous newspaper story in the spring.

"Perhaps you'd like a drink. I know I would," she said.

"Yes, I'd love one. A brandy would be nice, if you have it."

He watched her intently as she picked up a crystal decanter, her black dress sketched dramatically against creamy skin gilded by lamplight.

They faced each other across the fire, and as she handed him a glass he clasped her hand. "Shannon, there's so much we still have to talk about, so much to say."

If she avoided the conversation she could sense was imminent, Zan would disappear from her life forever, Shannon realized. It seemed up to her to decide the course of their future. What had begun spontaneously between them years ago in Koonwarra had evolved into an intricate relationship that now included their son as well. Somehow the simple life they had dreamed of and longed for had grown complex and confused, like a house that had been added to over the years until it rambled aimlessly in every direction. She came to the instant decision that they owed it to Patrick to give their love another chance. She felt an undeniable need to lay everything before him, to strip her every emotion bare, conscious that false pride had been the source of many of their problems. Taking a deep breath, she said, "Come and sit down, Zan. I want to start at the very beginning."

As she let her buried thoughts escape, she felt herself freed from the burden of the past. Thirsting for a new level of truth and frankness, she unraveled the tortuous hidden history of her past, telling Zan all about her breakdown in Paris and how close she had come to having an abortion. She related how Amadeo had rescued her and protected her during her pregnancy, how he had offered her the chance to direct Galant. Determined to leave nothing out, she revealed the inexplicable physical attraction Amadeo had always held for her, confiding that even now, after all that had happened, she still harbored a lasting affection for the man to whom she owed so much.

"Are you in love with him?" Zan asked quietly when she had finished.

"No, but I was once, when I was younger. It took me years to realize that though we're total opposites in many ways, we could still remain close friends. Amadeo is incapable of the kind of constant love I need—there have always been so many other women in his life besides me." She paused. "And what about you? Is there anybody in your life? When I rang you this summer, in June, after I heard about Rosemary, a woman answered. I sensed that she was more than a friend, so I just assumed you were involved and didn't call back."

Zan's eyes wavered for a moment before he replied, "Yes, there was someone. It started after Rosemary died and everything was over between you and me. It wasn't intentional, but one thing led to another. I owe her a lot; she's been so very kind and supportive. But the minute I found out about Patrick I called her and told her we had to end it. She was upset, but when I get back I'll go to her and explain everything; she's married and has a child, and I think it's best this way for all concerned. But Shannon—if you have any worries about that, please don't. I've put it all behind me. Actually, what I'm saying is that I'm still here if you want me."

Shannon didn't reply for a moment but stared into the flames. At last she said, "You know, I've often regretted that

I came to England last May. I broke our unwritten code not to meet outside Seillans, and look what happened. On the other hand, if I hadn't, you and I would still be drifting on the same wayward course. The very air in that village was like a drug that led us into apathy. The truth is, we had become used to the situation. It might have gone on for years."

"God knows you're entitled to feel this way, but I must convince you otherwise. The bizarre string of events that ended in tragedy will always haunt me, Shannon. But believe me, I had every intention of leaving Rosemary. I was never so close to it as the week before Gilston's column broke. It blew my life apart in the cruelest way possible. But what else could I think when I saw those pictures of you, Patrick, and Benguela? Doesn't it seem incredible to you now that you hid my own son from me for over four years?"

She met his eyes unhesitatingly. "It was the worst mistake of my life, I know now. But Zan, things appeared differently to me then. I didn't want to blackmail you with a child. Can't you see that I wanted you to come to me from love, not from guilt or a sense of obligation?" She sighed. "Obviously I was terribly unsure of myself."

"Unsure of me, you mean. And my love for you." Rising from his chair, he took her hands and drew her to him. "Shannon, this may be too soon, but it's what I've come to say. I want more than anything else for us to recapture what we once had. For our sakes and for Patrick's. I know it's still there. What's between us is much too strong to be destroyed after surviving so much, and we mustn't throw it all away. I want us to be married as soon as you're ready. Say you'll come back to Kilgarin with me, now, this weekend."

"Oh, Zan, I want to try again more than anything," she whispered as he held her. "But it's not going to be easy. You'll have to be patient, because it's going to take time."

He hugged her tightly. "Shannon, darling, I'm so glad, so glad. I'm going to try and deserve you from now on. And Patrick—what a precious gift you've given me. He's still so young that we have a chance to start at the beginning."

She smiled up at him. "Did you see the look on his face when he came into the room? He didn't know what to make of you."

"He really is the image of you. I don't know how you've brought him up all on your own. You've been through so much."

"Zan, let's make a vow now to stop protecting each other, to always be as honest as we've been tonight." She seemed to see Zan with a new clarity: she no longer idolized him as she once had, but she didn't want to. "And promise me you'll never put me on a pedestal again. From now on I want to live with my feet firmly on the ground."

Tilting up her chin, he leaned down to kiss her. "Now you are asking the impossible," he teased.

It took Kerry a moment to recall where she was when she opened her eyes and glanced 'round the dimmed bedroom; at last she realized muzzily that she was at home, in Markham Square. When she had gone to bed, long past midnight, she had taken two sleeping pills, unable to bear another hour of consciousness. Now, as she awoke, everything she had been trying to forget came flooding back. She felt an uncontrollable spasm of nausea roil within her when she recalled Zan's phone call the previous day. In an apologetic, hurried voice, he had announced that their affair was over.

"I know what a shock this must be to you, Kerry, but there's no time to explain now. . . . Kerry? Are you listening? When I get back we'll have a long talk and I'll explain everything I should have told you before. I know this is a shabby way to treat you after everything you've done for me, but it's for the best. Mark would never have left you if it weren't for me, and I hope your relationship will knit back together again. . . ."

Crushing her pride, she'd begged him shamelessly, "No, no, you can't do this to me. Please!" Her cry had been that of a wounded animal.

"Please try to understand, Kerry. I'll have to go in a minute. I haven't got long, my plane's been called already."

Perceiving an undercurrent of turmoil in his voice that had nothing to do with her, she'd wanted to scream at him, cry and sob, but all she could do was listen in impotent anguish as his hurried words had ripped her world apart.

"Kerry, there's one other thing. This is going to come as a terrible disappointment to you, I know, but I must ask you not to come to Kilgarin as we planned. When I tell you more you'll know why. Please forgive me, but I really have to go."

Even twenty-four hours later Kerry couldn't quite comprehend that their glorious affair had come to an end as abruptly as her marriage to Mark had ended. When her husband had announced one evening at the end of July that he was leaving her, Kerry had received the news with total calm.

"You deserve someone better than me, a lot better, Mark," she had replied. When he'd admitted that he was involved with Penny, his secretary, she had responded sincerely that she hoped he would be very happy.

The moment he'd moved out, Kerry had experienced relief from the gnawing guilt of living with a man whose love she could never return.

The more time Kerry had spent with Zan, the closer they'd become. It had surprised her how quickly they'd reached that rare and blissful state of intimacy where they could communicate without the need for words. Having both married for the wrong reasons, they discovered together what it meant to share the simple, unhurried pleasures of life without the intrusion of the outside world. Yet in counterpoint to their easy domesticity flowed a physical chemistry that could be stirred up simply by the touch of their hands or a glance across the room. Moments later they would be together in bed making love with a ferocious tenderness that, for Kerry, laid bare the many facets of love. It seemed remarkable how they complemented each other on every level. Kerry's mocking humor leavened Zan's seriousness, and her American frankness cut through his British conventionality. And his undisguised need for her brought out a generous side of her nature that had always lain dormant. Zan's confidence, grounded surely on his unshakable position in the world, granted to Kerry a new tranquillity. She didn't have to climb anymore. She had arrived, slipping quietly into the safe harbor of her dreams without fanfare or drama. But it was love, not wealth or position that had proved to be her aim. That was where fate seemed to be taking them. With every passing day she sensed Zan's guilt over Rosemary's death recede, felt him regain his desire to live life to the full. Kerry had begun to feel so sure of herself, so certain of her position in Zan's life, that she allowed herself to forget the chilling telephone call from Shannon in June.

When Zan had finally invited her to be by his side for the first weekend of the new hunting season at Kilgarin, Kerry knew that this public acknowledgment of their relationship meant Zan no longer doubted that they belonged together, that he was beginning to return her love. All summer he had been indecisive about whether the hunt ball at the castle, planned by Rosemary in the spring, should proceed; but at Kerry's urging he had decided to go ahead. She had argued that the weekend would give an opportunity for Zan to rally his closest friends around him and clear the shadow that hung over his name.

She curled up in bed, feeling her heart race with panic. Of all the shocks she had sustained during the past months, this was by far the most devastating. Recalling Zan's voice, she raked his every word for clues. Why had it happened at that particular moment?

As she sifted through her memory, it came to her with sickening clarity. There was only one possible explanation for Zan's abrupt change of heart—Shannon. It had to be her. Somehow she had wormed her way back into Zan's life, exercising the fatal attraction that had always mesmerized him in the past. Her mind leapt to that phone call in June, to the voice she had been certain was Shannon's. She had gotten through to him at last, after waiting a respectful time, to reclaim her place as his future countess. Shannon the sorceress had even managed to soothe the troubled waters churned up by the scandal, no doubt convincing Zan that the dark little boy who obviously belonged to Amadeo was really his.

Tears of frustration stung Kerry's eyes. How well she understood the power of suggestion a male child exercised over a man. The idea that his own flesh and blood was waiting to be claimed had appealed romantically to any man, as Kerry knew so well from her own experience. Even a strong man like Lindy Van Buren could be reduced to a worshiping slave at the suggestion there existed a living replica of himself. When Lindy had heard of her breakup with Mark, he had pledged continued financial support, simply because he was little Lindy's father.

The question was, how could she combat the formidable combination of a woman and her child? "Well, I won't give up, I won't," she whispered defiantly.

In a few moments Kerry rose from bed, her devastation overcome and transformed into her old determination. Throwing on her dressing gown, she hurried downstairs to look for the guidebook she had taken with her to Ireland the weekend she had bought Criterion. Tomorrow was the day she was supposed to leave for Ireland to join Zan at Kilgarin. All the arrangements had been made, and she had no intention of changing them. Mark was going to take Lindy, Theresa would have the weekend off, and she, Kerry, was going to Ireland.

Dashing back upstairs, Kerry threw open the curtains, admitting the gray morning light of London. Sitting tensely in a chair by the telephone, she dialed the number of The Swan and Shamrock in the village of Dooley, near Kilgarin. If she couldn't stay in the castle, she would stay in a pub. She would win Zan back; shock him into the realization that he loved her. Her spirits rallied as she charted a course to claim what was hers, driven by passion to cross the Irish Sea to southwestern Ireland near Limerick, in the wilds of Kerry—her namesake.

The day after Zan's quest to Paris, he returned to Kilgarin with Shannon at his side. As they drove to the castle, Shannon's anticipation at the fulfillment of a dream she had harbored for so long was colored by an unexpected apprehension. Sensing her uneasiness, Zan reached over to squeeze her hand reassuringly.

All the way there, she had taken in the powerful landscape of Ireland, intrigued by its beauty and its lurking strangeness. It was a land of contradictions, with factories alongside fine Georgian houses and a wild, lush countryside that dwarfed small farm holdings of incredible poverty. She had seen a donkey cart driven by a gypsy tinker, full of black-eyed, barefoot children who seemed to belong to another century. The handsome faces of the people, marked by both hardship and humor, had made a deep impression on her, and she was poignantly reminded of Brendan's Celtic magnetism.

They drove due west, past sharp green country that melted into distant mauve mountains rising out of a sea of mist. Passing whitewashed cottages where smoke curled from chimneys tucked into the thatch, they crossed a stone bridge spanning foaming amber water, then suddenly reached the acres that surrounded Kilgarin. Zan slowed down as they approached the entrance gates.

"Well, it's not far now, darling."

"I know—the suspense is agony," she said with a nervous laugh.

433

At last, there it was—Kilgarin Castle, which had lived at the heart of her imagination for years. Through a veil of fine rain she stared at the dark rectangle pierced by narrow windows. They passed under the gaze of two huge stone dragons and into the graveled courtyard.

"Parts of the towers are the original sixteenth-century structure, but the central part was restored after a fire in the early nineteenth century," Zan told her.

They got out of the car, and Shannon paused to gather her impressions of this great mansion rising darkly against the sky, its hewn stones softened by moss and vines. She looked at the ramparts set in a sloping green landscape; they recalled a feudal era, when arrows would have rained down on an approaching stranger.

A stout, graying Irishwoman with ruddy cheeks came out to meet them.

"Shannon, this is my housekeeper, Mrs. Flaherty."

"Welcome to Kilgarin. I hope you enjoy your stay with us, to be sure." In one sharp glance she took in every detail of Shannon's appearance, measuring her up for the role of the new countess. "We thought with the weather you might be delayed. There's hardly been a morning for a month that it hasn't rained," she announced cheerfully. "But it's good for the land and for the complexion. Will you be taking tea in the drawing room, m'lord, by the fire?"

"What would you like to do, darling? Do you want to see the castle first, or have tea?"

"Oh, let's see a bit of the castle. I can't wait."

Zan ushered Shannon into the galleried great hall, its leaded windows casting dim squares of light onto the floor below.

"Come and have a look at the family tree," he said, putting his arm around her shoulder.

Shannon stared up at the huge tree, done in petit point, representing the ancestry of the earls of Kilgarin, its branches reaching back to Elizabeth I.

"Look up near the top, can you see an O'Falaon? Mary O'Falaon married Cedric, brother of the second earl, in 1635. Falaon was changed to Faloon in the seventeenth century. So you see, we might be related."

"You could be right," she said with a laugh, examining the tapestry. "How amazing."

"While you're here we must ride over to the ruins of Castle Shannon, a few miles from here. You can see where your ancestors lived."

They went into the huge formal drawing room overlooking landscaped gardens, where Shannon's attention was captured by the portrait of a young man whose devil-may-care smile and strong features reminded her of Zan. It had been painted in the 1920s, and the artist had posed his subject against the drawing room fireplace.

"That's my father," said Zan when he saw Shannon looking at the portrait. "It was painted long before he met my mother. Her portrait is over there, above the sofa."

Shannon crossed the faded Persian carpet to look at Zan's mother, a pretty young woman in blue, with pale, dreamy eyes and fawn-colored hair.

"There's a slight resemblance between you. I think it's your eyes."

"There are still a few things to be done to this room. Some of the chair covers, and the new curtains haven't been hung yet. They were especially commissioned to match the old brocade that's been here for a hundred and fifty years."

Shannon looked around her, fascinated. Silk panels hung on the walls alongside mellowed old paintings, the perfect complement to a room filled with fine furniture. Every table or chest contained some memento collected by generations of Kilgarin earls—from fine Regency clocks and porcelain to Victorian bibelots. She paused to study a group of snuffboxes displayed on a boulle cabinet, along with miniatures of children painted on ivory in enamel frames.

"That was presented to my grandfather by the maharajah of Cooch Behar when he was tiger-hunting in India," Zan remarked as Shannon inspected a jeweled sword in its scabbard. "What do you think of the drawing room?"

"It's lovely, Zan, so elegant, so full of history. Yet I can imagine closing the curtains and curling up in front of a fire on a cold evening," she said, linking her arm through his. She tried to picture what it would be like when Patrick joined them in a month or so.

As they proceeded into the book-lined library, he said, "This room is supposed to be haunted by a Kilgarin who committed suicide in the eighteenth century because of gambling debts."

"Are there any other ghosts?" she asked as they swept into the long gallery.

"Yes, in fact. Come and have a look." He led her to a tall, rain-spattered window that overlooked the gardens on the other side of the castle. A sweep of clipped lawn was cut by a wide path, lined with sculptured yews, that ended dramtically at the lake.

"You're supposed to be able to hear the sound of silk gowns sweeping the gravel on midsummer's eve, and the echo of a harpsichord playing on a windless night."

"Do you know, I think this is my favorite room so far," she said, looking 'round. The long gallery had an air of frivolity and romance that was missing from the other imposing rooms of the castle. The windows hung with pastel silk curtains seemed to transform the gray light of Ireland into a honeyed softness.

"It looks a bit chaotic. They've already started preparing it for the ball on Saturday."

At the mention of the party Shannon hugged his arm for an instant. She was unnerved at the thought of meeting so many people so soon; but she had finally agreed to come to Kilgarin when she realized how much it meant to Zan to have her at his side. All the guests who would be coming on Saturday would have known Rosemary, and Shannon would be regarded as an interloper.

"The orchestra will be on a dais, just there," Zan said, gesturing. "This room was added especially for a splendid ball given in honor of Queen Victoria, when she came to see the Lakes of Killarney. In fact, the workmen were still gilding the ceiling an hour before the party started, so the story goes."

"I hope we won't be in the same boat on Saturday," she said, and they laughed.

Taking her hand, Zan whirled her around the floor in a waltz for a moment, then paused to kiss her lightly. "Come on, let's go and have some tea. Tell me, does Kilgarin live up to your expectations?"

She sensed how proud he was of his property, a house fit for the lord he had become. "It's much grander than I thought it would be. But honestly, Zan, I never allowed myself to dwell on Kilgarin too much."

"But do you like it?" he persisted.

"Of course I do. Who wouldn't? But to be honest, in my mind it's always been a symbol of what kept us apart."

"I know. But from now on things are going to be entirely different. Kilgarin is going to be home for all of us: me, you, Patrick, and Saffron, as well as the rest of the family when they come along."

They had never touched on the subject of having children, and now, in the wake of their new openness with each other, it had taken on a new importance.

"Do you want more children?" she asked.

"I want as many bright-eyed beautiful children as you'll give me," he whispered, kissing her ear.

They had tea by the fire in the sitting room upstairs, containing a fine breakfront bookcase filled with leather-bound books and hung with old prints of famous Irish houses—Castletown in County Kildare, Ballantry House in Waterford, Dunboy Castle in West Cork—all names familiar to Shannon.

"Maybe you'd like to take a tramp in the garden before it gets dark."

"Yes, why not, if it's stopped raining."

"I think it has," he said, crossing to look out the window.

Shannon watched him as he stared outside, silhouetted against the glass pane. When they had finished talking in the early hours of the previous morning at her flat, they'd gone to bed exhausted and had chastely slept side by side until morning. What would it be like when they made love after all this time? she wondered, feeling nervous at the prospect. From the moment they'd arrived at Kilgarin she had found herself wishing they hadn't made this hasty decision but had waited until they could escape to Seillans; then she'd realized she was falling into the same old trap. London and Kilgarin were the reality of their life together, not Seillans.

Later they were walking down the graveled path to the lake, discussing Zan's plans for Kilgarin and expanding the farmland that surrounded it.

"I guess that means you'll be spending more time here—I mean we, darling," she corrected herself.

"I suppose it would, eventually. Would you find that so awful?"

"It would be sheer torture," she said in mock horror as they approached the lake. The path ended in a flight of steps that led to a terrace. Adorning the front, two winged horses in stone reared toward a statue of Poseidon rising from the lake.

Shannon leaned thoughtfully on the balustrade and watched as beeches, elms, and willows shed their leaves on the dark water. She hadn't yet had time to think how she was going to sort out her own life and fit it in with Zan's, even though it was something she'd had years to consider. She had begun her break with the past by writing Amadeo a letter, which she had given Fiona to deliver, relating the news of her impending marriage to Zan. As the two of them gazed at the lake she was reminded of that autumn day at Les Tourelles, when she had told Amadeo with such conviction that she and Zan would end up together one day. Now that it had come true, she knew she never could have foreseen how difficult it would be to tell Amadeo; already she had begun to regret the bubbling optimism of her letter. It left no room for going back. She had kissed her life good-bye without a backward glance, and she wondered if her tone had been too smug, too triumphant, but it was too late now to change it.

Later, as they walked arm in arm back toward the castle, the significance of it came home to her: this was the seat of the earls of Kilgarin, and someday her son would be one of them.

That evening they had supper in the pale rose dining room, under a glittering chandelier that cast splinters of light on the linen and the old Spode china. The two of them sat at the end of the vast table, Zan in a smoking jacket, Shannon in a long dress of coral cashmere. She looked down the long, empty table that tomorrow would be set for the banquet before the ball. Everything about Kilgarin was oversized. It was a house that needed to be filled with laughter, friends, and children.

"What are you thinking?" he asked affectionately, filling her glass with port.

"I'm just thinking how different Kilgarin is from Seillans. It seems so strange to see you dressed up like that. I keep picturing just the two of us at the little table in the kitchen."

"You know, I felt exactly like that about you when I arrived in Paris last night. It seems ages ago, doesn't it? I was struck speechless by your glamour. I suppose it was foolish of me, but I half expected to find a girl in jeans with an apron wrapped around her—the one I used to know."

"She's still here. She's just on holiday for the moment," Shannon murmured as Zan kissed her hand.

"Shannon, I've been thinking. Let's announce our engagement tomorrow at the ball. Some of my oldest friends are going to be here, and I think it's time I brought you out of the cupboard. I want everyone to know about us and put an end to all the speculation that has been going on since May. The sooner the better for Patrick's sake, as well."

"Oh, Zan, don't you think it's still too early?" she hedged. He was saying the words she had been waiting years to hear, yet she found herself reluctant to agree. "We haven't even had a chance to get used to the idea ourselves."

"I don't know about you, but I have," he said tenderly. "Shannon, you looked so worried. Please, darling. I know what you're thinking. All that rubbish in the papers, that's it, isn't it? But people's memories are very short, believe me. They'll be enchanted by you. Look at Mrs. Flaherty and the rest of the staff. They adore you already."

"I suppose Flaherty will get you anywhere," she retorted.

"That's a terrible pun, but I still love you, anyway," said Zan with a kiss.

Laughing, they rose from the table and went out the door arm in arm, upstairs to the bedroom next to Zan's, where Shannon had tactfully been installed. When he had closed the door behind them he took her in his arms, his mouth seeking hers in an ardent prelude to lovemaking. As they embraced she felt his hands unfastening her dress. When Shannon slipped out of her clothes a strange apprehension overtook her, smothering the desire that had fueled her existence for so long. Zan was waiting for her in the big four-poster bed, and as she slipped between the cool sheets next to him, she felt him naked against her for the first time in more than eighteen months. As they began to kiss she found herself searching for the source of the mutual adoration that had always made their lovemaking so effortlessly sublime. Instead, moving with a sense of slow motion, she was trapped by a bruised recollection of the past that made her feel an unaccustomed shyness. As his hands intimately explored her body, she felt desperation rather than passion, torn by the realization that all their hopes were pinned on this moment.

When it was over and Zan dozed in her arms in a light sleep, Shannon lay awake thinking. Where had the passion gone? she asked herself. She had to admit that the act had been only a pale copy of the joyous celebration of love that had marked their reunion every year in Seillans. The fire had gone out, as if it had been left untended too long. Would it come back? There was no way to know whether learning to love again took time, or if once extinguished, passion never returned. Before she fell asleep Shannon thought of Amadeo. He would be back in Paris by now and had surely read her

439

letter. Sighing, she moved closer to Zan, brushing her hair absently with her fingers.

Feeling Shannon's gentle touch, Zan pretended he had fallen into a doze, fearing she would want to talk. Since Paris she seemed to have the disturbing need to examine, to analyze the reasons that lay behind every emotion, and now he knew he had no answers for her. Staring into the darkness, Zan felt as if he had climbed to the top of a mountain expecting a golden view, only to find the landscape obscured by mist. This wasn't how he'd imagined it would be on the great day he brought Shannon home to Kilgarin. The communication between them was strained, empty, and vague, utterly lacking the magic they had relived each spring in Seillans; their lovemaking had been almost dispassionate, impersonal. Zan knew that Shannon had feigned arousal and that their act of love had verged on a performance, a realization that engulfed him with confusion. He had been counting on that moment of supreme intimacy to bring them back together again.

To his shock, he found he had been fantasizing about Kerry as he'd made love to Shannon. The memory of Kerry quivering with pleasure in his arms had sprung involuntarily to his mind. He pushed it away, but it returned again, the recollection of a flowering desire that had eclipsed everything he had ever known. He tried to tell himself not to be deceived by an illusion. Here he was, fulfilling at last the dream of a decade—Shannon, the mother of his son, at his side. Yet he knew he wasn't happy. Surely all they needed was time.

Chapter V

County Limerick, Ireland, 1985

Kerry had risen from the hard, narrow bed in the beamed room under the eaves of The Swan and Shamrock, and now she stood ready for the day's hunt. Tucking her hair back severely into a net, she searched her own reflection in the beveled glass speckled with age. There was a tautness about her mouth that she couldn't dispel, and her usually direct gaze was clouded by nervous preoccupation. Going to the little window, she pulled aside the lace curtain, trying to take courage at the sight of the green hills of Ireland. By four o'clock that afternoon she would know where her future lay.

The first thing Kerry had done on her arrival the previous day was to drive to a local livery stable to find a suitable mount, arranging for the groom to meet her at the gates of Kilgarin Castle on the morning of the hunt. Then, returning to the pub, she'd gone downstairs for supper, hoping to gather information. She'd sat unobtrusively in the corner of the smoky room, watching the knot of men drinking and smoking 'round the bar, and it wasn't long before she'd heard comments exchanged about Lord Kilgarin.

"He'll not be wasting any time. Wicked, I call it. The young countess hardly cold in her grave," said the publican's wife.

"Don't be so hard-hearted, Molly. He's not yet got an heir. He's young and healthy and ought to be marrying again as soon as he can."

"There's talk that he'll marry the one that he brought with him yesterday. Moira O'Brien saw her this morning and said she's as dark as a tinker's daughter and a beauty. Nothing like the first countess, a real English rose if ever there was one."

The telling description—dark like a tinker's daughter—made Kerry's mouth go dry, confirming her worst fears. Who else could they be referring to but Shannon?

"She'll be the one in that newspaper scandal, I'll be bound. She's been his fancy lady for many a year," came the sour comment.

"Downright sinful, I'd say," someone remarked.

"Let him do as he pleases and be done with it," was the reply. "Another round, Molly. . . ."

The conversation had changed, and unable to bear another minute in the claustrophobic little room, Kerry had hurried away, leaving her cottage pie half-eaten.

Kerry picked up her riding crop and left the pub; outside, a group of farmers were drinking pints of Guinness in a patch of weak sunshine. Pulling the veil down from her bowler hat and tucking it determinedly under her chin, she felt the men's bold stares as she passed. Their eyes, full of curiosity and condemnation, reminded her unpleasantly for an instant of the groups of men who used to loiter on street corners in Wishbone, their piercing gaze challenging every woman who passed. Glad to get away, she leapt into the hired car and zoomed down the treacherous, narrow-walled road that led to Kilgarin.

To her relief she saw the groom was waiting as arranged at the castle gates, holding the reins of the powerful bay with white markings that she had chosen from among half a dozen other horses. She parked her car off the road and greeted the groom with an air of brisk self-confidence that disguised the tension gnawing at her.

"Morning, missus," he replied, touching his cap. "Dandy here is full of spirit and waiting to go. He knows when the hunt's on, right enough. He'll give you a good run, won't you, Dandy boy?"

Kerry looked over her shoulder, barely listening to his banter, desperate to get away before she saw the flash of a pink coat coming down the lane.

"Give me a leg up, will you?" she said tersely, anxious to get on the horse. Taking command of the reins, she veered the horse around without another word and trotted through the high gates toward the castle.

Releasing a pent-up sigh, she slowed the bay to a walk along the drive, needing time to get her bearings. The trees and shrubbery surrounding the castle were dripping with an early autumn mist that hung in a cloud of vapor. Her heart slammed violently against her chest when she caught sight of the weathered outline of the castle, where two dozen or more riders and as many followers on foot had already assembled. Hearing the pounding of hooves behind her, she looked askance as a group of local gentry rode by dressed for the hunt, the ruddy-faced men touching their hats as they smiled in her direction. When they had passed, she urged her bay to a trot. Her timing was perfect: servants were just lifting their silver trays to collect empty stirrup cups from the riders. She slipped her hand into her pocket to feel for the note she had composed that morning. The moment she reached the fringe of the gathering, she called to a footman and handed him the envelope. In a low, urgent whisper she said, "Would you please give this to Shannon Faloon, the lady who is accompanying Lord Kilgarin?"

Adrenaline shot through her as she watched the footman thread his way toward an elegant woman on horseback at the edge of the castle forecourt. It was Shannon, her flawlessly beautiful countenance blurred by a veil, and Kerry was crushed by a suffocating jealousy when she identified Zan at her side. She saw him cast Shannon the same private, reassuring smile that had been for her alone these past few months.

Kerry turned away the moment she saw the footman hand Shannon the note, leading her horse to the fore of the hunt, where the whippers-in were gathering the restless hounds in preparation for the first blare of the huntsman's horn.

Later that day, as the hunt disappeared ahead of her into a copse of trees, closing in for the kill, Kerry lagged behind, then truned to retrace her path on the soft ground torn by hoofmarks. Crossing a little bridge that spanned a muddy stream, she headed for her rendezvous. There was no sign of Shannon, and she urged her horse forward, anxious to be the first to arrive. She trotted under the ancient archway that marked the entrance to Castle Shannon, glad to see the ground was unbroken. The sweet, living smell of earth damp from rain calmed her feverish emotions as she dismounted and led her horse behind a half-crumbled wall, feeling an inexplicable need for concealment. If Shannon did keep their appointment, she wanted to take her by surprise. This time, Kerry intended to have all the advantages.

But would Shannon come in answer to her anonymous summons? And if she did, what did she, Kerry, intend to say? Crossing the threshold of the great hall, she gazed at the central staircase climbing to a blue sky smudged with clouds. Her footsteps resounded hollowly as she walked to the far side of the ruined hall, intending to conceal herself in the shadows while she waited. The Faloons, she thought ironically, would gather once more in their castle. Hearing the crush of footsteps in the undergrowth, Kerry gasped softly when she saw Shannon pass through the doorframe and into the arena where their future would be determined.

To the fore of the hunt, Zan galloped alongside a clutch of eager riders who followed the staggered line of hounds streaking after the fox. The huntsman's horn resounded through the thicket to the thud of hooves on wet earth and the labored breathing of horses. Casting a backward glance, Zan could see no sign of Shannon—or Kerry—among those who had ridden with the hunt to the end. He brought his horse to a rolling halt and waited as the muffled sound of the hunt died away, then turned back as an uneasy presentiment overtook him. Scanning the landscape glazed with patches of late afternoon light, he could see no sign of any horse or rider. With every mile that drew him nearer to Kilgarin, his misgivings increased. Shannon must have left the field early, but where was Kerry? And why had she come? When he had recognized her in those fleeting moments before the hunt began, there had been no time to make any decision. In his confusion and embarrassment he realized his callous rejection of her had been ungentlemanly, but at the time there had seemed no way out of his dilemma. His first duty had been to Shannon and the son he had never met, and he hadn't stopped to consider the consequences of his rash behavior. How could Kerry be expected to know what was at stake between him and Shannon, and why should she care? he asked himself. The moment he got back to London he would have to explain everything to her—unless, he thought uneasily, she forced a confrontation in the interim, here at Kilgarin.

Arriving at the line of stables beyond the castle, Zan absently greeted several of his guests who were staying overnight for the ball, but his only concern was to discover whether Shannon had returned. Dismounting, he called to the head groom, who was crossing the yard:

"Connors, has Miss Faloon come back on Empress yet?"

"No, not to my knowledge, sir. But Shaughnessy sent a message down to say that when she got back I was to tell her a telegram had arrived for her this afternoon."

"A telegram?" said Zan, puzzled. "Thank you, Connors. When she does come, tell her I've gone up to the house."

The castle was in a fever of last minute preparations. In the hall Zan politely acknowledged one of the village girls, who was carrying a huge bouquet of flowers. She bobbed her head in return and continued on to the dining room, where Mrs. Flaherty was overseeing the laying of the table for the buffet supper to be served at midnight. Then, on his way to his office, he had to step aside in a narrow corridor as a member of the band hired from London struggled past with a bulky instrument case. There were many things he knew he ought to be attending to, but a mounting sense of urgency made it impossible to concentrate.

"Shaughnessy, there you are," he called, seeing the estate manager coming out of his office. "I understand there's a telegram for Miss Faloon."

"Ah, yes, m'lord. Let me pop in and fetch it." He returned a moment later and handed it to Zan. "It came just after half-past two, and I was wondering if I shouldn't send out someone to look for her. But as it was so near the end of the day I kept it by. I'll be in the ballroom helping set up chairs, m'lord, if you need me."

"Thank you, Shaughnessy," Zan replied absently, heading back to the stables to wait for Shannon. For a moment he was unsure whether or not to open the telegram, but common sense told him he must read it without delay in case it was urgent. Only Fiona knew where Shannon was, and the telegram could have something to do with Patrick. Ripping it open, he read Amadeo Benguela's message to Shannon, feeling as if a knife had passed through him.

"Connors," he shouted, breaking into a run, "saddle me a fresh horse."

Shannon crossed the threshold of the ruined castle and looked around suspiciously at the remains of the once proud Faloon kingdom, wondering if she should have come. The flick of a lighter as Kerry lit a cigarette caused her to whirl around.

"You startled me," she said with a sudden intake of breath. "Who are you? Was it you who sent me that note?" As she approached the woman standing in the shadows, the feeling grew within Shannon that she knew her face from somewhere.

"Don't you recognize me, Shannon?" asked Kerry, her smile full of provocative defiance.

Shannon peered at her for a moment before it dawned on her who she was. "Kerry! Is it really you? But I don't understand. What are you doing here?"

"You might say that I've come to claim what's mine."

"What on earth are you talking about?"

"Zan, Shannon. He belongs to me. Hasn't he told you?" Kerry said with bloodless determination. There was a weighted pause while each of them surveyed the changes the years had wrought on the other.

445

Shannon found it hard to believe that this self-possessed, compellingly attractive young woman was her sister. The only thing about Kerry that had remained unchanged was the challenge in her eyes, no longer the rebellious belligerence of an adolescent, but the naked will of a woman of character. Shannon sensed uneasily that Kerry was about to reveal something she would rather not hear. They resisted the revelation that would bring them into conflict, and there seemed nothing Shannon could do to stop the storm threatening to break in Kerry's green eyes.

"I simply don't understand what you're talking about, or why you asked me to come here," said Shannon defensively, beginning to tremble with cold and the shock of seeing her sister.

"Now you know exactly how I felt when I heard that you'd come back into Zan's life."

"What do you mean?"

"Zan and I have been having an affair, Shannon. In fact, I woke up on Wednesday morning thinking we were still lovers. That was the day you decided enough time had gone by since Rosemary's death and that it would amuse you to pick up with Zan where you had left off."

"Kerry, you don't know what you're talking about," said Shannon, her head spinning as she realized her own sister must be the woman Zan had told her about. "Zan and I have been involved for years."

"Oh yes, I'm aware of that. I know everything about you since you left Australia. I know why you left home—why you abandoned me to rot at Koonwarra. And I know everything that's been going on since."

"You've got it all mixed up. That's not what happened. Zan and I didn't have anything to do with each other until ages after I left Koonwarra, after I became a model. But there is something that you're not aware of, Kerry, and that's that I had Zan's child four and a half years ago."

Kerry's look was scathing. "All of England knows about that. I saw the pictures in the papers like everyone else. Oh, yes, don't look so surprised. I've been in England for a year, long enough to know everything about you both. But I didn't believe that story for a minute."

"That's up to you," said Shannon coldly. "I kept Patrick's birth a secret all those years to protect him. I didn't want Zan to come to me out of loyalty, out of duty. But that's something you wouldn't understand."

446

"How noble of you," scoffed Kerry. "Tell me, where was all this nobility when I was *begging* for money at school? Do you have any idea what I went through? As if you gave a damn. Well, I made it anyway, no thanks to you."

At this Shannon's eyes sparked fury. "And who do you think paid for your education at Braemar? My gigolo, as you called him in that charming little letter you wrote me when I was down and out myself. Yes, that's right. Amadeo Benguela, and I paid him back. If you don't believe me, I'll send you the bank records to prove it. I didn't tell you, Kerry, because I thought your pride couldn't stand it."

"What do you mean?" cried Kerry. Through her disbelief she caught a glimmer of the terrible truth. If what Shannon said was true, then she owed Lindy nothing—she never had. The whole course of her life had been determined by a staggering delusion that she had been manipulating him. She had been too clever for her own good, assuming that it was she who was in control, when in fact Lindy had been using her all along. Her anger at her own blindness was followed by a wave of inexpressible shame at the wrong she had done Shannon. Shannon had continued paying her way at Braemar even after that scathing letter. It was an act of profound loyalty that now ripped through Kerry's vanity and self-deception. She might never be able to admit her own treachery—the betrayal that had caused Shannon such heartbreak and had resulted in Rosemary's death—but she would always carry it on her conscience. Yet, facing Shannon, Kerry knew that no amount of guilt could ever make her give up Zan.

"Do you know, Kerry," Shannon continued, "when I realized who you were, I was struck speechless for a moment at what a beautiful, sophisticated woman you've become. But now I see that underneath you're a striving, grasping bitch, eaten up with envy. I haven't done anything to you. You've done it to yourself."

Kerry flinched at this harsh judgment, but she summoned the courage to say, "I love Zan, Shannon. And what you don't realize is that he loves me. . . ."

"He told me there had been someone. But when he said it was all over I believed him. So that's the end of it. I don't know why you're here, but—"

Kerry interrupted her. "You missed your chance, Shannon, but even if you hadn't, he would have been all wrong for you. Zan and I complement each other. He needs the strength of a woman like me. He may never have loved Rosemary, but by God she was strong! That's why he never left her for you. You were just a fantasy, an escape. And today you took my place. I should have been by his side this morning. That's what we planned for weeks."

Shannon tried to shield herself against the unswerving conviction in her sister's voice, as she struggled to hold on to her fragile belief in Zan.

"Is it really true that you were supposed to be here today, with him?" she murmured.

"Shannon, Zan's not for you. You belong with a man like Amadeo Benguela."

Shannon regarded Kerry dispassionately. "What do you know about him? You'd say anything at this point to plead your cause."

"I was at the polo match at Smith's Lawn last spring, Shannon, watching from the sidelines. Do you really think that a man like Benguela would risk his reputation, his life even, on a whim? You're a fool. He's obviously in love with you and always has been. You say he put me, your little sister, through college? Why? And everybody knows the story behind Galant. Benguela put the world at your feet because he loved you. But he's protected you so well that you've lived in a dream. You were free to indulge yourself one week a year because you didn't dare love in the fullest sense. Unlike me, you risked nothing. I'm risking everything at this moment because I love Zan, because I don't want to live without him. I would never be content to be with Zan just one week a year—never. I want him for keeps, for always." Kerry's declaration rang out proudly in the empty shell of the once great hall.

Shannon hesitated. Her sister had cruelly put into words all the misgivings she herself had experienced in the last forty-eight hours. It was true. She was afraid to love, afraid of loss, of feeling pain, of making a fool of herself. Regarding Kerry, who vibrated with the force of her own convictions, Shannon felt ashamed. Unlike herself, Kerry was unfettered by pride. She had pursued Zan with fearless tenacity, risking public humiliation if he rejected her—something Shannon never had the courage to do.

Shannon pressed her hands to her temples in a gesture of hopelessness, not knowing where to turn. "You're forgetting one thing," she said at last. "If Zan and I don't marry, our son Patrick will remain illegitimate. We'll be depriving him of his birthright. You have a little boy yourself. You must understand. Could you live with yourself if you had disinherited him, if you hadn't given a relationship every chance for his sake? Tell me, what would you do in my place?"

"I've been in your place, Shannon," she replied, recalling her formidable battle with Lindy in New York; how she had fought and how she had won.

The look they exchanged, as they realized what was at stake, united them in their dilemma, much as the common bonds of joy, fear, and hope had always tied them irrevocably together in childhood. Then, they'd had only each other to turn to. The knowledge of how much they still needed each other came home, reviving the embers of passionate loyalty that had been their protection against the slings and arrows of fortune.

"Help me, Kerry. What am I going to do?"

Kerry moved toward Shannon and put her arms around her affectionately, sensing that her sister's unhappiness was as deep as her own.

"It's your decision, Shannon. You're the one who has to make it," she said calmly. As they held each other tightly, searching for an answer, a fierce protectiveness toward Shannon was unleashed in Kerry.

"Oh, Kerry, it's so good to have you back in my life again, to be able to talk to you this way. There's still so much to say, so much we don't know about each other. What fools we've been. Let's try not to hurt each other again. I don't know how we're going to work this out, but we'll do it somehow."

Looking at her sister, Shannon was reminded of the Kerry she grew up with, the anguished little girl who saw everything she wanted desperately slipping through her fingers. At that moment Shannon felt the last remnant of her desire to hang on slip away. Zan's hold over her had mysteriously vanished; it had gone long ago, though she hadn't realized it. Now, as she fathomed the image of lasting love in Kerry's eyes, she couldn't summon the desire to pursue their dream any further. At that moment she relinquished her claim. Like a bird released from a cage, it soared into the blue, its wings catching the sun until it disappeared from sight.

When they left the ruins of the castle, their arms entwined, Kerry sensed that Shannon had made her decision, but she was afraid to know the outcome.

On the path they turned to look back. The sun had broken through, streaking the gray horizon with gold that burned like coppery fire on Castle Shannon, its crumbling towers cast in gilt relief against a patch of blue.

"Is it like you thought it would be?" asked Shannon.

"Not really. What about you?"

"I don't know what I expected. But just imagine how grand it must have been once. I was always sure this was just another one of Dad's stories."

"Were you?" said Kerry, surprised. "I wasn't. I always knew it was here."

"Well, you were right all along," said Shannon with a wistful smile. "Don't you wish that Dad were here now? I can hear him say, 'Girlie, when are you going to learn to listen to your old dad? He knows a thing or two.'"

Kerry shook her head in amusement. "I can just see him striding around as if he owned the place, proud, but determined not to admit it."

"I suppose we'd better be getting back," said Shannon reluctantly. "Everybody will wonder what's happened to us. Come on, I'll race you to Kilgarin," she called with a mischievous smile as she untied her horse.

"You're on," retorted Kerry, darting to fetch her mount.

They cantered down the hill and across a lush paddock, where they could see a rider approaching. As he drew nearer they recognized Zan. When the three of them had converged, Shannon attributed the troubled look on Zan's face to Kerry's unexplained presence.

"Kerry, what are you doing here? I don't understand. What's going on? Do you two know each other?" Running his hands through his tousled hair, he looked from one to the other as a memory slowly surfaced from the recesses of his mind. "Good God, it can't be. Kerry—of course! Kerry and Shannon Faloon." He regarded them for several moments with a look of complete astonishment. "But why didn't you tell me in the first place? The whole thing is incomprehensible," he said in bafflement.

In the awkward pause that followed, Shannon looked from Zan to Kerry. In the ruins of the castle she had seen clearly what she had to do; but now, face to face with Zan, she wondered where she was going to find the courage to tell him that she was no longer in love with him and that they could never be married. She wondered if he had already sensed the change in her when she saw him staring at her with a deeply serious expression.

"Why don't we all go back to Kilgarin?" Shannon began.

"Just a minute," Zan interrupted. He withdrew a telegram from his pocket and handed it to her. "This came for you this afternoon. I opened it immediately because I was concerned that something might have happened to Patrick, but don't worry, everything is all right." His voice was cold.

As Shannon read Amadeo's long telegram the words clashed violently together. She had to read it over and over again to make sense of it all. It was full of medical jargon, quoting a letter from a Dr. Darlan in Paris and stating in dry, precise terms a revelation that rocked her life apart. She folded it and met Zan's eyes.

"Is it true?" he whispered.

"I don't know, but it is possible," she replied simply. Though the chances of Amadeo being Patrick's father seemed infinitesimal, she couldn't deny it. She had never even paused to wonder if Amadeo might be Patrick's father—she hadn't wanted to. From the tone of his telegram, it seemed obvious all he wanted was to clear up a deception that might someday cause incalculable harm.

Dazed, she turned to Kerry. "It seems that Amadeo Benguela has incontestable proof that Patrick is his son. I must go back to Paris immediately. If the two of you don't mind, I'd like to ride ahead and sort things out in my mind. I'm sure you have a lot to talk about. I'll see you at Kilgarin in a few moments." Urging her horse forward, Shannon took the muddy lane to the castle.

For several moments Kerry and Zan rode silently beside each other. When they came to the crossroads, Kerry reined in her horse. Turning for a last look at the landscape, she shivered from the chill that had descended over the countryside with the oncoming dusk. Taking a deep breath, she said, "Well, I guess I'd better leave you here. I'm supposed to have the horse back by five, then I'll have to go and collect my things from The Swan and Shamrock." Leaning forward in the saddle, she held out her hand. "Good-bye, Zan."

He leaned across and took her hand, a smile playing at the corners of his mouth. "And just where do you think you're going, Kerry Faloon Van Buren?"

"Back to London." Her heart leapt, but she didn't dare look at him.

"No, you're not. You're coming back to Kilgarin with me. You seem to have forgotten that there's a party on tonight."

She stared at him speechlessly for a moment, and then the shadow of a flirtatious smile stole across her face. "Well, in that case how can I refuse?" she replied, resisting the temptation to tell him she had packed a gorgeous gown of kelly green in the wildly improbable event that she might need it.

Shannon let herself quietly into her apartment late that evening, setting her suitcase down in the hall. Taking off her coat, she was surprised to see a shaft of light coming from the open doors of the drawing room. When she went in she was startled to see Amadeo in his shirt-sleeves, slumped in a chair by the fire, a glass of brandy in his hand. Hearing her footsteps, he looked up. Everything about him seemed completely out of character, from the haggard expression of his unshaven face to his listless posture. During the long journey from Kilgarin to Paris she'd had ample time to think of all the things she should have considered so many years ago. Eventually she'd come to the conclusion that had she listened to her most profound instincts, she might not have deluded herself for so long. The pain she now saw in Amadeo's eyes gave her the courage to acknowledge that she belonged to him with all her heart, and always would, though she feared it was too late. She walked to him tremblingly, humbled by her own blindness and stupidity.

"I've been such a fool, such a fool," she said fighting back the tears. She had the right to ask him why he hadn't told her about Patrick before now, but she knew why—she was so headstrong and impulsive that he had been afraid of losing her and his son.

He rose slowly, gazing intently at her; and as he read the adoration in her face, he seemed to emerge from a long tunnel of despair.

"Shannon—I love you," he whispered. "*Je t'aime. Te quiero*," he repeated joyfully, gathering her in his arms.

452

She held him as she had held no one before, pouring out the love that he had been waiting so long to receive.

"Can you ever forgive me?"

"I can forgive you anything, as long as we spend the rest of our lives together, Shanita."

ABOUT THE AUTHOR

JUSTINE HARLOWE, much married and much traveled, lives in Chelsea, London, with her seven children and three cats. Her interests include painting, photography, exploring, entertaining, and following the stock market.

The stunning sequel to
Barbara Taylor Bradford's
A Woman of Substance

Hold The Dream

With ambition, brains, courage, and an unconquerable will, Emma Harte rose from extreme poverty to build an empire. In retailing, banking, newspapers, oil drilling and energy production, and in real estate, Emma Harte commanded the family business and was as awesome, respected, and feared as any woman in the history of the world. But Emma Harte was nearly eighty and it was time to ensure that what she had given her life to build would be carried on in her spirit after her death.

HOLD THE DREAM is the story of two heroines: Emma, whose understanding of her family must guide her in her bequests, and Paula McGill Fairley, Emma's granddaughter and true heir in every way that matters—in business, in leadership of the family, and in that driving will that will never let her settle for anything less than the best—in work . . . and in love.

HOLD THE DREAM is a story you'll wish
would never end.

on sale March 26
from Bantam Books